'Miller slapped the table hard with it.
"Never! We're left with a half-built bridge and you're asking us to pay almost the full price for it. We've got the contract. We'll take you to court and force you to finish it yourselves rather than pay that sort of money."

Emma Jane heard herself saying in a clear, resounding voice, "I'll finish it then." Everyone, including Johnstone, stared at her.

"I beg your pardon?" asked Miller.

"I said that I'll finish it. I'll take on the responsibility for my father's contract and finish it. I've got the plans – I can hire engineers. I shall complete it and hold you to the contract."

Johnstone had been thinking of her as little more than a child dressed up like a woman of fashion in her purple clothes, but the way she was speaking now made him reassess her, and he realised there was more to the mousy-looking, shy girl than first appeared.

She saw she was wearing him down and pressed her advantage by saying, again not completely truthfully, "I know all about it, and I want it to be built exactly as he intended. If we leave it to them it'll end up a cut-price version . . . This will be my father's memorial, and it's not done to skimp on the cost of a memorial, is it? I'll build his bridge. I'm quite sure I can do it."'

Elisabeth McNeill was born in Fife and brought up in the Borders where most of her books are set. After working as a newspaper reporter in Edinburgh, she lived, with her husband and four children, in India for ten years before returning to England and working as a freelance journalist. She writes articles for various magazines and newspapers and has broadcast on *Woman's Hour*, as well as writing a weekly article for *The Scotsman*. Elisabeth McNeill now lives in the Border village on which she based the village in *A Bridge in Time*.

By the same author

The Shanghai Emerald
Lark Returning
A Woman of Gallantry
The Mistress of Green Tree Mill
Perseverance Place
St James' Fair

A BRIDGE IN TIME

Elisabeth McNeill

ORION

An Orion paperback
First published in Great Britain by Orion in 1994
This paperback edition published in 1994 by Orion Books Ltd,
Orion House, 5 Upper St Martin's Lane, London WC2H 9EA

A CIP catalogue record for this book is available
from the British Library

ISBN 1 85797 406 9

Typeset by CentraCet Limited, Cambridge
Printed and bound in Great Britain by
Clays Ltd, St Ives plc

To my granddaughter
QKIKI-ADI

PROLOGUE

The ancient village of Camptounfoot nestles on the sunny lower slopes of a trio of hills called the Three Sisters which rise, stark and high, out of a wide spread of woods and pastures bordering the river that runs southwards to become the boundary between England and Scotland. The hills look like watchful women, standing close together for comfort and reassurance, staring out in all directions, eternally vigilant on behalf of the people who have lived at their feet for centuries. Travellers approaching from many miles away use the hills as a guiding point for, in a mystical way, the Sisters draw the surrounding world into themselves, gathering up roads and paths like tangled skeins. Those skeins end in Camptounfoot, which claims to be the oldest village in Scotland. It is there that this story begins . . .

One bright spring morning long ago, when Christ's followers were still alive and travelling the world with stories about their Master, a Roman general rode over the saddle between two of the Sister hills and stared down at the lush river valley below. As he gazed, he realised he had found the perfect site for a camp, and cantered down the slope to begin his great project. Ditches were dug; long rows of barrack-houses and stables were built and were soon followed by villas for the officers and temples for the gods. For a hard-fought century the Romans held on to their camp, which they named Trimontium after the trio of towering hills above them, but local tribes finally drove them out and the place they had built returned to its old wildness – grass grew between huge paving stones, brick walls crumbled, gods and goddesses tumbled from their marble plinths.

Over the following centuries the Roman soldiers were forgotten, but they left behind them a legacy in the form of a community of craftsmen and artisans which huddled at the camp's gate. These people had learned many things from their foreign masters, and when the army marched away, they stayed on in the place called Camptounfoot – a proud and independent brotherhood who handed down their skills from father to son. Unlike most of their neighbours, the people of Camptounfoot acknowledged no overlord and looked to no great man for protection. Because they had skills to sell, they were democratic and independent, not bonded to anyone but capable of earning their bread as weavers, sculptors, stonemasons or builders. Unusually in a district where most of the land belonged to a great man, they owned their own properties in perpetuity. Out of natural good manners they curtsied or touched their caps to the local aristocrat, the Duke of Allandale, but he didn't own them in the same way as he owned people and property in the other villages round about.

When the Romans left, the villagers of Camptounfoot did not move into the deserted camp, for they feared the grandiose gods who ruled over the tumbledown buildings there, but being practical people, they systematically plundered the campsite in order to build their own village. By the nineteenth century, it was a well-established place of eighty stone-built cottages with steeply pitched thatched roofs. The floors of the rooms and the pathways running from house to house were laid with hard-baked red tiles or huge Roman paving stones. In the structure of the walls were incorporated old altar stones, grave markers, carved pillars and arched pediments – relics of the forgotten past. From their flowerbeds and vegetable plots village people often dug up bronze statuettes, rusted weapons, bright blue melon beads or broken bangles. They rubbed the dirt off their finds and took them inside to decorate the sooty mantelshelves of their kitchens, or gave them to their children to use as toys.

This community created out of relics clung together, both materially and psychologically, as tightly and close-knit as the cells in a honeycomb. Their homes clustered together like an intricate and convoluted puzzle, one behind the other, each in its neighbour's shade as if frightened to stand alone. Every house had a garden and often an orchard as well, surrounded by tall walls, some rising to above ten feet in height. These walls were symbols of the village's attitude to the outside world, for they showed a determination to stay apart and enclosed.

The villagers kept secrets. They hid any real treasures they found in their fields or gardens, and they did not talk about the ghosts which haunted their narrow alleys that ran between their high walls. On windless evenings when grey wreaths of mist drifted over the surface of the ground, groups of men in strange clothes, glittering with shining armour, were sometimes to be met, marching soundlessly along the paths between the houses, still talking about events that had occupied their minds so many centuries ago. These marching men were Camptounfoot's secret, and they were not feared for they menaced no one, and even the most timid child who caught a glimpse of them knew not to be afraid.

Camptounfoot was secure. The people who lived there did not want anything to change, and little had done so since Roman times. The cycle of life seemed unchanging – villagers were born, grew up, married, had children and died in a never-ending sequence within the clustering cottages. Generation after generation talked about the same topics – the weather, the crops, who was sick, who had died, who had hit bad times or been blessed with unexpected good fortune. The inhabitants peered through their shuttered windows as strangers rode along their main street; they heard about the death of kings and the defeat of armies, but they stayed apart from conflicts. They knew that was the way to survive.

Essentially nothing changed until 1853, when rumours

began to spread from house to house that a railway was going to be built through Camptounfoot. This caused consternation for a while, but most of the villagers secretly felt sure that such a thing would never happen . . .

CHAPTER
One

Halfway up the steep and twisting village street sat a low-roofed alehouse, that was not only a woman-free meeting place for the men of Camptounfoot, but also served as the official centre of gossip. William Strang the village blacksmith, his neighbour Tommy Rutherford, a weaver, and Black Jo the undertaker and carpenter, were sitting by the fire with mugs in their hands one cold spring night when Hughie the alehouse-keeper looked up and asked them, 'Where'll they build the station, do ye think?'

They had been discussing the railway rumours a few minutes before and knew what he was talking about. The blacksmith shrugged and laughed. 'In Rosewell, I dare say. They'll no' build it here. What for would they build a railway through Camptounfoot?'

Hughie shook his head. 'That's no' what I heard. Rosewell might be getting a station but we're getting a junction . . . and a great big bridge over the river down there by Craigie's last field.'

His customers laughed. 'Away you go! The railway'll go to Rosewell because it's four times as big as Camptounfoot. And the river bank's lower there; they'll cross it at Rosewell, beside the road-bridge. What for would they be coming along here, where the river banks are high to cross the river?'

There was a solemn air about Hughie as he cautioned them, 'You wait. A customer was in here today saying that some railway man from Edinburgh's been down to speak to the Duke about laying the line across his land at Rosewell, but the Duke saw him off apparently. And you ken as well as me that he owns most of the fields around

Rosewell. They'll not get to cross the river there. They'll be lucky if they even get a station. It's causing a terrible rumpus.'

There was a little window in the back wall of the alehouse that looked across the river to the lights of the town of Rosewell glittering a mile away, and Tommy Rutherford, the grey-haired weaver, stared out at those lights which sparkled like diamonds in the frosty night as he asked, 'What sort of a rumpus?'

Hughie told him. 'Half the Rosewell folk are mad that the railway's no' coming, and the other half are mad that it might . . . The Duke and his friends are whipping up opposition to it. They don't want anything to change, but the shopkeepers and the mill men are angry because a railway would have brought them business. Now it's going to run down through Maddiston apparently, and they're feared all the trade'll go there.'

William Strang took a swig of his ale and said in a joking tone, 'They've managed all right in Rosewell till now, haven't they? They're just greedy.'

The weaver looked sharply at him and asked, 'Are you not for the railway, then?'

'Oh, I've nothing against it, providing it doesn't run past my door but I don't think it will so I'm not bothered.'

'But it'd bring work and it'd bring money. Look what's happened to other places where they've built railways. Camptounfoot would benefit. There'd be more houses and more jobs for folk, visitors would ride in on the trains, somebody could open a hotel . . .' Hughie's eyes were sparkling at the idea.

William stood up to his impressive, well-muscled height of six feet two inches and said, 'This village is fine the way it is. We're not needing more houses or hotels. My folk have been here for as far back as anybody can remember, and it's aye been a great place to live and die in. I don't want anything to change.' His tone was vehement and he was no longer joking. Laying his empty mug on the table top he said, 'I'm off home now. I just hope all this talk comes to nothing. There'll be a rumpus here too if they try to bring a railway through this village.'

His friends were silent as they watched him go but once the door had closed behind him they began to talk again. 'William's old-fashioned, but then the Strangs have aye lived here,' stated Jo the undertaker.

'So have the Rutherfords,' the weaver reminded him. 'We've been in our cottage for seven generations that I know of, but I can't make up my mind if I'm for the railway or not.' His brow was furrowed as he pondered the problem.

Jo said, 'It might not be good for you. It would mean the mills in Maddiston get an edge on you. If they take over any more of the weaving trade you'll be frozen out.'

Tommy Rutherford nodded sadly. 'That's true, but maybe our days're finished anyway. When I was a laddie there were ten families of weavers in this village but now we're the only ones left.'

The others nodded in agreement. They had watched as, one by one, the weaving families of Camptounfoot sold their homes and moved away to the mill-towns that were starting to spring up along the banks of local rivers. Sometimes these displaced villagers came back on visits, and then it was clear to see how they yearned for their old free way of life – but they had condemned themselves to labour like ants in an ant hill for an exacting employer who was never satisfied with the amount of work they put in. Tommy Rutherford alone remained independent, working at a loom set up in his downstairs room. His wife worked along with him and they hoped their children would soon start weaving as well. They had managed to survive because their webs were exceptionally fine, so good that a middleman was prepared to make a special journey every month to Camptounfoot to collect the lengths of woollen cloth they weaved. But for how long would that go on? Even if no railway came, the mills of Maddiston would probably take away the Rutherfords' customers eventually. Tommy shook his head sadly and

Jo said in sympathy, 'I ken. It's a bad time, isn't it? Everything's changing.'

Hughie was gathering up dirty mugs and he snorted. 'It's all right for you, Jo. Folk'll aye keep on dying – you'll never be out of a job. But I think a railway would be a good thing. It would open up the world for the folk of Camptounfoot.'

Tommy stood up, for it was his turn now to go home. 'Do we want the world opened up for us, though? We've managed fine till now.'

Jo glanced at him and said, 'Don't worry, Tommy. It might never happen. It's probably all talk.'

In the street outside, the oil lamp set high on the wall at the corner of St James' Wynd was casting a pool of light on to the gleaming cobbles when the weaver stepped out of the alehouse door. He looked up and down the steep street, noting the candles gleaming in his neighbours' windows. There was one behind the glittering panes of Mr Jessup's sitting room overlooking the street, and Widow Blackie's window shone too. He was glad to see her light, for when she had been ill recently, her house had been in darkness every evening. She must be feeling better if she was still up, he thought.

On the other side of the road, the window of the schoolhouse was glowing as brightly as a beacon, and the weaver knew that Mr Anderson the schoolmaster would be entertaining his friends, for he was a hospitable man who liked nothing better than to spend an evening in conversation with his neighbours. On impulse, Rutherford turned back to knock on Anderson's door and find out if he knew anything about this railway business.

Mrs Anderson opened the door and invited him in. As he'd expected, there were four or five people already sitting around the fire. Among them he recognised his neighbour Tibbie Mather, William Strang's widowed sister, and her bonny daughter Hannah. They moved aside to make a space for him on the wooden settle facing the blaze and he sighed as he sat down. 'I've just seen your brother in the alehouse and he was talking about this railway business,' he told Tibbie.

She turned her pink-cheeked, chubby face towards him and asked, 'What was he saying?'

'He'd heard they might be going to build a railway through this village and a bridge over the river as well. There's talk of it in Rosewell apparently.'

The others stared back at him apprehensively and Mr Anderson nodded. 'We've just been talking about the same thing. Hannah here heard something at her work. She's been telling us about it.'

They all looked at Tibbie's eighteen-year-old daughter who seemed to glow and glitter in the firelight like a goddess, for her mass of red-gold hair caught the light like a golden crown. She leaned forward and said, 'They were gossiping about it in the kitchen today at Bella Vista. The Colonel's all for it, they say. He's investing money in the railway company that's going to build it.'

Six months ago, Hannah had taken her first place as a kitchen-maid in the recently finished mansion Bella Vista, which was owned by her employer, Colonel Augustus Anstruther, late of the East India Company army, who had come home with a vast fortune and built himself a fine house overlooking the village from farther up the nearest of the Three Sisters. The village took pride in the fact that one of their girls was working for this magnate, and Hannah brought a great deal of fascinating gossip home with her when she came to visit her mother, which she did almost every day.

Now Tibbie snorted, 'The Colonel would be all for it! He's just an incomer, isn't he? He doesn't know how local folk think.'

Mr Anderson shook his head. 'Oh Tibbie, maybe a railway'd be a good thing for us.'

She was shocked. 'How can you say that! Maybe in Rosewell or Maddiston, but not here. We're not needing a railway in Camptounfoot.'

Old Jock the village postman, who was in the party, nodded sagely. 'That's right, Tib. We're not needing a railway. All that noise and carry on, and what about the building of it? That'll be some turn-up.'

Everyone looked at him in alarm, for this was something they had not considered. Mrs Anderson, who was a great reader of newspapers, chipped in, 'You're right, Jock. If they build a railway here, they'll have to bring in navvies and they're awful men, real savages. The papers are aye full of terrible things they do.'

'What sort of things?' asked Tibbie.

Mrs Anderson rolled her eyes. 'Fighting and drinking, sometimes even murder. Terrible things. Attacking women too. There won't be a woman safe in the district if the navvies come.'

Tibbie looked at her lovely daughter in alarm and half-rose from her seat. 'Oh my God!' Hannah was in the habit of running back and forth from the village to Bella Vista even in darkness. She was going back there that very evening.

Hannah guessed what her mother was thinking, but she was not worried; she laughed as she put a hand on Tibbie's arm and said, 'Sit down, Mam. They're not here yet and they'll probably never come. It's just one of those rumours. Even if they do built a railway down here, it probably won't come near Camptounfoot.'

As they talked on, it soon became obvious that there were two schools of thought about the coming of a railway. Older residents like Tibbie, Mrs Anderson and Postman Jock were totally against the idea but the schoolmaster and Hannah were more receptive. Mr Anderson, whose imagination had always been sparked by tales of travel and distant lands, welcomed the opportunity that a railway would give to his pupils, and Hannah, young and high-spirited, was in favour of anything modern and new, though she took care to hide her eagerness from her worried mother. For Tibbie was of the old school. She had been born in Camptounfoot; married a man also from the village and spent her subsequent life in a cottage that had been owned by his family for hundreds of years. She had no wish to live anywhere else, for she was sure that there was not another place on earth more beautiful or peaceful than her native home. Like her brother William the blacksmith, she did not want anything to change – and even the suggestion of upheaval frightened her.

Now she rose from her seat and took her daughter's arm. 'Come on, Hannah. It's time you went back to Bella Vista and I went home. It's getting late.' As Hannah stood up, the firelight gilded her fine skin and highlighted her delicate features. Everyone in the party was struck again by how lovely she was. She smiled at her mother without argument for she realised how the talk was upsetting Tibbie.

Tommy Rutherford stood up with them and said, 'I'll have to go too because my wife'll be wondering where I am. I'll walk up the road with you, Tibbie.'

Outside, the night sky had deepened to dark purple and the stars glittered like chips of ice. Hannah kissed her mother and ran off down the hill while Tibbie and Tom climbed the slope past Widow Blackie's door. When she saw the light in the window, Tibbie paused and said, 'Meg's still up. I'll look in at her and see she's all right.'

Rutherford stopped too. 'Her light was on when I passed and I thought it was strange. She's usually asleep by this time, isn't she?'

They knocked at the door and when there was no reply, turned the handle and went inside. The door opened directly into a low-roofed room with a fireplace at the far end and a bed recess down one side. Tibbie stepped into the flickering shadows cast by the candle and called softly, 'Mistress Blackie, Mistress Blackie, where are you?'

A feeble voice came from the bed. 'I'm here, Tib. Oh, I'm glad to see you. I'm sick, awful sick.'

Tibbie gestured to Rutherford. 'Run home and get your wife, Tommy. I'll maybe need some help.' He did as he was bid and only minutes later his wife was in the old widow's cottage with a basket of food on her arm. The neighbours of Camptounfoot always stepped into the breach in emergencies, and now they had everything in hand. It was midnight when Mrs Rutherford went home again and when she did, her husband was waiting to hear her news.

'The poor old soul's dying,' she said sadly as she took off her shawl. 'But Tibbie's with her and I'll go back in the morning.'

Tom shook his grey head. 'That's Camptounfoot for ye – that's what living in a village like this means. Tibbie and William are right: I hope no railway comes here to change things and spoil what we've got.'

When the first grey streaks of light began to appear in the sky, old Mrs Blackie died peacefully with her hand in Tibbie Mather's. Her neighbours washed and dressed her in the white cotton gown she had laid aside for her shroud, and then Tibbie ran up St James' Wynd to rap on Jo's door and call out, 'Widow Blackie's gone!'

Jo shoved his head out of the upstairs window and told her, 'I'll be down right away.' The age-old way of doing things went on without effort. Next day the old lady, whose only son had been killed at Waterloo, was buried by her neighbours in an ivy-lined grave dug in the burying-ground beside the ruined gable wall of an ancient chapel that long ago went out of use when French monks came and built a huge abbey at Rosewell on the opposite bank of the river. Though the villagers of Camptounfoot worshipped in Rosewell, they still buried their dead in the village.

Tibbie Mather stood beside the grave with her sister-in-law Effie and her friends Mrs Anderson and Mrs Rutherford, and they wept gently for their dead neighbour. They'd known her all their lives; she had been grey-haired and bent when they were girls, and now it seemed right that they should be mourning her death in the graveyard where their own ancestors lay, and where one day they would be buried themselves.

The village remained silent and subdued for twenty-four hours as a mark of respect, but next morning things were back to normal. Children shouted in the school playground; William's hammer could be heard clanging on iron in his smithy at the end of the Wynd; a woman called out a cheerful greeting to her neighbour as she passed up the street. Life was flowing on as usual. Neat and tidy in a crisp white apron, Tibbie Mather stood at her front door and listened with her head cocked to one side like a sparrow. Her dread of innovation, her fear of a terrifying railway thrusting its way into the middle of their little community gradually disappeared. In a way, she found the death of the old widow a sort of reassurance because it made her feel that village life flowed like a river and, like a river, Camptounfoot would never change.

It was just as well that Tibbie did not know about a meeting being held that very morning at an elegant office in Edinburgh's Rutland Square. Five men sat around a large table poring over maps and papers spread out over its polished surface.

'Just look at all that empty land and not a mile of railway line on it!' exulted the most enthusiastic of them. His name was Sir Geoffrey Miller and he was the Chairman of the recently formed Edinburgh and South of Scotland Railway Company, which had been inaugurated by a special Act of Parliament only a few weeks before.

His colleagues leaned forward and followed his pointing finger with their eyes. 'Look at all those mill-towns, growing like mushrooms and hardly a decent road to any of them. The woollen trade's booming and they're desperate for a way to ship their goods out. They're mad for us to open our line. We'll make a fortune!' cried Miller, although he was not normally given to expressions of excitement.

'*If* we can get it built,' demurred a cautious banker called Thomas Munro.

The others round the table made similar doubting sounds but Miller was unabashed: 'Of course we'll get it built! The mill-owners are backing us – they're all eager to put money into the line. We've got two local landowners, Anstruther and Raeburn of Falconwood, nibbling too. I'm going down there soon to see them and I'm sure we'll have them behind us. They're both sharp businessmen and this is a sure-fire success.'

'What about young Allandale? I've heard he's against it,' came a voice from the back of the room. The speaker was John Smith, a canny financier who liked to have everything cut and dried before he invested as much as a pound. The new railway company needed his backing and he knew it.

'His sort are always against the railway but that hasn't stopped them being built in other places, has it? The dukes and the earls don't want their power base to shift but they've ruled their little kingdoms for too long and if manufacturers grow powerful, the old aristocrats will be threatened,' said Miller, staring over the heads of his colleagues at Smith.

When their eyes met, Smith countered with, 'He could still stop your plans in their tracks. He owns too much land down there.'

Miller gestured with his pen. 'Come and look at this. I know exactly how much he owns. This and this and this . . . all the ground south of Rosewell, unfortunately, but he doesn't own this – or this. That part's Anstruther's, and that narrow stretch on both sides of the river belongs to Raeburn. We'll take our bridge across the river on Raeburn's land.'

Smith stepped up beside him and leaned over his shoulder. 'Anstruther's a parvenu but does Raeburn know what you're planning? Is he brave enough to defy his Duke?'

Miller laughed. 'For hard cash he'd defy anybody. I've offered him a seat on the board and two thousand a year . . . He's got land but not much capital. He'll come.'

Smith laid a finger on the map. 'It's all very well getting his land, but where do you go from there? The Duke owns the area behind it.'

Miller had an answer to that as well. 'He doesn't own the land behind this village here, though, and it marches with Raeburn's. We can run our line along its boundary. Anstruther bought that ground five years ago from the Duke for a house and a park. He's built the house, but he's ready to sacrifice part of his park if what I hear is true. It's perfect! The line will run down from Edinburgh to Maddiston where the big mills are, then it'll go on to Rosewell where we can build our station on the north side. After that it'll cross the river by Camptounfoot and head for the south. Eventually it'll end up at Berwick.'

His colleagues stood nodding their heads as the line was traced for them. It was untapped country indeed. 'It'll revolutionise trade,' said one of them, but Smith's brow was still furrowed. 'I know that part of the country,' he said slowly. 'I used to fish the river there. Isn't the bank by Camptounfoot very high? Surely that's a bad place to try to build a bridge?'

Miller shot him a glance. 'It's not the easiest,' he admitted grudgingly, 'but it's the only place available to us because of Allandale. If we build our line at all, we've got to use Raeburn's land and we need Anstruther's too. I'm sure I can persuade them.'

'No doubt, no doubt,' said Smith smoothly, 'but who's going to build it? That could prove a costly enterprise.'

'Oh, I don't think so. There's not much railway-building going on just now, and contractors all over the country are eager for work. We can drive a hard bargain. I've put out notices for tender – they'll be flooding in soon. Are you coming in with us or not, Smith?'

The financier leaned over the papers for a long time before he finally straightened up and stuck out his hand. 'It has possibilities, I think. Yes, I'll back you, providing you arrange certain things to my satisfaction.'

'And what may these be?' enquired Miller confidently.

'The first is that you rope in Anstruther and Raeburn and have their agreement in writing. The second is that you find a bridge-builder capable of tackling a project like this, and I can tell you before it starts that it won't be easy. I'm not going to back any scheme for a bridge which falls down before it's finished. Get the best man for the job and then I'll put in my money.'

The prospectus for Camptounfoot railway viaduct arrived on Christopher Wylie's office desk in Newcastle the next day. Wylie pored over the papers for an hour and then sat back with his hands over his eyes. 'Can I do this? Can I take this on?' he asked himself. Standing up, he stretched his arms high above his white head and felt his aching bones creak with the effort. He was getting old. A few years ago, nothing would have stopped him from putting in an offer to build the Camptounfoot bridge but he was fifty-six years of age and he'd lost his enthusiasm. His only son was dead and there seemed to be no point in striving so hard any longer.

He turned and walked towards his office window and stared out across the River Tyne at the boats lined up along the busy wharves. Newcastle was booming. With every year that passed, more ships came up the river; more money flooded into the city. Wylie remembered when he'd been able to walk the streets and greet most of the people he saw. Now those streets were full of strangers, prosperous and busy, confident and bustling – people who did not recognise him and whom he did not know.

His eyes ached with the effort of reading the closely printed prospectus in dim light, and he rubbed them with his knuckles. Behind him he heard the office door open. 'Is that you, Claud?' he asked without turning round.

'Yes,' said the gravelly voice of his old assistant and secretary Claud Cockburn, who had worked with him since he first started up his contracting business some thirty-four years before. Like his employer, Cockburn was growing old and anxious to retire.

Wylie still did not turn. 'Did you read the papers about that bridge?' he asked.

'Yes,' said Claud, none too enthusiastically.

'What do you think?'

'I think you could do it. You're probably the only contractor in the north who could.'

'You don't sound too keen,' grunted Wylie, finally turning round.

'I don't know if you want to put yourself through all that again,' said Claud slowly. A little hunchbacked chap with a deeply lined face, he looked like a gnome from a fairy tale.

'I don't know either. I'm getting too old . . . it would have been different if James was still alive,' sighed Wylie.

Claud nodded. 'I know. But if you don't mind me saying so, you could do with the money. You've not had a contract for eighteen months and you lost a lot on Hudson's collapse. You can't afford to retire yet, Chris. You need one last big job to recoup your losses.'

'How bad are things?' asked Wylie.

His old friend shook his head. 'Bad enough. You owe the bank a packet, and if you don't start making some money soon they'll foreclose on you.'

Wylie groaned. 'That's what I've been afraid of. My God, I used to be the biggest railway contractor in Newcastle – everybody came to me with their work. What's happened?'

'There isn't any railway work at the moment. Everybody's scared off because of what happened to Hudson. This bridge is the first thing that's come in for a year.'

Wylie stared at the old man's face. 'You mean I should try to get it?'

Claud nodded. 'You *have* to get it if you're not going to go bust,' he said. Then he sighed. 'But I'm too old to help you any longer. I'm sixty-seven, Chris.'

Wylie straightened his broad shoulders and turned away from the window. 'I know. I'm going to pension you off, old man, but let's sit down and go through the prospectus together. Light the lamps, Claud. Give me the benefit of your help one more time. I hope you're not in a hurry to get home tonight.'

'I'm never in a hurry to get home,' Claud sighed. 'There's nobody waiting for me, not like you.'

Wylie sighed too as he thought about his once bright and cheerful wife, reduced now to a weeping, hysterical wreck because of the death of their beloved son. 'Send the carriage home with a message for Arabella to say I'll be back late, and then come and help me work out what it's going to take to secure this project,' he instructed his faithful old clerk.

CHAPTER

Two

Tibbie Mather lived in a stone-built cottage with a thatched roof that was situated by the side of the main road opposite the opening of St James' Wynd. Overlooking the street, it had a green-painted front door, one window with tiny opaque panes, and a wooden gate that opened into a disused stable. At the back were two bigger windows facing south on to the sheltering hills, and a door into a garden that was full all summer with flowers, neat rows of vegetables and old-established herbs. A well covered with a wooden lid stood in one corner of the garden and at the other was a little lavatory, the walls of which were washed down with white lime every spring.

The cottage was a warm and cosy place even in the most bitter weather, for its walls were five feet thick and its thatch was one of the thickest and oldest in the village, so deeply covered with grass and houseleeks that even in the middle of winter it looked as green as a lawn. This thatch was home to hundreds of birds, who made their nests there and rustled companionably through the nights, listened to by the people inside the cottage as they lay in bed.

Tibbie's late husband Alex had been a stonemason, and when they married he had carved a sundial and erected it above the back door. It bore their entwined initials and the date of their wedding, 1829. When Alex died in 1843 of the lung disease that plagued men who hewed away at dusty red sandstone, their child Hannah was only eight years old, but Tibbie was not left badly off because her husband, being twenty years older than she, had saved his money carefully during his working life. Also, the proud

24

and self-protective Society of Master Masons in Camp-tounfoot ran a benevolent fund which was distributed to their widows and orphans. When Alex died, Tibbie received a gratuity of ten golden guineas, and every New Year's Day a half-guinea tied in a silk handkerchief was left on her window-ledge.

She was a proud, erect little woman in her late forties with a smooth-skinned plump face and brown hair tinged at the temples with silver strands. Even in middle age there was a kittenish quality about her that was infinitely appealing, and she looked at the world through round, innocent eyes that seemed always to be pleased with what they saw. If anyone in the village was in trouble, Tibbie would turn up on their doorstep with offers of help, food and sometimes even a few coins from her savings. People told her their secrets because there was no viciousness or malice in her, and they knew she would not condemn them as silly or feckless, even when they were.

When Alex died she grieved, but the delight she took in her home, her garden, the village where she lived, the friends who surrounded her and most of all her bonny daughter, healed the hurt. On this bright spring morning, as she opened her door and stepped into the garden to look at the snowdrops that were thrusting their green spikes through the dark earth, she would have said to anyone who asked that she was a truly happy woman. She had no idea how much everything was about to change . . .

The sky was a very pale shade of blue, almost the colour of pearls, really, and there was a stillness in the air that meant the overnight frost had not yet lifted. The nearest hill looked very close and the gorse-bushes which marked its sides stood out as black as charcoal against the red sweep of withered bracken.

Tibbie pulled her black shawl off the back of the kitchen door and draped it over her shoulders. She kept her head lowered and her breath spiralled out in front so that she looked like a busy little black dragon as she emerged into the open air. The path on which she stood was lined with snowdrops growing together in big clumps, their delicate

25

white heads nodding on the ends of fragile stems. She gazed down at them in delight, for their annual emergence always seemed to be a miracle after the bleakness of winter. Then she was startled to hear voices coming from the field on the other side of her cottage wall.

She straightened up and stared. A party of men were walking along the hedgerow. Some of them carried long poles over their arms and others were consulting sheets of paper, pausing and assessing the lie of the land as they went. She did not recognise any of them and felt her heart leap with fright as she watched their progress along the field boundary.

A tall man in the front of the party saw her and lifted a hand in greeting. 'Good morning,' he called.

Her mouth was too dry to reply at first and she had to swallow before she could speak. 'What are you doing?' she shouted.

'We're surveying for your new railway,' he sang back cheerily.

Tibbie swayed. All of a sudden the cold seemed to bite into her bones. 'You're not putting it there. Not through the field!' she exclaimed. The strip of rough land was the common property of the cottagers whose houses over-looked it and who used it to graze a cow or a horse. Tibbie herself ran a few hens on it and augmented her income by selling eggs.

The friendly man walked slightly closer to her and called reassuringly, 'No, not through the field – down by the hedge. We'll build an embankment and the line's going to run along the top.'

She stepped back in alarm, clutching her shawl to her throat. 'Oh no, don't do that. We don't want trains coming through this village,' she cried in horror.

Back inside the kitchen, she leaned against the closed door and tried to stop the shaking in her legs. She felt as if a nightmare had become reality; the railway which she envisaged as a fire-breathing monster would run within touching distance of her beloved home. She could see it in her mind's eye, snaking along the thorn hedge throwing out showers of red-hot cinders, terrifying the animals and the people. People had said it would never happen, but now they were actually planning the line. She had to talk to someone – she had to have reassurance from her neighbours that it wouldn't be allowed.

Ignoring the surveying party who were still pacing the hedge, she dashed back into the garden again and out through her wooden gate into a narrow path that ran behind the cottages. It was a struggle to keep her feet on the slippery paving stones which were rutted down each side by the passage of old wheels – first chariot-wheels and then farm carts – but she moved with determination because she knew where she was going. Her destination was the village shop, the centre of Camptounfoot life. Everything that went on was known about there.

Its brass bell tinkled when she stepped inside and Bob, the shop-owner, shoved his head round the edge of the door that divided the counter area from the back parlour where he and his wife Mamie lived. He held a steaming cup of tea in his hand and was obviously none too pleased at being interrupted in his breakfast. Tibbie knew she had to buy something to explain her presence, so she looked hurriedly around at the stock, searching her mind for a purchase that would not cost very much. 'I'm needing a ball of string,' she gasped finally.

Bob's wife Mamie appeared at his shoulder and raised disapproving black eyebrows to her hairline as she said, 'You must be needing string awful bad to be out this early. It's not eight o'clock yet.'

'I'm an early riser,' said Tibbie, but it was impossible to keep the real object of her visit a secret any longer so she burst out, 'I've just seen some men walking the field behind my house. They say they're surveying for a railway line!'

Bob nodded his head sagely. 'So they are, so they are. Dinna you worry though, they'll no' harm you, Mrs Mather.'

'I'm no' feared of the men,' snapped Tibbie, 'but I

27

don't like them speiring the place out. We don't want a railway coming through Camptounfoot.'

Bob was rummaging in a drawer below the wooden counter for balls of string. His shop was a cluttered wonder but he always knew where everything could be found. Heavy working boots for adults and children swung by their knotted leather laces from nails hammered into the roof-beams. A black umbrella hung beside them. It had been up there for ten years at least and was delicately draped with spiders' webs, for it had not been moved since the day he put it up. No one had ever shown any interest in buying it because, when it rained, sensible folk covered their heads with shawls or pulled their working caps on more firmly. As her husband searched for Tibbie's string, Mamie stood with her hands resting on the counter beside bars of bright green soap, a big yellow cheese and a tempting-looking ham which was half-sliced and showing succulent pink flesh frilled with white fat. At the far end of the counter she kept a box of sticky sweetmeats for children, though few of the mothers of the village could afford such luxuries often. Behind her were black japanned tins full of tea and sugar and shelves of scouring powders and metal polish, for which there was a big demand, and dark blue bottles of patent medicines, the labels of which proclaimed their miraculous powers in curing a variety of ailments, from nervous collapse to impotence and child-birth pains. The air was full of mouthwatering smells, somewhat spoiled by a strong whiff of paraffin that drifted in from the back premises every time the door was opened.

The pair of them stared hostilely at their flustered customer as Bob at last emerged red-faced from floor level brandishing a ball of string in his hands. 'You might not want a railway Mrs Mather, but there's other folk not of the same opinion. There's some that think a railway'll bring business to Camptounfoot.' He slapped the ball of string on the counter top and said, 'That'll be a penny farthing.'

She paid reluctantly, took the string and asked again, 'It's definitely going there, then? It's not just an idea?'

'They're surveying for the railway line,' said Bob.

It was obvious that the shop-keeper was very much in favour of the idea and Tibbie felt a pang of fear at the realisation that this could split the village into two opposing camps, but she couldn't stop herself from saying, 'Oh, I hope somebody stops them from bringing a railway to Camptounfoot.'

'It's what this place needs,' said Mamie sharply.

'But it'll change everything. We're grand as we are – we don't need a railway,' cried Tibbie frantically.

Behind her, the shop-bell tinkled again and Black Jo the undertaker bent his head to pass under the low lintel. 'Are you on about the railway? You're right, Mrs Mather. We dinna need sic a thing in Camptounfoot. It's the invention o' the devil.'

The others turned and stared at him in alarm, for they knew that from time to time Jo was liable to be seized by strange attacks of religious fervour allied with other peculiar symptoms.

A bachelor in his forties, he lived with his mother in a tall stone house that looked like a decrepit tower at the corner of St James' Wynd, with his workshop eccentrically situated on the first floor. When he finished making a coffin, the rough wooden box had to be manoeuvred out of the workshop window and lowered on ropes to the ground.

His sinister occupation, combined with his long, gloomy, cadaverous face and the grubbiness of his attire, made him an object of dread to the adults as well as the children of the village; when one of his religious fits took him, Jo loudly preached Biblical texts from his open window in the middle of the night or prowled around his neighbours' cottages, peering through uncurtained windows at women living on their own. A raucous widow called Bella Baird was one of his favourite victims, but she knew how to treat him and, if she heard a scuffle at her window while she was washing herself before the kitchen fire at night, she turned to show her ample, uncovered breasts to the spy and cried, 'Tak' a good look, Jo! Tak' a

29

good look and then awa' hame to yer mither.' Other village women were not so bold, however, and went in dread of Jo. Now he loomed large and dark in the shop door, shaking his head and declaiming, 'We're no needin' any railways. It's the devil that's sent it to plague us.'

Bob looked at him with scorn. 'Don't be daft!' he snapped. 'It'll bring business. There'll be more folk for you to bury. Progress is what this place needs, it's stuck in the past. Naething's happened here for hundreds of years and you a' need shakin' oot o' yersel's.' Bob was proud of the fact that he had been born and brought up in Edinburgh and had only come to Camptounfoot to open his shop ten years before.

'We'll be overrun wi' evil! Is that what you call progress?' demanded Jo. 'There'll be godless navvies rampaging up and doon the street. Is that progress?'

Mamie laughed. 'Navvies'll be good for business if they come in here. We'll be selling baccy and clay pipes all day long.'

'You'll repent! You'll be sorry you welcomed the devil,' intoned Jo in a voice that sounded as if it came from the depths of the tomb.

Bob's patience snapped. 'What is it you're wanting?' he asked roughly and Jo hurriedly bought a small square of yellow soap then beat a quick retreat. When he went away, Bob was moved by a feeling of pity for the worried-looking Tibbie, and told her in a gentler tone, 'Don't you worry, Mrs Mather. Maybe a railway won't be as bad as you think. Maybe you'll not mind it when it's built. This is eighteen fifty-three, after all, and the world's changing. We cannae be left behind. Just think, you'll be able to get on a train at your ain back door and go anywhere you want.'

Tibbie looked stricken and there were tears in her eyes. 'I don't want to leave here. I've never wanted to leave here. I don't want anything to change,' she said with a tremor in her voice. Then she grabbed the ball of string and fled.

Behind her, Mamie shook her head and said to her

husband, 'Do you think she's all right? Maybe she's losing the place.'

It's a local colloquialism for going a bit silly. He did not agree. 'Och no, she's just like some of the other folk here, stuck in their ways and feared of change. But they'll get used to it. They'll have to.'

'What can we do? Who's going to help us? We're powerless, we're only little people who haven't any influence,' ran Tibbie's angry thoughts as she walked up the steep village street. A cold sun had risen and was gilding the tops of the walls and striking sparks off the glass of uncurtained windows overlooking the road. Voices called out greetings as she passed open doors revealing sparsely furnished interiors, but she answered abstractedly. Women paused in the task of sweeping dust off worn red sandstone doorsteps and greeted her with, 'Grand day, Tib.' She called back, 'Aye, grand day, Mary . . . Grand day, Meg . . . Grand Day, Rose . . .' but the gravity of her expression made them stare after her and a few asked, 'What's up, Tibbie?' When she told them about the railway, some agreed with her that it would be a terrible thing, but she could see from others' responses that they secretly welcomed its coming. Already the village was being split in two over the issue.

The main street was long, and twisted in a sinuous S-shape uphill all the way to Tibbie's cottage. It was so steep that older people were forced to pause halfway to draw their breath and calm their beating hearts. She stopped at the gate of the village school, a long, narrow building like a cowshed with a tiny playground at one end. In it children were running around, fighting, playing peeries, screaming and shouting as they waited for the day's lessons to begin. Schoolmaster Mr Anderson was standing in the doorway with a big brass bell in his hand and he called, 'G'morning, lass. You're out early.'

She turned her head towards him and said, 'They've started surveying the railway line. It's going at the back of my house.'

31

From their previous discussion she knew he was not against the new project, but he remembered her fear of innovation and dread of change so he came to the playground railings to say softly, 'It might not be a bad thing, Tibbie. It'll open up the world for our bairns.' Too often he'd watched gifted children being forced by long-established custom to follow the menial occupations of their fathers because there was nothing else they could do. Perhaps, with a chance to travel, they'd go out into the world.

She gazed at him with disappointment in her eyes. 'Oh, why should they want to go away from here? And think how much our village'll be changed!' she cried.

He still tried to console her. 'Change isn't always a bad thing, Tibbie.'

She obviously did not believe him and when he began clanging his bell, she hurried on to the narrow mouth of St James' Wynd where the Rutherfords' cottage sat back behind a high garden wall. As she passed its gate she could hear the clack of flying shuttles. On impulse, she pushed open the gate and walked up the cobbled path to the open window. Leaning on the sill she looked in to where the weaver and his wife were sitting at their looms. 'I've just seen men walking the new railway line,' she told them.

Mr Rutherford looked up. 'I heard it's starting soon. It's got nearly as far as Maddiston and it'll be here by the end of the year, they say.'

Tibbie gave a sob and the weavers looked at her with sympathy.

'Dinna take on so, Tib,' comforted Mrs Rutherford. 'We'll all get used to it in time. We've been praying about it. God'll look after us. It might not be as bad as we think.'

Tibbie drew her head back and wiped her eyes. The Rutherfords were very Christian people who prayed about any problem in their lives. She wished she had the same consolation but that was denied to her.

Her next destination was the house where she had been born at the top of St James' Wynd, the blacksmith's cottage now occupied by her brother William and his wife Effie. His forge adjoined the house. As she turned into the Wynd, Tibbie saw smoke rising like a silver plume from the chimney and knew that William would be heaving on the huge bellows beside the forge to bring life back into the previous day's fire. She went to his workshop first and stood leaning her arms on the open half-door, watching him at work as she used to watch her father. William's broad back was covered with a clean white shirt, already marked by a triangular patch of sweat between his shoulder blades. A pair of braces crossed his shoulders and his breeches were held up by a broad leather belt that was cinched around his waist. He was so intent on his task that he did not know she was there until she knocked on the door with her fist. Then he turned and a smile lightened his solemn features.

'Oh, it's you, lass. I'm just blowin' up the fire. I'll not be a minute and then we can go ben for a cup of tea with Effie.' He gestured towards a little door in the end wall that led from the forge to the house.

Tibbie nodded acceptance. 'I smelt baking when I was coming up the Wynd. Effie's making bread, I think.'

William laughed as he wiped his hands on a piece of dirty cloth. 'Is that what brought you out?'

His sister shook her head. 'No, I came to tell you that the railway men are walking along behind my cottage. They're going to build the new line there.'

William nodded soberly. 'I've heard talk of that. Come and have some tea and we'll talk about it with Effie. Now don't take on, Tibbie. It might not happen.'

Tibbie's sister-in-law Effie was a wonderful house-keeper, the sort who could make a shilling do the work of a guinea. Everything in the cottage sparkled and shone, and what was most comforting to the distraught Tibbie was that nothing seemed to have changed since she was a child: the same pair of brass-bound bellows glittered on the hearth, the same plaster ornaments decorated the mantelshelf, and the same flowered china cups were hanging on hooks in the open-shelved cupboard by the fire. It even seemed that the same tabby cat slumbered in the big chair. A new addition since Tibbie's last visit, however, was a large coloured lithograph of Queen Victoria and Prince Albert hanging in a prominent position over the kitchen table.

Struggling to contain her emotions, she concentrated on the picture. 'Is that new, Effie?' she asked, peering at the glass. She didn't really care for it. The Royal couple stood stiffly to attention, a bulging-eyed Queen clinging tightly to her husband's arm while he gazed straight ahead like a man in a trance.

'I bought it from a pedlar last week. Isn't she bonny?' asked Effie, who was a passionate lover of Victoria.

Tibbie tried to be kind about the tubby little figure in the picture. 'Er, yes,' she said doubtfully.

William interrupted, 'Tibbie didnae come to talk about the Queen. She's seen the men from the railway company walking the field at the back of her house.'

Effie shot him a glance. They had obviously known about this and kept it from Tibbie. 'It'll not make much trouble for you, Tibbie. It'll just be noisy for a wee while,' she said softly.

Tibbie shook her head. 'It's not only me that I'm worried about, Effie. It's what a railway'll do to the whole village. It'll no' be the same once it's built. Camptounfoot's always been a sort of separate place, secret in a way. That's what I wanted to talk to you about. Isn't there any way we can stop it?'

'Apparently not. There was a meeting of some of the men of the village last night, and the Duke sent his factor to speak to us. He's against the railway, but he's not been able to stop it either. There's a lot of folk for it, you see, even in this village. They think that if we're against it, we're old-fashioned,' said William glumly.

Tibbie snapped, 'But don't they know what'll happen? Camptounfoot'll change.'

Effie was pouring the tea and she said, 'But maybe they want it to change. They say we need progress.'

Tibbie rapped the table sharply. 'If I hear another

34

person talking about progress, I'll scream. What's progress if it brings noise and racket into our village, trains rattling along day and night! Nobody's asked people like me what we want. Half of this village would say the same thing as I do, I'll be bound.'

'I don't want it either but I can't stop it,' said William. Then seeing how upset his sister was, he put an arm around her shoulders and gave her a hug. 'Oh, don't take on, lass. It might not be as bad as you think.'

There were tears sparkling in Tibbie's eyes again as she choked out, 'I'm so worried. I've a terrible feeling – I'm sure something bad's going to happen to us over the head of this. I just feel it.'

William tried to be matter of fact. 'Now stop getting those fancies of yours. You've been like that ever since you were a bairn, always having dreams and seeing things.'

She bridled. 'It's not dreams – I *do* see things. And I see the marching men though I ken fine you don't like me talking about them. I'm not the only person in this village to see them either.'

'All right, all right,' William consoled her. 'I believe you. You've not seen them recently, have you? That's not what's bothering you?'

Tibbie shook her head. 'No, but I'm feared that if the navvies go digging up the place they might go away. They won't like disturbance.'

'My God, they'll have seen plenty of disturbance in their time,' joked William. 'Drink your tea and calm down.'

His wife Effie had more tact than her husband, and with sympathy she eventually succeeded in calming Tibbie and diverting her mind from the threat of the railway to the subject closest to her heart – her daughter. 'How's Hannah getting on up at Bella Vista?' she enquired, and Tibbie immediately brightened.

'Oh, she's doing very well. They've made her a table-maid now. The housekeeper said she was wasted in the kitchen!'

Effie threw up her hands. 'That was quick! Trust

Hannah. That lassie's going a long way, you mark my words.'

Tibbie smiled at last. 'She's quick, that's true. She came home yesterday to tell me that they're paying her an extra five pounds a year now! Isn't that grand?'

'She'll be a lady's maid before you know where you are,' Effie said with pride. She was the mother of three sons and the achievements and beauty of her niece was a matter of family pride to her as well as to Tibbie.

'It's a good place,' said Tibbie with satisfaction. 'I'm glad she was taken on there because I didn't want her to go to work on the land. She's more likely to meet a good husband in a well-run household like Bella Vista than working on a farm.'

'Oh, you needn't worry about Hannah meeting a husband!' Effie laughed. 'All the lads in this village are daft about her. She could have her pick of them right now.'

Tibbie frowned. 'I know, but there's not one that I'd really want for her. She'll maybe have to look outside Camptounfoot for a man, I think.'

Both William and Effie laughed at this. 'Now that's an admission, coming from you. You usually think Camptounfoot folk are the best in the world.'

'Oh, Hannah's special. It's going to take a grand man to match her,' said Tibbie, and then she added, 'I wouldn't really mind if she went as far as Rosewell or Maddiston to find a husband, as long as he was good enough for her.'

Effie leaned over and hugged her sister-in-law. 'That'll be a grand day, the day our Hannah gets married,' she exclaimed and Tibbie beamed.

'Aye, won't it!' she agreed, and the happy thought made her forget the railway for a little while.

Even before the plans for a railway were officially announced, the village of Camptounfoot was riven by disputes about it. Two camps quickly formed. Old friends fell out; members of the same family quarrelled. Bob and Mamie found that half of their customers stopped coming into the shop when the couple openly announced their support for the pro-railway faction. Some of the women from the oldest-established families in the village now preferred to walk a mile to Rosewell rather than go to the local shop. The Rutherfords, who were against the railway, fell out with their old friends the Armstrongs who were for it, because Alex Armstrong was a mason who foresaw plenty of work coming from railway construction, especially when he heard that a large bridge was to be erected across the river at Camptounfoot. Postman Jock, anti-railway, stopped speaking to his pro-railway brother, Big Will, who was also a mason. Mr Anderson had some sharp words with his wife when he told her to stop agitating against the railway line, and he was deeply distressed one morning when he had to break up a playground fight between two factions of for and against railway-ites among his pupils . . . There were few residents in the eighty households that made up their little community who did not hold a strong opinion one way or the other. The alehouse-keeper tried to keep the peace but few people listened to him when he reminded them, 'It doesn't really matter what you all think – you can't do anything about it!'

Though she watched the field behind her house with close attention every day, Tibbie did not see the surveying party again, and she was beginning to relax her fears a little till one afternoon, when she was walking up the street towards the outskirts of the village where she knew the primroses grew, she saw someone coming out of the tall farmhouse that stood right on the village boundary, as bleak and forbidding as an armed guard. The farmer Craigie Scott, spying her in the roadway, raised an arm and came thundering down over the cobbles with a black and white collie dog running at his heels. 'Hey, Tibbie, wait a minute!' he was calling as he ran.

In an unconscious gesture of self-protection, she crossed her arms on her breast and awaited his approach. His tousled hair was standing up like a mop all round his head and his face was red and tense-looking. He was shabbily dressed and did not look prosperous, though village people knew that he was very rich indeed. There were rumoured to be leather bags full of money and other treasures stacked in secret places all over his farmhouse, but he was famous for his meanness and reluctance to spend any of it.

Apart from its legendary secret hoards of treasure, Craigie's house had two other distinctions. One was a stone set over the front door which was carved with a bull's head crowned by a wreath of laurel and surrounded by strange writing that no one could interpret. It had been dug up by a ploughman in 1584 and that date was carved on it too but it was much older, for it had originally been an altar stone in the Roman temple of Mithras that stood in the middle of what was now Craigie's hayfield. Unknown to any of the villagers, the words carved on it were in Hebrew.

The farmhouse's second distinction was the enormous orchard which surrounded it. This was the biggest and most productive in a village of orchards, walled to a height of twelve feet and full of ancient apple, pear and plum trees that showed a springtime frothing glory of blossom over the tops of the walls. There was no way into this paradise except through Craigie's house or by a little locked wooden gateway in the stone wall. The door was studded with big iron nails but some of the planks were warped and split by age so that passers-by could put their eyes to the gaps and peer into the forbidden world, where rosettes of pink and white flowers decorated the trailing tree branches and snowdrops and primroses spangled the grass. In autumn the fruit ripened and fell to the ground where it lay, a temptation to village children who lusted after Craigie's fruit although there was plenty in their own gardens. It was a rite of passage, like the manhood ceremonies of primitive tribes, for boys to stage raids on the farm orchard, but Craigie guarded his fruit assiduously and had been known to let off a blast of buckshot at the backsides of running boys when they breached his walls. This of course made the stealing of his apples and pears even more of a challenge.

Now the guardian of this paradise hurried towards Tibbie. His tacketty boots made a ringing sound on the stones of the road and he lifted his long stick in half-threatening salutation. Suspiciously she watched his approach. They were always polite to each other but she was afraid of him and with reason, for just before her marriage to Alex she had been stopped in the street by a furious Craigie, who shouted angrily at her that she should have married *him*.

'But we never walked out, you never asked me,' she protested, knowing full well that even if he had, she would not have considered it.

'I picked you out. I want you. You led me on, you made me think it was possible,' he yelled intemperately at her.

After Alex's funeral, to her horror and anger, Craigie came knocking at her door late one night. 'Let me in,' he whispered through the wooden panels and she replied roundly, 'Go away. Go away and don't ever come back or I'll set my brother on you.' He did so, but she was always conscious of the way he looked at her whenever they met.

Craigie never married anyone else. He lived with his two unmarried sisters in the big farmhouse and the girls, as they were still called though both were now nearing sixty, were even more peculiar than he was for they never went out at all and were loathed for their extreme greed and obsessive secrecy. No one was ever invited into their house and the door was guarded by the vicious, snarling sheepdog. If they were owed money, even by the poorest of the poor, they insisted on instant payment of the last farthing and never gave anything away, even unwanted rotting fruit. They would rather leave any surplus unused, and it was said that they crept out at night to pour milk into the village burn rather than give it to poor families who needed it.

All this ran through Tibbie's head as she watched Craigie running towards her. 'What does he want?' she asked herself, for she knew he was not one to waste time on idle pleasantries.

He was panting when he stopped beside her and his first words were, 'I hear you're against the railway too.'

She nodded her head. 'I don't want it.'

'I've warned the bastards off my land,' he said, as if expecting her to congratulate him. This was not unexpected: Craigie hated trespassers.

'They weren't on your land when I saw them,' she said.

He looked at her sharply. 'They're surveying for that railway line. They'll have to cross my land to get at it. I told them I'd shoot the first man to put a foot on my ground.'

Tibbie wondered how much money the railway company had offered him. His anger was perhaps a ploy to raise the price – she wouldn't put it past him. He was shaking slightly as he spoke, however, and was obviously under a great deal of strain. 'No navvies are going to cross my land. I told them that,' he repeated.

'What did they say?' she asked.

He grimaced. 'They said they'd come in from the other side, from Falconwood's land. He's given his permission, they told me.'

Tibbie's heart chilled as she remembered that only part of the land around the village belonged to Craigie, but nonetheless he'd be a formidable opponent and he had plenty of money to finance a fight. 'Maybe they'll move it away to the south if they know you're against them,' she suggested.

'Not a chance,' he said. 'South's the Duke's land and he's warned them off as well. It's the only time in fifty years that a duke's opinions and mine have agreed.' He laughed a strange cracked laugh that was very far from humorous.

'I'm like you. I don't want our peace to be destroyed by a railway,' she ventured.

He glared at her. 'Peace? I don't give a damn about peace. It's my land that worries me. I'm not having them digging it up. I'll shoot any bastard that puts a toe on it,' he shouted. His eyes were bloodshot and a line of dried spittle marked his lips.

She took a step away and tried to calm him by saying, 'Be careful, Craigie. If you try to shoot somebody they'll hang you.'

He did not even hear her, for his head was raised to the sky and he was shouting, 'I hope they're listening! I'll shoot every bastard one of them, that's what I'll do.'

Tibbie turned to flee. It terrified her to think that she and Craigie were on the same side in this dispute. She did not want to be associated with him. For the first time she began to question her attitude to the coming of the railway, but when she was back in her garden looking out over the empty field towards the serene hills on the horizon, she imagined what it would look like when the ground was cut across by a railway line and her fears came flooding back. The peace, the tranquil beauty of the Three Sisters and the dreaming valley would be ruined. 'Oh no, oh no,' sobbed Tibbie.

CHAPTER

Three

The kitchens at Bella Vista were the last word in modernity. Other country houses in the district had smoky, airless kitchens in the basement, but Colonel Anstruther's were high-ceilinged and gleaming, tiled from roof to floor in glossy white, and situated in a separate wing jutting out from the back of his mansion.

In fact the house he had built for himself when he returned from India was very unusual indeed. While the kitchens met with great approval from servants and a place at Bella Vista was greatly sought after among them, in the opinion of other landowners, Bella Vista was grotesque. Where their taste ran to gracious Palladian or Adam mansions, Anstruther had commissioned a pink stone Rajah's palace with turrets and minarets, pointed window-frames and a castellated walk laid out around the top of the roof. While it was under construction, carriages full of curious upper-class neighbours turned up every day to watch the emergence of this monstrosity, but when it was finished and the Colonel and his lady moved in, society studiously stayed away. A man who could live in a house like that wasn't quite their sort, they decided.

It was therefore unusual for the Anstruthers to hold parties but when they did, hospitality was lavish and the care taken immense. From dawn, the servants were whipped up into a frenzy of excitement by the butler Mr Allardyce, who was such a taskmaster that by noon several of the maids had collapsed into hysterics.

Hannah Mather was not the hysterical type, however. While chaos reigned in the kitchen, she remained outwardly calm, nodding her head when given a barrage of orders and keeping a smile on her lovely face. It was the first time she was to help at table for a large dinner and though she was slightly nervous inside, she managed to conceal how she felt.

The housekeeper, Mrs Clayton, who was Camptounfoot born and a friend of Hannah's mother, whispered in her ear, 'There's nothing to worry about. You'll be as right as rain. Just stand by the wall looking bonny and pass Mr Allardyce the dishes when he asks for them.'

Hannah smiled her serene smile and Mrs Clayton was glad she'd suggested this girl for the table-maid's place. Not only was Hannah a sensible lassie but she possessed a rare beauty that graced any room. Nor did she clump around like some of the other maids but moved smoothly and silently like a dancer, always gentle and discreet. Now she stood tall, willowy and straight, in the dark gown that made a stark contrast against the gleaming white kitchen wall. Her red-gold hair was pinned up high beneath the stiff lace cap, and two long streamers fell down the back of her neck. They tickled against her skin but Hannah was well aware that she must ignore the irritation. 'You're an asset to us,' whispered the housekeeper before she moved down the line of servant girls to chivvy the red-faced second table-maid Jessie for allowing her hair to come out of its pins.

At that moment Allardyce, the excitable butler, came charging into the noisy, frantic kitchen and clapped his hands to drive his army of maids up to the dining room. 'They're going in soon, they're going in now. Get to your places, hurry, hurry.'

The girls climbed the stairs, giggling among themselves about him, and as Hannah lifted her skirts to negotiate the steps she felt a surge of excitement. She had never attended a grand occasion before and was looking forward to it as eagerly as she would have done if she had been a guest and not a servant. She was determined to notice everything, remember every detail, so that she could regale her mother with the full story tomorrow. Tibbie loved hearing about the doings at Bella Vista. The

Anstruthers were like characters in an on-going novel to her.

Seven maids were lined up along the dark-green wall facing the long table when the double doors between the salon and the dining room were thrown open by two footmen and the procession of diners advanced. Mrs Maria Anstruther, plump and straining the seams of her pink satin crinoline gown, led the way on the arm of a tall, supercilious-looking man in his mid-forties. This, the maids knew, was an Edinburgh gentleman called Sir Geoffrey Miller who was guest-of-honour and was staying with the Anstruthers for a few days. Behind the leading couple walked Colonel Anstruther himself in his scarlet and gold military uniform. On his arm leaned Lady Miller, a whey-faced, feeble-looking woman who, the kitchen gossips knew, travelled with two maids, a nurse and an enormous box of medicines and potions for her various ailments. The other guests filed in at the back of their host and hostess – four dark-suited men from Edinburgh who had arrived without their wives and, the only recognisable local faces, Raeburn of Falconwood, the next-door estate, with his jolly wife who had a very loud voice and a great liking for claret.

Hannah eagerly watched the advancing procession as the ladies were handed into their chairs. She was disappointed at the lack of fashion or style among the three women. Lady Miller was wearing dull grey that matched her skin, while Mrs Raeburn was in a shabby blue gown that looked none too clean. Mrs Anstruther outshone them all, not by her unsuitably girlish pink gown, but because of the jewels with which she was richly adorned. Tonight she was wearing rubies and diamonds – hanging from her ears, clasped around her neck, pinned to her bosom in a huge brooch, and made into bangles for her plump wrists. The value of the stones that glittered from her must have been immense.

The appointments of the dining room, one wall of which was lined with tall looking glasses and the other with long windows overlooking the gardens, were all contrived to echo the hostess's ostentatious display of wealth. Tubs of palms and white-trumpeted daturas filled the corners, and the long table stretching down the middle of the floor was draped in white linen and adorned with heavily chased silver ornaments. Beside the Colonel's chair stood a massive silver wine cooler containing half a dozen bottles of champagne, and another urn, almost as large, stood in the middle of the table full of tropical flowers that scented the air with a heavy sweetness. At every place was lined a battery of wine glasses in varying sizes, and cutlery that looked too heavy to lift. What Hannah most admired was the cunning way the napkins were folded so that they looked like little castles. It seemed a pity to her when the guests opened them carelessly, shook them out and draped them over their knees.

When everyone was seated, the first course, pale jellied consommé, was carried in and gilded plates reverently placed before the diners. Spoons were raised and voice hushed, when suddenly the solemn atmosphere was shattered by the sound of a coachman's horn and the crunch of horses' hooves and carriage-wheels on the gravel outside the windows.

The Colonel dropped his spoon with a clatter and an exclamation. 'Who the hell is that, arriving at this time of night? Go and send them packing, Allardyce.'

Before the butler had time to do as he was bid, however, the dining-room door flew open and a young man came bursting in. With both arms extended he advanced on Mrs Anstruther's chair while the servants and other guests stared open-mouthed. The hostess sat goggling for a few seconds, then she stood up and held out her arms as well. 'Gus, my darling Gus!' she cried, and burst into tears. After that she stared up the table at her husband and called out, 'It's Gus, my dear. It's Gus – back from Bombay!'

The Colonel was on his feet. 'Good God, so it is. We didn't expect you, Gus.'

The newcomer was beaming. His resemblance to his mother was marked, for both of them had the same tightly curling blond hair, flushed complexion and round cheeks, the same blue eyes set in folds of fat. They looked like a pair of happy porkers as they hugged each other. When the hugging stopped a woman's lilting voice came from the doorway. 'Introduce me to your parents, Gus dear,' it said. All eyes swivelled to the darkness of the hall, where the slim outline of a female figure could be seen silhouetted against the candlelight cast down by the wall-braziers.

This stranger stepped forward and revealed herself to be a dark-haired young woman dressed in a well-cut, claret-red travelling costume and a little hat with a swirling feather that lay against her cheek. Romantic Hannah, who was closest to the door, blinked at the sight of this apparition, revealed as dark-haired and ivory-skinned with merry triangular eyes above prominent slanting cheekbones and a sweetly curving mouth. She was by far the best-looking young woman anyone in the room had ever seen.

Gus stepped towards her and announced without much enthusiasm, 'This is my wife Bethya.' The young woman beamed on the company. It was obvious that she had boundless confidence and was not a bit abashed at being introduced to her new parents-in-law in such an unconventional and half-hearted way.

The Colonel was the first to speak. 'Well done, boy! She's a beauty,' he said. Then he walked across the floor and took the girl's hand. 'Welcome to our home, Bethya. Come and sit down. You must be hungry after your journey. Allardyce, bring more chairs. My daughter-in-law will sit by me. D'ye like champagne, my dear?'

She flirted at him from her lovely eyes. 'I adore champagne,' she said, peeling off her ivory-coloured gloves and unpinning her little hat, which she handed to Hannah who happened to be standing nearest. With the hat off she looked even prettier because her hair was thick, very black and glossy, tumbling round her neck in glorious ringlets which she tossed back to fetching effect not wasted on the open-mouthed men around her.

One person in the company was not impressed, how-

46

ever. Gus' mother sat staring bleakly at her son's new wife with her eyes narrowed and her mouth pursed tight. Bethya smiled down the table and walked its length to plant a kiss on the pink cheek but Mrs Anstruther flinched at the contact between them. This insult did not seem to make any impression on the pretty stranger, who swept back to her seat beside the Colonel and sat herself down prettily in the chair that the servants carried in for her.

It said a lot for Allardyce's organisational abilities that the dinner was re-started and ran as smoothly as clockwork. Throughout it, the new Mrs Anstruther chattered and flirted, smiled and conquetted, casting her spell over all the guests except her mother-in-law. The more Maria Anstruther gazed at the stranger the more her eyes hardened, and from time to time she patted her son's hand as if in commiseration. 'Where did you meet her?' she whispered to him at last.

'Bombay,' he said in reply.

His mother sat back. 'I thought so. Oh Gus, you shouldn't have done it.' He said nothing but lifted his wine glass and swigged down an immense draught of best Bordeaux before calling for the glass to be refilled.

Meanwhile, at the other end of the table Bethya had everyone under her spell, drawing them out with artful, innocent questions, never appearing challenging or clever but always eager to listen to the opinions of those older and wiser than herself. When the man opposite her was introduced as Falconwood, she smiled and said, 'What a pretty surname. I've never heard it before.'

'Oh, it's not our name. It's the name of his place. We're called Raeburn,' said Falconwood's wife, leaning forward.

'Raeburn – like the painter?' asked Bethya, but it was immediately obvious that neither of the Raeburns had ever heard of their famous namesake.

Sir Geoffrey Miller, sitting two places up from Bethya, was an art connoisseur, however, and his eyes glittered with interest as he asked her, 'Are you interested in art, Mrs Anstruther?'

'Oh, very much so,' cried the girl, clasping her hands.

'I'm so looking forward to touring the exhibitions. I hear there are some very good galleries in Edinburgh. I didn't have much opportunity to see great European art in India, but I'll remedy that now I've come home.'

At this point Mrs Anstruther senior spoke in a sarcastic voice. 'Home? Which part of the country do you come from exactly, my dear?'

Bethya's smile did not falter but she knew the knives were out between them. Coolly she replied, 'My papa comes from Somerset and my mama's family are from Wales.'

'That explains your accent,' said Maria. 'I expect you know Wales well.'

'I've never been there,' said Bethya flatly.

The Colonel's lady lifted an eyebrow. 'So you grew up in India?'

'Yes, in Bombay. I was born there.'

'And your mother?'

'She was born in Bombay too . . .'

'Aaah, I thought so. Two generations Bombay-born . . .' Mrs Anstruther sounded pleased. A dangerous light flashed in Bethya's eye but her sweet smile remained in place. Like a dog worrying a bone, Gus' mother returned to the attack. 'Tell me about your family,' she said in honeyed tones.

Bethya's face became serious. 'I've five sisters and my parents are both alive. I miss them all very much.' There was genuine sadness in her voice as she spoke, for to even think of her absent family gave her a pain in the heart that took all her ebullience to conceal.

'Your father is Army?' asked Mrs Anstruther.

A shake of the head was the reply. 'No, he's a merchant.'

'Selling what?'

'Carpets.'

'*Trade*.' It was spoken like an accusation. Then Mrs Anstruther furrowed her brow. 'But how did you meet Gus? Trade and military don't usually mix.'

A tinge of colour rose in Bethya's pale cheeks but she

48

maintained her coolness as she said with a fond smile at her silent husband who had done nothing to prevent his mother grilling her, 'Dear Gus and I met at a military review. We were introduced by my cousin's husband who is in Skinner's Horse.'

The situation was saved by the Colonel, who attempted to end the inquisition by crying out, 'Skinner's Horse? A great regiment! I once met Skinner himself when I was a young chokra!'

His wife glared at him. 'It's an irregular regiment. It's not a regiment for gentlemen.' Then she sat back, satisfied.

Colonel Anstruther could see how the situation was developing between his wife and his new daughter-in-law. He glanced at Gus who sat slumped in his chair, head down, determinedly drinking wine. It was obvious he was not going to step in to prevent Bethya from being savaged by his mother. The Colonel's eyes were sharp as he detected signs in his son that he would have counted against any junior officer in his regiment – the slack mouth, the pouched eyes, the shaking hands, all signs of a drunkard. The last time they had met, Gus was a junior officer fresh from school but even then, his father had to admit, he was idle and slovenly. Now, he told himself bitterly, his only son was a wastrel. That was why he had come home without any warning. 'I wonder if he was told to go?' he asked himself uneasily. 'I wonder if he was cashiered? And why has he come home with this pretty piece, when he appears to have no interest in her at all?'

The remainder of the meal went off smoothly because the Colonel's wife caught a glance from her husband that warned her to draw in her claws, and since he was the only person in the world of whom she was afraid, she behaved more temperately until, as dessert was being served, her son suddenly slumped forward in his chair and his face fell into the creamy confection on his plate.

The Colonel's wife gave a half-scream. 'Poor Gus has fainted! He's tired out, that's what's wrong.'

Allardyce the butler rushed forward and righted the unconscious figure. He knew very well what was wrong

49

with Gus. Singlehandedly the Colonel's son had managed to dispose of a bottle of champagne, three of claret and two of port. His expression gave nothing away, however, as he indicated to the footmen to lift Gus from his chair and carry him out of the room while his father, who had also been noting his son's intake of alcohol, watched with unconcealed distaste.

Gus' collapse was a signal for the women to leave the table and they clustered in the doorway while the men stood up. 'We're going to discuss business now so perhaps it would be best if you don't expect us to join you in the drawing room,' said the Colonel. Most of them didn't mind at all. Lady Miller looked exhausted, Bethya was tired and Mrs Anstruther furious. Only Raeburn's wife was disappointed that the evening was to end so abruptly, but she put a good face on it by saying cheerfully, 'I'll take myself off home, then. Come when you're ready, Raeburn old boy.'

When they were all in the hall bidding goodnight to each other, the footmen staggered past bearing Gus' lifeless body and Bethya turned to give them orders. 'Put him in a dressing room or somewhere on his own. That's how he usually sleeps it off.'

No one else had admitted that Gus was drunk, and his mother glared at the girl in fury but all the young woman did was smile sweetly, bid them good night and run upstairs after her drunken husband as if Gus collapsing in the pudding was an everyday occurrence. She was jubilant at having discomfited the horrible woman who had taunted her so cruelly throughout the meal.

Once inside her bedroom however, Bethya stood stock still for a moment and then raised both clenched fists above her head in a furious gesture. Her eyes were flashing and she radiated a kind of electrical energy that filled the air around her. 'I hate that woman! I really hate her. I wonder if this has been worth the trouble. Perhaps Papa was right,' she hissed.

Her dark-clad maid was standing at the toilet table where she had been arranging her mistress's brushes, combs and unguent bottles. She looked up and revealed a strange, triangular-shaped face with very wide-set eyes, a long flaring-nostrilled nose and a tiny mouth. When Bethya first saw Francine she thought the maid looked like a cobra, and some long-forgotten racial memory of reverence for snakes stirred in her. Out of all the demure girls sent for her inspection by the London agency when she and Gus had disembarked from the ship that carried them home, the reptilian-looking young Frenchwoman was the one she chose. It proved to be a good choice, for the two rapidly became friends, and were far more intimate than would usually have been the case between maid and mistress – but Bethya was lonely. Her husband ignored her, she had no friend and she sorely missed the company and confidences of her sisters. Francine became the only person she could talk to.

Seeing her mistress fuming in the middle of the room, the maid asked in her strongly accented voice, 'What did your father say when you wanted to get married?'

'He told me not to marry Gus. He said I'd regret it.'

Francine nodded. 'But you married him anyway. Did you think you were in love?'

Bethya calmed down a little and looked at her maid as if she were simple-minded. '*Love*? Of course not. You don't imagine I could fall in love with someone like that, do you? Anyway, I think love's just a feeling silly women have for equally silly men. Gus is my *laisser passer* to the great world. I'm a Bombay chi-chi girl, so who was going to marry me and take me out of India? Nobody. They'd bed me quick enough, they'd make me a mistress but they wouldn't marry me. He married me because he had to find a wife quickly to save his face. There was some scandal about drummer boys and talk of him being disgraced. What with the drink and the other things, he was in deep trouble. Oh, don't look like that. I knew what I was doing. I wanted to go to a place where people wouldn't point a finger at me and whisper "coloured", "half-Indian", "chi-chi". God, I hate that word! You know what it means, don't you? It means dirt, shit – *merde* in your language. That's what they call us in India. Indians and whites both call us that. It's so horrible and unfair. If you could see my lovely sisters and compare them with those women downstairs and hear them called chi-chi!' The fists went up in the air again in an impotent gesture.

Fervently the maid said, 'But you're so beautiful! How can they call you a name like that?'

Bethya shrugged. 'There's girls as beautiful as me walking the streets of Bombay as whores. When I was fifteen I looked in my mirror one day and I saw that the way I look is all I've got, and I swore then that I was going to use it. I'm not going to stop using it till I've got where I want, and Bella Vista with Gus Anstruther is only a small step on the way. I wish I could tell his hideous old mother that. She might not be so horrible to me if she knew I've no plans to stay around for long.'

'What did she say to you?' asked Francine curiously.

'The usual memsahib type of things. Where do your parents come from? Why do you speak with such a funny accent? Insinuations, jabs. She more or less said that I was a native.'

The maid raised her eyebrows. 'But . . .'

'You're going to say I am. But nobody here knows nor cares – only her. The old man likes me – he'll be no trouble. She's a bitch, though, a typical Colonel's wife – down on everything and everyone.'

Calmer now that she had unburdened herself, Bethya sat down on a stool before the looking glass and the maid began unpinning her wonderful hair. As she worked Francine said, 'The servants downstairs have been telling me that your husband's father is very, very rich. Perhaps his mother thinks you married her son for his money. They say the house is full of treasures brought home from India, some very wonderful things.'

Bethya nodded. 'They're right. I've seen some of them already, and I knew Gus' father was rich. Colonel Anstruther was famous in India for his avarice. He took bribes from all the princes – jewellery, gold, ivory, silks –

anything that was valuable. He was a byword in the Army: 'As greedy as Anstruther or a man-eating tiger', they used to say. Of course I married Gus for his fortune! Even a girl who looks like me can't make her way in the world without money. I have to get some before I start, and I'll get it from Gus.'

She knew she should not be talking like this to a maid, but even though they had only been together now for a month, she trusted the strange, quiet French girl completely. They were allies. Putting up a hand she touched the maid's arm and said confidingly, 'Stay with me, Francine, and you'll share in my fortune – I promise.'

A starry look came into the maid's large eyes. 'I'll stay with you,' she said. Her hands stroked the torrent of glossy hair and she added, 'I'm sure you'll succeed. You'll take the fashionable world by storm. Look at your hair – it's glorious, so thick and glossy and such a wonderful colour.' She held up a strand that shone like blue-black silk in her fingers.

Bethya laughed. 'I'm lucky. When I was small my ayah used to rub coconut oil into my head every Saturday night. I hated the smell and the way it felt, but it worked. My sisters wouldn't let her do it to them and their hair isn't nearly as thick as mine.'

'I'll rub oil into your hair if you want,' said her maid eagerly but Bethya shook her head.

'Oh no, there's no need for that now. What you can do for me is gather all the gossip you hear in the servants' hall. Tell me everything. Information is always useful.'

'Of course,' agreed the maid, and bent to her task of brushing out the lovely hair. The expression on her face was like that of an acolyte at the temple of a pagan goddess.

After the ladies left the dining room, Colonel Anstruther's manner changed and he became again the formidable character who had cut a swathe through many Indian battlefields and squeezed gold out of countless reluctant princely fists. 'Don't let's dicker about any longer. You came here to talk about the railway, didn't you? What's in it for me if I decide to throw my hand in with yours?' he abruptly asked Sir Geoffrey Miller.

Their eyes met and Miller looked at the line of tired-looking serving maids. Anstruther beckoned the butler. 'Let the girls go, man. Only keep what you need to serve our wine, and make sure they're discreet.'

Allardyce ushered his staff out of the room and told them, 'I need one maid and one man to help me. Who'll volunteer?' It was a rhetorical question for he'd already made up his mind who he wanted, a quick young lad called Allan, and Hannah Mather, the bonniest and brightest of the maids. He pointed to them. 'You and you, come back in with me. I'll make it up to you. You can both have a day off tomorrow.'

When they returned to the dining room, the men were smoking cigars and the Colonel was asking the party from Edinburgh, 'Let's get started. What sort of bundobust have you got to offer me?'

Miller's eyebrows went up. He did not know the meaning of the Indian word and he wished Anstruther would speak plain English. The Colonel saw his confusion and repeated, 'What sort of deal will you offer for my land?'

'A very good one,' said Miller.

Anstruther leaned forward with his sharp little eyes fixed on his opponent's face. 'Tell me exactly why I should throw in my lot with you and not join up with my aristocratic neighbours to freeze you out.'

'We'll give you a directorship. We'll give you shares. When it's finished, this line will be one of the most profitable in the country because there's no opposition and the manufacturers in Maddiston are crying out for a railway. So are the big farmers – they want to reach more markets.'

Anstruther nodded. 'How many shares for me? I'm not going into anything where I'll only be a toady bacha. I want to be one of the main men in the company. I want to be a major shareholder.'

'You can always invest in us,' said Miller sharply, and Anstruther grinned sardonically. 'Why buy something that you might be given?' he asked. The qualities which had amassed him a fortune in the East were very obvious in him now. 'I could invest or I could stay out, and if I stay out there won't be a railway line down here. You need my land for the next section.'

'We have Falconwood's land,' said Miller, pointing to his neighbour at the table.

'Falconwood only has a strip. You can build a bridge on his land but without my spread, it'll lead nowhere.' Anstruther was obviously enjoying himself.

Miller changed his tactics, leaned back and smiled. 'Of course we are very aware of your value to our enterprise. We'll make you a director and as part of your emolument you'll have thirty thousand shares.'

Anstruther smiled back, all aggression gone. 'And how many are there altogether?'

'Five hundred thousand.'

'Not bad. It's almost enough for me to agree to make my family social pariahs, because that's what we'll be when it gets out that we've sided with you. The Duke and his toadies will cut us dead.' He didn't say that they'd cut him already anyway and he didn't care a fig.

'Would forty-thousand shares soften the blow?' asked Miller.

Anstruther threw back his head and laughed. 'I wonder if my new daughter-in-law would rather be rich, or patronised by the aristocracy?' he asked aloud. Then he answered his own question. 'From the look of her, I'd say she'd rather be rich. I'm in.' Then he reached down to the floor to haul up another bottle of champagne from the cooler and beckoned to the red-haired maid to bring more glasses.

Hannah moved quietly, not drawing attention to herself and making sure that the keen interest she took in what was being said went unremarked. Though she was tired and her back ached with the effort of standing stock-still, hands folded, by the wall, she was glad Mr Allardyce had chosen her to help him. What was being discussed, she knew, was the fate of her village and her heart ached with sympathy for her mother for, though she herself was not against the coming of a railway, she knew how much it upset Tibbie and others like her.

Her ears were pricked as the Colonel started discussing the building of the railway bridge. 'That's going to be your biggest hurdle,' he told Miller. 'It's going to have to go at a difficult place if it crosses Falconwood's land. Who's going to build it for you?'

Miller looked up from his glass and said, 'I know of the very man. His name is Christopher Wylie.'

'I've heard of Wylie,' said Falconwood, turning in his chair. 'He's famous. Didn't he build the big bridge at Berwick? He'll not build our bridge unless we pay him a fortune.'

Miller nodded. 'Yes, he built that bridge and he's also the man who put in a fortune with George Hudson and lost the lot. He's desperate for money now. My cousin Thomas Munro is his banker in Newcastle and I know to a penny what he owes. Wylie'll build our bridge – and he'll build it at our price.'

'That's what I like to hear,' Falconwood gloated. 'I'll leave the organising to you. We have a deal then, have we? I'm in if you are, Anstruther.'

The stout little Colonel stood up and struck out his hand. 'I'm in too. You've got a railway, gentlemen – just make sure it's finished quickly and starts bringing in money as soon as possible. Now it's time to go to bed, it's past midnight.'

It was almost noon next day when Hannah arrived at her mother's front door. When she turned the handle she found to her surprise that it was locked. No one locked their doors in Camptounfoot unless they had something to hide, so she ran to the little window overlooking the street and rapped on it with anxious fingers, shouting, 'Mam, Mam, let me in. What's wrong?'

When Tibbie unlocked the door her daughter asked,

'Why were you locked in? Has Craigie been bothering you again?'

'No, I'm feared of these navvies that folk say are moving into Rosewell.'

Hannah giggled, 'You're the limit. If it's not one thing, it's another.' Then she remembered the bad news she was bringing and said more soberly, 'Come and sit down while I tell you what I heard last night. I don't want you to get too upset, but they are going to build the railway line through here – and they're building a bridge as well. The Colonel's going in with them.'

Tibbie's face was stricken. 'Then it won't be stopped now, will it? Where's the bridge to go?'

'Across the big field where Craigie grazes his bullocks. They had plans of the land with them last night. They said that's the best place.'

Tibbie gasped, 'My God, that bonny field! Craigie'll be taking pot shots at anybody who even puts a foot on it. We're in for awfy trouble, I feel it in my bones.'

Hannah sighed, 'Apparently that's not Craigie's field – he only rents it from Falconwood. That's why they can take it back. A man called Wylie's going to build it for them. I heard them talking about him. He needs the money, so they say.'

Her mother stood listening and wringing her hands. 'Oh Hannah, everything's going to change. Nothing'll ever be the same again.'

Hannah clasped Tibbie round the waist. 'Oh Mam, don't worry. It won't be as bad as you think, I'm sure it won't. What are you so scared about?'

Tibbie shook her head. 'I'm feared of the trains and I'm feared for the village. I've not seen the marching men this year and I think I may never see them again ... I'm feared that something bad's going to happen. I don't know what – I've just got this awful feeling.'

Hannah shook her gently. 'Stop it now, Mam. Nothing bad's going to happen. You mustn't think like that, it's unlucky.'

'Oh Hannah, you're young,' Tibbie wailed, 'you don't

understand what an upheaval this means to us older folk. There's people in this village that have stopped speaking to each other over the head of it. It's splitting us up and that's only the start.'

Hannah tried to laugh. 'Does it matter much if you don't speak to Bob and Mamie any more? Come on Mam, be sensible. It's not like you to act the goat. You're not like daft Craigie or silly old Jo . . .' She pulled some faces and eventually succeeded in making her mother laugh a little. Then Tibbie looked into her girl's frank and honest brown eyes that shone with common sense and sympathy. 'Oh, you're the kindest girl that's ever walked the world. I am being silly, amn't I? Why do I worry about the village so much when the most important thing in the world for me is you!' she cried and hugged Hannah close.

They spent a peaceful gossipy afternoon together and Tibbie was regaled with every detail about the dinner party and the dramatic arrival of the Colonel's son and his lovely, exotic wife. She couldn't hear enough about Bethya and had to be told again and again what she looked like, and what she wore.

Hannah had good powers of description and recreated the scene with panache, saying dreamily, 'Oh Mam, you've never seen such a bonny woman in your life. She's got the blackest hair and her face looks as if it was carved from ivory. All the servants are saying they can't imagine why she married that fat hulk, young Mr Gus. He never gives her a kind look either.'

Tibbie, fascinated, shook her head. 'There'll be trouble there then, mark my words.' They gossiped and speculated until it was four o'clock and Hannah had to leave. Her mother waved her off from the front door, calling after her, 'Next time you come we'll go for a walk, Hannah. It's a long time since we had one of our walks.'

'All right, next time . . .' came Hannah's voice, echoing back along the empty street. She knew her mother wanted them to walk the old paths that might soon disappear under the new railway.

CHAPTER
Four

A smart carriage bowled up to the front door of a large, imposing bank at the end of Newcastle's Neville Street, and a fine-looking gentleman emerged from it to stand on the pavement and stare up at the building's windows for a second. Then, pulling down the sleeves of his jacket with a determined air, he approached the bank's door with its gleaming brass handles and enormous knocker. Christopher Wylie was deadly tired, both in mind and body, but he knew he must not show it, especially today, for he had a very important appointment with Thomas Munro, his banker.

Munro was waiting for him. He stood up when Wylie entered the room, but his demeanour was grave and there was no welcoming decanter of sherry and gleaming glasses on the desk top. Only customers who were in credit were treated to sherry. Munro surprised his caller, however, by walking round his desk and coming forward with one hand out-thrust. 'I was sorry to hear about your tragedy,' he said solemnly.

Wylie's handsome face wore a stricken expression but only for a moment. Recovering his composure he said, 'Thank you. We all found it hard to bear. My wife's still not come to terms with it . . .'

'I lost a son when he was small – younger than yours, though. My lad was nine.'

Christopher nodded. 'James was twenty-five. It's a tragedy at whatever age.'

'Sit down,' said Munro, pulling out a chair, 'and tell me what I can do for you today. Your letter said you'd a proposition for me.'

The caller nodded. 'I have. I've been given the chance to bid for a big contract in the north. There's good reason to believe that it's mine for the asking, but I need the money to finance my offer.'

Munro knew as much if not more about the contract in question than his caller, but he kept his face impassive and nodded his head slowly. 'How much money do you need?' he asked.

Wylie raised his white head and fixed pale-blue eyes on the banker's face. 'I need ten thousand pounds now and another ten later.'

The banker sat back in his chair and shook his head. 'Not possible, old man, not possible. You're in to us for ten thousand already. I can't double your debt, far less treble it. The shareholders would never stand for that.'

'You'll be paid back with interest in two years. You know me, I'm an honest man. I only owe money because of Hudson's crash. I'll pay it all back when I get this bridge job.'

'What if you don't?'

A flash of anger showed in Wylie's eyes. His proud spirit hated being put in the position of a beggar. 'I'll pay my debts anyway. I'm not finished yet. There's other bridges to be built and I've a good reputation.'

Munro hastened to agree with him. 'The best, the best, I don't doubt it.' He knew the history of the man before him. Christopher Wylie was a self-made man, born in Newcastle to a poor family, who'd succeeded through enterprise and incredibly hard work. Starting when he was still in his teens, he'd prospered through the years of Railway Mania, building bridges and stations, viaducts and embankments. His reputation was impeccable – he played fair and gave good value for money. It was not his fault that he was short of money at a time in his life when he should have been contemplating retiring to a life of ease. He'd invested with his old friend, George Hudson, the Railway King, and when Hudson crashed, many of his friends went down with him – Wylie not as far as some of the others.

'Tell me about this bridge,' said Munro in a more mollified tone, and Wylie leaned forward with his hands knotted on his lap.

'It's not going to be easy,' he admitted. 'I've seen the specifications and it's to go on a very difficult site. But it'll be a challenge. I think it'll be my last bridge and I want it to be my best.'

Munro smiled. 'Then it'll be something very special, for you've built a lot of fine bridges in your career.'

'Oh, it will be special, it will be! I'm probably the only man in the country who can build it and I've an idea in my mind that'll make it very special indeed.' Wylie unlocked his hands and spread them out in a wide gesture. He wasn't boasting idly and both of them knew it. His genuine enthusiasm even infected the cautious man on the other side of the desk.

'I'd like to help you,' said Munro, 'but are you sure you'll be paid fairly and on time?' He wished he could drop his mask and lean across the desk to tell Wylie, 'Watch out for Miller. He may be my own cousin, but he's as slippery as an eel.'

'Oh, I'll be paid,' was the reply. 'The bridge is being built over the Tweed by a consortium of local landowners and railway men from Edinburgh. They're crossing untapped country so it's bound to do well. They've hit on a money-maker, but they need this bridge and they've come to me for it.'

He wanted to say to Munro, 'Please back me. This is my last chance and I know it. If I can get this job I'll be able to recover some of my lost position and leave my family comfortable when I die. Listen to me, listen, listen.' But he was a proud man and he recoiled from too much self-revelation.

'Twenty thousand is a lot of money,' said Munro cautiously.

'But it won't be just any bridge. This is going to be a thing of beauty,' said Wylie with conviction.

The banker sank his head in his hands. 'Oh God, man,

you can't afford a thing of beauty. Why don't you just build them an ordinary, workmanlike bridge?'

Wylie shook his head. 'But I've told you – this is going to be my last bridge, my swan song. I want to go out on a high note and this is my chance to do it. How much will you back me for?'

Munro looked up. 'Ten thousand, only ten thousand. No second instalment.'

Wylie jumped to his feet, as agile as a man half his age, 'That'll have to do, then. When can I get it?'

'When do you need it?'

'I'm going to Scotland tomorrow to talk terms and see the site. I'll come back next week and tell you whether or not they're going to sign with me. Don't worry, you'll not lose your money, and I'll build a good bridge, even if I have to kill myself in the attempt.'

Munro felt admiration for the man as he stood up to shake hands once again. 'I hope very sincerely you don't kill yourself, Mr Wylie, and get a good safe contract with the railway company. Don't leave any loopholes or they'll catch you out.'

'At least I've warned him,' he thought, 'but business is business and every man must watch out for himself.' Whatever happened the bank would get its money, for what he had not told Wylie was that he and his fellow directors were also shareholders in the Edinburgh and South of Scotland Railway Company.

When he found himself on the pavement again, Christopher Wylie tilted his head to stare at a patch of blue sky that showed above the towering roofs of recently erected buildings. He'd made his first fortune here and lost it again, but now he intended to make another. 'I must, I must,' he told himself. 'I can't die and leave my family victims of the bankers. I can't leave them penniless when they think they're rich. I'll recover my position,' he vowed to himself.

Haggerty the coachman, who'd been with Wylie for thirty years, was waiting in a side street, and when he saw his employer come round the corner, he lifted the reins and sat up straight with a quizzical look on his face. Climbing in behind him, Wylie said, 'Your job's all right for another six months. I got the money.'

Haggerty grinned, showing broken teeth. 'Well done, Chris,' he said. As was the case with Cockburn, there was no master-and-servant constraint between them when they were alone, but Haggerty would never have acted so familiarly if anyone else had been present.

'Take me home,' said Wylie, slumping back against the cushioned wall and closing his eyes. It was a relief to have a smart carriage to drive about in, for a man had to keep up appearances and he was glad that he did not have to make his way home by public conveyance. He could sit back, doze a little and let Haggerty do the driving. His bones ached and his head throbbed. He felt very old indeed. In fact he'd felt that way for the past nine months, ever since the terrible day they'd laid his son James in his grave. James, his only son, his heir, his successor. It was to James that he had intended to pass down his business. Now there was no one to take it over, but he could not stop working himself till he'd put things back on a firm footing, made it worth selling to one of his eagerly watching rivals.

Home was Wyvern Villa, a redbrick house built in the suburb of Jesmond. It stood in the middle of large gardens, its façade topped with a tower like an Italian campanile that ended in a big iron weather vane. The windows in the tower had little leaded lights that cast patterns of bright colours over the floors inside, and the front door was studded like the gate of a mediaeval castle and adorned with an iron knocker in the shape of a mailed fist. Mrs Wylie loved Wyvern Villa but Christopher much preferred the old Georgian, flat-fronted house near the docks where they had lived until she persuaded him that their growing prosperity meant they ought to move to a better district.

'After all, we've a daughter to marry off and she must move in the right society,' his wife had said.

Wylie was asleep when the carriage rattled to a stop at

his front door. Haggerty turned round and poked him on the shoulder with his whip at the same time as the door opened. A thin, pale girl came running down the steps and opened the carriage door. 'Oh Papa, you do look tired. Come in at once and I'll bring you some tea,' she told him.

'Make it a brandy, Emma Jane,' he said as he climbed out. 'I'm celebrating because I think I'm going to get that bridge I've been bidding for.'

She clasped her hands in pleasure. 'That's wonderful! I know you want to build it. It'll give you something to take your mind off James, won't it?'

All he said was, 'Yes, that's right. It'll keep me busy. Now lead me to the brandy.'

In the first-floor drawing room his pretty wife Arabella was lying on a long divan with a Paisley shawl draped over her legs. Her plump face was strained and a handkerchief dangled from the hand that hung slackly down towards the floor. Wylie paused in the doorway and smiled at her but she only smiled faintly back. His heart filled with love and pity for he knew she could not come to terms with losing James.

'How are you this evening, my dear?' he asked, walking softly across the floor.

She gave a sob as she answered, 'I was thinking about James. Do you remember the day he went into the fields and gathered a big bunch of flowers for me? At least he thought they were flowers but they were weeds really. He was such a sweet boy.'

Her husband nodded bleakly. 'I remember. You must stop thinking about him all the time Arabella, you're making yourself ill.'

Piteously she sobbed, 'I can't stop. He's in my mind day and night. I wake up thinking about him and I fall asleep thinking about him. It's so cruel. He was so young, he had everything to live for. Oh, I wish it was me who'd died and not him!'

In anguish Wylie knelt by the side of her couch. 'My dear, it was an accident. There's nothing we could have done to prevent it. His horse threw him and he broke his neck. It was God's will. All we can do is endure and take care of his wife and daughter.'

She wiped her eyes with the sodden handkerchief. 'Oh yes, I agree, but Amelia doesn't seem to want to be taken care of. Sometimes I think she's forgotten about James already. I heard her laughing and actually singing in her apartment this afternoon. I had to send Emma Jane to ask her to keep quiet and respect my mourning.'

He remonstrated gently with her. 'My dear, Amelia's only young. You can't expect her to mourn forever. You can't expect her to die of grief.'

Arabella looked up with tear-filled eyes. 'Oh Christopher, of course I don't. It's just that we can't seem to be able to talk to each other. Anything I say she takes the wrong way.'

He frowned, for he knew that Arabella tended to speak before she thought and might well have hurt Amelia unwittingly. 'I'll speak to her for you,' he offered and she gripped his hand as she said, 'Oh Christopher, please do. It's awful having an atmosphere in the house. It's so bad for poor little Arbelle.'

He stood up and looked around. 'Where is Arbelle? I'd like to see her.' At that moment the drawing-room door opened and his daughter Emma Jane appeared carrying a tray with the brandy decanter and his favourite glass on it. She put her burden down on a side table and he nodded, indicating with two outspread fingers how much brandy he would like poured. When that task was completed Arabella said, 'Fetch poor Arbelle for your Papa, Emma Jane. He hasn't seen the little darling today.'

Emma Jane smiled and hurried away to do her mother's bidding. Christopher noticed how her impassive little face was transformed by a smile. When solemn she looked quite frumpish, but a smile turned her into an impish little thing with a scattering of freckles over the tops of her cheeks and across her nose. The way she wore her hair scraped tight back from her pointed face added to the elfin look.

She was still smiling when she came back a few moments later with a doll of a child hanging on to her hand. This was four-year-old Arbelle, daughter of the dead James and his wife Amelia. All the Wylies were convinced that Arbelle was the prettiest, cleverest, most entrancing little girl in the world. When she saw Christopher she dropped her aunt's hand and ran to him with both little arms held out, her golden curls flying, and lisping, 'Oh Grandpa, Grandpa, what have you brought me? Is it a thugar mouse?'

Three pairs of female eyes looked expectantly at him and he said defensively to them, 'Oh my dear, I've been at my bank. They don't sell sugar mice in banks.'

Arabella bent towards the little girl and said in the high, fluting voice she always used when addressing the child, 'Isn't Grandpa naughty? He's forgotten your sugar mouse. Will we send the kitchen-maid out to buy you one?'

'I want two,' pouted Arbelle.

'Two then,' agreed her grandmother.

At that moment another voice spoke up from the open drawing-room door. 'She don't need no sugar mice. She'll be puking up all night if she eats two of 'em.'

Mrs Wylie hoisted herself up from her cushions and said in a ladylike voice that contrasted with the strong Northumbrian accent and lack of grammar of her daughter-in-law, 'Oh, a sugar mouse will do poor Arbelle no harm, surely, Amelia?'

'Yes it will. She'll be as sick as a dog,' said the child's mother, advancing into the room and shaking a finger at her daughter. 'I told her she weren't to 'ave any sugar mice today and she knows it.'

'Oh poor Arbelle,' sighed Mrs Wylie, sinking down again and rolling her eyes.

Arbelle's little face squeezed up and the tears began to flow. Her mother, however, was unaffected by her grief. She grabbed her daughter's hand and said, 'You were trying it on, weren't you? You're a little monkey.'

The likeness between mother and daughter was striking.

Both had faces like flowers – pink-cheeked and round – both had blue eyes and full lips, and both had tousled golden curls that they could toss with devastating effect. Amelia was already beginning to grow plump, but she still gave off a strong aura of sexuality which made her father-in-law realise how hard widowhood must be for her and why there was so much trouble between her and his wife. Arabella meant well, but she was basically a simple woman innocently unconscious of the deeper, darker forces within others.

When he saw that buying a sugar mouse might cause another family explosion, Christopher Wylie put his money back in his pocket. Then he steered the conversation into less dangerous waters by asking the little girl, 'What have you done today, Arbelle? Did you do your lessons with Emma Jane?' he asked.

Emma Jane answered for the sulking child. 'Yes, she did and she reads well. She's very clever.'

From Arabella's sofa came a deep sigh. 'Her father was clever at reading when he was small. Very clever.'

'I was a good reader when I was at school too,' said Amelia defiantly.

'Were you, my dear? How long did you attend school?' asked her mother-in-law tactlessly.

Emma Jane leapt into the conversation now and announced hastily, 'And Arbelle can count to ten. Count for Grandpa, my dear.'

The prodigy wiped her eyes and started to chant, 'One-two-three-four-five-theven-thix-eight-nine-ten.'

'That's wrong. It's five, six, seven, eight, nine, ten . . .' corrected her mother and Mrs Wylie sighed again.

'Oh poor Arbelle. You did very well, dear – you're only four, after all.'

At this Amelia's temper snapped. 'Don't call her poor Arbelle all the time! She's *not* poor.'

Mrs Wylie's face went bright pink as she argued, 'Not poor? Of course she's poor. She's fatherless, dear little thing. She'll not even remember James when she grows up.'

Amelia's face was blazing as she shouted back, 'I miss him too, you know. And my dad died when I was seven and I wasn't poor. Lots of bairns lose their dads and survive it. Don't call her poor!'

Seeing her advantage, Arbelle ran to her grandmother and was hugged close in a tearful embrace. 'Oh poor Arbelle, you're a sensitive little girl. Poor Arbelle,' sobbed Arabella, cradling the child's golden head on her breast while the others watched helplessly and, with an exclamation of disgust, Amelia flounced out of the room.

After the tears were shed and dried again, it was Emma Jane's task to take the little girl back to her mother's apartment in the west wing of the house. She found Amelia curled in a big armchair by the window, her chin in her hand. She only grunted when her daughter was returned to her. Emma Jane stood awkwardly in the doorway and said, 'I'm sorry about what happened, Amelia. Mother's so distraught about James she doesn't know what she's saying sometimes.'

Amelia stood up. 'Then she should think a bit more. Sometimes I wonder if she's trying to get rid of me. She's always thought I wasn't good enough for her son because I was only a housemaid. I don't know how you stand her, Emma Jane, she's always complaining.'

Emma Jane's face was stricken as she replied, 'Oh Amelia, she's so sad. I understand how she feels – I'm sorry for her. I wish I could do more to cheer her up but I can't take James' place. He was always her favourite but I don't mind.'

Amelia sat down again and sank her face in the cushions. 'We all miss James, make no mistake about that, Emma Jane. But weeping and wailing won't bring him back. Life goes on, you know. Don't sacrifice your own life to looking after your mother. You should be getting married yourself soon. You're old enough now.'

'I'm twenty-two,' said Emma Jane stiffly.

Amelia looked up bleakly and said, 'Find yourself a husband as soon as you can. If you wait too long you'll never get away. You'll still be here looking after your mother when you're sixty.'

Emma Jane walked away with the words ringing in her head. She didn't want to think about what Amelia had said because she was very afraid that her sister-in-law's prediction might prove true. Compared with the vivacious Amelia, who had started attracting suitors again even though she had not been widowed for a year yet, Emma Jane felt plain and unappealing. She was quite sure that no man would ever want to marry her, and that she'd end up as Arbelle's adoring maiden aunt – a figure of fun and pity.

That same evening, Christopher Wylie ate an early dinner then retired to bed. His had been a happy marriage until James died, for he and Arabella were friends as well as husband and wife, and they loved lying side by side in bed in the darkness quietly talking, sometimes until the early hours of the morning. He had always discussed all his business affairs with her but now, because her grief was so absorbing, he did not want to worry her with his problems. Yet that night he almost yielded because as he lay down beside her, she reached out and took his hand. 'You look so sad now, my dear,' she whispered.

His heart ached. How he wished he could tell her about Munro, about the difficult bridge, about his crippling money worries but that would be too cruel. 'I am worried,' he admitted.

'Is it about this new project?'

'Yes, it's not going to be easy. I may have to be away for long periods of time. Will you be all right when I'm in Scotland?'

She sighed. 'Oh yes, you mustn't worry about us. Emma Jane will look after me.'

He frowned to himself. 'Emma Jane's a worry, too. She doesn't have much of a life since . . .' He was going to say 'since James' death,' but bit the words back.

'I know,' his wife said sadly, 'but I can't take her out into society, Christopher, I'm not capable of seeing people yet. When I am, I will try, but she's so shy! She doesn't say a word when we have company. I think she's worse than she used to be.'

He ventured, 'Perhaps Amelia could accompany her to things – tea parties or concerts, wherever young ladies go these days.'

That suggestion was not met with approval. 'Oh my dear, Amelia's friends are not the sort of people Emma Jane should know! They're all ex-servants. I don't expect Amelia will be with us for much longer anyway. I'm sure she'll marry again soon. She's the marrying kind – not like Emma Jane.'

He closed his eyes and remembered his daughter as a little girl. Even when she was tiny she had been solemn and anxious to please, always running along behind her handsome, dashing brother, always trying to catch up with him. 'Perhaps we've not been entirely fair to Emma Jane,' he murmured as he drifted into sleep.

Next morning he rose before dawn and was eating breakfast in his silent house, when he was surprised to see his daughter come slipping into the dining room with a long shawl wrapped around her shoulders. She sat down opposite him at the table, leaned her chin in her hands and asked, 'Where exactly are you going today, Papa?'

He looked up, surprised at her interest. Normally she seemed indifferent to his business affairs, and he had only ever talked to her of them in generalities, not as he had done with James, who had had his complete confidence.

He smiled at her as he said, 'Today I'm going to Edinburgh to speak to the railway company directors. I hope to get them to confirm that I'll get the bridge contract. I've only had vague promises so far, but now I want it in writing. Then, if I'm successful, I'll go to a little town on the Tweed called Rosewell. That's where this bridge is to be built.'

She smiled her impish grin and he noticed that her eyes seemed to glow like amber in the candlelight. 'I do hope you're successful, Papa,' she said.

'Could I unburden my worries to this girl? Would she

understand what I was talking about?' he pondered. But then he decided that to do so would be unfair. Why saddle her with the knowledge that her apparently prosperous father was teetering on the brink of bankruptcy? She had enough to concern her with looking after her mother and teaching Arbelle. He had to maintain his front of the all-powerful parent, so he patted her hand and said reassuringly, 'Oh I'll get it, my dear. I'm quite confident of that.'

Her eyes were sad as she looked at him and for a moment he wondered what she saw that made her so pensive. 'I hope you'll not tire yourself out when you're away. I hope you'll eat properly and not stay up late poring over your papers,' she told him softly. It sounded as if she was a mother worrying about a careless child.

He laughed. 'Don't worry, I'll do all the right things. After I've been to Edinburgh, I'll take rooms in Rosewell and when I'm established there, I'll send my address. I may have to be away for several weeks, my dear. I've already warned your mother about that. You'll be in charge here and I rely on you to let me know if anything happens ... if your mother is ill or anything like that. Don't hesitate, write immediately.'

'Oh course,' she replied gaily. 'You mustn't worry – we'll be perfectly all right, but we'll all miss you. Have you any idea how long you'll be gone, Papa?'

He shrugged. 'I can't say. There'll be a lot to do to get this project off the ground. After I've been to Edinburgh and Rosewell, I'm going to look for a certain man I'll need to help me with this job. He's working in Scotland – I'm not sure where, but I've got to find him.'

She looked interested. 'He must be very special if you want him so badly. Who is he?'

Her father buttered another slice of toast and smiled slightly as he said, 'He's an Irish navvy called Tim Maguire. The best in the business, believe me.'

'A navvy! According to the newspapers the navvies are all like animals,' she exclaimed.

'Oh, some of them are wild men, that's true, but not all. There's good men among them too. On a big job like this the navvies can make or break it, and I'll need them on my side.'

'And this man Maguire will do that for you?'

'Yes, I think he can. He and his father have worked for me in the past. I heard the other day that the father's dead but Tim's on his own, working in the north. I'll just have to go round the navvy camps until I find him.'

Her face was solemn as she listened. 'Do take care, Papa. I wish I could help you like James used to do. If he was still alive, you wouldn't need this Maguire man, would you?'

Wylie was ready to go now so he stood up from the table and rang the bell to alert Haggerty. 'Ifs and buts butter no bread, my dear. You will help me very much by keeping this household going and looking after your mother.'

He travelled from Newcastle to Edinburgh by train, crossing the high bridge that he had helped to build across the River Tweed at Berwick. It was the first big contract he had ever undertaken, and it had made his reputation as well as his first fortune – the one he'd just lost. 'How strange that again I'm investing my hopes in another bridge across the same river,' he thought as he stared out at the rippling waters of the Tweed estuary far below the carriage window. In some strange way his fate lay down there . . .

Christopher was proud to have been associated with the wonderful expansion of railways that had transformed the land and the lives of people living in it. When he was born, a man could travel no faster than the speed of a galloping horse and he could remember stagecoaches full of exhausted people clattering into Newcastle. Yet here he was, sitting in a comfortable train swaying and speeding towards Edinburgh – a journey he would accomplish in only a few hours when it used to take more than two days. He had the zeal of a Jesuit about wanting to convert people to a belief in railways, but he knew there were still those who were afraid of them and wished they had never been invented. These people were only simple and misguided, he thought; they'd change their minds in time when they saw the benefits that the iron horse could bring them.

It was raining when he alighted in Edinburgh, and he drew his thick overcoat around him as he trudged up the hill from the station to Princess Street. Mist hung over the brooding castle in the middle of the town, and people passing him on the street wore grim, suffering expressions; the cold bit into his bones. It was not a good omen for what lay ahead, but when he reached Rutland Square where the railway company had its offices, his attitude changed for he was shown into a sumptuously furnished room with a bright fire blazing in the hearth beneath a carved marble mantelpiece. Sir Geoffrey Miller, whom he had met on previous contracts, advanced towards him with an outstretched hand and a friendly smile on his face. 'Take off that wet coat, Wylie. You've arrived on a typical Edinburgh day. Sit down and have a drink – will whisky do?'

Whisky suited him very well, and when he had taken a sip he felt warmth flow back into his body and hope into his heart. Now he was sure that everything was going to be all right.

There were several other men in the room and he was introduced to them by Miller. 'This is Colonel Anstruther of Bella Vista, Mr Raeburn of Falconwood, Sir Rupert Caldecott of Marchhouse, Smith, one of our directors . . .'

The man called Smith laughed and said, 'I'm Smith of Edinburgh – the only one who's not a big landowner in the Border country.' 'Then you're the money man,' thought Wylie. 'You're the one to watch.'

On a long gleaming table in the middle of the room lay large sheets of paper, plans and drawings. He walked across to them, and asked, 'Are those the survey details?'

Smith stepped up beside him. 'Yes, it's a difficult site: high precipitous river banks and a wide valley to cross.'

Wylie looked directly at him. 'Is there no other place for the bridge to go?'

Smith shook his head. 'No, it must be here.' He laid a hand on the papers. 'There's no alternative – it's the only place where we have access to sufficient land. The other landowners are trying to block us out, you see. We need a contractor who can build a bridge in a difficult place.'

Behind them Wylie heard a warning cough. Smith had been indiscreet. 'If you don't feel you can do it, Mr Wylie, we'll find someone else who can,' Miller said smoothly from the fireside.

Wylie did not turn round but only bent to examine the plans more closely. 'Oh, I can do it,' he announced curtly, 'and if I can't, no one else will be able to either. But it's going to be an expensive job, worse than I anticipated from your tender prospectus. I can see that it's going to need at least eighteen piers to carry the line over the river, and some of those will have to be sunk in the riverbed and the others on what looks like very sloping land.'

There was a silence behind him before Miller asked, 'What sort of outlay do you think it will need?'

'A lot. You want a decent-looking bridge, don't you? You don't want an iron skeleton that'll rust and erode within a few years. That valley gets hard weather in winter and iron might not last long. You'll need a stone bridge because stone lasts forever.'

He had brought a document case with him and now he bent to pick it up off the floor. 'I've already made a few drawings from what I heard about the site. I brought them for you to look at.' On top of their plans he spread his own and flattened them out with the palm of his hand.

The men clustered round and stared for a moment in silence, then Smith said, 'It's very imposing, very grand.'

Miller coughed. 'Grandiose, I'd say.'

Wylie looked hard at him. 'This bridge will give your railway distinction,' he said.

'Can we afford such distinction, though?' said Miller.

Wylie started to fold up his plans. 'If you can't, you don't need me. I only build fine bridges. Perhaps you should look elsewhere for your contractor.'

The way they reacted to this told him that they had

74

tried others, and been disappointed. 'Come, come, don't be hasty. We haven't turned down your plan yet. I like the look of it myself. How much do you suppose a bridge like this will cost?' The speaker was the man introduced as Anstruther. He had a scarlet face but shrewd little eyes that sparkled with intelligence when he looked at Wylie.

'I don't know exactly but it won't be cheap. I'll have to go down there and estimate more exactly. A lot depends on how long it's likely to take.'

'We know the answer to that: it must be finished and operative within two years. We've budgeted for that.' Miller's voice was sharp.

Wylie shook his head. 'That's not very long. It's May now – let me have until the end of eighteen fifty-five and I shall give you your bridge.'

'And at what price?' asked Smith.

Wylie stalled. 'I've to buy in stone and bricks . . . I don't know what that's going to cost.'

The man called Caldecott leaned forward and spoke for the first time. 'I own a quarry about five miles from the site. Part of the deal is that any contractor for the bridge buys the stone from me.'

Wylie looked at him. 'At your price?' he asked, and Caldecott nodded. 'The carve-up begins,' thought Wylie. 'What's going to come next?'

Now the hard talking began. Smith was in charge and he told Wylie, 'If we can fix a price today, we'll give you the contract. We are prepared to pay thirty-five thousand pounds for the finished bridge, but you will have to take half of the price in railway shares.'

Wylie knew they were hedging their bets. They were telling him, 'Build the bridge and then get your profit.' It was the donkey and carrot principle.

'How many shares will I get at the end?' he asked.

The other men in the room looked at each other. 'We thought ten thousand. They're pound shares and we'll each contribute a proportion of our own holdings for you,' said Smith.

Wylie folded up his plans again. 'Make it twenty

thousand in cash and twenty thousand shares and I'm your man.'

Miller stepped forward and stuck out a hand but this time he was not smiling. 'Done! Twenty thousand in cash and twenty thousand shares. The shares will be handed over on completion of the project, but we must insist on a fixed completion date. It has to be the first of August, eighteen fifty-five. That way, we'll have our line operating before winter.'

Wylie shook the extended hand, slightly surprised at the ease of the negotiation. A niggling worry plagued him and he could not rid himself of the feeling that he'd been savaged by a pack of gentlemanly wolves. 'I'm afraid I'm in for a shock when I see that site,' he told himself.

CHAPTER
Five

The navigators, or navvies as they were popularly called, lived in a huge camp of wooden sheds, turf huts and tents in a valley just outside the town of Penicuik. Some of their dwellings were more solid and weatherproof than others, and these were the ones that the men moved with them as they went from job to job. Only a few travelled with their wives and children and had their own little houses, sometimes adorned with its name burned in pokerwork on the front door. Navvy humour showed by naming their houses *Laburnum Villa*, *Mon Repos* or *Blarney Castle*. In the Penicuik camp there was even a lean-to shanty with the nameplate *Buckinem Palas*.

House-owners and heads of families were, however, the exception rather than the rule and the majority of the men lived in bunkhouses, each one run by a slatternly woman who provided their food, made desultory attempts at keeping the hut clean and acted as a prostitute for the lodgers. Fights and sometimes murders were common in those huts, and nights in the camps were made horrible by the screams and yells of battling men and women, for a navvy camp always acted like a magnet for the lowest prostitutes of any district where it appeared. Navvies were highly paid and tough, men who used women in the same utilitarian way as they used their picks and shovels but with less regard. A favourite shovel was always referred to as a 'navvy's prayer book' and kept oiled and rust-free. For most of them, there was no such thing as a favourite woman – and the idea of cherishing one was completely alien to them.

Tim Maquire, twenty-five years old and as tough as

tempered steel, with a mop of black curly hair and a threatening dark stare, lived with seven other men in a shed run by a woman called Major Bob. No one knew her real name but she had been given her nickname because of her constant references to her husband – 'my Major Bob' – who, she said, had served in the Peninsular War with Wellington. How she descended from being an Army officer's wife to keeping a hut for navvies was anyone's guess, but her fondness for brandy was certainly at the back of it. It was unusual to find her sober after midday.

To most of the navvies Major Bob acted in a high-handed and truculent manner, but she was in awe of Tim Maquire who, like his workmates, was always called by a nickname. His was Black Ace – which suited him, because he had a reserved and solitary air. Even the most reckless did not play the fool or try to take a rise out of Black Ace.

He was lying on his cot with one strong arm across his eyes to shut out the light when she walked tentatively up the narrow passage between the beds and whispered to him, 'There's a man outside wants to speak to you, Black Ace.'

He lowered the arm and squinted at her. 'I was working all night – I'm tired. What sort of man is he?'

'A gentleman by his clothes and his voice, but he seems to know his way about.' Major Bob was a crashing snob and could spot a gent a mile off. When she pronounced the word 'gentleman' she did so in her most refined voice. She had not yet started drinking but when she did, her standards and her articulation would both slip.

'Tell him to go away. I don't have any dealings with gents,' said the man on the bed, replacing his arm across his eyes. Major Bob lingered, however, because the stranger had promised her a florin if she introduced him to Black Ace.

'I think you should see this one. He's not the ordinary type of gentleman,' she persisted.

Irritated, Tim lifted his head from the pillow to shout at her and saw that the light from the door was blocked out by a tall thin figure who stood leaning negligently against the jamb.

'He can go away. I don't know any gentleman. The likes of me doesn't keep that sort of company,' he snarled in the very marked Irish accent that he always used when he was annoyed.

The man in the doorway was undeterred. Instead of going away, he strolled along the passage towards Tim's bed and drawled, 'You're quite right, old boy. You don't know me but really I'm not as bad as I look.' His voice was excessively smooth and well-bred, and would have told more sophisticated listeners that he was a produce of a famous English public school. When he came nearer Tim could see that he had a long, lean, cleanshaven face with strongly-marked features and a wide, thin mouth. His fine, corn-coloured hair was worn long and was so glossy that it looked as if it were woven from silk. The most arresting thing about him was his eyes, for the lids half-covered his pupils and gave him the look of a predatory hawk. These strange hooded eyes often made people think he was secretly laughing at them. All his life he had got into a lot of trouble because of his eyes.

'I don't know you,' said Tim Maquire shortly.

The hawk grinned and nodded. 'That's right – you don't, but we know people in common.'

'Like who?' Tim sounded disbelieving.

'Like the Tiger and Billy Bouncer.' On site, navvies all used aliases. They preferred to keep their real names secret for a variety of reasons, not all of them creditable. When a stranger came to a site, the ganger would often give him the nickname of a man who had died or moved away, and in that way some men travelled the country under a variety of aliases but the Tiger and Billy Bouncer were well-known throughout the navvy community as straight fellows and not trouble-makers or rabble-rousers.

'Did they send you?' asked Tim curiously, eyeing the stranger's clothes which were obviously expensive although well-worn. His long-tailed coat was dark blue and his trousers cream. His feet were shod in highly polished brown leather boots that looked as comfortable as gloves, and in his hand he carried a long cane with a silver knob, and a cream-coloured tall hat. He looked a perfect swell – but one who had fallen on hard times.

'When the Tiger and Billy Bouncer told me to look you up, they said you might find me a place in your gang. They said you always run the best gang on any site where you are working,' this vision said, leaning his weight on his cane in the attitude of one watching a sporting event.

'Did they now?' Tim guffawed. 'You don't look like a navvy to me.'

The stranger grinned with satisfaction. 'No I don't, do I? No bright cravat, no monkey waistcoat, no nickel watch and chain . . .'

Tim bristled, for like most navvies, he had a weakness for bright brocade waistcoats and flashy neckerchiefs. To dress up when you weren't working was one way of cocking a snook at ordinary working men, and showing that you were a member of the labouring aristocracy, the highest-paid working men in the world.

'What's wrong with coloured waistcoats and neckties?' he asked defensively.

'Oh nothing, dear chap, nothing at all, but a well-tied and well-laundered white cravat does look smarter, don't you agree?'

'No, I damned well don't,' said Tim, getting up off his bed. 'And there's no call for well-tied cravats in my gangs.'

The stranger laughed. 'Don't let's fall out over sartorial niceties. I'm looking for a place in a good gang and your friends told me that you run the best. I want you to take me on.'

Maquire was on his feet now with his well-muscled arms crossed on his chest. There was a tattoo of a shamrock entwined with roses on his right forearm. After the newcomer made his request, the dark shadowed eyes stared at him for a moment and then Tim threw back his head and chuckled. 'Don't be half-witted! If I took you on, the men would laugh you off the site. Anyway, you're too late – the job's finished up here. We're going to have to move away tomorrow and find other berths. There's not a lot of railway work going on at the moment, and we might have to travel a long way.'

The other man drew himself up to his full height. He was as tall as Maquire but he was more slimly built. 'I know where there's work,' he said coolly. 'I saw the digging going on when I was coming up from the south.'

'Where?' asked Maquire, but the stranger only grinned. 'Take me on and I'll tell you.'

'Oh piss off,' was the angry reply as the ganger turned away. 'I don't need toffs like you to lead me around by the nose. I'll find work myself. I've always found it in the past without any help from anybody.'

The other man still stood his ground. 'Don't lose your temper, Black Ace. And don't let your eyes deceive you. I might not have a big gut but I'm strong and I'm a good worker. The Tiger wouldn't have put up with me if I wasn't, would he? Look at it this way: take me on and I'll add a dash of culture to your gang.'

Tim whipped round with his eyes burning bright blue in his weather-beaten face. His hair was tousled and because he had not shaved for a couple of days, his chin was dark and stubbled. He looked dangerous.

'I've already told you. PISS OFF!' he shouted. As he spoke he shoved the cheeky stranger in the chest with one extended hand. He thought he'd used enough force to make him tumble backwards but he was disappointed because the other man did not budge an inch and the chest he pushed against felt as hard as iron.

In retaliation the stranger even had the nerve to push Tim back and say, 'Don't resort to violence, old boy, if you don't want it to become quite nasty.'

Maquire was furious. 'I don't like you or the likes of you. I wouldn't have you in my gang if there was no one else to hire. I don't need some toff sniggering at me and using fancy words that he thinks I can't understand.'

The stranger was contrite. 'Oh don't misapprehend me, I wasn't trying to patronise you. That's just the way I talk – it's a habit I've got into. The Tiger called me Gentleman

Sydney because of it. What can I do to show that I'm capable of pulling my weight? I really want to work with you. They say you're the best and I only like the best in everything.'

Some of the other navvies had come into the shed during the altercation and now stood at the door watching. When Gentleman Sydney asked what he could do to convince Tim, one of them, a saturnine individual with a fierce squint whose nickname was Frying Pan, shouted out, 'Fight him! Take him on! Black Ace is a great fighter.'

'Yeah,' laughed the others, 'fight him for a place.' They nudged each other in anticipation of a spectacle.

Surprisingly, the stranger agreed. 'All right,' he said, and began peeling of his smart coat. Underneath it he was wearing a pristine white shirt with wide sleeves and a pintucked front. With a grin he rolled the sleeves up to his elbows and then struck a prize-fighter's attitude before Tim. 'I'll fight you for a place. First blood wins, all right?'

Tim hesitated, but only because he did not want to hurt a man who had been sent to him by his friends. However, the yells of the other navvies convinced him that he had to accept the challenge and, with a lift of the shoulders, he said, 'All right, first blood. I hope I don't kill you.'

The words were hardly out of his mouth when a sharp jab from his opponent's fist caught him on the eyebrow. He reeled and shook his head, then went in like a bull. Fists flailing, he hammered away at the other man's ribs but there was no retreat. When he lifted his head to see how Sydney was taking his punishment, another quick punch caught him on the jaw and made him see stars. This was serious. He couldn't let himself be beaten before his men. He drew back a fist and swung through with a massive punch which threw his opponent's head back. Sydney staggered against a bed, half-collapsed but quickly got up again and stepped forward once more. 'By God, you're tough,' thought Tim, just as a fist hit him full on the mouth and, to his horror, he tasted blood on his tongue.

He wiped a hand across his face and when it came away

it was stained with gore. Both of them stopped fighting and stared at the red smear. 'First blood,' said Sydney, as casually as if he was making a remark about the weather.

Tim nodded. 'You've won. Well done. Who taught you to box like that? I never saw it coming.'

'A sadist of a master at my old school taught me,' Sydney said wryly. 'He called it the manly art – huh! But you're some boxer yourself. You really hurt me – I'll be black and blue tomorrow. Do I get a place now?'

'Go on, Black Ace, you've got to take him on,' called Frying Pan and Tim grinned. 'All right, you've earned it. I hope you've been on navvying jobs before and all your talk isn't hot air.'

'I've navvied before – in France where I met the Tiger and then in the Midlands, that's where I met Billy Bouncer. When I said I wanted to see Scotland, they both told me to look up Black Ace and give him their regards.'

Tim nodded, only half-believing, but another look at his bloodstained hand convinced him. 'Oh all right, come here at half-past six tomorrow morning and help us load the hut on to a cart. I want to be out of here before the others. There's not a lot of work around.'

'Do you want me to tell you where there is work?' asked Sydney.

Tim sighed. 'I see I'm not going to be able to stop you. Where is it?'

'At a place called Maddiston. They're cutting a line southwards from there to the Scottish border. There's going to be a lot of work on that line for at least two or three years.'

'Well, I suppose we'd better head for Maddiston,' said Tim. 'Now push off and come back tomorrow. I've had enough of you for one day.'

At five o'clock next morning, when it was still dark, the men in Major Bob's shed were awake and dismantling their dwelling. From frequent practice they knew how to take it apart like a child's model, for each bit, each plank and spar slotted into place. It was not long before the outer walls were loaded on to a long dray drawn by two horses which Black Ace had hired to carry them to their next stopping place. They were piling on the beds and chairs when their ganger paused and said bitterly, 'I knew that toff Gentleman What's-His-Name wouldn't show up.'

The words were hardly out of his mouth when they heard a voice calling out to them, 'Good morning, good morning,' and Sydney strolled up through the rising grey mist. He was wearing a long dark overcoat with huge pearl buttons that glittered in the half-light like carriage lamps. Over one shoulder was slung the strap of a battered leather satchel out of which his silver-topped cane jutted. His high hat was tipped forward on his head and he was grinning broadly as he stood looking at them.

'You're late,' said Tim shortly.

'I know. I slept in an hotel last night and the chambermaid didn't awaken early enough to give me my morning call. Silly girl. And to think I kept her in my bed all night to make sure she wouldn't oversleep,' said the latecomer.

The men stared at him for a second before the inference of what he'd said sunk in. Frying Pan gave a short barking laugh. They all joined in and even Tim permitted himself a smile as he worked. 'All right, take an end of this if you've any strength left,' he grunted, heaving away at the big iron stove which had stood in the middle of the hut. Its long pipe was already dismantled in sections and lay on the grass.

When everything was at last aboard, the men clambered on top of the load. Dressed in their best and brightest clothes, with clay pipes in their mouths, they settled down to enjoy their trip through the countryside. Whenever they came to a village or hamlet they waved cheerfully to people gaping at them. It was like a triumphal progress.

Major Bob travelled with them, seated in a wooden armchair at the end of the cart. When she climbed aboard, she said to Tim Maquire, 'I'm not coming with you all the way this time. Drop me at the first railway station you come to. I'm retiring. My daughter, the one that's married

84

to the clergyman in Liverpool, wrote to me and invited me to stay with her. She's very respectable, you know.'

This did not seem to make much impression on Black Ace, so every time she caught his eye, she'd say again, 'Remember and take me to a station, I'm giving this up.' Frustrated by his lack of response, she then started telling the other men, 'Don't let Black Ace forget about me. I want off at a station.' To Sydney's surprise none of them paid much attention to her either and eventually he whispered to Frying Pan, beside whom he was sitting, 'I hope you're going to do what the poor woman wants. It's not a life for a woman of her age after all, trailing around from navvy camp to navvy camp.'

Major Bob's voice was growing louder. 'I think I won't go to Liverpool after all. I'd rather go to London to stay with my son. He's a lawyer and very respectable.' She leaned perilously down from her chair to look at Sydney over a pile of mattresses and said in a very ladylike voice, 'Do you know London well, Mr Sydney?'

He smiled. 'Yes I do, madam. It will be very pleasant there now – flowers in the parks, all that sort of thing . . .'

'That's where I'll go then,' said Major Bob, and slipped off into a peaceful little doze.

On the other side of Sydney from Frying Pan was a younger man with a thatch of bright yellow hair that stuck out all around his head like an overblown dandelion. He was laughing as he saw the expression on Sydney's face. 'Oh don't listen to her,' he said. 'She's always like that when we move, always leaving, always going to London or Liverpool, but if she does have any children, they'd run a mile if she turned up on their doorsteps. She never goes anywhere but with us.'

Every now and again Major Bob would waken and ask loudly if they'd found a station yet. When they assured her that there was one around the next corner, she took a black bottle out of her capacious holdall, unscrewed its cap, took a long swig, then did it up and replaced it in its hiding place before going back to sleep. Sydney was afraid that eventually she'd topple off her chair altogether so he climbed up to sit beside her and hold on to her when that moment arrived. He then had the opportunity to take a good look at her. She was the ruin of what must once have been a striking-looking woman with black hair and arching dark eyebrows over large and imperious eyes. In spite of the ravages of time and debauchery, her features still showed traces of gentility, although the cheeks were mottled with broken veins. When she woke and saw him watching her she gave him a surprisingly sweet smile. 'I'm going to London, you know,' she told him. 'It will be nice to be with ladies and gentlemen again, not with this riffraff. They don't have any manners, you see, but you can't really blame them because they've all come from rough homes. Now my dear husband, the late Major Bob, he was in Spain with Wellesley before they made him a Duke. My Major Bob was a gentleman. He would eat his heart out if he could see me now. That's what having no money does to a woman, you see.'

Tim, in the front of the cart, turned his head with a laugh and shouted back, 'You mean that's what having a drouth does to a woman. If you stopped drinking brandy you'd have plenty of money. You charge us enough for looking after you.'

Major Bob bridled like an angry horse. 'Brandy? What do you mean, brandy? I hardly touch a drop, just a little now and again for my nerves. And what was that about looking after *me*? I look after you. You're an impudent Paddy, Black Ace. I don't know why I stick with you and your gang of hooligans.'

Tim didn't take any offence at this but still laughed as he told her, 'You stick with us because we look after you and we're the best-behaved gang you've ever been with. Besides, we all pay our dues every Friday and don't borrow any of it back from you on a Saturday, like most of the gangs.'

'Then let's see how you can get on without me from now on,' she said stiffly. 'Just drop me at a station and I'll take a train to London – or is it Liverpool? I forget.'

It took four hours for them to travel from Penicuik to

Maddiston, and by the time they were nearly there, Major Bob had given up all pretence of leaving. Now and again she would waken, uncork her bottle and take a long draw. Sometimes she offered the bottle to Sydney, but never to any of the others. He always shook his head and said courteously, 'No thank you, my dear lady, I'm not a brandy-drinker.'

This seemed to astonish her. 'Not a brandy-drinker and yet in a navvy gang? What do you drink?'

He thought for a moment and told her, 'I like claret and porter now and again. But what I really enjoy is champagne – or plain water.'

She was shocked. 'Oh, don't let them hear you talking like that,' she whispered.

'Don't you think they'd approve of champagne?' he asked, equally quietly.

'It's not that. It's the water they wouldn't approve of.' By this time her face was flushed and her speech less precise. When she next fell asleep, her bonnet slipped down over her eyes and she made loud snuffling sounds like a dozing dog. She was still sleeping when their cart rolled into the main street of Maddiston, so when they stopped Tim and Sydney lifted her out of the chair and laid her flat on top of the mattresses to sleep off the effects of her journey.

As they stood looking at her recumbent figure, Tim said fondly, 'Oh well, once again Major Bob's staying.'

Sydney grinned back and said, 'She's a bit of an old soak, isn't she?'

The answer was another laugh but not an unkind one. 'She's all right if you learn to close your ears to her. If you stay with us you'll have to do the same as we do – pay her five shillings a week and she'll cook for you, clean your corner and do your laundry.'

Sydney looked taken aback. 'I'll send my shirts to a local laundry – I always do that. But I'll be glad to pay my five shillings.'

'That's all right then,' said Tim. 'I'll tell her you're on

the roll, but don't try making up to her. She's not like the other women – she's not a whore.'

Sydney visibly reeled. 'I assure you, old boy, I wouldn't dream of it,' he said fervently.

Maddiston was a long narrow town meandering along the bed of a river. Lades leading off the river's main flow were diverted by stone-lined culverts into tall mill buildings which contained floor upon floor of looms, all clattering and rattling away at once. The town echoed with the noise and the air in the streets smelt oily from the raw wool that was shipped in by hundreds of cart-loads to keep the looms working. The navvies' dray stopped in front of a long narrow inn on the outskirts of this busy place where the thirsty men jumped down and ran inside, eager for beer. Major Bob was left sleeping peacefully on top of the load.

The inn was packed full of working men – some navvies and others more soberly clad. When the navvies saw Tim Maquire, they sent up a cry, 'It's Black Ace! Have a drink, Black Ace!' Soon he was swallowed up in their midst while his companions stood together with their beer mugs in their hands. Gentleman Sydney watched him go and said to the young lad at his side, 'He seems to know everybody in the navvying trade.'

His companion, the young man with the thatch of yellow hair, nodded. 'Aye, he does. He's been working the lines since he was eight years old.'

Sydney's jaw dropped. 'Eight! Good God – I was sent to school at eight and I thought I was being badly treated.'

The lad looked at him sharply. 'Where did you go to school?'

Sydney only laughed. 'No history, no history, old boy. What's your name?'

'They call me Jimmy-The-New-Man.'

'Is that because you're a newcomer too?'

'Not really. I joined the gang a year and a half ago. They didn't know what to call me and the name they used has just stuck. I came down from Inverness to work. I left home because my father beat me – and I'll never go back, never, not if I live to be a hundred. I was lucky that Black Ace gave me a place. He's a grand fellow.' Hero worship shone out of his eyes as he spoke.

Sydney nodded sympathetically. 'I could tell from your accent you're from the Highlands. All the others are Irish, aren't they?'

'All of them except me – but I'm a Roman too, so that's all right,' Jimmy told him. 'Are you a Roman?'

Sydney grinned. 'I'm more of a Greek, I think. No, I'm not a Roman – I hope they won't mind. Tell me their names. I've only met Frying Pan and you so far.'

In turn Jimmy introduced him to the brothers Gold Tooth and Pea Head, to the massively muscled and confused-looking Brick Wall, to a long-faced man they called the Parson and finally to a sprightly-looking little leprechaun of a fellow who jumped forward with his hand extended and chirped, 'Me name's Naughten-The-Image-Taker.'

'That's a strange name,' said Sydney.

Naughten laughed. 'They call me that because I make their images. For a florin I'll draw your likeness and you can send it home to your family. I'd make a good job of those eyes of yours. Have you a florin? If you have I'll do it now.' As he spoke he fished a block of paper and a few stubby pencils out of his coat pocket.

Sydney shook his head. 'No, thank you. I've no wish to see my face on a sheet of paper, and I'm sure my people wouldn't want to see it anyway.'

'That's a pity, that's a pity,' said Naughten, but he was undeterred and was soon pushing his way through the crowd offering to execute images for anyone who wanted to be preserved for posterity. He had several acceptances and the sitters sat self-conscious and stiff on a chair brought from the inn kitchen while the chattering Naughten drew away. Sydney stood at his shoulder watching him at work and saw that, while he had a certain naïve facility with the pencil, he was no artist. What he could do, however, was to give his wooden-looking portraits some undeniable characteristic of the sitter – a squint, a large nose, a pendulous lip, even a treasured watch and chain, all were copied faithfully but with no aim to flatter except in the matter of the watch and chain. One man who commissioned his portrait looked at the finished product and cried out angrily, 'By God, man, you've made me look as if I'm dead.' He passed the paper back to his friends, who all burst out laughing. 'True enough, you look like a corpse!'

Naughten, swiftly pocketing his florin, acted outraged and said with professional pride, 'The trouble with you is that you don't recognise real art. Take a look at that picture: isn't that your own long horse-face to the life there? Your mother, if she's honest, won't ever mistake that for anybody else.'

A serious altercation was prevented by the return of Black Ace, accompanied by a shifty-looking stout man wearing a tight black jacket and a dusty bowler hat. 'This is Jopp,' said Tim to his men. 'He's overseer with the railway company that's building the new line. He says if we go down to Rosewell, about four miles south, there's a camp being set up and we'll get work there.'

'Who's the contractor?' asked Frying Pan suspiciously, because there were some employers that knowledgeable navvies avoided at all costs.

Jopp was reassuring. 'There's a good man hiring for a squad to build a big bridge. I've forgotten his name but he has a fine reputation. Men are going down there already because they've heard he's got the contract. You'd better hurry if you want a place with him.'

They rushed back to their cart and as they rode out of Maddiston they passed the place where the town's new station was being built. Huge heaps of red sandstone blocks and piles of earth like pyramids scarred the field. The air rang with the sound of masons' chisels and the steady thump, thump, thump of steam engines. The modern age was creeping into a part of the world that had changed little since Time began.

The countryside became pretty and rural again soon

after they left the station site behind. The road meandered slowly by a river that tumbled over stones as big and as white as roc's eggs. On the banks, purple balsam and white meadowsweet bloomed beside huge stalks of hogweed that towered as high as trees. Swifts dashed and swooped over the surface of the water, playing an eternal, joyous game.

Rosewell, when they finally reached it, seemed to be dreaming, caught in a long-past era. Their first view of it showed the town spread out before them on a rising piece of ground overlooking a large meadow beside the confluence of the river from Maddiston with the Tweed. Between the meadow and the town stood the stark but lovely ruins of an ancient Abbey, half-roofless but with the delicate traceries of glassless windows still showing in high walls against a cloudless sky.

The drayman steered his horses into the middle of the town, passing the Abbey gate and negotiating a narrow street lined with ancient houses until he reached a wide square surrounded by prosperous-looking shops with their proprietors' homes on the upper floors. In the middle of the square was a tall red sandstone pillar topped by a lion *couchant*, and several old men were sitting at its foot. The driver leaned forward and called out to them: 'Where's the navvy camp?'

'We're not wanting any navvies in Rosewell,' said one surly ancient.

The driver was an Edinburgh man who scorned countrymen. 'You might not be wanting them but you're getting them. Where's the camp?' he snapped.

Another man stood up and pointed along the street that headed westwards. 'It's out there. They've taken over a field on the side of the hill. They'd better stay there too or we'll put the police on them.'

'That's what I like to hear, a friendly welcome,' called Sydney in his most gentlemanly voice as they trundled off.

The camp was in a large field bordered by a low drystone wall and with a thick clump of trees in the top corner. Already the grass was marked by big patches of churned-up mud, especially at the watering place beside a little burn that came chattering down from the hillside. By the gate, horses' hooves had torn up the ground as they hauled in carts that were parked here and there over the field. There was a group of slatternly women standing gossiping by the gate while ragged children and skinny dogs cavorted around them. Men were busy building the huts and sheds in which they would live for the duration of the work in Rosewell.

Once more people waved when they recognised Tim Maquire. 'Hey, Black Ace, so you're on this job too – that's good!' they called. He was obviously well-respected among them.

Tim stood up in the front of the cart beside the driver and looked for a good stopping place. 'Go up to the side of the hill near the trees,' he instructed. 'When it rains it won't be so muddy there.' As soon as the cart came to a stop, he vaulted to the ground and started giving more orders. Major Bob wakened too, miraculously sobered by her sleep. Without another word about London or Liverpool, she set to work with the men, hauling off bags and baskets and piling them up on the ground.

They had been working for over an hour when there was a cry from the foot of the field and a man came walking towards them with his arm raised, calling out, 'Tim Maquire! Tim Maquire! It's a miracle that I've found you here. I've been looking for you everywhere.'

Tim straightened from his task of hammering in posts and wiped his sweating brow as he stared at the approaching figure. 'Hey, it's Mr Wylie,' he called. Then he dropped his hammer and ran down the field shouting, 'It's good to see you, sir.' When they met the two men clasped hands with a beaming enthusiasm that Tim had not shown when greeting anyone else.

Wylie was the first to speak. 'I've been all over the place looking for you. Yesterday I went to Glasgow to that line that's going north, and this morning I was at Penicuik – but they told me you'd left and no one knew where you were going.'

'Yes, I kept that quiet,' Tim grinned. 'I didn't want them flooding after me and taking all the work. Aw, don't tell me this is your contract, Mr Wylie! I can't be so lucky, can I?'

'It is Tim, it is, and I'm lucky too because the man I want to run my labour force is you. Will you be my chief ganger? There's not another man can match you.'

They shook hands again. 'Of course I'll work for you, Mr Wylie. You've always been a good boss for me and for my father . . .' As he said this Tim's face became more solemn and he added, 'I was sorry to hear about Mr James. He was a good lad, a promising lad. He'd have carried on where you leave off.'

Wylie nodded, his eyes stricken. 'It was a terrible thing to happen – an accident, God's will. But you've had a loss too since we last met. I heard about your father and I'm sorry. He was a fine man.'

Tim's face was grim. 'That was an accident, too – in Preston. A falling block of stone caught him; he was too old to get out of the way. Thank God it was instant, though.'

'I'm sorry,' said Wylie again. 'I never knew a man I respected more than him. He had dignity as well as strength. I always felt he had a story to tell if he chose.'

Tim nodded. 'Aye, and a sad story too. We once owned a farm in Ireland, but the English came and took it off us. Then they rented it back to my family again, but one day the landlord sent men to drive us off. It was the famine time. My mother died of starvation and my father and I came to England because he heard there was work on the railways. His dream was to make enough money to go back a rich man; one day I'll do it for him.'

Wylie put an arm round the young man's shoulders as they walked up the slope towards the half-built hut. 'Stick with me, Tim, and I'll see you make your pile,' he said firmly. He always called Tim by his real name and never Black Ace, because he'd known him since he was a lad fetching and carrying for his father on various sites.

Tim grinned. 'I'll stick with you, Mr Wylie, and so will

93

my men. Now tell me what you're going to build here. It's a bridge, isn't it? You're the bridge man.'

'Tomorrow when you've finished your hut and got settled in, we'll take a drive to see where the bridge is going. It's a bad place, but we'll do it. I'm sure of that now I've found you,' said Wylie in an optimistic tone.

After he left the navvy camp, Christopher Wylie took rooms at the Abbey Hotel in Rosewell. It had once been the gatehouse of the old Abbey and its walls harboured thriving colonies of bugs that were ravenous for new blood. Amazingly, bug-bites, plus the sleep-disrupting tolling of the Abbey bell which was rung at eight o'clock in the evening, at midnight and at six in the morning, failed to depress Wylie's spirits. He woke full of good cheer and when he arrived at the camp to collect Tim Maquire next morning, he looked years younger than he had done on the previous day.

'We're going on an expedition,' he announced as they walked to the waiting hackney carriage he had hired.

'Where to?' asked Tim, who was not averse to the idea of an outing.

'First of all we'll look at the north bank of the river, and then we'll go over to the other side where the main supports of the bridge will be built. I warned you it'll be a difficult job: now I want you to see it for yourself.'

Tim smiled happily. 'I like challenges.'

The first place they stopped was a mile downriver from Rosewell. They climbed out and stood looking over the edge of a sheer precipice to where the river sparkled far below. Tim glanced at Wylie and asked, 'Must it be built here? Couldn't it go on flatter land?'

'No, apparently not. All the flat land belongs to the Duke of Allandale and he's very anti-railway. He's doing all he can to stop it, but two big landowners are holding out against him. The bridge has to be here because this is the only route that can cross their land. A man called Raeburn who's on the railway company board owns this ground and that meadow on the other side of the river.'

'I see, so the line goes here . . . But it's a sheer drop of forty feet at least!'

'Fifty, actually,' said Wylie, 'but I've taken that into account. I'm going to throw my bridge high across from here on tall pillars to that rising land behind the big meadow, which belongs to the second railway company man, Colonel Anstruther. Then the line will run along the back of that little village you can see on the top of the hill.'

Tim nodded and asked, 'What do the villagers think about it?'

Wylie shrugged. 'I don't imagine anyone has asked them. Anstruther owns the land behind the village and we have to use that.'

Tim shaded his eyes with one hand and stared hard down into the valley. 'It's a difficult one, right enough. How many piers will you need to carry the bridge?'

'Nineteen – all tall and narrow like slim tree trunks. That'll be a good bit to build on. I've a vision of it in my mind.'

Tim looked into the older man's face and said slowly, 'This'll make you famous, Mr Wylie. Even more famous than you are already.'

Wylie laughed, and the flash of white teeth and the way his eyes crinkled showed how handsome he had been as a young man. 'You've hit the nail on the head, Tim lad. I'm after fame: I want to build a bridge that'll take people's breath away. I'm glad it has to go on this site because although it's difficult, it has tremendous possibilities. Not many men would attempt it. Look over there and picture it – piers as thin as wands with arches soaring to the sky. I saw an illustration in a book once, showing an aqueduct the Romans built in France: I'm taking that as my inspiration.'

Tim was solemn. 'Thin as wands, eh? They'll have to be strong, though. You don't want to be remembered as the man whose bridge fell down, do you?'

'There's no danger of that. My piers will be built of stone and they'll be as solid as rocks. Come on, let's go over to the other side and I'll show you where they'll be built.'

They walked back to the carriage which conveyed them again to Rosewell, where it turned south in the square and headed for an old stone bridge across the river. This bridge was only wide enough to admit one vehicle at a time and there were two little stone bays built into each side, jutting out like balconies over the fast-flowing river. In those bays, pedestrians could take shelter from the passing traffic.

The road-bridge was squat and very strong, built on two arches over the Tweed and supported on three stubby piers, all as solid as bastions. On each side of the bridge, facing outwards, were two carved shields in bas-relief showing vases with lilies spraying out of them. Wylie and Maquire were interested in the bridge's construction from a professional point of view and leaned from the carriage to look back at it when they reached the other side. The driver saw their interest and said over his shoulder, 'Did you notice the foundations? They only show when the river's low. You're lucky we've had a dry spell and they're showing today.'

'What do you mean?' asked Wylie, and the driver laughed. 'Folk don't notice 'em. I'll show you.' He drew on the reins and pointed with his whip. 'Look down at the water level. What do you see?'

Tim screwed up his eyes. 'Bags of cement. How old is this bridge?'

'More than a hundred years. It was built when my father's father was a wee laddie and he would've been a hundred and fifteen if he was still alive.'

Tim shook his head. 'I didn't know they were using cement like that then. It's amazing it's lasted so long in water.'

'That's because it's no' cement: it's wool.'

The driver achieved his desired effect, for his listeners looked first at the bridge and then at him in disbelief. '*Wool*?' asked Tim.

'Aye, bags o' wool. My grandfather used to say he

helped lay them down in the river bed, and when they get wet they go as hard as stone – harder in fact. The piers are built on top. It's an old trick and it worked a treat.'

Tim looked at Wylie and laughed. 'Don't try it, Mr Wylie – don't even think about it! Stick to the way you know.'

On their way to the southern side of the planned bridge, they drove through Camptounfoot which was looking its best under the sunshine, with early flowers blooming in the cottage gardens and fruit forming on the orchard trees. Its tranquillity gave no hint of the trouble behind the closed front doors, for dissension over the railway continued to divide the people.

The first house in the village was the mill, and its moss-covered wooden wheel was slowly creaking round as they passed. The miller and his family were traditionalists who did not want a railway. Two old men stood leaning against the mill's whitewashed wall and looked bleakly at the carriage as it drove by. 'They don't seem to like strangers here,' said Tim soberly.

The village street was cobbled so their wheels made a ringing sound as they rode around the corner where the little shop stood. Mamie's face showed at the window and she smiled at the sight of them, as did the man sweeping the doorstep of a low-roofed alehouse, but women carrying buckets of water from the well stared bleakly in the direction of the strangers. Cottages clustered close to the road edge, with doors opening right into it, and the travellers caught sight of skirt-flounces and pinafore-ends as the women ran back inside, dragging children out of the way of the carriage. 'It's a pity it's so unfriendly,' said Mr Wylie, and the garrulous driver was a mine of information here too. 'They're canny folk here. They believe in keeping themselves to themselves. It's certainly a queer place to drive through on a winter's night, I can tell you. Funny things have been seen here.'

Tim was interested and asked, 'What sort of things?'

'Apparitions, but the locals don't talk about them. They keep their secrets.' By now they were at the top of the village and open country spread before them again. Only one house remained to be passed, a tall building that stood like a gatehouse at the end of the street. None of them noticed a strained white face staring down at them from a tiny bull's-eye window on the gable wall.

The field where the bridge was to be commenced lay only a few hundred yards beyond the village boundary and the driver said cordially, 'Take your time, gentlemen. I'll put the carriage under those trees and wait for you there.' He pointed to a beech copse at the top of the road where he intended to have a quiet doze.

The pair climbed down and headed for the river, where they stood with their boots in the shallows, picking up stones and examining the consistency of the ground. 'I wonder what would happen if I floated my piers on woolsacks?' mused Wylie, but Tim shook his head.

'Stick to cement and stone. At least we know they won't shift.'

'But the wool didn't either, did it? Maybe the old bridge-builders knew something we don't.'

'Their bridge wasn't going to carry a train – yours is,' Tim reminded him and Wylie laughed.

'I'm surprised to find you being so conservative, Tim,' he said.

They walked the ground carefully, pacing it out while Wylie consulted the plans in his hand. They took soil samples, they drove sticks into the earth to test the depth of the covering, they stared all around taking their bearings, estimating and discussing. They were so engrossed that they did not notice a figure slipping over the adjacent field and lying down behind a hedge that ran along its boundary. It was when Wylie was climbing the ridge to get a better view, that the spy jumped out at him. Tim was in the lower part of the valley and all he heard was a fearsome yell.

A man was screaming, 'I'll kill you, you bastard! You're not going to take my field! You're not going to build your bloody bridge here!' Craigie Scott was standing up behind the hedge with a gun in his hand, his face distorted and

98

his hair flying. The gun was pointing at Wylie, only a few feet away. 'I'm going to kill you. That'll stop them!' he yelled again.

Wylie straightened his shoulders. Strangely, he was not afraid as he looked down the barrel of the old-fashioned gun, but he did not have time to say anything or fully realise how close he was to dying because Tim suddenly burst into view, running fast with his head down. He charged straight into Craigie's back, threw him to the ground and fell on top of him. The gun was pointed to the sky as it went off, blasting shot into the empty air and making crows rise squawking out of the trees in alarm.

Tim was yelling too. 'I'll kill you first – I'll snap your neck like a chicken bone.' His hands were round Craigie's thin throat and he was banging his head up and down on the hard ground. 'Kill you, kill you, I'll kill you,' he was grunting, and did not stop until a concerned Wylie pulled him off.

'Stop it! If you kill him, they'll hang you, not him. Stop it, man, stop it. I'm all right – he didn't shoot me.'

Tim was transported with fury. He rarely lost his temper but when he did he was uncontrollable. However, Wylie's entreaties eventually succeeded in calming him and he let go of Scott, who crawled away sobbing, 'You cannae tak' my field. We've farmed it for a hundred and fifty years.'

'You can still farm it,' said Wylie, picking up the gun and carefully unloading it just in case. 'When the bridge is finished, you can farm it again.'

Scott was sitting on the ground shaking his head. 'No, not after it's been dug up, not then. It'll be spoilt. Everything'll be spoilt. I should have shot you.'

Tim hauled him to his feet, shaking him like a stuffed doll. 'Stop that! Where do you live?' he demanded.

The carriage-driver, who had heard the shot, came running up and shook his head at the sight of the three of them. 'Oh God, it's Craigie Scott! Aren't you going to take him to the police? Did he try to kill you?' he asked Wylie, who shook his head. Navvies had as little to do with the police as they could. 'No. Tell us where he lives and we'll take him back. He's drunk, I think,' he told him.

'He's no' drunk. He's too damned mean to get drunk, but if that's what you want we'll drive him back to his house. His sisters'll take care of him,' said the driver.

As they headed for the farmhouse, with Craigie sitting between Tim and Wylie in the back, he began raving again. 'You cannae tak' my field. What's going to happen to this village? It's the work of the devil to bring a railway here . . .' His voice, high and shrill, went echoing down the street and made people throw open their doors in alarm to see what was going on.

At the farmhouse, Tim hauled the distraught man out of the carriage and handed him over to a wispy-looking little woman who appeared in the doorway. 'Here, take him in and keep him out of trouble. You're lucky we didn't hand him over to the police,' he told her, and then ran back to the waiting carriage which set off at a good clip downhill.

As they were driving past the next cottage, its door opened and the most beautiful girl Tim had ever seen stepped out into the road. The sun made her red hair glitter like gold and the face she turned up to the passing carriage was oval and perfect, with enormous brown eyes that stared straight into his and turned his heart over in his chest. He gave a startled gasp because he had never seen such a lovely girl in his life before. He was sure she was a vision.

Because it was a fine day, Hannah had run the short distance home from Bella Vista to spend a few hours in the afternoon with her mother. They were chattering happily in the kitchen when their peace was disturbed by the sound of shouting coming from the street. Running to the front door, Hannah opened it and found herself staring into the eyes of a stranger who gazed back with a terrible intensity. When she looked up at the dark face, Hannah felt a curious leaping in her heart, a sort of recognition or precognition, but there was no time to think about it for in her ear her mother hissed, 'What an evil-looking devil! Oh Hannah, I think he must be yin of thae navvies.'

The carriage passed and the two women ran out into the roadway to stare at Craigie, who was gesticulating and shouting at the top of his lungs: 'I should have shot him! You'd all have thanked me if I'd shot him!'

His frantic sisters and his two female farmworkers, the bondagers Big Lily and Wee Lily, were hauling at him, attempting to force him into the house. Eventually they succeeded, and only his manic screams could be heard echoing over the orchard wall. '*I should have shot the bastards! I should have shot them both and then there would be no railway here . . .*'

When the noise finally died down, Hannah and her mother looked at each other with disquiet. 'I told you Craigie would start shooting folk,' whispered Tibbie.

'But that's not even his field where the bridge is going. He only rents it from Falconwood,' said Hannah in bemusement. All this to-do about the railway was beginning to oppress her. She thought the villagers of Camptounfoot were being very stupid.

'But they've rented it for years. His father had it before him so he thinks it's his. Big Lily was telling me the other day that when Craigie got the letter saying that Falconwood was terminating their agreement, he went about mad. I think there's something in that field he wants to keep for himself,' Tibbie said.

Hannah asked, 'What do you mean? What can there be? It's just an ordinary field, isn't it?'

Tibbie shook her head. 'None of the fields round here are ordinary, you should ken that by now. Funny bits and pieces even turn up in our garden. If we find them here, what can Craigie find in the fields when he ploughs? You ken that cottage down by the burn, the one Jimmy Thomson bought and calls Fortune Cottage? How do you think he got the money to buy that?'

Hannah shook her head. 'I've no idea. Maybe somebody left him a legacy.'

Tibbie snorted. 'Jimmy dug his legacy up, that's what.

Folk in this village have been digging things up for generations. I mind my father telling me about a golden sword he once found; there's even those bonny blue beads you came across in the hayfield when you were a bairn. I think Jimmy Thomson found a pot full of money when he was ploughing for Craigie, and they shared it between them. They're maybe still finding stuff – that'd be a reason Craigie's so keen to keep the railway off his land. If they start excavating the earth, there's no telling what they'll find – and you know how grippy Craigie is. He cannae stand the idea of anybody else getting something he thinks should be his.'

Hannah pulled at her mother's sleeve. 'Come on, Mam. I'm due back at Bella Vista by six o'clock – what about that walk we promised ourselves? It's a fine afternoon and it'll take your mind off all this nonsense.'

'It's not nonsense, my girl,' Tibbie objected sadly, but she went inside nonetheless, and a short while later she and Hannah were back on the street with heavy boots on their feet and shawls across their shoulders.

'Which way will we go?' asked Hannah, staring around at the peaceful landscape.

'This way,' said Tibbie, pulling her daughter in the direction of Craigie's house. It was ominously quiet as they walked past it – not even the normally vicious dog came out to bark at them. Tibbie marched on purposefully towards a narrow lane that branched off the main road beyond the farmhouse. There, the lane was sunk between high hedges of holly, elder and ash, so deeply walked down by generations of feet that it seemed like a tunnel into the Underworld.

'I know where you're going – you're as bad as Craigie,' said her daughter accusingly, but Tibbie did not pause. She walked on with her head down and a set expression on her face.

'It's a long time since I've seen it,' she declared.

'But it always makes you greet,' protested Hannah.

'I like greetin' sometimes,' said Tibbie.

The lane led as straight as an arrow to the eastern

horizon, where another hedge crossed it in a north-to-south direction. When they reached that, the village was left well behind them, and the only trace of it was the smoke from its chimneys spiralling up into the clear sky. They paused beneath a big ash-tree that reached its branches high and creaked mournfully as the wind blew through it. Tibbie gazed around. 'This is where they'll be running the railway line, I think. I hope they don't spoil it,' she said softly.

Hannah took her mother's hand and pointed into a little wooded glade through which a burn softly chattered. 'It's down there, isn't it?' she asked.

Tibbie nodded. 'You're right, lass – that's where it is. You've a good memory and I've only brought you here twice, I think.'

Hannah shook her head. 'Three times. I've never forgotten it. I thought it was so sad.'

Tibbie hugged her. 'Oh Hannah, it's not sad really. It's life – it's history.'

'All right, I'll remember to tell you that when you start greeting,' said the girl with a little smile. As they spoke, they were climbing a bank and pushing their way through the second hedge, ignoring the springing young bramble-bushes that grabbed at their shawls. Then they half-ran, half-slid down into the burn. Its banks were soft and spongy and Hannah made a face as her feet sank into the morass up to the ankles. 'Oh, my new stockings!' she protested, but her mother did not seem to hear her because she was already scrambling up the other bank towards a big elder-bush that sprouted out of a shelf of rock over-hanging the burn.

'It's in there,' she panted. 'That bush has grown up around it since the last time I was here. Elders grow like weeds – three feet a year,' she gasped as she struggled upwards.

'Take your time, Mam,' cautioned Hannah, but as she spoke her mother was snapping branches off the elder-bush and feeling around with her hands on the mossy ground.

Then she cried in delight, 'Oh, here it is, Hannah! It's still here!'

Hannah climbed the bank to join her and wrinkled her nose as she too bent down. 'There's a fox been here as well – I can smell it,' she said.

'Well, it's safe enough for the summer. The Duke and his hunters won't be back till the winter comes again,' said Tibbie with satisfaction, also sniffing the air. She was piling broken branches on the bank and scraping with her hands at what looked like an outcrop of rock, 'It's all covered with ivy,' she told her daughter. 'We'll have to clean it.'

There were several broken fingernails as they scraped away at the clinging ivy and the lichen that covered the surface of the stone. 'Why don't we just leave it?' asked Hannah, halfway through the task, but Tibbie demurred.

'Oh no. I want to see it again.'

'You just want a weep, that's what's wrong with you,' teased Hannah, but she went on helping to clean the surface of the stone.

At last her mother sat back on her heels and said in satisfaction, 'There they are, the poor souls.'

Hannah squatted down beside her. 'Yes, there they are,' she breathed with a sad note in her voice, for what their work had revealed were the carved outlines of a woman and a child. The woman was shown with her head bent as if she was talking to the child, and one hand was laid lovingly on its shoulder. Both of them were clad in long loose robes, and the woman's cloak was pulled around her throat as if to protect her from the cold. 'She'd feel awful chilly up here if she came from Rome,' said Tibbie softly.

'You don't know she came from Rome,' said Hannah.

'I'm sure she did. When my father found this stone, he got the old schoolmaster from Rosewell to take a look at it and he read the writing on it. He said her name was Flavia and the wee girl was her daughter Corellia. They died at the same time and the schoolmaster said the stone was put up by Flavia's husband, Titus. He must have been broken-hearted when they died.'

There was a catch in her voice as she spoke and her daughter patted her shoulder. 'I knew you'd greet. It always does that to you.'

'I'm not greetin,' sniffed Tibbie, but her eyes were wet.

The slab had sunk into the ground; one side was lower than the other, so that the mother's fond leaning towards her child was accentuated. Large crude letters were inscribed along the top, and Hannah traced them with her finger. 'I wish I could read what it says,' she told her mother, who replied, 'I don't know anybody with the Latin any more. I don't think even Tommy Anderson would be able to read it. Anyway, it's best if we keep it a secret.'

Hannah sighed. In spite of her determination to stop her mother from becoming emotional, she also found the stone very affecting and had to force herself to sound brisk when she said, 'That's the trouble with Camptounfoot – everything's always got to be kept secret.'

Her mother looked up in surprise. 'But it's aye been like that,' she protested. 'When my father found this stone, he showed it to me and William, and to the scholar from Rosewell, but he didn't tell anybody else. We've respected it.'

Hannah gave a little frown. 'How do you know there's not other people in the village keeping things like this secret? Maybe even keeping this to themselves!'

Tibbie sniffed. 'I'm sure there's lots of secrets in Camptounfoot. Like I told you, that is what's bothering Craigie, but I'm not greedy like him. I don't want to dig this up and sell it to some museum. I just want it to stay where Titus put it to mark the grave of his wife and bairn. Like I said, it's a matter of respect. Come on, help me clean it up a wee bit. Poor souls, we cannae leave them all dirty like this. I wish I'd brought a brush to give them a scrub, but I didn't think it would be so overgrown.'

She began rubbing at the surface of the stone with the corner of her apron and Hannah helped as well. After they had been at work for a while, the figures on the stone emerged more clearly and they could see that the woman had some sort of ornament in her hair and a sweet smile on her face. The child looked angelic. Tibbie paused at last and said softly, 'Well, that's the best we can do. I hope they go on lying in peace here for a long, long time. My father said this stone was put up about the same time as Jesus was alive. Imagine that! It fair breaks my heart to think of them lying hidden here for so long. Poor Titus. I wonder what happened to him after he buried them.'

The poignancy of the little glade affected Hannah too and there were tears in her eyes as she laid an arm over her mother's shoulders and hugged her close. 'It's sad, that's true, but it all happened a long time ago. Don't upset yourself, Mam. I'm sure nobody's going to move it. Come on, let's cover it up again and go home. I've got to be back at Bella Vista soon because there's a big dinner tonight and young Mrs Anstruther's maid says that her mistress is going to look a perfect picture in a new gown she's had sent up from London.'

They pulled the undergrowth back over the partially cleaned stone and when it was once again well hidden, re-traced their footsteps through the fields and down the lane. Hannah's ploy to divert her mother worked, for Bethya was always a great distraction. Tibbie said in a disapproving tone, 'That young Mrs Anstruther seems to spend an awful lot of money. She's aye getting things sent up from London, isn't she?'

'Yes, practically every week, but I don't blame her. It can't be much fun being married to Mr Gus. He's never sober, not even in the morning. He reels about the house with a glazed look on his face and then falls into a chair and snores so loud that you'd think he was trying to bring the roof down.'

'Does nobody stop him?' asked Tibbie in amazement.

Hannah laughed wryly. 'Stop him? Quite the opposite. His father has washed his hands of him – the Colonel hardly ever looks at him. His mother doesn't see anything wrong with him – she thinks he's perfect – and Mrs

Bethya passes him a drink any time he asks for it. She just smiles and hands him the bottle. The butler says she's trying to make her husband drink himself to death so's she can marry again.'

'Just imagine!' gasped Tibbie with round eyes. She was being entranced by Hannah's descriptions of Bethya's new costumes, when two figures emerged from a field-gate ahead of them and stepped into the lane. One of them raised an arm and called, 'Hey, Tibbie!'

'It's Big Lily,' said Tibbie, grasping Hannah's arm. 'She'll be wanting to talk about what happened to Craigie.'

Hannah nodded. 'Then don't let it go on too long, Mam. Remember I've got to be back at work soon.'

With Big Lily, the bondager, was her daughter Wee Lily. Both of them were dressed in the uniform of women farm-labourers – an ankle-length striped skirt, men's boots and a flat black straw hat that was tied on to the head by a triangle of sprigged cotton. They stood side by side, nodding like automata as the other mother and daughter approached. Big Lily was obviously bursting with gossip and could hardly wait for them to get into earshot before she started talking. 'My, wasn't that a terrible thing that happened to Craigie? He's got a black and blue patch in the middle of his back as big as a kailpot. That's where the navvy butted him wi' his heid.'

Hannah said, 'He shouldn't have been trying to shoot people.'

Big Lily shot her a baleful glance. 'You're getting awful grand-sounding, Hannah. Is working in the big house turning you into a lady?'

Tibbie leapt to her daughter's defence. 'She has to talk proper or they wouldn't ken what she was saying up there in Bella Vista, would they?'

Wee Lily, who was slightly simple-minded, was standing grinning vacuously beside her mother and she said happily, 'They'd never understan' me nor my mither then, wid they?'

Big Lily snorted. 'I wouldna want to work in a hoose

anyway. Penned up a' day at their beck and call, never able to get out into the open air.'

'Hannah gets oot. She's oot now, isn't she?' protested Tibbie.

'But she's no' her ain boss, is she? You should have got her a job on the land, Tibbie, it's far healthier.'

Hannah had heard this discussion many times before and was determined to put a stop to it. 'I wouldn't want to work outside,' she stated firmly. 'I don't like getting wet. I'd hate to go out in bad weather.'

Wee Lily looked shocked. 'Och, weather's guid for ye, Hannah. But I think you're too bonny to be a bondager. Maybe in a big hoose you'll meet a fancy gentleman and get merrit to him.'

Hannah giggled. 'Maybe I will, Lily. If I do I'll ask you to the wedding.'

At that she felt her mother pulling at her sleeve and heard her saying, 'We'll have to be off. Hannah's got to go back to Bella Vista now.' Tibbie practically hauled her daughter away, leaving the two Lilies with their red-hot gossip about Craigie still burning their lips, and when they were out of earshot she hissed, 'What did you mean by saying you'd invite them to your wedding? I'd not have them there at any price.'

Hannah was amused. 'I knew that would annoy you. They're all right, Mam, they're innocent enough.'

By this time they were at the cottage door and Tibbie flounced inside, saying over her shoulder, 'If that's what you call innocent, you and I have different meanings for the word.'

Hannah was surprised at her mother's vehemence. 'I know they're bondagers, and bondagers get a bad name but there's never been any scandal about the Lilies except for when Wee Lily was born.'

Tibbie was thrusting the blackened kettle into the middle of fire. 'Exactly,' she snapped.

'Oh Mam,' said Hannah. 'Lots of lassies have a bairn before they're married. There's at least ten in this village alone.' Tibbie sniffed and her daughter went on, 'Anyway, nobody knows who Wee Lily's father is. If it was Jo like people say, you can't blame Big Lily. Jo's queer as queer can be.'

'It wasnae Jo that fathered Wee Lily,' said Tibbie shortly.

'Then was it Daft Andie the loonie at the mill-house?' asked Hannah curiously.

Tibbie shook her head. 'Not him either.'

'How do you know who it is?' asked her daughter suspiciously.

'I know because I helped Big Lily when she was in labour. She came in from the field one afternoon and I heard her groaning in the hay-shed when I was passing. She told me who the father was then.'

'In that case, having led me on so much, you've got to tell me too. Who was it?' asked Hannah.

'It's Craigie Scott,' threw out Tibbie, pouring boiling water from the kettle into her teapot.

There was a silence behind her as Hannah stared at her with horrified eyes. 'But Mam, everybody says that Craigie and Big Lily are half-brother and sister. Big Lily's father was Craigie's father, too. Her mother was his bondager.'

'That's true,' said Tibbie.

'And Craigie fathered Wee Lily?' asked Hannah in disbelief.

'He did – and that's why she's the way she is. Bairns born like that are often short of a shillin'.'

Hannah's face flushed. 'Oh, poor things. That's a terrible story and I don't think it's Big Lily's fault. What could she do? She's only a bondager. You know how they're treated.'

Tibbie nodded. 'There's something in that, but Big Lily didnae seem to think there was anything wrong with it. She told me she'd never need go to a hiring fair if she's got Craigie's bairn.'

Hannah was genuinely shocked. 'That's awful. He treated her like an animal and she's grateful!'

Tibbie furrowed her brow. 'Well, Big Lily's an idle

besom really and so was her mother. She'd not find it easy to get another good place.'

Hannah thumped the table. 'Do you think being at Craigie's is a good place? Those two women live in a shed that's worse than anything he'd use for his cattle. It's Craigie I blame, not Big Lily. That he'll never send her away isn't any excuse for him. I've never liked him and I like him a lot less now. I'm glad that navvy butted him. I wish he'd broken his ribs!'

CHAPTER
Six

When the Abbey bell struck midnight, Christopher Wylie woke in a cold sweat and lay trembling in bed for a few minutes before he realised what was wrong with him. He had wakened up to the full knowledge of how close he'd come to being killed that day. The narrowness of his brush with death made beads of sweat stand out on his forehead and waves of nausea sweep over him. When he had stared down the barrel of Craigie Scott's gun he had been calm and controlled, for he had not let himself think about what was happening. It was only now in the silence of the night that terror gripped him. Shaking, he rose from the lumpy, creaking bed and padded over to the window to breathe fresh air. There was a huge moon floating like a full-sailed ship across the sky, and its rays illuminated the stark Abbey ruins in an eerie way so that they looked as if they were brushed with silver and made the shadows they cast as black as coal. Christopher was not normally a fanciful man, but tonight he imagined he saw dark figures flitting to and fro between the broken columns.

He passed a shaking hand over his face. Part of his anxiety was that he knew if he had died that afternoon, he would have left too many things undone. If he had been shot, his dependants in Newcastle would have found themselves penniless and embroiled in a contract which would be impossible for them to fulfil. All his available cash was committed to the bridge. His wife and his daughter would have been left paupers. He felt that he had been given a warning that it was irresponsible to ignore. 'I must do something about them. I must make them safe,' he said to himself. The time had come for him to go back to Newcastle and put his domestic affairs on a firm footing.

Next morning he felt too ill to eat breakfast and called for the carriage early. Before he could get into it, however, Tim Maquire appeared in the hotel. There was an anxious glint in his eye as he looked at his employer. 'I came to tell you to take things easy today, Mr Wylie,' he advised. 'You had a bad shock yesterday. It was a close call. I couldn't sleep all night myself for thinking about it.'

Wylie nodded. 'I didn't sleep either, but I've decided to go back to Newcastle today because there are things I ought to organise.'

Tim's look of concern deepened. 'You shouldn't travel today. You're very pale – go tomorrow.'

'No, I've made up my mind,' Wylie told him. 'It must be done now. When I'm away, try and find me a decent lodging, Tim. This place is bug-ridden and noisy and I won't be able to stand it for two weeks, far less two years. I'll be back before the end of the week and when I return we'll start on the first piers of the bridge. I'll leave it to you to get a good gang of labourers together.'

The hired carriage took him to the railway junction, and on arrival at Newcastle, he went straight to his lawyer Mr Johnstone and stayed closeted with him for three hours. During that time a message was sent out to tell Haggerty to come to collect his master. From the lawyer's office, Wylie called on Munro in the bank and finally, when it was almost dark, he climbed into his carriage for the final leg of his journey to Wyvern Villa. He was dog-tired and could see from the look on Haggerty's face that his exhaustion was obvious. 'You want to take it a bit easier at your age, Chris,' said the coachman solemnly.

'Just one more job, Haggerty. One more job and then I'll retire to a life of leisure. When all this is over I think I'll go to the South of France. Arabella and Emma Jane would like that, wouldn't they?'

Haggerty said nothing but looked back over his shoulder with a sad expression on his face.

Arabella was sitting with her daughter and granddaughter when he stepped into the drawing room. Amelia was not present. At the sight of them he made a conscious effort to stand up straight and smooth the haggard expression from his face, for he did not want to worry them.

When she saw him, Arbelle dropped her toys and ran over to grasp him round the legs. 'What have you brought for me, Grandpapa?' she asked.

He absently put a hand on her head and said, 'Nothing, my dear. You shouldn't ask for presents all the time, you know.' It was the only time he had ever been so abrupt with her.

Then he went over to kiss his wife and told her with undisguised relief, 'You're looking much better, darling.'

She twinkled at him with something of her old appeal. 'I do feel better, Christopher. Emma Jane's been taking great care of me. I've even been out driving this week.'

'Where's Amelia?' he asked, and his wife and daughter exchanged a glance over the child's head.

'She's gone to Hexham to visit her sisters,' said Emma Jane. 'Mama and I are looking after Arbelle till she comes back tomorrow.' He could tell from the tone of her voice that there was more to this than met the eye and that he'd hear it all later when Arbelle was in bed.

'Good, good,' he said. 'I want to see her when she returns.'

His wife looked at him curiously. 'What about?'

'Oh, just things,' he said vaguely. 'I was thinking the time had come when she might want a house of her own. When the bridge is finished I'd like us to go travelling, perhaps to France for six months or so. We could close up this house or even sell it and move elsewhere.'

Arabella clasped her hands. 'Oh Christopher, that would be wonderful! That's something for us all to look forward to, isn't it?' He was delighted by her response, and the burden on him seemed to lighten a little.

Later, when Emma Jane went off to put the child to bed, he and his wife were left alone together and he again said how much the improvement in her health and spirits pleased him.

'I have something to look forward to now,' she said with her old smile. 'I've got France to think about. Where will we go? I know – let's go to Menton. I've heard it's beautiful there. Mimosa grows wild . . .'

He took her hand and continued '. . . and lemon trees, and grapes on the vine . . . and the sun shines every day.'

'Perhaps things are getting better for us,' she whispered. 'And there's news about Amelia too. I think she's planning to marry again.'

His face changed. 'Is she? Who to?'

Arabella was surprised by his reaction. 'I thought you'd be glad! She hasn't said anything to us, but Arbelle's let some things drop. There's a man called Dan who's been paying court to Amelia whenever she goes to Hexham, and she's been there a lot recently. I'm half-expecting her to make an announcement when she comes back tomorrow.'

Wylie stood up, frowning. 'She can't do that yet.'

His wife said, 'Oh Christopher, she's not the sort to stay long without a man. You've only to look at her to see that.'

He shook his head. 'It's not that. It's just that there are certain matters I have to arrange with her – about my estate and Arbelle's future . . .'

His wife nodded in understanding. 'But you can do that even if she does get married, my dear. You can still make a settlement on Arbelle, surely? The only thing that worries me about Amelia getting married again is that we won't see the poor little darling so often. I don't think I can bear that. She's such a joy to me.'

'I'll ask Amelia to make sure you see plenty of Arbelle,' he reassured her. 'I'm sure that can be arranged. You mustn't worry, my love. You must keep on growing stronger – that's the most important thing.'

'Oh, but I am stronger. I was even able to go out calling three times last week with Emma Jane. She's so shy and awkward, Christopher, that it made me realise how I must make a greater effort for her sake. She hardly ever opens her mouth when she's with strangers and I'm sure my friends think she's a mute or very stupid, when you and I know she isn't. How could we have produced a daughter like that – you're so handsome and I was the belle of Newcastle when I was young.' Arabella had been the most sought-after girl in the city – a lovely young thing with a laughing face and high spirits when he married her, and Wylie sighed at the memory.

'It can't be easy being the daughter of the belle of Newcastle,' he ventured, and she dimpled.

'You old flatterer. But seriously, Christopher, I'm worried about that girl. If a young man speaks to her, she panics.'

'Emma Jane's just shy and she hasn't met many young men,' he said gently. 'If you treat her tactfully she'll grow more confident in time. She's very young for her age. I still think of her as a child in a way, so perhaps it's our fault that she's so retiring. When she gets to the South of France, she'll change, though . . .'

Arabella laughed happily. 'Of course, so she will! Oh, that's going to be lovely. I'll dream about it every night till we set out.'

'Oh Arabella,' he thought. 'I wish I could really talk to you. I wish I could tell you how I felt after that madman tried to shoot me.' But he did not broach the subject because he was afraid that hearing about it might throw her back into weakness and depression.

After dinner, when he went into his library, he was surprised to see his daughter already there, bending intently over the papers spread out on his desk. For a moment he thought she was spying on him, finding out about his complicated financial affairs, but when she spun round he could see from her face that she was innocent of such duplicity. 'I was looking at your plans, Papa. I think they're splendid,' she announced excitedly.

'Yes, they are, aren't they?' he said proudly, walking over to stand beside her and spread the plans out flatter with his open palm. 'This is going to be my swan song, Emma Jane, my best bridge ever.'

She looked up with shining eyes. 'Then it'll be magnificent. You've built some lovely bridges.' He was surprised because he was not aware that she knew of anything he'd done. He was about to roll the plans up when she stayed his hand. 'Tell me about it, Father. How high is it going to be? How long will it take to build? What do all those lines of figures down the margin mean?'

'It's going to be over one hundred and fifty feet high in the middle, and it'll take more than two years to build. I've agreed to have it finished by the beginning of August eighteen fifty-five. The figures in the margins are my calculations about stress resistance and weight-bearing, that sort of thing.' He was flattered that she was interested but did not take her seriously. He thought she was only being tactful.

Then she surprised him again by saying, 'I think the design's very elegant and I recognise it. I saw a bridge just like it in one of the books in your library. It said the Romans built it near Avignon. Is that where you got the idea?'

'Yes, it is.' Impressed by her perspicacity, he pointed to one of the plans and said, 'Look, I'm going to build nineteen piers. Maquire thinks they're too spindly, but they're not – they'll carry it.'

She nodded as she leaned over the plans beside him. Then she said, 'So you found your Mr Maquire, did you?'

'Yes, and thank God I did. He's recruiting a good squad of men for me now. He'll have it all done by the time I get back.'

'Oh Papa,' she sighed, 'I wish I could help you. The idea of building something like this thrills me.'

'It's not women's work Emma Jane,' he said amused. 'And to prove it, I've something to tell you that you mustn't repeat to your mother. Yesterday, a man tried to shoot me.'

To do her credit she did not react hysterically. All she said was: 'Why?'

'Because I'm putting the bridge on a field which he uses to graze his animals.'

'For that he tried to shoot you? It's so trivial.' Her tone was horrified and disbelieving.

'It's not trivial to him. The people in that part of the world are very territorial and stuck in their ways. There's a village beside the bridge where people turn their heads away when railway-workers pass through it. They don't like us spoiling their peace and tranquillity.'

She nodded slowly. 'That's very sad, but I can understand how they feel in a way. A railway must be very frightening to people whose way of life hasn't changed for centuries. But please take care – you're very precious to us, Father.'

He was gratified by her concern. 'When the man tried to shoot me it had one good effect,' he admitted. 'It made me aware of how difficult it would be for you and your mother if I was to die suddenly. I came home to organise my affairs.'

Her solemn amber eyes were fixed on his face as he went on: 'I've told my lawyer to make arrangements for you.'

'For me? But I'm all right.'

'I've bought you an annuity so that you'll always have an income. It's not large, but if things work out the way I plan, I'll buy you a bigger one later. In the meantime you'll at least have something.'

She didn't ask for any details but he gave her them anyway. 'I've bought a three per cent annuity that will give you one hundred and fifty pounds a year.' As he spoke the words, he reflected that it cost him more than that for the annual upkeep of the gardens alone at Wyvern Villa.

His daughter was making different calculations, however. 'Five thousand pounds is a lot of money to spend on me, Papa,' she protested.

He stared at her in astonishment, for he had no idea she could do mathematical calculations. When she had attended a girls' school in Newcastle, she had received an undistinguished record. Her reports always stressed her amenable nature, but said little about her academic abilities and achievements.

'It'll give you an independent income, my dear,' he said, and she surprised him by suddenly throwing her arms round his neck and planting a kiss on his cheek.

'Thank you so much, thank you,' she cried, as if he'd given her five thousand a year.

'Your first payment will fall due next week, and I want you to buy something pretty to wear with it,' he told her.

Her face fell. 'But I don't need any new clothes, Papa.'

'Every young lady needs new clothes and your mother wants you to go out into society more,' he said, but it was obvious that this idea depressed her. He persisted, however. 'It helps Arabella to get out. You must go with her, Emma Jane, because she can't go alone.'

The shuttered look came down over her face again. 'Of course I'll go, Papa,' she told him, but it was obvious that she would not enjoy herself.

Next day, when he was poring over his papers in the library, his daughter-in-law Amelia arrived home. He had told Emma Jane that he wanted to see James' wife as soon as possible, and within a short time of her arrival, she appeared beside him. Her look was cautious as she asked, 'You wanted to see me?'

He smiled. 'Yes I do, my dear. Sit down. I've a proposition to put to you.'

'A proposition?' The word made her even more wary.

'I want to buy you a house.'

'Oh yes?' Her eyes were searching his face, trying to discern his motives.

'There's a pretty little cottage for sale along the road. You may have seen it. I would like to buy it for you.'

Amelia bluntly asked, 'Why?'

'I want you to keep this to yourself, but I've had to pledge the deeds of Wyvern Villa to my bank as security for a loan and money I already owe to them. If anything happened to me before I could pay it all back, this house would belong to the bank. Emma Jane and my wife would have nowhere to live and no money – they'd lose everything. If you had a house, however, they could go there.'

Amelia's eye was sharp as she looked at him. 'Would they want to live with me? Besides, I've a problem about this plan. I'm thinking of getting married again. I was going to tell you all soon—'

'That won't make any difference. I've told my wife that when the bridge is finished we might sell Wyvern Villa, and I'd like to set you and Arbelle up in a place of your own but close by. If you get married again, your husband would probably be quite happy to get a wife with a cottage as her dowry.'

Amelia shook her head. 'The man I'm marrying won't care about any dowries. He lives in Hexham anyway and that's where I'll go when we wed. But we're not rushing into it. I know I'll have to wait till James has been dead for at least a year. That's why I've been taking it slowly about telling you all. There's no hurry.'

Christopher's face was worried but at this he cheered up a little. 'In that case, I can still go ahead with this plan. It would put my mind at rest, Amelia. If things go well with the bridge, you'll have your little house forever or be able to sell whenever you choose. In a way, I'm taking out an insurance policy by buying you a house.'

It was difficult to explain to himself why he was talking so plainly to this girl when he could not do so to either his wife or his own daughter, but there was a level-headedness and shrewdness about Amelia that reminded him of his own mother, who had come from a similiar background as the girl James had married. Amelia might look like a doll and sound like a servant-girl, but she was far from stupid.

She nodded and said, 'You're putting a house in my name so that if you crash, it won't be taken by your creditors. Why don't you buy it in Emma Jane's name?'

He shook his head. 'I can't buy the house for Emma Jane or Arbelle because if my estate was to be seized, that might be taken too. If the house is yours, though, that would be different. I'll provide the money and you can buy it in your own name, but I have one request. Please don't keep Arbelle away from her grandmother when you marry and go to Hexham. We all love the child so much.'

Amelia smiled. 'I know that. I wouldn't be so cruel because she loves all of you too, but I wish you weren't so soft with her. You're all spoiling her. She'll turn into a brat if she's not watched.'

He nodded in agreement. 'I know that's true, and we will try to be firmer with her. When you go to live in the cottage, let her see her grandmother every day as well.'

'Oh I will,' Amelia promised. 'But I have something to ask in return. Please tell your wife *not* to call my daughter "poor Arbelle". It really cuts me to the heart when she calls her that. I miss James and so does Arbelle, but I don't want us to be pitied because he's gone. It hurts my pride and I don't want my daughter to be made to feel that way either.'

'I promise you I'll tell my wife she must stop calling her that. I'll make sure she understands that it could be bad for the child,' he told her.

Amelia smiled her thanks but made no move to leave the room. Instead, she leaned forward in her chair and directed her most dazzling smile at him. 'Now we've two secrets between us, haven't we? My wedding to Dan and your worry about the house. I won't let you down, Mr Wylie, and I hope you don't mind me marrying again.'

'You've a long life ahead of you. You should get married again. I don't mind at all,' he said sincerely, thinking that no one in their right mind could expect a young woman like Amelia to stay a grieving widow for the rest of her life.

When he returned to Rosewell after only one week away, Christopher Wylie was astonished by how things had advanced in his absence. In search of Tim Maquire, his carriage took him to the navvy camp which he saw had already quadrupled in size, nor was its growth yet finished, for approaching along the road from the north came a long line of heavily laden carts that looked like an army on the move. This influx of people had turned what was recently a pasture into a shanty village of narrow streets, running east to west along the face of the slope, with one broad alley bisecting it from north to south. Smoke rose from a forest of chimneys sticking out of the jumble of roofs, some made of tarpaulin, others of turf or wood. There was a constant background din of shrieking women, crying children and barking dogs. Somewhere in the distance, someone was playing a trumpet.

Wylie was not the only person in the district to be impressed by the rapid growth of the navvy camp. It had obviously become a local landmark, for parties of smartly-dressed ladies and gentlemen had ridden out in gigs or phaetons to stare at it, loudly exclaiming among themselves over the ramshackle look of the huts, the villainous aspect of the women and the insolence of the dogs and children. They gawped with the same thrilled horror that people in cities experienced when they went to look at bedlams.

On hearing that Mr Wylie was back, Tim, resplendent in a scarlet pillbox hat with a long golden streamer flowing from the top of it, came running down the broad middle path. As he reached the carriage Wylie asked him, 'This is quite a change. How many men are here now?'

A grin flashed across the dark face. 'Over two hundred and fifty, but they're not all mine – yours, I mean. Jopp sent down a squad from Maddiston two days ago to start building the station here, and there's a line-laying gang moving in. They're extending the track from the north; it's past Maddiston now.'

'Who have you got for our job?' asked Wylie, and Tim pushed his hat to the back of his head as he rubbed a hand over his face.

'Let's think. As well as my own gang I've got the Donegal boys – remember them? And I brought in Benjy because he's a good carpenter. I promised them all five shillings a day and no truck. I've taken on Bullhead and his boys too. I know they're wild, but there's nobody faster than Bullhead when he gets his teeth into a job.'

Wylie pulled a face. 'But he's a trouble-maker – you'll

have to watch him. At the first sign of a riot, he's off the site. Remember the battle he caused at Preston? In the end they had to call out the Army!'

Tim nodded grimly. 'I've already warned him. I told him I'd wrap his prayer book round his neck if he causes any upset. The people round here don't like us anyway, and they'd be down like a ton of bricks at the first sign of trouble.'

Wylie laughed because he knew that when he talked about wrapping Bullhead's prayer book around his neck, Tim was referring to the man's huge earth-moving shovel. The navvies called their shovels 'prayer books' because they said they stared into them so much.

Now he nodded in approval. 'Anyway, you seem to have found some good men. Five shillings is top rate but these men are worth it. Well done, lad.'

Tim was pleased to have earned his boss' congratulations. 'The men are always ready to work for you, Mr Wylie. It's not just because you pay fair wages either, but Jopp's men are already grumbling because they're being paid half their wages in truck. He's buying in cheap food and paying them with that. He'll have trouble with them soon if he doesn't improve the quality of his supplies. The butter is rancid in the barrel and the meat's got worms in it.'

Wylie looked disgusted. 'That's a pity. If Jopp's men get restive, they could cause trouble among the others.'

Tim wasn't worried. 'Our men won't listen to them, they're all old hands. But there's still one thing I haven't done – I haven't found you other lodgings yet. I've tried all over Rosewell but nobody'll take in a man connected with the railway. They're all afraid of coming out in favour of it because the Duke of Allandale's the local landlord and they're scared of offending him.'

Wylie grimaced. 'Ah well, it's back to the bugs then,' but Tim told him, 'No, don't give up. There's one place I haven't tried yet – that village near the bridge. There must be somebody there who'll take a lodger.' He didn't say that he had taken to walking to and fro to the bridge site by way of Camptounfoot in the hope of catching another glimpse of the beautiful red-haired girl; so far, however, he had not seen her.

'Don't you think I might get murdered in my bed there?' Wylie asked, only half-joking. 'Remember our friend with the gun.'

'They can't all be mad in that place,' Tim objected, 'but I'll sound it out, Mr Wylie. I'll enquire at the alehouse tonight.'

As Wylie was driving away from the camp gate after speaking with Tim, a man he recognised as Colonel Anstruther, on a big bay horse and accompanied by a very pretty woman on a sweetly-pacing grey mare, rode up.

'Morning Wylie,' said Anstruther, for his sharp little eyes missed nothing, and though he'd only met the contractor once he immediately knew who he was. He reined in his horse beside the other's carriage and asked, 'When's the bridge going to begin?'

'Tomorrow, I hope. My men have already marked out the site of the north pier and we cut the first sods at dawn tomorrow.'

'Well done, that's quick work. I'll come over and watch. You've some fine-looking men, but there's a few villains among them, I can tell. It must be like managing an army, running a gang of navvies. It's difficult to control men like that.'

Wylie shrugged. 'I'm used to it. I've a good ganger to help me and most of them have worked for me before.' He sounded more confident than he really felt, for the prospect of two more years at the work-face secretly depressed him. 'I'm too old to go on like this much longer. Thank God for Maquire,' he thought.

Colonel Anstruther had a fair idea of the enormity of the effort that loomed in front of Wylie. They were about the same age and he knew that he would not like to have to shoulder the other man's responsibilities. The mechanics of railway-building fascinated him, however, and he had already got into the habit of riding over from Bella Vista every day to the camp to see what was going on.

A few days after she arrived in his house, his new daughter-in-law had offered to accompany him on his morning ride, and now they were making it a daily outing. The pair of them quickly struck up an unlikely alliance. The Colonel enjoyed Bethya's company, for his wife would not go near the navvy camp and his son was worse than useless as a companion. Gus never rose before noon and when he did, his first concern was to call for the brandy decanter, but Bethya was always eager for an outing because time hung heavily on her hands and, what was even more important, she took a vicarious pleasure in watching the magnificently muscled men who strode like gods around the navvy camp. On days when the sun shone, they took off their shirts and strutted about naked from the waist up. Bethya, who admired goodlooking men, loved those sunny days best of all.

Now the Colonel turned in his saddle and told her, 'If they start on the bridge site tomorrow, we'll go down to watch, my dear.'

She sparkled at him. 'Oh yes, Bap, let's! What a lufrah that'll be!'

When they were alone together they used many Anglo-Indian words which had quickly become part of their ordinary conversation, but which met with raised eyebrows of incomprehension at Bella Vista. The Colonel talked away happily to his daughter-in-law about burra pegs when he meant double whiskies; double roti when he meant bread; gharris instead of carriages; wallahs instead of men; chokras instead of boys ... Because she was so beautiful and exotic, because she awoke in him memories of lovely Indian princesses in shadowy palaces, he gave her the affectionate name of Begum and in return she called him Bap. Once or twice, a servant would hear her addressing him in this way and the news soon got back to the kitchen that young Mrs Anstruther called her father-in-law by the local word for a bread roll which was what Bap meant in the Borders. The scandalised servants did not realise it was also an affectionate Indian word for 'Father'.

'Yes, we'll come back tomorrow my dear, that'll be a sight to see, but we'd better go home now. That crook Miller's coming to luncheon,' the Colonel told her as they rode away.

When they reached Bella Vista, Francine was waiting in Bethya's chamber with steaming water in a Chinese *rose famille* bowl and a flounced muslin dress lying on the bed ready to be stepped into. Flapping her hands excitedly she said, 'You must hurry and dress. Sir Geoffrey has arrived in very good speereets. You must look as pretty as possible.'

Bethya sighed, 'I wish he was more attractive. I've been up at the navvy camp with Bap and those men are thrilling, Francine! They're wild and rough and so male. They turn my stomach to water just to watch them.'

Francine sniffed. 'They're animals. You must find yourself a gentleman. If you are clever with Sir Geoffrey you will have him on a string. The servants say that his wife is very sick now. She has not long to live, apparently. And he's very rich—'

'I know. He's also a bore and as pompous as a pandit but – don't say it – he's a baronet as well. And it's not as if I have much choice round here. No one ever invites us out except terrible rustics like Falconwood. I thought we'd move in society. I want to meet people like the Duke of Allandale – he's a bachelor, they say – but because of the railway, we've thrown our lot in with the wrong set. If I'd known how dull life was going to be here I'd never have married Gus.' Bethya sighed and stuck out her pretty feet for the maid to slip on her satin shoes. 'I have all those beautiful clothes and no one to admire me in them. I'm young and healthy and I need love – but what do I get? Gus, who doesn't even share a bed with me, not that I want him to, I must admit. The only thrills I have are from watching the navvies. I'm beginning to fantasise about being raped by one of them, I really am.'

Francine did not approve at all and her face showed her

distaste. Bethya leaned down and stared at her. 'I don't understand you. You're a woman, you're young and striking-looking but you have no beau, do you? Haven't you seen the navvies? Don't they make you long for them – with those muscles and the swaggering way they walk? They're real men. I thought French girls liked real men.'

'I think the navigators are very coarse,' said Francine, rolling her 'r's' in emphasis.

Bethya laughed teasingly. 'I love the way you say that word – *navigators*! You're a snob, that's what's wrong with you. But of course I am too. I might enjoy a navigator in my bed but I'd never marry one. And yes, you are right – I must concentrate on Sir Geoffrey and put the navvies out of my head. Where's my pearl necklace? It should go well with this dress.'

A few minutes later Bethya swept downstairs in a cloud of scent, with golden bracelets jangling on her elegant arms. She paused on the bottom step in full view of the drawing room, just long enough to give herself an advantageous entrance. When everyone was looking at her, she kicked back her skirt and stepped through the open door. Gus curled his lip as she advanced first on him and planted a kiss on his cheek. 'Good morning, darling,' she chirped. 'Are you feeling better today?'

His mother, sitting stiffly on the other side of the room, snapped, 'He'd be better every day if you didn't encourage him to drink so much.'

Bethya opened her lovely eyes very wide and said, 'Oh Mama, you mustn't say things like that. I love Gus but I can't stop him doing anything he wants to do. He's very headstrong.'

Mrs Anstruther's irritation was so overwhelming that she even forgot Sir Geoffrey was in the room. 'Don't Mama me,' she spat. 'I see how you're twisting my husband round your finger. I've heard you calling him Bap – but you're not going to call me Mama!'

Knowing full well that she was being watched by their guest, Bethya wisely said nothing. By acting meekly she had the advantage. The Colonel and Sir Geoffrey were both overwhelmed with pity for her and Anstruther resolved to remonstrate with his wife as soon as they were alone for bullying the poor girl so unmercifully.

Sir Geoffrey defused the situation by saying in an excited voice, 'I've brought good news today. The station at Maddiston's almost finished and the line's laid all the way between there and Edinburgh. We're going to open it officially next month, on the tenth actually, and can you guess who will perform the ceremony?' He looked around the room hopefully, encouraging one of them to hazard a guess.

'Your wife,' said Mrs Anstruther in a nasty tone while looking at Bethya.

Sir Geoffrey ignored that. For once he looked really animated. Bethya was laughing inside, wondering how he'd react if she suggested Genghis Khan or Christopher Columbus, but she fixed admiring eyes on his face and remained modestly silent.

Gus took a swig from his glass and muttered in a surly voice, 'Oh come, Miller, we could be guessing from now till Christmas. You'll have to tell us.'

'Queen Victoria herself!' said Sir Geoffrey, sitting back in his chair and slapping both hands on his knees.

The reaction was all he desired, even from the senior Mrs Anstruther. Her face went scarlet and she gasped, 'Is the Queen really coming to Maddiston? Will I meet her?'

'Of course you'll meet her, my dear lady. You'll be in the reception party, and so you will you, Mrs Bethya. She's coming on the tenth of August and you'll all turn out in your finery to greet her. She's doing us a great honour. She'll come down from Edinburgh by train and open the station. Then she's going to take a tour of the district before travelling back by our train again. Just think, the local gentry will have to turn out to meet her. They can't ignore such a visit. They'll be forced to acknowledge that the railway has arrived in the Borders. What a victory for us!'

Bethya played up for all she was worth. Half-swooning, she fanned her face with her open hand as she gasped,

'Oh I'm overcome, such a surprise. The Queen! How clever you are, Sir Geoffrey. I'll count every day until the tenth of August.'

Sir Geoffrey's predictions about the reaction of the people who opposed the building of a railway line were accurate. On the day the news was broken at Bella Vista, the Duke of Allandale, a tall, good-looking bachelor of twenty-eight, arrived back in his mansion Greyloch Palace that occupied a magnificent position on the southern slope of the Three Sisters. He had been travelling in France and Italy, and had returned with crates and boxes full of antique treasures picked up on his travels. He was furious to learn that the railway plans were so well-advanced and, worst of all, that the Queen herself was going to give her sanction to them by opening Maddiston station.

He shouted at the factor who brought him the news: 'Goddammit, I'll have to go and meet Her Majesty off the train! I'll be forced to mix with all that riffraff backing the railway.'

'They're not all riffraff. The Chairman of the Board is Sir Geoffrey Miller,' protested the Duke's man of business.

The Duke glared. 'Never heard of him! Which Miller is that?'

'An Edinburgh Miller.'

The Duke shrugged. Edinburgh Millers were beneath his notice. He asked, 'When is the Queen coming? We'll have to entertain her, I expect. You'd better tell my mother. She'll want to make the arrangements.'

The Duke's formidable mother was in charge of all his local social life. She lived at Greyloch Palace throughout the year and was far more feared by the neighbours than was her son. His chief activities when he was at home consisted of hunting foxes, shooting grouse, or fishing for trout and salmon, and it greatly irked him that his sporting properties were about to be disrupted by a railway line. The intrusion of modern times was not to his taste at all. After his factor was sent off to see the old Duchess, the Duke called for a horse and headed for the rising ground above the river to spy out where the bridge was to be built.

When he found an advantageous viewing place, he drew a spy-glass from his pocket to inspect the men working in the meadow below him. He was scanning the ground closely when a voice spoke up behind him. "Mornin', Your Grace. It's a sin what they're doing over there, isn't it?'

He turned in the saddle and saw a man dressed in working clothes and leaning on a tall stick behind him. It was Craigie Scott. 'It's an upheaval we could do without,' he agreed.

'Can't you stop it?' asked the man in a passionate voice.

'I'm afraid I can't. I've kept them off my land but I can't ban them from land that belongs to other people.'

'That field down there was my best grazing field. My family rented it for fifty years from Falconwood and now he's taken it back to build his bridge on it. I went to my lawyer but he's in Falconwood's pocket. He said I couldn't do anything. What's the law if it can't protect us from things like this?' Scott shook his stick furiously in the direction of the valley.

'You might get your grazing back when the bridge is finished,' suggested the Duke, but that was not well-received.

Scott leaned towards the mounted man and said, 'It's what they'll find in there that worries me. I've unearthed things you wouldn't believe when I was ploughing it.'

The Duke was interested. 'What sort of things?'

Craigie's eyes took on a crafty gleam. 'Wonderful things – helmets and breastplates and a golden mask, which I've got in my shed. I'll show it to you if you like, sir.'

'If you found a golden mask on Falconwood's land you should have given it to him.'

Craigie snorted. 'I paid a good rent, why should I give him what I dug up?'

The Duke had not expected to be arguing Falconwood's case but now he said sternly, 'Because it's the law.'

Craigie lifted his stick and shouted angrily, 'To hell

with the law! It doesn't help folk like me. I curse them. They'll all suffer, you see if they don't. I hope their bridge is never finished. I hope it lies in a pile of stones for evermore. The old Dukes wouldn't have let this happen. They'd have driven them off the land.'

The Duke saw the man was beyond reason. 'Things have changed, I'm afraid, but if it's any comfort to you I don't want this railway either. I'm having to make the best of it too.'

Craigie Scott lifted contemptuous eyes and said, 'Then I'll curse them for you as well.'

The Duke rode hurriedly away, chilled by the knowledge that he had met a madman and unsure whether the curses were not directed at him as well. When he reached the road, he was close enough to see the features of some of the men labouring in the field. He gazed at them without curiosity at first, but suddenly started when one man in particular caught his attention. He brought out the spyglass again and put it to his eye. 'It can't be,' he said aloud, dropping the glass. Then he took a second look and laughed. 'What a strange thing to imagine. As if he would be there!' he said, before folding up the glass and shoving it back in his jacket pocket.

When the day's work was over, Tim Maquire mopped his brow and, pointing over the hill, said to Gentleman Sydney, 'I'm going to the alehouse in that village over there. Do you want to come with me?'

Sydney, who missed nothing, grinned and replied, 'You've been making a habit of patronising that place. What's so special about it?'

'Nothing, but the ale's good enough and it's not crowded like the Rosewell alehouses. Come and see for yourself.'

They walked slowly up the hill to Camptounfoot and into the alehouse, where the locals around the bar went quiet as soon as they stepped inside. Sydney called out a greeting but no one spoke in reply. Tim, however, did not seem to care about the hostility. He walked up to the wooden counter and laid down the money for two mugs of ale which he and Sydney carried outside to drink sitting on a wooden bench set against the wall.

'Not very friendly, are they?' Sydney remarked.

Tim shrugged. 'It doesn't matter – at least they don't get nasty. I want you do me a favour. I'm trying to find rooms for Mr Wylie here but there must be something about the look of me that scares people because they slam their doors in my face. I thought if you asked, they might listen. You sound like a gent.'

'My dear man,' said Sydney with a laugh. 'I *am* a gent! No, but seriously, why should they listen to me? And even if they did, that doesn't mean they'll do what you want.'

'Talk to them – explain what a decent man Mr Wylie is. I'm sure someone will take him in. That Abbey Hotel's worse than the navvy camp. It makes Major Bob's shed look like a mansion. He can't stay there. He was looking grey in the face today and I'm worried about him,' said Tim solemnly.

Sydney nodded. 'You do worry about him, don't you?'

Tim looked up from the mug in his hands. 'Yes, I do. He was kind to me when I was a lad. He needs somebody to help him now and I want to be the one that does it.'

'All right, let's go back to the camp and put on clean clothes before we go in search of lodgings. Take a tip from me, Black Ace: wear a white shirt and a black coat, and forget the fancy waistcoats and red hats. They just scare the locals.'

The sun was lower when they returned to Camptounfoot by the river path. They stared down into the shot-silk rippling water flowing past their feet and Sydney suddenly said, 'In a way, you can't blame the people round here for not wanting anything to change, can you?'

'But things change all the time, don't they?' Tim objected. 'Even the water's changing now, isn't it?'

His friend clapped his shoulder. 'You're a homespun philosopher. Come on, we'd better hurry up and get to Camptounfoot or all the landlords and landladies will be abed and they certainly won't open their doors to us then.'

Once again they bought some ale and sat on the bench facing Tibbie's front door. Tim kept his eyes on it and his face was impassive. He was wondering about the girl he'd seen there. Was she married? She'd haunted his thoughts since he caught that glimpse of her. She'd made him think of the old Irish songs he'd heard sung long ago when he was a child, songs of love with lilting melodies that now ran through his thoughts like the river he'd watched with Sydney.

'I think I'll ask in the alehouse about lodgings,' he announced, standing up. Over the door hung a wilting bunch of greenery, which was the sign that ale was sold inside, and the leaves brushed his head as he went back into the dimness. As usual the other drinkers fell silent at the sight of him. Tim wasted no time in pleasantries. 'I was hoping there might be a household in the village that wouldn't be averse to making a bit of money by taking in a gentleman. He's looking for two good rooms and some decent food,' he told them all.

The men looked at each other, impressed by his directness. 'He's no' a navvy, is he?' asked one of them, finally.

'He's a building contractor, a gentleman from Newcastle who's used to a good way of living. He's in the Abbey Hotel now but it's not good enough for him,' said Tim.

'Can't say I blame him. It's a filthy hole,' muttered one of the men, who was a mason and not averse to the bridge-builders. He looked at his companions. 'Jo's mother might take him.'

Another man laughed. 'Aw, come on. If he's a gentleman he'll not want to go there!'

'Who else is there, then? Big Bella? What about Tibbie? She's got room now that her Hannah's working up at the big house.'

The others nodded. 'Aye, Tibbie Mather might take him.'

Only the alehouse-keeper demurred. 'She'll no' do it. She's dead against the railway,' but the others disagreed: 'At least he can ask. She can only say no.'

Tim stood listening to them and then he said, 'I'll ask this Tibbie. Where does she live?'

One of the men pointed out of the window. 'Over there, that's her house right opposite. Run and chap on the door and see what she says – or I'll go, if you like.'

But Tim was already halfway through the door. 'No, no, I'll try. I'll be back in a minute.'

As he stood on Tibbie's doorstep with his hand on the knocker, he was thinking, 'I wonder if that red-haired girl I saw here is Tibbie, or maybe she's Hannah? I like that name. It's pretty, like she is.'

A motherly-looking woman answered the door. Her eye went up and down the dark stranger and she said suspiciously, 'What would you be wanting here?' She recognised him at once and it took all her courage, and the knowledge that Hannah was behind her in the kitchen, not to slam the door in his face.

He was very polite, however. 'I'm looking for rooms for my employer, Mr Wylie, and I was told that you might consider taking him in.'

A figure stepped into the space at her back and Tim's heart rose when he saw it was the same girl he had glimpsed before. She was even prettier than he remembered.

'What are you saying to my mother?' she asked grimly. He repeated his request and she took hold of the older woman's arm, pulling her back from the door. 'Don't worry, Mam, I'll take care of this.' Then she stood firmly in the doorway and said, 'We don't take lodgers. I don't know who could have given you the idea that we do. They must have been playing jokes. We're not a lodging house. There's a place in the village that takes men but I think it's full.'

He did not go away. 'It's not a common lodging house I'm looking for. Mr Wylie is a gentleman. He's got a big house of his own in Newcastle but he's needing a place to stay while the bridge is being built.'

Behind the girl, Tibbie gasped, 'That'll be the man

Craigie tried to shoot. Oh my God, we're no' going to tak him in. I don't want Craigie bursting in here with a gun.'

Tim backed away, saying, 'I'm sorry for bothering you but he's a gentleman, a good man, I've never met a better. I'm looking for a comfortable place for him because he's not so young any more and can't take the rough life . . . I'm worried about him. Maybe you know someone who'd take him.'

There was an urgency in his tone that softened Hannah. She stepped out and pointed down the road. 'Look, do you see that big white house there, the one jutting out into the road? That's Mr Jessup's house and he lives there with his sister. Sometimes he takes people in during the summer from Edinburgh, but there's nobody there at the moment. Go and ask him, but please don't come back and bother my mother. She's nervous and navvies worry her.'

When the girl closed the front door of the cottage, Tim heard her turn the key in the lock but he was not offended. His head seemed to be swimming and there was a funny haze before his eyes. 'That beer must have been stronger than I thought,' he told himself as he ran across the road to summon Sydney from the bar-room where he was regaling the customers with some tale that was making them laugh.

'Come on, I've been told where to go to find a lodging for Mr Wylie. It's down here,' he said, setting off downhill towards the house the girl had pointed out. Its gable-end protruded into the roadway like the prow of a ship and it was as tall as the farmhouse, but not so gloomy. There were four little windows like ship's gunholes scattered here and there in an apparently haphazard manner in the wall overlooking the street, and a large stone sundial that had lost its metal prong jutted out of one corner. The entrance was down a little alley and through a double gateway under a stone arch, in the middle of which was set a weatherworn and featureless stone head. When Tim pushed on the gate, it swung easily and they found themselves in a paradise of a garden, full of fruit trees and beds of multi-coloured flowers. Along a far wall ran a little burn with tall yellow flag irises and wild mint growing along its edge. The front door to the house was up a little flight of steps and when Tim knocked on it, an apple-cheeked, middle-aged woman answered and smiled at him. Her mannerisms were birdlike, for she cocked her head to one side and fixed his face with brightly sparkling eyes as she asked, 'What can I do for you, young man?'

When he explained his errand, she went on smiling but held up a hand and said, 'It's my brother you want. He lives here too. I'll fetch him.'

As if she'd given a secret signal, a head popped out of a window above the door and another bright voice called out, 'Come up, come up and we'll discuss your business, but I can't hold out much hope. We don't want to offend our neighbours, you see.'

Tim and Sydney entered a tiny hall and climbed a precipitous staircase that was little more than a ladder leading into a long room filled with the rays of the dying sun, for there were windows in every wall, small and paned with old green glass and all admitting a flow of faintly-coloured light. A bright fire crackled in the burnished hearth, making reflections of the flames glitter and gleam on brass fire irons. An open piano, with music on its stand and a stool pulled up before it, stood against one wall; a cat slept on a mat under one of the windows. When the strangers entered, the animal opened a speculative eye and stared at them. Tim felt sure that it was also considering their proposition and had decided against it.

'I'm Mr Jessup,' said a spindly-legged old man, coming towards his visitors with a hand extended. 'Good to meet you, gentlemen. I heard what you said to my sister. We do rent rooms but as I told you, there's bad feeling in the village over the railway and we don't want to cause any trouble. It's best to be neutral.'

Tim looked around the friendly room and pleaded, 'But Mr Wylie is a gentleman like yourself, sir. He's not a navvy – he won't offend anybody. They'll not even know he's here. He's badly in need of a comfortable place to stay.'

Mr Jessup laughed. 'It's impossible to keep a secret in this village. If I took in a dormouse to spend the night, someone would know. But tell me about your Mr Wylie. I'll ask Matilda to bring us some biscuits and a glass of wine while you sit down and tell me the story of your lives. I love stories.' The two navvies looked at each other in surprise. That was the last thing either of them intended to do, but they politely sat down, accepted wine and biscuits and listened while Mr Jessup told them the story of *his* life. 'Matilda and I are city people really, from Manchester, would you believe! We came here on a visit fifteen years ago, saw this house, bought it and stayed. I teach the piano to young ladies, but there's not a great demand for that in Camptounfoot. However, I sometimes go to the big houses round about and give little recitals. Would you like me to play for you now? Matilda plays too. She's a violinist.'

Tim was about to protest that they ought to leave soon but Sydney interrupted to say, 'How delightful – I love music. What will you play? How about a little Mozart?'

Mr Jessup clapped his hands together in delight. 'Mozart for a summer evening! Perfect, perfect! Matilda, we're going to play a little Mozart for these gentlemen . . .' His sister immediately appeared in the doorway, violin in hand and smile in place. She took up her position beside the music-stand while her brother, flicking out his long coat-tails before he sat, plumped down on the music stool and off they went, launching themselves into music that twirled and twined a magical way through the long room.

Sydney sat back with his eyes closed and one finger gently keeping time. When they finished, he opened his eyes again and said, 'Masterly, masterly. I've never heard that piece played better.'

'Have some more wine and then a little Haydn,' cried Mr Jessup, refilling their glasses before they could protest.

It was dark before the impromptu concert ended. As they said goodbye, Mr Jessup shook their hands and remarked, as if a bargain had already been made, 'When will we expect Mr Wylie? Tomorrow – is that all right?'

In the street once more Tim shook his head like someone who'd been entranced, for his ears were ringing with music and his stomach was full of sweet wine and biscuits. 'My God, I thought they were going to keep us there forever,' he said.

Sydney only laughed and replied: 'They're actually very good musicians, you know – very skilled. Poor things, I don't expect they get much chance to play to an audience like they did tonight. And you got what you wanted – you got Mr Wylie a comfortable berth, didn't you? They wouldn't have taken him if they hadn't relaxed like they did with their music. That's what did the trick.'

'It probably did,' agreed Tim. 'I only hope he likes music, too.'

CHAPTER
Seven

'How are you settling in with the Jessups?' Tim Maquire asked Christopher Wylie on a bright morning about six weeks after he had moved into the lodgings at Camptounfoot.

'Every morning I waken up I can't believe my good fortune at being so comfortable. Thank you so much for finding me such a pleasant place to live,' was the heartfelt reply. Wylie's face was less harried and he looked far more relaxed and healthy than he had done for a long time. He stared around at the scene of activity on the high ground where the bridge embankment was being heaped up by navvies pushing barrows and wielding picks and shovels. Horses straining before huge, heavily-laden waggons were carrying in load after heaped-up load of red earth; the air was filled with the thud, thud, thud of steam engines and the shouts of labouring men.

'I don't like tempting fate but strictly between ourselves, Tim, this job's going far more smoothly than I anticipated,' said Wylie, pointing over the river valley towards more men who could be seen labouring on the point of land where the first pier of the bridge would soon be built.

Tim nodded. 'They're working well because they want as much as possible done before the Queen comes. Jopp told me that they're bringing her up here to look at the place where the new bridge is to be built. Are you going to Maddiston station to meet her, Mr Wylie?'

'Yes, but I'm not keen on that sort of thing. They expect me to be there, though.'

Tim glanced at him and asked, 'Is your wife coming

from Newcastle for it? Women usually like that kind of affair, dressing up and everything.'

The answer was a shake of the head. 'My wife's too unwell to travel far. She's not over James' death, you see – and my daughter has never travelled on her own.'

From the way he talked Tim imagined that Wylie's daughter was still a child and he said, 'Ah, that's a pity. You must have been hoping you could show this place to them.'

Wylie stared out over the valley, his eyes distant under furrowed brows. 'Yes, but that's not possible.' He was thinking of James and the sorrow returned to his eyes but he shook himself and said briskly, 'Anyway, I'm pleased it's going so well. Our troubles seem to be disappearing one by one. Even in Camptounfoot people are nice to me now. They're getting used to the idea of having a railway at their back doors.'

'And they like the money,' Tim said less charitably. 'I've got twenty Camptounfoot men on the wage roll now. They're making more money in a week than most of them made in three months before we came here. Today a young fellow called Rutherford arrived looking for work. He's a likely enough lad so I hired him.'

'Yes, Mr Jessup told me about him,' Wylie said thoughtfully. 'Robbie Rutherford's his name and his family are the village weavers. Apparently they were very much against the railway, but the lad's clever and he's decided he wants to be an engineer – that's why he's come to us. Jessup says he's only sixteen, so keep an eye on him, Tim.'

'I'll do that, Mr Wylie. And now will you come on down to the river bank with me? The men are starting to dig the first foundations in the water and I want you to make sure they're right.'

On the morning of the royal visit, the sun rose in a cloudless sky and larks were singing in cornfields that made patches of gold on the lower slopes of the hills. In houses large and small throughout the district, people were in a state of high excitement for, since the days of the

Stuarts, it was rare for a ruling monarch to be seen on the Border roads.

William Strang's wife Effie was up at first light scouring every corner of her cottage till it gleamed and sparkled. When he came in for his breakfast from the forge, her husband looked around in gratification. 'My word, Effie, this place is looking awfu' bonny.'

'That's because the Queen's coming,' she told him, tying on her largest and whitest apron.

'But she's no' coming in here, is she?' he asked.

Effie bridled. 'She's passing by the end of the lane. She'll be driving through Camptounfoot. It's up to us to make sure the place is looking its best.'

William lifted his tea cup in a genteel fashion and said, 'My word, they're great folk these royals. I didnae ken they could see through walls, though.'

His wife bristled anew. 'You're as bad as that sister of yours! I told her about the Queen and she said she didn't think she'd bother going out to see her. And her front door opens into the street too! I said, "Tibbie, if you don't open your door and look at the Queen, you'll regret it for the rest of your life."'

'What did she say?' asked William.

'Oh, she only laughed but I'll get her out when the procession comes by. I'll make sure I do,' said Effie with determination.

In Bella Vista the Colonel and his family were preparing to mount their barouche for the drive to Maddiston. The two males in the party were resplendent in military uniforms, booted, spurred, gold-trimmed and laced, buttoned, sashed and be-medalled. At least the Colonel was be-medalled. His son was merely bemused – and already half-drunk. The senior Mrs Anstruther was dressed in a gown of Prussian blue with a deep-brimmed bonnet from which trailed three enormous ostrich feathers dyed the same shade as her dress. Her jewellery was magnificent and even though it was not yet noon, she sparkled with diamonds. There was a brooch in her bonnet brim, another on her breast and a massive choker encircling her neck with huge droplets nestling on her comfortable bosom. She was considerably annoyed because the Colonel had given his daughter-in-law her pick of the family jewellery as well, and Bethya had chosen long emerald earrings surrounded by tiny seed pearls. The colour of the stones matched the bows and loops on her ivory silk gown which had been specially ordered from a London modiste and had arrived in a box the size of a small house. With it she wore a cheekily cocked hat in green that made her artfully arranged curls gleam like a raven's wing. In her hand she carried an ivory silk parasol to keep the rays of the sun from her face. In its shade her eyes leapt and danced with excitement.

After they had driven off, Allardyce the butler told his staff, 'The Colonel said you're all to have the day off so that you can go and see the Queen. When the family return they'll go straight to bed.'

Madge the kitchen-maid nudged Hannah and whispered, 'Then we'll be able to go to the dance at Rosewell, won't we? Ask him, Hannah.'

'Can we go to the dancing, Mr Allardyce?' asked Hannah shyly.

The butler was in a good mood. 'If all your work's done, you can go,' he acceded. 'It's not every day the Queen comes, is it?'

The girls rushed back into the house giggling at the prospect of an unexpected holiday. Not only could they put on their bonnets and watch the Queen pass by, but they could go dancing as well. For weeks everybody in Rosewell had been talking about the big dance to be held that night. All the unmarried lads and lassies wanted to be there. Only Francine showed no excitement as she walked behind the other maids and Madge turned to say to her, 'Will you be coming with us, Francine?'

Jessie, Madge's friend, jeered, 'She's no' the dancing kind.' Jessie always made a butt of the French girl, imitating her accent, teasing her about her devotion to her mistress and criticising her reserve.

'I'll stay to put my lady to bed,' said Francine stiffly.

'But we won't be going down to Rosewell till half-past nine. She'll be in bed by then,' said kind Hannah.

'You never ken, she might even have company. Maybe that husband of hers'll get in beside her for once,' said Jessie wickedly.

They all laughed and Madge joked, 'That'll be a special occasion – as rare as the Queen's visit.'

Francine went red but made no reply and Hannah said diplomatically, 'You'll enjoy the dance, Francine. Come with us – there's grand music.'

But Madge interrupted, 'Dancing's not for the likes of her. She'd rather stay here and comb her mistress' hair. She's not normal.'

Stung, Francine whipped round and shouted, 'I am normal! I'm perfectly normal. What do you know about it?' Her large eyes were fixed furiously on Madge's face and Hannah stepped in to make the peace.

'Oh Madge, that's not fair. Francine's just shy.'

'There's a difference between being shy and hating men. That yin hates men. You've just got to watch her speaking to them to see how she feels. She backs off as if they're going to bite her. I tell you, she's not normal.' Madge's temper was up too by this time.

'That's a terrible thing to say,' sobbed Francine.

She was furiously angry and Jessie challenged her: 'If you're so normal then, come to the dance.'

Hannah reassured the shaking French girl. 'There's nothing to be feared of. I'll stay with you and make sure nobody makes fun of your accent. Come to the dance, Francine. You can walk down with me when Mistress Bethya's gone to bed.'

'She'll not come, she'll not come,' chanted Madge and Jessie, dancing about like impish children. Francine let loose a flood of angry French words.

'What's she saying?' sniggered Madge, but nobody could tell her and she went on: 'I know – she's saying she won't come to the dance because she'd rather hide here where nobody can see her funny face and queer ways.'

'I will come. I'll come and I'll dance just to show you

I'm normal.' Tears glittered in Francine's prominent eyes as she spoke, and Hannah's pity was evoked.

'Oh, don't take on, don't listen to them. You stay at home if you want. I'm sorry now that I asked you to come.'

But Francine's face was set. 'I will go to the dance with you, Hannah, if I may. I'll meet you in the kitchen at half-past nine. Please wait for me.'

Jessie couldn't resist having the last word. 'You'll have the bonny Bethya settled in bed by then, will you? You'll have her curls all combed out and perfume on her pillow? I bet you wish you could get in beside her but it's men she likes . . .' It was her last tease, for Francine hit her full in the face with an open palm. The blow left a red mark on Jessie's fair skin and she jumped forward with her fists clenched but the other maids and Hannah held her back.

'You asked for it, Jessie. That was a terrible thing to say,' Hannah told her struggling friend.

Francine stalked away as if nothing had happened and called back over her shoulder, 'I'll meet you here at half-past nine, Hannah. I shall go to the dance.'

The cheering began even before the dark-green and gold-painted engine hauling two green and gold carriages stopped at Maddiston station. The welcoming party, seated on a sort of dais on the platform overlooking a broad red carpet, all sat forward in eager anticipation, all that is except for Gus Anstruther, who reached into his pocket, withdrew a silver flask and applied it to his lips. The door of the first carriage swung open and a magnificently uniformed equerry jumped down to the ground. He held the door back and revealed a tubby little figure in pink with a fussy bonnet decorated with roses. She looked like a cook on her afternoon off. The cheering grew hysterical and drowned out the oom-pah-pahing of Maddiston Brass Band which was attempting to play *God Save The Queen*.

The little person stepped down on to the platform, accepted a pair of golden scissors from Sir Geoffrey Miller who rushed forward with them in his hand, and smartly snipped in half a long red ribbon that had been stretched across the middle of the platform. 'I declare this station open,' she intoned in a high, fluting voice. The cheering began again and the Duke of Allandale, with a long-suffering air, walked elegantly along the stretch of carpet to show the Queen and her husband Albert, who had appeared at her back like a threatening stormcloud, to his carriage which was waiting to convey them round the local beauty spots. Sir Geoffrey was left, staring at the trailing ends of ribbon, with a disconsolate look on his face. The Queen took the golden scissors with her, smartly slipping them into her reticule, a shirred pink satin affair, before she paused on the steps to admire the baronial-style station. 'Very nice,' she said, and climbed into the Duke's carriage. Then they drove off to even more deafening adulation.

The sun was shining as they headed for the baronial mansion built by a famous novelist on the banks of the Tweed. Albert was particularly interested in the novelist's collection of antiquities, especially the things he had picked up from the battlefield of Waterloo, and the Duke had to cool his heels while these were minutely examined and commented upon. It was after midday when their cavalcade headed for Greyloch Palace, going through Camptounfoot on the way.

'What a picturesque old place,' said Queen Victoria, leaning forward in her seat. Seated at her side, her attentive husband pulled her shawl back over her shoulders. Once again she was in what was euphemistically called 'an interesting condition', and he always took great care of her when she was pregnant.

'People say it's the oldest village in Scotland,' the Duke told her. 'It's always been a village where masons live. They've left their legacy behind, too. Look at all the sundials on walls, ma'am.'

'Ah, tempus fugit,' sighed Albert, who had an excess of Germanic gloom but his wife was more cheerful.

'I think it's very pretty,' she said, waving to some women who were standing at the side of the road.

One of them shouted out, 'God bless you, ma'am,' and fell down in a faint, overcome by patriotic emotion. It was Effie, and the woman beside her was Tibbie, mortified by her sister-in-law's loss of control.

'Pull yourself together woman, pull yourself together,' she was urging in a whisper as she chafed Effie's hands.

Seeing the woman fall to the ground, the Queen ordered her carriage to stop and leaned down from her seat to enquire after the casualty. 'Is she all right?' she asked.

Tibbie looked up and bobbed her head. 'She's fine, ma'am. There's nothing to worry about,' was her reply.

Then, when the Queen's retinue had rolled on its way, Effie opened her eyes, stared up at the sky and heaved a sigh of sheer delight as she whispered, 'I'm in heaven. I've died and gone to heaven. The Queen asked if I was all right!'

'You're a daft besom,' snapped her exasperated relative. 'Get up. You fair black affronted me.'

The Duke ordered his coachman to drive along the road from which the works of the emergent bridge could be seen. 'You'd better see this,' he advised the monarch, 'because they're sure to ask if you noticed it when you go back to Maddiston.' With a disapproving expression he pointed out the earthworks that were beginning to scar the horizon but Albert was very interested.

'That's a considerable project,' he said in his heavily accented English. 'Could we perhaps drive a little closer and take a better look at it?'

'We'll have to go over on to the other bank of the river again,' said the reluctant Duke, but Albert's wish was law and they retraced their route through an empty-looking Camptounfoot and back by the road-bridge to the area where the navvies were working. At the sight of the line of carriages, the men raised their loud huzzahs in honour of Victoria, throwing their hats and caps in the air as they did so. The Duke looked at the cheering gang in disgust and then turned his head away but as he did so, he once more caught a glimpse of the man he'd seen through his spyglass. The fellow was cheering more loudly than the others and, by God, he was the spitting image of his old schoolfriend Godders! The only difference was that this navvy chap was leaner and harder-looking, more burned by the sun. 'If I ever see Godders again, I'll pull his leg about having a double who works on a navvy site,' resolved the Duke.

It was after five o'clock when the royal progress was finished and Albert and Victoria were driven back to Maddiston to reboard their train for Edinburgh. Once more the official party were in their places on the dais, less immaculate than they had been in the beginning in some cases. Once more the band played stirring music and the gathered populace cheered as with a thump and a shriek, a shudder and a shake, the royal train started up and pulled the gleaming carriages out of the station. The great day was over and Maddiston station was officially open for business. Christopher Wylie, who had been given a place at the back of the dais, climbed wearily down to ground-level and found himself beside Sir Geoffrey Miller, who deigned to smile at him and say, 'Well, that's that, Wylie. All we've got to do now is get the line down to the bridge and over the river. Then the project is completed, isn't it?'

'That's right,' agreed Wylie. 'It's not going to take too long.'

'Good chap, good chap, then the money'll start rolling in,' said Miller, clapping him on the shoulder.

By the time Colonel Anstruther and his party arrived back at Bella Vista, only Gus was cheerful because, as usual, he was drunk. The others were tired and short-tempered, anxious only to seek the solitude of their rooms where corsets could be unlaced, shoes taken off and pent-up frustration unleashed. When Bethya reached the sanctuary of her chamber it was a relief to see Francine, as cool and remote as ever, rearranging the bottles on the dressing table. The strain of keeping a sweet expression on her face all day had exacted a heavy toll on Bethya and she was ready to lash out. 'For God's sake stop tinkling those bottles like that . . . Fetch me some hot water and wash my face. I'm exhausted, utterly exhausted, and my head is throbbing fit to burst,' she gasped as she threw herself on to the bed. Silently Francine did as she was bid, washing her mistress' face and hands and then sponging her brow with a piece of flannel soaked in aromatic liquid.

'Ugh, that's stone cold. What is it? It'll make my headache worse,' complained Bethya, who was lying with closed eyes accepting these ministrations but Francine said, 'No, it will help. It's *rose vinaigre*. We use it in France for headaches. Lie still and the pain will go away.' As she spoke she laid a cool hand on top of Bethya's head and in time the response was a remorseful sigh.

'You're right, it does. You're a magician, Francine. I don't know what I'd do without you. I've had such a horrible day, sitting for hours in the same carriage as Gus and his mother. It's "Dear Gus" this and "Dear Gus" that all day long. She was the only person in the whole gathering who couldn't see he was rolling drunk.'

'She's his mother . . . Did Sir Geoffrey like your dress?' asked Francine.

'Oh yes, I think so. He kept looking at me, anyway – and so did several others including the Duke of Allandale. What a smart-looking man, Francine – so very elegant and well-bred! I wish I could get to know him. The others are far too easy. I feel like a big-game hunter going after rabbits when I turn my charms on Sir Geoffrey and his friends.'

Francine said, 'I saw the Duke with the Queen and her husband when they drove past our gates. You're right, he is a good-looking man but haughty.'

'At least he's a real man,' Bethya mused. 'Oh, how I wish I had a lover, Francine. You've no idea how I wish for one. I saw the maids all getting ready to go out to meet their beaux tonight and I wished I was going with them, I really did.'

Francine said softly, 'I'm going to the dance, madam. If I find a nice man, I'll bring him back for you.'

Bethya laughed. 'What a strange idea! How naughty. If you find a nice young man, Francine, you keep him and enjoy him and tell me about it later. I console myself with the idea that Gus can't last for ever. His liver must be almost worn out by now. With any luck I'll be a widow soon, a rich widow, I hope, and I can go man-hunting on my own behalf. Then I might not have to settle for Sir Geoffrey – I might set my sights higher. But are you really going dancing, Francine? That's not like you.'

'The other maids asked me to go with them.'

'What will you wear?' Bethya had never seen her maid in anything other than a plain black dress with a white crocheted collar.

'I don't know,' said Francine, frowning. 'I thought I'd go in this dress with a shawl.'

'Oh my dear, that won't do at all. You must dress up if you're to catch a beau. Take your pick of my gowns, borrow any one you like. Show those girls downstairs how pretty you can look.'

That was the telling remark. With the words ringing in her head, Francine busied herself preparing her mistress for the night. It was after nine o'clock when Bethya had eaten her supper off a tray carried up from the kitchen and slipped into her bed. When her mistress was asleep and breathing deeply, Francine began her own toilette.

The three girls sitting at the big deal table in the kitchen had their eyes fixed on the large clock on the end wall. 'When is she going to make an appearance? It's half-past nine already. I'll bet she doesn't come,' said Madge.

'Give her another five minutes. If she doesn't come then, we'll go,' said Hannah, but before the time was up the kitchen door opened and a vision in cerise satin stood framed in it. Francine's dress was cut low on the shoulders, showing a generous spread of naked chest and emphasising her tiny waist. It fitted well because Bethya and her maid were almost the same size. Francine's hair was dressed in two long ringlets falling flirtatiously down each side of her strange face and she was carrying a large ostrich-feather fan which she opened coquettishly and held up before her face. The girls round the table were all astonished.

'Oh bless my soul! I'm no going out wi' a freak like that! What'll folk think? She's like one of them street women in London,' gasped Madge. She stood up and backed away as Francine advanced on her with the fan held out like a dagger.

'You invited me, you challenged me. I'm going to the dance with you,' she said.

Madge and Jessie looked at each other and clucked in terror. 'But it's no' that kind of a dance. It's no' a ball,' they protested. 'It's only a dance. Folk don't dress up like fashion plates for it.'

Hannah was giggling in the background and in a spluttering voice she said, 'You look very grand, Francine. That's one of Mrs Bethya's gowns, isn't it?' Then to Madge and Jessie she added, 'You asked for it. This is your own fault. Come on, let's go or we'll be too late.'

The maids pulled black woollen shawls over their sprigged cotton gowns but Francine produced a long, multi-coloured Paisley shawl which she draped over her shoulders. Like a peacock with farmyard hens, she set out to walk to Rosewell with her reluctant escort. Madge was running alongside Hannah and whispering, 'You can look after her if you're so keen for her to come. I'm not going to stay with her. The minute we get into the hall, I'm off.'

'Please yourself,' said Hannah. 'She's playing a game with you and I think she's the winner.'

It was already growing dark when they reached the middle of Rosewell and the square was crowded with young people, most of whom knew Hannah, Madge or Jessie and greeted them with waves and calls. When they saw Francine, their jaws dropped and some of the girls started giggling behind their hands. 'Who's the Duchess?' a bold lad enquired of Hannah as she passed, but she shot him a baleful glance and swept on her way. As the four of them approached the hall door, Hannah noticed out of the tail of her eye that a party of men on the far side of the square were watching everything that was going on. They were noticeable because of their clothes – bright coloured waistcoats and neckerchiefs. Some of them wore skullcaps with tassels and embroidery around the edge. 'There's some navvies,' whispered Madge, who had seen them too and was impressed by their muscular nonchalance. She drew herself up and pranced along with her head held high, for she was a pretty girl and well aware that she drew men's eyes.

Tim Maquire's gaze was fixed on the red-haired girl he'd seen at Camptounfoot and who had haunted his thoughts ever since. Suddenly he turned to his companions, Sydney, Naughten-The-Image-Taker and Jimmy-The-New-Man to say, 'I feel like dancing tonight, lads. Let's go in there.'

Jimmy grimaced: 'They'll not let us in, Black Ace. Sure, they close the door against navvies. Look, there's a policeman standing there. He'll turn us away.'

'Let's try anyway,' said Tim and, with Sydney close behind him, he made for the door. Their way was barred by a held-up hand and the words, 'Nae navvies.' Before Tim could protest, however, Sydney stepped forward and said in his purest tones, 'My dear man, what makes you think we're navvies?'

'Your get-up. Only navvies dress like that.'

Sydney threw back his head and laughed. 'It fooled you, didn't it? I'm down here staying with my friend Dicky Allandale and we had a wager that we'd dress up like navvies and get into the dance. Come on, help us win it. There's half a sovereign in it for you.'

He drove a hand into his breeches pocket and pulled out a golden coin which he adroitly palmed into the constable's fist. 'You're a friend of the Duke?' stuttered the guardian of the door. Sydney nodded and bent his head towards the constable's ear. Then he whispered into it. The constable laughed. 'Oh, all right. In you go, but see you cause no trouble. The local lads might think you're real navvies and try to pick a fight with you.'

Sydney clapped him on the shoulder. 'The last thing we

ever do is fight, old chap. Come on, you fellows . . .' In they went, all of them except Sydney looking somewhat sheepish.

'It's a good job he didn't speak to any of us. Our accents would give us away. What did you say to him to make him change his mind?' whispered Tim.

'I pretended I'd been the Duke of Allandale's fag at school. I told him the Duke's nickname.'

'And how did you know that?' asked Tim suspiciously.

'My dear chap, I made it up. I just said the first thing that came into my head. He wouldn't know the difference.'

The Corn Exchange hall was long and narrow with a platform at the far end on which were grouped two fiddlers and a woman playing a battered piano. They were just finishing a rousing reel when the girls entered. Immediately they were inside, Madge hissed in Hannah's ear, 'Well, I'm off. You're on your own wi' her,' and grabbing Jessie by the hand she fled to the back of a cluster of giggling, red-faced girls who were grouped like penned sheep on the left-hand side of the room. The air was heavy with anticipation as bashful-looking males, wiping their brows after the last exertion, lined up along the other side staring at the girls. One or two of them had got their eye on Hannah Mather and brightened considerably.

Madge and Jessie were giggling and whispering to their friends, pointing out Francine and describing her strange ways. The French girl stood beside Hannah with her head high, pretending not to notice or care what an object of derision she was. If she rued the wearing of such a noticeable gown – for it stood out among the simple cotton dresses of the other girls – she did not show it. Tender-hearted Hannah tried to help her. 'Do you want to sit down, Francine?' she asked, indicating a line of benches along the wall on which one or two wallflowers were sitting all forlorn.

'I will stand,' was the stoical reply. Francine was determined to show Madge that she was capable of coping with this experience, though privately she found it horrific.

When the music started again, she stood staring bleakly

out at the hustling crowd as men converged on the girls in a rush to get the best partners. Three swains were heading for Hannah when they were thrust aside by a tall, dark-haired man dressed like a navvy. As he approached he could see from the terror in Francine's eyes that she thought he was going to ask her to take the floor with him, but his glance swept over her and landed on Hannah. 'Will you dance with me, please?' he asked.

She held out a hand and took his. It was a gesture of natural grace and when their fingers made contact, the colour flooded into her cheeks making her face glow like a summer rose. Then she smiled her tranquil smile that seemed to make time go more slowly. 'I'd like to dance with you,' she said.

All around them people were scampering on to the floor, for dancing was a wonderful release from the strictures and uneventful tenor of their days. Milkmaids danced with masons, cooks with carpenters, ploughmen with girls who served behind the counters of Rosewell's shops. In a far corner Hannah saw Wee Lily stamping her feet and giving staccato 'hoochs' of delight as she whirled round in the arms of an orra man from Falconwood's farm.

She knew that the man she was dancing with herself was the one who'd been with the bridge contractor when Craigie tried to shoot him, the same one who had asked her mother to take Mr Wylie in as a lodger; she speculated on how outraged Tibbie would be if she knew her daughter was taking the floor with such an object of terror. But what was the harm? Anyway, she realised with delighted surprise, he was a wonderful dancer.

Tim Maquire had romance in his soul. When dance music began, his feet itched and something joyous wakened deep within him; an innocent sense of joy and delight, the optimism and wonder that had been suppressed in him after he left Ireland as a bewildered eight-year-old and which he had since kept well-hidden. It was only when fiddlers struck up and he could swing a pretty girl around in giddying circles that he forgot to maintain his usual dour façade. Smiling, he stepped and swayed, took Hannah's hand and guided her around the floor. She was a good dancer too and moved with him like a flowing river, bending and swaying as elegantly as he. They made a striking couple, black head and red head inclining towards each other, for Hannah was tall and he did not have to bend to look down at her. They did not speak, they only danced, their bodies communicating vibrantly with each other. When the sweating fiddlers drew their brows over the strings in a last crescendo, Tim stopped dead in the middle of the floor, surprised at how much he had forgotten himself. He wished he could go on dancing with her all night. In a strange way he felt as if he knew her, had known her for a long time.

'Dance the next one with me too,' he asked urgently, but she shook her head.

'Oh no, I can't do that. I'm promised to other people. Come back and ask me in a little while.'

For the next three dances, he did not take the floor again but stood watching from the door with his brow-lowered expression back in place. He observed Sydney skipping like a dervish with one girl after another, his elegantly booted feet flashing and his arms in the air. Sydney was still a mystery to Tim for, though he had integrated completely with the other men and did as good a day's work as any of them, he was obsessively secretive and told them nothing about himself. Normally when men worked together in a gang and lived together too, they picked up facts about each other's lives but next to nothing had been revealed by Sydney. Tim noticed that his clothes must all have been very expensive when bought new, and his boots had the labels of a Parisian boot-maker stitched inside the mahogany-coloured tops. He also owned leather-bound, gold-tooled books which he occasionally brought out of his satchel and lay reading. They were strange books, full of poetry, but when one of the men asked him what the poems were about – for navvies loved yarns and yearned to be told stories – Sydney only laughed, closed the book and put it away. Looking at him now, whirling in the middle of the hall with his lean face laughing and his strange eyes glittering, you would not have thought him anything more than a joker, a jackanape.

Tim's eyes sought out his other friends. There was that silver-tongued devil Naughten spinning the tale to a round-eyed girl who looked like a housemaid. Tim knew what he was saying. 'I'm a travelling artist, so I am, and if you sit for me I'll draw you a likeness that'll bring tears to your mother's eyes, it'll be so lifelike and natural.' The girl was nodding and staring at him, her eyes filled with uncomprehending admiration. Tim hoped for her own good that she didn't have a silver florin in her pocket, for she might lose that as well as her virtue.

Tim started searching the dancers on the floor for Jimmy. He always felt responsible for that lad, for Jimmy was a vulnerable and credulous youth. To his surprise he eventually located him dancing with the odd-looking girl who had been standing beside Hannah when Tim took her on to the floor.

In fact, when Tim first made his bee-line for Hannah, Jimmy-The-New-Man had followed him across the floor heading for the same girl, but Black Ace got there first, so soft-hearted Jimmy extended his hand to the strange, frightened-looking girl who stood beside the red-headed beauty because he felt sorry for her. She accepted him silently, but as they danced he had the feeling that she was trying to keep as far away from him as possible. 'I don't bite,' he told her with a laugh but she did not laugh back until they danced over to the top of the hall where they found themselves beside a group of giggling girls. They all seemed to know Jimmy's partner. 'Give him a kiss, Francine!' called one of them in a jeering voice, and that seemed to have a miraculous effect on Jimmy's partner. She stepped closer to him and put an arm round his neck. He was so surprised that he nearly fell over backwards. After that he could not get rid of her, for she fawned over and flattered him all night, fluttering her eyelashes and patting his hand like an accomplished flirt.

He could not believe his luck, for though she was an oddly-dressed lassie and spoke very queer, there was a strange allure about her and she seemed besotted with him. Jimmy was a shy lad, but quite successful with women, and in the past he'd enjoyed some tender adventures. This, he thought, might be another one waiting to happen.

When the hands of the big clock on the back wall of the hall neared midnight, Tim Maquire walked over the floor and positioned himself beside Hannah. 'I've come for my dance,' he said with a smile. She stood up, smiling too, and said, 'You took your time.' She knew he'd waited till the last dance, for whoever took a girl on to the floor for that had the privilege of walking her home. The band played a waltz with a wistful theme and as they moved around the floor, Tim found he was thinking about Ireland. A wave of terrible nostalgia hit him and he longed to be able to talk to the girl in his arms about the thoughts that filled his mind. Astonishingly, at that moment, she glanced into his eyes and said softly, 'You look sad. Are you homesick?'

'Homesick? Me, of course not!' he robustly replied. He did not know why he denied his inner self but he was still keeping up his hard exterior, not yet ready to let her see what was inside, and he shivered at the thought of how nearly she had exposed him. 'Can I walk you back to wherever you're going?' he asked her but she shook her head.

'I've come quite a long way and there's four of us. We'll all walk back together.'

Tim looked over the tops of the dancing heads and asked, 'Did you come with that girl in the red dress?'

Hannah nodded. 'Yes, I did.'

He grinned. 'Well, from the looks of it she'll not be walking back with you. She's got a stranglehold on my friend Jimmy.' He whirled Hannah round at that moment so she could see Francine with her arms tightly clasped round a blond-haired navvy and her dark head lying on his shoulder.

'Oh my heavens, I thought she was feared of men,' gasped Hannah, totally amazed, for this was a side of Francine that she had never dreamed existed. Then the idea struck her that the French girl might be drunk. The man could have been plying her with alcohol – things like that did happen. 'Is that man your friend? He's one of the navvies, isn't he?' she asked her partner. 'Is he – is he safe?'

Tim bristled. 'You mean because he's a navvy you think he's some sort of devil?'

Hannah was embarrassed, though that was almost what she had meant. 'Of course not,' she protested. 'It's just that Francine's foreign and a bit strange. She might not understand . . . She doesn't usually act that way.'

Tim glowered. 'She's putting on a good act, then. Of the two of them I'd say it's Jimmy who has the most to worry about. We're navvies but we're not all wild animals, you know.'

Hannah was not easily put down. 'I didn't say you were,' she snapped and walked away from him.

When Hannah with Jessie and Madge emerged from the hall, they had their arms linked and were giggling together about the things they'd seen and heard during the evening. At the door Hannah drew back. 'I must find Francine,' she said. 'We can't leave her to walk home on her own.'

'Oh, you needn't bother about her. She set off earlier with a yellow-headed navvy and said to me that we weren't to worry about her,' said Madge. Then she added, 'My word, she changed her tune tonight. Did you see her, grabbing at him as if he was the first man she'd laid hold of in years? I still think there's something odd about her, though. She doesn't act natural.'

Hannah felt concerned. 'I hope she's all right. I feel responsible for Francine. She wouldn't have come with us if you hadn't gone on at her like you did, Madge.'

'Maybe I've done her a favour,' giggled Madge and clutched at Hannah's arm again. 'Come on, hurry up. It's late.'

They were turning a corner in the East Port of the town that led to the road towards Bella Vista when a dark figure stepped out of a doorway and faced them, blocking the narrow roadway. 'I'll escort you girls back home – just in case there's any wild animals about,' said Tim Maquire's voice.

Madge giggled. 'The wildest animal round here is my mither's dog.'

'Never mind, I'll walk with you anyway,' said Tim. Hannah did not protest but neither did she speak as they walked the mile and a half to the big house, though Madge and Jessie prattled on. When he left them at the servants' door of Bella Vista, Tim said nothing about meeting Hannah again, and though she had given him no encouragement, his failure to do so made her angry and disappointed.

'Ssh, don't make a noise. If Mr Allardyce hears us, he'll give us a terrible talking-to for waking folk up,' whispered Hannah when the three girls crept into the dark kitchen.

'I hope he didnae hear that navvy speaking out there,' Madge whispered back. The maids were not meant to bring back 'followers', and transgressions could be punished by dismissal if the butler was in a liverish mood. Hannah said nothing to that so Madge added, 'That one has a real notion of you, Hannah.'

'He's too cheeky for his own good. I wonder where Francine is?' said Hannah in a worried tone but Madge replied, 'She can look after herself. Don't worry about her.'

What they did not know as they slipped up the backstairs to the attics where they slept was that Francine was standing in a corner of the kitchen corridor listening to them. Her heart was racing and her fists were clenched so tightly that the fingernails cut into the fleshy pad below the thumbs. She was waiting for them to go to bed so that she could run up to Bethya's bedroom.

When all was quiet, she slipped like a shadow up the main staircase and silently opened her mistress' chamber door. Bethya lay as she had done when Francine left, hair spread on the white pillow and one arm thrown out by her side. A little candle in a glass holder burned by the bedside. Bending down, Francine breathed softly into Bethya's ear, 'Madame, madame, wake up, wake up.'

Bethya stirred and slowly opened her eyes. She stared at the maid's face for a few moments as if she was having trouble remembering who she was, and then she yawned and said, 'It can't be morning yet. It's still dark.'

Francine's eyes were glittering strangely. 'Madame, waken up. I've brought you a present.'

'A present?' Bethya turned in her bed and yawned again. 'What sort of a present? Do go away, Francine, I'm sleepy.'

'Madame, I've brought you a lover. He's down in the summerhouse now, waiting. I brought him specially for you. You'll like him.'

Bethya was wide awake now and she stared at her maid in disbelief. Then she said, 'Go to bed, Francine. You've been drinking.' There was indeed a smell of alcohol coming from the maid, who had needed its help to brave the dance.

She did not go away, however. Instead she pleaded almost tearfully, 'But you said you wanted a lover so I went to the dance and brought one home for you. He's young and strong and very handsome with bright yellow hair. He's a navvy, one of the men you've seen working on the bridge site.'

Bethya was shocked. 'How could you even think of such a thing? I wouldn't take a navvy as my lover! I might admire them, but I'm aiming higher than that. You can't seriously imagine that I'd get up and go out to meet a completely strange navvy in the middle of the night, do you? You're mad. Go to bed.'

'But he's waiting for you,' pleaded Francine.

'If he is, get rid of him. Don't let him wander round the house. We might all get murdered in our beds,' snapped Bethya and shoved her head under the pillow.

Francine ran back down the stairs and out through the open kitchen door. The moon was shining brightly and the trees surrounding the huge lawn cast velvet black shadows on the grass. She flitted over the expanse like a wraith till she came to a white-painted summerhouse set in a grove of trees by the side of a little ornamental pool. There was a man sitting on a low seat with his head in his hands and when he heard her approaching he stood up and stepped towards her, intending to embrace her as soon as she stepped into the summerhouse's sanctuary. But she paused on the grass before the threshold and hissed like a cat, 'Go away! Go away this minute and never come back.'

Surprised, he sat down again and gasped, 'But you told me to wait for you!'

'Go away, go away!' There was a note of hysteria in her voice and she did not seem to understand what he was saying. In a furious voice she went on, 'I want you to go away. If you don't, I'll rouse the menservants and have you thrown out.'

'You're mad!' he shouted back. 'You're raving mad. You were all over me half an hour ago – leading me on, promising me things. Now you're a different woman.'

She clenched her fists as if she wanted to hit him. 'I hate you. I hate all men. Go on, go away and never come back.' The silver moonlight lit up her face and turned it into a primeval mask. He was awed by her exotic, fearsome beauty, for in rage she did look beautiful.

'Aw, don't be like that now. If this is some sort of a game, I'll play it. Just let me hold you again,' he pleaded but she gave a strangled scream.

'Go away – go away. There's nothing for you here. GO AWAY.' Then she turned and ran back over the grass. He watched until she disappeared into the house with a flash of skirts.

A little later Tim, wandering back along the moonlit lanes with his hands thrust deep into his pockets and thinking about the red-haired girl, was surprised to hear running feet coming up behind him. He turned, alert and defensive, but his shoulders relaxed when he saw Jimmy bearing down on him. The young navvy was running as if he was being pursued by the devil and there was a look of fury on his face.

'That cock-teasing bitch,' he gasped when he drew up beside his friend. 'You wouldn't believe how bold she was, Black Ace, but when we got back to the house, she went all funny on me – acted as if she'd never seen me before, shouted and told me to go away, said if I didn't she'd get the men of the house to throw me out.'

Tim was interested. 'That odd-looking one, was it? She's a funny piece.'

Jimmy nodded. 'Sydney said she's French. She kept calling me "cherry" or something. Maybe all the French are like that – loving one moment and hating the next.' He was totally confused by what had happened to him.

'Forget about her,' advised Tim.

But Jimmy shook his head. 'I can't. She made a funny sort of impression on me. In a way I was sorry for her – I want to know why she's behaving like that.'

Tim paused and put a hand on his arm. 'Believe me, it's best to put her out of your mind. You'll just get into trouble if you follow it up,' he said earnestly, but the moonlight and the strangeness of Francine had enchanted Jimmy.

'She was like a witch – I think she's put a spell on me. I want to see her again.' he said.

CHAPTER
Eight

The month of August was brilliant. The sun shone almost every day, turning the harvest to deep gold in the fields and drying out the grass in the hedgerows so that it stood up stiff and straight and tinged with brown. Rowan berries darkened to a deep shade of scarlet, rose hips glowed like rubies in the hedges and the elder trees started to bear heavy flourishes of purple berries that the women of Camptounfoot went out to gather for the making of jellies and cordials which would be used as medicines in the coming winter.

On the cliff overlooking the river, Tim Maquire looked down on his army of labourers in the meadow below. The river ran along the valley foot like a sheet of watered silk, sparkling and glittering in the sun, its edges decorated with long trailing flourishes of white spangled water weed. On the hottest days, when the temperature rose to over ninety degrees, some of the men stripped off their clothes and splashed naked in the shallows. This was a sight much relished by Colonel Anstruther's daughter-in-law if she arrived at the right time to see them. She came daily, mounted on her smart mare and clad in a riding habit of cream-coloured linen with a tip-tilted hat and veil, to view the work in progress with her ever-admiring Bap.

After the night Francine brought Jimmy home, the matter was never mentioned again between mistress and maid. Bethya, as generous as ever, continued to give Francine presents and gossiped about what went on in the house and kitchen, but refrained from talking of her burning sexual frustration or telling the maid how the sight of the frolicking navvies exacerbated it. Sometimes she wondered, as she looked at the half-naked men labouring on the embankment that was rapidly taking shape on the northern bank, which one it was that her maid had procured for her, but she never asked.

Then, in the middle of the month, Francine burst into the bedroom one evening and said, 'The post has just arrived with a letter from Sir Geoffrey for the Colonel! The butler was there when he opened it and the Colonel said Lady Miller has died so Sir Geoffrey won't be coming to tour the workings as he had intended to do this week.'

Bethya clasped her hands together, her eyes shining. 'If he's going to make a move for me, he can do it now. He's been very attentive recently. He spoke very meaningfully to me the other day and said he couldn't imagine why I stay with Gus.'

Francine nodded. 'The servants are saying that the last time he was here his valet was telling them that he doesn't care at all about his wife so he'll not be grief-stricken, far from it. Lady Miller has been ill for a long time and he was hardly ever at home. He'll have to observe mourning, though, but apparently he intends to come down to Bella Vista as soon as possible. He might speak then.'

'Oh yes, so perhaps I'll soon be Lady Miller! Gus won't make any trouble about divorcing me – though I don't think he'd let me divorce him. He's so worried about his reputation – after all, that's the only reason he married me in the first place. If he divorced me though, he'd be the innocent party and he'd like that,' said Bethya, her face glowing. 'Now, let's look out my prettiest gowns, but none that are too brilliantly coloured. I'll have to be very discreet.'

Bethya did not expect Sir Geoffrey to come down to Bella Vista immediately, and knew she would have to wait for him to preserve a pretence of proper mourning, but when several weeks had passed and there was still no news of him, she began to feel impatient. Every day she prowled her bedroom, snapping at Francine and fretting. 'Has there been any word from him? Has the Colonel had a letter? How long is it now since his wife died?'

'It's three weeks. It's a month . . . he's bound to come soon,' consoled the maid who, when she was not looking after Bethya, hung around in the kitchen listening to the gossip. She even made herself endure the taunts of Madge and Jessie: 'Going dancing again, Francine? What happened to your bonny young navvy, then? What did you do to him? He's never come back looking for you and you seemed that keen on him!' Then they'd go off into peals of laughter, leaning against each other and hiccuping with mirth.

One evening, about a month after the dance, Madge came running into the kitchen with her eyes popping out. 'I've just seen him! I've just seen Francine's navvy in the shrubbery,' she gasped. 'He was hiding behind a tree and watching the hoose.'

Francine, who was sitting at the end of the staff dining table, seemed to freeze like a statue but Jessie went off into wild laughter. 'Och Madge, you're a caution.'

Madge turned on her. 'I'm no' joking! I did see him, keeking out from behind a tree and watching the kitchen door. He's looking for her, I tell you.'

Francine stood up and backed towards the door. Her face was white and her eyes staring. She looked as if she'd seen a ghost. Mr Allardyce saw how affected she was and said soothingly, 'Don't worry, Mademoiselle. I'll send some of the men out. If he is there, they'll run him off the place.'

No one was found in the shrubbery, however, and when this was reported to the butler he summoned Madge to his pantry and gave her a stiff talking-to. 'It's very cruel to tease that poor French lassie the way you do. It's got to stop,' he ordered.

Madge protested, 'But he was there – I swear he was.'

'That'll do,' said Allardyce. 'I don't want to hear any more about it.'

The fuss about the spying navvy was forgotten next morning when a letter arrived to tell the Colonel that Sir Geoffrey Miller intended to make a visit of inspection to the railway workings in three days' time, and hoped he could take advantage of the Colonel's hospitality to stay for a few days at Bella Vista.

Francine went running up the stairs to her mistress' room and with difficulty restrained herself from charging headlong through the door. 'He's coming, Madame, he's coming,' she whispered urgently when she drew back the curtains that draped Bethya's bed.

Bethya sat up, pushed the hair out of her eyes and asked, 'When?'

'On Thursday. The Colonel received a letter. It went in with his breakfast tray and he's told Allardyce to prepare for Sir Geoffrey's visit. I'll press all your dresses again. Which will you wear for him?' The pair of them descended on the wardrobe and spent a happy hour deciding which of the gorgeous gowns would be most likely to entrance Sir Geoffrey.

For the next two days they changed their minds at least a dozen times and when they were not debating about clothes, they discussed between themselves how it would be possible for Bethya to extricate herself from her marriage to Gus. 'I suppose I could threaten to talk about what happened in India. I could tell his father why he had to leave the Army and come home. That's grounds for divorce if nothing is,' she said.

'But you weren't married to him then,' protested Francine. 'It would be better if you threatened to make a scandal about the way he's carrying on with the boys up at the stable now. The servants talk about it all the time. They think I don't understand them but I do. They are very coarse.'

Bethya's eyes were fixed on the maid's face. 'What do they say?'

'They say he is a pederast.'

'How long have you known about that?' asked Bethya.

'Several months. It started soon after you came here. Some of the boys complained to the butler but there were others who didn't, and they're still there. The complainers left. The Colonel paid them to keep quiet so there's no point in threatening to tell him about your husband. He knows.'

Bethya's face was solemn. 'I thought Gus learned his lesson in India, but apparently not. Why didn't anyone tell me?'

'I suppose they thought it might hurt you. I thought it would upset you, that's why I said nothing.'

Bethya snorted. 'Upset me? I don't give a damn about Gus. I'm only glad to have some weapon against him. I could get a divorce from him for his unnatural habits. He's never slept with me, you know, not once, but to divorce him for non-consummation would be very shaming. It would make me look stupid. People would think I stayed married to a man like that because I didn't know any better! I'd look a fool and a failure – I couldn't bear it. This way is much better. When Sir Geoffrey speaks to me, I'll tell Gus that we must be divorced quietly or I'll bring a case against him and make his peccadilloes public knowledge. Thank you for telling me, Francine. Thank you very much.'

When Sir Geoffrey and his fellow directors from the Edinbrugh and South of Scotland Railway dismounted from the train at Maddiston, they found grooms waiting with a party of riding horses that Colonel Anstruther and Falconwood had arranged to be sent to the station. It took three hours to cover a few miles of workings and emergent excavations between Maddiston and Rosewell because they were continually stopping, conferring, examining and asking questions. At Rosewell they met up with Anstruther's party and set out to inspect the work on the bridge which was pronounced to be proceeding well though Miller took care not to sound over-enthusiastic before Wylie. It would not do to let the contractor think he was too satisfied. Instead he said warningly, 'You'll have to go on working very hard to keep up your schedule. The rest of the line's advancing faster than we expected. It'll be here from the north by next winter, that's certain, and the line from the south won't take much longer. You don't want to be the one who holds everything up, do you, Wylie?'

Christopher Wylie's face showed strain but he nodded confidently. 'We won't hold you up, Sir Geoffrey. We'll finish on time.'

'It would be good if you could finish early, considering the progress made by the other contractors. Perhaps if Jopp and his men moved in to help you, things might go along faster?'

The sly-faced Jopp was sitting on his horse behind Sir Geoffrey and a spark of something – malice or ambition – flared in his eyes. Wylie shook his white head vigorously. 'This is my contract: I've undertaken to finish it on a specific date and I will. There's no need to bring in another contractor. That would only confuse the operation.'

Miller's voice was as smooth as whipped cream as he looked down into the valley floor once more. 'That's splendid, just what I like to hear. Anyway, if you're late you lose money . . . so you won't be late, will you?'

Two deep lines were etched down the sides of Wylie's mouth as he nodded in reply. 'That's true,' he admitted. 'That's why I won't be late.'

At Bella Vista, Bethya had been in a frenzy since morning. She'd wanted to ride out with the Colonel when he went to meet his colleagues, but that idea was pooh-poohed as inappropriate. 'We'll be talking business, Begum, it's an all-male occasion. You stay here and make yourself pretty for when we come back,' said her father-in-law in a kindly tone.

She seemed to accept this but in her chamber, she raged to Francine, 'He's taken Gus with him, and Gus has no more idea of what's going on in the railway workings than a two-year-old child. He's not interested, he never rides out with Bap in the morning. I do, I've seen the work from the beginning but he won't take me. Isn't it unfair?'

Francine shrugged. 'He's a man – they are all the same. Now come, what will you wear? The party is returning at tea-time so I've put out your plaid taffeta gown, the one you had sent up from London and haven't worn yet.'

It was spread on the bed, a flurry of stiff material above a hoop of frilled underskirts. The glossy taffeta was patterned in squares of purple, pink, rose-red and palest mauve, and when she put it on, Bethya glowed. At four o'clock, her maid arranged her hair and tucked into one of the luxuriant coils a tiny nosegay of roses. 'You look lovely. He will not be able to resist you,' she said with satisfaction as she stepped back to contemplate her handiwork.

Now Bethya rose and listened at the door. 'I think I hear them coming. When they're all in the drawing room, I'll start going down the stairs.'

The effect her entrance created was everything she desired. The men standing around with tea cups in their hands seemed to freeze as she paused in the doorway. All eyes were fixed on her. She smiled her sweetest smile and walked into the company, heading for her father-in-law. 'Dear Bap, I hope you're not tired out. It has been a long day for you,' she sighed.

Behind her she heard her mother-in-law crash a tea-spoon down into a fragile saucer but the Colonel beamed. 'Not at all, my dear. It's been most interesting. The work's going well and Sir Geoffrey's very pleased, aren't you, Miller?' He turned to his chief guest who stepped forward from the fireplace and took Bethya's hand in both of his as he stared meaningfully into her eyes which glowed back at him full of adoration.

'My dear lady, how delightful to see you again. One of the things I've missed most during my absence from Bella Vista has been the chance to talk with you,' he said archly. Her hand lay confidingly in his and her eyes promised him paradise. Then, from behind, came the voice of Gus's mother . . .

'Sir Geoffrey was just telling us his good news,' she said in a tone of great satisfaction.

Bethya glanced over her shoulder at the speaker and

then back at the man who was holding her hand. 'Good news?' she queried sweetly.

He dropped her hand as if it had suddenly burned him and stepped back while Gus' mother continued, 'Yes, he's just announced his intention of marrying again.'

It was an effort for Bethya to maintain her brilliant smile but she had a long training in hiding her true feelings. 'You're marrying again?' she asked lightly, but with an undertone of surprise that implied this was a precipitate thing to do since it was such a short time since his wife had died.

'Ah well, dear lady, sometimes grief can only be assuaged by alleviating loneliness. My wife-to-be has also been widowed recently and she feels as I do . . .' he told her.

There was a strange hammering noise in Bethya's ears as she nodded apparently sympathetically and then turned, still smiling, to walk to her chair. She knew that Maria Anstruther was watching her every move with glee. The old harridan then said, 'Tell us the name of your future wife again, Sir Geoffrey. I'm so forgetful.'

He was obviously highly pleased with himself as he intoned the name. 'Lady Mary Brightwell. Her husband Sir Arthur died three months ago. He had large estates in Lincolnshire . . .'

Mrs Anstruther nodded. Her favourite reading was the Court News in *The Times* and ladies' magazines that provided information about the aristocracy. 'Yes, it's an old family. She has no children, I believe?' she prompted.

Miller looked sharply at her. 'That's right – she's childless. It's been a great grief to her.'

'Perhaps that can be rectified now,' said Mrs Anstruther coyly, but Sir Geoffrey shook his head.

'Oh no, dear lady, my future wife and I are both beyond that stage of life. We're marrying for companionship in our later years. We were both devastated by the loss of our partners and it was coincidental that they should die at almost the same time.' He heaved a sigh but the light of satisfaction in his eyes belied his false melancholy. Sir

Geoffrey had landed a major coup and all of the people in the room knew it.

Later, Bethya wondered how she managed to get through that tea party without breaking down or starting to scream. Sir Geoffrey sat beside her and flirted outrageously, taking her hand and smoothing the back of it with his long fingers. It was obvious that he imagined their teasing relationship might well continue although he was marrying again. Once he bent his head to whisper in her ear, 'I see your husband has not improved his ways . . .'

She fixed him with a sharp eye and said, 'Poor Gus, I love him so. I keep hoping that things will improve one day. Miracles do happen, don't they? After all, look at what's happened for you, Sir Geoffrey!'

She knew now that he had never had any intention of marrying her. If he could safely seduce her without being found out, he would and still hoped that he might, but he was far too much of a snob to compromise his position by involving himself in a divorce suit or by marrying a girl of mixed race. Bethya's tempestuous blood surged in her veins and she felt capable of murder, but for an hour and a half, in the lavishly furnished drawing room with Persian carpets on the floor and gold-embroidered silken hangings draped down the walls, she sat drinking tea, making innocuous conversation and stifling her feelings.

When she at last reached her bedroom again, Francine was waiting with the *rose vinaigre* and a brandy decanter. 'I heard the news – the kitchen's full of it. They say his new fiancée's ten years older than he is and very, very rich . . . She's also very snobbish and treats him like a parvenu but she's marrying him because he's rich as well.'

Bethya, set-faced, said nothing but swept one arm along the table top and sent decanter, glass, bottles and china ornaments smashing on to the floor. 'I hope she leads him a hellish dance. I hope she makes him wretched. I hope he finds that her estate's entailed and he can get his hands on none of it,' she hissed.

'Hush, hush, don't let anyone hear you,' whispered her maid, bending down to pick up the smashed glass.

'I don't care who hears me,' cried Bethya, pitching a heavy crystal scent bottle at a large painting of dogs chasing a stag over a heather-covered hillside. The glass shattered, spraying the floor with shards.

'Oh Mon Dieu!' cried Francine, standing back with her hands clasped in front of her mouth, but Bethya was pitching another bottle at the companion picture which depicted the stag dying in a welter of blood.

'I've always hated those pictures,' she yelled as the second painting plunged from the wall. Its fall seemed to satisfy her orgy of destruction, however, and she picked her way among the breakages to her bed, where she collapsed in a flood of tears. 'I've been a fool,' she sobbed. 'I thought it wouldn't matter here that I was half-caste but it's just as bad as Bombay. He's been laughing at me all the time, leading me on, hoping he'd get me into his bed. He never had the least intention of marrying me though he certainly made me think he might. What a fool I've been, what a fool!'

Francine, busy clearing up the débris, agreed. 'Men, they are all like that. I hate them – I really hate them!' There was a fierce note in her voice that made Bethya sit up and look at her maid sharply.

'I can't honestly say that I hate them, but I don't trust them, that's certain. Oh God, am I condemned to live here with Gus forever? Do I have to go on dressing up and acting like a doll while he plays around in the stables with a lot of little boys?'

Her maid stood up and said, 'You must use what you've got. If you can't get a man to marry you, you will have to utilise your assets another way. You must look for a rich protector, someone to take you away from here. Even if he doesn't marry you, he'll take you into society – only the demi-monde, perhaps, but look what happened to Lady Hamilton. There's many others like her too, especially in France. I used to watch them driving in the Bois but I've never seen one as lovely as you.'

Bethya sighed, 'What chance have I of finding a gentleman protector here?'

The maid was quite serious, however. 'There are many well-to-do people living round about. We're surrounded by huge estates. You must get to know the better-class people, cultivate the gentry.'

Bethya nodded. 'That's more difficult than it sounds, as I have found out.'

'You're a clever woman. You'll find a way if you really try,' consoled Francine.

When young Mrs Anstruther went down to dinner that night, she was as lovely and light-hearted as ever, making jokes, flirting, waving her fan and entrancing all who saw her, with the usual exceptions of her husband and mother-in-law. Mrs Maria Anstruther eyed her son's wife suspiciously, searching for signs of grief or swollen eyes but without satisfaction. Eventually, filled with irritation at Bethya's ability to hide what she was feeling, the Colonel's wife leaned over the table and asked, 'What was that terrible noise coming from your rooms this afternoon, my dear?'

Bethya opened her exquisite eyes very wide. 'Noise, Mama?'

'There was an awful noise of breaking glass, shouting and thumping about. I was trying to have a nap and it woke me up.'

Bethya laughed. 'Oh, that! My maid knocked over a scent-bottle. It was one of my favourites and I shouted at her. I'm sorry we kept you awake. You must have very acute hearing.'

From that day, however, a hardness entered Bethya. She was as bright and beautiful as before, but inside she harboured a fierce desire to escape from the tedium of her life at Bella Vista. Because she felt that Sir Geoffrey had treated her shabbily, she made up her mind that when she left Gus, she would move into a glittering world that made Sir Geoffrey's seem pedestrian.

During the last glorious days of that autumn, Tim Maquire began behaving oddly. He had never been a heavy drinker, but his friends noticed that in the middle of every afternoon, he would suddenly develop a thirst and announce his intention of walking into Camptounfoot for a mug of ale. If anyone offered to go with him, he'd find reasons for telling them to stay where they were. He liked to drink alone, he said.

Frying Pan, who had known Maquire for a long time, worried over this behaviour. 'He's never been a drinker. I hope he's not getting a taste for it,' he fretted, for he'd seen many good men wasted by their thirsts.

Naughten shook his head. 'He's never away for very long and he's always sober when he gets back. It must be a woman. He must have found a woman in that village.'

'If he has,' Sydney joked, 'she's not getting much out of it. He's never gone for more than fifteen or twenty minutes.'

They started timing him, and what Sydney said was true. Every day Tim set off walking to the village in mid-afternoon and he'd be back in about the time it took to swallow a pint of ale and walk the distance to and from Camptounfoot. Sometimes when he returned he'd be looking pleased with himself, but mostly he seemed doleful.

'Is the ale in that place very good? You seem to like it,' asked Naughten innocently one afternoon.

Tim was in a melancholy mood. 'It's not bad,' he said. He did not tell them that it was not ale that took him to Camptounfoot but the chance of catching a glimpse of the red-haired girl Hannah who, he had discovered, was often going to or from her mother's house in the middle of the afternoon when she had a few hours off work.

Hannah saw him the first day he took up his seat opposite her mother's cottage. She glared fiercely when she stepped out of the door for he was staring straight into her mother's window. Next day he was there again and the day after that. She did not understand why she did it but she always took care to be coming or going at about the same time. It was as if they had a secret rendezvous, yet for a long time they never spoke. At least she didn't. He always touched his hat to her and said, 'G'day.'

She did not want her mother to realise that she knew

this man, but in time his persistence wore her down and one afternoon, coming out on her way back to Bella Vista, she returned his greeting. He immediately stood up and said, 'Can I walk with you?'

She bristled. 'Of course not.'

'Just down to the corner,' he said.

She hissed at him, 'Don't let my mother see you. She doesn't like navvies.'

'Does that mean you'll walk with me?'

'No, it does not. Stop staring at me.' She flounced her skirt and hurried off. She felt sharply conscious of his eyes following her until she turned the corner at Bob and Mamie's. She wished that she could look back at him but she knew he would take that as encouragement.

Next day, to her strange relief, he was on the bench again when she walked up the street. He tipped his hat over his eyes when he saw her and said, 'I'm not looking at you.'

She laughed, she couldn't help it, and he looked up laughing too. Very white teeth flashed in his dark face and something jumped in Hannah's heart. She remembered the exciting feeling it had been to dance with him. 'Oh, what a fine-looking man he is,' she thought. 'What a pity he's a navvy but my Mam would go mad if I started walking out with a navvy . . .'

'I wish you wouldn't sit there every day,' she said softly.

He looked innocent. 'Why not? It's quiet and peaceful here. All I'm doing is drinking a mug of ale and watching the world go by. There's no law against that, is there?'

She shook her head. 'Well, don't sit here waiting for me to walk with you,' she said grimly.

'Oh, to be sure I know that'll never happen,' he said in his lilting accent, then he grinned again and added, 'But it brightens my heart just to look at you.'

Flushing scarlet she started to run and disappeared into her mother's house as if a battalion of dragoons were on her heels. From the bench by the wall she heard him laughing.

*

Brilliant sun beamed down on the beautiful Borderland for over a month, and every day Tim sat by the alehouse waiting for Hannah, but one Monday morning, a heavy, threatening bank of purple clouds covered the sky and in the distance thunder could be heard rumbling. By noon a terrible storm descended on the valley. Jagged forks of lightning flashed across the sky and rain lashed down in torrents that seemed capable of cutting through cloth. The corner outside Bob's shop was flooded by the little burn coming down from the hillside which now tried to find a new course through his parlour. Mr Jessup's garden was awash and the few people who were brave enough to go out found that they were forced to wade through pools of water that in places were waist-deep.

Work on the railway stopped. With his shirt soaked through and sticking to his skin, Tim ran around the site putting tarpaulins over half-dug holes or over rising pillars of stone. Navvies huddled in their huts smoking their pipes and watching the lashing rain through the open doors. They earned no money while work was suspended and the hold-up frustrated them sorely, driving some to drink and others to gambling. In the camp there were fights and disagreements; women dragging buckets to the swollen burn quarrelled noisily and the soaked dogs fell snarling on each other's necks.

In Major Bob's hut, the landlady took out her brandy bottle and began drinking. By mid-afternoon on the second day of the rain she was incapable of speech and had to be carried to bed, where she lay snoring loudly. Tim Maquire looked at her with stern disapproval. 'She's on a bender,' he said. 'She won't be capable of cooking anything for days. We'd better start foraging for ourselves.'

'I'll cook,' offered Naughten, but the others all shouted, 'Oh no, not you!' The last time he'd done the cooking they'd been served charred beef and watery cabbage.

'I'll cook,' came Sydney's drawl. 'I'll make a ragoût.'

'A what?' asked Frying Pan.

'A stew,' said Sydney.

'If that's what it really is. We don't want any of your foreign muck,' was Gold Tooth's contribution.

'Then make it yourself. As far as I know, all your countrymen can do is boil potatoes,' snapped Sydney.

Tim groaned aloud. He could foresee trouble and did not want to be there when it happened, so he took his coat off the peg by his bed and said, 'I'm going to walk over to Camptounfoot to see Mr Wylie. I'll leave you to it.' He didn't think Hannah would be abroad in this weather but he was going over just in case.

As he stepped outside, the rain hit him with the force of a whip but he put his head down and strode along paths that had turned into liquid mud. Within minutes it squelched over his boot-tops and soaked between his toes. Men standing in hut doors hailed him. 'Where are you going in this, Black Ace?' they asked.

He paused to speak to some of them and heard the same from all, a tale of irritation and ennui that was taking its grip of the whole camp. 'There's been a terrible fight in Bullhead's hut. He half-strangled Panhandle,' he was told by one man. Then Tim swore. 'Damn Bullhead, he's always ready to cause trouble. I'd better go and have a word with him.' Bullhead could cause a lot of damage, and Tim did not want any of the men to be disabled or out of action when the rain stopped because they would have to work twice as hard as usual to make up for lost time.

Bullhead's hut was one of the filthiest in the camp. When Tim opened the door he was assailed by the stink of stale tobacco smoke and frying fat. From somewhere at the back of the shed came the sound of strangled choking and coughing. Bullhead was sitting by the stove in the middle of the floor with another two navvies. They were all very drunk. Putting his hands on his hips Tim glared at them. 'I hope you're all going to be able to work tomorrow,' he said.

'And how do you know it'll not be raining tomorrow?' asked Bullhead belligerently. When drunk he was always ready to pick a fight with anybody about anything.

'I don't, but it's bound to stop some time and judging by the way you're going on, you'll be drunk then too,' said Maquire.

'Damn you, Black Ace. You're a cocky young bastard. Just because you're Wylie's right-hand man you think you're God, but you can't push me around. You'll take on more than you can cope with if you even try.' Bullhead rose to his feet with his fists up and took a swing at Maquire's head. The blow went wild because he was too drunk to stand up and Tim ducked it easily.

'Oh sit down, you silly sod. Sit down and keep out of trouble and don't go injuring any of my men or I'll put you off the site. I'll make sure you don't work for anybody else either. You're a troublemaker,' he shouted at the weaving Bullhead before he turned and went to go out of the shed. He heard the racking coughing again and wondered if the sounds were made by Panhandle, recovering from Bullhead's attempts to strangle him.

The woman who looked after Bullhead's hut was an evil crone called Squint Mary and she was huddled in a corner by the door, taking cover from her drunken lodgers. Tim paused beside her and asked, 'Is that Panhandle who's coughing? Is he all right?'

She looked up at him. One of her eyes was purple and she'd obviously been beaten up recently. 'Panhandle's fine,' she spat. 'He ran away after the fight. That's young Dogface who's coughing. The infection's all over the camp – haven't you got it in your hut yet?'

He shook his head. 'No, we haven't. Who else is ill?' Illness was only an irritating hold-up as far as he was concerned.

Squint Mary frowned and reeled off a list of names. She finished up with: 'They say Benjy's just about dead. He was never very strong at the best of times but this cough's really done for him.'

Benjy was a good, quiet workman and a skilled carpenter, one of the best in the business. Tim had known him a long time, and his work was always done correctly. Besides, Benjy was a decent little fellow. Worried, he hastened through the mud to where he knew Benjy had erected his neat little house. Among the wild navvies Benjy was a sort of a joke because he was so uxurious, a good family man, a loving husband to his quiet wife and a doting parent to their two small children. When he went from job to job, he took his house with him. It was a wooden shack, painted dark green with white trim around the window and doorframe. On the lintel he had carved the name *Benjy's*, and his wife painted the white trim with multi-coloured flowers every time Benjy gave their home its annual refurbishment. It had been redecorated when they came to Rosewell and was still gleaming with bright paint and prettily painted flowers through the grey and driving rain.

As he drew near, Tim's heart gave a lurch for he heard the unmistakeable sound of Irishwomen keening over a death. He had heard that noise too often in his childhood to mistake it for anything else. Above the background noise soared the voice of one woman who was not weeping because she'd been beaten, nor because a child was ill – she was weeping because her man was dead.

The door was ajar and Tim put his head round to look inside. Benjy's house was as he would have expected, neat and scrupulously clean. Three women were sitting round a table in the middle of the floor with their heads in their hands as they wailed and a fourth was standing by a bed in the corner beating her breast. Her fair hair was flowing wildly round her face which was lifted to the roof as if she was addressing the deity. 'Oh God, why've You taken my Benjy? My Benjy's dead. I've lost him. Oh, my Benjy's dead. I've lost him,' she howled over and over again. Two frightened-looking children were sitting on stools by the fire watching their grief-stricken mother. The oldest, a boy of about six, held his little sister in his arms. Tears streaked both their faces.

When Maquire stepped into the house, the women at the table looked up and one of them sobbed bleakly, 'There's been a death here, Black Ace.'

He nodded, looking at the shape of a body lying on the bed beneath a patchwork cover. 'Benjy?' he asked.

The dead man's wife, whose name was Mariotta, turned round and ran towards him. 'What's to happen to me and my bairns now, Black Ace? What's to happen to us?' she cried in anguish.

A second woman stood up and put an arm round the frantic woman. 'Hush, Mariotta, hush. Take a sip of brandy and that'll make you feel better. You're upsetting the wee ones.'

Gulping and hiccupping, Benjy's wife accepted a tea cup with brandy in it and swallowed down the fiery liquid, but her grief was unassuaged. 'Oh my Benjy, my dear Benjy. What'll I do without my man?' she howled again.

One of the women, the wife of an older navvy and a devout Christian, gestured Tim towards the door so that she could talk to him out of earshot. 'I'll take her bairns to my house tonight. Will you fix up the funeral?' she asked.

'What happened? I'd no idea he was even ill,' said Tim, who was unnerved by the terrible scene being enacted in the hut. Mariotta was still howling and it seemed as if her yells echoed and re-echoed across a cold and unheeding world.

'He had the consumption. He'd had it for a long time – had been coughing blood for about a year, but this last attack did for him. Poor Benjy. He didn't think he was going to die, though. I wanted to send for a priest but he wouldn't hear of it. He thought if a priest came, that would be the end for him,' the kindly woman wept.

'Yes, I'll arrange the funeral,' said Tim. It was customary among the navvies for a man's colleagues to pay for his burial and to make a collection for his family if he had one.

'I'll look after the lassie. Poor soul, she's distracted. She's got no family, nobody except Benjy. They met about eight years ago when he was working on the same site as her father. She was just a young lassie then. Never been with a man or anything like that. Her father was killed by an earth-fall, so Benjy took her,' said Mariotta's friend. Tim nodded. He knew how women were passed from one kind of protection to another among the navvies. Some were luckier than others but Benjy was a good man so Mariotta had been lucky.

The woman beside him was still talking. 'She's a decent, God-fearing lassie, not like most of the trollops in this camp. Never drinks or swears or takes other men. It's always the good folk that get the heaviest blows though, isn't it? Poor lassie and those poor bairns. She's brought them up like angels. What's going to happen to them now, Black Ace?'

Tim shook his head. 'We'll raise some money to pay the fare for her and the bairns to go back to Ireland. She's Irish, isn't she? She must have family there. I'll see what I can do.' By now it was dark and he knew he'd missed the chance of meeting Hannah so he hurried back to Major Bob's to tell his friends about Benjy's death and to collect some money for the widow.

It was still raining next morning when they buried Benjy in an unmarked grave at the back of the Abbey burying-ground in Rosewell. The Kirk session would not give permission for a Roman Catholic navvy to be laid to rest among the townspeople, so Benjy had to be put into the section set aside for suicides and other outcasts. A party of strong navvies carried his plain, pine coffin down from the camp to the Abbey, and stood with their hats in their hands while a priest intoned the burial ceremony. Mariotta and her children were the chief mourners, accompanied by the women who had been with her when Benjy died.

At the conclusion of the short ceremony, Tim Maquire waited by the gate of the burying-ground for the widow to appear, and handed her a purse of money that he had collected from the dead man's workmates. 'It's seven pounds and ten shillings,' he said, 'and Mr Wylie's going to pay for you and the children to go back to Ireland.'

She raised bloodshot blue eyes to his face and whispered, 'Why should I go there? I don't know anybody in

Ireland. I was born in London and I've lived all my life in navvy camps.'

She was thin and bird-boned with a peaky white face. Her huge trusting eyes gave her an air of fragile prettiness like a broken flower. Her hair was fair and parted in the middle, drawn down in two curves over her ears. As he looked at her, Tim wondered how old she could have been when she took up with Benjy, for she was little more than a girl now and yet her son was six years old. He estimated that she was probably no more than twenty-two or three – and a widow already.

'There must be someone in Ireland you know,' he persisted. 'Your father was Irish, wasn't he?'

She nodded. 'And my mother too, but I've no idea where they came from. I've no birth or death certificates or anything like that, for they couldn't read or write – neither can I.'

Tim looked hard at her. 'Go back to Ireland,' he said gently. 'You can't stay here.'

'I know,' she said. 'Mr Jopp came this morning and said I must be off the camp by the end of the week. There's no place there for women without men. He offered me five pounds for my house to save me shipping it away.' Her voice was despondent, and it was obvious that she had no idea what she was going to do. Her children clung to her skirts, looking up at her with fear in their eyes.

'I'll speak to the priest about you,' said Tim, who was filled with a terrible pity for the three of them. 'I'll send him round to your house tonight – he's sure to have some ideas. And if you need more money, I'll make sure you get it. Just let me know how much you want.'

'Aw, sure you're a good man, Black Ace,' she whispered.

That night he was sleeping in his cot when he felt a hand shake his shoulder. He opened his eyes and in the light of the moon shining through the window, he saw Major Bob bending over him. 'Wake up, Black Ace! I've a proposition to put to you,' she hissed in his ear. He could tell from the smell of her breath that she was drunk.

'Go away, it's the middle of the night,' he groaned, and turned over to avoid her.

She pulled at his shoulder again. 'Get up, Black Ace, and come with me. Mariotta sent me to fetch you.'

'You want to lay off the liquor,' he said sternly, but rose from bed, pulled on his trousers and jacket, reached under the bed for his boots and stuck his feet in them. While he was doing this she stood swaying at the open door of the hut, gesturing to him to hurry up. To his relief, when he reached Benjy's hut, Mariotta was not drunk, but she was the only one of the gathering of women who was sober. 'What's all this about?' he asked as he stood in the doorway, looking at them sitting round the stove with empty bottles littered at their feet. Mariotta occupied a chair beneath the window. She had been crying again.

'We've just been telling this lass what she ought to do,' said a tall blonde woman with raging eyes who rose from her seat when Tim appeared. He glared at her and she went on hurriedly, 'We've told her she ought to look for a new man.'

'Aw, never!' he exploded. 'She only buried her last one this morning.'

Behind him Mariotta gave a gulping sob and stammered, 'The priest says I'll never be able to keep my bairns. He says I should go to the nuns, and the bairns to an orphanage. He doesn't approve of me and won't help me because they're bastards. I wasn't really married to Benjy. We just joined up together – you know how it is.'

He nodded. The blonde woman by his side gave him a jab in the ribs with her fist and said, 'So she's looking for another man. If she finds one in this camp, she won't have to leave here. He'd just move in with her and her bairns.'

Then he knew why they'd sent for him. They were all watching him, eager-eyed, and Mariotta's eyes were the most pleading of all. He backed away. 'I can't. I'm not marrying anybody. I'm saving up to go back to Ireland and buy a farm.' As he spoke he realised how little he'd thought about his dream recently. He'd spent more time thinking about the girl with the red-gold hair. She was another reason why he couldn't take on Mariotta and her children, no matter how much sympathy he had for them.

'I told you I'd get you more money if you needed it,' he said, turning to the forlorn girl who only shook her head and said sadly, 'I told them you wouldn't take me on but they wanted to send for you. It wasn't my idea . . .'

Major Bob turned on him like an angry terrier. 'Don't be a miserable rat, Black Ace! You've no other woman, you've plenty of money and this is a poor lassie who'll have to prostitute herself if someone doesn't take her on. What else is there for her? When a navvy dies, his woman's left to fend for herself as best as she can – and we all know how that is! She either goes whoring or she finds another husband.'

Raddled-looking Squint Mary groaned and said, 'That's what happened to me.' She looked after a shed containing ten men and slept with them all and as she got older, she was forced to take in the least desirable men, the brutes and basest drunks no one else would accept.

Tim groaned just as loudly and said, 'I know. I'm sorry but I can't take Mariotta.' He turned to her and urged, 'Go to Ireland. You can get a job in a big house or something and keep your bairns with you. People are kinder there.'

Major Bob gave a cracked little laugh. 'Don't you believe it. Not for women they're not.'

Mariotta was weeping silently and in desperation she stood up to hold out her arms in a wide gesture. 'I'm not old. I'm not sick. I'm very clean and I keep a decent house. I can have more bairns, plenty of bairns. And I've never had any other man but Benjy!'

He was shocked for her. 'Stop it, stop it,' he shouted. He couldn't bear to hear her pleading like that. Repelled, he stepped back into the open air and tried to explain. 'I'm not looking for a wife. I don't want the responsibility. It's not you, Mariotta – I'd say the same about any woman.' That was a lie and he knew it. If Hannah asked him, he'd be mad with joy.

She sat down on her chair again and her face was set so

that she looked as she would if she lived to be an old woman. 'Then I'll have to find someone else,' she said.

'Think about it, don't do anything in a hurry and take care who you pick,' he told her, but she only smiled sadly.

'It doesn't matter really, does it?' she said dully. 'I've a feeling my life's finished anyway. If it wasn't for my bairns I'd go down to the river and drown myself.'

The rain continued to fall and the river to rise for another forty-eight hours. A concerned Wylie arrived in his hired carriage from Camptounfoot and hurried up through the camp to find Tim Maquire. 'We've got to go over to the south side of the bridge and look at the foundation holes. I'm sure they'll be washed away by now,' he said.

Half an hour later, after having driven through pools of water that rose about the hubs of the carriage-wheels, they stood at the top of the field and gazed at a scene of desolation. Part of the river bank where it had been intended that the first pier on the south side should go, had been swept away completely, and the freshly dug foundation holes had caved in because of water running down from piles of earth higher up. All the work would have to be done again.

Wylie groaned and knuckled his brow. 'Oh my God, this is going to set us back for more than a week – and that's only if it stops raining now.'

Tim looked up at the pewter sky that still gave no sign of brightening. 'We'll make it up, Mr Wylie, don't you worry. My men and I'll make it up,' he promised.

When he reached the camp again he was drenched to the skin and walked wearily up the path to Major Bob's hut. Standing at the door waiting for him was Mariotta, holding a child by each hand.

She smiled sadly at him and said, 'You're very wet. I'll wait out here till you dry yourself a bit. I've something to tell you.'

Inside the hut he grabbed a rough linen towel, wiped his face with it, stripped off his soaking coat and walked quickly back to the door to hear what she had to say. He wanted her to go away as soon as possible, for the sight of her made him feel guilty as if he had committed some sort of sin by not taking her when she offered herself to him.

She was still standing at the door, sheltering the children from the rain under her outspread cape. When he stepped out beside her, she looked up and asked, 'Would you like to buy my little house, Black Ace?'

Relief shone out of his face. 'Ah, you're going away then after all, Mariotta. That's good – I'm glad. But I thought you said Jopp had offered to buy your house?'

She shook her head. 'He did – he offered five pounds, but when I went to him today to say I'd accept, he backed down, said he couldn't pay more than three. That's because he knows my week's up the day after tomorrow. I've to be out of the camp by then.'

Tim hissed under his breath, 'That's Jopp for you!'

Mariotta was looking anxiously at him. 'The house is worth more than five pounds. It's watertight and very snug. It's a lovely wee house. I'll leave the furniture in it too. All I'll take are our clothes.'

'Goddammit, I'll pay you ten for it. Wait here and I'll go and get the money.' He ran inside and hauled his bedding off his cot. His savings were in the mattress. Major Bob was watching as he took the money out but he didn't care because he guessed she'd always known where he hid it and had never touched it.

When he thrust ten golden guineas into Mariotta's hand her fingers closed over them and she said softly, 'God bless you. This'll pay for the care of my bairns for a long time. It'll keep them for a year.'

He was taken aback. 'Why, where are they going?'

'There's a woman in Rosewell called Mrs Rush who says she'll take them in. She'll be good to them and I can see them every day while I'm here.'

Something in her tone chilled him. 'While you're here? Where are you going?'

'I don't know. Where does any navvy camp go? I'll have to move on eventually but I'll worry about that when it happens.'

He put out a hand and laid it on her shoulder. 'Who's taken you, Mariotta?' he asked.

She flushed. 'Bullhead,' she whispered.

'Not him! Oh my God, not him! Don't you know they say he killed his last wife because of the beatings he gave her?'

'I heard that, but he came to my house last night and offered to take me. Because he wants me he won't let any other man offer for me. It's him or nobody – I haven't much choice. But I don't want him to have the children, that's why I need the money for their keep in a decent house. I told him what I was going to do. He said it doesn't matter. He's promised to treat me well. His last wife drank, he said, that's why he hit her . . .'

'You didn't believe him, did you?'

She stared at him with enormous, hopeless eyes. 'I have to believe him, haven't I?'

'Listen,' he almost said. 'Don't go to Bullhead, come to me,' but he couldn't. 'Listen,' he began again, 'if Bullhead ever gives you any trouble, tell me and I'll bring him back into line. He's afraid of me. Don't let him hit you. Don't let him sell you to other men . . .' She looked terrified but he knew that Bullhead had done that with his women before and felt he ought to warn her. Her life with Benjy could not have prepared her for the brutalities of a man like Bullhead. 'If there's any suggestion of that, come and tell me,' he insisted and she nodded, looking like a child again.

I'll tell you,' she promised, and reached into her skirt pocket to draw out an iron key. 'This is the key to my house. I hope you're happy in it,' she said as she handed it over to him.

CHAPTER
Nine

By next morning, the rain had abated and Tim led the navvies who were sober enough to work, along the road to the bridge site. By the time he had assigned them all their daily tasks and seen that everything was going well, Christopher Wylie had still not turned up, and Tim knew something must be wrong, for by then it was past midday. In a great hurry Tim ran up the slope of the field and along the road to Camptounfoot, not even slackening his pace when he drew level with the alehouse. He was going to the Jessups' and had no time for dalliance.

Mr and Miss Jessup was sitting at their table with solemn-looking faces when he knocked on the door. They were relieved to see him. 'Poor Mr Wylie's very unwell. I want to send for a doctor but he won't let me. Perhaps you can persuade him that it would be a sensible thing to do. He's fevered and has a terrible cough,' said old Jessup anxiously.

They took Tim upstairs to the top-floor room where Christopher Wylie lay with a flushed face and closed eyes. His cheeks were sunken and he looked like an old man whose strength had left him. Tim put a hand on the wrinkled forehead and felt fever burning beneath the skin. Wylie opened his eyes at the touch and murmured, 'Oh it's you, lad. I'm glad you came. I've a bit of a chill and I won't be at the site today . . .'

'I'll see to things,' Tim told him reassuringly.

Wylie coughed rackingly and turned his head weakly on the pillow. Tim remembered Benjy and made a quick decision. 'I'm going into Rosewell to fetch you a doctor,' he said.

Wylie was so ill he didn't even protest, just closed his eyes again. The Jessups were waiting on the landing outside the bedroom and when he emerged Tim asked them, 'How long has he been like this?'

'Two days. He won't eat and he coughs all night. I'm not much of a hand at nursing and my sister's very shy. We haven't been able to help him much,' said the old man.

'I'll bring a doctor,' said Tim, hurling himself down the narrow stairs. 'I won't be long.'

As luck would have it, when he ran into the street he almost collided with Hannah, who smiled and paused as if ready to speak but he could not spare any time. The memory of Wylie's stricken face haunted him so he only paused long enough to touch his hat and ran on past her. She stared after him in surprise, wondering if she had offended him so much on their last meeting that he would not speak to her again. Then she shrugged and pulled her shawl tightly over her head. That was his loss, she told herself.

Dr Stewart, who practised in Rosewell, was a great snob and could only be persuaded to attend Wylie when he heard that the patient was the bridge contractor, and not a navvy. He rode to Camptounfoot in his gleaming carriage but did not offer Tim a lift, so when the navvy reached the Jessups' again, the doctor was already preparing to leave. Pulling on his gloves he said to Mr Jessup, 'He'll need careful nursing. I've left a prescription for him – make sure he takes it, sir. He's a very sick man.'

Tim came crashing through the door at that moment and asked, 'What's wrong with him? What can we do?'

The doctor looked at him icily. 'He has severe congestion of the lungs. His heart's rather feeble too. He must stay in bed until the cough goes away.'

'How long will that be?'

'As long as it takes – there's no way of telling. Some people recover quite quickly, some never recover at all. If he's to get better he'll need careful nursing.'

When the doctor drove away, Tim and the Jessups

stared at each other. 'Do you want me to take him away?' he asked them.

Mr Jessup shook his head. 'Oh dear me, no. Where would he go? Anyway, moving the poor man in this state might be very dangerous, but we can't nurse him really. Neither of us are young . . . Quite frankly it takes me all my time to look after my sister.'

Miss Jessup was looking frightened and suddenly Tim realised that her childish ways were not affectation. She only managed to function because she had her brother telling her what to do all the time.

'I'll find a nurse for him, and we should write to his wife in Newcastle asking what she thinks ought to be done. Perhaps she'll come up and nurse him herself,' said Tim.

Mr Jessup nodded. 'I'll write the letter – I know his address there. I'll send it off today.'

When the missive addressed in a spidery, old-fashioned hand was brought to the breakfast table at Wyvern Villa next morning, Emma Jane eyed it with apprehension. Without opening it, she knew it contained bad news but it was addressed to her mother and had to be carried upstairs on Mrs Wylie's breakfast tray before she could find out what was in it.

After her husband went away to Scotland, Arabella Wylie had slowly relapsed into the melancholy and hypochondria that had held her in its grasp after James' death. She could not be shaken out of it because the only person with the power to do that was Christopher, and he was far away. She missed him dreadfully and wept every evening at the time when he would normally be returning home. Helplessly Emma Jane watched and tried to cheer her mother, but to no effect. Arabella stopped going out, stopped receiving visitors and took again to her bed while her daughter passed her time teaching little Arbelle and reading her father's engineering books in his library. This solitary life did not worry her. In fact she rather liked it, since it meant she was not faced with the frightening prospect of going into society. The only exciting thing that had happened recently was when Amelia brought a man called Dan Peel to meet her mother-in-law and Emma Jane.

It had not been an easy meeting because Dan was awkward and over-awed by the elegance of the Wylie home and by the reserve of Mrs Wylie, who did not like the idea of another man taking her son's place. It was obvious that, though Amelia did not say so, this was the man that she was preparing to marry.

Poor Dan sat stiffly in a velvet-covered chair and twirled his hat in his hands while Amelia and Emma Jane attempted to make conversation around him. He said little but if he did speak, his accent was thickly rural and Mrs Wylie's eyebrows went up in disapproval. When he went away she said to Emma Jane, 'He's very ungentlemanly, isn't he? What will your father say if Amelia marries him!'

'He seems a pleasant enough man and he's got a good carter's business according to Amelia, so he's not poor,' ventured Emma Jane.

Her mother shook a sad head. 'It's not Amelia I'm worried about, but Arbelle. How is she going to turn out, living in that sort of society? I wonder if your father could persuade Amelia to give her to us to bring up as a lady?'

Emma Jane did not think it at all likely that Amelia would agree to such a suggestion, but she said nothing. Whatever her mother felt about Amelia's lack of breeding, there was no denying her love and care for Arbelle.

These concerns were thrust aside, however, as Emma Jane stood on the upstairs landing waiting till her mother read the mysterious letter that had been taken in by Mrs Haggerty who was the head indoor servant at Wyvern Villa. Within moments there was a pitiful wail from the bedroom. 'Emma Jane! Oh, Emma Jane . . .'

When the girl went in her mother was lying back against her pillows with a wan face. She held the letter out and sobbed, 'Read that, Emma Jane. Oh, what will I do? I can't go to him – I can't even walk!'

Emma Jane's eye ran down the single sheet of elegant writing. '*Dear Madam,*' it said. '*Your husband has been taken* ill with a severe chest complaint. I must hasten to assure you that his illness is not life-threatening but he must remain in bed with careful nursing for some time. His assistant Mr Maquire has found a woman to care for him so you must not worry, but we thought it best if you were informed of the situation. I will send you a daily bulletin about his health and assure you that he has the affection and attention of myself and my sister . . . John Jessup.'

'You're father's ill. What are we to do?' Mrs Wylie sobbed.

'I'll go to him. I'll go today!' said Emma Jane with sudden resolution. She knew she was the one who had to go. Cockburn was too frail to travel now and her mother could not either. Arabella sat up. 'Yes, go at once. Oh, I wish I could go with you but I can hardly move, I'm so unwell. Oh Emma Jane, why has this happened to us?' And she burst into a storm of weeping that took some time to assuage.

When Emma Jane ran down to the cottage to tell Amelia what had happened, she found her sister-in-law at breakfast wearing a long flowing wrapper with dozens of ribbons down the front that made her look like one of the dancing figures from Botticelli's painting *Primavera*. On hearing the news, Amelia asked, 'Will you be able to go all that way on your own, Emma Jane? Do you want me to come with you? Mrs Haggerty could look after Arbelle while I'm away.'

'No, thank you all the same but I'll manage perfectly well, I'm sure. I came to say that I'm going, that's all. When Papa is well enough I'll tell him about you and Dan, Amelia. I'm sure he'll be very pleased.'

Tears sprang into Amelia's blue eyes. 'Oh, that'll be good of you, Emma Jane. I've been worried about how you'd all feel about Dan. I did love James, you know – I love him still. It's been a real surprise to me that you can love two people like that . . . I don't want you to think I've forgotten him.' Her voice broke then, and Emma Jane noticed that when she was distressed or excited, Amelia's vowels seemed to break up into two parts – 'don't' became 'do-an't' as if she was sighing in the middle, and the sound was very endearing.

Amelia reached out a hand and grasped her sister-in-law's. 'I know you haven't forgotten him, and Papa will too. So does Mama really but she's so sad about James herself that she can't think clearly,' she whispered.

Amelia collected herself quickly. 'When are you going? What can I do to help? Wait till I dress and I'll come back with you and help you pack a bag. And don't worry about your mother when you're away. I'll look after her so you can stay as long as your father needs you.'

When the two girls got back to Wyvern Villa, however, Mrs Wylie was in the middle of another fit of hysterical weeping. This time, the cause was Emma Jane. 'I'm so worried about you, my dear,' she sobbed. 'How will you manage to travel so far when you've never even gone to Newcastle alone before? Perhaps I should send for one of your cousins from Harrogate to come and travel with you.'

Mrs Wylie's sister Louisa had married a doctor in Harrogate and had two supercilious girls and a haughty son whom Emma Jane loathed. She stepped back in alarm. 'Oh no, Mama, that *won't* be necessary. Anyway, Amelia has offered to come with me and I've said I don't need anyone. There's no time to wait for someone coming from Harrogate. I have to go now.'

Her mother sighed but was slightly calmer. 'Oh my dear, I'll have to write out a list of things you must do and things you must ask your father when he's well enough.' When, an hour later, Emma Jane was about to leave, her mother summoned her to the bedside and inspected her with a critical eye. 'You need a thicker wrapper – that one's too thin. And perhaps you should wear my bonnet. The one you've put on looks a little tired and the blue ribbons are too bright. Take my one with the black trimming. You're still in mourning, after all. Now here's my list for your father. Make sure he gets it and there's no need for you to look at it. It's private between your father and I. Have you taken some jars of calf's-foot jelly from the larder and his favourite jam? Have you that bottle of good port and one of brandy? Make sure he gets egg-whip with brandy every morning – that's good for chest trouble. Oh, goodbye my dear, and God bless you. Give me a kiss before you go.' She held up her pale cheek and Emma Jane kissed it. 'This is what it must be like for soldiers being sent into battle,' she thought.

An equally fussy Haggerty drove her to the Central Station and installed her in a corner seat in a Ladies Only compartment. When at last he assured himself that she was secure, he bustled off down the platform and she breathed a huge sigh. For the first time in her life, at the age of twenty-two, Emma Jane Wylie was going some-where alone. The train gave a rattle and a lurch. There was a piercing whistle and a whoosh of released steam from its tall funnel. The carriage began to rock gently and very gradually pulled out of Newcastle heading for the north. As the speed built up, she sat forward in her seat and started to rummage in her reticule. Out of it she pulled a closely written sheet of instructions which her mother had given her before she left. They told her not to speak to anyone, even innocent-looking women; not to eat anything offered to her by fellow travellers, and to sniff her sal volatile the moment she felt faint or panic-stricken. She read all the notes very carefully, then folded the page in half, and started tearing it into pieces, first into halves, then quarters, then eighths and sixteenths . . .

When she was satisfied that the page had been reduced to the tiniest fragments possible, she dropped the window-glass and scattered them into the breeze so that they sailed off like snowflakes. She laughed and leaned out, staring at the flying paper and the passing world. What joy it was to be travelling so fast and so freely! She felt like an intrepid explorer as the wind whipped her hair out of its neatly-arranged bun and blew it around her face. She was still laughing when she drew back into the carriage again and caught sight of a pink-faced young woman in the mirror above the opposite seat. 'That's me!' she thought. For a moment she hadn't recognised herself.

The train was late in arriving at Maddiston, which made Emma Jane frantic to reach Camptounfoot as quickly as possible. The nerves which had beset her when she thought about how to get from the station to the village where her father was lying sick, miraculously disappeared as she walked along the platform and summoned a hired carriage from the forecourt. She was not aware that she was speaking with brisk authority when she told the driver, 'Take me to Camptounfoot – and fast, please.'

He helped her climb aboard, stowed her bag in with her, then mounted his box, cracked his whip and they were off. Once or twice he looked back over his shoulder at the girl sitting stiffly in the middle of the seat behind him and, because he was incorrigibly curious, started to question her in a roundabout way. 'It's bonny country round here when it's fine but you're not seeing it at its best,' he told her. She looked out at the drizzling rain and made a noncommittal sound.

'You know the district?' he asked.

'No, I don't,' she said shortly. He wondered where she was going in Camptounfoot, for she looked as if she might be some sort of upper-range servant, a lady's maid or a governess perhaps, though she was very young.

'You're sure it's Camptounfoot you want?' he persisted.

'Yes.' The tone was decisive.

There weren't any houses in the village grand enough for a lady's maid, however, so he raised his eyebrows and was finally forced to ask, 'Where in Camptounfoot exactly?'

She glared at him with eyes that reminded him of a startled cat. 'I'm going to the residence of Mr Jessup.'

It was obvious that she did not want to expand on the reason for her visit and the driver felt quite intimidated by her so for the rest of their journey they rode in silence.

Mr Jessup's face was blank when he opened the door of his house to an unknown young woman. 'Is this where Mr Wylie lives?' she asked. He told her it was. For a moment he thought it was another nurse sent by Tim Maquire, who had already recruited a good-living navvy wife to nurse the sick man, but she had children and a husband of her own at the camp so she had to keep running to and fro.

The girl smiled and her grim expression was transformed. 'Oh, I'm so glad I've found the right house. I'm Mr Wylie's daughter. May I see him, please?'

Christopher was asleep but he was gently wakened by a hand on his shoulder and a voice saying, 'Papa, Papa, wake up. I've come to look after you.'

His eyes blinked open and his first smile for days lightened his features, 'Emma Jane. Bless you, my dear child,' he whispered and Mr Jessup noticed that his words made the girl glow as if she had been given the gift of a fortune.

When the nurse came back after seeing to her own children, she was met by Emma Jane in a white apron who thanked her for her work, gave her a generous tip and said it would not be necessary for her to come back any more. The woman was relieved because she had not liked walking through Camptounfoot where hostile faces and hard eyes stared at her from cottage windows and people turned their heads away rather than speak to her. She was not to know that their dislike was not for her personally, but for the fact that she was a navvy's wife and therefore associated with the hated railway. Even the people whose men had taken jobs digging the bridge foundations avoided her because they were afraid of antagonising their more anti-railway neighbours. The village was fighting among itself now, gossiping virulently about who had taken railway money, who had given in.

On her way back to the camp the woman met Tim Maquire hurrying into the village to check up on Mr Wylie. He looked at her with concern. 'Where are you going?' he asked.

'A woman's arrived from Newcastle. She paid me off and said she's going to nurse him,' was the reply.

Tim speeded up his footsteps: he was convinced that the stranger would be Mr Wylie's wife, and he wanted to reassure her that he would do everything he could to help while she nursed her husband back to health.

Mr Jessup was looking worried when he let Tim in. 'I don't know where she can sleep,' he whispered.

'Perhaps we can put up a truckle bed for her if she can't share his,' was the reply.

'Oh, I don't think that will do,' said Mr Jessup, wringing his hands.

'She won't mind. She'll realise it's an emergency,' Tim told him comfortingly and hurried up to the sick man's room. The woman who turned and looked at him when he stepped inside, however, took him by surprise because she was only a girl. This couldn't be Wylie's wife, he surmised, because he remembered young James who had been in his twenties when he died and this girl wasn't even as old as that, from the look of her.

He paused in confusion and she asked, 'Who are you? What do you want? My father's asleep.'

My father! Of course, this was Wylie's daughter. But from what her father had told Tim about her, he had assumed that she was still only a child, barely out of the schoolroom. This was a solemn-faced young woman with scraped-back dark hair and fierce yellow eyes which stopped him in his tracks. He took off his hat and said awkwardly, 'I'm Tim Maquire, your father's ganger. I've been seeing to things for him.'

She smiled and her face changed completely. 'Oh yes, I've heard about you. My father thinks highly of you, Mr Maquire. I'm very pleased to meet you. Father's asleep and I don't want him disturbed, so perhaps we could go on to the landing and talk?'

Outside the bedroom door he told her that he would bring anything she needed from Rosewell. All she had to do was tell Mr Jessup, who would send a village urchin to the bridge site to fetch him. Mr Jessup's head was poking up from the stairwell and he nodded vigorously at this, but Tim knew he wanted the subject of where Emma Jane was going to stay broached.

'Er, where will you sleep?' he asked her.

She looked down at Jessup and realised how much of an imposition she must be for him and his sister. 'Oh dear,' she gasped, 'of course. Perhaps I could hire rooms in the village?'

Tim shrugged. 'No one'll have you. I had the devil's own job getting this berth for Mr Wylie.'

Emma Jane looked at Mr Jessup and pleaded, 'I'll sleep on the floor. I won't need anything, I really won't. I'll look after myself entirely. But I must be able to take care of Father . . .'

Jessup's kind heart prevailed over his reservations again. The girl was so obviously genuine. 'There's a little cubbyhole just off his bedroom. It's only a big cupboard really but we might make up a bed in there,' he said doubtfully.

'Oh, I'd be happy to sleep in the cupboard,' cried Emma Jane, 'and I'll pay you for my lodgings, of course.' She was very glad indeed that she'd had the sense to bring all of her allowance money with her, and even more grateful that she had not spent any of it on fripperies. Then she looked at Tim and said, 'I understand the doctor's coming every day to look at Papa. We'll be quite all right now. Thank you so much for your help. You mustn't worry about my father any longer. I'll send you a message if I need anything.'

More than slightly discomfited, he withdrew, for she'd dismissed him without knowing how much she'd hurt his feelings. It was an innocent mistake, for to her he was only one of her father's workmen and she thought it unfair to burden him with her troubles. She did not realise how close he was to her father, nor how much he had worried and worked when Wylie fell ill. She had no idea that it was Tim who had arranged for the doctor to come and the navvy's wife to nurse Christopher Wylie, but it seemed to him that she was taking everything out of his hands and he resented her attitude very much.

Over the days that followed, the kind Jessups took Emma Jane to their hearts and found pleasure in feeding her the same delicious food as they provided for the invalid – boiled chicken and apple puddings floating in cream; river trout and flummeries; soup made from vegetables grown in their garden; boiled mutton with caper sauce. She grew sleek on their regime and they secretly congratulated themselves in the change they saw in her. As Christopher improved in health too, they once more started playing their music again in the evenings and Emma Jane drifted off to sleep in a sea of rippling notes from the piano and violin of her host and hostess. She did not know what she was listening to, but felt as if she were being carried down a silver river like the one that flowed in the valley between Camptounfoot and Rosewell. While she slept, she dreamed that she was a mermaid, slipping between the fronds of waterweed like a fish.

The happiness that filled her when she heard the music, grew as her father's strength returned and eventually he was able to drive out in the hired carriage to see his precious bridge. Tim had looked after things so well during his boss's illness, that there was plenty to look at and exclaim over. All the foundations for the piers had been dug and the northern bridgehead was rising like a castle bastion on the far side of the river. Wylie sat in his carriage and beamed. 'Well done, well done,' he congratulated his ganger. Then he pointed out to his daughter, 'Look at that, Emma Jane – isn't that a great bridgehead? It could carry four bridges.'

'It certainly looks very strong,' she agreed and her father said, 'It has to be: it's carrying a huge weight – and I can't take risks with it.' Then his face sobered a little. 'The stone's costing more than I bargained for, though. The quarry was forced on me by the directors. I could have got stone that was just as good and just as durable from a quarry at Rosewell or on the side of one of those hills behind Camptounfoot for half the price.'

She said the right things, nodded in the right places and watched while her father and Maquire talked to each other. Only then did she realise how the two men related to each other; how devoted the younger man was to her father and how her father admired him. She began to have some inkling of the mistake she'd made in her treatment of Tim Maquire. This was no ordinary navvy; this was someone who was very special to her father. To make amends she smiled at him and made some innocuous remarks but he fended them off impassively. It was obvious that he had not forgiven her for cutting him off from her father and probably never would.

One afternoon when they were making their inspection visit, their carriage was overtaken by a couple cantering along on horseback. The first rider, a red-faced old man with a halo of white hair, turned in his saddle and called out, 'Good to see you out and about again, Wylie!' He was followed by a beautiful young woman in a cream linen riding outfit which fitted her like a second skin, who smiled but did not speak.

When they had passed, Christopher looked at his daughter and said, 'That's Colonel Anstruther, one of the railway directors, with his daughter-in-law. He's Edinburgh's spy, I think.'

Emma Jane raised her eyebrows. 'Edinburgh's spy? Why should they spy on you, Papa?'

'Because the railway chairman Miller is crafty. He's hoping I fall down on the contract, but not too soon. He wants me to run out of money or enthusiasm when all the hard bits have been done but the job's not completed – then he won't have to pay me, you see. My contract's for a finished bridge. I won't get paid if it's only half-done. He'll bring in a squad of cheap labour and finish it off himself.'

She leaned forward and patted his head. 'You'll finish it, Papa. Don't worry – you'll finish it.'

His eyes gleamed with reborn enthusiasm as he told her, 'Yes, I will, and it'll be my best bridge ever, my legacy, my swan song. It's coming along magnificently thanks to Maquire, and I'm coming along well thanks to you, Emma Jane.'

That night, after another of Miss Jessup's delicious little suppers, he was strong enough to stay up late and talk to Emma Jane, the longest conversation they had ever had together. In the room below, the music of Chopin ebbed and flowed as they got on to the subject of Amelia and Arbelle.

Very tentatively she told him about Dan, for she was afraid it would upset him to hear that his son's wife was planning to re-marry, but he did not seem surprised. 'Amelia's right to marry again. She's not the sort to stay a widow long. When's it to be?' he asked.

'Soon – next month, I think. Mother's very upset about it but she's trying to stay calm. She's worried about Arbelle, really. She thinks Amelia won't bring her up like a lady when she goes to live in Hexham. She thought you would ask Amelia if you and Mama could adopt Arbelle.'

Her father looked hard at Emma Jane and said, 'I wouldn't even suggest it. Your mother must remember that Arbelle is Amelia's daughter as well as James'. If this situation is handled with care, there will be no breach between us, but if it's handled badly we might never see Arbelle again and that would break my heart as well as your mother's. I wish I could go to Amelia's wedding but there's too much for me to do here. I want you to go for me and represent the family – show Amelia we understand and that we don't mind her marrying again. She's a good girl and she's already promised me that we'll always see a lot of Arbelle. If we play fair by her, she'll play fair by us.'

'Mother's worried about the cottage too. She thinks it a waste of money for you to have bought it just when Amelia was planning to re-marry,' said Emma Jane.

'She needn't concern herself with that,' said her father firmly. 'Tell her Amelia and I have an arrangement about that cottage. Amelia is an admirable young woman: James knew what he was doing when he married her.'

Emma Jane sat up straight and for the first time spoke the thoughts that had been in her mind for some time. 'I think it might not be a bad thing for Arbelle to be away from us for a bit, Father. Mama spoils her. Perhaps what she needs is a more natural life, growing up in a village with other children, living an outdoor life. In Wyvern

Villa she's like a hothouse plant, forced before her true season.'

He looked at her with respect. 'I didn't realise you thought that too, my dear. Every day you surprise me more. You've proved to be a pillar of strength during this illness and I'm very grateful, but now that I'm better I want you to go back to Newcastle, buy yourself a pretty dress and dance at Amelia's wedding.'

She smiled. 'I will, but not yet, Papa. I want to be sure you're completely recovered before I leave you.'

When she woke next day the rain was pouring down from a leaden sky and at breakfast her father said, 'There won't be much chance of work today. I hope the river doesn't rise too high. Maquire said yesterday that he's planning to start on the stonework of the foundations next.'

She looked up at him and said, 'If you're not going out, Papa, why not get out your plans and show me the bridge? Now that I've seen the site, I'll be able to appreciate it more.'

He looked pleased. 'All right, I'll do that. Come down to the parlour and we'll work there.'

All day long the rain poured down; all day long their two heads were bent over the plans. When Emma Jane showed understanding of a complex point, her father would give his big laugh, throw down his pencil and say, 'You're a wonder, my girl. I never thought you'd be able to understand that.' He showed her how to calculate stresses; he sketched for her how he hoped to lay the bricks around the high arches on top of the piers. He explained his calculations of how many bricks would be required . . . 'Three hundred and ninety-five thousand at least,' he said, 'and that's only for one side. To finish the bridge, I'll have to double that figure.'

'Where will you get so many bricks?' she asked.

'I've got all that arranged. They're coming from a brickworks at Wallsend – it's one I've used before. I've gone there because they make salmon-coloured bricks that'll blend in beautifully with the red sandstone of the piers. I'm looking on this as a work of art, you see,' he said jocularly.

She sat back in her chair and sighed in admiration. 'I see what you mean. It is a work of art. I think it's going to be beautiful.'

For the next three days, while the rain went on falling, father and daughter pored over maps and plans for the bridge. Emma Jane's interest was so keen and intelligent that Christopher forgot she was only a girl and he talked to her as he would have done to James. She realised this and her soul expanded with a pride in herself that she had never experienced before. Then, on the fourth day, a letter arrived from Mrs Wylie announcing the date of Amelia's wedding. It was only three weeks away and the letter said that Arabella's nerves had collapsed under the strain. If Christopher was well enough to be left, Emma Jane must come home.

'I won't have you travelling to the station in this rain,' she said firmly to her father. 'It's still very wet and you could catch another cold. I'll be quite happy going to Maddiston alone.'

He would not hear of that, however. 'If I can't take you to the station, I'll ask Maguire to do it,' he said.

Though she protested, he was adamant and young Robbie Rutherford, who had become a friend of Emma Jane's during her time in Camptounfoot, was sent to fetch Tim, who quickly arrived. When he heard the task he had been assigned, his face showed dismay but Christopher Wylie's wish was his command. 'Of course I'll put Miss Wylie on the Newcastle train,' he said, but without any marked enthusiasm. Then he looked at her with expression and asked, 'Are you ready to go now, miss?'

She nodded; he made her tongue-tied. She kissed her father and climbed into the waiting carriage, taking care to sit as far away from Maguire as possible in case he thought she was bold. The feeling of intense maleness that came from him disturbed her. For his part he was aware of her withdrawal and felt that she disapproved of him so he sat grimly in the opposite corner and stared out at the passing countryside while they drove along. Neither of them spoke.

The road from Camptounfoot took them over the bridge into Rosewell, and halfway across it, they drew level with a tall slim girl standing in one of the pedestrian bays. All of a sudden Tim Maquire seemed to come alive. His face was animated and almost boyish as he leaned down from the carriage to ask, 'Where are you going? Can I take you there? It's bad weather to be walking.'

He had not seen Hannah since Christopher Wylie was taken ill and now she stared up at him out of wide brown eyes, the lashes of which were wet with raindrops. His heart was beating fast as he looked down at her but she did not return his smile. She stared calmly at him, looked at Emma Jane and then back at Tim again before she replied, 'It's perfectly all right. I'm only walking into Rosewell on an errand for Mr Allardyce. The town carter will take me back to Bella Vista.'

Emma Jane saw that the girl who had such a marked effect on Maquire was a real beauty. Her hair, which was partly covered by a shawl, was a wonderful shade of red-gold, and her skin was as white and soft-looking as satin. She made Emma Jane feel like a little mouse as she sat huddled in her mother's black shawl and unbecoming bonnet. She was embarrassed too because she could feel the sexual tension that flowed between those handsome people. It reminded her of how awkward she used to feel sometimes when she was with her brother James and Amelia. She could see that the girl thought Maquire was escorting her – which he was, but not in the way the girl thought, of course. Hannah was jealous but tried not to show it. Pulling her shawl over her head, partly obscuring her face, she stepped out of the bay and strode across the bridge, forcing the carriage to go slowly behind her till she reached the far bank of the river.

It was agony for Emma Jane to be hustled on to the platform at Maddiston by Tim, who took his commission from her father seriously. The train steamed in, late again. He would not leave her till he saw her safely into her seat though she pleaded with him to go for she could tell that he longed to rush back to Rosewell and find the red-haired girl. In a way his confusion made him more humane and likeable in her eyes, and she began to feel more sympathy towards him. As the train drew away from Maddiston she gave him a little wave with her gloved hand, and to her surprise he waved back, but then she saw him starting to run along the platform to where the carriages waited. It made her feel very lonely and unloved.

A deep depression settled on Emma Jane during that journey back to Newcastle. In spite of having to sleep in a cupboard, she had enjoyed every moment of her time in Camptounfoot and wished she could have stayed longer. During their days together she and her father had struck up a rapport that had not existed between them before and she found the work on the bridge fascinating. It interested her far more than the needlework and watercolour painting that her mother considered to be suitable pastimes for a young lady. But now Wyvern Villa awaited her: home, with its atmosphere of mourning and illness, its silences, its ineffable boredom. 'How am I to endure it?' she asked herself in a panic as she stared bleakly out of the train window at a grey world.

Haggerty was waiting when she alighted from the train. As he opened the carriage door he said, 'My word, miss, you're looking well. That Borderland must agree with you. You're quite changed.'

Surprised, she asked, 'Am I? It must be all the wonderful food I've been eating.'

Haggerty's awkward compliment cheered her, and as they rolled along the thronged street that led from the station, she remembered what her father had said about buying a pretty dress for Amelia's wedding. She knew in a flash that if she left the picking of a gown to her mother, she'd end up in the same subfusc clothes as she had been wearing ever since James died. She leaned forward and said in the coachman's ear, 'Haggerty, you know that dressmaker where Mrs James used to go for her gowns? Madame Rachelle was her name, I think.'

He turned his head. 'Yes, I used to take her there, Miss Emma.'

'Take me,' she said.

He looked amazed. 'You? Now?'

'Yes. I want to order a gown before I go home. Take me there now, please.'

It was an order, not a request.

Madame Rachelle occupied an opulent suite of rooms on the first floor of a new building in Neville Street. When Haggerty stopped the carriage at its wide front door, he turned and stared at Emma Jane in disapproval. 'You're quite sure you want to go in there, Miss Emma?' he said. 'That woman's a robber. Can't I take you to your mother's dressmaker?'

With a determined air Emma Jane stepped down and told him, 'No, this is the place I want. Just wait for me, Haggerty, I won't be long.' He gazed after her departing back with concern as if he feared she'd taken leave of her senses.

A tall thin saleslady with a supercilious smile summed up her new customer in one glance, and obviously was not impressed with what she saw. Some governess looking for a dress to change her life, she thought. She was about to say that Emma Jane might have come to the wrong establishment when the small person in the black-trimmed bonnet lifted two unnerving golden eyes and looked straight at her with a commanding stare. 'I would like to speak to Madame Rachelle herself,' she said.

The saleslady backed away. 'Who will I say has called?' she asked.

'Tell her I am Miss Emma Jane Wylie and I have come at the recommendation of my sister-in-law Mrs Amelia Wylie.'

Amelia was well-known in the salon for her lavish spending when James was alive and because of her open, unsnobbish manner. She had been one of the salon's favourite customers, so Madame Rachelle appeared at once when she was told who wished to speak with her. She was a large lady with a bosom like the prow of a ship, and on her commanding nose was perched a pair of gold-rimmed eyeglasses that flashed and glittered in the diffused sunlight coming through the lace-curtained windows. The eyes behind the glasses were black and shrewd and missed nothing. 'How is Mrs Wylie? Well, I hope?' she intoned in a booming voice with a strange accent that she had long cultivated in the belief that sounding French gave her business an added cachet. Her real name was actually Rachel Wormington, but Rachelle de la Tour sounded so much more impressive.

'Amelia is very well. I've come to you on her recommendation,' said Emma Jane. It was not strictly true, but she had always heard her sister-in-law enthuse over Madame Rachelle's gowns and certainly Amelia looked well in them – but she would probably have looked well in anything. Now Emma Jane wanted to change her life and a new wardrobe seemed a good way of starting.

'You are marrying?' asked Madame Rachelle curiously.

Emma Jane shook her head. 'No, but I'm going to a wedding and I want to look my best.' There was something about the drably-dressed little person that appealed to Madame Rachelle. She could transform this ugly duckling into a swan.

'What is it exactly you require?' she asked in a kindly tone.

Emma Jane twisted her gloved hands and said, 'Well, the first thing I have to find out is, how much it will cost for you to make me a gown. I haven't a large allowance.' In her skirt pocket she had what was left of her quarterly stipend, twenty-one pounds and sixpence. She'd spent the rest of it in looking after her father and travelling to and from Maddiston. He was so accustomed to having money in his pocket that he hadn't thought to enquire how she was financing herself, and neither did her mother, who was used to Christopher paying for everything.

Madame Rachelle was no fool. She knew this girl was Christopher Wylie's daughter and that he was one of the biggest building contractors in Newcastle. 'Miss Wylie, your Mama would pay for your dress,' she said but Emma Jane shook her head.

'I don't want her to,' she announced firmly. 'My mother is . . . my mother likes to have her own way. I want a dress that I've chosen, and paid for myself.'

Madame Rachelle actually laughed, a deep throaty gurgle that made her sales staff all turn round in surprise. 'People do not often start by negotiating a price with me,' she said, 'but depending on what you want, I can probably fit you out for a wedding for under ten pounds.'

Emma Jane smiled. 'In that case, I'd like a dress that will be useful for things other than just going to a wedding. I'd like something that I could wear for travelling.'

'You have plans to travel?' asked Madame Rachelle. This little sparrow amused her.

Emma Jane nodded her head. 'Father's talking about going to Menton soon. I think I might acquire a taste for travel,' she said solemnly.

Madame snapped her fingers and a girl rushed forward with a pattern-book through which the proprietrix ruffled before she stopped at one page and handed it open to Emma Jane. 'That,' she said, 'would suit you. In that you could travel to France and all the women would look at you and think, how *chic*. In fact, I think you'd be far more appreciated in France than here in England, as you've a very French style about you. It's the eyes, I think. Yes, it's the eyes.'

Emma Jane was surprised. 'I've no foreign blood at all, I'm afraid. English as roast beef on both sides.'

Madame Rachelle laughed. 'Maybe it comes from the Norman Conquest, in that case. But first, what about the colour for your costume? Garnet red would suit, I think.'

Emma Jane shook her head. 'Oh no, I can't wear red. I'm still in half-mourning for my brother.'

'Full mourning from the looks of you,' said Madame Rachelle disapprovingly. 'But it's more than a year since he was killed, isn't it?'

'Yes, but my mother is still wearing black.'

'My dear, your mother will probably go on wearing black for the rest of her life but not you, I hope.'

'She wouldn't mind if I wore grey,' suggested Emma Jane, who had a picture in her mind of a discreet grey coat and skirt.

Madame Rachelle shook her head. 'Not at all. Grey is not your colour. You are too small – it would make you look like a sparrow. I won't permit grey. Take off that bonnet and let me look at you properly. Stand over there in the light.' While Emma Jane stood stock-still and stiff with embarrassment, the dressmaker prowled around her until at last she paused, snapped her fingers and said, 'I know! I've just the colour for you. You will wear violet: it will be most flattering for your eyes. They are your most arresting feature.' She dragged out the word 'arresting', rolling her r's like a real Frenchwoman.

Emma Jane stared. 'My eyes?' All her life she had been warned by her mother and her school-teachers against her tendency to look 'stony' or 'hostile', and so she had come to believe that her eyes were particularly unattractive.

But Madame Rachelle was nodding her head enthusiastically and saying, 'You have remarkable eyes, my dear – very arresting and a most unusual colour. They look golden in this light. You should emphasise them.'

No one had ever talked flatteringly to Emma Jane about her appearance before, and now on the same morning she had been complimented by Haggerty and now Madame Rachelle. She felt confidence grow within her. How glad she was that she'd come to consult Madame Rachelle. The dressmaker was bustling around, giving orders to her girls, and one of them came running in with a swatch of material in her arms. Rachelle pulled at one end and held it against Emma Jane's face. 'That's it, that's your colour exactly. I'll make you something lovely out of this.'

Emma Jane gazed down at the soft cloth. It was the colour of Parma violets, flowers that she had always loved. 'It's very pretty,' she sighed.

Madame Rachelle was brisk. 'Of course it is, and now for the style. Something military but feminine, I think. No crinoline, they're outdated now. A flowing skirt. And you must have a hat, sitting forward on the front of your head. It will draw attention to your eyes as well.'

'I don't think I can afford a hat. Perhaps I can make do with one of my old bonnets?' suggested Emma Jane but Madame Rachelle was outraged.

'What! You're going to spend your money on one of my lovely creations and top it with an old-fashioned bonnet like that thing you were wearing when you came in? That I will not permit. Emily, bring the Parisian purple hat out of the stockroom.'

The girl called Emily ran off and came back with a cheeky little hat about the size of a saucer. It had a curling feather sticking up from the back and a tiny swathe of veil in front. Madame Rachelle perched it on Emma Jane's head and then turned her round so that she could see herself in the mirror. 'Can you look at yourself in that hat and not want to buy it?' she asked.

The girl who stared back from the glass was not Emma Jane Wylie but a stranger who looked confident and cheeky. A pair of large golden eyes gazed levelly out through the veil, and Madame Rachelle was right – they *were* arresting eyes. 'I'll buy it,' said Emma Jane, without thinking about how much it cost.

'It's two pounds ten shillings,' Madame Rachelle told her as she removed the long steel pins that held it in place on Emma Jane's thick hair. 'If you can't afford it, you can pay me later – I'll give you credit. I can tell that you're honest. And remember, when people ask where you bought your outfit, you must always say Madame Rachelle of Newcastle. You'll be an advertisement for me.'

Haggerty was fidgeting and irritable when Emma Jane finally emerged from the salon. 'You've been in there for two hours. Your poor mother will be frantic,' he said accusingly.

She looked surprised. 'In that case, I'll say I missed the train. All right, Haggerty, drive me home. I've done everything I want to do.'

*

Being back in Wyvern Villa was as bad as Emma Jane had feared. Her mother lay in bed all day, weeping and even more helpless and pathetic than she had been immediately after James' death. When Amelia appeared she was grim-faced and resentful at the way her mother-in-law refused to accept or even discuss her remarriage. Both of them poured out their woes and justifications to Emma Jane, who often felt that her head would burst with the effort of listening to them and sympathising tactfully. Yet in spite of her efforts, Amelia stormed through the house like a thundercloud and Mrs Wylie continued to be completely unreasonable. Then the news came that Claud Cockburn had died. It fell to Emma Jane to write to her father with the bad news.

When she went to bed at night she wished she was back at Camptounfoot, and remembered with regret how the sweet bedtime music of the Jessups used to soothe her into slumber.

It took considerable guile to escape from Wyvern Villa for her fittings with Madame Rachelle, but she swore Haggerty to secrecy and managed to persuade her mother that she had developed a passion for visiting art galleries, something Mrs Wylie considered very suitable for an unmarried young lady.

Emma Jane found the fittings traumatic because she hated looking at herself in Madame Rachelle's long pier glass, for it seemed to emphasise all her worst points. The violet-coloured outfit was lovely, however, and she watched its emergence from the swatch of cloth with admiration and delight. At last it was delivered to Wyvern Villa in a striped box accompanied by the little hat nestling in a bed of tissue paper in a bandbox all of its own. These treasures were smuggled to Emma Jane's room from the kitchen door by Mrs Haggerty, who was in on the secret of which she approved more than her husband. 'Miss Emma's quite right to buy herself a pretty dress. She hasn't much fun in her life, poor little soul,' she told him.

Upstairs, Emma Jane untied the string around the

boxes with a sinking heart. 'What if they're a disaster? What if I look terrible in them. I'll have wasted my allowance for nothing,' she told herself. The dress was in two parts, a bodice and a skirt. She put on the skirt first. It swept the floor with a wonderful fall and made her feel regal. Encouraged, she slipped on the bodice and did up the line of frogged fasteners which Madame Rachelle had said would give her the impression of being bigger-breasted than she actually was. It fitted perfectly and she pulled down the cuffs of the sleeves with even more satisfaction. Now only the hat remained. As she lifted it out of its packaging, she was struck by how frivolous it looked. She could already hear her mother's voice saying, 'Good heavens, what a ridiculous hat!' Without looking at herself, she perched it unsteadily on her head but you can't put on a hat without looking so she turned round and faced the glass. Though her hat was at the wrong angle, what she saw astonished her. The girl who looked back at her was not mousy Emma Jane Wylie, she was – she was what? She was arrresting, very *arrrrrresting* indeed.

'How do you do?' said the new Emma Jane to herself, and smiled a mysterious, challenging smile. She turned her head and admired her profile, she turned her back and looked over her shoulder at the elegant person in the glass. She held an animated conversation with this stranger about things she'd read in the newspaper, and laughed at her own wit. 'I must be very characterless if clothes can make such a difference to me,' she thought, but her worry disappeared when she realised that in her Madame Rachelle outfit she felt capable of coping with any people, any problem. It was as if she had donned a mask which made it impossible for the outside world to recognise her, and she suddenly understood how it was that people in revels could act outrageously. They thought they could not be recognised.

She slipped off her new finery and hung it carefully in her wardrobe before going back to care for her curious mother. Later that day she said casually, 'I've bought a new gown to wear for the wedding, Mama.'

'A new gown, Emma Jane? That's good,' said her mother listlessly. She refused to discuss anything to do with Amelia's wedding so the existence of Emma Jane's new dress was glossed over. This relieved her because she was afraid her mother would not like the purple dress and she did not want any criticism to mar her secret delight.

Amelia went to Hexham a few days before her wedding, leaving Arbelle with the Wylies. The little girl was to be taken to Hexham by her aunt Emma Jane on the eve of the ceremony.

When it was time for Haggerty to drive Emma Jane and her niece to the station, Arbelle burst into a flood of weeping and ran to her grandmother with her arms held out, crying, 'Oh Grandmama, Grandmama, I don't want to leave you! I don't want to go to Hexham.' They clung together sobbing and promising each other that their separation would only be a short one. In the end Emma Jane had to haul an hysterical Arbelle down the front-door steps and carry her into the carriage. Watching from the drawing-room window was her mother's distraught face.

All the way to the station Arbelle sobbed heartbreakingly, causing great upset to both Emma Jane and Haggerty, who wondered how they could be so cruel as to separate her from her beloved grandmother. Once the train had started, however, the child's attitude changed completely and she dashed from side to side of the compartment, exclaiming about the view from the windows and the comfort of the seats. Her tears were completely forgotten and when she eventually arrived at Hexham, she ran up to her mother waiting on the platform, sank her face into Amelia's skirt and cried out, 'Oh Mama, how I've missed you. I never want you to leave me again, never!' Emma Jane looked at her with amazement. 'How can someone so young have learned such wiles and be able to act them out so well,' she wondered, 'when I'm so much older but as transparent as water?'

Amelia looked blooming even though she was wearing

her plainest clothes – a dark skirt, simple cotton blouse and a long shawl. Her head was bare and she had heavy walking shoes on her feet. She saw Emma Jane looking at them and laughed. 'Quite a change from satin slippers, an't they? But after tomorrow I won't have much call for fancy clothes. Dan's a working man and I'll be a working man's wife. Tomorrow's my last day of finery.' She took Emma Jane's arm and led her out of the station to a cobbled yard where russet-faced Dan Peel was waiting with a flat cart drawn by a shaggy cob. 'Climb on the back, Emma Jane, and hold on to Arbelle but don't worry, you won't fall off, Dan'll drive very slow,' instructed Amelia as she climbed on to the box beside the driver.

Amelia's family cottage crouched like an animal on the watch on an outcrop of rock near the ruins of the Roman wall. It was long and low and roofed in huge stone slabs that fitted closely one on top of the other. There were no thatches up here. They wouldn't have withstood the gales that blew over those high bare moors. Inside, the cottage was warm and cheerful, full of people all a'bustle because of the preparations for the wedding. Everyone was given a job to do, even Arbelle who, after she'd been kissed by her other grandmother and several aunts, was given a bowl of peas and told to shell them. Amazingly she did it without protest.

Emma Jane was overawed by the sight of a table in the kitchen piled high with food – legs of lamb, cooked chickens, enormous hams, bowls of eggs and pitchers of cream. 'Are you expecting many guests? There's such a lot of food,' she said to Amelia, who laughed.

'Well, we're cooking for the dance as well,' the young woman said teasingly. 'There's to be a dancing after the wedding, you know.'

Emma Jane's heart sank. She was always at her worst at dances, for she felt too awkward to act naturally and never knew what to say to any man who asked her on to the floor. Every time she'd been at a dance, she went home feeling like a social failure and a severe disappointment to her mother.

'I didn't know you were having a dance. I didn't bring a ballgown with me,' she lamented, but Amelia only chuckled again.

'Bless you, we don't wear ballgowns up here! I'll lend you a frock of mine if you haven't anything suitable, but we dance in plain dresses and if our shoes pinch, we take 'em off and dance barefoot. This won't be one of your Newcastle dances, don't worry about that.'

When Emma Jane climbed into a big bed with a downy feather mattress in a room that also housed three of Amelia's sisters, she was dog-tired and sank under the heavy quilt with a feeling of utter happiness. The house smelt of woodsmoke, apples and bread dough and, as everyone settled to sleep, the old floors creaked reassuringly while outside a wind rattled against the windows and sent clouds chasing each other across a clear night sky. 'I'm so glad I took Father's advice and came to 'Melia's wedding,' was Emma Jane's last conscious thought.

The ceremony was at noon next day and the morning was passed in a flurry of female excitement. The church was within walking distance and at a quarter to noon, the family all waited at the cottage door for Amelia who appeared at last, looking as beautiful as a fairy queen in a dress of pink voile and lace, rosebuds and ribbons, that set off her flaxen beauty to perfection. On her head was a flat straw hat with ribbons down each side and tied under her chin. It too was decorated with enormous silk roses.

At the sight of her Emma Jane clapped her hands and exclaimed, 'Oh 'Melia, you look lovely! What an exquisite hat.'

'You look very well yourself. I hardly recognised you, Emma Jane. That's a Madame Rachelle outfit, isn't it? No one else in Newcastle makes hats like that.'

When the newly-married pair stepped out of the church door an hour later, rain had begun to fall but no one cared. Kirtling up their skirts, the women splashed through puddles back to the cottage where the real fun of the day began.

The feast was gargantuan. Dish after dish was borne in by Amelia's two elder sisters Betty and Jen who both resembled their pretty sister but had the look of fading full roses instead of Amelia's glorious high flowering. With the food they served demi-johns of home-made ale that had the miraculous power of releasing Emma Jane's tongue and making her see the world around her in an entirely new light. Everything seemed bright and optimistic, everyone was witty and handsome, including Emma Jane herself. When Betty, in response to a compliment about the size of the cake that had been baked, said with a great laugh, 'Oh well, anything that'll keep can be stored for the christening. That won't be long – six months, I reckon,' Emma Jane felt not a twinge of disapproval or shock. 'What was the use of waiting, eh?' Betty asked with a knowing eye and Emma Jane found herself nodding in vigorous agreement. 'No use at all,' she said.

When it was growing dark, the band arrived, two fiddlers and a man who played the small Northumbrian pipes which he tucked under his arm and blew at with a will. The moment the music struck up, the tables were shoved back and the guests began dancing, not ordered quadrilles or well-behaved polkas, but arm-raised twirlings and shoutings that filled everyone with a wild enthusiasm. They all danced, children and aged crones, men with walking sticks and even the dogs. Emma Jane plunged into the revelry, dancing first with one partner and then with another, laughing and joking and throwing back her head in complete unselfconsciousness.

By ten o'clock she had acquired a swain, a fair-haired farmer who plied her with ale and, while they took a rest from the dancing, informed her that he had a fine house and £500 a year and was in search of a wife.

'You're a Newcastle lass, aren't you?' he asked.

'I am,' she agreed and he leaned towards her.

'Do you know the Wylies?' he asked. 'Amelia's lucky to get away from them, if you ask me. They say the old woman's a terror and the daughter's a poor little thing, a real old maid.'

Emma Jane nodded solemnly. 'Is she? Poor girl,' she said, and hoped that no one told the unfortunate fellow who she was.

To her surprise he took her hand and asked, 'Are you in search of a husband?'

She looked sympathetically at him. 'Not at the moment, but perhaps soon,' she said.

'Then when you are, remember my name: Tom Featherstone of Hillslaphead. Remember – Featherstone, that's me.'

She laughed and pulled him to his feet. 'Come on, let's dance again. I'll remember your name. I don't think I'll ever forget it.' After all, he had just given her the great compliment of her first proposal and he'd obviously thought it impossible for her to be the sour little spinster Miss Emma Jane Wylie.

On the morning after the wedding, Emma Jane was up early and dressed in her plain travelling clothes for the trip back to Newcastle when Amelia popped her head round the bedroom door and said, 'If you like, you can take Arbelle back with you. That would please your mother. I'll collect her next week when Dan and I come down to take some of my things out of the cottage.'

Emma Jane walked towards her sister-in-law and hugged her. 'Amelia, I want to tell you how very sorry I am about the way Mother has behaved. She's just so upset about James still she's not thinking correctly. I hope you'll forgive her.'

'Of course I do,' Amelia reassured her, 'but I don't want her to think I'm being greedy in keeping the cottage. There's a reason for that, Emma Jane.'

'A reason?'

Amelia nodded. 'If you don't know I can't tell you, and I hope it comes to nothing but believe me, there *is* a reason. Just trust me, that's all. It doesn't bother me what your mother thinks but I want you to trust me. I'm keeping the cottage till your father says I've to give it up.'

'Father? What's he got to do with this?' asked Emma Jane, but Amelia put up a hand to stop her.

'No more talk – I want to give you a bit of advice. I saw you last night, and you weren't the Emma Jane I've always known. You should get away from your Mama. If you stay with her too long, you might grow like her.'

Emma Jane groaned. This was too close to her own secret thoughts to be comfortable. 'How can I leave Mama? Who would look after her if I went away?' she asked.

'But she's using you. She's not sick, not really. She just needs you and your father to think she is.' Amelia's voice was vehement and she grabbed Emma Jane by the shoulders to give her a little shake. 'Listen. In just over a year your father will have built his bridge. When that happens, go away. Travel abroad, find a husband, take a lover, do anything you want, but go as far away as possible from Newcastle.'

Emma Jane was learning how much she would enjoy freedom, but she knew it was unlikely that she would ever have the opportunity to seize it. Amelia seemed to sense her inner doubts and gave her a fiercer shake. 'I do-ant know why I bother about you, I really do-ant! Listen to what I'm telling you,' she urged.

When she parted from her mother at Hexham station, Arbelle launched into one of her histrionic performances, weeping, wailing, throwing herself at Amelia and pleading to be allowed to stay. Amelia and Emma Jane had a fearful struggle to get her into the carriage, where she lay on the seat sobbing till the train drew out of the station. Then she sat up, ready to start enjoying herself, but she found herself staring into her aunt's eyes. They looked fiercer than she had ever seen them, and she shrank back.

'Look at me,' said Emma Jane between clenched teeth. Arbelle looked, and kept on looking like a mongoose hypnotised by a snake. Her aunt leaned over towards her and said very quietly, 'If you throw one of those weeping fits ever again with your grandmother or your mother, I'm going to tell them what you're really like. I will. I'll tell them that the moment you're out of their sight, you wipe your eyes and forget all about them.' As she spoke

Emma Jane was deliberately making her gaze as fearsome as possible, summoning up strength and the will to dominate from her innermost soul.

It worked. Arbelle, who had never been dominated before, nodded meekly and said, 'All right, I won't do it again, I promise. Please don't look at me like that, Aunt Emma Jane. It's very frightening.'

Emma Jane sat back against the cushions with joy filling her heart. 'I can do it! If I can frighten Arbelle, I can do anything,' she said to herself.

CHAPTER
Ten

The rains were followed by a period of beautiful late-autumn weather when leaves made Persian carpets of glowing colour around the trunks of the bare trees; herons fished in the peaceful shallows of the river which bore no resemblance to the raging torrent it had been only a few days before; cheeky robins made their appearance in village gardens where they intended to pass the winter. and the last fruit fell from the black branches of the apple trees. In a field outside the village, Craigie and his bondagers gathered in their potato crop. The women walked half-bent along the turned rows of earth, picking up the yellow potatoes and putting them into shallow cane baskets which Craigie then collected in his horse-drawn cart. He sat impassive on the seat with his face like a carved mask. Nowadays he spoke to no one, looked at no one, only kept up a strange muttering to himself as he guided his horse up and down the field.

'He's in a bad way, is Craigie,' said the villagers to each other as they watched him. 'He'll go like his father, see if he doesn't.'

Village people didn't mention Craigie's father before strangers because like a big family, they tended to stick their communal skeletons in a cupboard and not look at them unless forced to do so, but now the gossips whispered to each other about how old Scott had ended up a raving lunatic, how in the end he was confined in a private hospital after he had tried to slit his throat with a razor. As the villagers remembered him they saw him again in his son. They felt sorry for Craigie because they knew what had driven him to such a pass, but they avoided the farm and no one would walk past the orchard wall at night.

Tibbie heard the talk and felt pity for all the Scotts. It seemed tragic to her that the peaceful life of Camptounfoot had been torn apart by the coming of the railway that seemed to be creeping nearer and nearer every day. One by one her neighbours accepted the inevitable; only a few still held out against the change and she and Craigie were among them. She thought of the others as a flock of sheep being harried by a snapping dog towards a gate. They might not want to go through; they might have put down their heads and shown resistance at the beginning, but in the end they did as they were told. Even the Rutherfords, who had been strong opponents of the railway in the beginning, were won round because their Robbie was now an apprentice builder who came striding proudly back into the village each night at finishing time with his head high and ambition shining out of him.

Another thing that won some people round was the fact that the bridge contractor was living with the Jessups and had proved himself to be a decent and gentlemanly person. When Tibbie voiced her fears about the change a railway would bring to village life, and her dread about what would happen when the work and the navying gangs drew nearer to Camptounfoot, people only laughed now and said, 'Och, it's not near so bad as we thought.' They were even talking of day trips to Edinburgh or Newcastle when the railway line was finished. They did not seem to care that what they were witnessing was an end to the old way of life altogether. 'You're too old-fashioned, Tib,' they said. Even William and Effie said it, so she learned to hold her tongue and keep her fears to herself. On nights when mists swirled eerily along the bed of the lanes, when white owls swooped overhead hunting little mice in the dying grass and the moon shone overhead like a huge red ball of blood, she sometimes went out hoping to catch sight of the marching men, but was always disappointed. They were staying away and she was afraid that they had gone forever.

When she spoke to her daughter about her worries, Hannah was as brisk and matter-of-fact as the rest of the villagers. 'You're being silly, Mam,' she said. She tried to divert Tibbie with tales of Bella Vista but without much success. The saga of Bethya's endless purchasing was beginning to pall.

It was palling with Bethya too, but she had set herself a target of amassing as much in the way of assets as she could before she finally left Gus. She was piling up money, clothes and particularly jewellery like a squirrel hoarding against winter. The Colonel indulged her unashamedly, bringing out piece after magnificent piece for Bethya to wear, and never insisting that she return them to his strongbox after use. This was all much to his wife's wrath. She kept warning him, 'That girl's milking you, Augustus. One day she'll take off from here with all your jewels and what will you do then?' He paid no heed to her, for he could see no fault in Bethya.

As the days dwindled into winter, Tim Maquire was lovesick; Hannah seemed to be avoiding him and he was too engrossed in work to hang about waiting for her as she came and went in the village. Sometimes he caught a fleeting glimpse of her, always tantalisingly just going out of sight. He did not have time to brood, however, for Mr Wylie was back on the site and working like a demon to get as much done before the bitter winter weather stopped operations.

As soon as his daughter went away and there was no one to restrain him from overdoing things, Wylie had come back to the bridge site. He was pleased at how work had gone in his absence, but he noticed that Miller's toady Jopp was now much more in evidence than he had been in the past. He was on the site, in the navvy camp, riding up and down the workings. Wylie knew only too well that Jopp had been detailed to watch him, to pick his brains, to work out exactly what he was intending to do and prepare his own forces for stepping in. At some point, when the moment was ripe, Sir Geoffrey hoped to oust Wylie, who guessed accurately that the shrewd but straight-dealing Colonel Anstruther and the bovine-brained Raeburn were unaware of what was brewing. Anstruther especially wouldn't like it because, although he had enriched himself in India by a variety of devices, he had always given something, protection or promotion, back in return for his bribes. In his own way he was a gentleman.

When he went back to the work-site on the valley floor, Wylie said shortly, 'Watch out for Jopp. Keep an eye on him and don't tell him anything.'

Maquire laughed. 'I've been doing that from the beginning. He's a rat. I've been on jobs with him before and I know what he's like. He's a company man, always ready to ingratiate himself at the men's expense.'

'This time it'll be at *my* expense. He's up to something with Miller,' said Wylie slowly.

'I don't like Miller either. He's got a shifty eye,' agreed Tim. 'Don't worry, Mr Wylie, we won't work for anybody else but you.'

Wylie was grateful but he added, 'If bad weather sets us back, I'll be in real trouble.'

Maquire told him, 'All right – while it's fine, we'll work round the clock to make up for lost time. I'll tell the men tonight. Go back to your lodgings and have a rest, Mr Wylie, you look tired. Leave it to me.'

That night in the camp, he gathered his men and told them what was planned. 'The bad weather's coming soon and we're behind schedule. We've got to make up time. I want half of you to work through the night. The building of the lower piers has to be done before the frost comes.'

Bullhead, in the front of the crowd, called out, 'There'll be extra money for night-work, won't there?'

'I didn't think that would be necessary,' hedged Tim, but Bullhead walked away, saying over his shoulder, 'I've just got myself a new woman so I've better things to do with my nights. I'm not going to work unless you make it worth my while.' His friends laughed and catcalled in approval. Tim remembered that Mariotta was the new woman. He'd seen her slinking around the camp like a beaten dog since she moved into Bullhead's hut and dreaded to think what her life must now be like. In his pocket he still carried the key to her old house. He'd never even gone to look at it. Somehow it didn't seem right.

'All right, Bullhead, don't work. Will anyone else volunteer?'

Sydney was the first and he was followed by Jimmy-The-New-Man, who was worrying Tim because he was rapidly sinking into drunkenness and lassitude. His old innocent cheerfulness and optimism had vanished and he had taken up with bad company – Bullhead and his gang of ruffians. It wasn't uncommon or unexpected for young navvies to go to the bad, but somehow Tim had not thought it would happen to Jimmy. 'Good, that's good,' he said approvingly, thinking that if the lad was working at night and Bullhead during the day, they'd not come across each other so often. Jimmy, who was the youngest member of Tim's gang, seemed to have no one in the world to care about what happened to him.

For the next week Tim hardly slept at all; he supervised both day and night-shifts, exhorting the labouring men, listening to complaints, imbuing them with his sense of urgency. He took up a pick and worked alongside them so no-one could accuse him of being a slacker. In the light of the flaring lamps one night, Gentleman Sydney leaned on his shovel-handle and said, 'Tell me, Black Ace, do you happen to know if any of your ancestors were the fellows who cracked whips over the backs of galley slaves?' Tim only laughed and went on digging.

By dint of superhuman efforts, nine foundations were laid in the deep holes along the face of the field. On the morning of the eighth day, snow began to fall from a pewter-coloured sky but the navvies went on digging. Maquire went in search of Wylie who was in a little shed on the side of the bluff poring over his plans by the light of a flickering oil lamp. It was bitterly cold and the white-haired man was wearing an overcoat, a muffler and thick gloves as he worked. He looked terribly ill. 'We've done it, Mr Wylie,' Tim announced triumphantly. 'We've laid the stone in all the bases. When this snow stops, we can starting building them up.'

When Wylie looked up he was smiling, but the light of the lamp showed that his face was deathly white. Concerned, Maquire stepped towards him and said, 'You'll ill again, sir. You've been doing too much. I'm going to take you home.'

Wylie sank into his chair with a gasp and admitted, 'Yes, I am tired, Tim, but you must be too. We're well ahead, though, and it's nearly Christmas. Give the men a couple of days off because we can't do anything in snow. You've all done a magnificent job. Tell them I'm grateful.'

When Tim returned from telling the men that they were to have paid leave, he found Wylie slumped in his chair and put out a hand to help him to his feet. 'I saw your carriage waiting up on the road. The driver will take you back to the Jessups'. You should be in bed.' He rolled up the plans on the table as he spoke and added, 'Take the plans with you. We don't want Jopp casting his eye over them.'

Wylie did as he was told without protest but added, 'Come to the Jessups' with me and have a glass of something to celebrate the season, Tim. I think we deserve it.'

The snow drifted round them like a curtain as they rode into the village. Wylie lay against the cushions with his eyes closed, knowing that Tim Maquire was watching him with concern. When at last they rolled up to the Jessups' gate, Maquire jumped to the ground and half-lifted the other man down, saying, 'I won't come in after all. I'm tired too. Go to bed, Mr Wylie. I'll come back when the weather changes but it looks as if this has set in for a while.' As he spoke snow was settling on his bare head like a cap.

Before Wylie would go in, however, he looked up at his carriage driver and said, 'Take Maquire back to the camp at Rosewell, please. It's too far for him to walk in this storm.'

Tim gazed up at the grey outline of the hill towering

over the village. Its top was shrouded in snow, and white sheets of snowflakes were blowing around the lower slopes. The roofs of the village houses were already covered, and only two marks in the white surface of the road showed where a cart had passed along before them. The air was full of the comforting smell of woodsmoke from nearby chimneys, and he longed to warm himself before a blazing fire. He shuddered as another gust of snow caught him and cut through to his skin. Gratefully he climbed aboard the carriage box and the cabby cracked his whip over the old horse's back. 'Won't take long,' he said, hunching his shoulders beneath his thick coat.

The horse was slithering and slipping round the corner by Bob's shop when Tim caught sight of a dark-clad figure standing back against the wall to allow the carriage to pass at that narrow point. Wondering who was abroad on such a terrible evening, he leaned forward in his seat and then caught sight of the flash of Hannah Mather's red hair under the hood of her cloak.

'Hold up, hold up,' he told the cabby, and leaned down to say to Hannah, 'What are you doing out in this? Go home. You'll catch your death.'

'I've got to get back to my work,' she said, looking up at him. Her cheeks were bright pink with the cold.

'Go home to your mother and wait till this storm's over,' he said shortly but she shook her head.

'I can't. I've to be back by half-past six because the housekeeper's mad at me. I was late yesterday too. If I'm not back in time I might lose my place, and if I don't go now I won't be able to get through later.'

'Get in. We'll take you to Bella Vista,' he said.

The coachman heaved a heavy sigh and groaned, 'You've awful good at giving lifts in other folks' carts.'

But Tim told him, 'It's not far. Drop me there too and I'll walk back to Rosewell. That'll save you going too much out of your way.'

When Hannah saw that this suggestion met with agreement, she did not argue but put her booted foot on the metal step and jumped into the back. As they started up again, her glowing face was pressed to the little window between the front and the passenger seat as she thanked them. 'This is kind of you. I didn't realise how bad the weather was getting. I don't want to lose my place. It'd be hard to find another as good so near home.' She seemed to have forgotten her hauteur against Tim and her laugh was like a tinkling bell as she settled into her seat. The sound of it made him smile and he was still smiling when the carriage stopped at the gate of Bella Vista. Hannah hopped out, pretending to act the lady, and said, 'Thank you, kind sir.'

She was about to start running up the drive when he put out a hand and stopped her. 'Aren't you going to thank me properly?' he asked.

Behind them they heard the noise of the departing carriage-wheels in deep snow but they stood very still staring at each other for a few moments before she said, 'But I did thank you. Didn't you hear me? I said "Thank you, kind sir" in my very best voice.' There was a suppressed giggle in her tone which showed she was not a bit afraid of him though he loomed large beside her in the grey light.

'Is that all you're going to do?' he asked her.

'What else do you suggest?' she countered.

'You could give me a kiss,' he said. She said nothing but her eyes searched his face, taking in the square chin with a deep cleft in the middle of it; a wide mouth with a surprisingly soft and feminine upper lip that was broader and more curving than the lower; deep-set eyes that looked thoughtful and brooding; cheeks darkened by the stubble of two days without shaving. She knew the bristle would scrape her skin if she put her face to his and she suddenly longed to feel it. He was having a most peculiar effect on her.

'You're a brazen fellow asking a girl for a kiss when she thought you were a gentleman who'd saved her from being frozen to death in a storm,' she said cheekily and he laughed. Tiny wrinkles appeared around his eyes giving him an unexpectedly boyish and merry look. He was not nearly as old as she had thought. 'You should laugh more often,' she told him seriously.

He didn't reply to that, however, for he was holding her hand and saying in his soft Irish voice, 'Aw come on, one kiss isn't a lot to ask for saving your life, now is it?'

She pretended to ponder the question, putting a finger to her cheek and frowning. 'Now should I give this man a kiss or not?' she teased aloud. 'No, I don't think so. I'm not in the habit of kissing strange men I meet on the road.'

'Ah, you know me. I've been chasing you for months. I'm not a stranger,' he coaxed even more softly. Then he put out a hand and lifted her chin so that she was staring directly into his eyes. His grim look was back as he said, 'I'm your fate, I think. Give me a kiss and find out.'

Surprised, she did not draw away but stood still staring at him while he gently rearranged the wet hood around her neck and wiped fronds of hair out of her eyes. His touch was very gentle. She didn't breathe while he took her chin between his finger and thumb and held her face very still as he bent towards her. She liked the smell of him – soap, wet cloth and tobacco – and it seemed to take a very long time until she felt his lips on hers. Both of them closed their eyes when their mouths met and stood very still, not daring to breathe. His lips were cold and dry; hers warm, sweet and moist. They only brushed each other at first but when she did not draw away, he became bolder and put an arm round her shoulder, pulling her closer as he kissed her with growing urgency. There was magic between them now and behind their closed eyes they were both seeing flashing lights, shooting stars, huge glowing circles of blazing fire amid velvet blackness . . . When they could no longer breathe they stood apart and looked shakily at each other.

Hannah was the first to speak. 'Have I paid my fare to your satisfaction now?' she asked.

When he nodded and spoke, his voice sounded very distant. 'Indeed you have,' he told her. The snow had made his curly hair fall down over his forehead into his eyes and he blinked as if he was having difficulty seeing.

Without thinking, she put up a hand to wipe it away. 'You're very wet. It'll be you that's catching your death, not me,' she whispered softly.

He caught her hand between both of his and said fiercely, 'I love you. Come with me.'

Hannah stared at him, for a moment frightened at the thought that she had sparked something into life that she might not be able to control. 'I can't come with you,' she told him.

'You can. Come with me – I've got my own house. The key's here in my pocket. I promise on my mother's honour that I won't harm you. Just come and see my house. I've not been in it myself yet. I was waiting . . . Come and see my house. I'll bring you back here, as safe as an infant in its mother's arms: that I promise you. Come with me, please.'

As he said 'please' his voice was very soft and he gently dropped her hand so that it hung by her side. Then he stroked the soft skin on the back of it with one finger as if he was stroking a kitten. 'Please,' he whispered again.

She could not understand what had got into her but she heard herself saying, 'All right. I'll come.' It felt as if she were two people, one standing back and warning while the other went rushing headlong into trouble. 'You'll have to bring me back though,' she told him and he nodded.

'Of course. And I'll speak to the housekeeper and tell her that I captured you. I'll say it wasn't your fault.' He was joyous as he took her arm and, oblivious to the blizzard that was blowing around them, they ran down the road in the direction of Rosewell.

Hannah had only seen the navvy camp from the distance though she had heard a lot about it; little of what she'd heard was good but when she found herself in its broad middle road, she was surprised that it was not all a huddle of pigsties as she'd been led to believe. Under the snow most of the huts looked trim and weatherproof, with chimneys smoking and windows shuttered against the storm. Some of them had names painted above the doors, or pictures adorning the whitewashed walls. The only signs of life were a few dogs which skulked about in the spaces between the buildings.

When Tim Maquire slackened his pace and reached into his pocket for his key, she saw that they were standing in front of a neat little wooden house with a steeply pitched roof. It was painted dark-green, with broad white strips round the window and door. In these strips were painted multi-coloured flowers – buttercups, rosebuds, cornflowers and scarlet poppies, with green leaves twisting about them. 'Oh, what a bonny wee place! Is it really yours?' she exclaimed in delight.

He was having difficulty in getting the key into the lock because his hands were frozen, but at last he succeeded and threw the door open so that she could enter. She stepped inside and gazed about with shining eyes. It was like being in a doll's house, for it was small and compact and Mariotta had left it immaculate.

The floor consisted of scrubbed white planks and in the middle of it stood a pot-bellied iron stove that glittered like jet with blackleading. Beside it was a bucket full of dry twigs for kindling. There was a wooden table, two upright chairs, a run of empty shelving along one wall and in the far corner, a built-in bed with a blue and white ticking mattress. The frame of the bed was painted with the same flowers as the outside window and door. Throwing back her hood, the red-haired girl stood in the middle of the floor and gazed around. It seemed to the watching Tim Maquire that light radiated from her and lit up the dark corners.

On the table stood a battered metal candle-holder with a stub of candle in it. He struck a light from his watch-chain tinderbox and lit it. The faint light it cast flickered and danced on their faces as they looked at each other. Very slowly they moved across the room, drawn together by a force they could not resist. He put his arms around her and held her close with her head resting on his chest.

They stood like that for a while until she whispered, 'Who was Benjy? I saw the name on the door.'

His face was against her hair, breathing in its wonderful, spicy smell. With an effort he told her, 'Benjy built this house. He died a little while ago and his widow sold it to me.'

Hannah sighed, still not lifting her face. 'That's sad. Did Benjy paint on the flowers?'

Tim shook his head. 'I don't think so. I think his wife did that.' He could hardly speak and his voice sounded strange and croaking in his own ears.

'Poor soul, she must have loved this little house. It feels as if someone loved it,' whispered Hannah.

'I love you,' said Tim. His heart felt as if it was bursting as he held her and the words could no longer be contained.

She did not reply but stood away from him and became very brisk. 'If you're going to sleep here tonight, you should light the stove. It's cold outside and those walls are only wood, you know.'

Without speaking, he lifted the candle and held it to the scraps of paper that were stuffed into the bottom of the stove. Then he lifted its lid and threw in several handfuls of twigs and a big log that he found in the bottom of the bucket. There was a whoosh and a comforting crackle, and soon a few red embers dropped on to the stone slab that formed the stove base. They stood side by side looking at it with their hands held out to the heat and their faces gilded by the glow. Without switching his gaze, Tim asked, 'Did you hear what I said then?'

'Yes, I heard you. I'm thinking about it,' was her reply.

'Oh God, don't think. It doesn't need thinking about. It's just happened. I don't know how . . . but it's happened.' He turned and put out his arms towards her as if he was asking for comfort. She shook off her wet cloak and stepped into his embrace.

'Don't think, don't think,' her inward self was saying as she was swept along on this dangerous and exciting voyage into a world that she had never visited before.

As the twigs in the stove burned down, the lovers sank

to the floor in front of it, using Hannah's cloak as their carpet. Lying side by side they kissed and clung together as if their whole survival depended on being together. Both of them felt the urgency of their bodies beneath the strictures of their clothes. They longed for the silken touch of skin on skin but just when Tim was tearing off his shirt and pulling it over his head, Hannah stopped him. 'No, no! I've got to go back to Bella Vista. I can't stay here like this . . . no, no.' Her protests dwindled and disappeared, however, as he began to kiss her again. She rubbed her hands down the smooth slope of his back, feeling the long pads of muscles down each side of the spine and the bony projections of his shoulder blades. 'Ah,' she sighed and relaxed beneath him with her mouth against his shoulder.

When he unbuttoned her blouse, she made no protest but lay like an odalisque while he sat up and admired her. 'Oh, you're lovely, you're so lovely,' he sighed in adoration but then, as if consciousness had suddenly returned, the rapt look in his eyes disappeared and it was his turn to become brisk. 'Aw, Hannah, I can't do this. You're too good a girl. You'll have to get up and get dressed. Don't lie there like that, it's more than I can bear.'

She didn't move, only went on lying very still with her face turned to the fire and her fingers trailing down his forearms. He was sitting up and saying fiercely, 'Hannah, did you hear me? I'm not the marrying kind: I'm a travelling man. Life with me wouldn't be right for you. Oh God, get up and put your clothes on, Hannah.'

He jumped up and walked towards the window. Through the glass he could see that the snowflakes were still swirling around like mad dancers. The ground outside was thickly covered. 'I'll take you back now. Soon you won't get through,' he said harshly as he stared out. He did not dare turn round and look at her.

Then behind him he heard her saying, 'Come here, Tim Maquire. Come here and lie down beside me again. I don't want to go back – I want to stay here with you. Don't you want me to stay?'

He tried to resist but her calling was like a siren song. Eventually he went over and knelt beside her on the spread-out cloak. 'Hannah, I don't want to get married,' he said.

She shook her red-gold head. 'I don't care. I love you too, Tim Maquire. I want you too. I can't get up and leave you now.' Then she raised her long white arms and pulled him down beside her, turning so that her face was against his, her lips moving on his cheek as she spoke. 'Don't worry, I won't blame you. I want it as much as you do,' she whispered.

Early in the morning he was the first to waken and for a few seconds found it hard to remember why he should be lying in a tumble of abandoned clothing in front of the still-burning stove. Then steely light coming the window showed a naked Hannah asleep in the crook of his arm, curled up like a baby with her face against his shoulder. He lifted a tendril of her curling hair and with a look of adoring wonder on his face wound it around his forefinger. Gently he touched her shoulder and said, 'Wake up, wake up, my flower. It's half-past six.' He possessed a strange and useful facility for being able to tell the time accurately without consulting a watch.

She rolled on to her back and stretched out like a big golden cat, her long toes all pointing out like fingers as she tensed her muscles. Then she opened her eyes and stared into his face. The first look that came into her eyes was tenderness, and she stroked his stubbled cheek with a soft hand. Then more mundane considerations came to her mind and she sat up, saying, 'Oh my God, half-past six! I've lost my job, that's for sure. What's my Mam going to say? Oh my God, you must have bewitched me.'

He lay proud in his nakedness and watched her as she ran around crying out, 'Where's my boots, where's my cloak? Oh dear, I've lost my place as sure as I'm alive and it was a good place – I'll never get another as good. What'll I say to my Mam?'

'I'll tell your Mam it was my fault. I'll tell her last night was the most wonderful night of my life. Don't spoil it by having second thoughts now, Hannah.'

She was hauling at the clothes under his back, saying crossly, 'Get off my petticoat, you big thing you. Oh, I should have been up and working in Bella Vista half an hour ago.' Her concern was genuine and he could see that there were tears in her eyes as she scrabbled around looking for her clothes. Her naked skin shone like silver in the early-morning light and her hair tumbled around her shoulders like a golden waterfall. He could have looked at her like that forever. When he rose and went over to comfort her, she stopped her fretting to stare at him. He was broad-chested, narrow-hipped and magnificently muscled, with a strip of curly black hair starting just beneath his breastbone and spreading out till it became his pubic bush. He made no attempt to cover his maleness and she gazed at him with admiration. 'Oh my word but you're a bonny man, aren't you?' she sighed as she stepped into his embrace once more. Without premeditation they were back on the cloak on the floor, all cares and responsibilities forgotten. It no longer mattered a fig to Hannah Mather that there would be no maid to serve the food in Bella Vista's breakfast room that morning.

They stayed in their snug little hideaway till afternoon, before they realised that it was Christmas Eve. Outside, the snow still drifted from the sky though not with the same fury as it had done the previous day, but the paths and roads were packed with drifts. Travelling any distance would be very difficult, which made Hannah glad because she knew her mother would not expect her in such weather. She and Tim lay cosily in bed with their clothes piled up on them as coverings. There they stayed in each other's arms, laughing, talking and making love until hunger hit them. Not an apple core, not a rusk of bread could be found to eat in the hut so Tim pulled on his clothes and said, 'I'll go down into Rosewell and buy us some food.'

Hannah popped up and cried, 'I'll come with you,' so

they dressed with many kisses, and arm in arm waded out into the snow giggling like children. First they called at the coalyard and bought a bag of best coal which Tim shouldered while Hannah went into the shops around the square and bought bread and cheese, bacon and apples, a twist of paper full of tea and a pat of golden butter. When she came out they put their heads together and talked about her purchases before she went back in again and bought a tin of black treacle, a stone bottle of beer, a paper bag full of potatoes and a bundle of mistletoe tied with a red ribbon. Their last call was at the butcher's shop, where they purchased a leg of lamb at considerable expense. Then, laden with their provisions they went back to their hut.

As Tim unlocked the door, Hannah looked at the word *Benjy's* and said, 'You'll have to change that now, won't you? You'll have to put *Tim's* on it.'

He shook his head. 'No, I think I'll put *Hannah's*' he said. With a tender look she reached out a hand and touched his as they went into the warm darkness of the interior. Their stove was still burning as a welcome for them.

If Hannah had paused to think, she would have immediately realised that the news that she had been seen buying provisions in Rosewell, in company with a big, black-haired navvy, would reach Camptounfoot almost as quickly as she and Tim were safely back at Benjy's.

Tibbie was washing clothes in the little wash-house at the back of her cottage, happily humming away to herself as the fire crackled up beneath the big metal boiler while sheets rolled and bubbled away inside it in a sea of frothing soapsuds. 'Hey Tib,' came a voice from the door and she turned to see Big Lily standing in the trodden-down snow.

'Hello Lily,' she said. 'Give me a hand with this sheet, will you?' She stuck a long pole into the middle of the water and attempted to fish a wet sheet out with it.

'Can Hannah no' help you wi' that?' asked Lily.

'Hannah's not here. If she was she'd help me of course,' snapped Tibbie.

'If she's no' here, why's there a man from Bella Vista chapping at your front door and wanting to know why she's not been at her work since yesterday?' asked Lily.

Tibbie froze. 'She left here yesterday afternoon to go back to Bella Vista,' she said wonderingly. Then she put a hand on her heart and gasped, 'Oh God, she went out in that storm. I hope she's all right, Oh, I hope she's not been murdered. Maybe one of those navvies has got his hands on her.'

'Aye, that's what I heard,' came another voice, and Tibbie's sister-in-law Effie appeared in the wash-house door with a very disapproving expression on her face. Tibbie and Lily stared at her in amazement and she nodded grimly. 'I cannae imagine what she thinks she's doing, buying legs of lamb in Rosewell with a navvy.'

Tibbie was near tears. 'Legs of lamb? What's this about legs of lamb? Hannah's gone missing. She's not been at her work.'

'She's not been that far either,' Effie informed her, 'because I've just been told she's prancing around Rosewell spending money like it's gone out of fashion and she's got a navvy with her.' This time it was Tibbie's turn to faint.

When she came to, she was half-lying in a chair in her own sitting room with several village women around her. They were all talking at once and the subject that engrossed them was Hannah: 'Shopping in the square with a big black-haired navvy, the same one that comes here to see Mr Wylie at the Jessups'. Buying all sorts of things – even a tin of treacle and mistletoe if what they say is true.'

Another woman spoke up from the back. 'The housekeeper in Bella Vista's hopping mad. She won't have her back, she says. Where did she go last night, that's what I'd like to know, and her poor mother that respectable!'

Wee Lily, who was listening to all that was being said

with a very solemn expression, chipped in: 'Hannah's a nice lassie. Dinna say anything against Hannah.'

Her mother, Big Lily, descended on her and bustled her out into the road. 'Away you go and feed the hens,' she ordered. When she came back she was shaking her head and saying, 'She picks up everything. Aw, dinna tak' on like that, Tibbie. At least she's no' been murdered.' For Tibbie was sobbing and weeping as if her heart would break.

'Now just stop that. I'm away home to get William. I'll make him go up to that navvy camp and find out where she is and who she's with. Stop greeting this minute and drink this cup of tea,' ordered Effie, before she marched out of the cottage in search of her husband.

After Hannah and Tim went back to their house, they cooked and ate the food they'd bought and then set about making their bed. Tim went up to Major Bob's and brought back a bundle of thick covers, but they had no sheets and Hannah wrinkled her nose when she felt the roughness of the blankets. 'My Mam has a box of the grandest big linen sheets you ever saw in your life. I wish I had a pair of them here now,' she sighed, and then gave a gasp. 'Oh, my Mam! I'll have to go home soon and tell her what's happened. As soon as this snow melts I'll go.'

'What will you say to her?' asked Tim with a laugh.

Hannah twinkled back at him over the top of their tumbled bed. 'I'll explain that I've gone stark staring mad and run off with a navvy. But I don't think she's going to like it . . .' For the last few words her voice became very solemn.

He dropped his end of the blanket and walked over to her. Taking her hand he asked, 'Would your mother like it better if you went home and said you'd married a navvy?'

She looked up at him and he asked again, 'Would she like it better if you and I got married, Hannah?'

'But I thought you said you're not a marrying man. You told me that last night before—'

'I thought I wasn,'t, but I've changed my mind. There's

nothing I want more in the world than to marry you. I never thought this would happen to me but now that it has I'm not going to let it go. If you won't marry me, I'll haunt you.'

She held out her arms and hugged him. 'Och, there'll be no need for that. Of course I'll marry you, Tim Maquire.'

They were building up the stove with coal for the night when there was a terrible thumping at the door and when Tim opened it, in the opening stood Hannah's Uncle William, his eyes flashing and his beard bristling. He drew back a fist and was about to hit Tim on the jaw, when she ran up and cried out, 'Oh Uncle Willie, don't hit him. We're getting married.'

William was not actually a violent man and he dropped his fist with relief. But his glare was still ferocious as he stared at Tim. 'When are you getting married?' he asked.

'As soon as I can find somebody to do it,' was the reply.

William's gaze went into the candlelit room and lingered on the made-up bed. 'You'd better find somebody soon then,' he said. 'Her mother's in a terrible state. Don't you go home till you're married, Hannah. That's the least you can do for your poor mother now.'

Then he turned to go but Hannah, in tears, grabbed his arm. 'Tell her not to worry, Uncle Willie. Tell her I'm all right. I'm very, very happy. But I'd like her to be at my wedding. Can't I go and ask her?'

But William looked down on her with hard eyes. He'd always been fond of Hannah, had cast himself in a father's role for her ever since Alex died, but now he thought that she'd done something completely out of character. 'I've told you, she'd prefer it if you go home with a wedding band on your finger. She's a very respectable woman, your mother. Don't go to tell her anything till you're respectable too – and you'll only be that when you're married.'

The moment William left, Tim began pulling on his jacket again. 'Come on,' he said to Hannah. 'We'll have to find somebody to marry us.'

Hannah gasped, 'So late?'

'We'll try anyway,' he said firmly. William's lecture had gone home with him.

The minister of Rosewell lived in a pleasant, ivy-covered house near the Abbey ruins. His housemaid, who answered the door, knew Hannah and looked in amazement from her friend to the man beside her. She half-pulled the door to behind herself and whispered, 'What do you want, Hannah? Mr Patterson is in a bad mood tonight.'

'We want to get married,' Hannah whispered back.

'Oh dear me, that's going to cause a to-do. Wait here and I'll go and ask him.'

In a few seconds the minister's voice was heard in the hall and he strode up to the door where he eyed the bedraggled pair. He obviously had no intention of inviting them inside. Hannah he recognised and nodded briefly at, but he eyed Tim up and down suspiciously. 'Can't this wait till tomorrow?' he asked.

'We'd like to get married tonight,' said Tim firmly.

The minister sniffed when he heard the Irish accent. 'What religion do you adhere to, young man?'

'If I'm anything I'm a Papist,' stated Tim.

Mr Patterson stepped back as if he'd been told his caller was carrying the plague. 'You'd better leave now. I've no intention of marrying a girl who I know is a member of the Church of Scotland to a Papist. And I'm surprised at *you*,' he added, turning his head to Hannah.

She opened her mouth to protest but Tim pulled at her sleeve. 'Come away, Hannah, come away. He'll not help us.'

Their next call was at the lodgings of the priest who ministered to the navvy community. When he opened his door he smelt strongly of spirits but ushered them inside with an affable expression. On discovering that the would-be bride was a member of another church, he did not seem too put out and only asked, 'Are you prepared to convert?'

'I hadn't thought about it but I don't think my mother

237

would want me to and she's not going to be happy about this in the first place,' demurred Hannah.

The priest patted her hand. 'You go away and think about it. If you'll convert, I'll marry you. But if you won't, I won't either.'

It was pitch dark and all the shops where they'd made their joyous purchases were shuttered and dark when they found themselves back in Rosewell Square. Linking arms they trudged through the snow up the steep hill back to the navvy camp and *Benjy's*. 'I wish I could go home and tell my Mam what's happened but she's not going to let me into the house unless I've got a bit of paper to say we're married,' groaned Hannah.

'I didn't think it was going to be so difficult. I should have told lies to that minister. I should have said I was a member of the same church as you,' sighed Tim. He put his arm around Hannah and hugged her close as he whispered, 'It doesn't matter to me that we've not got any papers, though. I love you paper or no paper.'

She laughed and snuggled closer. 'It doesn't matter to me either. Aren't we awful?'

They were near the camp-gate when a tall dark figure in a billowing cape overtook them. Looking back over his shoulder Gentleman Sydney recognised Tim and laughed, 'This is an unusual sight, Black Ace in thrall to a woman. What's happened to you? I thought you were the original woman-hater.'

Tim chuckled back; 'You were wrong, then, weren't you? This is Hannah Mather. She and I have been down in Rosewell trying to get married, but nobody'll do it for us.'

'Oh trust you. Black Ace. Never a man to do anything by halves, are you? It's marriage now, is it? Who did you ask to marry you?'

'The Minister at the parish church and the priest,' said Tim in reply.

'We want a proper certificate to show my Mam, you see,' explained Hannah.

'But I could give you that,' said Sydney.

'I know you can do lots of things,' joked Tim, 'but you're not an ordained clergyman, are you?'

'No, I'm not, but that doesn't mean I can't marry you. In this country it's legal to be married without a priest or a minister. All you need are three witnesses.'

'Are you sure it's legal?' asked Hannah suspiciously.

'Perfectly legal, and if I was one of the witnesses I'd even give you a certificate – better than anything you'd get from that drunken whisky priest, anyway.'

Tim glared at Sydney and said, 'I hope this isn't one of your jokes.'

'On my word, old man, it isn't. I've a cousin who ran away and married at Gretna Green in the blacksmith's shop and my uncle couldn't do a thing about it. That's how I know.'

'You said we need witnesses. Who will we ask?'

Sydney was greatly taken with the idea and suggested, 'What about Major Bob?'

Tim shook his head. 'Not her. She'll be drunk by now anyway. Go and find Naughten and Frying Pan – they can be the witnesses. Bring them to *Benjy's*. Hannah and I are there.'

'You've anticipated the starter's flag, then?' Sydney grinned. 'All right, I'll come to *Benjy's* with the witnesses in ten minutes.'

Their little house was warm and comforting, with a red glow in the half-open gate of the stove. Hannah rushed about putting out food while Tim stoked up the stove again, and they hadn't finished their tasks when the door opened to admit Sydney with the witnesses. Naughten was beaming broadly and hopping about from foot to foot like an imp. In his hand he carried a bundle of pencils and a roll of paper. 'I'll make you a good certificate,' he chortled, waving the paper at Tim.

Sydney threw off his cape, put his hat on the bed and eyed the pair of lovers sternly. 'I hope you've both thought about this very seriously, that it's not just a sudden whim and that you're not going to repent tomorrow. Most of all

I hope that neither of you have ever been married before, or this won't be even half-legal.'

Tim spoke first. 'We've thought about it hard – it's no whim. I love Hannah and I think she loves me. And you know perfectly well I've not been married before. You called me a woman-hater, didn't you?'

Sydney nodded, and turned to Hannah, who whispered softly as she stared at Tim, 'I love him. I've never been married before, either.' Then she smiled gently and reached for his hand.

Sydney said very solemnly, 'In that case, tell each other that you'll marry and that you'll stay together for as long as you live.'

'I'll marry you and I'll stay with you forever,' came Tim's voice with ringing conviction. Tears spangled Hannah's eyes as she watched his face and then she repeated the words without faltering.

'Good. Now tell each other that you're man and wife,' said Sydney.

'You're my wife ... You're my husband ...' They grasped hands and stared at each other as if there was no one else in the room. Naughten, standing by the door, shuffled his feet in embarrassment as he looked at them.

Sydney broke the spell by becoming very brisk. 'That's that, I think. We've all heard you say it. You've taken each other as husband and wife: you're married. I'll write you out a certificate and we can sign it.' Then he anxiously asked Frying Pan, 'I didn't ask if you can write. Can you?'

The big rough man flushed. 'I can write my name, if that's what you're asking.'

'Good, good. Now come on, Naughten, let's have that bit of paper and we'll write all this down.'

While Tim and Hannah held hands like people entranced, Sydney leaned over the table and rapidly penned words on the large sheet of paper Naughten produced. 'What's your name, my dear, and where do you live?' he asked Hannah over his shoulder and she told him. He didn't take long and quickly handed the paper over for them to peruse. It read: *'This is to certify that on this day December 24th, 1853, Timothy Maquire, bachelor, of the house called* Benjy's *in the navvy camp above Rosewell, in the presence of myself as chief witness and the other witnesses here-signed, took Miss Hannah Mather of the stone cottage next to the farm at Camptounfoot in the county of Roxburgh, spinster of that parish, as his wife. Signed Sydney George Frederick Algernon Godolphin.'*

When Tim's eye reached the bottom of the sheet he looked up at Sydney with disbelief. 'That's never your name?' he asked.

'Believe me, it is. And none of you had ever better let it out. I've spent years living it down,' was the sharp reply as Sydney shoved a pen into Frying Pan's fist and pointed to the foot of the page. 'Sign there where it says Witness . . .'

The navvy's signature was a scrawl of awkward-looking capital letters, but Naughten's was a flourish of carefully-penned italics. When he had completed his elaborate signature to his satisfaction, he looked up at Tim and said, 'Let me make a drawing along the top for you.'

Tim was anxious to secure the precious paper and put it in his pocket but he agreed. 'Oh all right, but nothing fancy – just a little one.'

'That's right,' laughed Sydney. 'Do something quick. Can't you see they want us out of here as quickly as possible? Have a little tact, man.'

Naughten dashed away with his coloured crayons and when he stood back, they all leaned forward to see what he'd done. Along the top of the paper was a frieze of lover's knots, rosebuds and crossed shovels. Sydney threw back his head and laughed, 'Navvy's prayer books. Very appropriate!'

The reason why Tim and Hannah were anxious for their guests to leave was not as Sydney had jocularly supposed. Tim knew that Hannah was worrying about her mother and as soon as the door closed behind their witnesses, he urged her. 'It's not too late. The snow's melting and we can go to Camptounfoot now. It's better to get it over.'

When they went out again, the air was sharp and crisp.

The world had become very still and peaceful, sleeping under a night sky that was spangled all over with thousands of stars. The dark outlines of the three guardian hills loomed on the southern horizon like a theatrical backdrop when they crossed the stone bridge, and the lights of Camptounfoot could be seen strung along the ridge ahead of them as they walked towards it, following the course of the river that glittered beside them like a silver ribbon.

Tibbie was sitting by her kitchen fire when she heard her daughter rapping gently on the window-glass. She knew who had come so late. The door was unlocked and Hannah slipped in. 'At least she has the grace to look abashed,' thought her mother, as she stared up stony-faced. They gazed silently at each other for a few seconds until Tibbie said, 'You've lost your place at Bella Vista, you know.'

Hannah nodded, her glorious hair glittering in the candlelight. 'I know. It doesn't matter.'

'Doesn't matter? It was a good place.'

The girl stepped into the circle of light cast by the fire in the unlit room. 'I'm a married woman now, Mam.'

Tibbie dropped her head into her hands and moaned, 'Oh, not to a navvy! Have you any idea what these men are like? They're animals.'

'Tim isn't an animal. He's a fine man and I love him, I really love him. You've got to believe me.' Hannah's voice was anguished as she pleaded.

Her mother's look was still stony. 'That was quick work – you didn't even know him yesterday. And does he love you? Where is he? Has he sent you back here on your own?'

'No, he hasn't. He's at the door waiting. And I did know him yesterday. I've known him for a long time really. I met him at the dance the day the Queen came.'

Tibbie flinched. 'That railway has a lot to answer for. Craigie was right: it's made my lassie a navvy's whore.' Her voice was bitter and she said a word that she would not normally have used, but the strain on her was intense.

The effect it had on Hannah, however, was to make her angry. 'Don't call me a whore! You're my mother and you know I'm not that. I'm telling you I've married a man whom I love, just as you married father because you loved him. Remember what that was like, Mother.'

Tibbie looked up, stricken. Already she was beginning to regret the violence of her reaction. 'But does he love you, lass? These men leave women behind them wherever they go,' she groaned. She loved Hannah dearly. There had only been the two of them together for so many years and she knew in her heart that no matter what her daughter did, she would never repudiate her but she was angry, as much at the fact that this had been sprung on her as anything else.

Hannah saw how her mother was softening, and knelt by the chair to ask, 'Can I bring Tim in to speak to you, Mam? Then you'll see that he's not what you think.'

Tibbie neither said yes or no. Instead she fixed her dauther with a sharp eye and asked, 'When you say you're married, who did it? I can't think any Minister round here would marry you without asking me what I thought first.'

Hannah stood up. 'Tim's got the certificate with him.' she said. 'I'll bring him in and he'll show you.'

It did not really surprise Tibbie that the man her daughter brought into the room was the same one as had saved Mr Wylie, the bridge contractor, from being shot by Craigie. There seemed to be a strange inevitability about what was happening. She felt she was being carried along by a force she could not control. He stood in the middle of her kitchen floor with his queer-looking hat in his hands and she asked him, 'I hope you're not playing around with my lassie?'

He shook his black head. 'I love Hannah, Mrs Mather.'

Tibbie was not softened. 'She says that you've got married but I can't see how that's possible. Have you a proper certificate?'

He handed over his precious paper which she read with a wrinkled brow, sceptically eyeing the decoration of flowers and spades. 'This doesnae look very legal to me.'

He stepped forward to assure her, 'But it is. The man who signed it there says it's a perfectly legal irregular marriage. That's what they call it . . .'

She snorted. 'Irregular! That's about the word for it. What's his name – God what? It sounds as if he made it up. Where did you find him?'

'Godolphin, his name's Godolphin.'

'What sort of a name is that?' It was obvious that Hannah's mother suspected the whole thing was a pretence. She turned to her daughter to demand, 'And what are you going to do about Bella Vista? Are you going to ask them to take you back?'

Tim and Hannah looked at each other and the same question was in their minds: 'Has all this taken only twenty-four hours to happen? Have our lives been turned outside down in such a short time?'

It was Tim who answered. 'Hannah won't have to go back to Bella Vista. I earn enough to keep her.'

'You cannae live here,' said Tibbie defensively. 'I'm against the railway so you cannae live here. And I cannae answer for what Craigie Scott would do if he knew you were living here – probably shoot the pair of you. He's gone real soft in the head over this railway.'

Hannah said softly, 'We don't want to live here. We've just come over to tell you that we were married and to wish you Happy Christmas. We've got our own wee house.'

Tibbie cocked a suspicious eye. 'Your own house – where?'

Hannah beamed, pleased that at last her mother was showing some curiosity. 'It's in the camp. Tim bought it. You'll have to come up and see it.'

But Tibbie was shocked. 'You'll be living in that navvy camp! What a place for my bairn to be. I've heard plenty about what goes on there – drinking and fighting and that's not the worst of it.'

'It's not all like that,' protested Tim, but he might as well have saved his breath because Tibbie was shocked and said that there was no way that she would ever consider going into the navvy camp, not even if her beloved daughter was living there.

When Hannah at last kissed her mother goodnight and asked for her forgiveness, Tibbie clung to the girl and let her genuine feelings show. Her tears flowed in a cataract as she sobbed, 'Oh Hannah, Hannah, what a Christmas this is. I used to dream what it would be like when you got married. I imagined us all in the church, you and me and William and Effie and all the neighbours . . . I never thought it would be like this. Oh, bairn, I hope you're happy and that you've not made a terrible mistake. But I'll have to give you a wedding present. What would you like?'

Hannah looked at Tim over the top of her mother's head and gave a little half-smile. 'Oh Mam,' she said through her own tears, 'I'd like a pair of your linen sheets.'

'Isn't that strange? I washed some of them today. Just go up and take a pair out of my big box. Take the ones with the embroidered ends.'

When her daughter was out of the room, Tibbie turned to her new son-in-law and said fiercely, 'That lassie's the best lassie in the world. I hope you ken that. She deserves a fine man to take care of her. I hope you're able to look after her right.'

His face was solemn as he looked down at her. 'Mrs Mather,' he said. 'you mustn't worry. As long as there's breath in my body, I'll love and respect Hannah.'

After they left *Benjy's*, Sydney and the other witnesses walked together through the crisp snow up the camp and paused at the place where two main paths crossed. 'That's a bonny lass Black Ace's got,' sighed Frying Pan with a forlorn look on his face. He was rocking his feet a little because he had been drinking when Sydney found him to witness Tim's wedding.

'Go home and sleep it off,' laughed Naughten, slapping him on the back and hurrying away as he had some clients for likenesses waiting for him. Sydney was left alone, wandering along with his hands thrust deep in his pockets, when he became aware that someone was moving quickly up the path in front of him. It was Jimmy-The-New-Man, scuttling along furtively like someone anxious not to be seen. For some time, Sydney – like Tim – had been concerned about young Jimmy, who was beginning to show the effects of his nightly debauches with Bullhead. His features were thickening and his youthful slimness had disappeared.

Sydney ran and soon caught up with his quarry. 'Where are you going at this time of night?' he asked.

Jimmy whipped round, taken unawares. He looked the picture of guilt. 'For a walk.'

'I'll walk with you,' offered Sydney, but Jimmy shook his head violently.

No, no, I don't want company. I'd rather go by myself.'

'You shouldn't drink so much, Jimmy,' said Sydney quietly.

'What I drink's my own business,' came the sharp reply, and Jimmy strode away in anger. As Sydney watched him go something infinitely forlorn about the disappearing figure struck him, and instead of going back to Major Bob's he decided to follow to see where Jimmy was headed.

To his relief, he soon realised that the lad was not heading for Bullhead's hut but in the opposite direction. Striking out for the camp boundary, he shinned quickly up the stone wall that surrounded it, paused on the top, balancing himself on the uppermost stones, and them jumped down, landing on his hands and knees in the snow at the other side. Standing up, he then ran off into the wood that crowned the hill. If he had not been travelling in such a hurry and making such a noise as he crashed through the undergrowth, it would have been difficult for Sydney to follow him, but he took his lead from the sounds of Jimmy's passage and soon emerged on the far side of the wood in time to see the lad running across a field towards the grounds of Bella Vista. 'Why's he going there? I hope he's not intending to do something stupid like trying to break into the place,' thought Sydney. He resolved to follow and perhaps step in to prevent trouble if necessary, for he knew that Jimmy was drunk and capable of irrational behaviour.

Bella Vista's white lawn was surrounded by a wood; the tree branches were weighed down by the snow on them. It looked like a wonderland. Silently, Sydney slipped between the trees and kept Jimmy in sight for he was easy to spot because of his dark clothes against the expanse of pristine white. As Sydney watched, his quarry crept stealthily near to the house and lay down beneath the low-lying branches of an old yew tree. He was spying on the place and seemed to know his way around for obviously he had used that hiding place before. It was well chosen because it gave a sight of both the front and back doors of the big house. Sydney, sitting beneath another tree farther back in the shrubbery, saw that the windows of the rooms in the front of the house was ablaze with light, and there was much coming and going from the back courtyard. He and Jimmy stayed watching for some time till the lights in the front were extinguished downstairs although those in the first-floor bedrooms blazed on. A pair of menservants came out of the kitchen courtyard, laughing and pushing at each other as they headed for their quarters above the stables. A woman shooed out a pair of cats and slammed the back door on them. Still Jimmy did not move. 'What's he planning to do, the young fool?' thought Sydney, and wondered if he should make his presence known and take him back to the camp.

At that moment, two women came round the corner of the house. They were heavily cloaked against the cold and were walking arm in arm, laughing and talking together. One of them swung a glass lantern to and for as she walked. Suddenly one of them broke away and ran into the middle of the unbroken snow of the lawn, scooping it up in her hands and throwing it around like a child. 'It's wonderful! It's lovely! I've never touched snow before,' she cried as she ran. The other woman followed the path that led to a grotto and a summerhouse situated in a grove of ornamental trees in the shrubbery facing where the watching men were hidden.

To play in the snow was a release for Bethya. Her life at Bella Vista was becoming almost insupportable, and coming out late at night with her maid into this silver wonderland was a great escape for her. The snow made her fingertips tingle as she lifted it to her face and rubbed it into her cheeks, making them throb as well. She'd read about snow, of course, but had never seen it before and was as happy as a little child to play in it while Francine sat in the summerhouse smiling indulgently. Bethya's cavortings took her close to the place where Jimmy lay hidden. She bent down and lifted a huge handful of snow while she called to her maid, 'Come on, Francine. Let's have a snow-fight. Come out and join me!'

The maid rose, dark in her cape, and walked across the snow. Her footsteps could be seen in its surface like the track of a spectre. When she was close to her mistress there was a sudden flurry in the shrubbery and, as if released by a spring, Jimmy leapt up from his hiding place and ran towards them. At first they did not see him, but hearing Sydney's warning cry, they turned round in alarm just as Jimmy was about to throw his arms around the maid and bring her to the ground. She had the lantern and she swung it at his head, hitting him above the eye and making him reel back with a howl of pain.

Sydney was now running down the path too and the second woman turned towards him with both hands out. 'Don't touch us, leave us alone. Go away. I've nothing worth stealing,' she shouted.

'I'm not going to touch you. I'm trying to stop him hurting you,' gasped Sydney grabbing Jimmy who was staggering about with his hands to his face. 'Hold up that lantern and let me see what's happened to him,' Sydney ordered the first woman, who was sobbing and gulping as if she was about to have a fit of hysterics.

Her more composed companion snatched at the lantern, saying, 'Give me that, Francine, and pull yourself together.' When she held it up they could see that blood was seeping through Jimmy's fingers and splashing red into the snow at his feet.

'Is it your eye?' asked Sydney sharply, but Jimmy shook his head.

'No, its my brow. She cut my brow.' He dropped his hands and the light of the lantern showed a deep but clean cut on his left temple.

'Sit down and I'll tear a bit off your shirt to tie it up. What did you think you were playing at? You're lucky she didn't knock you out completely,' snapped Sydney.

The women stood behind, the frightened maid still sobbing but the mistress utterly composed now. 'Will I send in for some brandy?' she asked.

The maid cried out, 'No, Madame, no! Send him away. It's the man who's been following me. I've seen him in the garden several times.'

Bethya stared at her. 'What does he want?'

Francine was gulping out her words. 'He's the one I brought back to the summerhouse – the one I sent away when you said – he's been following me ever since . . .'

Bethya cut her off with a noise like a spitting cat. 'I told you that would cause trouble!' Then she turned on Sydney and demanded, 'Take him away out of here. I don't know what the pair of you think you're doing, but there's nothing here for you. Go away before I call the men. If they get hold of you, you could be hurt.'

Sydney wanted to tell her that he was on her side, but she didn't give him the opportunity. Stamping her foot she shouted, '*Toom Jao*! Go away! Be quiet! Get out and don't come back. I won't have my maid terrified by the likes of you. Get out!' She looked magnificent as she pointed towards the gate. Her lovely face was like a cameo against the dark hood of her cloak and her eyes were flashing fire in the light of the lantern. She was obviously not a woman with whom it was safe to argue.

'Come on, Jimmy. Lean on me, old chap,' said Sydney, pulling at the injured man's arm.

As they limped away Bethya shouted furiously after

them, 'You're lucky I haven't sent for the policeman. I will if I ever see either of you here again.'

Sydney turned his head and laughed then, for in her angry voice he had caught the note of shrill India, the sound of the chawl. She knew why he was so amused and coloured a furious shade of red at having let down her guard.

When they were clear of the garden, Sydney said to the groaning man beside him, 'What the devil did you think you were playing at? You deserved what you got, you know.'

Jimmy mumbled painfully, 'I love her – I'm mad about her. I've been watching her for weeks, ever since that dance.'

'She'd never look at you, even though she's a half-breed,' drawled Sydney. 'Don't you know she's Anstruther's daughter-in-law!'

'Not her,' Jimmy said irritably. 'The other one – the maid. She took me back with her from the dance as sweet as honey and promised to sleep with me. Then she went into the house and when she came back she was like another person, shouting and yelling for me to go away like that one did tonight.'

Sydney shook his head. 'She's playing games with you, Jimmy old man.'

But Jimmy wouldn't believe it. 'She kissed me as sweet as sweet, she kissed me and put her hands on my cheeks and said such nice things in her funny voice. I love her, Sydney, I really do. I can't get her out of my head. I keep thinking if only I could speak to her, ask her what I did wrong . . . it's driving me mad.'

'Forget about her. Find another girl,' was Sydney's advice but Jimmy kept shaking his roughly-bandaged head and saying, 'No. I only want her, just her.'

The snow started melting that night, and by the afternoon of the next day it had almost disappeared. Tim went round the navvy huts to tell his men, 'It's work again tomorrow, boys.' Then he and Hannah walked to Camptounfoot where she went up to sit with her still-grim mother and he called at the Jessups' to see Mr Wylie.

'You're looking better, sir,' he said with relief when he noticed that the old man's face had regained its normal colour.

'I feel better. Merry Christmas, Tim – I hope you've had a good one.'

Maquire laughed. 'The best in my life, sir. I got married.'

Wylie was astonished. 'Quick work, my lad, but sometimes that's the best way. I knew I wanted to marry my Arabella the moment I laid eyes on her. What's the name of your new wife? Where did you find her?'

Like a boy Tim leaned forward in his chair and poured out the story of himself and Hannah – how he had hung about the village looking for her, how beautiful she was, how everything about her was perfect. 'I've never felt so happy in my whole life before. I used to think I'd not be happy till I was back in green Ireland, but now I know I was wrong. All I look forward to is going back to my hut and being with Hannah. Oh, Mr Wylie sir, I feel as if my heart's so full it could break open in me chest!' He was not superstitious so he felt free to acknowledge the delight he was experiencing.

Wylie, listening and watching him, felt an involuntary twinge of envy. 'Maquire is at his peak, he has all his life before him, with so many joys still to come,' he thought, 'but my life is finishing and there is not much left to look forward to.' But he drove his melancholy away and jumped to his feet to shake his ganger's hand. 'May you live in happiness with your Hannah forever. I'm glad for you, as glad as I would be if you were my own son!' Then he threw an arm around Tim's shoulder and gave him a huge hug. It was an emotional gesture for both of them and it bonded their friendship forever.

When toasts were drunk with Mr Jessup, Wylie suddenly announced 'This is not the way for a family man to spend Christmas, away from the people he loves, is it? I've made up my mind to take a short holiday from the bridge, after all. I'll leave everything to you, Tim, because I know you can do it as well as me. Tomorrow I'll go down to Newcastle and surprise my family. It's been too long since I saw my wife, and what you've told me about your Hannah has made me realise how much I miss her, and how much she must be missing me.'

Next day, before he went to the station, he drove by the bridge site. The snow had gone and the re-emerged grass looked very green against the piles of red sandstone that lay in huge heaps along the slope. Every day these piles grew bigger as carts laden with huge blocks of stone came trundling down the hill. While the bright winter sun warmed their backs the men laboured with a will, singing in unison as they wielded their picks and shovels or chipped away with their chisels at the ruby-coloured stone.

Standing beside the biggest heap of stone, Christopher Wylie stared up into the pale vastness of the sky above his head and had a vision of what his bridge would look like when it was finished. Transfixed, he stared into the emptiness where soon there would be soaring arches, outlined with pale-pink bricks. He blinked his eyes and the vision disappeared but he knew he'd seen into the future and his spirits rose. His bridge would stand there one day. There was no doubt any longer. He was building his memorial and he felt like an Egyptian Pharaoh overseeing the creation of his own pyramid.

He turned and grinned happily at Maquire by his side. 'It's coming on well, Tim. We'll finish on time now. Everything's going our way, isn't it?'

Tim grinned back and eagerly agreed. Everything was ideal, that was for sure. Not only was the work going smoothly but he and Hannah were as happy as children in their little house. Love had come to him, and that was something he had never expected or even believed was possible.

The mild weather lasted for most of January, and Christopher Wylie did not come back so Tim spent all the daylight hours at work and when he was out, Hannah walked to Camptounfoot every day to visit Tibbie. Although she pleaded with her mother to come and visit *Benjy's* there was no relenting. 'I will not set foot in that camp,' Tibbie said vehemently when Hannah suggested it. Nor did they discuss Tim, for when Hannah mentioned his name her mother seemed to go deaf. Tibbie preferred to act as if things were still as they had been when Hannah used to run down from Bella Vista. This annoyed the girl, but she could do nothing about it and resolved to let things go quietly until her mother came round of her own accord.

In the afternoons when the light began to fade, Hannah always glanced at the little clock on the mantelpiece and said, 'I'll have to go now. Tim'll be home soon and I want to have his supper waiting.'

One day Tibbie had been labelling bramble jam and she suddenly asked, 'Does he like jam?'

'Though she still hasn't spoken his name, at least she's referred to him,' thought Hannah, who nodded and said out loud, 'Yes, he does.'

'Take him that jar then,' said her mother, passing her a basket with a glowing red glass jar in it. It was her way of acknowledging that Hannah was now running her own domestic establishment and that she had a husband to feed – a huge concession.

They were embracing fondly on the front doorstep when Craigie Scott came striding up the street. At the sight of Hannah, he paused and called out, 'Aren't you ashamed to have a daughter that's a navvy's whore, Tibbie Mather?'

Tibbie's face went white and then scarlet. She stepped out into the roadway and faced up to him with her fists on her hips. 'Don't you call my lassie a whore, Craigie Scott. You're not in a position to point a finger at anyone, and anyway my Hannah's a legally-married woman with a paper to prove it.'

Hannah came out to stand beside her mother and pull at her shoulder. 'Ignore him, Mam. Come away,' she cried, for she was afraid that Craigie would lift his stick and hit Tibbie with it. He looked capable of anything, for the muscles of his face were twitching uncontrollably and his lips were frothing as if he was having a fit. Never a dapper dresser, he had degenerated into a scarecrow figure with long, grey-streaked hair down to his shoulders and a thick stubble of beard on his chin.

He pointed at Hannah and called out in a terrible voice, 'She's betrayed her forebears. She's taken up with one of those devils that're cutting into our land. She'll pay for it. I curse her and her black stallion.'

By now, scandalised people had appeared at the village doors and Craigie's two sisters came running down from the farmyard to try and calm him. They grabbed his arms but he shook them off like a dog shaking fleas out of its coat. 'No good will come to a navvy's whore,' he yelled.

Tibbie was almost as transported by rage as he was. 'How dare you talk like that about my girl! She's a respectable lassie and so's her man,' she cried. In her fury she reached into Hannah's basket and grabbed the jar of jam which she heaved at Craigie's head. If it had hit him it could have cracked his skull, but he dodged and it smashed to pieces on the cobblestones at his feet. That silenced him. Everyone stared at the broken jam jar and then at Tibbie, who was weeping and embracing Hannah.

'Don't listen to him, my lamb. Away home to your man and be happy. He's a good man and I'm glad for you. Craigie Scott's mad and he doesn't know what he's talking about,' she sobbed. Then to Craigie's sisters she shouted, 'Get him home. Keep him there. If you don't he'll end by getting locked up like his father.' It was a shocking thing to say, she knew, because village people didn't throw secrets like that at each other in the open air but she didn't care. He had miscalled and menaced her beloved Hannah and she felt capable of killing him for that.

One good result of Craigie's intemperate outburst was to remove the constraint between Hannah and her mother. Next day, Hannah did not use any of the little back lanes when she came into the village but walked proudly up the middle of the main street with her head held high. Her mother, who had been watching for her daughter, came out to meet her and they walked round to the back of Tibbie's cottage arm in arm. That day too Tibbie was prepared to talk of Tim for the first time and Hannah was able to tell her mother how happy she was in her marriage. They parted with much affection.

Next day, though Tibbie waited anxiously till it was dark, Hannah did not appear, however, and by the afternoon of the day after that, she could contain her anxiety no longer and set out to walk to Rosewell and the navvy camp. There was a feeling of ice in the wind so she wrapped up warmly in two shawls for the journey. As she walked along she could see the gradually-encroaching line of the railway cutting, and reflected that her feelings about the despoilation caused by the railway would never change but she was prepared to relax some of her hostility towards the navvies, at least towards Tim Maquire whom her daughter loved so much. She hurried along with her head down worrying about Hannah, for she knew there had to be some serious reason why she had not visited Camptounfoot for two days.

She did not know what she really expected to see when she reached the navvy camp. Her imagination was filled with Biblical-style scenes of degradation like Sodom and Gomorrah, with lecherous drunken men and lascivious women reeling about. The reality was an anti-climax, for the camp into which she stepped looked quite orderly. The field was full of a huddle of buildings, some neat and trim but others with straggling turf roofs and tip-tilted chimneys. As in Camptounfoot, the doors of each house contained lounging women and ragged children, all shouting and eyeing the stranger with curiosity. Tibbie stepped primly up a muddy track until she came to a shed in which there was a shop, for through its open door she could see a long counter and barrels and sacks lined against the walls. She was not to know that she had found the hated truck-shop where the navvies employed by Jopp were forced to spend their pay. The man in charge was a red-faced old drunk who cheated the customers and short-changed the children. When Tibbie put her head in the door and asked him, 'Where does Mr Maquire live?' he only shrugged and said, 'Never heard of him.'

There were some women grubbing through potatoes in a big barrel, looking for the few that were not rotten or sprouting, and one of them lifted her tousled head to say wearily, 'If you mean Black Ace, I know where he lives.'

'Take the lady there,' said the shopkeeper shortly, and when the woman straightened up, Tibbie saw with shocked surprise that one of her eyes was closed by a terrible contusion and her cheek was purple and yellow with bruising. Her upper lip was also badly split and bleeding slightly. 'Come on, it's this way,' she said, stepping out into the open air and gesturing with her hand.

Tibbie trotted along beside her asking anxiously, 'What on earth happened to your face? Your lip's bleeding.'

Her guide wiped a hand over her mouth as if she was surprised by Tibbie's concern. It seemed she was half-stunned and not fully aware of what was happening. 'Have you had an accident?' asked Tibbie again, but the only reply was a sigh. 'Oh, no accident. Just bad luck, that's all.'

Tibbie put a hand on her arm and said, 'You should have that face cleaned and dressed. Come with me to my daughter's and I'll do it for you.' When she was close to the woman she smelt a strong whiff of gin but that did not repel her, for the poor soul was obviously suffering. On looking closer, she could see that the woman was young, not much older than Hannah. She had also once been pretty, and moved in a surprisingly graceful way.

'Is it your daughter that's married to Black Ace?' asked the girl, and when Tibbie nodded, she went on, 'Oh, she's lucky. He's a good man, not like the one I'm with. Mine did this to me.'

Tibbie was shocked. 'That's awful! It looks as if he might have broken your cheekbone. Is it very painful?'

'Yes, it is a bit, but the gin helps.'

Tibbie patted her arm. 'It'll do more harm than good

in the long run. Lead me to Maquire's hut and I'll take care of your face.' They were in a narrower path now and the woman paused to point down it to a hut at the far end. A snake of smoke was rising from its single chimney.

'That's Maquire's house. It's bonny, isn't it?' she said. It was bright with paint and gleaming among the duller huts like a little jewel. Tibbie felt proud for Hannah as she looked at it.

When she walked towards the hut door, her battered guide turned to go but Tibbie reached out and pulled her back, saying, 'Don't run off. I've offered to help you. I can't stand to see anybody suffering like you are.'

'I can't pay you. I've no money,' said the other woman stiffly.

Tibbie was outraged. 'Who said anything about being paid? I don't want any money – I like helping people. Come on in here and Hannah and I will look after you. My name's Tibbie Mather, by the way. What's yours?'

'Mariotta.'

Tibbie knew it would have seemed stupid to say, 'What a pretty name,' but that was what came into her mind. 'Come in here, Mariotta,' she said gently, pushing open the door to Hannah's little house. It seemed to her that the girl still hung back but she pulled firmly on her arm and finally succeeded in hauling her inside.

Hannah was in bed, sleeping with her hair tumbled over the pillow. Her face was very white and her mother was momentarily distracted from her first patient by finding herself with another. 'Oh Hannah, are you sick, bairn?' she called out anxiously and Hannah woke, sitting up and staring at Tibbie as if she was a vision.

'Oh Mam, I was feeling awful sick but I think I'm a bit better now,' she said, swinging her legs over the bed and stepping on to the floor.

Tibbie's face was a picture. 'How sick? What kind of sickness?'

'Just sick. I couldn't eat. It was the same yesterday morning and my breasts are sore . . .'

Tibbie clasped her hands in delight. 'You're pregnant, bairn! She's pregnant, isn't she?' she asked Mariotta.

The battered girl nodded bleakly. 'It sounds like it,' she agreed.

Then Tibbie remembered why she'd brought this poor injured person into Hannah's house. 'You lie back in bed, Hannah, and tell me where you keep your medicine chest. I met this lassie on the road and she's needing a dressing on her poor face. Did you ever see anything like it? Her man hit her.'

Hannah watched while her mother bustled about, dipping pieces of clean white cloth into various potions and brews which she'd given Hannah herself and which now came in useful much sooner than she'd expected. Mariotta's face was bathed carefully and Tibbie's cool little fingers gently touched the damaged places. 'What kind of a brute would do this to a woman?' she asked herself as she worked. By this time Hannah was feeling better and had dressed herself in a gingham gown and a long apron. She stood beside her mother and held the basin of water while their patient sat and silently endured the treatment. All the time Tibbie was still speaking. 'Two of your teeth are broken but things aren't as bad as I feared. Your cheekbone's not broken after all, but that lip's badly cut. It'll take a while to heal. What did he hit you with?'

'A stick,' said Mariotta bleakly.

'A stick? Don't you go back to him – run away! Haven't you any parents you could go to?'

'No, I've nobody.'

'Oh, you poor soul. Stay here with Hannah and I'll go back to that shop and buy a wee bit of beef to put on your eye. It'll take the terrible swelling out of it. I didn't think much of what that place was selling – it stank – but since you're not going to eat the beef it won't matter.' As she spoke Tibbie was pulling her purse out of her pocket and counting the coins it contained.

Mariotta put up a hand. 'Oh, don't spend money on me – I'm not worth it. Anyway, he'll just hit me again tonight and black the other eye.'

'Then we'll get Hannah's man to talk some sense into him,' said Tibbie firmly and bustled out. When she came back she put a neatly trimmed bit of beef on Mariotta's eye and she and Hannah succeeded in persuading their patient to lie down in the bed for a little while. Soon she was fast asleep and they sat talking quietly together about what she'd told them. 'Isn't that awful?' whispered Tibbie, and Hannah nodded.

'I know there's some rough people in the camp but Tim and I keep to ourselves and never hear them.'

'Ask him to do something about that man. He must be a terrible bully to hit a wee woman like her. She's no bigger than a bairn,' said Tibbie with deep pity as she looked at the frail figure on the bed.

'This place isn't like Camptounfoot,' said Hannah wryly and Tibbie waggled her head in agreement.

'I can see that! Why don't you come back and live with me in the cottage till you have your bairn, Hannah?'

Her daughter laughed. 'We're not sure I'm having a bairn yet, Mam.'

But Tibbie nodded. 'Oh I'm sure, all right. You've got that look in your eye women always get when they're carrying. Come home with me and I'll look after you.'

'Oh, Mam, I can't come home. I wouldn't leave Tim.'

'But he could come too.' It was a tremendous concession and they both knew it.

Hannah took her mother's hand. 'Don't be upset, but we can't come and stay with you. Think what Craigie would do if Tim moved in next door to him! Anyway, Tim has to stay in the camp to be with his men and we're awfully happy in this wee house.'

Tibbie accepted her daughter's arguments, especially the last one, with good grace and was so pleased to think that she was about to become a grandmother that when Mariotta awoke some hours later there was a festive air in the little house. A kettle was boiling on the stove and Tibbie was frying pancakes on a big black griddle. When she saw that her patient's eyes were opened she turned with a smile and asked, 'How do you feel now, my dear?'

Mariotta sat up. 'A lot better.'

'That's good. Now have some tea and a bite and I'll take you home.' But Mariotta would not accept the offer of an escort through the camp though she drank the tea and ate three pancakes. When Hannah and Tibbie waved her off from the green and white painted door, Tibbie called after her, 'Take care of yourself, lass.' But even as she heard herself say the words she realised how meaningless they were.

When Tim arrived home that night, he found his wife in a high state of excitement.

'You'll never guess! My Mam's been here – walked in as if it was something she did every day.'

'That's grand,' he said. He was pleased for Hannah because he knew how much Tibbie's consistent refusal to visit *Benjy's* hurt her.

'And not only that,' Hannah was saying as she clattered the kettle on top of the stove, 'but she brought someone with her.'

He laughed as he sat down at the spread supper-table. 'Not Craigie Scott?'

Hannah grinned at him over her shoulder but then her look became more sober as she went on with her tale. 'No, she brought a woman she met in the road out there. The poor soul had been beaten by her husband. You should have seen the state she was in! Her face was black and blue. He must be a brute to hit a woman like that, and she was little, not nearly as big as me.'

Tim looked up from the table. 'What was her name?'

'Mariotta. Isn't that a pretty name? Poor thing. Mam put medicine on her face and then made her lie down and have a sleep in our bed.'

Tim sank his head in his hands. 'Oh Hannah, that must have been cruel for her. This house was hers before her first husband died. She lived here with Benjy and her bairns. I bought the house from Mariotta.' He decided against saying anything about his refusal of Mariotta's offer to give herself to him. The story was bad enough without that.

Hannah was looking at him with her eyes wide open and stricken. 'And we made her come in and lie down in her own bed! I'd no idea. I wouldn't have done that if I'd known.'

Tim got up from the table. 'You weren't to know, and I don't suppose she'd want to say anything. I'll go and speak to Bullhead – that's the man she's with now. He'd better listen to me.'

It was supper-time and the camp was crowded and noisy as Tim hurried between the huts to the one where Bullhead still lived. As he approached it he saw that there was a woman cowering by the open door and sure enough it turned out to be Mariotta, sitting on the ground with her head sunk in her hands. Though the night was chilly she was only wearing a thin green cotton dress that could not keep out the cold. He bent down beside her and said softly, 'Mariotta, Hannah told me what happened at *Benjy's* today. I'm sorry. She didn't know it was your house.'

She lifted bleary, bruised eyes and he saw the extent of damage Bullhead had inflicted on her. In only a short space of time she had become almost unrecognisable as the girl who had given him the key of *Benjy's*. Her face was battered and swollen, and most of her teeth had been knocked out or broken. Her fair hair, once so neatly combed, was straggling and sparse as if some of it had been torn out by the roots. He could not hide his shock. 'My God! I told you not to go to Bullhead,' he gasped. She tried to rise to her feet but she was very drunk and could hardly stand. Tim put a hand under her elbow and said urgently to her, 'Go away! Go down into the town and take a room in an inn for the night. Sleep it off and in the morning, collect your bairns and go away. I'll give you the money for your fares.'

But she was beyond understanding, beyond organised action. All she could say over and over again was, 'That's a nice lassie you've taken up with, Black Ace. Nicer than me. What a kind lassie and a kind mother too. They washed my face and gave me tea ... in *Benjy's*. It's a bonny wee place, isn't it?'

He gave her a little shake. 'Go and hide yourself from Bullhead. I've come to talk to him and you'd better be out of the way when I do.' She at least did what she was told this time, and went staggering off up the path. He hoped that she was heading for some other hut where she would be given sanctuary, but then he realised that she was going towards the woods. It was a cold night and she had no coat. She'd probably freeze to death if she lay in the open without a covering so he ran after her, pulled off his jacket and draped it over her shoulders as he said, 'Go and sleep it off some place safe. And when you wake up, don't go back to Bullhead.'

When he entered the hut his anger was burning inside him like a fire. Bullhead was as usual lording it over his friends. To his disappointment Tim saw that Jimmy was among them. He walked up to the group who were throwing dice by the reeking stove and put a rough hand on Bullhead's shoulder, pulling him to his feet with a fierce grip.

'Get up you swine,' he growled between clenched teeth.

Bullhead shook Tim's hand off. His brows were lowered and his eyes burning. 'What's the matter with you now, Black Ace?' he asked.

'I've come about Mariotta. I've just seen her – she's in a terrible mess. How could you do that to a woman?'

Bullhead leered, 'Oh so there *was* something between you and her, then. The bonny redhead's not enough for you, is she? You can have that woman of mine if you like. Just give me a shillin' and take as long as you like.'

Without warning Tim drew back his fist and bit the big man straight in the mouth. He felt one of Bullhead's teeth shatter beneath the blow and that gave him infinite satisfaction. Bullhead shook his head and blood spattered out on to Tim's shirt-front. 'Why'd you do that?' he gasped, wiping his face with his hand.

'You don't like it, do you? She doesn't like that sort of treatment either, and you've been handing plenty of it out to her, haven't you? You're a pig, Bullhead, just a pig. You're the sort that give navvies a bad name. If I hear about you hitting Mariotta again, I'll break the rest of your teeth and your neck as well.'

Bullhead was a coward as well as a bully and he backed down without making any effort to fight back. Instead he sank back on to the floor and would not look up at Tim as he stormed away. When his assailant had gone, however, he glared at the men around him and sneered, 'He thinks he's big, but he can't push me around. I'll do what I please with my woman – and next time I give her the back of my hand, she's going to learn that she'd better not go running with any more tales to Black Ace . . .'

CHAPTER
Eleven

The euphoria that Emma Jane felt at Amelia's wedding did not last. When Arbelle went back to her mother, Wyvern Villa became a house of grief and illness, with maids tip-toeing through the corridors and the only excitement being when Mrs Wylie's doctor called to see his patient. Emma Jane passed her days in the library, surrounded by leather-backed tomes. She found that she could understand her father's textbooks more easily now that she'd seen the bridge site and listened to his explanation of the plans. The evenings were spent reading to her mother or writing letters to her father at Camptounfoot. As she wrote she visualised the village and felt something of the regret that the villagers experienced when they heard that modernity was to fall upon them and trains were to run past their doors. That was all the more reason, she thought, for her father's bridge to be a really beautiful one. If Camptounfoot was to have its serenity disrupted, it should be given something of distinction to make up for it.

Christmas was very sad. Her father had written to say that he could not take time off to come home, and only a few friends of her parents called to give the Wylies the compliments of the season. They spoke in soft, concerned voices as they stood in the drawing room taking their farewells. 'Your poor Mama's far from well. Her nerves are in a shocking state. Let's hope the winter doesn't prove too much for her. You'll have to take very good care of her, Emma Jane,' said Mrs Morrison, Arabella's oldest friend.

'Oh, I will,' said Emma Jane with sincerity, but when

she was alone she sat with her head in her hands and wondered if the whole of her life would be given to nursing her ageing parents. Amelia's words, 'Travel, find a husband, take a lover . . .' ran in her mind and she wondered if she would ever do any of those things. Then she chided herself for selfishness and went upstairs to sit by her mother's bed. It was a wet, drizzling afternoon and as she sat on the window seat looking out into the garden, the melancholy of the view almost overwhelmed her. Everything looked sad and rain poured like oil over the glossy, dark-green leaves of the evergreen shrubs below the window.

'You should go out more, my dear,' said her mother's faint voice from the bed. 'When I was your age I was the belle of Newcastle.'

'I know, Mama,' said Emma Jane, for she had heard this many times before.

'Mrs Morrison's son is home from the Navy. I understand he's become very dashing. They're giving a soirée tomorrow evening and she asked if you would like to go,' Mrs Wylie said, and Emma Jane backed against the window glass in panic.

'Oh, I don't want to, Mama,' she said hurriedly. 'Besides, I can't leave you.'

Her mother's voice quavered as she said, 'I feel as if I'm such a burden to you, darling. You must start looking for a husband and Alfred Morrison is going to do well in his career. He'd be very suitable.'

Her daughter's expression, however, was not optimistic – for Emma Jane knew that her capacity for being 'fetching' was very limited. When her mother fell asleep she went and surveyed the contents of her wardrobe. There was little in it that seemed likely to fetch her a beau, for everything looked so dull, with grey, fawn or black the predominant colours. Only the purple dress made by Madame Rachelle glowed and she stroked its skirt, delighting in the softness of the material. Now she could not imagine how she had had the enterprise to pick such a colour. She'd probably never wear it again. Twelve pounds, six shillings and eightpence wasted. Black was more indicative of her present mood and circumstances. When she looked at her reflection in the long glass, it seemed to her that she resembled a nun.

The doctor who came to the house each day arrived just then and Mrs Wylie was wakened so that he could look at her tongue, stare down her throat, pull down her eyelids and sound her chest. Then with a solemn face he walked downstairs to confer with Emma Jane in the drawing room. 'I can't find any signs of organic disease, but she seems very anaemic and low in her spirits,' he announced, 'Perhaps a change of air would help – a change of air and a rich diet. Give her a glass of sherry at eleven o'clock every morning and make sure she eats plenty of cream and butter, glasses of milk, that sort of thing. She's painfully thin. She's still grieving and she's lonely. She'll be better when your father comes back.'

This advice, which Emma Jane had known anyway, was costing five shillings, but she said politely, 'Yes, Doctor.'

'You must look after her, Miss Wylie,' he said as his farewell shot, and she nodded, thinking how everyone was always telling her what to do, but no one seemed to wonder what – if anything – she herself wanted from life. To them she was the unmarried daughter with her future mapped out for her – as carer for her ageing mother.

The doctor's recommendations didn't help. Arabella's tears kept flowing and when her groaning food tray was carried upstairs, she turned away from it with an expression of nausea. 'I hate cream, Emma Jane, you know I do! Please may I have some plain boiled fish with nothing on it,' she implored but her daughter wrung her hands and said, 'The doctor prescribed cream. You must eat it, Mama. Do try.'

Because Emma Jane's exercise was limited to walks around the garden, she was never truly tired and couldn't sleep when she went to bed at night. She lay staring at the ceiling trying to blank out her thoughts, and when she did drift into sleep, she was plagued by terrible dreams – of running headless through deep forests with unseen pursuers crashing behind her and catching up on her all the time. Just as they were about to reach out for her, she woke, sweating and shaking.

On the day she felt at the end of her patience, the sound of carriage wheels was heard on the gravel and her father jumped down from a hired cab. Emma Jane burst into tears at the sight of him and rushed out to be clasped in his embrace.

'I couldn't stay away after all, my dear. Don't cry. Everything's going to be all right,' he told her.

'Oh Papa, isn't this awful? Mama's so sick, the weather's so terrible and I'm so unhappy.'

He gently patted her hand. 'Stop crying. I'm back now and I'll do my best to make this a happier time for you. Now let me see your mother.'

The doctor had predicted that Arabella's health would improve when her husband came home, and he was right. Within hours she was sitting up in her flowered bed-jacket and positively coquetting with Christopher, who sat by her bed holding her hand and complimenting her. Standing in the doorway, Emma Jane saw them like this and felt unwanted. They were so engrossed in each other, so obviously in love. She backed away with the glass of medicine she was taking to her mother still in her hand. The presence of her husband would do the patient much more good.

Next day Arbelle arrived with Amelia, who was rosy-cheeked and blooming in advanced pregnancy. The pair hovered over the sickbed with the awkwardness that the healthy always feel in the presence of the ill, then quickly made their escape into the drawing room where Emma Jane waited for them. Amelia shot her a look. 'You're well and truly tied, ain't you? Don't let it become a habit. When your father's finished his bridge, you've *got* to go away, and I'm going to tell him so.'

She was as good as her word. Before she went away, leaving Arbelle behind for a week to cheer up her grandmother, she said sternly to Christopher, 'How long are you going to stay at home?'

He shook his head. 'I'm not too sure. I can't leave the bridge for long.'

Amelia pursed her lips. 'They need you here, too, you know.'

'I do know – and it worries me a lot. Already Arabella is better now that I'm home.'

The girl fixed him with her bright eyes and said, 'You must take more heed of Emma Jane. She deserves a life besides playing nursemaid to her mother.'

Wylie was immediately contrite. 'Oh, I know that, Amelia. I'm very grateful for everything Emma Jane does, both for her mother and for me. I'll make it up to her when all this is over, I really will. What do you think she'd like?'

Amelia laughed. 'The best thing you can do for her is to open the front door and push out. She won't leave unless you do so.'

While Wylie was away visiting his family, the snow began to fall again at Camptounfoot and this time it froze and blanketed the ground for days on end. Local wiseacres who could forecast the weather said it would not melt for a month, so Tim wrote to Wyvern Villa advising Wylie to stay where he was until the thaw came. Work on the bridge was impossible in such hard frost.

While the navvies could not work they lounged around the camp with time hanging heavy on their hands. There were fights – numerous disputes about money lost or won at gambling, and rows over whores. Two jealous women had a screaming, hair-pulling fight in the middle of the road, watched by a gaggle of men who laid bets on the eventual winner. Even the dogs fell to scrapping, snarling and biting over morsels thrown out on to the dirty snow around the hut doors.

Jopp's truck-shop was ransacked by a group of angry women who were tired of being sold rotten meat and weevilly flour, but the quality of the provisions did not improve and the atmosphere in the camp thickened and grew more threatening with every day that passed. It took all of Tim Maquire's strength of personality to maintain some sort of order, for it was the custom among the navvies for gangers to police the camp themselves. They preferred to keep the local constabulary out. Even if there was a murder in a navvy camp, the men sorted it out themselves and policemen in the towns near camps preferred to look the other way unless the peace and security of local people was threatened.

The snow pleased Hannah very well because it kept Tim at home. The pair shut their hut door and cuddled in bed or huddled over their stove like children, while outside the big flakes floated down past their window. When he went out to check on his men, she took the opportunity to do her chores or run to the burn that flowed down by the boundary wall with her bucket and fill it with fresh water. On the second day of the snowstorm, she met Mariotta and told her, 'I'm sorry that I didn't know about you owning *Benjy's*. You must have thought my mother and me very unfeeling, forcing you to come in like we did.'

Mariotta, who was sober, shook her head. 'I could tell you didn't know,' she said. 'You were very kind to me – and your husband helped too. Bullhead hasn't touched me since Black Ace warned him off. I'll bring his coat back soon but I'm still wearing it. The cold's so awful just now.'

After that they met every day and chatted for a few minutes, but Mariotta still didn't bring back Tim's coat as the weather hadn't lifted. Then one morning, when the sky was lighter and it seemed that the cold was abating, Mariotta said to her new friend, 'I'll bring your man's coat tomorrow.'

'Come in the afternoon and have some tea with my mother. She's coming and she'd like to see you again,' said Hannah.

'I will. I'll come tomorrow when I see Black Ace going out to do his round of the huts,' said Mariotta, nodding her head.

That night, however, the frustration of a week without work burst out in a terrible fight involving over fifty men. Roaring drunk, they rampaged up and down the roads of the navvy camp, howling and shrieking like dervishes. It was the first time Hannah had seen a real outbreak of disorder and she was terrified, but Tim had to go out and leave her. Armed with a thick cudgel, he stormed into the darkness, calling back to her as he went. 'Lock the door behind me and don't open it to anyone till I come back. Not to *anyone*, Hannah – not even your own mother. Someone could try to rush in. Don't open it until you're sure it's me.'

She huddled beside her stove, listening to the yells and screams for over an hour before she heard a strange sort of scrabbling at her door. It sounded as if a dog was trying to get in. She rose and walked across the floor on her tiptoes, put her ear to the keyhole and whispered, 'Who's there?' The scrabbling went on. Now it sounded as if someone was scraping fingernails down the paintwork. Frightened, Hannah called out, 'Go away, go away!' The scrabbling dwindled away and finally stopped, much to her relief.

When Tim came home, wiping his brow on his shirt-sleeve, he said, 'That took some sorting out. Thank God, Sydney and Panhandle and some of the others were sober. We got order at last but it wasn't easy, I can tell you.'

Hannah's eyes were wide with fright as she told him, 'Someone came to the door when you were out. They tried to get me to open up. It was so strange, the way they scraped at the paint . . . as if they were lying on the step. Oh, I was scared.'

He stared hard at her. 'You didn't open it, of course?'

She shook her head. 'No I didn't, but it was so strange. I felt I ought to open the door because it sounded as if the person out there was hurt and needed help. I felt bad about turning them away.'

He hugged her tight. 'Don't think about it, my love. It was probably a drunk.'

The next morning, however, when Hannah opened the

door, she saw a scrap of green material lying in the slush by the step. She bent down and picked it up. It was the same cotton as Mariotta's thin dress, and one she always wore. The door swinging open behind her had marks on the paint, down near the ground. It looked as if a hand had scraped its fingernails down the wood. With a cry of anguish she ran back in to Tim, holding out the cloth. 'Look what I've found! That's Mariotta's isn't it? That's the colour of the dress she always wears.'

He didn't recognise it but he knew that Hannah was quick about things like that so he said, 'It might be.'

'Oh Tim, it must have been her at the door last night. I think she was trying to get in. I hope that brute hasn't been hitting her again, and I turned her away!'

Tears were running down her cheeks and he took her in his arms, cradling her head against his chest. 'Hush, Hannah, hush, you'll upset the bairn. Mariotta's coming to see you and your mother today, isn't she? Help her then. And tell her to get out of this camp. She doesn't listen to me.'

Tibbie's brow was furrowed when she arrived at Hannah's later in the day. 'When I walked down the hill I was wondering where the railway line's going to go when it reaches Camptounfoot. Will it run up the little burn where Flavia's stone is?' she asked her daughter.

Hannah shook her head. 'I don't know. I'll ask Tim.'

'Make him promise not to break that stone. It would be terrible if anything happened to it,' said Tibbie.

'Don't worry, Mam. I'll take Tim for a walk up there and show it to him. He'll make sure it's safe if I ask him.' Hannah was bustling about, happy to be playing at houses. Then she told her mother, 'I asked Mariotta to come and take tea with us. I'm a bit worried about her. I think her man's been beating her again.'

The two of them spent a happy afternoon together but their visitor never came. When Tibbie was preparing to leave Hannah said, 'Isn't it strange about Mariotta not coming? She seemed so pleased to be asked. I hope she's all right.' She did not tell her mother about the scrap of green cloth and the strange noises at her door in the night because she did not want Tibbie to worry about her daughter living in a camp where fights like that could happen.

Tibbie dismissed her worries. 'Och, don't worry. You'll see her again soon. She probably forgot to come if she was drinking. There was a strong smell of gin on her that day I met her.'

'No, she was sober when I spoke to her,' Hannah said. 'She looked as if she was trying to stay sober too.'

'It doesn't take long for some folk to change their minds,' was Tibbie's sharp reply.

When Hannah went out to fill her water-bucket she met two other women and asked about Mariotta. Neither of them had seen her but one said, 'She's Bullhead's woman, isn't she? You could ask Squint Mary about her.'

'Who's Squint Mary?'

'She's the hut-woman for Bullhead and his boys. That's her hut up there – the one with the turf roof.'

On impulse, Hannah headed for the hut where she had been told Mariotta lived. Close to, it looked ramshackle and filthy and she could hear raised voices coming from inside. She was about to turn and leave when an evil-looking woman came out of the door and glared at her. 'You're Black Ace's woman, aren't you? What would you be wanting up here?' she asked.

'I'm looking for Mariotta,' said Hannah.

The woman stepped back and her face seemed to close up. 'She's not here. She went away.'

'When did she go?' Hannah was not displeased to hear this because she remembered what Tim had said about advising Mariotta to leave.

'Two days ago, I think,' said Mary.

'That can't be right. I spoke to her yesterday.'

Squint Mary snapped, 'She went yesterday, then. What matters is that she's not here now.'

Hannah hurried back down the hill worrying about Mariotta, and when Tim came in, she unloaded her worries on him. 'If she was going away, why did she say she'd come here to see Mam? And what about that bit of cloth I found at our door? Oh, I wish I'd opened it! I wish I'd not been so scared.'

Tim tried to calm her. 'I'll tell you one thing: she wouldn't go far without her bairns. She was devoted to them. They're staying with a woman called Rush in Rosewell. She told me that once.'

'Nanny Rush! I know her. She keeps a dame school. I'll go to see her tomorrow,' cried Hannah.

Mrs Rush was a sweet-faced woman with curly grey hair pinned back in a bun from a round face that looked like an ageing kitten's. She had chubby red cheeks and sparkling brown eyes, and always smelled of vanilla. For many years, since having been left widowed and childless at a young age, she'd run a school for the children of local tradespeople in a room opening into the street on the narrowest part of Rosewell's East Port. Hannah had never been one of her pupils but Nanny and Tibbie were old friends, and when she opened her door she recognised the tall girl on her doorstep immediately.

'My word, Hannah, you're looking bonny. I heard you were married – it obviously suits you. Come in, lass, and tell me your news,' she cried, holding the door wide and revealing five boys and four little girls sitting round a deal table by the fire with books in their hands.

Hannah looked at them closely, trying to work out which, if any, were Mariotta's children but without success. Some she recognised but at least four were strangers to her. She whispered to their teacher, 'I've come to ask if you've seen my friend Mariotta. She left her bairns with you, I believe.'

Mrs Rush nodded. 'Aye, she did. Lovely, good bairns, little angels both of them.' Unlike some dame-school mistresses, Nanny genuinely loved children and always thought the best of them.

Hannah's face looked solemn. 'Has Mariotta been here to take them away?'

Nanny shook her head. 'No, they're still with me. She was last here three days ago – yes, that's right, she came on Monday – and she didn't say anything about going away. She hasn't been down since, and I was a bit surprised because she comes every day, even through all that snow. She loves those bairns.'

'Which are hers?' asked Hannah, surveying the cherubs around the table.

Nanny Rush pointed to a boy and a girl sitting together. 'That's them, Tommy and wee Marie. Come and say hello to them.'

Hannah bent down by the blond-haired little things and told the boy, 'Hello, Tommy, I'm a friend of your mother. She sent me down to see if you're all right.'

He nodded. 'We're well, thank you. Is our mother well?' He was so solemn and adult-sounding that it was difficult to believe he'd been born and raised in a navvy camp. Hannah had seen other children running wild in the camp, filthy, bare-legged, swearing and shrieking like devils, and she knew Mariotta must have had a hard job keeping her children away from them. 'When my baby's big enough I'll make Tim find a proper house,' she resolved.

'She's well,' she assured the children, both of whom were staring at her with eyes behind which unspoken anxieties showed. Filled with pity for them, she stood up and said to Mrs Rush, 'How was Mariotta when she came the last time?'

Nanny pulled at Hannah's sleeve and led her into a little parlour behind the schoolroom. 'I've been worried about her. When she came to me first and brought the bairns, she was so decent and good-living – that was just after her poor man died. Then she brought the money for them and insisted on paying me a whole year's board at once. She said she was afraid to keep the money in case it was taken off her by somebody up at the camp. But after that she was different. She's sometimes the worse for drink when she comes but always loving and kind to the bairns, always sweet with them. Once or twice she's looked as if she's been in a fight, though. I've never seen such a change in a woman in such a short time.' There was no condemnation in Nanny's voice, only pity. Mariotta's pathetic state had touched her heart as well as Hannah's.

'She's living with a brute of a man,' Hannah told her and Mrs Rush nodded in reply.

'I know, she told me. I asked her why she stayed, and she said it was because of her bairns. They're happy here and she didn't want to move them, especially since she'd nowhere else to go.'

'But the woman who lives in the same hut as Mariotta told me she has gone away,' whispered Hannah.

'I don't believe it. She'd never leave without coming to tell me and the bairns where she was going.' Mrs Rush was adamant about that.

Hannah frowned. 'I don't believe it, either, but she might have had to get away fast. Maybe she means to write to you . . . if you get a letter please send a message to my Mam and she'll pass it on to me.'

The kindly woman nodded. 'I'll do that, and don't worry about her bairns. I'll take care of them. I'm growing real fond of them anyway. I never had any bairns of my own, you know . . .' Her voice had a yearning note in it and Hannah could tell that Mariotta's children had taken the place of the grandchildren Nanny Rush would never have.

When she went home and reported to Tim what she had found out, he was also concerned. 'Poor Mariotta, I wonder what's happened to her. She'd have to be desperate to run away without her children. They were the only reason she put up with Bullhead in the first place.'

Hannah's eyes were full of tears as she cried, 'If only I'd opened the door. I can't help thinking this is all my fault.'

But Tim told her firmly, 'Of course it isn't. If it's anyone's fault, it's Bullhead's. I'll go up to his hut right away and ask him about Mariotta.'

Squint Mary's hut seemed strangely subdued when Tim stepped through the door, and he heard the men whispering to each other, 'It's Black Ace . . . It's Black Ace.' He gestured to Bullhead who was lying on a tumbled cot by the door and stepped outside to wait for him to appear.

'What have you done with Mariotta?' was Tim's first question.

Of course Bullhead blustered, 'What d'ye think? What does anybody do with a woman like that?'

Tim glared. 'Where is she?'

'How do I know? She ran away. I didn't ask her where she was going and she didn't tell me.'

'When did she run away? Was it the night of the big fight?'

Bullhead became suspiciously co-operative. 'Yes, that's when it was. I was drunk that night and she ran away.'

'Had you been abusing her, knocking her about?'

'No.'

'Did anybody else see her go? Did she take anything with her?'

'How do I know? She's pushed off, that's all I can say. She was a mean, moaning bitch – she'll not be missed. What's it to you, anyway?'

'I don't like to see plain bloody cruelty, that's what it is to me,' snapped Tim, turning away. Back at *Benjy's* he told Hannah that Mariotta had left the camp after a row with Bullhead, but he himself was not convinced and resolved to ask around to try to find out what had really happened to her.

As the weeks passed, however, he had no success. People he asked about Mariotta wrinkled their brows as if they doubted her existence. It was as if she had been spirited off the face of the earth. The more he was stone-walled, the more suspicious Tim became. He did not tell Hannah of his misgivings because he was afraid of upsetting her in her pregnant condition. He did everything he could to please her, and in time she stopped agonising about Mariotta. As the baby grew within her, she took on the wonderful bloom of a healthy young woman preparing to give birth.

When the snow disappeared and the frost lifted, Christopher Wylie returned to his lodgings much improved in health. Little by little the days lengthened and the sun seemed to give out extra warmth. Spring was coming: there had been a miraculous rebirth.

'Come and see something,' Tibbie invited Hannah when, as had become her habit, she appeared at the cottage on a bright morning in early April. They walked into the little garden where only shrivelled strands of dead brown leaves showed that clumps of flowers and vegetables had flourished there during the summer. Reverently Tibbie bent down and lifted a low-growing branch on her lilac bush to reveal a hidden cluster of snowdrops. One or two of them had already opened and their fragile heads swung as she pushed back the branch that had shielded them from the cold.

Hannah clapped her hands in delight. 'Oh, they're out again! It's like a miracle every year, isn't it? Spring's here. It won't be long now till summer.'

Tibbie laid a gentle hand on her daughter's swelling belly and said, 'And it won't be long till the baby comes. You're still all right, aren't you? You're still feeling fine? Is the baby moving much?'

Hannah beamed. 'I feel better than I've ever felt in my life, Mam. I can walk for miles and I've enough energy for ten women. The baby is kicking all the time. I love the feeling. I can hardly wait for it to be born. You'll come and help me when it starts, won't you?'

Tibbie frowned. 'I was hoping you'd come here for the birth. That camp's a rough place.' But she was wasting her time.

'Oh no,' Hannah exclaimed. 'I want my baby to be born in *Benjy's*.' She wanted to have the child in the little house where it was conceived, but she did not say that to her mother.

'Why do you still call it that? Benjy was the name of that poor soul's husband, wasn't it?' asked Tibbie and Hannah nodded.

'Yes, it was Mariotta's husband's name. We thought about changing it but we didn't. *Benjy's* suits it, somehow.'

Tibbie's face became more solemn as she asked, 'Have you heard anything more about that poor lassie?'

Hannah shivered. 'Mariotta? No, nothing. She's just disappeared. Tim's asked lots of people about her but none of them know anything. Sometimes I think I must have imagined her. Nanny Rush's got the bairns but I don't know what'll happen if Mariotta doesn't get in touch with her before the money for their keep runs out.'

Tibbie shook her head vigorously. 'You needn't fash yourself about that. Nanny Rush has a good heart. She'll keep those bairns for nothing – she told me that herself. They're safe enough with her.'

The mention of Mariotta had depressed Hannah. 'I don't like thinking about her,' she said in a stricken voice, and her mother put out an arm and hugged her.

'Don't you go getting fancies, not at this time. What are you going to do today?'

'I thought I'd go down to the bridge and meet Tim at dinner-time. He said he'd take a break and go with me to see Flavia's stone. I want him to know where it is so it's not dug up or broken like you said when the line goes by there.'

Tibbie approved of that plan. 'If you take him there, make sure nobody else sees. If one of those antiquarian folk get a sight of it, they'll have it howked up and sent away to some museum or other.' The bridge site had been plagued recently by visits from antiquarians and collectors, who offered the navvies money for anything interesting that turned up.

'Don't worry, we'll keep it a secret,' said Hannah, with a smile. Her good spirits returned as she anticipated the walk through the dell to the bonny wee burn where there should be other snowdrops spangling the banks. Flavia's husband had chosen a fine place to bury them.

It was not far from her mother's cottage to the bridge and she paused on the top of the hill to stare with wonder at the sight that spread before her. What had been a green and empty valley, with sheep and cows grazing by the river and only the occasional fisherman casting a line into the water, was now a scene of great activity. The whole place was transformed. In the broad riverbed, stumps of rising pillars had been built and on up the meadow, so that the bridge looked like the skeleton of a beached leviathan or a line of headless soldiers marching up the brow of the hill. Hannah stood on the ridge along which the railway line linking the bridge with Camptounfoot and Rosewell would soon run, and huge piles of raw earth marked its course. Squads of labouring men were building up a tall embankment on which the line would be laid.

Some of the men working on the bridge were Camptounfoot folk, who waved or called to Hannah as she passed with her bonny hair flying. Tim and Wylie were standing in the shadow of one of the tallest piers. The white-headed man shook Hannah's hand cordially and asked, 'Have you come to take my chief helper away?'

She brandished a little basket she was carrying in her hand. 'Oh no, I've only brought him something to eat. There's plenty for two. You must have some of·it as well.'

Wylie shook his head. 'Thank you, but it's almost noon. I go back to Miss Jessup's for my meal. She's always mortified if I don't eat it all up – she thinks something's wrong with it. No, you two sit down here on the bank and eat your dinner.' To Tim he said, 'I'll be back at two. We'll talk about what to do with that pier base then.'

As Hannah watched him go she said to Tim, 'What a sad face that man's got. Is he worried about his bridge? It looks as if it's going up fast to me.'

Her husband nodded. 'It is. It's going very well. He's worried and sad about other things, though. His only son died not long ago and his wife's sick all the time.'

Hannah had a tender heart and she clasped her hands in shocked surprise. 'Oh, poor soul! No wonder he's sad. What's the matter with his wife? Can't she be cured?'

Tim shrugged. 'I don't know. His daughter, the one that was here, looks after her. He says when the bridge is finished he's going to take them both to the South of France. He thinks the sun'll be good for them.'

Hannah gave a little giggle. 'Oh, I remember the girl –

a wee thing in a black bonnet. I was that jealous when I saw her in the carriage with you. Do you remember?'

He took her hand. 'I remember. There wasn't anything for you to be jealous about. I don't even remember what she looks like. She was a quiet sort of girl ... mousy. Nobody could call you mousy, my beauty. Come on, let's go so that you can show me this Roman stone you've been going on about. How will I keep the diggers away from it if I don't know where it is?'

There were still a few pockets of snow lying in darkened hollows behind the field walls where they walked. The burn was tinkling like crystal over multi-coloured stones, and to Hannah's delight there were hundreds of snowdrops growing on the banks. She gathered some and carried a posy as she walked along with one arm linked in Tim's. 'It's not far,' she told him. 'We've just got to climb that bank and go under that elder tree and it's there.'

He looked at her anxiously. 'You're sure this is all right. You're not going to do yourself an injury?'

'Don't be silly,' she laughed. 'I'm as strong as a horse. Come on, it's up here.' She dropped his arm and clambered up a steep bank to a little overgrown ledge where she began scrabbling with her hands among dead leaves and pads of green moss. 'Here it is. Look, Tim.' She was holding back a lot of sharp and leafless elder branches to show him a pale-coloured stone with carving on it. 'It's a gravestone to a woman called Flavia and her wee girl. The husband put it up,' she said solemnly.

'When?' he asked.

'Oh, a long time ago,' came the reply, 'but my Mam and I love it. We think it's awful bonny and awful sad, and we're worried in case it gets dug up when the railway goes through.'

He stood up straight and gazed around, taking his bearings. 'The line might well be coming along here. If it does, I'll dig up the stone myself and give it to your mother.'

Hannah looked stricken. 'Oh, that's awful! We don't want it to be moved. Flavia was buried here and this is where her stone should stay. Look at her and her bairn, Tim. Aren't they lovely?'

He bent down again and stared at the carved figures. They were worn and chipped but he could see what it was about them that touched Hannah's heart. Softly he told her, 'It's not up to me to say where the line goes, but if I can miss this place, I will. Don't worry about it, Hannah. It'll not be broken or thrown away. It'll be treated with respect.'

She slid like a child back down the slope and put her arms round his neck. 'I knew I could trust you, my Tim. I can always trust you,' she whispered.

They parted on the road that ran along the face of the hill, the road that would one day run under the last arch of Wylie's bridge. She turned and waved two or three times before she finally disappeared over the face of the hill on her way to her mother's cottage. When she had gone, Tim slithered down the muddy slope to the river where Wylie was standing staring at the river that ran fast and strong around the stubby piers. 'I'm not happy about that last one. There's always movement in it. We'll have to wait till the river falls and start it again,' he said disconsolately.

Tim frowned. 'Do you remember what that cabbie said about the old bridge being floated on wool?' he mused.

Wylie glanced sharply at him. 'Funny you should say that, Maquire – I was thinking the same thing. Will we give it a try?'

Tim pondered. 'We might, just with that one pier, but I think we should do a belt-and-braces job – woolsacks and concrete as well. It's got a lot to carry, more than the old bridge.'

Wylie was enthusiastic. 'You're right – it's worth a try. I'll drive up to Maddiston and buy a couple of cartloads of woolsacks from one of the cloth-mills. I'm keen to see what happens when we put it in water.'

'I'll carry on here,' Tim told him, glancing up at the sky. 'The weather's changing again and it looks as if the snow might come back. We'll do what we can and then we'll stop for the day. If you leave the cashbox I'll pay the men for you.'

He was right; the Border climate, which could be sunny in the morning and storming by night, was playing tricks on them again. By four o'clock, the sky was as dull as lead and the first flakes of another snowstorm were drifting in the rising wind. Men shuddered and leaned on their spades until Tim yelled, 'That's it! I'll pay you out now. Stop working.'

When his men were lined up in front of him, he called their names in turn and handed them their day's money. At last he came to Jimmy-The-New-Man's name, but no one stepped up to claim the money. 'Where's Jimmy?' he asked and Panhandle said, 'He didn't come out today.'

'Is he sick?' asked Tim, looking at Gentleman Sydney, whom he knew shared his concern about their youngest worker.

Sydney shook his head. 'Drunk again,' was all he said.

On their way back to the camp, he and Tim walked together and Sydney explained, 'That young fool Jimmy's gone to pieces. First it was the French maid up at Anstruther's house. He thought he was in love with her because she led him on at the dance, but now he's got some sort of religious mania. He drinks himself silly and then starts praying and carrying on. When we came away this morning he was raving at Major Bob about mortal sin.'

'Because of the maid?' asked Tim in bewilderment.

Sydney shook his head. 'Nothing so simple as good old healthy lust, I'm afraid.'

'I'll go and see him straight away. He can't keep his place in our squad if he's not going to pull his weight,' snapped Tim.

In Major Bob's the stove was burning brightly and there was a pleasant smell of new-baked bread. Sydney sniffed the air and said to Tim, 'She's been baking – that means she's sober. It's amazing, she's been sober for five days now but really I think I prefer her drunk. When she's sober the hut's clean and the food's good, but she talks all the time. If I hear another word about the marvellous Major Bob I'll have to hit the bottle myself. At least when she's drunk, she's silent.'

When an irreproachably clean and tidy Major Bob saw Tim she greeted him like a prodigal son but he cut into her transports of delight with a curt question. 'Where's that idle young sod Jimmy?'

She nodded her head grimly. 'Him! He's up at Bullhead's – that's where he spends his time now, and that's what's got him into all this trouble. He's got delirious terminus, you know,' she said sagely, adding in explanation, 'That's a disease you get when you drink too much.'

'Really?' said Sydney, suavely raising one eyebrow. 'Did you know about delirious terminus, Black Ace?'

But Tim was in no mood for jokes. 'I'm going to find Jimmy,' he said, and strode out of the hut.

Squint Mary didn't want to let him into Bullhead's hut but he unceremoniously lifted her up and set her aside. Then he stood in the doorway and yelled, 'Jimmy-The-New-Man, I want to see you straight away. Come out this minute.' Through the reek made by the smoking stove he saw a weaving figure heading towards him and went out into the open air where it was easier to breathe. When Jimmy emerged he looked terrible. His eyes were bloodshot and half-closed, his mouth hanging slack like the slobbering mouth of a lunatic. 'What have you done to yourself?' demanded Tim. 'You should be ashamed. You can't stay on my squad unless you pull yourself together.'

Jimmy swayed on his feet and gave a convulsive sob. 'Aw, Black Ace, I'm sorry. I'm a terrible sinner – I've done awful things. God's going to punish me, I know it.'

'I'll leave that to Him,' said Tim. 'What's worrying me is if you're not able to do your work. I don't carry passengers. I took you on because you were strong and willing – and you've let me down. Are you going to pull yourself together or not?'

Jimmy was weeping, knuckling his red-rimmed eyes. 'I'm a lost soul. I don't know what to do.'

Tim had seen men taken over by religious mania before, especially when drunk. 'For God's sake, don't burble on like that. You used to be a sensible laddie. I don't want to see you going to the dogs. If I throw you off the site, you'll be in prison in a week.'

Jimmy was anguished. 'Don't throw me off, Black Ace. I'll try harder.'

Tim screwed up his face in disgust. 'If you're not at work tomorrow, you're off my gang!'

He was about to leave when Bullhead came storming out of the hut waving his fists and shouting, 'Let the lad alone. Why are you bothering him? He doesn't know what he's saying.'

Tim swung round on him and rapped out: 'It's you I blame for this. He was a good lad before he got mixed up with you.'

Bullhead was pushing Jimmy back into the hut, saying, 'In you go, there's a bottle in there for you.' Jimmy disappeared without a backward glance.

Next morning, the lad did not turn up for work and with a deep feeling of disappointment, Tim sent Panhandle up to Bullhead's hut with the possessions Jimmy had left at Major Bob's. 'Tell him he's off our squad and out of the hut,' was all he said.

When Panhandle came back he told Jimmy's old workmates, 'Bullhead says it doesn't matter that Black Ace's got rid of Jimmy. They're both moving out of our camp and going to join one of Jopp's gangs up at Maddiston. Jimmy's as drunk as an organ-grinder's monkey so he's no loss.'

Snow fell again that night but it was a typical late-winter storm that carpeted the ground for two days and then disappeared completely, a symbolic end to winter. Like a jack-in-the-box popping up for the second time, spring returned and this time it stayed. On the anniversary of the first day she'd seen surveyors walking along the hedge behind her house, Tibbie Mather stood again in her garden with daffodils budding at her feet and thought about everything that had happened. A huge new bridge was rising at the edge of the village, the once-contented community around her was split and quarrelling among themselves about the railway, and her daughter Hannah was the wife of an Irish navvy with a baby soon to be born to them. All in twelve months! She could hardly believe so much had happened in such a short time.

She looked up at the nearest guardian hill and saw sheep and lambs grazing on the lower slopes. They had just been let loose from the in-bye fields where they had been kept all winter until they lambed. Now they were free to roam miles of wild hill country and would not be gathered in again till autumn. As she stared, she saw the figure of a shepherd with two dogs walking among his flock. It was the Duke of Allandale's shepherd, whom she knew well by sight. Her keen eyes followed him till he disappeared over the saddle between two of the Three Sisters and then she turned to go indoors and put on the kettle in anticipation of Hannah's daily visit. Had she stayed out and watched a little longer, she would have seen the man and his dogs come running down the hill again and head for Rosewell, for he had made a grisly discovery.

The Rosewell policeman had a little office in a narrow road that led from the Square to the Abbey Hotel. He was sitting there with his feet on the fender and his pipe in his mouth when the Duke's shepherd came tumbling in the door, gasping, 'There's a body on the hill, Johnny!'

The policeman removed his pipe and asked, 'What kind of a body?'

'I think it's a woman. It's got yellow hair and it's wearing a gown.'

'How do you mean, you "think"? Is it a woman or isn't it?'

'My God, man, it's been half-eaten by foxes, and it's been up there for a while from the look of it. Och it's a terrible sight. My dogs came on it – if it wasn't for them I'd never have seen it. It's been stuck under a big whinbush.'

'There's naebody missing from Rosewell as far as I ken. This'll hae something to do wi' these damned navvies, mark my words,' said the policeman, moving ponderously across the floor towards the door. 'Come on, I'll get some men and a stretcher. Show us where it is.'

Two hours later, the remains of what had once been a woman lay on the floor of the police office, below an old blanket donated by the officer's wife. The finders stood around and scratched their heads. 'I'd better get Doctor Stewart to have a look at it before I write my report,' said the policeman. He was very much out of his depth because there had not been a mysterious death like this in Rosewell during his whole tenure of office, some seventeen years.

Summoned from his luncheon table, the doctor screwed up his face in distaste at the sight of the corpse. 'It's a woman all right and she's been dead for months, I'd say. Her head's bashed in and her ribs are broken, so's her left leg. The foxes have made a bit of a job of her, though. You'll have to try to identify her from her clothes.' He lifted a scrap of green cotton between finger and thumb and asked, 'Was this all she had on?'

The policeman reached behind him and lifted down a man's black jacket. 'This was over her when Allandale's man found her,' he said.

'Have you looked in the pockets?' asked the doctor.

The policeman shoved his hand in two deep side pockets and found nothing. Then he turned the jacket inside out and at last cried, 'Here, what's this?'

Like many navvies, Tim Maquire had been a dandy in his bachelor days. He liked to buy good clothes and patronised the best tailor in any town where he was working. In Preston, where he'd had this jacket made, the tailor was a craftsman with an eye for detail. When he stitched on his own label, he also sewed under it the name of his client in delicate stitches of scarlet thread. *Mr T. Maquire* was what he'd sewn.

The policeman and the doctor read the name with interest. 'Maquire, an Irish name – a navvy, I'll be bound,' they said in unison.

Tim was up on the embankment when the policeman arrived looking for him. 'Are you called Maquire?' he asked.

'I am.'

'I'd like you to come with me.'

'Why?'

'To assist me in establishing the identity of a body we've found.'

'What sort of a body?'

'A woman's body.'

Tim went green. 'It's not Hannah? It's not my wife?' he gasped.

The policeman shook his head. 'I don't know whose wife she is. She's been dead a while. We're hoping you'll be able to tell us something about her.'

Tim felt his heart steadying. He'd seen Hannah only half an hour before. 'All right, I'll come with you,' he said, though he was baffled as to what this was all about. As he strode off up the road with the policeman, a blaze of gossip and suspicion spread out behind him.

In the police office a gang of hangers-on were waiting around the body. The policeman looked at Tim and said, 'I hope you've a strong stomach.'

'Pretty strong,' was the reply, but even Tim tasted bile in his mouth when the blanket was flung back and what was left of Mariotta was revealed.

'Your jacket was over her when she was found. Who is she?' asked the policeman.

Tim wiped his face with his hand and said, 'Her name's Mariotta. I recognise her hair, really. It's hard to tell from anything else.'

'Mariotta what?'

'I don't know. She used to be married to a man called Benjy but he died and then she took up with Bullhead. He might know what her full name is.'

'How did she come to be found with your jacket on her?'

'Because I gave it to her one night. She was going off to sleep in the wood and I put it on her for fear she'd die of

287

cold. You'd better ask Bullhead how she came by her death. I've a strong suspicion he'll know something about it.'

'Where's this Bullhead then?'

'I'll take you to him,' said Tim. He was filled with a terrible burning anger, for he was sure that the brute of a man had killed Mariotta.

Bullhead was a pulley-man on the line out of Maddiston. When the police party found him he was hauling on a thick rope pulling barrow-loads of earth up from a cutting that was sunk deep in the side of a hill. The Rosewell policeman looked with apprehension at the muscles of the man's huge arms as he asked, 'Are you the one who has – had – a wife called Mariotta?'

The answer was a grunt. 'No wife, woman.'

'Do you know where she is now?'

'Don't know and don't care. The bitch took off with my money and if I find her I'll tan her hide.'

This was the first mention Bullhead had made of Mariotta stealing money, and when Tim opened his mouth to say something about it, the policeman silenced him with a glare. He asked Bullhead, 'Were you in the habit of striking her?'

The navvy dropped the rope and his load hit the ground with an earth-shattering thud. 'What's all this about?' he growled.

'We've found a body that's been identified as your woman Mariotta and we're trying to find out who killed her.'

'How do you know she was killed?'

'Because her skull was smashed in.'

Bullhead showed no emotion. 'Useless bitch,' he said, lifting the rope again. Then he turned his bullet head and added, 'I'd nothing to do with it. She took off one night with my money and I've not seen her since.'

His protests did not stop him being marched back to Rosewell, however, where both he and Tim were locked in the only police cell. They sat on opposite benches, staring at each other but saying nothing. Outside, the news of their arrest spread like wildfire. When Hannah heard, she went running into Rosewell. At the police-station door she met Christopher Wylie. Grabbing his arm she sobbed, 'Oh, sir, they've arrested my Tim! They think he killed Mariotta. I know he didn't.'

He patted her hand soothingly. 'Of course he didn't, and I'm going in there now to tell them so. Calm down, my dear. Come in with me and we'll speak to the officer. There's been a terrible mistake of some sort.'

Their protestations on Tim's behalf were listened to with sympathy by the policeman, who knew Hannah well, but eventually he held up a hand and said, 'I've got to keep him here because his jacket with his name in it was found wrapped round the body.'

Hannah sobbed in relief. 'Is that all! But he gave it to her one night when she was going to sleep in the wood and he was afraid she'd freeze to death. He came home and told me. She said to me afterwards that she'd bring it back but she never did.'

'Can you remember when that happened?' asked the policeman. For a miracle Hannah could remember exactly. The progress of her pregnancy had made her very time-conscious, and she had got into the habit of marking off the days on a wall calendar. Sometimes she wrote events on it, too, and she had marked down the day she had invited Mariotta to tea.

When she told the policeman this, he grinned. 'That's grand, Hannah.' He'd already been told that the day of the big fight was the last time anyone could remember seeing Mariotta.

Wylie interrupted, 'In that case, you've no reason to hold Maquire, have you? I'll stand surety for him. He's an honest and honourable man. He'd never do a thing like this.'

But they could not secure Tim's release until the policeman had conferred with the town magistrate and the doctor, so they were told to wait outside the office while this conference was going on. Wylie stood on the doorstep holding Hannah's hand and trying to reassure her while inside, the powers of the town were in deep discussion.

'We've no witnesses to anything except when she was last seen. No one'll admit to knowing anything about her, though it seems to have been fairly general knowledge that her man beat her up – but that's not unusual among the navvies,' said the policeman.

'Has anyone said they actually saw him beating her?' queried the magistrate, but the policeman shook his head.

'No, sir, but they saw her with black eyes and bruises, things like that. This man Bullhead says she got the injuries from other men. She was a prostitute, apparently. His theory is that she got involved in the fight in the camp and then crawled off up the hill to die.'

'With a cracked skull, broken ribs and a broken leg?' asked the magistrate sceptically.

Stewart was studying his elegantly-buffed fingernails, and he said in a bored voice, 'She's not been much of a woman, by all accounts – a prostitute, living with a man without being married to him and a heavy drinker into the bargain. She's no great loss to humankind. I think we should just write it off as accidental death and forget all about it.'

Which is what they decided to do. The cell-door was unlocked and the men inside were told, 'Off you go, and don't come back. The quicker you and your women are out of this town the better. We don't like your sort.'

'What about Mariotta?' asked Tim.

The policeman was not an unfeeling man and he looked shamefaced as he said, 'The town'll bury her. The doctor thinks she must have crawled up the hill to die. There's no way of proving anything else.'

Bullhead gave a little snort of agreement at this and Tim turned on him. 'I know you did this, you bastard. Even if they can't prove it, I'm sure you did it, and one day you'll pay for it,' he vowed bitterly.

Smartly the policeman stepped between them. 'Now, now, none of that. You two had better keep the peace if you don't want to get into more trouble – and don't try to bolt either because I'll go on asking questions about this. I'm not really satisfied myself.'

When he pushed them out of the door, Hannah and Christopher Wylie rushed up to Tim. He reached out and hugged his wife to him, but Bullhead gave a jeering laugh. Stepping out of punching distance, he shouted, 'Does your lassie know what went on between you and Mariotta? Have you told her why you're so worked up? There was more between you than a jacket, wasn't there?'

When Tim looked at Hannah he saw a flicker of doubt in her eyes and he spoke vigorously. 'It's not true, Hannah – it's not true. He's lying. I was sorry for her when Benjy died. She wanted me to take her but I wouldn't. I was already in love with you.'

'Why didn't you tell me that?' she asked.

He shook his head. 'I thought it was bad enough that we were in her house.'

She shuddered. 'Poor Mariotta. How awful she must have felt about me. I wish I'd known it all. You should have told me everything.'

While they were talking, Wylie turned and walked away. It was best to leave them to themselves at such a time, he reckoned.

In confusion and anguish Hannah looked around the familiar street as if she were seeing it for the first time, and then a thought struck her. 'The children! What about her children? They're living up there with Mrs Rush.' She pointed to the narrow opening of the East Port. 'Someone'll have to tell Nanny Rush what's happened,' she said.

'I'll do it,' said Tim grimly. Together they walked to the dame-school door and knocked.

Mrs Rush answered, but her ready smile faltered as she saw the stricken expressions of the two people who looked back at her. 'What's the matter?' she asked.

'It's about Mariotta. Are her children with you just now?' asked Hannah.

'Yes, they're in the back room,' said Mrs Rush, pulling

the door closed behind her to shut out the sound of their voices.

'Mariotta's dead, probably murdered, though they're not going to do anything about that,' Tim said savagely. 'Her body was found on the hill. She'd been there for a long time – about three months.'

Mrs Rush was shocked but not too surprised. 'I thought something terrible had happened to her. She was so good about coming to see her bairns. They've been worried about her, especially the wee boy. The wee girl's a bit too young to worry for long. Oh, what'll I tell them?'

'You'll have to tell them the truth,' whispered Hannah.

Mrs Rush looked doubtful. 'I'll tell them she's dead, but not how it happened. They needn't know anything about that. I'll say she died of a fever.'

'What's going to happen to them now?' asked Tim.

'She left me a good bit of money,' Mrs Rush said quietly.

Hannah remembered the two fair heads side by side at the deal table and tears rushed to her eyes. 'I hope they're not separated. We'll help you – we'll give you money if you need more.'

But Nanny Rush shook her head. 'By the looks of you, you'll be having a bairn of your own to care for soon. We're all right just now. We'll manage fine. I'm not poor – I've got the school and they're good bairns. I'll not give them up, don't worry. They'll not end in the Poor's House or an orphanage if I can help it.'

Mariotta's broken body, wrapped in a shroud, was buried next day in the pauper's communal grave by the Abbey wall. Tim was working but Hannah went and stood beside the only other mourners, Mrs Rush and the two weeping children. When the earth was thrown in on top of their mother, she knelt on the grass and gathered them in her arms, 'Your Mother's in heaven now,' she said, swallowing back her own tears. 'She's watching you from up in the sky. She doesn't want you to be too sad for her.'

'Oh, but I miss her, I miss her,' sobbed the poor little

boy and his younger sister, frightened, put her face against his shoulder and wept too. When Hannah left them in Mrs Rush's cosy parlour, she walked back to the camp with many different emotions fighting inside her – grief and anger and confusion among them. She kept hearing Bullhead's jeering voice: 'Does your lassie know what went on between you and Mariotta?' Was she feeling jealousy? If she was, she must put it out of her mind. But she was also feeling terrible pity for Mariotta, and for her children. Along with that pity she felt anger at whoever had killed her for, like Tim, she knew that Mariotta had been murdered. And worst of all, she felt remorse. 'Why didn't I open my door that night? Why was I so scared?' she asked herself over and over again, because now she was certain that Mariotta had lain on the step, scratching with her fingernails at the door she had painted with flowers, imploring to be let in and kept safe from a terrible death.

The news that a woman's body had been found on the hill, and that she was one of the inhabitants of the navvy camp – a prostitute, even, said the rumours – swept the district and was discussed with shocked horror in farmhouses, cottages and mansions alike. For some time a few of the local wealthy ladies had operated charitable schemes for the more miserable navvy families, and Mariotta's murder accelerated their kindly impulses. Appalled by the hopelessness and brutality of the lives of some of the people inhabiting the camp, they decided to form an evangelising committee to bring love and Christianity to the navvies.

Mrs Maria Anstruther, ever generous in her donations to good causes, was asked to be on the committee – an honour she eagerly accepted because it meant that her family was at last accepted into the inner circle of Border society. Realising that she would need all the help she could get, if she was not actually to exert herself, she struck up a sort of armed alliance with Bethya ... 'You help me and I'll help you,' was the hidden message. If Bethya assisted her mother-in-law on the committee, Mrs

Anstruther would see to it that her son's wife was launched into good society. It was an offer that the younger woman could not afford to refuse and they both knew it, for Bethya's dreams of finding a man to take her away from Gus and Bella Vista would never come true until she moved in a wider circle. Her mother-in-law was well aware of her ambitions and by now silently concurred with them. Anything that might remove Bethya from her life, she would foster.

So they sank their differences; dressed in their most glorious gowns they held fund-raising tea parties for charity. Their hospitality was so lavish and their house so magnificent that invitations to these parties were the most sought-after in the district. Word of them eventually reached the ear of the old Duchess. Intrigued, and slightly annoyed that someone was usurping her position as chief mover in such affairs, she summoned the Anstruthers and their fellow committee members to Greylock Palace for tea.

When Francine heard about the Duchess' invitation, she clasped her hands together in excitement. 'This is the beginning! How wonderful. What will you wear?'

Bethya glittered with anticipation. 'My green silk – with a bonnet. It's an all-woman affair and I must look elegant, but not too fashionable or dashing.' She was already establishing a local reputation as a leader of fashion, and other women waited to see what she ordered from London for each season before instructing their seamstresses to copy it. She made friends by being generous in lending patterns and fashion magazines which were sent to her from Paris and, most of all, by not minding when other ladies turned out in blatant copies of her own clothes.

The old Duchess was indifferent to fashion, however. She still wore the elaborately ruffled, beribboned and tightly corseted satin dresses that had been in fashion when she was a bride. She even stuck a black beauty spot in the shape of a sickle moon on her cheek if she was trying to be very smart. Bethya's magnificence was there-fore wasted on her, but anyway she was not concerned with costume. There were more important things on her mind as she rose to address her guests in the long drawing room overlooking the loch that gave her home its name.

'I expect you've all heard about the body of that poor woman being found on our hill,' she began. The Three Sisters were almost part of her garden as far as she was concerned. A murmur of voices told her that they had: 'Dreadful, shocking, horrific sight, I believe,' they said.

'Of course I was against bringing navvies into this part of the world from the beginning, but they are here now and we must do our best to help them. They're drunken and godless so it's up to people who have been more carefully nurtured to try to save those who are prepared to listen.'

Her audience stared at her, wondering what remedy she was about to suggest to cure the navvies' social ills. Bethya, who had seen poverty in India that made the navvy conditions seem salubrious, was suddenly struck by the contrast between the Duchess' glorious sitting room and the turf-roofed huts in the field outside Rosewell. Greyloch Palace's drawing room made the salon in Bella Vista seem vulgarly opulent because its style was that of well-tended antiquity. The furniture gleamed with a silken patina of age; the walls were covered with family portraits going back three centuries; the silk of the French hangings was worn so thin that they were almost transparent but they hung beside paintings worth a king's ransom.

The Duchess was well-launched into her speech. 'I have had a number of texts printed and the younger women among us must take over the task of distributing those among the navvies and their families. When they do this, they must also invite these people to a soirée in the Rosewell Town Hall, where the Parish Church Minister will preach to them and try to point out the error of their ways. I don't expect we'll save many of them, but at least we'll be able to give them a good meal – and many of those women and children look as if they could do with it.'

Bethya warmed to the imperious old woman then; the

Duchess was no fool. Behind her there was a rustle and servants began passing among the guests, handing out sheets of paper. One was put into her hand and she saw that it contained several quotations from the Bible and a homily about leading good, clean, Christian lives. At the bottom of the sheet was an invitation to the soirée in Rosewell Town Hall in two weeks' time.

When every woman had been given her paper, the Duchess rallied her troops. 'Now each of you must take twenty of these and pass them out among the navvies and their people. Make sure they get into the right hands. Don't leave the work to your servants because they'll probably just stick the sheets under a hedge. Pass them out yourselves.' She spoke with the authority of one who had never had an order questioned or disobeyed, and her audience dutifully folded up the papers and put them into bags or reticules, though from their expressions it was possible to tell that many hearts sank at the task which had been laid on them.

Normally when they were forced to go out together, Bethya and her mother-in-law travelled in stony silence, but the Duchess' tea party overcame Mrs Anstruther's habitual taciturnity and as soon as she was in their carriage, she burst out, 'What nonsense! What good does she think that's going to do? They'll never read those texts. I've seen her sort going around preaching to the Indians. They just eat the free rice and then go back to worshipping their own foul idols again.'

Bethya enjoyed needling Gus' mother so she said innocently, 'But we'll be spreading the word of God. It won't fall on stony ground, I'm sure. I think the Duchess is quite right: these poor people need to be told that they've been living the wrong way and there's another road they can take.'

Mrs Anstruther shot a glance of suspicion at the bright young face beside her but Bethya only widened her eyes to make them look more innocent. 'Humph,' she snorted. 'I doubt if it'll work, but we have to do what she wants or we won't be asked back. You can take my texts with yours and spread them around. I'm too old for that sort of thing.'

When an open carriage full of smartly dressed women stopped on the road under the towering embankment, the navvies labouring on top of the earthen mound all stopped work, leaned on their spades and started cheering. Not for them the diffident attitude of most working men towards the employing classes.

Mrs Stewart, the wife of the Rosewell doctor, who had been roped in by Bethya to help distribute the texts, went pale.

'Why don't we just leave them here by the side of the road and tell the men to pick up one each when they finish work?' she pleaded, brandishing her bundle of paper.

Bethya fixed her with a scathing eye. 'The Duchess was most emphatic that each text should find its way into a navvy's hand,' she said uncompromisingly.

'The Duchess doesn't have to do it though, does she?' groaned Mrs Stewart, and the other two ladies in the carriage made agreeing noises. They didn't want to get out and walk the gauntlet of cheering navvies either.

'You are being silly,' said Bethya, standing up from her seat, adjusting her bonnet and waiting for the liveried coachman to open the door for her. When he did, she stepped to the ground with an air of royalty. The navvies' cheers grew in volume. She was sorely tempted to sweep them a curtsey but knew that would cause great scandal to the respectable Rosewell ladies whom she had dragooned into helping her.

'What a good thing the Duchess has chosen to do this during the fine weather,' she thought to herself as she proceeded in stately fashion down a stony path towards a group of men working around a rising pillar of stone. She opened her cream-coloured silk parasol as she went and twirled it gently behind her head. In the bag that swung from her wrist she carried a sheaf of texts. The men stopped what they were doing and stared. As she drew closer she saw that one of them was the man who had been with the crazy young fellow who had tried to attack Francine in the grounds of Bella Vista. 'Thank heavens he's not in the working party at least,' she thought. The memory of his crazy attack made her step falter slightly but she gathered her courage and went on.

The tall blond man she recognised stepped forward with a smile on his face. 'Good day, mum. Is there someone special you'll be louking for?' he said in a strange countrified accent. She frowned. Surely he hadn't talked like that before? She seemed to remember he had sounded quite civilised.

'I'm a member of the Rosewell and District Ladies' Temperance Society,' she said with her most fetching smile. That was what the Duchess had decided they should call themselves. 'Temperance in *all* things,' she'd said when deciding on the title.

The navvy raised his eyebrows almost to his hairline. Was she imagining it, or did his hooded eyes glitter with malice? But she must be wrong for he was smiling very sweetly as he asked, 'What did you say the name woz?' in an even thicker accent.

She flushed. 'The Rosewell and District Ladies' Temperance Society.' This time her tone was slightly sharper. 'I've brought you some texts and an invitation to a temperance soirée in the Corn Exchange next Sunday evening.'

She thrust a couple of sheets of paper at him and he seemed to be overcome with gratitude. 'Oh dear lady, how kind of you. Give me some more and I'll take 'em to me friends.' Then he turned his head and cried out, 'Here lads, this lady's come to invite you to a temperature party.'

'Temperance, a *temperance* party,' she interrupted, and he beamed brightly back at her.

'Oh, of course, a *temperance* party. It's just that I'm ignorant, so I am. Thank you, mum. We'll be there.'

She thrust the rest of her bundle of paper at him and, scarlet-cheeked, hurried back to the carriage. She knew very well that he'd been making a game of her and she was furious but did not want to show it.

Mrs Stewart, cool under a green parasol, leaned forward and asked, 'What happened? We saw you talking to that tall one in the white shirt. Did you give him the texts? You're very brave, my dear.'

Bethya leaned back and smiled. 'Of course I gave him the texts, and he said that he and his friends will certainly attend the soirée. Now let's go back to Bella Vista for tea. I've done enough for one day.'

Texts and invitations were distributed in the camp as well and put to various uses by the people into whose hands they were pressed. Hannah was given one by an earnest lady in black as she stepped out of the gate one day on her way to visit her mother. When she returned home to *Benjy's* that night, she found it in her pocket, smoothed it out and put it on the shelf beside the ornamental china. Tim came in later, saw it, picked it up and said, 'Sydney's been passing these out. He's keen on the idea of us all going to the soirée. He's up to some devilry, I think.'

Hannah liked Sydney but she commented: 'Oh, he shouldn't do that. They're only trying to help after all.'

Tim glared at her. He hated the idea of being an object of charity. Memories of the time when his mother was dying in Ireland after they lost the farm were too painful. He knew what it was like to be dirt-poor and hopeless. Then they'd needed charity and, though he was only a child, he'd sworn to himself that he'd never need it again. 'They can keep their damned help,' he said hotly. 'I'm not going and neither are you, Hannah. We're decent-living people. I earn good money by the sweat of my brow and I don't need the likes of them telling me how to behave!'

Hannah was tired and irritable. It had been a very warm, humid day, her back ached in a funny way and though she could not admit it to herself, the memory of Bullhead's jibe about Tim and Mariotta still rankled. 'You're always the best, aren't you, always perfect,' she stormed. 'You don't think they might be acting out of kindness. You might not need charity and help but there's plenty of others in this camp that do. I think it's kind of them to bother.'

He was tired too. His eyes were flashing as he turned on her. 'You're not going, Hannah. You're not to go to be looked down on by them.'

She flounced across the floor, or as near flounced as she was able to in her condition. 'I'll go if I want to. My Mam and I always used to go to the Ladies' Church soirées at Christmas for the widows and orphans of the two parishes. This isn't any different.'

Furious, he shook her arm. 'Don't go, Hannah. Don't dare to go.'

'And what would you do? Hit me – like Bullhead hit Mariotta? You surely wouldn't do that. You worried about her enough.' Then, appalled at what she had said, she stopped and stared at him.

He dropped her arm and turned for the door. 'I'm going to see Sydney,' he said, and left the house. When he came back an hour later she smelt beer on his breath. Neither of them mentioned what had happened and were scrupulously polite to each other for the next few days until the memory of their first fight began to fade.

When Sunday came neither of them mentioned the soirée. Hannah had been subdued all day and at about three o'clock she rose from her chair with a sigh and said to Tim, 'I think I'll go and lie down in bed for a little while. My back aches.'

He lowered the newspaper that he had been studiously reading in an attempt to make her believe that he'd completely forgotten about the soirée. 'I'll rub it for you,' he offered, and she smiled her old smile at him.

'You would too, wouldn't you?' she said, then sighed, 'But we can't make love any more. Is that why we've been arguing? I feel so heavy and ugly. Will I ever be pretty again?'

He stood up and hugged her. 'You're beautiful. I've never seen you look so beautiful. I love to see you like that with your round little belly sticking out in front. I feel I ought to be down on my knees worshipping you. Don't worry, you'll be back to your old self soon and then you won't be able to stop me getting into bed with you, morning, noon and night just like it used to be.'

She laughed and laid her head on his chest. 'Ah, that'll be lovely,' she whispered.

They were standing like that when the door opened to admit Sydney and Naughten, both dressed in their best with their hair plastered down. Sydney was sporting a scarlet neckerchief instead of his usual white stock and Tim cocked an eye at it. 'Going out in navvy gear, are you? What about the well-tried stock, then?'

'I don't want to disappoint the dear ladies,' drawled Sydney. 'They expect us to dress like this, you know, and to spit and swear and sing dirty songs. I wouldn't wish to let them down. Aren't you two coming with us?'

Hannah and Tim looked at each other and she said. 'No, I'm tired and I want Tim to stay at home and keep me company.'

'He seems to be doing that very well,' commented Sydney, wryly. 'All right, we're going and so are Panhandle and Gold Tooth and about twenty of the others. I've even persuaded Major Bob to turn up. I hope she doesn't get saved or she'll talk my ears right off. They're all on their way to Rosewell now. When it's over I'll come back and tell you what happens.'

Hannah waved an admonitory finger at him. 'Don't you go causing trouble. Those ladies mean well. They're trying to help and there's a lot of people in this camp who need it.'

Sydney put a hand on his white shirt-front. 'Me? Cause trouble? Never, my dear. I'll be the soul of – the soul of what? Never mind, I'll be the soul they're looking for. I'll let them save me.'

'I don't like the sound of that,' said Tim as Sydney's laughter died away.

In Bella Vista Francine was fussing around her mistress, pulling out the edges of her lace fichu, fluffing up her curls. 'But I'll be all crumpled by the time I get there,' said Bethya sharply. 'I wish you'd come with me. The other ladies will have their maids to help them.'

Francine's face went stiff. 'I can't come, Madame, please don't ask me. I'm terrified in case I meet that man again.'

'How silly. What could he do in a crowd like that anyway? I'd look after you. You can't hide from men all your life, Francine.'

The maid whipped round. 'I wish I could. I hate them. I hate the way they look and I hate the way they smell. *I hate them!*' There was such fury in her voice that Bethya was genuinely startled. She hadn't taken Francine's reclusiveness too seriously before, for she thought her maid was only shy and that one day she'd meet a man who would change all that because she was a striking-looking girl.

'Goodness, how violent you are. Why do you feel like that?' she asked in a wondering voice.

Francine's hands were shaking as she rearranged the ornaments on the dressing table. 'I hate them, that's all. I've had some bad experiences,' she said in a trembling voice.

Bethya patted her on the shoulder. 'Haven't we all, my dear. All right, I won't argue with you any longer. I'll go to the soirée with Gus' mother, the old dragon. I wonder if that odd man who always seems to be laughing at me will be there? I hope not, he makes me feel so uncomfortable.' Francine's eyes, as she listened to her mistress, took on a wary look but she said nothing.

Rosewell Square was crowded with carriages when the Anstruther barouche drew up. Everybody who was anybody had come to help at the Duchess' charitable occasion. Inside the hall were a line of long tables loaded with buttered bread, scones and colourful cakes. Ladies in lovely gowns rushed about with cups of tea in their hands, pressing them on bewildered-looking women and ragged children. There were far more helpers than those needing to be helped.

The Parish Church minister and his prim-mouthed wife

stood with the Duchess at the end of the hall surveying the gathering. The Duchess looked formidable in a scarlet gown and a huge bonnet, out of which a purple aigrette rose in the air like the favour of a mediaeval knight. 'I hope more than this will come,' she said in a ringing tone. 'There's only women and children here. Where are the men? They're the ones who need saving.'

At that moment the hall door was thrown open and in marched a body of at least thirty navvies, all in their best and brightest clothes. Some of them were genuinely interested, but Sydney's little group of ten or twelve were only out for a joke and were looking to him with his cruel wit to provide it for them. He walked in last of all and surveyed the crowd with an imperious eye. The first person he noticed was the beautiful young Mrs Anstruther, whose glorious dark hair and alabaster skin excited his admiration. He thought she looked like an exquisite doll but he felt he had her measure. He knew she was an adventuress through and through. This was all going to be much better fun if she was watching.

He started by marching up to the Duchess, elbowing the minister aside and grasping her gloved hand in his. 'God bless you, mum. God bless you,' he said in what he hoped was an authentic rural Shropshire accent.

Taken aback, the Duchess drew away from him but he kept her hand pinioned in his. 'What you're doing is a saintly thing,' he said loudly, gesturing with his chin at the tables of food. 'All this grub and us starving.'

She rapped him firmly over the knuckles with the handle of her parasol and he let go of her hand. 'Please go and sit down, young man,' she said. She was thinking, how strange – it was as though she knew him from somewhere, but that was impossible ... A feeling of disquiet filled her, as, with an exaggerated bow that would have seemed fulsome at the grovelling court of Louis XIV, Sydney retired.

While the Minister was saying Grace, there were heavy sighs and sounds of enthusiastic agreement from Sydney's part of the hall, but mercifully he stayed quiet during the tea, which was eaten with relish by the guests, especially the children. After the plates were emptied, the Duchess stood up from her place and with a sharp tap of her parasol on the floor, announced, 'Ladies and gentleman, Mr Patterson, our minister at Rosewell Paris Church, will now give an address.'

Silence fell. Mr Patterson stood up and launched into his talk in a mellifluous, pious-sounding voice. 'Dear friends,' he began, 'I hope you do not mind me calling you my friends, because you *are* my friends. This delightful event which Her Grace has so generously provided for us all has proved that. Dear friends, I have come here today to ask you to consider your ways. To ask you to wonder if you are doing the best with your lives, to ask yourselves if, when you answer to Our Father in Heaven, you will be able to say, "I tried my best, I did everything I could, I behaved well . . ."'

The devil entered into Sydney then. With a dramatic flourish he gave a strangled sob and sank his head in his hand. The Minister looked across at him with sympathy but went on: 'Some of you will have knowingly or unknowingly committed sins. These sins may be small or they may be great, they may be sins of omission or sins of commission, but when you come to the Day of Judgement, they will all be added up in your account. Do you drink? Do you take the Lord's name in vain? Do you tell lies? Have any of you – ' dreadful pause – 'committed even more serious sins? Have you stolen something that does not belong to you? Have you committed adultery?'

Sydney sobbed again, more loudly this time. Heads turned to look at him. Bethya saw who was making so much noise and her eyes widened in alarm for she had an intuition that Sydney's remorse was not genuine. She knew the object of the soirée was to persuade navvies to lead better lives, but she suspected Sydney of playing games. 'I hope the Duchess doesn't see through him, too, and never finds out that I was the one who invited him here,' she thought in a panic.

The Minister was well launched into his theme now,

elaborating on the evils awaiting sinners in hell compared to the pure delights of heaven. He concluded by telling his listeners, 'All you have to do is repent, stiffen your resolve to withstand evil. Swear today that you will repudiate evil, but most of all that you will never again touch a drop of alcohol! If you make that pledge, God will be on your side.'

There was a stricken silence in the hall while he paused and held up both hands to give his final blessing, but before he could get the words out, a man came dashing from the back of the crowd and threw himself at the Minister's feet. It was Sydney, of course. He was thoroughly enjoying himself playing the fool.

'What a magnificent address. You've made me see the light. I've been a terrible sinner. I've dallied with women, I've sworn and gambled and drunk fifteen mugs of beer a day for the past five years but now I'm going to stop. You've shown me the way, oh thank you, thank you!' he howled.

His performance was so histrionic that even Major Bob thought he was serious. She stood up from her seat and gasped, 'Oh, poor soul – he's not that bad! What's happened to him? I'll stop drinking too. I'll give it all up and go to live with my daughter in Liverpool who's married to a lawyer.'

Sydney could hardly believe his luck when he heard her. He moved back and let Major Bob go forward to the Minister who took her hand in his, glad that his preaching had fallen on fertile ground. The Duchess was more sceptical, however. Her eye was on Sydney and she saw the mocking expression on his face.

At that point her son the Duke arrived at the hall door. He had come to put in an appearance at his mother's soirée and to escort her home. He strode towards the platform just when the Minister was about to bless Sydney, and as he stepped up beside the sobbing man, he gave a start of surprise. Sydney looked up, met his eyes and had the grace to look abashed. 'Godders!' exclaimed the Duke, in a tone of total astonishment.

Sydney rolled his eyes and gave a heartrending sob, put his hands over his face and backed away, choking out in his rustic accent, 'Me sins are too great, m'lud. I can't bear it.' While the gathering watched in amazement he fled for the door and disappeared.

The Duke looked up at his astonished mother and asked, 'What's going on? What on earth was he doing?'

Mr Patterson spoke first. 'He was repenting of his sins, Your Grace.'

The Duke turned and stared at the half-open hall door. There was no sign of Sydney. He shook his head. 'I doubt it. I really do.'

'So do I,' said his mother acidly. 'Do you know him, Richard?' If the Duchess had not been so discomfited by the strange behaviour of the navvy, the look in her son's eye would have alerted her to the fact that he was keeping something from her.

'I thought I did, Mother, but I must be wrong,' he said.

The disruption meant that the impact of the Minister's address was lost, and the guests began drifting away with only a few taking the temperance pledge. Major Bob was among them, however.

To her own surprise, Bethya found that she was shaking with nerves when the affair ended, so rattled that she could hardly join in when her friends began speculating about the navvy's strange behaviour.

'Do you think he really had some sort of revelation?' they asked each other, but Bethya only shook her head and said, 'I've no idea. It was so strange ...' Inside, though, she was fuming. She felt that part of Sydney's charade – for she was sure it was a charade – had been directed at her, and this made her furious.

'What have I done that he wants to make fun of me like that?' she asked Francine when she reached home at last.

The maid shrugged. 'Perhaps he is mad.'

'He didn't look mad. In fact, he looked as if the whole thing was a huge joke to him. It made me very angry.'

'It is best to avoid him,' Francine counselled her grimly.

'Of course I will,' cried Bethya. 'I hope I never lay eyes on him again.'

After the soirée, summer came into its full glory. From early morning till late at night the sun shone down from a cloudless sky and the river which ran like a raging torrent in winter dwindled into a mild little stream that was possible to ford in places. Local people crossed it on stilts, a custom that was copied by the navvies who were now working on both banks. In the river bed, huge boulders, some only seen once in fifty years, stuck up starkly, and around the foundations of the old stone bridge, the hard-packed woolsacks of the foundations were clearly visible.

It was the most magnificent summer in living memory. The navvies stripped to their waist and laboured under a tropical blaze that turned their skin to the colour of mahogany. The sun dried out and cracked into wide fissures the earth they were digging; water spilled on it scattered like diamond droplets and then disappeared. It was as if the thirsty soil gulped them down.

The vista up the valley was half-obscured in a perpetual heat haze, with hill-tops seeming to swim above the ground like islands in a dreamy sea. When evening came the sky presented a pyrotechnical glory of purples, oranges, yellows and reds that filled it like a huge canvas. As day after brilliant day went by, gardens grew parched and leaves on the trees drooped grey and colourless because they were coated with a fine film of dust. People dragged buckets of water up from wells and rivers to slake the thirst of their flowers and vegetables, but the crops stopped thriving. They needed a downpour from heaven.

Camptounfoot was lucky, for it had many wells, sunk centuries before by the Romans and still in daily use. Almost every garden had one, neatly lined with blocks of red sandstone and covered over with a wooden lid, which, when lifted off, showed a green and glittering surface far below. Through all the days of drought, the wells still smelt sweet, though it took longer and longer to lower the buckets and a harder haul to pull them up again. Never in living memory had Camptounfoot's wells run dry, but after six weeks without rain wiseacres shook their heads and predicted that a calamity might occur if the dry spell did not break soon.

In spite of its name Rosewell did not have so adequate a water supply as Camptounfoot. The monks who built the Abbey had led piped water into it and to the houses that surrounded it, and later a big well was dug in the town square. Cottages along the river bank relied on its flow or its tributary streams for their water supply, but now that was running dangerously low too and the demands on the town well increased. The town magistrates imposed a time limit for bucket-filling – from six in the morning till half-past eight, and from six till eight at night. With moderation, they reckoned, the water supply would hold out till the rains came, as come they must. Now every morning people stood in the gardens and scanned the cloudless sky in hope of seeing a drift of white above the hills but they were disappointed.

The navvy camp was badly hit by the lack of water. The stream which was its main supply had dwindled to a trickle and women had to walk to Rosewell Square with their buckets to fill them at the town well, much to the annoyance of townspeople who resented what little water was left being drawn off by the navvies. When Hannah told him about the water available in Camptounfoot, Tim Maquire organised a daily water-cart to trundle from the village to the camp where its liquid load was given out at the rate of half a bucket per person.

The water problem did not greatly concern Christopher Wylie, who wanted the good weather to continue for as long as possible. He couldn't believe his luck in being blessed with such fine working conditions, and urged his men on to get the piers finished before the weather broke and the river became a torrent again. Daily the stonework rose, line upon line of neatly hewn blocks, gaining height but dwindling in thickness as they reared towards the sky. Wylie watched from the bank, fanning his face with a shady hat. On the day the first of the piers attained the height of one hundred feet, he threw this hat in the air and cheered like a boy. The next two were not long in reaching that height as well but the fourth pier – the one in the river that had given so much trouble – finally had to be redug; more cartloads of woolsacks arrived from Maddiston to be laid on rocks and concrete at the bottom of the huge cavity. Down they went, one upon the other, while Jopp and other sceptics eyed the work with disbelief.

'That'll never stand the first flood,' they said, but Wylie refused to be discouraged.

'I think it will, but I'm not going to take any chances. We'll only build the bottom of this foundation. We'll make it solid to above water level and then we'll leave it over the winter. If it withstands the floods, it'll withstand anything, and next spring we'll build the pier up to the same height as the others,' he announced. His absorption in his work allowed him to forget his anxiety about Arabella. Emma Jane's letters informed him that she was making a slow recovery, so at least she was not any worse. He wrote back and promised that when the good weather broke, he'd take some time off and travel to Newcastle to see them all.

The demands on him also closed his mind to his own state of health; he was almost too tired to eat Miss Jessup's delicious food when he finally made his weary way home at night. From time to time he saw Tim Maquire looking strangely at him, and more than once the young man advised him to take things easier. 'This weather's tiring enough for young men, let alone someone of your age,' he said warningly, but Wylie always shook his head.

'I've got to finish this bridge as fast as I can, and everything's going well at the moment so I'll run with it. I'll rest when it's over – then it's off to Menton with my wife and daughter to sit in the sun with my feet up like a gentleman.'

Tim laughed. 'I hope you do, but knowing you I wouldn't be surprised if you didn't go off and start building something else. We'd have to put you in leg-irons to make you stop, I think.'

During the hottest weather Tim had his own worries:

for Hannah who was finding it hard to bear. No longer could she walk to her mother's every day, and carrying heavy buckets of water from the cart or the burn to *Benjy's* was almost beyond her, so Tim paid one of the camp urchins to fetch and carry for his wife. The child was idle and had to be continually chivvied, which was tiring and annoying for Hannah.

'Why don't you go to stay at your mother's now?' he anxiously asked her on a morning when he saw her walking slowly across the floor with one hand pressed hard against the small of her back. There were few women in the camp he would trust with helping his precious wife when she went into labour.

Hannah was unwilling. 'Not yet,' she said.

'I think you should go now. Go back with your mother when she comes to see you today,' he told her, and worry made his voice sharp.

She frowned. 'You're very anxious to get rid of me, aren't you? It's not time yet, I tell you. I haven't even had a twinge and people say you always get plenty of warning. I'll go when that happens.'

'But what if it starts when you're alone – before your mother comes or when I'm out?'

She laughed and patted his cheek. 'You think it all happens in a few minutes, don't you? My Mam said she took two days to have me. I'll walk to Camptounfoot when I feel the first twinge. Walking's good for you when it's starting. It hurries it up.'

'Hannah, don't argue, just do what I tell you for once. Go to your Mam's,' he said, but he had no conviction that she would obey. Hannah was like that: she did as she pleased.

That meant all the time he was at work, he was on tenterhooks expecting to be summoned by Hannah's mother, but when evening came and he hurried home, his wife was always there, sitting in the sun by their door with her eyes closed and her huge belly resting on her knees. He liked to pause for a second to take a good look at her before he woke her up for she looked so wonderful, so peaceful and full of burgeoning promise.

One night Naughten-The-Image-Taker was sitting beside Hannah, drawing her, when Tim came home. She sat very still with her chin raised and her eyes fixed dreamily on the hills behind the camp as he sketched away. 'I'm doing a likeness of your lady, Black Ace,' said Naughten. 'She's got a lovely profile so I want to do her sideways on. You'll like it. It'll be her to the life, just wait and see.'

Tim looked over the crouching man's shoulder. Though Naughten was not skilful enough to give his drawing life, it was unmistakeably Hannah with her mass of curling red-gold hair and her proud high-bridged nose. 'Don't forget the pretty way her mouth curves – don't forget that,' he said, and Naughten cast a cheeky glance at him.

'If you're so critical, maybe you should draw her yourself, Black Ace.'

Tim grinned. 'I can do lots of things but not that. Make a good job of it and I'll pay you two florins.' Naughten's normal rate for a likeness was one florin, though he always started by asking for more. 'Done, two florins,' he said, and scribbled more colour into Hannah's cloud of hair.

When the drawing was finished and Naughten had been paid, he skipped off happily. Hannah held her likeness on her hand, staring at it intently. 'Do I really look like that?' she asked, and Tim leant his chin on her shoulder to scrutinise Naughten's work.

'In a way he has got you. He's got your hair and your lovely dreamy eyes and your mouth . . . but he's not got your soul, Hannah. It's not possible to draw that,' he told her.

She turned and put an arm round his neck. 'You've got my soul, Tim, and my heart too. Don't ever forget it.'

While the sun blazed down with ever-increasing force, even the most enthusiastic sun-worshippers tired of its relentlessness. On a day when the temperature rose to over one hundred degrees at noon, Christopher Wylie felt very faint and tired and told Tim that he was going back to the Jessups' to put his feet up.

'I'll come with you,' offered Tim, who was worried by the wan look in his boss's eyes but Wylie shook his head.

'No, stay here. Make sure the men on the sixth pier keep the line straight. I'll be all right – I won't walk fast, I'll take my time.'

The sun was beating down on his back like a relentless flail as he toiled up the hill that seemed steeper than ever before. The muscles of his calves ached strangely and he had pins and needles in his hands. All he wanted to do was lie down and close his eyes. The jutting-out wall of the Jessups' house reared into his sight at last and he headed for it with the feeling that once inside he would be safe. Through the gate into the shady garden he staggered and leaned panting against the garden wall. Miss Jessup was sitting beneath one of her apple trees playing with a kitten and she looked up in surprise at the sight of him.

'Oh Mr Wylie, what a colour you are. Come in and sit down. I'll fetch you some port. My brother's out but he'll be back directly,' she cried, jumping to her feet.

Wylie could only gasp through blue lips, 'Help me up the stairs, please, Miss Jessup. I must lie down.'

She was a simple soul who operated best when told exactly what to do, so he headed her for the house and leaned on her arm as they progressed slowly up the stairs. It seemed to take a very long time till they reached the top, but once there she held the door open for him to go through into his cool bedroom. He fell on to the coverlet and she bent over him to whisper, 'Would you like tea? I'll bring you tea.'

His voice sounded strange and faraway as he whispered, 'No, no. Just take my boots off, please.' She untied the laces and slipped them from his feet. 'Now leave me to sleep,' were his last words, telling her to tiptoe away.

Half an hour later, she returned and peeped round the door to see if he needed anything. His head was turned towards her and his blue eyes were wide open and staring but he did not reply when she spoke to him. Frightened, she closed the door quickly and went back to the garden where she stood wringing her hands and wondering what to do. Her brother took every decision in their lives and he was in Rosewell giving a music lesson. She did not even know which house he was visiting. Frantic, she opened the big gate and hurried into the street in search of someone to advise her. The first person she saw was Tibbie Mather, who was returning from visiting Hannah in the navvy camp.

Tibbie brushed the hair from her damp brow and paused when she saw Miss Jessup dithering about in the middle of the cobbles. She was obviously trying to block Tibbie's passage and something was bothering her but she couldn't get the words out. Sensing her confusion Tibbie said gently, 'It's a hot day, isn't it?'

Miss Jessup gulped before she replied. 'Yes, it's very hot. I'm awfully worried about Mr Wylie. I don't think the heat's suiting him either.'

Tibbie put her basket on the ground. 'Is something the matter with him?'

'I don't know. I'm not sure, Mrs Mather. He's lying in his bed with his eyes open but he's not speaking. Maybe you could have a look at him. My brother's out, you see . . .'

Something in the woman's voice warned Tibbie that this was serious. She tried to sound calm and reassuring as she said, 'I'll come in and speak to him if you like.'

Miss Jessup led the way, talking all the time. 'He's up in the big bedroom. It's a bonny room with a window looking into the garden. He likes that. He sits up there in the evening and smokes his pipe, poor man. He's fond of his pipe.'

The nervous flow of talk went on till they reached the bedroom door, where Miss Jessup paused and looked at the handle as if to touch it would burn her. It was obvious she meant her companion to open it but Tibbie rapped on the wood with a bent forefinger and called out softly, 'Mr Wylie, sir, are you all right?' When there was no reply, she called again, 'Can we come in?' Still no reply so she turned the brass handle and peeped inside. It only took one quick look before she closed the door again and took Miss Jessup's arm gently, saying, 'Come on back down-stairs, my dear. There's not much we can do for him.'

'Is he still asleep?' asked Miss Jessup.

'I'm afraid it's worse than that,' Tibbie told her. 'The poor man's dead. I'll go and fetch Jo. Now you sit down here under the tree and keep calm.'

As she hurried out into the street again and ran towards the opening of St James' Wynd, the hot spell suddenly ended – for the first drops of rain began to fall, splashing in huge drops on to the dry, dusty cobbles.

CHAPTER
Twelve

For several weeks, since the beginning of the good weather, Arabella Wylie had been improving in health and spirits. Every afternoon she was helped downstairs by Mrs Haggerty and Emma Jane to the garden, where she lay in the shade of leafy trees on a long wickerwork chair. She hated to be left alone, and if Emma Jane rose to fetch a book or tried to take a turn around the lawn, her mother would cry out, 'Stay with me, my dear.' She was not a querulous or ill-natured patient, for she was unfailingly grateful for everything that was done for her and frequently told Emma Jane how good she was. Patting her hand she would whisper, 'I don't know what I'd have done without you during this terrible time, my dear child. This illness would almost certainly have killed me if it wasn't for you . . .'

The doctor still came every day, and Emma Jane tried periodically to find out exactly what ailed her mother – but he remained very vague in his diagnosis. 'Hysterical . . . neurasthenic . . . highly emotional,' were his usual phrases. When Emma Jane asked directly, 'Will she ever get better?' he replied in a bright tone of voice, speaking loudly and clearly as if addressing someone of limited intelligence. 'Of course she will, my dear Miss Wylie. You must not worry about that, but it could take time.' His attitude infuriated Emma Jane and made her deeply depressed. 'What do you mean by "time"?' she wondered as she stared after his well-tailored back. 'Do you mean my mother will be like this until I, too, am old?'

She could talk to no one about her deep unhappiness, of the feeling she had of being a prisoner inside Wyvern

Villa, condemned to a sentence from which there was no release. In the evenings, she sometimes walked to the gate and watched couples strolling past arm in arm and envied them with a deep burning envy, which she felt was selfish and something of which she ought to be ashamed. Day after day she struggled against the terror that her life was passing without being lived, running out like an emptying basin, a relentless flowing away that she could neither channel nor stop. It was worst at night, when she lay sleepless in bed shuddering over nameless fears with tears sliding down her cheeks and soaking her pillow for no reason that she could pinpoint, only her conviction that she had to go on living in a long dark tunnel that had no way out, an unremitting trudge to the bitter end. The memories of how happy and carefree she had been at Camptounfoot and at Amelia's wedding were so cruel that she did not allow herself to dwell on them.

In August, Amelia came down from Hexham with Arbelle and the new baby – a fat, pink-cheeked little boy called Alfred. Emma Jane's mother managed to summon up some energy during their stay and delighted in the little girl who was, amazingly, growing into a sweet-natured and well-mannered child. 'Sit by Grandmama,' she coaxed Arbelle in the afternoons, and while the two of them were taken up with each other, Emma Jane was allowed a little freedom to take short walks with Amelia and the baby. On the last day of their stay, Amelia paused in the middle of a leafy path and, hoisting her sleepy baby up on her shoulder, she turned to face Emma Jane and say, 'You're miserable, aren't you?'

'Of course not. Mama's getting better every day. I mustn't be selfish . . .'

'Don't be silly. What sort of life is this for you? Who do you ever see?'

'I don't want to—'

'Don't you tell me no lies, Emma Jane Wylie. I saw you at my wedding dance. When are you going to tell your father to hire a nurse for your mother so that you can have a life of your own?'

'Mama wouldn't like a nurse.'

Amelia shrugged. 'I don't suppose she would. No nurse would do for her what you do. She's well enough to be left with Mrs Haggerty for a few days. I'm going home tomorrow. Come back with me for a bit – it'll do you good.'

Emma Jane protested, 'Oh no, she's not ready for that yet. We mustn't rush things.'

'I'll ask her if you like.' Amelia could tell from Emma Jane's expression that the thought of getting away even for two days appealed to her, so when they walked back to the garden, she said to her mother-in-law, 'I'll leave Arbelle with you for a few days if you like.'

Arabella looked up with a smile. 'That would be delightful! She's such a joy to me. I miss her so much now that you're not living here any more.'

Amelia smiled back. 'And I'll take Emma Jane in place of her.'

Mrs Wylie's eyes went to her daughter. 'But what will I do without Emma Jane?' Her voice sounded quavery and scared.

Amelia was matter of fact, however. 'You'll manage very well, like you did when she went to Scotland. The maids will look after you and Arbelle, and it'll only be for two or three days.'

Amazingly, Mrs Wylie stopped protesting and agreed. 'Of course. Emma Jane deserves to get away from my sickbed for a bit. Arbelle will keep me company, won't you, darling?'

The child put out a hand and took her grandmother's. They looked very like each other as they sat in the dappled shade, and watching them, Emma Jane felt sure that when Arbelle's day came, she too would be the Belle of Newcastle.

The arrangements were easily made. Emma Jane packed a little bag and went to bed early so that she could waken and be ready when Dan arrived with his big cart to take his wife home, but during the night, a frantic Mrs Haggerty came banging on Emma Jane's bedroom door.

She was crying out, 'Miss, Miss! Your Mama's bell's been ringing. She's not well. I've sent Haggerty for the doctor.'

When the doctor had been and a gasping Mrs Wylie was settled in bed, Emma Jane told Mrs Haggerty, 'He says Mama has a mild heart murmur. It's not serious, but it's worrying for her. I won't be going to Hexham with Amelia after all.'

The maid looked at her with a sagacious expression but all she said was, 'I'm sorry, Miss.' She did not explain what exactly it was that she felt sorry about, though later in the kitchen she told her husband and the other two maids, 'It's a terrible pity that the mistress relies on Miss Emma so much. She can't seem to see how unfair it is to keep her stuck at home like this.'

Haggerty shrugged. 'The mistress has always been spoiled. When Chris comes back, things should get better, though. Miss Emma needs a bit of freedom. She was a different girl when she came back from Scotland.'

Solemnly they sat at the kitchen table and talked about how they had hardly recognised Emma Jane after she returned from Camptounfoot, but one and all agreed that her flowering burst of youth and high spirits had been short-lived. Once more she was the old shy, self-effacing Emma Jane. They felt sorry for her.

The heat intensified. No one could sleep at night and Emma Jane got into the habit of sitting up in her nightgown at the open bedroom window till the small hours of the morning, when a misty coolness crept over the garden. Then, happy to be shivering slightly, she crawled into bed and fell asleep. When morning came she often slept on because of those late-night vigils, and the maids did not disturb her till after nine o'clock.

She was sound asleep on the morning a telegraph message was delivered to Wyvern Villa while dew still sparkled on the grass of the lawn. Slowly drifting into consciousness, her feeling of peace was cruelly ripped apart by a long wail like the howling of a banshee which rang through the silence of the house. She sat bolt upright and felt the hairs rise on the back of her neck at the

318

terrible sound. Leaping from the sheets she ran, still in her nightgown, out on to the landing, where she found Mrs Haggerty standing outside Mrs Wylie's bedroom door with both hands over her mouth and her eyes round in horror. From the other side of the door came hysterical weeping, the same wails and sobs as had echoed through the house on the awful day that James was killed. Emma Jane felt that time had turned back. They were living through that nightmare all over again. She stared at Mrs Haggerty, whose face was crumpled up like crunched paper and from whose open mouth no sounds came. Then she heard her mother's voice calling out, 'Oh Christopher, my darling, my darling, what will I do without you? Oh Christopher, oh Christopher.' Emma Jane swayed and leaned against the wall for in that instant she knew that her father was dead.

Then, as soon as she collected herself, she ran into the big bedroom and cradled her sobbing mother in her arms. One by one people came. She sent for Amelia; she despatched messengers to their lawyer and her mother's doctor; she wrote letters to her Aunt Louisa and her father's sister. The friends who came to commiserate or help were met by Emma Jane, whose eyes looked enormous and seemed to burn like golden lamps in her peaky face. She was unnervingly calm as she told them. 'A message came to say that Papa's dead.' She was too shocked for tears. Amelia came that afternoon and burst into the house like a whirlwind, but Emma Jane greeted her with the same calmness and the same words she had used to greet everyone else. She only began weeping when her sister-in-law put both hands over her face and sobbed, 'Oh no, oh no, not him. He's such a good man – not him, it's not possible.'

It was as if her open grief was permission for Emma Jane to grieve, too, for she had been staying strong to help her mother who was inarticulate with weeping. The two young women clung together and cried as if their hearts would break until Amelia lifted her head at last and asked, 'How did it happen? How did you find out?'

'We got this,' said Emma Jane, bringing out of her pocket the paper with the awful news that had fallen from her mother's bed on to the floor that morning. Amelia puzzled over it. 'But it doesn't say what happened. Do you think it was an accident?' she asked, but the message was stark and uninformative. It only said: *Regret to inform you that Christopher Wylie died today. Await instructions. John Jessup.*

'Instructions – have you sent any? What are you going to do?' were Amelia's next questions.

Emma Jane stuck out her chin and said, 'I've been waiting for you to come so that I can go to Camptounfoot.'

Amelia shook her head. 'Oh no, you can't do that. It has to be a man. I'll send Dan.'

Emma Jane argued quietly, 'But Dan doesn't know Father. They've never met, have they? It wouldn't be right for him to go. I'm going – I'll leave now. There's a late train that'll take me to Maddiston. Haggerty's harnessing the horses to carry me to the station. I've been to Camptounfoot before – I know the village and I know the Jessups. It's my place to go.'

'But – but – someone must go with you. If you wait till one of my sisters comes from Hexham to take care of the children, I'll go too,' protested Amelia but Emma Jane was not even listening to her.

'You must stay here with Mama and try to calm her a little. I'm going now and I'm going alone because I can't waste time waiting for someone to escort me. Please don't argue, Amelia. Try to help instead. Stay here till I come back with . . . with Father.'

'You're bringing your father back here?' whispered Amelia.

Emma Jane looked surprised. 'Of course. Where else should we bury him except in his own family grave with James?'

Even Haggerty thought it was a bad idea for her to go to Camptounfoot. Twice she had to order him to bring round the carriage and when he finally did, he stood in the hall and argued with her. 'There's plenty of men up there at the bridge that'd bring your father home. He has that good assistant Maquire, hasn't he? He'd bring him back.'

She was impervious to objections. White-faced but completely calm, she stepped down to the carriage. Then Haggerty put his hand on her arm. 'I'll come with you, Miss Emma. You can't go alone.'

She turned on him and snapped like an angry little dog. 'Haggerty, I'm going and I want to go on my own. I insist *on going alone*. Besides, you'll be needed here. Stay and do your job.'

At the station he put her into an empty ladies' compartment as if she were a child, tucking a rug around her legs and standing looking anxious on the platform as the train pulled out. She gazed bleakly back at him through the smeared glass, not waving, not smiling, her eyes huge and her face very white. 'This is a nightmare,' she was thinking. 'This isn't happening – I'm dreaming. Any minute now I'll wake up and find it isn't true.' But she didn't wake up. The train pulled out of Newcastle and with a shrill scream started to build up to its top speed of thirty-five miles an hour, going in the direction of Morpeth and Berwick with its heartbreaking bridge. Bitterly she remembered how much she had enjoyed the journey the first time she'd done it, how she'd stared out of the window at the line of white dunes and gun-metal-coloured North Sea, but this time it was dark outside and the windows were streaked with driving rain. The world looked as if it was in mourning.

There was a little corner of her mind that simply did not believe her father was dead, and she secretly hoped that when she got to Camptounfoot she'd only find him ill again perhaps, or injured in an accident but alive. He couldn't be dead, just like that. He couldn't have gone from his family without saying goodbye. The journey seemed interminable. The lights of little villages and isolated farmhouses slipped past the window and she watched them with a distant stare. If they'd all been burning down, her blank expression wouldn't have flickered. She was totally outside her own body, unaware of how she was feeling physically, only concentrating on her thoughts and these were directed towards her father. She didn't wonder what was going to happen to her mother and herself in the future, she only throught about the next thing to be done and that was to get to Camptounfoot.

The train was late in arriving at Maddiston and the town looked grey and miserable beneath sheets of rain that seemed to be trying to make up in hours all that it had denied the earth during the weeks of drought. Clutching her bag, for she had brought little with her, Emma Jane descended a flight of steps from the platform to the station yard and held up a hand to summon a cab from the waiting rank. The man she got was not her old driver but a stranger. 'Where to, Miss?' he asked.

'Camptounfoot, the village beside Rosewell.'

'I know it. I'll have you there in half an hour.' He glanced back over his caped shoulder at the girl in his cab and thought what a po-faced little madam she looked. Not one to make conversation with, or flirt a little to. It was very dark when they left the town; rain was still falling and trees, houses, even the animals in the fields, seemed to swim in a sea of grey mist. Lights twinkled from cottages and farmhouses with a diffused watery glow so that they looked like friendly islands in a hostile world, and Emma Jane felt very alone and lonely as she rode past them. Then she saw the lights of Rosewell clustering close together. The town was deserted, for it was after midnight when the cab rattled past the stark ruins of the Abbey, black against the grey sky, and over the cobbles of the Square, passing beneath the glow of the wall-mounted oil lamp that illuminated the narrow entry of the East Port. Now it was only a short drive to Camptounfoot and her heart began to beat fast and her teeth to chatter at the anticipation of what she was about to endure. 'Oh God, don't let me collapse. Help me through this,' she prayed, and gritted her teeth so tightly that the cabbie heard the grinding noise and looked round in surprise.

The Jessups' house was in darkness from the street side,

but when she went through the gate she saw a lamp shining out of the first-floor window which she knew had been her father's room. Her heart gave a leap and she thought, 'He's up there looking at his plans. He's not dead after all!'

Mr Jessup in a nightgown and nightcap answered her knock and gazed at her in amazement. 'Miss Wylie! We didn't know you were coming.'

'I'm sorry, there wasn't time to let you know.' She was shivering visibly so he opened the door wide and said, 'Come in. Where are you staying?'

She shook her head in a bewildered way. 'I don't know.'

'You'll have to stay here but my sister's been badly affected by this. She's had to take to her bed . . .'

'I won't need looking after, Mr Jessup. I just want to see my father and hear what happened to him.' Her voice cracked as she spoke because now she knew that her father was indeed dead. Touched by her distress, John Jessup took her into his little sitting room, blew up the fire and thrust a glass of port into her hands before he told her as gently as he could about Wylie's unexpected death. She listened quietly with her head down and when he had finished, she looked up and asked. 'Where is he?'

'In his old room. Jo, the village undertaker, is keeping watch with him.'

'Can I see him, please?'

'Of course, my dear.' The girl was still silent but Jessup saw tears pouring down her cheeks. He put out a hand to help her to her feet and led the way to the stairs.

A sinister figure dressed in black was sitting at the foot of Wylie's bed. Emma Jane flinched at the sight of Jo because he looked like the Grim Reaper, and his presence brought home to her with terrible clarity the truth that her father had really gone. The body seemed very long as it stretched out beneath a white crocheted blanket, but mercifully the face was covered. She thought if she'd had to look at it now she would have collapsed in hysterics.

Fighting to stay in control, she whispered, 'He didn't suffer, did he?'

The black-coated man looked up to reveal lantern jaws, unshaven cheeks and deepset eyes like burnt holes in his face. 'The doctor from Rosewell said it was instant. His heart just stopped. The weather's been awfy hot and he was down on that site day and night for weeks. He was too old for it.'

She stood in the doorway. 'Where's his assistant, Maquire? Does he know Father's dead?'

The undertaker nodded. 'Aye, he does. He's been here but his wife, Tibbie Mather's lassie, has gone into labour a month early and he's had to go back to the camp. Ane goes oot and ane comes in, that's what they say. It never fails.'

Emma Jane shuddered. It seemed to her that the low-roofed room was full of listening shadows, people who had lived and died there before. Perhaps her father was among them now. She wished she could tell him of her grief, assure him of her love, console and comfort him as he left the life he had loved so well.

Mr Jessup was standing behind her on the landing, and from the way he put his hand on her arm while he said, 'Come away, Miss. Come away and lie down,' she guessed that her appearance was ghastly. Suddenly that awareness brought on a wave of such weakness that she had difficulty in staying erect but swayed and had to support herself by leaning against the wall. Mr Jessup's face became even more worried, and it was obvious that he feared having yet another casualty on his hands. 'Come, my dear, you can sleep in the same little room you had before. Come now . . . you're in no fit state to do anything more tonight. Jo's going to sit up with your father and I'll be here too. Tomorrow's plenty of time for everything else.'

When she woke next morning she had no idea where she was, and lay staring around the white-walled closet in amazement for several seconds. The cot-bed was shrouded in white muslin curtains, and high up in the wall a tiny square of window with four minute panes like a doll's-house window let in a narrow shaft of light. The light was cold and grey, and told her that the weather was gloomy outside. Then the terrible realisation of where she was and why she'd come there swept over her like a cold wave. Shuddering, she quickly rose from bed, pulled her travelling shawl over her nightgown and hurried through to her father's room. The black-coated undertaker was still there, head nodding as he dozed in a chair by the bedside. A guttered candle flickered on the table and filled the air with the smell of burnt wax. The lamp in the window had gone out.

Very quietly Emma Jane walked across the bare boards of the floor and lifted the corner of the blanket. Her father was dressed in his best dark-grey suit, with a pristine white cravat tied beneath his chin, but a handkerchief was bound round his head to hold his jaw in place, and two copper coins rested on each closed eyelid. His skin was a pale-grey colour like chamois leather, and his neatly-combed white hair fanned out around his face like an aura. He looked like someone she had seen in a crowd, only vaguely familiar. It was his elegant hands, crossed on his chest, that really unlocked her grief. How often as a child, she'd hung on to those hands, how often she'd watched with admiration as he unrolled his plans and pointed out things to her with those long fingers. On the third finger of his left hand he wore a gold ring with a flat black stone set in it, and the sight of it was too poignant to bear.

She took his beringed hand in hers and started to cry, great heaving sobs of pain that racked her body and made her chest ache. The agony and grief that had been so long penned up inside her flowed out as if a dam-gate had opened. She did not care about disturbing Jo or anyone else in the house, she did not care who heard her, but sobbed on and on till she felt cleansed and strangely free. In a peculiar way she was weeping not only for her father but for many other things that had blighted her life for too long.

When her weeping started, Jo woke, jumped from his chair and left the room, leaving her to mourn alone but the Emma Jane who eventually wiped her face was a different girl from the one who'd arrived at the Jessups' house the previous night. By giving vent to her grief she had exorcised some of the demons that haunted her.

She kissed her father's ice-cold cheek and was gently pulling the blanket back over his face when a tap came on the door and Mr Jessup's voice asked, 'Can I bring you a cup of tea, Miss Wylie?'

To her amazement she felt very hungry when she heard this. 'Thank you,' she said. 'I'd like some tea but don't bring it in here. I'll come downstairs to drink it.' She was sorry for being a nuisance to him because she knew he was very harried by looking after his still-shocked sister as well as having Emma Jane's dead father and his weeping daughter to worry about.

Her trim and business-like behaviour in spite of her swollen, tear stained face was an intense relief to her host when she stepped into the neat little parlour. 'Jo's gone home for his breakfast. He'll come back with the – er – he said he'll come back with the coffin in about an hour. He always keeps one ready, half-made I mean, you see,' he told her.

'That's good,' she said and sat down at the table, grateful that he'd provided bread and butter as well as tea for she was starving and tried not to eat too voraciously. Hunger did not seem correct in her circumstances but Mr Jessup pushed the plate towards her, saying, 'Eat it up, please. What do you intend doing now?'

'I'm taking my father home to Newcastle. I'll need to hire a cart to drive us to the station. I told our coachman Haggerty to meet every train at Newcastle from noon today till I arrive, and he's bringing a hearse as well.'

Impressed, Jessup asked, 'Do you want somebody to travel with you? I can't leave my sister, but Jo'd go to Newcastle if you wanted, and he'll bring out his cart to take your father to Maddiston.'

She looked confused. 'Thank him for the use of his cart but it won't be necessary for him to come to Newcastle with me.' Her tone was very definite because the idea of making the train journey with the Grim Reaper by her side was too horrifying to contemplate.

Mr Jessup went off to pass on her wishes, and when she was finishing her third slice of bread, the door opened. Tim Maquire stepped into the room. His chin was dark with stubble and his curly hair disordered. He looked exhausted, and he glared at her out of red-rimmed eyes as he said, 'Mr Jessup tells me you're taking Mr Wylie home. Do you want me to come with you?'

She stared at him in surprise. 'But the undertaker said that your wife's having a baby. Has it been born yet?'

He shook his head. 'Not yet. It's not due for another month really but she started last night. It could go on or it might stop, the women say . . . Her mother's with her.' He was distracted with anxiety about Hannah, who had been seized with labour pains in the middle of the night, and he hated the idea of leaving her in travail, but he felt as if he was being hauled in two for he was fond of Christopher Wylie and had loyalties to him as well. The sudden death had come as a tremendous shock to him, and he wanted to express his feelings by helping Wylie's daughter. For the first time in his life he was totally confused, torn between worrying about Hannah and shocked about Wylie.

The girl sitting coolly at the table eating bread and butter did not seem to appreciate what he was implicitly offering her. She looked up now and told him: 'It's kind of you to offer Mr Maquire, but no, thank you. The undertaker said he'd come but I refused him too. Everything's arranged at the Newcastle end. I'll be perfectly all right.'

She sounded as if she were talking to a casual acquaintance, not to someone who felt as close as a son to Christopher Wylie, Tim thought angrily. She didn't appreciate that he too might be grieving and want to give practical expression of his grief. 'Poor old Wylie, if this hard little piece is his daughter,' he thought. He glared at her and she was taken aback by his evident hostility. In her surprise at Maquire's reaction she returned her most intimidating look, the one that even quelled Arbelle. He was good at intimidating stares too, and gave her one back of equal ferocity.

The atmosphere in the room froze. 'I'll go home right away. Hannah needs me more than this cold bitch,' he thought. Then he remembered that he had not paid the customary respects to the dead man. He was not going to say he was sorry to her, but what he could say with honesty was, 'I had the greatest respect for your father, Miss Wylie. He was good to me. Everyone here will miss him but me most of all. I know I'll never see his like again, as a builder or as a man.'

She dropped her head to hide from him the fact that she was in danger of weeping again. 'Thank you. I'll tell my mother what you've said. Now if you'll excuse me, I'll have to start getting ready to leave.' She stood up from the table and pushed her chair back. He was flustered and surprised that she did not say anything about what was to happen to the work in progress. She'd never mentioned the bridge or said who was to take over from her father.

'Do you want his men to go on working?' he asked roughly.

She looked surprised. In all her grief and confusion, the matter of the bridge had not yet concerned her. 'Yes, of course. Yes, the men must go on working,' she said. She cast her direct glance at him again and asked, 'Will you do the same as you've always done?'

He was stiff and ready to take offence at anything she said, but for Wylie's sake he replied, 'Of course I will. I'd do anything for your father and I know what that bridge meant to him.'

Through the window she saw the black shape of Jo coming up the path. That was the signal it was time to go. 'That's good, thank you. I'll let you know what's going to happen when I know more myself,' she said and turned to leave the room. He stared after her in disbelief. Not a word about who was to take over the contract, not any enquiry about how the work was getting on. His heart surged with anger at her disregard of the work that had engrossed, and killed, her father.

Jo spied Tim standing in the parlour and called out, 'Give us a hand with the coffin, lad.' He had another two men with him, weedy-looking specimens who were none too keen on work, and they stood back while Tim and Jo negotiated the coffin round the bend in Mr Jessup's stairs. Then the black-painted box was laid on the flat bed of the cart and covered with a drapery of black velvet rimmed in tarnished gold, the village mort cloth that had covered every Camptounfoot coffin for nearly two hundred years. At that point, Emma Jane came out of the house carrying her holdall and a large folder with all her father's plans for the bridge. Tim stared at them and without thinking, asked abruptly, 'Are you taking those away? I might need them.'

She looked surprised at his objections. 'But I want to look at them too. I'll bring them back as soon as possible. Just do what you know he's sanctioned in the meantime.'

'My God,' he thought with rage, 'she's treating me like any navvy, like a spadesman. I helped to draw those plans up, but she doesn't know how much I've done on the bridge and she doesn't care either.'

He stood with his hat in his hand as the cart drove away. He wanted to go to Maddiston with it; he wanted to see Mr Wylie off on his last journey but she didn't ask him and he didn't offer. Though he'd have gone with Emma Jane if she'd needed him. he was glad not to be put to the test because he was in an agony of anxiety about Hannah.

Her labour had started the night Mr Wylie died, and as he looked back on the events since, he felt bemused by the obtuseness of fate in making everything happen at the same time.

When Miss Jessup and Tibbie found Wylie dead, the first thing they did was send one of the little Rutherfords from the village to bring Tim, who came running up from the bridge. He was overcome with grief at the sight of his dead employer and friend, but soon wiped his eyes and became practical. Though Emma Jane did not know this, it was Tim who had gone and found Mr Jessup in

Rosewell; it was he who had organised the sending of the message to Wyvern Villa and had fetched a doctor. Then he went home to check on Hannah, whom he found well and happy, before returning to sit through the first night with the corpse, grateful that the weather had turned and the rain had cooled everything down. Early in the morning Jo arrived to measure for the coffin and Tim went home again. Though it was early, Hannah was already up and feverishly scouring the floor of their little house.

'What are you doing?' he asked in disbelief.

'I couldn't sleep. I've a bad pain in my back and I kept thinking about poor Mr Wylie so I decided to get up and clean the house. That way it'll be perfect when the baby comes,' she said.

He'd heard that women sometimes got a burst of energy before giving birth and his eyes were anxious as he asked, 'Has it started? It's too early.'

She shook her head. 'I don't think it's started. It's just that I have this pain—'

Her face contorted as she spoke and he grabbed her, asking, 'How often do you get the pains? Are they regular?'

'I'm all right. It's just backache,' she insisted, and made him lie down on the bed where she lay beside him and the pair of them slept for a couple of hours. When they woke, she said her backache had gone and he went to the bridge. All the men had heard about Wylie's death and some were working but others were not, so it fell to Tim to chivvy them back with assurances that everything would go on the same as usual. The bridge had to be finished. He felt he owed it to Mr Wylie to see that it was.

He was walking from group to group promising that their wages would be paid, when the little Rutherford from Camptounfoot came racing down the field calling out, 'Your wife's started. Mrs Mather's gone to the camp to help her.' Once more he was running over the fields, and did not slacken his pace till he reached the door of *Benjy's*, which was firmly closed. As he was about to open it he heard a terrible groan coming from within, and his heart dropped like a stone into his stomach.

'Dear God, look after my Hannah,' he prayed aloud.

Tibbie saw his anxious face looking in and waved to him to stay where he was. In a few minutes she came out and told him, 'I'm fair mad at her. She must have had those pains for at least a day but she held off from telling us. I think she did it because she wants to have the bairn here.'

He understood. He knew Hannah wanted to have the baby in *Benjy's*, in their bed, surrounded by the things they'd bought with such love and enthusiasm. 'Is she all right?' he asked.

Tibbie clapped his shoulder. 'She'll be fine – just leave it to me. I've sent down to Rosewell to a friend of mine who delivers babies. She's the best in the town.'

'Get the best, the very best. I don't care what it costs,' said Tim. 'Should I go to fetch the doctor?'

'Heavens no, everything's normal. I'll tell you to get a doctor if there's any problems but I don't think she'll need him. Now you go back to work and keep your mind off it. Leave this to the women.'

He went back to the Jessups' to find out what was happening, but everyone there was waiting for news from Newcastle and there was nothing he could do. He returned to the bridge but found it impossible to concentrate, and was glad when the time came to stop work and he could walk back to the camp with Sydney. With every step he took he thought, 'When I get home I'll find Hannah's had her baby . . .'

But she hadn't. Tibbie and her friend were looking more harassed than before and shooed him out of *Benjy's* with no ceremony at all. Before he went he saw Hannah lying in bed with her hair plastered around her face. The sight made him frantic with anxiety.

Sydney was outside and put a hand on his arm. 'Come up to Major Bob's for a bit of supper and we can have a hand or two of cards.' Tim enjoyed card-playing and was skilled at it, but tonight concentration eluded him. All he could do was sit by Major Bob's stove and stare out at the steadily falling rain between forays down to *Benjy's* to check on Hannah.

'Why's it taking so long?' he asked every time he came back, and Major Bob laughed at him.

'How long's it been?' she enquired. 'Only since this dinner-time? That's not long. Some women labour for days. I remember one woman . . .'

'BOB!' said Sydney in his most ringing tones. 'That'll do. We don't want any of your horror stories, thank you. It's a pity you're teetotal now or you could have uncorked the brandy bottle and knocked this poor suffering expectant father out.'

At dawn next morning, before going to the Jessups', Tim was at the door of *Benjy's* again with a headache that felt as if an army of gnomes were driving spikes into his skull. His mother-in-law opened the door and shook her head. 'Not yet . . . it's sort of stopped,' she said in a weary voice.

'Oh God,' he cried, putting his hand to his eyes. 'I can't stand this. What's wrong? This can't be normal.'

Even Tibbie looked worried. 'She's getting tired,' she whispered as she pulled him into the room.

Hannah's face was being washed by the midwife but she saw him and called out his name in a voice that broke his heart in two. Anguished, he rushed over to her and took her in his arms. 'Oh Hannah, my darling Hannah, it won't be long now. I love you, Hannah. Oh God, I wish this had never happened.'

She put her hand on his head and whispered. 'Tim, oh Tim. Don't worry.'

He felt Tibbie pulling at his shoulder and stood up. She spoke softly in his ear. 'Wait outside. We're going to have a look to see what stage it's at. I'll call you when we know.'

When she finally appeared, he said impetuously: 'I don't care what you say, I'm going to fetch a doctor for her. This can't go on.'

But she was shaking her head and looking more cheerful. 'There's no need for that. The doctor would only haul it out – he's very impatient in birthing cases. She's farther on than we thought. It won't be long now – we've just got to be patient. I was like her. It took me a long time, too, because we've both got narrow hips but she'll do it, don't worry. Go away for a couple of hours and when you come back you'll be a father.'

He was in an agony of worry while he was with Miss Wylie at the Jessups', and by the time the cart drove off with her and her father's coffin, more than two hours had passed. He could not get back to *Benjy's* quickly enough, running and tripping over stones as he went, careless in his haste. The door was still closed but this time he did not knock, only charged through it as if the devil himself were at his heels.

Tibbie and the midwife were standing by the stove gazing at something wrapped in a white shawl in Tibbie's arms. They looked up at him and his mother-in-law said in a faltering voice, 'You've got a daughter.'

He didn't stop or make any comment. Instead he threw himself at Hannah's bed and knelt on the floor beside her. She was lying with her eyes closed but she opened them when she heard him saying, 'Hannah, I love you. I love you more than anything or anyone in the world. I nearly went out of my mind at the thought of losing you. I don't care if we never have another baby. I don't want to go through all that again.'

'Oh Tim,' she said reprovingly. 'Take a look at her and you won't say that.'

He turned as Tibbie held up the baby and put it into his arms – a little doll, so small and fragile in his big hands that he was afraid he would hurt it. But as he looked down at the little face a warm river of love flooded into his heart. 'My daughter, my own wee girl,' he gulped and walked across to Hannah again, laying the child down on the cover beside her. 'Oh, thank you, Hannah. We're a family now. Nothing'll ever separate us,' he said and burst into tears, for once not caring who saw him weep.

*

While Tim and Hannah were adoring their new daughter in bright and cosy *Benjy's*, Emma Jane's train was pulling into Newcastle station which was dank and smoke-filled, a suitable setting for misery and mourning. Haggerty was waiting by the platform gate with Christopher Wylie's lawyer, Mr Johnstone, and a cousin of Emma Jane's called John Alexander, the son of her father's sister in London, whom she had not seen for several years. They all rushed towards her as she walked along the platform, their faces anxious.

'You should have waited till I came. You shouldn't have gone alone,' said John, taking her arm. He was a pleasant-faced young man with bright ginger hair, and sharp brown eyes which scrutinised her face with concern.

'I couldn't wait, I had to go,' she told him sadly and he nodded in sympathy as he hurried her to where their carriage was waiting under the station portico. Obviously he was intent on getting her out of the way before her father's coffin was unloaded. With a sigh she gave herself up to his ministrations. It was a relief to feel that things were out of her hands now. She was immensely tired, too tired to weep, too tired to speak, too tired to think.

Wyvern Villa had taken on a sinister and intimidating look. Every blind in the house was drawn; the knocker was muffled in black crepe, and a funeral wreath made of black ribbon and dark-green bay leaves decorated the front door. Inside there was even denser gloom and silence – total silence. The footsteps of Emma Jane and her cousin seemed to echo in a most unsuitable way in that house of mourning. Mrs Haggerty came tip-toeing over the hall to open the door to them and she whispered, 'Your Mama's asleep. The doctor's been. Mrs Amelia's in her cottage with the children but she's coming back in half an hour.'

'Is Mama any better?' asked Emma Jane. The maid shook her head.

'Oh no, she's very poorly. Worse than she was over Master James, much worse.'

Emma Jane shuddered. The memory of her mother's grief at that time came back to her with awful immediacy.

She quailed at the thought of coping with it again. 'Should I go in to her?' she asked but Mrs Haggerty shook her head.

'Not yet – let her sleep. The doctor's given her valerian. You look tired, Miss. I've prepared your bed and I'll make you some tea. Go and lie down for a bit.'

The fact that she was being treated with kindness and consideration broke Emma Jane's strength of will and she started to cry, swaying in the hall with her hands over her eyes, sobbing and sobbing as if her heart would break. John and Mrs Haggerty had to half-carry her upstairs. When John was descending the stairs again, Amelia appeared in the hall and looked up at him. 'How is Emma Jane?' she asked.

'Terrible – she looks like a walking corpse herself. She's not going to be able to stand much more of this, I'm afraid. Heaven knows what we're going to do with her and her mother,' he said, shaking his head.

Amelia did not look too despondent, however. 'I think there's more to her than people imagine. She's not the little mouse she looks. You'll be surprised by Emma Jane,' she told him.

After three terrible days of mourning and waiting for the funeral, Christopher Wylie's cortège moved away from his house in splendour, attended by a line of fifteen black carriages full of mourners, for he was a well-known and highly respected man. The only flowers decorating the hearse were huge white trumpet lilies, and the body had been transferred from Jo's rough box into a coffin of black ebony decorated with silver, which was carried in a glass-sided hearse drawn by two pairs of black horses with magnificent black ostrich-feather plumes nodding from the polls of their heads. Their harness was made of black patent leather studded with silver bosses. It was a sight to chill the most insouciant heart, and people on the streets stood still with their hats off or heads bowed in acknowledgement of mourning even though they did not know who it was that had died.

Mrs Wylie was too distraught to attend the funeral and

remained in bed, attended by her sister Louisa who had arrived from Harrogate and her sister-in-law, John's mother, who anxiously dispensed medicines to her and vainly tried to soothe her continual weeping. In the absence of her mother, Emma Jane, as principal mourner, rode in the first carriage with Amelia, Dan and her Cousin John. She was totally silent during the journey and sat as stiff as a statue in the corner of the carriage, draped in black crepe with a thick veil obscuring her face. Her mind was numbed. She felt as if she was watching a performance on stage with herself as one of the actors. Consistent thought was beyond her but strange mental pictures kept flashing into her mind – sometimes she had a glimpse of her father's room in the Jessups' house, the room in which he had died. Then she remembered holding his hand and walking in a field of flowers when she was very small; but most often she kept seeing the bridge, not as it was now, half-finished and surrounded by piles of raw stone and heaps of bricks, but soaring and high, a magnificent creation. That must be how he had imagined it. 'I wonder if I'm picking up his thoughts,' she asked herself as she stared through the mesh of her veil at the coffin on the carriage in front.

Did they bury him in the huge graveyard on the outskirts of the town, or did she imagine the whole thing? Had she stood with her family at the church door and shaken the hands of the mourners as they filed out – or was that imagination, too? Did they all return to Wyvern Villa for glasses of sherry sipped in great solemnity?

As he was leaving the house after the grimmest day of her life, Mr Johnstone, the lawyer, shook Emma Jane's hand and said gravely, 'I'll come back to see you tomorrow, Miss Wylie. There's a geat deal to discuss, of course, and this is not really the time.' She could tell by his tone that what he had to impart would not be good news.

He arrived at eleven, and when Mrs Haggerty had shown him into the drawing room, where John was waiting, Emma Jane came shakily downstairs, holding very tight to the banister. There was a strange weakness in her legs and she was mortally afraid of falling. Mr Johnstone and John both rushed forward to help her to a chair when she stepped into the room. The lawyer, who was looking worried already, frowned even more deeply as he watched her, wondering how this frail girl was going to cope with the news he had to deliver.

'I'm sorry Mother can't come down,' said Emma Jame softly when she was settled in her chair.

The lawyer nodded sympathetically. 'I was told that she is very ill with grief,' he said solemnly, 'but what about you, Miss Wylie? Are you sure you can stand a business discussion today?' The girl seemed to be shivering with cold although the room was oppressively hot.

She stared up at him wide-eyed as if in surprise. 'Oh, I'm all right. Tell me what you came about, please. Is it Father's will?'

Resolving to get this business over with as quickly as possible, he whipped a spectacle case out of the pocket of his coat and perched gold-rimmed spectacles on his nose. 'Yes, it is. There are several things to explain to you. Do you wish Mr Alexander to stay with you while I go through these matters?'

She looked at her solicitous cousin and leaned towards him. 'John, would you mind if I heard all this alone, at least in the beginning?'

John did mind, but he stood up immediately and said, 'Of course not. I'll wait in the library – call if you need me.' It struck him that her shivering might not be caused by cold but by apprehension. She was bracing herself for bad news and wanted to hear it unobserved by anyone else. Poor Emma Jane, he thought, for he had a better idea than she did of the fraught state of his uncle's finances.

When John had left the room, Mr Johnstone sat forward in his chair and brought out a folder of papers from his case, saying in a matter-of-fact tone, 'Then let's start. It shouldn't take long – your father left a very simple, uncomplicated will. After your brother's sad accident, he made a new will and left the bulk of his estate to your mother. On her death everything reverts to you, of course; she has only a life rent of it. There are one or two small legacies as well: five hundred pounds to your coachman Haggerty, for instance; fifty pounds to Mrs Haggerty; a thousand pounds to your niece Arbelle, and some personal things like pictures and furniture to your sister-in-law Amelia.'

He was accustomed to defensiveness or outrage when people heard that things in their home had been bequeathed away from them, but Emma Jane only gave a little smile and said, 'That's good – Amelia deserves a legacy. But what about her cottage?'

Mr Johnstone shot a quick glance at her as he said, 'The cottage is hers outright: your father gifted it to her. It is not part of his estate – just as your annuity is yours entirely. The capital was bought in your name.'

She sat back with a sigh of relief. 'I was wondering what would happen about my allowance.'

'It's not a large annuity but at least it is secure,' he said, and a certain note in his voice made her open her eyes wide and stare into his face.

'What do you mean?' she asked fearfully.

'Miss Wylie, what I have come here to say is that your annuity is the only sure income you and your mother possess at the moment. I don't know how to tell you this, but your father's affairs were very confused when he died. I'm afraid he could not have gone at a worse time as far as his family is concerned.'

To his amazement she did not seem surprised. 'How bad is it exactly?' she asked, but before he could reply she hurried on, 'I hope there's enough to pay the outside legacies?'

He nodded. 'We'll manage to find the money for the Haggerties, and to pay for the funeral. There are also several tradespeople and sub-contractors who owe your father money from various projects in the past. I'll put pressure on them to pay up, but I don't expect to bring in much more than will cover the immediate outstandings. Larger sums like your niece's legacy will have to wait.'

She made no comment, only fixed her yellow eyes on his face as he went on, 'There's also a problem about this house, Miss Wylie.'

'What do you mean?'

'Your father pledged the deeds of it against a loan from the bank to finance his work on the bridge. He made an arrangement with your sister-in-law that you and your mother should go to live in her cottage if his loan was ever called in ... That agreement was verbal and will only work to your advantage if your sister-in-law honours her promise. There is nothing in writing.'

'Amelia's a very trustworthy person,' Emma Jane told him, and then: 'Are you telling me we have to give up Wyvern Villa? Mother's too ill to be moved. Can't we wait a little while?'

He looked at her with surprised respect. He'd expected tears, protests, complaints – but she was taking it with admirable calm. Perhaps she didn't understand what he was saying?

'It is likely that you will lose this house – perhaps not immediately, but soon. I've arranged a meeting with your father's railway clients and his bankers the day after tomorrow, and I'll let you know what's decided as soon as possible. You see, the only tangible asset the estate has, is the half-finished bridge. When it is completed, there is a considerable sum of money due to your father's estate, but not until then. It will pay off his debts easily but the bridge must be finished first,' he concluded.

Now he was ready to leave, for he thought he'd told her enough bad news for one day, but Emma Jane stood up and halted him with an outstretched hand. 'I know – I've been thinking about that. Perhaps it will be possible to hire someone to finish it for us. The bridge was very important to Father. I'd like to accompany you to that meeting,' she said.

'Miss Wylie, it may last quite a long time. It may also become quite – argumentative, shall we say? I'll have to fight for everything I can get. Bankers are not sentimentalists – they're not moved by sympathy, only by balance sheets.'

'This is something of immense importance to me, Mr Johnstone. I want to take part in whatever is decided. Can I go as my mother's representative? Is that possible?'

He looked at her sharply. 'Mrs Wylie is the person who is likely to suffer most through this. If she designates you as her representative I don't suppose there will be any problem about you sitting in on the meeting.'

She nodded. 'Where is it to be held and when?'

He told her and she said, 'I'll be there, with Mother's authority. Thank you for coming to see me, Mr Johnstone. This must be very difficult for you.'

He turned in the doorway and said in a heartfelt way, 'It is. I was an old friend of your father. Fate's been very cruel, taking him at this time when he didn't have a chance to sort out his problems as he would have done, I'm sure. I'm sorry, Miss Wylie.'

When he left, Emma Jane put on a heavy cloak and set out to visit Amelia. Though the distance was little more than 200 yards, she felt strangely weak and ill before she got there, and in Amelia's little parlour sank into a deeply cushioned chair with a trembling sigh. Her sister-in-law was angry with her. 'You're in a state of shock. You shouldn't have come here. You should have sent Haggerty to fetch me.'

Emma Jane shook her head. 'We can talk quietly here. At home the aunts are always running in and out, never giving me any peace. Listen, Amelia, the lawyer's been to see me. He says Father's financial affairs are in a real mess. We'll have to sell Wyvern Villa.'

Amelia was not surprised. 'It's that bridge – he'd sunk everything into it,' she said sadly.

'It's not nearly finished yet, either, and I don't know what I'm going to do about it. We'll have to sell the contract, I expect,' said Emma Jane.

'The bridge is somebody else's business. What matters

as far as you're concerned is that there's no money.'
Amelia was, as always, very practical.

'It's even worse than that, I think. I got the feeling that
Mr Johnstone wasn't telling me everything. There might
be lots of debts. I'm going to the meeting he's having with
the bankers, then I'll find out exactly how things stand,'
Emma Jane told her.

'That's a good idea. At least you'll hear what's what.
It's always best to know the facts,' agreed Amelia.

'They won't take me seriously unless I go as Mother's
representative, though. She has to appoint me to act for
her.'

The two young women stared at each other. 'Even if
she was able to write it she probably wouldn't. She doesn't
think women should dabble with business matters. She'd
tell you to leave everything to the men,' said Amelia.

'That's what I was thinking,' agreed Emma Jane.

Another silence fell till Amelia announced, 'It's a pity
I've not got much of a way with handwriting.'

'I have,' said Emma Jane.

'Then write it yourself. Write it and sign it. No one'll
ever know.'

Which was exactly what they did.

Since Madame Rachelle measured Emma Jane for the
purple costume she had lost weight, but in spite of that it
still looked impressive when she put it on and turned
slowly before her mirror. She knew she ought to be in full
mourning, but she was sick in her soul with always
wearing black. This outfit gave her confidence, and that
was something she would need in abundance before the
afternoon was over. Besides, she intended to leave the
house without anyone, especially her Aunt Louisa, seeing,
so her lapse from mourning etiquette would go unnoticed.

Haggerty drove her to the offices of the bank in the
middle of Newcastle. She had been there before but the
awesome solemnity of its marble hall with porphyry pillars
supporting a domed glass roof always made her quail a
little, and she was quaking even more than usual as she

341

walked over the gleaming inlaid floor to Munro's office, where she was admitted by a sepulchral-looking young clerk in a black suit. When the door swung wide she was ushered into an enormous room with a Turkey red carpet, upon which stood massive mahogany furniture glittering like glass. Johnstone was there, so was Munro and beside them were several men who were introduced to her in turn . . . Sir Geoffrey Miller of the railway company, Colonel Anstruther, Mr Raeburn, Mr Smith the financier and Sir Rupert Caldecott. Only Anstruther was familiar, for she remembered seeing him riding round the bridge workings with his daughter-in-law. The other names she had heard her father mention, and knew he'd had deep reservations about Miller in particular

Mr Johnstone showed her to a chair and told the gathering, 'Miss Wylie has come as the representative of Mr Wylie's heritors, gentlemen.' They nodded. Some smiled – two looked across at her and expressed their sympathy about the death of her father. She nodded back, murmured her thanks and crossed her gloved hands in her lap, demurely waiting . . . It did not take long before the purpose of the meeting emerged. The main matter of concern was the bridge. How much remained to be done and who would do it? What it would cost? Had Wylie's death caused much of a setback?

She listened with growing dismay as they debated, making it obvious from what they said that her father's death was only a side issue to them. Her lawyer kept trying to steer the discussion back to his client's concerns but with little effect until, losing patience, he snapped, 'How much will you pay Miss Wylie to relinquish the bridge contract, then?'

Sir Geoffrey Miller turned his head, lifted his eyebrows and gave a deep sigh. '*Pay*? My dear sir, Wylie's contract with us was quite specific. If he failed to finish the bridge, there would be no payment. He took a gamble on that and he was to be paid partly in cash and partly in shares. Because he was in need of capital to buy materials and pay his workforce, he received most of the cash when the work began. I suppose you could say that he owes *us* money.'

It was obvious to Emma Jane that this development was not welcomed by her lawyer. He said sharply, 'That was a very hard contract, gentlemen. Surely you're not going to hold Mr Wylie's estate to it?'

Miller's eye was steely. 'A contract is a legal undertaking, Mr Johnstone,' he replied.

The antagonists looked hard at each other. Colonel Anstruther opened his mouth to say something, and Emma Jane had the feeling that in spite of his red-faced, bluff appearance, he was kinder and more chivalrous than the others, but Miller quelled him with a look and went on, 'We are not the only people with claims against Wylie's estate, are we? The bank holds promissory notes for a great deal of money, does it not? Mr Munro the banker is one of our directors on the railway company board.'

The implied threat was apparent and Johnstone sighed, 'What do you propose?'

Miller smiled slightly and joined his hands together in an upturned 'v' with the fingertips touching and the wrists apart. 'We will write off the debt to us – what the bank does is the bank's business – if we can take over the bridge lock, stock and barrel. We'll put in our own man to finish the job. Luckily he's there now, organising the labour on the line between Rosewell and Maddiston, so he knows the ropes. We will need Wylie's plans and specifications, of course . . .'

'That means you get more than half of a bridge free,' said Johnstone wryly.

'Hardly free. We made an advance, remember – and there was a contract.'

Johnstone was angry and his eyes were blazing as he protested, 'What you have paid in advances wouldn't buy you one quarter of the work that has already been done, and you want all his plans as well. That's robbery, gentlemen.' Emma Jane, leaning forward in her seat, felt her own anger rise. She wanted to chime in and support

343

him, but knew it was more politic to keep quiet. Her mind teemed with angry thoughts of the days and nights her father had laboured over his plans, the love and dedication he had put into them and the dreams he wove around this, his last great project. 'We can't just give it away to those rogues,' she told herself.

She could see from the look on Mr Johnstone's face that he was thinking the same thing, but at that moment Munro the banker leaned across the table and pushed another sheaf of papers in his direction. 'These are the details of Mr Wylie's indebtedness to the bank,' he said coldly.

Johnstone picked them up, turned the pages rapidly and put them down quickly. Though he said nothing, Emma Jane could tell that what he read had discouraged him. He looked in her direction and then said to the other man, 'Could I have a few moments with my client, please? We'll go into the anteroom.'

'Of course,' said Sir Geoffrey in his most courtly manner, rising and opening the door. The others rose too as Emma Jane walked out behind her lawyer with her head in a whirl.

Johnstone took her arm and steered her into a smaller room next door where he stood with his finger pressed against his forehead, saying, 'I cannot imagine what possessed your father to sign that contract. It's highway robbery. He never told me half of its restrictions, nor about what he owed either. Those debts must have been building up for years. It's much worse than I feared, Miss Wylie. I had hoped to salvage something for you and your mother, but that is looking less likely now.'

She stared at him from level eyes and said fiercely, 'I know it would be sensible to give up the contract, but I hate the idea of them taking over his bridge like that. It meant so much to him.'

'Oh, they'll finish it,' he assured her. The emotional aspect of the affair meant little to him.

'But it won't be *his*. I remember he said that he wanted it to be his memorial . . . now it'll belong to someone else.'

Johnstone looked at her in surprise. 'What's more to the point, my dear, is that you and your mother are being cheated out of your inheritance. That's what worries me most.'

'They're threatening us, aren't they? Perhaps we're stronger than we think. I've got the plans, after all,' she said.

Johnstone stared at her. 'Have you? Have you everything? There are no copies anywhere else?'

'Father didn't make any copies. He just kept working over and over again on the same plans. I helped him when I was staying in Camptounfoot, and so I understand them perfectly. Everything's noted down – specifications, stresses, all that sort of thing . . . I brought them back with me when I brought his body home. I knew he wouldn't want me to leave them.' Her voice was sad as she remembered gathering up the scattered papers in his room at the Jessups'.

Johnstone suddenly became jubilant. 'My dear girl, that was a stroke of genius! That may be the first ray of light in this whole dirty business. Now let's go back in there – and leave this to me,' he cried.

The others were waiting, confident that everything would go their way. Johnstone kept his face solemn as he sat down again after Emma Jane had been ceremoniously re-installed in her chair. 'Let me hear your final proposals, gentlemen. Surely you will be prepared to pay Miss Wylie and her mother something?' said the lawyer.

Again Miller was the spokesman. 'We'll take over the half-built bridge and put our man Jopp in charge of the work. Because we don't want to be too hard-hearted, we will pay the Wylie estate two thousand pounds. We feel that's very generous under the circumstances.'

Johnstone looked at Munro and asked, 'How much money exactly is outstanding against Mr Wylie?'

Munro shuffled his papers. 'At this moment, fifteen thousand, five hundred and ninety-two pounds.'

Johnstone switched his stare back to Miller. 'Two thousand won't go far in paying that off, will it?'

Miller snapped, 'He owed most of that before he ever got involved with the bridge. I know he owed ten thousand at least.' Johnstone gazed pointedly at Munro, who had the grace to look down. There was only one place that information could have come from – and they all knew it.

Then Johnstone addressed them, and this time, his voice was full of confidence. 'Miss Wylie has in her possession her father's plans, gentlemen, and she and her mother, as his heirs, have inherited his contract with you, especially since there is money still to be paid to them for it. I suggest that your offer to her should be more realistic before she does anything about giving up the plans or the bridge contract. If she so chose, she could hire another contractor to complete the bridge, and then claim her dues from you.' Having said his piece, he sat back and awaited their reactions.

Miller was the first to speak. 'This is nonsense. The bridge is half-finished and the contractor is dead. It is of paramount importance that the work be completed as quickly as possible. The lines from the north and the south have nearly reached the river: they'll be there by next spring. We don't want the opening of the line to be held up for months. Every day that passes means we lose money.'

Now, for the first time, Emma Jane took part in the discussion. 'The bridge is ahead of schedule – I can see that from the plans,' she broke in. 'If my father had lived, he would easily have finished on time.'

Miller shot her a look of open dislike. 'But he *didn't* live, did he? We could call in our own men and build an ordinary bridge quite quickly, but your father's grandiose scheme is already too far advanced. For myself, I'd be sorely tempted to pull it down, but by this stage that would cost more money than continuing with the thing.'

She stared at him aghast. 'But it's going to be the most beautiful railway bridge in the country! He designed it with that aim in view. You can't pull it down and put a stumpy little, ordinary-looking bridge in its place.'

He leaned forward and said with cruel deliberation, 'If

it wasn't for the fact that those high embankments on each side have already been built up, and the stone piers laid, I would. But it'd mean making deep cuttings at each side of the river and that would take another year. I never liked the damned thing from the start, I can tell you. Now my concern is getting it finished.'

Johnstone stepped in again. 'Give Miss Wylie and her mother fifteen thousand pounds and they'll hand over the plans.'

Miller slapped the table hard with a clenched fist. 'Never! We're left with a half-built bridge and you're asking us to pay almost the full price for it. We've got the contract. We'll take you to court and force you to finish it yourselves rather than pay that sort of money.'

Emma Jane heard herself saying in a clear, resounding voice, 'I'll finish it then.' Everyone, including Johnstone, stared at her.

'I beg your pardon?' asked Miller.

'I said that I'll finish it. I'll take on the responsibility for my father's contract and finish it. I've got the plans – I can hire engineers. I shall complete it and hold you to the contract. It'll be quite lucrative in the end, won't it, Mr Johnstone?' She looked at her astonished lawyer who had been shaking his head, trying to make her stop talking.

'Yes, it will. There's a big share offer, and when the line's running you'll be able to sell them at a profit, that's certain,' he was forced to say.

'Enough to clear the estate debts?'

'Oh yes.'

She looked back at Miller. 'Then I'll finish the bridge. I'll honour the contract.'

Again Johnstone asked for privacy to discuss the problem. Again he and Emma Jane went to the anteroom. Johnstone's kindly face was creased with concern as he said to her, 'I hope you're only trying to wheedle more money out of Miller, Miss Wylie. You don't know anything about building bridges.'

'Oh, I'm quite serious. I'll easily find people who do

know about bridge-building. Father had a very good assistant and he's still up there continuing with the work. What's more, I helped my father with his plans. He explained everything to me and I'm sure that with the right labour force, I could do it. The plans are very specific, you know. Father was most meticulous.'

'How old are you?' Johnstone asked her. He had been thinking of her as little more than a child dressed up like a woman of fashion in her purple clothes, but the way she was speaking now made him reassess her, and he realised there was more to the mousy-looking, shy girl than first appeared.

'I'm twenty-five,' she lied.

'I'd no idea Christopher's daughter was as old as that,' he said.

She saw she was wearing him down and pressed her advantage by saying, again not completely truthfully, 'After James died, I helped Father with his plans and drawings, especially on this bridge. I know all about it, and I want it to be built exactly as he intended. If we leave it to them it'll end up a cut-price version. You can see that, can't you?'

'Perhaps a little less lavish expense might be a good thing from your point of view,' he suggested but she shook her head.

'Oh no. This will be my father's memorial, and it's not done to skimp on the cost of a memorial, is it? I'll build his bridge. I'm quite sure I can do it.'

Johnstone groaned, 'I don't think I should be allowing you to do this. What will your mother say?'

Emma Jane reached into her reticule and brought out the paper she and Amelia had concocted. 'She's given me complete control. If this is what I decide to do, no one can really stop me, can they?'

Half an hour passed before they went back to the big boardroom, and during this time, Miller had changed his attitude from aggressive to oily. He pulled out a chair for Emma Jane, enquired if she would take a glass of sherry or should he send for tea? She declined both and sat with her unsettling eyes fixed on his face so that he was forced to fidget with his papers as he began, 'We've discussed your problem and we think that if the Wylie estate wishes to continue with the contract that is acceptable to us – with qualifications. To safeguard ourselves we must insist that our own engineer Jopp works with your men, Miss Wylie, and we must also ask that you confirm in writing the finishing date stipulated with your father. When you do this, we also want you to agree to a penalty clause covering us against late or non-completion. There will be a financial deduction from your final payment for every week overdue – let's say five hundred pounds – and if you fail to complete, we pay you nothing. *Nothing*.' He looked at Johnstone and added, 'As you know, a time-clause is normal business practice.'

Johnstone stared back. He thought: 'Miller's sure she'll not be able to do it. He's gambling on her using the plans to get the project over a sticky stage, but falling down at the end.' He turned his head to look at Emma Jane, trying to tell her with his eyes not to agree. He wished he could say to her, 'We've got Miller on the run. In a moment he'll up his cash offer for the plans and let you out.' To his horror, however, the girl was sitting forward in her chair with her eyes shining. She looked transformed, almost unrecognisable, not the wan little thing who had come into the room two hours before.

'I'll accept that. I'll finish on time,' she said.

Outside, her carriage was waiting and as he handed her into it Mr Johnstone looked as if he was about to burst into tears. 'I shouldn't have allowed you to do such a disastrous thing. I blame myself entirely. I should have insisted that you settled for cash. He'd have gone to ten thousand in the end, you know.'

She patted his arm consolingly. 'Please don't worry, Mr Johnstone. I'm quite sure that the bridge will be built – and built by me. In a way I think this is what my father wanted me to do. Perhaps that's why he showed me his plans and told me so much about the bridge. Oh, by the way, what will we do about the money we owe to the bank? Do you think they'll insist on it being paid back immediately?'

Johnstone nodded. 'I thought of that too. I've a meeting with Munro again tomorrow. I'll let you know what's decided afterwards.'

She opened her mouth to suggest that she attend the meeting with him, but he held up a constraining hand, 'Munro and I will be best left to talk it out ourselves, Miss Wylie. Have confidence in me – I've your best interests at heart.'

Amelia was waiting at Wyvern Villa, sitting in the drawing room with Arbelle and the baby in a basket by her feet. Not even the plain black gown she wore as mourning for Christopher Wylie could dim her glorious life force and vibrancy. Her eyes were alive with interest as she looked at her sister-in-law. 'What happened, then? Did you manage to screw some money out of those railway men?'

Emma Jane took off her Madame Rachelle hat and put it carefully on an empty chair where it lay like a deposed crown. She felt that some of her confidence went with it and she said in a scared tone, 'Oh 'Melia, I'm wondering if I've done the right thing. I've said that we won't give up the contract for the bridge but that I'll finish it on Father's behalf. That's the only way we'll ever end up with any money at all, you see. And even then it won't be much – just enough to keep Mother in modest comfort for the rest of her life, really.'

Even Amelia was surprised. 'You're going to finish the bridge, Emma Jane! But you don't know anything about bridge-building, and you'll have to go up there and live. You'll have to work with those navvies!'

'I know, I thought of that. I'm not worried about going up there. I've been before, remember. I'll write and ask the Jessups if they'll give me Father's old rooms. The navvies don't worry me either – Maquire will see to them.'

Lights sparkled in Amelia's eyes. 'Well done, girl, well done. But what do you know about building bridges? Not much, I'll be bound.'

'Quite a lot, really. I helped draw up the plans. I've read a lot about it, too. I was interested, you see. I feel in my bones that I understand and that I can do it. I've got that sort of a brain.'

'But what about the men? They might not want to work for a woman,' suggested Amelia and Emma Jane nodded. She remembered Tim Maquire's lowering stare every time he spoke to to her.

'I intend to go up there and ask Maquire to be my site manager. If he says no, I'll find someone else. There's not much railway-building going on right now and there should be a lot of good men looking for work.'

Amelia rose from her chair and walked across the room to embrace the girl facing her. 'My dear, I knew you'd a lot of your father and James in you. If there's anything Dan or I can do to help, you've only to ask.'

Emma Jane laughed wryly and said, 'There is something you can do. I'm going to have to give up this house. The bank owns the deeds anyway and I can't afford the cost of keeping it going. I'll sell most of the furniture and silver to raise money for expenses while the bridge is being built, and I'll give the house to the bank to help repay some of Father's debts. They're much worse than we thought, 'Melia.'

Amelia nodded. 'I guessed they would be. He was a very worried man at the end. Do you want me to give you the cottage?'

'Yes, please. Just for Mother to live in. I'll give it back to you when I've finished the bridge and sold the railway shares they pay me with. I can't afford to pay Arbelle's legacy yet, either, but I will – I promise.'

Her sister-in-law laughed. 'Of course you can have the cottage.'

'You don't mind about losing it, then?'

'Mind? Of course not. Your father gave it to me so that if something like this happened, you and your mother would have a place to go. He and I talked it through. But bless us, Emma Jane, what are we going to tell your mother? She won't like leaving Wyvern Villa.'

'I'm afraid she'll have to. I've been working things out. I'm going to ask Aunt Louisa from Harrogate to take Mother south for a few months. Everything will be done by the time she gets back.'

Amelia threw back her head and guffawed. 'I'll make sure to be in Hexham that day, but I'm afraid I'll be able to hear the fuss she'll make even from that distance.' She turned to her daughter who was listening with round eyes and pointed a stern finger at the child as she said, 'If you breathe a word of this to your Grandmama, Arbelle, your aunt and I will eat you on toast for tea!'

Emma Jane was impressed to see that Arbelle's eyes widened at this ridiculous threat but she nodded with sincere obedience as she said, 'I won't tell. I promise I won't.'

Next day Mr Johnstone came back from his meeting with Munro and said that, to his surprise, the banker had been favourably impressed by Emma Jane and would not insist on immediate repayment of Wylie's debts in full, though he did want Wyvern Villa to be sold. Emma Jane took this in her stride and said, 'Yes, we'd already decided on that. Mama and I will make our home in Amelia's cottage. It's quite big enough for us now and Mrs Haggerty has said she'll continue looking after us. She and Mr Haggerty will live with us, though we won't be keeping a carriage. Haggerty will do the garden.'

The old coachman had never shown any interest in flowers or gardens before, but he had come to Emma Jane and said that he wanted to go on working for her, doing anything, and without wages. He'd even offered to lend her back his legacy, for he knew that things were going to be hard with her for a long time. Sometimes Emma Jane thought the Haggerties must have secret listening-places all through the house, because nothing ever happened without them knowing about it. She refused his money but gratefully accepted the offer of help, for the old couple had been with the Wylies all her life and to lose them would be like losing members of the family.

It seemed now that life was in a whirl. She spent her

time running up and downstairs to her mother's room, or conferring with Mr Johnstone and Amelia about the move to the cottage, arranging for the sale of the big furniture and pictures, the gleaming silver and the carriage with its pair of matching horses.

A letter arrived from Mr Jessup saying that of course he would be happy to have Emma Jane as a lodger, but only for a little while. He went on to explain that Christopher Wylie's death had brought on a severe mental collapse in his sister and she was not as capable as she had once been of looking after their establishment, which meant that the bulk of the cooking and cleaning fell on him. There was even a suggestion that, if her nerves did not recover, she might have to return to Manchester where they had relatives. '*I'm sure you'll agree that it's not seemly for a young lady like yourself to live in a house with a single gentleman,*' he concluded.

Emma Jane then wrote to Tim Maquire, addressing her letter to the navvy camp in Rosewell, and informing him that she intended returning to the bridge as soon as possible, and explaining her problem about accommodation. Perhaps, she asked, he could advise her where she might find more permanent rooms, because her stay at the Jessups' could only be for a few days. She hoped that the work was going well and said she looked forward to seeing all that had been done.

By the end of the week, her mother had agreed to be packed off to Harrogate with Aunt Louisa and when the still-unsold carriage drove off from the front door, Amelia and Emma Jane looked at each other in eager anticipation. 'Well, girl, this is it. This is when your adventure really starts. Good luck, good luck,' cried Amelia.

CHAPTER
Thirteen

When the Rosewell post-runner brought the letter from Newcastle to the door of *Benjy's*, Hannah, nursing her baby at her breast, looked at it with apprehension. 'Who's it from?' she asked, wondering if she ought to accept it, for neither she nor Tim had never received a letter before.

'How should I know? Just take it, Hannah. It's got your man's name on it,' said the postie, who was in a hurry.

She eventually stuck it up on the shelf beside the pretty china and laid her baby in a basket beside the bed. They'd called their daughter Kate, which was the name of Tim's dead mother, and both parents thought she was the most beautiful baby ever born. Hannah spent hours sitting in silent adoration of the child, softly brushing its silken cap of pale hair, curling and uncurling the little fingers and holding the warm little body close. When Kate slept too long, her mother was always in a fever of eagerness for her to waken so that she could nurse her again.

Today, the weather was strangely threatening and thunderous, with a dark grey sky and tension in the atmosphere that gave Hannah a funny feeling in her head – not a headache exactly, more a constant sensation of a headache about to arrive. Though the sun was not shining, it was very warm and her clothes stuck to her all the time. Everything that had to be done seemed to require tremendous effort, and she felt pity for Tim labouring down at the bridge. When he came home in the evenings he was always dog tired and grey-faced; even the effort of conversation was beyond him. Not that she herself was any more energetic. She didn't go out much because the walk to her mother's bearing Kate in her arms seemed too difficult.

She wished the weather would break and the crisp days of autumn could come, for it was early October, but still the heat persisted and the sky kept its purple colour. Thunder and lightning had always frightened Hannah, but now she scanned the sky, hoping for the dark build-up of clouds that would presage an electric storm because she knew only that would clear the air.

Her water-bucket was almost empty, so while Kate was sleeping she decided to walk to the burn and fill it. The little water that remained in the bucket had an oily film on top of it – a sinister, multi-coloured sheen. Wrinkling her nose, she poured the dregs out on to the pot of geraniums at her door and walked down to the watering place, where some of the other camp women were filling their buckets. They all knew her now as Black Ace's wife and greeted her with, 'Isn't this heat terrible?'

'I'm worn out. The bairns are all greetin' and the milk goes off in an hour. I wish it would rain,' said one of the younger women.

Major Bob was there too and she lifted her head to tell them, 'I don't like it. This is fever weather – I've seen it before. It can turn nasty. Don't keep food overnight: make sure it's fresh.'

The young woman snorted. 'Fresh – in this place? That truck-shop hasn't had fresh meat for a week and the butter stinks so strong that it would drive you out of the room.'

'I'm only telling you,' said Major Bob shortly. As she turned to walk away Hannah saw that her face looked yellow and waxen, and she wondered if the old woman was ill. Hurriedly she filled her bucket and rushed back to her house where, mercifully, Kate was still asleep. Her mouth felt dry and she was very thirsty so she dipped a cup into the water and drank it down. That was all that she wanted, for her stomach couldn't face the thought of food after the talk about rotten meat and rancid butter.

Tim was late coming back and the sky above the hills had turned to midnight grey when she finally heard his step at the door. The first thing he always did when he came in was to look at the baby, who was sleeping again after having been suckled, dressed in a clean gown and wrapped in its soft blanket. 'Oh, she's as bonny as ever,' he said with a little laugh and then looked at Hannah. 'And so's her mother.'

She reached for the letter. 'This came for you. What is it, do you think?'

He ripped it open with his fingernail and ran his eye down the words. 'It's from Wylie's daughter,' he said. 'She's coming up to Camptounfoot the day after tomorrow and she's looking for lodgings. Why can't she go to the Jessups'?'

Hannah knew the answer to that. 'Miss Jessup's fair out of her head these days. She was always pretty strange, but Mr Wylie dying was the last straw. She's gone like a bairn and her brother's awfy worried about her. He couldn't cope with a lodger as well.'

Tim looked up at her. 'Do you think your mother would take her? There's the Abbey Hotel, but Mr Wylie said it was full of bugs so we can't send her there. Ask your mother tomorrow and say it won't be for long. She's a city girl and she'll go back to Newcastle soon. She's probably only coming to tell us she's giving up the contract, anyway. Jopp's been going on about taking it over. I'm sick of listening to him.' Tim's tone was bitter and she could tell that he was angry and disillusioned.

She put a hand on his arm and said gently, 'Don't take on, Tim. You'll find another place to work. We don't have to stay here.'

'I know that, but I've put a lot into that bridge, just like Mr Wylie did, and look what happened to him – it killed him. It's a funny thing, but the stretch of line between Maddiston and Camptounfoot was called the Lucky Line because it hadn't claimed a life till Mr Wylie died. Now everybody's waiting for the next death. There's always more than one.'

Hannah shuddered. 'Oh, don't talk like that, Tim. Come and have your supper. Tomorrow I'll ask my mother about taking Miss Wylie. I don't know if she will, though – remember what she thinks about the railway. What's Miss Wylie like again? Mam'll want to know.'

Tim shrugged. 'You know. She was in the carriage with me on the bridge that day you took umbrage. You called her "a wee thing in a black bonnet". She's a fierce-looking little thing if you ask me, an old maid in the making.'

'Oh, that's cruel. She didn't look so bad. I was jealous of her because I thought she was your ladyfriend, remember,' protested Hannah.

Tim laughed. 'You were just being silly – playing me up. I know what you're like.'

In spite of the oppressive heat, which seemed even more suffocating next day, Hannah tied Kate into her shawl and walked to Camptounfoot. Tibbie was sitting in an arbour of honeysuckle with her cat on her lap and her knitting on the ground beside her. When she saw her daughter and granddaughter she held out her arms in delight. 'Oh, I was just thinking about you. I was going to walk to the camp to see you, as I was feared that you were sick.'

'I'm fine but this heat's terrible,' said Hannah, wiping her face.

'You've not got the fever in the camp, have you?' asked Tibbie anxiously.

'What fever?'

'They're saying that fever's broken out in Maddiston, and the folk in Rosewell are terrified of it coming there. I was afraid it might be in the camp. There's such a lot of folk there now and it thrives in crowded places.' It was true that the population of the camp had grown in the last few months as more and more men poured in to work on the lines that were advancing from two different directions. Mr Wylie's summer effort on the bridge had also meant that his labour force was doubled, and these men were still at work under the direction of Tim.

'I've not heard anything about fever in the camp . . .' Hannah said, but Major Bob's gloomy prediction came back to her mind and she resolved to take every precaution to keep their food fresh and free of flies. She'd heard tales about the fever killing people in their hundreds in big towns like Edinburgh, but Camptounfoot, with its deep clean wells, had never had an outbreak in her lifetime.

When she told her mother about Miss Wylie needing lodgings, Tibbie nodded her head. 'I know, Mr Jessup told me about her. He was fond of her father and he's sorry that he can't put the girl up, but his sister's away with the fairies these days. He's got to keep an eye on her all the time or she'd wander off and maybe get lost on the hills or drowned in the river. I asked him if Miss Wylie was likely to stay for a long time but he didn't know. I wouldn't mind taking her for a wee bit, but I'm not wanting somebody living with me all the time.'

Hannah was astonished at her mother's change of tune but wisely forebore from making comment on it. In fact Tibbie, like most of the people in Camptounfoot, had liked Christopher Wylie and had been shocked by his death. It seemed churlish to refuse to take his daughter in if she was only coming back to tidy up his affairs. Although she didn't admit it either, Tibbie had also become accustomed to the idea of a railway coming past the village. It didn't seem so bad now that it was almost upon them. Craigie was still raving on, of course, out in the street shouting curses in the middle of the night sometimes. He seemed to think that Wylie's death was some sort of justification for him, and that had lost him a great deal of sympathy, especially from Tibbie. She consoled herself by thinking that no one listened to Craigie any more. The villagers tolerated him as one of the local lunatics, just a bit more dangerous than Miss Jessup.

Tibbie could tell that Hannah wanted her to take the girl, for she was saying, 'Tim thinks she'll not be here long. He's got the idea that she's coming to tell him she's giving up the contract. After all, Mr Wylie's son's dead too and there can't be anybody left to run it. Tim's really upset because he doesn't like the man that'll take it over for the railway company. I don't think he'll work for Mr Jopp.'

Tibbie shot her an anxious look. 'You'll not be moving away, Hannah, will you?'

Her daughter shook her head in assumed cheerfulness, though the thought of leaving her native district worried her too. 'Och no, not for ages. If Tim leaves the bridge, he'll get hired by one of the other gangs working on the line. He's a good workman and they all know him.'

Tibbie nodded slowly, thinking about Miss Wylie. 'Tell him I'll take his boss' daughter for a wee while then.'

Hannah was pleased. 'Oh, that's grand! I know she'll be comfortable here. You'll be able to put her in the attic where I used to sleep. It's lovely up there. Let's go and sort things out now because she's coming tomorrow.'

They put the sleeping baby in Tibbie's box bed in the kitchen and climbed a steep ladder to the attic. Up there it smelt sweetly of stored apples and the dried lavender that Tibbie used for making a lotion she rubbed on sore backs and sprains. Over their heads the birds in the thatch were rustling and Hannah listened to them with delight, because that was one of the favourite sounds of her young life. The birds that shared her room had been her friends. A deep bed filled one corner, its mattress bare and the folded covers and feather pillows piled up at one end. 'I'll give you a hand to make it up, Mam,' she said and happily they shook out the home-made cotton quilts and spread them carefully over one of Tibbie's best sheets. Then they laid a rag rug on the floor and dusted a wooden box with a big metal hasp that did duty as a clothes-chest. When all that was done, Hannah said, 'I'll go and cut some flowers for a vase. They'll look bonny and welcoming for her.'

When she came back up the ladder with a bunch of yellow daisies in her hand she was white-faced, and sighed as she arranged them in the vase. 'I've got a bad headache that's just come on. I think I'll go home,' she told her mother.

'Oh bairn, I'll make you a drink of feverfew leaves. I'll go and pick some now. It's this weather that does it – I've had a headache myself for three days,' her mother told her. Together they went back down into the kitchen where the baby was beginning to stir in her pillow nest. For once, the feverfew tea did not cure Hannah's headache, and at five o'clock she set off for home, not telling her mother how her head was thudding and her vision swimming with thousands of flashing lights and black spots like tiny flies. All she wanted to do was to reach *Benjy's* and her own bed.

When Tim came home, he found her sweating like a sickly child. He soothed her, washed the baby for her and then laid it to sleep by her side in the big bed. When they were both asleep he went to sit in the open doorway to smoke his pipe, for Hannah didn't like the smell of tobacco in the house. He was sitting there when Sydney came striding down the path. 'Where are you going in such a hurry?' asked Tim.

'Into Rosewell for a doctor. Major Bob's in a bad way – I think she's got the fever.'

Something awful clutched at Tim's heart and for a moment he couldn't breathe. Then he asked, 'Has anyone else got it?'

'Naughten's not very well either, but not as bad as Major Bob. It's best to get a doctor for them, though. You never know.'

Dr Stewart lived in a stone house surrounded by a high wall in a narrow alley off the road leading down to the Abbey. He was playing chess with a friend when the maidservant told him that a 'gentleman' had asked to see him.

'Is it someone we know?' he asked.

The girl shook her head. 'No, sir.'

'Then ask him to wait in the patients' room and I'll be with him in a few minutes,' was the doctor's reply, for there was a cunning move he wanted to make before he left the board. He was smiling in triumph when he walked through the house to his consulting rooms at the back where the unknown patient awaited him.

Sydney had not troubled to change out of his working clothes of white shirt, black waistcoat and trousers tied with string just below the knees. He was sitting back in a wooden chair in a negligent attitude with his large-brimmed white hat hanging from his hand when the doctor arrived. Stewart's face changed when he saw that he had been summoned from his game to attend to a mere navvy and his tone was acerbic as he asked, 'What can I do for you, then? If it's gonorrhoea that's the trouble, I don't take these cases. You'll have to go to the charity dispensary in Maddiston.' Gonorrhoea was rife among the navvies.

Sydney stood up and said in his most polished voice, the one that had caused the maid to refer to him as a gentleman, 'Sorry, old man. I'm not your patient and I've not got the clap. I want you to come to the camp and look at a couple of people who have high fevers.'

The doctor was surprised and angered to be addressed as if he was some sort of superior servant. Sydney had turned the tables between them. 'Fever? In the navvy camp? I won't go near it. I wouldn't take the risk of bringing it down to the town. If there's fever in the camp, keep it there,' he snapped.

Sydney snapped back, 'You're a doctor, aren't you? You take some sort of oath about tending the sick, don't you? These people are sick and in need of help. I'm prepared to pay you any fee you require for your services.'

They glared at each other. The doctor's face was as red as fire, his jowls wobbling like the wattles of a turkey cock. 'I still have the choice of my patients. Who are you to talk to me in that tone of voice? Get out before I call the policeman.'

Sydney turned for the door and strode out through it without a word. In the street outside he stopped and looked around before heading for the police office. The policeman was sitting inside the little room smoking his pipe when a head came round his door. 'Is that man Stewart the only medical practitioner in this town?' he was asked.

The policeman removed his pipe and said, 'Aye, but there's another three in Maddiston.'

'Thanks,' said the stranger and withdrew. On his way to a livery stable to hire a horse for the ride to Maddiston, Sydney had to cross the Square. Standing in the middle of it was a fine barouche with the arms of the Duke of Allandale on the doors. Not only were there two fine grey horses harnessed in the shafts and a top-hatted coachman on the box, but an outrider in livery sat on a similar horse, waiting for the return of the barouche's occupant.

Sydney walked up to the outrider and asked, 'Where's your master?' The man pointed with his whip to the Corn Exchange. 'At a farmers' meeting in there.'

'Get off your horse and lend it to me. He won't mind,' said Sydney.

The man laughed, 'Go away. You're drunk.'

'Bloody fool,' snapped Sydney and strode into the door of the Corn Exchange. The Duke was sitting on the platform beside three other well-dressed men. The audience of farmers stared as a navvy strode up the aisle between the chairs and climbed the steps to the platform. There, without ceremony, he leant over and whispered urgently in the Duke's ear. The Duke looked astonished but then he nodded. The navvy turned and walked out. Seconds later the audience heard the sounds of a scuffle going on in the Square outside. The door opened again and one of the Duke's servants came running in. His master stood up and shouted, 'It's all right, Scott. I said he could have the horse.' Then he sat down and rapped a little hammer on the table in front of him to bring the meeting back to order. The sounds of a horse being galloped out of the Square came through the open door. No explanations were offered.

It was a good horse, far superior to any livery hack, so it covered the distance to Maddiston in record time. Slowing down as he entered the town, Sydney shouted to a woman sitting at a cottage door, 'Where's the doctor?'

'Which one? Is it young Doctor Robertson you're after?'

'He'll do.'

'He's just down there then. Third house on the left. The one with the rowan tree at the gate.'

The tree was heavy with scarlet fruit and Sydney tied his borrowed horse to its trunk when he alighted. Alex Robertson was new to Maddiston. He had arrived only a month before, fresh from hospital work in Glasgow, but because of the slowness of patients to come to him, he was beginning to think he'd made a mistake and should have stayed in the city. So far, the biggest number of patients he'd had were charity cases, and most of those were venereally-infected navvies attending the dispensary. None of the other doctors wanted to have anything to do with them.

When his door-knocker was rattled he answered it himself. The man on the step said abruptly, 'Have you any objection to treating navvies?'

Robertson shook his head. 'No, none at all.'

'Are you afraid to come to the camp with me to look at some cases of fever?'

'Of course I'll come. Wait till I get my case.'

'Have you a horse?'

'Yes.'

'Come on then, hurry up. This is an emergency, I think.'

Major Bob was raving, tossing and turning on her tumbled cot, clawing at the air with talon-like hands. One of the younger women from the camp was trying to give her a drink of water from a greasy-looking cup.

'She's awful dirty, Doctor,' said the woman apologetically when Robertson knelt by the bed to examine the patient, for Major Bob was lying in sheets stained with liquid excrement, but strangely enough there was little smell. He noticed this with disquiet. Cholera did not smell.

'How long has she been like this?' he asked.

'She was poorly yesterday,' said her attendant, 'but this . . .' she indicated the foul sheets . . . 'This only began tonight. She started vomiting and then—'

Robertson nodded, stripped off his jacket and rolled up his shirt-sleeves. He knew that he was in for a long battle, and one that he would almost certainly lose – for the woman was not young and the illness had her in its terrible grip. The strange man who had summoned him was standing by the curtain that divided the woman's cubicle from the rest of the hut. The doctor went up to him and whispered, 'She's in a bad way. The only hope is to give plenty of liquid and hope she manages to retain some of it. I'll give her an opiate in the hope of stopping the purging, but if it doesn't do that I'm afraid she'll die.'

'There's another one sick,' said Sydney, and pointed up the hut to where Naughten lay groaning. A bucket by his bed was half-full of foul-looking yellow vomit and his nut-brown, simian face was pouring with sweat. When the doctor and Sydney bent over him, he opened his eyes and groaned, 'Ah Sydney, I'm a goner. Send my things to my wife and little ones in Kildare ... the address is in my box.'

They pushed the beds of the sick people together at the end of the hut and tended them all night, but it was obvious that life was seeping away from them. As dawn was breaking, Panhandle rose from his bed and started to vomit as well. Sydney could not leave Major Bob, who was suffering terrible agony with stomach cramps, groaning and gritting her teeth when each one hit her. Her skin had turned a strange bluish colour and she croaked in a voice like a raven, 'Water, give me water ...' It was obvious that she was nearing her end, but she was not giving up without a fight for when Sydney asked her, 'Do you want a priest, Bob?' she shook her head and groaned, 'I'd rather have a brandy ...'

Sydney gave a wry grin. 'I knew your temperance oath wouldn't last, old girl,' he said, but he reached into his pocket for the flask he always carried and held it to her lips.

When her fingers touched the metal, she gasped, 'Silver, you can always tell quality.' Then she took a big gulp, coughed, closed her eyes and died.

Sydney pulled the edge of the filthy sheet over her face and walked down the hut to where the doctor was sponging Naughten's unconscious face. 'Major Bob's dead,' he said shortly.

Robertson looked up, surprised. 'Major Bob? Which is he?'

Sydney shook his head. 'That's what we called the woman. What'll I say she died of when I go to register the death?'

Robertson stood up. They were both about the same height. 'Say enteric fever, but I'm afraid it's cholera,' he whispered, so that the other patients could not overhear. Then he added, 'I'll only be sure if it spreads. Then there'll be an almighty panic and there's time enough for that.'

'How afraid are you?' Sydney whispered back.

'Almost certain. There's no smell from the faeces, you see – that's always a sign of cholera. And I've seen it before, in Glasgow, when I was a student. It's cholera all right. I wish to God it wasn't.'

Tim woke early before the sun rose and anxiously turned to look at Hannah who lay in the crook of his arm between him and the wall. She was sound asleep with the baby in her arms. In the dim light he stared at them with a heart so full of love that he felt a swelling in his throat. Kate was a tiny copy of her mother and he could not believe that these two beautiful people belonged to him.

When he rose, he pulled the cover carefully over them and whispered in Hannah's ear, 'I'm going to the bridge and then I've got to meet the Wylie girl off the train at Maddiston. Stay inside. There's fever in the camp.' She murmured a sleepy reply but did not open her eyes and within minutes he was dressed and out. He was well clear of Rosewall before the news of the deaths of Major Bob and Naughten-The-Image-Taker got about.

He did not go straight to the bridge site but called first at a cottage sitting high on the hill overlooking the river from the northern side. It was occupied by the family of a navvy called Bragging Billy, who did not like living in camps and always rented a house for the duration of any

365

project. Billy was awake and eating breakfast when Tim appeared at his door.

'What's up, Black Ace?' he asked, thinking there was some emergency on site.

Tim leaned on the jamb of the open doorway and said, 'Nothing's up. I've come to ask if you can take my wife and baby in for a while. There's fever in the camp and I want them out of it.'

'They've not got fever, have they?' asked Billy sharply.

'No, that's why I want them away. The baby's only a few days old and fever could be dangerous for her.'

'There's a room at the end we don't use. You can have it, providing they're not sick. I've bairns myself.'

'I wouldn't be moving them out if they were sick,' said Tim. 'I'll bring them over later.'

He then went to the site and got work started for the day. Soon it was time to leave for Maddiston and meet Emma Jane's train. Anxiety about his family and past resentments against the girl made him short and gruff when she finally arrived, for the train was late and he was desperate to get back to the camp and start moving Hannah and Kate. Miss Wylie walked up the platform with her black skirt rustling along the ground and said, 'Thank you for coming to meet me, Mr Maquire. I was afraid that you might not have received my letter.'

'I got it,' he said curtly. 'And I've found you a place to live. It's with my mother-in-law, Mrs Mather, in Camptounfoot. Mr Jessup's not up to having a lodger with his sister like she is.'

She nodded. 'I understood that from his letter. He was too polite to say so outright, though.'

He wondered if he should warn her that Tibbie did not expect her lodger to stay for very long, either, but decided to leave things to take their course. The porter coming behind her was only carrying one portmanteau so it looked as if she didn't plan on a protracted stay anyway. She volunteered no information on the matter, however.

He'd hired the same carriage as always carried her

father, and when she climbed into it he asked her hopefully, 'Do you want to go to Mrs Mather's first?'

To his dismay she shook her bonneted head. 'No. First I'd like to look at the bridge, if you don't mind. Has much been done on it since Father died?'

'Quite a lot,' he replied. 'The middle piers are almost built up to the beginning of the arches. The ones in the river will have to stand for the winter to make sure they won't be swept away by the water when it's running high. Your father floated one on woolsacks as an experiment, you see.'

She stared at him. 'On *woolsacks*?'

He sighed and started to explain the story to her. She watched him closely, apparently taking in what he was saying for she nodded her head from time to time. 'I hope it stands. That's why you're waiting, is it? To see if it's a success?' she asked.

'Yes,' he said. He wondered why she had come to see the bridge. If she was going to give up the contract, she could have done that by letter. He was determined to keep her tour of inspection as short as possible.

When their carriage went over the crown of the last hill and the valley opened out before them, she surprised him by standing up in her seat and shading her eyes with her hand. Her bonnet slipped off her head and hung down at the back of her neck by its broad black ribbon, but she ignored it. She was staring down at the line of the half-built bridge. 'It looks wonderful,' she said enthusiastically. 'Won't it be marvellous when it's finished?'

'It'll add to the view,' he said grudgingly, and jumped out of the carriage to the ground with his hand extended to help her out. She took it without comment. The men working on the site knew she was coming and stopped working so that they could take a look at her. Like him, they thought she'd come for a last sight of her father's project – a sort of sentimental journey.

She lifted her skirt with one hand and walked quickly down over the grass to the site hut. As she went, over her shoulder she asked him, 'Where's Jopp?'

His face went dark. 'Him! On the embankment. He came down from Maddiston to meet you.' Jopp had been throwing his weight about for days, boasting that he was going to take over the contract and interfering with what Tim was doing, questioning everything, countermanding orders and annoying the navvies with whom he was far from popular because of the truck business. They were afraid that if he was put in charge, truck would be imposed on them all.

Sure enough, Jopp had been watching, and now he came running down from the high embankment with his hand stuck out to shake Emma Jane's. She took it gingerly as he said effusively, 'I'm very pleased to make your acquaintance, Miss Wylie. Sir Geoffrey came down to see me at Maddiston yesterday and told me what's what.' He cocked an eye in Tim's direction as if there was a secret between himself and Emma Jane.

She frowned and replied, 'I understand that Sir Geoffrey wants you to share in the work on the bridge, Mr Jopp.'

He grinned. 'Yes, you and I will get along very well. Our aims are the same, aren't they? We want this bridge finished. Have you brought your father's plans with you?'

She didn't trust this man, not an inch, but she didn't show how she felt. 'I have his plans in a safe place,' she said coolly. 'Now tell me what's happening. I want to know exactly what stage has been reached.'

Jopp couldn't help her there, so Tim stepped forward and swiftly led her from place to place, indicating where there were or might soon be problems. She listened attentively, asked surprisingly sensible questions and when at last the tour was finished, she paused and looked at him as she said, 'You'll continue to work for me, Mr Maquire, won't you?'

'For you? Are you taking over the contract?' he asked in disbelief. He couldn't believe that she intended such a thing, in spite of all her interest and questions.

She bridled. 'Of course I am. I've got to finish it.'

'And where does Jopp come in, then?' he asked.

'The railway company has stipulated that I take him on as a sort of manager.'

'Jopp won't help you. He'll be more of a spy if you ask me. He'll only cause trouble,' said Tim.

She stiffened. '*I* don't want him – the railway people do. He's a safeguard for them, and I'm afraid he can't be dispensed with. He's part of the deal.'

'That's a pity,' replied Tim grimly.

'What I want to know is, are you still prepared to work for me in the same capacity as you did for my father? I know how highly he valued you. If you don't want to, please say so now because I'll have to find someone else,' she told him. She knew it sounded bald but he didn't appear to be making much of an effort to be polite to her either.

He glared. 'I'm still involved because I liked your father very much and I've been in on this bridge since the moment the first spade went into the ground. I take pride in my work. I'm as anxious as you are to see it finished.'

At last she smiled. 'That's good. Now perhaps you'll show me where Mrs Mather lives,' she said, turning back to the carriage, but the ice between them remained unbroken because there was something about Maquire that rubbed her up the wrong way. He seemed anxious to get her off the site and she felt sure he disapproved of her – that he disapproved of the whole idea of a woman giving him orders. Because of that she was all the more determined to appear matter of fact, and not show any weakness.

The cottage where he'd found her lodgings was smaller than the Jessups' house but she was pleased to see that it looked snug and cosy beneath its thick, green-covered thatch. Its walls were built of multi-coloured, misshapen stones, culled from the bed of the river long ago, neatly fitted together and piled one upon the other. The front door opened directly on to the cobbled road and beside it was a tiny window with eight little bottle-glass panes.

Tim knocked on the door before turning the handle and

stepping inside. 'Tibbie,' he called. 'I've brought Miss Wylie.'

A stout little woman with scraped-back grey hair and a sweet face stepped into the tiny entrance hall, wiping her hands on a white apron. She looked nervous, as if she was unsure that taking a lodger was the right thing to be doing. 'Oh Miss Wylie, I hope you'll be all right here. It's nothing fancy, you know. Not nearly as grand as Mr Jessup's. Maybe you should look some place else.'

Emma Jane smiled and her stiff little face was suddenly transformed. 'I think your cottage is lovely. It looks so old. And what a pretty garden!' she exclaimed, catching sight of the last of the summer flowers through the back window.

Tibbie's garden was her pride and joy and Emma Jane could not have said anything that pleased her more. 'Oh, it's old all right. My Alex's family have lived here for over a hundred years, maybe longer . . . nobody knows really. Do you like gardens, Miss Wylie?'

'I don't know much about them but I love to see them,' said Emma Jane in reply and then added, 'It's kind of you to take me in, Mrs Mather. It's so close to the bridge, so convenient. I hope it won't put you to too much trouble, though.'

Tibbie glanced at Tim but his look gave her no indication of how long Miss Wylie might be planning to stay. 'It's no trouble really,' she said, but she was still unable to hide the note of doubt in her voice. Then she rallied. 'Now come up the stairs and I'll show you the room. You'll be able to come and go as you like because I'll often be up at the camp with my daughter Hannah and her wee baby, Kate.'

Emma Jane looked quickly at Tim. 'Oh, I forgot to ask about the baby. She's thriving, I hope.'

His face darkened and he shuffled his feet but it was to Tibbie that he spoke. 'Don't go up to the camp today, Tibbie. There's been a couple of cases of fever there.'

Tibbie's hand flew to her face. 'Fever! How's Hannah? She had a bad headache yesterday when she left here.'

Tim hastened to reassure her. 'Hannah's all right and so's Kate. They were still in bed when I left this morning. I've told Hannah to stay inside and not go out. When I get back I'm going to move them to a cottage well away from the infection.' He didn't say that on the site he'd heard of the deaths of Naughten and Major Bob. As a result he was in agony, aching to get back to the camp as soon as possible, and his anxiety made him short-tempered.

'I'll leave you then,' he said brusquely to Emma Jane, who nodded.

'Yes, I'll be at the bridge early tomorrow. I'll bring the plans and we can talk more then.'

Tibbie put out a hand to clutch at his sleeve. 'Just a minute, Tim. Wait till I show Miss Wylie upstairs and then I'll come with you.'

'You've not to go into the camp, Tibbie,' he said sternly.

She kept hold of his sleeve, for she sensed something was badly wrong. 'Then I'll give you some medicine for Hannah – something that'll keep the fever away from her and Kate. You've got to take it, Tim. It works.'

'I'm in a hurry,' he pleaded, but she bent towards him and whispered, 'Then bring them here. We never have fever in this village.'

He patted her hand consolingly. 'No, I told you – I've got everything arranged. We're going to a cottage on top of the hill over the other side of the river. Don't worry. I'll come back and tell you when everything's been done.'

She could see that he was desperate to get away and she dropped her detaining hand but her eyes were terrified. Embarrassed, Emma Jane stood at the top of the stairs and wondered what she ought to do. When Tim left she came down and asked Tibbie, 'Would it be better if I went somewhere else, Mrs Mather? Then your daughter and granddaughter could come here.'

Tibbie shook her head. 'Oh, no. Tim's made his arrangements and I mustn't interfere. I hope they don't get the fever, that's all. It's been funny weather, real fever weather, and that camp's so crowded these days, but

Hannah wouldn't hear tell of leaving her wee house, not even when the baby was coming, would she leave . . .'

She was talking to herself as much as to Emma Jane, and the girl realised that the best thing she could do was to go upstairs and keep out of the way. In a little while Tibbie called up to her to come down and have some tea, and was pulling on her shawl as she indicated the tea-things on the table. 'Please help yourself, Miss Wylie. I'm going to walk to the camp. I can't wait any longer.' Her voice was distracted and it was obvious that she was racked with worry.

'But he said—' Emma Jane was going to say that Tim had advised against going there, but Tibbie's face was set.

'I know what he said but I can't wait here wondering any longer. I'd rather see for myself. You can look after yourself till I get back, can't you?'

'Oh yes, of course I can.'

'Good,' said Tibbie. 'I'll not be long.'

The village carter's dray was rumbling down the street taking a load of woven cloth from the Rutherfords across the road to Rosewell and he offered Tibbie a ride. 'Are you going to see Hannah?' he asked, and before she could reply, he went on, 'You should stay away from there, Tib. They say there's fever in the camp.'

She had to fight to stop her teeth from chattering. 'Oh no, it's only got as far as Maddiston,' she protested, but the carter shook his head.

'There's a rumour that twae folk died in Rosewell camp today.'

Tibbie could not stop herself from snapping, 'How do you know they died from fever? There's folk dying all the time from all sorts of things.'

The carter would have said more but he saw she was set on denying the possibility of fever so he shook his head and contented himself with, 'Well, you'll not get me going into that camp, that's one thing sure. See and not bring the fever back to the village.'

He dropped her a hundred yards from the gate, for he seemed to think that infection was hanging around it like a curtain. As she walked towards the camp, Tibbie was struck by the strange stillness that hung over it. Normally at that time of day the place was a hustle and bustle of activity, with tradesmen's carts going in and out, and busy women and fighting children milling about, but today there was not a cart or a human being to be seen and every door was closed. It looked like a place that was waiting for an onslaught of some sort – a place that was mortally afraid.

The sky was leaden above her head as Tibbie walked up the main path, and the unnatural silence made her notice things that she had not really taken in before. It was obvious that there were now far too many people living in the field for comfort or hygiene. Piles of rotting rubbish lay at some of the hut doors, and from the latrines dug at the back of the huts she caught stomach-churning stenches. Clouds of enormous bluebottles buzzed around the foulest lean-to sheds. In the central section of the camp there was no longer a blade of grass to be seen, for the most recent arrivals had pitched their tents across the paths that interlinked the original buildings. Tibbie was glad that the little house where Tim and Hannah lived was on the fringe of the camp, well away from the squalid inner section.

At last she could see the bonny painted door of *Benjy's*, with Hannah's tubs of bright geraniums on each side. That door was also closed, and the window curtains drawn. There were three men inside when Tibbie entered, and as her eyes became accustomed to the curtained gloom she saw that one was Tim, the second was his fancy-spoken navvy friend whom she'd often seen before, but the third was a stranger. He was also a young man and he stood with his shirt-sleeves rolled up and a worried expression on his face. They were all huddled together in the middle of the room arguing about something. Hannah and the baby lay in bed.

When Tibbie entered Tim turned towards her and said, 'You shouldn't come in here. The doctor thinks Hannah's

373

got fever.' His eyes were blazing as if he was furiously angry.

She pushed past him to reach the bed. 'Aw bairn, you'll be all right. You're a big strong girl,' she consoled.

Hannah's face was shining with sweat but she managed to reach out a hand and touch her mother's. 'I know, Mam, don't worry. I just hope the bairn doesn't get it.'

Baby Kate was lying in the crook of her arm and Tibbie reached out to pick the child up, but Hannah tightened her grip on the little bundle. The chubby infant face was very pale and from the laboured way Kate was breathing Tibbie could tell that she was also ill, perhaps even more ill than her mother. 'You lie there and keep quiet,' she whispered, and turned back to the men with an unspoken question in her eyes.

It was the stranger who answered her. 'I'm Alex Robertson, the new doctor from Maddiston. There's an outbreak of fever in the camp but as you said to your daughter, she's young and strong and well nourished.'

Tibbie's lips were dry and parched as she whispered, 'Fever?'

He nodded firmly and said very loud so Hannah could hear, 'Enteric fever.' But his eyes looking into Tibbie's said something else, something far more terrible. 'I'll look after your daughter,' he said next. 'Perhaps you should go home.'

'Don't be stupid,' she told him. 'I'm not leaving her – she needs me. Who'll nurse her if I don't?'

The doctor lowered his voice. 'You're not a young woman. Fever is more dangerous when the patient is older.'

'I don't give a damn,' snapped Tibbie, who never swore in normal circumstances. 'I'm not leaving Hannah.'

Tim was walking like a caged animal from one side of the room to the other, but now he whipped round and said roughly to the doctor, 'Let me take her away from here. I've got a place for her to go. It's up on the hill, well away from everybody else and from infection. She'll get better there.'

Robertson looked at him with pity. 'I'm sorry, I've told you already. I'd be breaking the law if I allowed you to move an infectious case of fever out of here. But apart from that there's another reason why she must stay. She's too ill to be moved, man. If you want her to survive this, you've got to leave her here and let us look after her as best we can. It's the only chance she's got!'

Tim stood in the middle of the floor like a statue and Tibbie's heart went out to him, for she could see that he was suddenly overcome by a sense of powerlessness. He had been sure he could snatch his wife and child away from danger, protect them by his own strength and ingenuity but now he had come up against this sinister enemy that he did not know how to fight. She ran over to him and put a hand on his. 'She's going to be all right. I'll stay here and nurse her. You go back to the cottage and bring me some things. I'll write down a list.'

In Camptounfoot, Emma Jane was still upstairs when she heard terrible crashing noises coming from the room below. She hurried down the ladder stair and saw Tim Maquire standing at an open wall-cupboard throwing bottles and jars on to the floor like a man gone berserk. 'What are you doing?' she asked.

He did not turn his head but went on searching among the close-packed jars on the middle shelf. Then he said, 'Help me, I'm trying to find all those things she wants. She said they were in here.'

Emma Jane entered the room and picked up a piece of paper that lay on the seat of a chair by his side. 'Is this the list?' she asked.

'Yes, I can't find them.' He was in too great a state of agitation to look properly, but it was not difficult for her to decipher the spidery writing on faded labels and quickly find each item on the list. She did not ask why he wanted all those things but guessed they were for his sick wife, for they were all either medicines or food like calf's foot jelly that would be suitable for invalids. When everything was gathered together she piled the bottles into a big wicker basket and covered them with a white cloth. He was by this time rummaging in a box beneath Tibbie's bed and hauling out folded white sheets. 'We'll need these too,' he said, shoving them under his arm, picking up the basket and leaving the house. He said nothing about going back to work and neither did she.

What she did call after him was, 'I hope everything's all right. I hope she gets better soon,' but she was not sure that he even heard her. Then she set about cleaning up the mess he'd left behind, for she guessed that it would be some time before she saw Tibbie again.

When Tim got back to *Benjy's*, the doctor and Sydney had left, summoned away to another sufferer, for the illness was manifesting itself all over the camp in a terrifying way. In almost every house or hut someone was affected – a child, a baby or an older person in most early cases during the first day. Tibbie silently put her finger to her lips to indicate that Hannah was asleep and started to lift the bottles and jars out of the basket, nodding with approval at everything he'd brought. 'Isn't there something you can go and do?' she whispered to him. 'She's sleeping now and it'll only worry you hanging about here. I'll look after her and if there's any change I'll fetch you. I'm sure she's going to be all right. She's never had a day's illness in her life, has my Hannah.'

He would not go far. For the rest of the day he paid hurried visits to the other huts, checking up with Sydney and Dr Robertson about the progress of the disease and always hurrying back to *Benjy's*. By afternoon Hannah seemed more peaceful and Tibbie remained wonderfully calm. When night fell, she told him with a smile, 'She's managed to feed the bairn. Kate suckled a wee bit so she must be getting better too. They're both still purging, but not so violently. I've rubbed turpentine on their bellies to ease the cramps and it's helped, I think. What's happening out there?'

He shook his head, not really wanting to tell her. 'It's bad. The town authorities have sent somebody up and they've decided it's cholera. There's no doubt any more. Robertson knew this morning but he tried to keep it quiet.'

She put her hands over her mouth, 'Oh God, cholera. That's what killed all those folk in Edinburgh last year, wasn't it?'

He didn't say yes or no but his harried eyes answered for him. 'Folk can get better from cholera,' he told her sharply. 'Robertson doesn't think Hannah has a bad case and like you said, she's strong. Those that have died already weren't as strong as her.'

'How many have died?' she asked.

'Forty-two.' His voice was bleak and she knew better than to show the horror that filled her. Cholera was cutting down the people in the camp like a harvester with a sharp scythe in a field of standing corn.

When the day's terrible toll was added up it transpired that Major Bob had been the first victim. Naughten and Panhandle followed her into death a short while later. By the time fifteen children of various ages, Squint Mary and Frying Pan and twenty-five others had also died, the Rosewell authorities were in a panic.

'We've got to keep this quiet,' said the Chief Magistrate to the Town Provost when the news was carried down to them in the Provost's office on the first floor of the Corn Exchange.

'It'll kill trade in all the shops if it gets out. And there's two big parties of tourists in town come to visit Sir Walter Scott's house. If they hear about this, they'll be out of Rosewell in half an hour and never come back,' mourned the Provost.

Dr Stewart, who was sitting in on their meeting, agreed heartily. 'And we've got to make sure that none of our people get it, so we'll have to seal off that camp.'

Colonel Anstruther, as a major landowner, had been summoned to the meeting, as were Falconwood and the Duke of Allandale. When they heard the terrible news, the Duke asked, 'How do you propose to confine the illness to the camp? People are coming and going all the time.'

The Provost had the answer. 'We'll guard the gate.

377

Nobody'll be allowed out till the danger of infection's past.'

The Duke looked at Dr Stewart and asked, 'How long is that likely to be?'

The answer was a shrug. 'In this weather, who knows? It's always worse in humid conditions. The period of danger of infection could be two weeks, even if there were no more cases after today.'

Anstruther leaned forward. 'Two weeks? The men in that camp are building the bridge. They can't stop working for two weeks.'

Stewart pondered that one. 'Well, they can go on working if they're able, providing they don't come into the town. They'll be told to go from the camp to the work-site and back again. We'll post notices telling other people to keep away from them.'

'But what about provisions for the camp? What about medicines going in? What about the bodies being brought out for burial?' asked the Duke. 'The people who haven't got cholera must eat — and we can't leave bodies unburied.'

The Provost had answers for these queries too. 'We'll send provision carts up for their truck-shop. There's a man called Jopp in charge of some of the work and he's not living in the camp, he's up at Maddiston. He's already been here offering to arrange for food to be sent in. He's got something to do with supplying the truck-shop, apparently.'

'But they don't all use the truck-shop,' protested Anstruther, who like the Duke was concerned for the welfare of the people penned up in the camp.

'They'll have to use it if there's nothing else,' said the Provost dismissively.

'And the burials?' persisted the Duke.

Dr Stewart had that in hand. 'A pit's being dug in the Abbey grounds now. We'll throw quicklime into it and all the dead will be brought down and put there within two hours of dying. We've also forbidden noisy funerals or great fuss. If possible, the bodies will be buried at night.

378

We don't want the townspeople upset: the less they know about this the better.'

Colonel Anstruther leaned forward in his chair with a worried frown. 'I've seen cholera in India – I know what it can do. This could be bad. By shutting sick and well people up together, we could be condemning a lot of them to death. And what about doctoring them? Who's looking after the ones who're sick? They don't always die, you know.'

Dr Stewart looked self-righteous. 'I've my patients in the town to consider. There's no way I can expose myself to such an infection. What if I brought it back to some innocent nursing mother or little child? Anyway, I'm led to believe that the young doctor who arrived in Maddiston a little while ago has gone into the camp. He'll manage, I expect. The other practitioners in the district can stand by in case the infection spreads outside. If it does, it's best that we're fit and able to cope.'

Most of the others made agreeing noises. Only the Duke and Anstruther kept silent. 'That young doctor must be a brave fellow,' was Anstruther's eventual contribution.

'Either that or a fool,' snapped Stewart.

To the intense relief of Tibbie and her son-in-law, Hannah and her baby seemed slightly recovered by nightfall. After a period of squirming and squalling, during which she passed copious watery stools, Kate became very quiet, not even whimpering but lying cuddled in her mother's arm with her eyes round and amazed as if she was seeing the world for the first time and was wondering about the beautiful things around her.

Hannah was able to talk a little and Tim held her head up while her mother gave her whey to drink. 'Ugh,' she said when she tasted it. 'You know I hate curds and whey.'

But Tibbie persisted in pressing the drink on her. 'It's an old cure for fever. You must take it,' she said. She was all the more insistent when her hand on Hannah's brow told her that her daughter was still burning hot. The fever had not left her.

At about midnight Dr Robertson and Sydney, both looking ghastly, came in for Tim and took him outside to whisper the latest news. 'There's been another ten deaths. It's rampant. We're taking the bodies down to the bury-ing-ground now and we need helpers. Can you come?'

Tim looked through the open door at the lamplit scene within. Tibbie was bending over Hannah who was pre-paring to sleep. The baby was also quiet. 'I'll come,' he said.

It was an horrific procession that made its way from the camp to the town that night. Pairs of men carrying makeshift stretchers with shrouded bodies lying on them walked in line down the main path of the camp beneath the light of a pale half-moon that swam in silver strands of drifting cloud. Owls hooted in the hedges which lined the road to the town, and surprised nocturnal animals scurried out of their way, for the men gave little warning of their approach. They were walking in silence and with measured treads.

When they reached the town square it was deserted. Oil lamps bracketed to the walls cast pools of light into the darkest corners, but not even a cat was out to watch them pass. If there were eyes behind the black panes of glass in the windows, they kept out of sight and gave no sign. The terrible procession crossed the square and headed down the lane to the Abbey. A lamp had been left burning in a bracket above the burying-ground gate, and in the grave-digger's hut the priest was waiting. When he heard the crunch of the boots of the first bearer-party on the gravel path, he stood up and came out.

'It's this way,' he said and walked in front, his white surplice fluttering round him like the robes of a ghost, leading them to a long, deep pit dug in a straight line beside the graveyard wall. The sharp smell of quicklime mixed with the strange sweetness of decay filled the air. One by one the stretcher-bearers tipped their burdens into the pit, and when all had been deposited, they grabbed the spades that were lying nearby and shovelled earth, mixed with more lime, on top. Then the priest asked the first bearers, 'Who were they?' They told him the names and he gabbled off a hurried litany of a series of pseudonyms; for Long Tom, The Music Man, Alfred-From-Hell, Lizzie who was Tom's wife and their child Little Billy . . . He prayed to his God to receive their souls in heaven and grant them solace after the misery of their existences on earth. There was no certainty that the people he was sending on their way to God had been Roman Catholics, but at least he was prepared to say prayers over them. The other clergymen of the town stayed well away.

Tim walked back to the camp after the hurried ceremony with the doctor and Sydney. He knew all of the men whom they had so unceremoniously buried, and also most of the women, and the lack of dignity that attended their end oppressed him. He glared at Sydney with his brows down. 'Your kind wouldn't bury their dogs like that,' he snarled.

Sydney was walking with his head bent and his hands shoved deep in his pockets. 'I know,' he agreed. 'This is terrible – I can't believe it's happening.'

The doctor told them, 'It's happening all right and it's going to go on happening. God knows when this'll end. I'm not a praying man but sometimes I wish I was. When I see people dying like that and I can't do anything to help, I feel impotent!' He stared at his companions from a face that resembled a skull, the eyes sunk deep in dark cavities.

'You'll have to sleep for a bit,' said Sydney anxiously. 'If you crack up we won't have anyone to help us.'

'Come into my house,' said Tim. 'I'll make a bed for you on the floor. It'll be quiet there. Hannah was sleeping when I came away.'

Benjy's was quiet. Tibbie lay asleep on a folded quilt at the side of Hannah's bed. The stove glowed red and a soft stream of steam rose slowly from the spout of the kettle that sat on top of it. Tim led the staggering doctor in and whispered, 'Lie down there by the stove. There's plenty of blankets.'

He then walked across to the bed where Hannah and the baby lay. Their eyes were closed and they both looked as if they were carved out of alabaster. 'They're going to be all right, aren't they?' he asked Robertson, who was laying himself down on the floor.

'There's a good chance, a good chance,' was the drowsy reply. In a little while everyone but Tim was asleep. He stayed sitting up in the wooden chair by the window, staring at the sky, waiting for dawn and wondering what new horrors it would bring.

In spite of his determination to stay awake, he fell asleep at about five in the morning but only slept for a short time before he was awakened by strange noises from the bed. It sounded as if Hannah was weeping and trying to call for help.

In a panic he jumped from the chair and ran across the floor to her. 'Hannah, Hannah, what is it?'

Her eyes were staring and her face deathly pale. 'It's the baby, it's the baby,' she groaned. Little Kate was silently convulsing, then straightening and convulsing again, drawing her tiny knees up to her chest. Her face was contorted in agony. The clothes she was wearing and the blanket that wrapped her up were soaking wet, and when Tim lifted her he could see that she was excreting water in copious quantities. It did not seem possible that her small body could contain so much.

The noise wakened Tibbie and Robertson, who ran to the bed as well. Robertson very gently held out his arms for little Kate and Tim placed her in them. When the first light of dawn came striking through the window, it showed him that his child's face was blue. As he watched, the awful convulsing stopped and the little limbs seemed to go limp. The doctor bent his head and put his face against the baby's. There were tears on his cheeks when he looked up at Tim and said, very softly, 'I'm sorry. I'm so sorry . . . she's dead.'

Tim threw back his head and was about to yell when

Tibbie put an urgent hand on his shoulder and hissed, 'Hannah, Hannah.'

His wife was lying on her side with her eyes fixed on the tableau in the middle of the floor. He walked across to her and leaned on the bedcovers. Oh God, they were soaking wet as well. Like Kate's, Hannah's life seemed to be seeping away. 'Doctor Robertson'll take care of Kate for a little while,' he said. Behind him he heard Robertson going out of the house with the dead child.

Hannah could not speak, for she too was beginning to writhe in agony – an agony far worse than she had experienced before. It was terrible to watch her. Tim sprawled on the wet bed beside her, trying to hold her down, and stroked the hair off her face as he whispered to her, 'I love you, Hannah. I loved you from the first moment I saw you. Do you remember? You were standing in the doorway of your mother's cottage and I rode past with Mr Wylie. Then I saw you at the dance with that French girl and I knew I was going to marry you. I love you. I love you. I love you . . .' Over and over again he told her, while she gripped his hand so tight that it hurt.

'Tim, ah Tim,' was all she could say. Her face looked shrunken and very small. When her struggling grew a little less he felt Robertson's hand on his shoulder. 'Let me look at her,' said the doctor's voice. It did not take more than a couple of seconds before he was standing up again with a terrible look on his face. 'These are rice-water stools,' he said, indicating the mess on the sheets.

Tim heard Tibbie give a convulsive sob and he stared at the doctor. 'What do you mean?' Hannah's eyes were now closed, and though her limbs were still twitching, it was unlikely that she could hear them any longer.

'It means she's dying,' said Robertson.

Frantically they tried to help her. They forced liquid in between her parted lips, they chafed her hands and wiped her face but death had too strong a grip on her. An hour later, at seven o'clock in the morning, Hannah Maquire died.

For several moments Tim stood still and very quiet in

the middle of the floor when Robertson told him Hannah was dead. Then he threw back his head and gave a cry of such anguish that everyone in the room felt their blood chill at the sound of it. 'Aw no, no, no, no,' he cried. Tibbie held her apron up to her face and wept into it; Robertson dropped his head like a defeated man and turned to leave, but Tim grabbed his shoulder to prevent him going. 'It's not true – say she's not dead! Do something,' he shouted.

Robertson did not turn and his voice was bleak and bitter as he spoke. 'I can't do anything. She is dead and so's the baby. I put it in the empty shed where the bodies are being collected. I'll have to go. There are others . . .'

Like a madman, Tim Maquire ran out of the house to the charnel-shed and found little Kate, who was lying on a bench near the door. Holding her in his arms and pushing people out of his way he went running back to *Benjy's* and laid the child beside her mother. 'There's your baby, my darling,' he told the body of his wife. 'Hold on to each other. Oh my God, I can't believe this. I can't believe it.' He sank to his knees by the bedside and buried his face in the foul and tumbled covers. Tibbie, weeping and grief-stricken herself, did not know how to help him. Timidly she laid a hand on his shaking shoulders and knelt beside him and they stayed like that, weeping together, for a long time.

At last he rose and pulled on his jacket. 'I'm going to get her a proper coffin. She's not going to be thrown into a pit wrapped in an old sheet like those poor souls last night,' he told the sobbing Tibbie.

At the camp gate, the two men on guard to prevent anyone going out and spreading the infection tried to stop him, but he pushed them each in the chest with his outspread hands and they went reeling away. He did not go to Rosewell but to Camptounfoot, to the man who had provided the coffin for Christopher Wylie. Jo was in his workroom on the first floor when he heard a terrible hammering at the lower door and stuck his head out of the window to ask, 'Who is it?'

'Hannah's dead. And so's our baby. I want a coffin for them,' shouted a man's voice.

Jo recognised Hannah Mather's husband and ran downstairs. There was genuine shock and horror on his face when he opened the door and exclaimed, 'Hannah's never dead! Not bonny Hannah!'

'I want a coffin big enough for them both. I want her to be buried with her baby,' said Tim.

Jo could see that he was half-mad with grief and hauled him inside. 'Sit down there a minute,' he said. 'I've got one that'll do. Is she in the camp? Have you got a cart to carry it?'

'No.' Tim ran a hand over his bare head in confusion.

Jo pushed him in the direction of William's house. 'Her uncle's next door in the smiddy. He's got a pony and cart and he'll lend it to you.'

When William was told about his niece's death he reeled and put a hand against the smiddy door to support himself. 'Oh my God, poor Tibbie. That lassie was all she lived for. Of course I'll give you my cart. I'll come with you, too. Somebody'll have to bring Tibbie home.'

'They'll not let you into the camp because of the cholera,' said Tim. 'Just lend me the cart.'

Everything was done in a great hurry, and in less than an hour Tim was back at the gate, standing up in the cart and driving on the fat pony like a charioteer. Again the men on guard knew better than to try to stop him, for he would run them down beneath the cart-wheels.

When he entered *Benjy's* again Tibbie had washed Hannah and Kate and dressed them in clean clothes. The foul bedding was bundled up in a corner. Hannah and her child looked beautiful and peaceful, all traces of their terrible agonies erased by death. Tibbie had combed out her daughter's lovely hair and it was tied in a loose knot on the top of her head. Kate, looking as if she were asleep, was cuddled into her mother's breast. Tibbie turned to Tim and wordlessly pointed at the bed to show what she had done. He stood in the doorway and stared. Then he groaned in renewed agony, 'Oh Hannah! Oh Hannah, how can you go away and leave me?'

At this moment Sydney appeared behind him, for he had seen the madly-driven cart going up the path to *Benjy's* and knew who was at the reins. Putting a hand on Tim's back he said, 'I'll help you put them into the coffin. I'm sorry, Black Ace. I'm so sorry.'

'Don't say anything, nothing, don't talk about it,' snapped Tim gruffly but he accepted the help.

When everything was done, Syndey said, 'You'll have to bury them in the cholera pit. They won't let them be put anywhere else.'

'I know that, but I'm not going to put them in like paupers when it's dark – not like the others. I'm burying my Hannah in daylight, and if anyone tries to stop me, I'll break their necks.'

They carried the coffin out to the cart and loaded it aboard. Tibbie walked behind with her black shawl draped over her head, and the three of them climbed on to the cart which Tim drove, more slowly this time, back to the camp entrance. Again the guards recognised him and, intimidated by his raging appearance and wild behaviour, stood back to let the cart through.

In Rosewell Square, people stared at the coffin on the cart without at first realising it had come from the camp. One or two of them recognised Tibbie and nudged each other, saying, 'That's Tibbie Mather sitting up there. What's she doing?' Then, when realisation dawned, they drew back in horror, and rushed into their houses or shop-doors with hands over their mouths. 'It's the fever, they shouldn't be allowed here,' they gasped to each other, for few of them could bring themselves to say the dread word 'cholera'. The town was still pretending to itself that the plague had not come upon the people living in its shadow.

The grim trio on the cart looked neither to right nor left as Tim urged the pony on through the traffic, which made way for it to enter the narrow lane that led to the Abbey. At its gate he and Sydney jumped down and gently lifted off the coffin, bearing it between them over the grass to the pit that waited beneath a covering of tarpaulin for its next occupants. There were some people there already, waiting with their hats in their hands. Tibbie looked up and saw her brother William with Effie by his side and Jo behind them. She rushed across and William hugged her close. 'We came because we knew you'd be burying her this morning. We didn't want you to have to do it without your family to help you,' William told her softly. Then he turned to Tim and asked, 'Have you a clergyman to bury them?'

'No. The priest's been blessing the other people that died but I didn't ask him. Hannah wasn't a Roman Catholic.'

'That's all right. I asked her own minister to come across,' said William. 'I'll go and fetch him now.'

The manse backed on to the burying-ground from the other side of the ruins of the Abbey, and he strode off across the grass with a purposeful air. The minister, when William had called on him earlier, had been reluctant to come but the blacksmith was an elder of the church and had stood his ground, 'My niece was a member of your church and I want her buried properly,' he said. It was a request that could not be denied to a highly-respected parishioner, but the minister was determined to conduct a short service from as far away as possible from any source of contagion.

Looking like a raven, he arrived in his black cassock and stood on a bit of rising ground twenty feet away from the open gravepit while he read from his prayer book. The words rang out with terrible solemnity and the wind ruffled his purple bands so that they waved around him like despairing hands, but what he said satisfied William and Tibbie. They were glad to know that Hannah was being sent on her last journey with the sanction of the church.

Tim, however, did not hear a word of the service. His mind was totally concentrated on the rough wooden box lying in the pit at his feet. He could not believe that it contained the bodies of the people he loved best in the world, the only people he had ever loved apart from his parents. He could not come to grips with the realisation that Hannah had gone and he would never see her again. When the minister raised his hands and proclaimed, 'I am the resurrection, and the life. Whoever believeth in me will live forever,' Tim gave a strangled sob and put his hands up to his face – for it was then that the full horror of the tragedy hit him.

The violence of his grief was terrifying. When Sydney put a hand on his arm to try to control him, Tim shook it off and turned to run headlong out of the burial-ground and along the riverbank. He did not know where he was going or what he was going to do, but ran as if he were being chased. The other mourners stood and watched him go in silence before William turned to his sister and took her arm. 'Come on home, Tibbie,' he said. The minister intervened, 'But Mrs Mather's been in the navvy camp. She shouldn't go back to Camptounfoot. What about contagion?'

William glared at him. 'Mrs Mather's going home. She's not going back to that camp that killed her lassie. If anyone tries to stop me taking her home, I'll not be answerable for what I do, Reverend.'

There was no answer to that. Anyway, the attempts at isolating the camp were already obviously futile. Every night, navvies and their families who were still well enough to travel were stealing away across country, running from the contagion. No one tried to stop them for fear of the consequences, and secretly, Rosewell was glad to see them go.

Stunned and silent, Tibbie hung on to her brother's arm. Sydney shook her hand and murmured something but she only nodded, for her mind was so confused that she was hardly able to understand him. Then he walked back to the camp. It did not seem to occur to him that he too could leave.

It was a just over a mile to Camptounfoot by the riverside path from the Abbey and Tibbie did not speak until the roofs of the village came into view, all huddled together in their comforting way in the fold at the bottom of the hill. She paused to look down on them and suddenly said in a stricken voice, 'The lassie's in my house.'

Effie thought she was talking about Hannah and patted her shoulder. 'Oh no, Tib, no she's not.'

'Where's she gone then? To the Jessups'?'

William and Effie looked at each other in surprise, but Jo chipped in with, 'Don't you remember? The Wylie lassie's in Tibbie's hoose.'

'Oh dear goodness, she canna stay there. I'll ask her to go away,' cried Effie, hurrying on in front but Tibbie called after her, 'Leave her be! I said I'd take her. I'll tell her myself.'

William gestured to his wife to come back and whispered, 'It'll be company for her. She'll need somebody in the house.'

'Another lassie?' questioned Effie.

He shook his head, warning his wife to say no more. Tibbie would do what she wanted about Miss Wylie, he reckoned.

As it turned out, Emma Jane was not in the cottage when they reached it but everything was neat and tidy; the fire was banked up in the grate and the cat alseep in its chair, though there was no visible sign that anyone else was living there. Tibbie looked around and told her companions, 'Just go away now and leave me, please.'

'Will you be all right?' asked Effie anxiously.

Tibbie did not answer but only shook her head. She felt that she would never be all right again. Her life was finished. Everything had happened so quickly that she was in a state of shock. 'Just go away, Effie. I ken where to find you. You've all been very kind, thank you very much, but I want to be on my own now.'

When they left she lifted the cat and sat in the warm cushion on the chair. Then she leant her head on her hand and let the deep, slow tears of heartfelt grief run unchecked down her cheeks. She did not sob, she did not cry out, nor did she shake or shudder; she cried as if the tears were coming from a bottomless well. It was afternoon when she saw a face at the window looking in from the garden. Rubbing her eyes to restore the blurred vision, she tried to make out who it was. The visitor rapped on the glass with bent knuckles and she beckoned to tell whoever it was to come in.

'Aw Tibbie, we heard about Hannah and we had to come and say how sorry we are,' said a voice, and Big Lily stepped through the back door, followed by her awkward-looking daughter. The sight of the pair of them, mother and daughter, grabbed at Tibbie's heart but she was too good a soul to envy Big Lily her child.

'It was brave of you to come, Lil,' she whispered. 'I've been in the camp, you know.'

Big Lily nodded. 'Oh aye, we ken about the cholera but we're no' feared. Is there anything we can do for you, Tibbie? Look, Wee Lily's brought you some eggs from Craigie's hens. He'll never miss them 'cos they've been laying in oor hedge.'

Tibbie rose and took the three brown eggs from Wee Lily's outheld hands. 'That's a kind thought,' she said brokenly.

Big Lily clamped a man-sized hand on her shoulder and said with genuine emotion in her voice, 'We're your neighbours, Tibbie. What else can neighbours do but try to help each other at a time like this?'

Camptounfoot proved its integrity to Tibbie Mather that day. When the two bondagers left, it was as if they'd made a breach in the wall of grief around her, and one by one the neighbours knocked at her door, some to give her their respects in lowered voices and others with offerings of scones or home-baked bread, a wee bunch of autumnal roses or a jar of home-made jam. Not one person acted as if they were afraid to be near her; not one said that she should not have come home in case she brought cholera to their village. They genuinely grieved for her tragedy and wept for Hannah Mather, whom they'd watched grow up.

The Rutherfords came, so did Bob from the shop with three slices of bacon wrapped in paper. Mr Jessup came and shook his head as he clasped her hand. He couldn't find words to express what he felt for her. The master mason who had employed Hannah's father came, still wearing his leather work-apron and with stone-dust in his hair. 'I've just heard about your Hannah. Oh my God, I wish it wasn't true, but don't you worry, Tibbie, I'll keep on sending your money at New Year. Alex was my best workman and I owe that to him,' he told her.

She always invited her callers into the house, and one or two came but most did not want to intrude on her grief. The last to arrive was the schoolmaster Mr Anderson, who had had to wait till the day's teaching ended and the bairns were turned loose to run up the street. Normally their letting-out time was marked by loud shrieks and shouts, but that afternoon the noise was subdued because he'd told them about Hannah's tragedy and asked them to be quiet for fear of upsetting her mother. Now he stood on her doorstep and said, 'I've come to say how sorry I am, Tibbie. Hannah was a lovely, happy lassie – one of the nicest I've ever had in my care.'

Tibbie was proud to hear her daughter being complimented, and nodded in agreement. 'Aye, she was a happy girl, wasn't she? Right to the end she was happy.'

Mr Anderson nodded sadly. 'A short and happy life – but that can't be much of a consolation to you now.'

Wordlessly Tibbie nodded. Nothing would ever console her for the loss of Hannah, that she knew.

It was dusk and the callers had stopped knocking on the door when she heard light steps on the cobbles outside and a tentative turn at the handle. A voice asked, 'Can I come in, Mrs Mather? I've only come to say that I've reserved rooms in the Abbey Hotel and I'll take my bag away with me now.'

Emma Jane Wylie stood in the kitchen doorway. She looked utterly exhausted and bedraggled. Her black skirt was dirt-stained and her fine leather boots covered with dried mud. Incongruously she still wore her unbecoming black straw bonnet.

'Oh heavens above, lassie, what have you been doing?'

Tibbie's surprise made her disregard for a moment her sorrow.

'I've been down at the bridge.' Emma Jane's voice was shaking and she was so tired she could hardly stand. All day she had walked around the site, sat in the hut, pored over her plans, asked questions, tried to understand the answers, ignored the curious stares and sometimes the derisive laughter of the navvies ... The day had passed so quickly that it was nightfall before she realised it, and then she felt terrible exhaustion overwhelm her. It took the last of her energy to climb the hill to Camptounfoot. Tibbie's kitchen glowed with warmth and comfort and she longed to sit down by the fire but she knew she could not stay, she could not impose herself on the sorrowing mother. She'd get to the Abbey Hotel somehow. It was a lie about reserving rooms but she was sure some would be available. The men at the site had told her Rosewell was empty because of the cholera in the camp.

'I've just come to fetch my bag,' she repeated, stumbling towards the stairs.

Tibbie's voice was sharp as she called after her, 'Are you feared I'll give you the fever?' Inwardly she was thinking, if it had not been for the railway coming here, her Hannah would be alive still, and she associated Emma Jane with the railway.

The girl turned in the hall and her face showed shock. 'Oh no, please don't think that! I'm not afraid of that at all. I just don't want to intrude on you. I'm so sorry about what's happened. It's a tragedy and I wouldn't blame you if you thought the building of the railway here was to blame for it.'

Tibbie stood up. 'If I thought that I'd be wrong, wouldn't I? This is God's will. For some reason He's taken Hannah and poor wee Kate and we can't do anything about it.'

Emma Jane nodded. 'Yes, that's what I thought about my father, and about James. Your daughter had a whole life in front of her. And to lose the baby, too – that seems so cruel.'

Tibbie waved a helpless hand as if to say, 'Don't talk about it. Don't say the things that I'm thinking inside my head.' When the villagers had come to console her, she'd kept her composure, she hadn't wept, but now, alone with this girl, the dammed-up tears began to flow again. 'I can't help it,' she sobbed. 'It hurts so much. I can't believe it.'

Emma Jane turned back and took the weeping woman into her arms. 'Oh, don't cry like that, don't cry. Let me make you some tea and then I'll go away. You haven't eaten anything, have you?'

She could tell from the room that nothing had been disturbed or moved since she'd left in the morning. Three brown eggs and an assortment of other food lay piled on the table. Most of it was wrapped in the paper that had covered it when it was handed over.

'Sit down,' she said, leading Tibbie to her chair. 'I'll boil you an egg and butter some bread for you.' She wasn't much of a cook because she had always been looked after by servants, but when she was small she used to watch Mrs Haggerty in the kitchen at home and knew how to boil an egg and make tea. At least she thought she did.

She pushed a pan of water on to the grate and let it boil, then was about to drop two eggs into the bubbling water when Tibbie remonstrated, 'They'll crack that way! Take the water off the heat and lower them in gently.'

Emma Jane looked over her shoulder. 'Oh, I'm sorry – I didn't know. I've a lot to learn, I'm afraid.'

'You'll never need to know, I don't suppose,' said Tibbie, but the girl turned to reply very seriously: 'Oh, I'm afraid I will. My father died in very poor circumstances, Mrs Mather. I'm trying to do all I can to salvage our fortunes but I'm beginning to think I'll not manage it.' The day she'd just spent had shown her the enormity of the task she'd undertaken, and her tiredness warned her that she might not succeed. In the firelight her face was white and drawn. Huge dark circles surrounded her eyes and there were lines of tension around her wide mouth.

Tibbie stood up. 'You're tired out, lassie. Here – let me make the tea. It doesn't look as if you've eaten much either.'

'Oh, I have. I don't need anything,' lied Emma Jane.

'You'll eat an egg with me. I don't want two,' said Tibbie, pushing her plate towards the girl who had loaded two eggs on to it. The egg did look inviting and so did the bread and butter. Emma Jane ate up without further protest. Then she went out to the little lean-to at the back door and washed the dishes in a tub of water that was kept there, dried them with a cloth and carried them in again to put them in their usual places on the shelf beside the fireplace.

Tibbie watched silently and then said, 'You're very noticing, aren't you? You know where everything goes.'

Emma Jane nodded. 'I took note before I used the things so's I could put them back in the right place. But now I'll have to leave, Mrs Mather. Is there anything else I can do for you before I go?'

Tibbie shook her head. 'It's awful late, isn't it? How are you going to get to the hotel?'

Emma Jane wore a little watch hanging from a bar-pin on her blouse. She pulled it forward and looking down at it. 'It's only nine o'clock. I'll be able to walk to the hotel in half an hour,' she said, trying to keep the dismay out of her voice but Tibbie noticed.

'You're not walking around on your own at this time of night. Stay up in your room tonight and we'll work out what's going to happen tomorrow,' she said.

'Oh, I can't stay. You must want to be alone,' protested the girl, but Tibbie shook her head and repeated, 'Please stay. I don't think I want to be on my own tonight.' It was true. Emma Jane's concern and tactful attention had showed her how much she would value company to get her through this terrible time.

It was a relief to them both that Emma Jane did not refuse the request. Though she was glad that she did not have to go out into the night in search of a bed, she was also deeply riven with pity for Tibbie Mather. She sat down by the fire facing her hostess and without artifice words began to flow between them. First Tibbie talked of her anger and disbelief at Hannah's death. She told Emma Jane how her daughter was buried with the baby in her arms, and wept again, but this time with less bitterness. Emma Jane listened and spoke when it was necessary, but made no attempt to stop the flow, for she could see that it was helping Tibbie to talk about what had happened.

When it was well after eleven o'clock, Tibbie sighed and told the young woman at the other side of the fire, 'I'm fair worn out with all this. I'll go to bed. I thought Hannah's man might have come tonight, but it's too late now. Oh the poor soul, you've never seen anyone so stricken as he was when they buried her and the bairn. I thought he'd gone mad. He ran off as if all the devils in hell were after him. I wonder where he went?'

'He didn't come to the bridge,' Emma Jane told her.

Tibbie shuddered. 'Poor soul, I hope he's safe. He loved Hannah, that's for sure. I'll have to try to find him tomorrow.' When she drew the window curtains she gazed out at the hillside, silvered in moonlight, and wondered where he was.

At that moment Tim Maquire was sitting on the side of the hill far above her head. He sat huddled in the shadow of a clump of whinbushes with his arms clasped around his knees, staring down into the valley. A fine mist was drifting along its floor and he felt chilled to the bone. By midnight the temperature had dropped to below zero, for once more the volatile local climate had played tricks. Yesterday it had been humid fever weather but now, only a few hours later, the frosts of autumn had come. They would drive away the fever, but too late to save Hannah and Kate, he thought bitterly. His tears were all shed but the pain in his heart was unremitting as he sat on the hillside and stared out bleakly at the twinkling lights of Camptounfoot and Rosewell. He could see flares where men were still working on the bridge but felt no curiosity

395

about what was going on. The only thing he wanted was to go away, as far and as fast as possible.

He stayed there, awake and pondering, till dawn, which burst with a glory that only happens in autumn after a night of sharp frost. Away to his right the first streaks of morning flashed across the sky like the brush-strokes of an inspired painter. They glowed in brilliant shades of orange, red and gold against a background of violet and then the huge sky above his head suddenly became awash with glory. He stood up and stared around.

The rising sun, sharp in the cold air, cast black shadows from the bushes and trees on to the ground. Somewhere in the distance he heard a cock crow and it was echoed by another and then another. Birds began to sing and their outlines spotted the clear sky. The beauty of the new morning could be taken as a mockery of his grief, but it might also be a reassurance. It seemed to him that he was being given some indication that Hannah and Kate had not been consigned to the ground, but that their spirits were soaring above him in heaven.

His clothes were damp with dew and his boots squeaked wetly when he stood up in them. Moving with determination, he turned his back to the dawn and headed across the flank of the hill in the direction of the camp.

Benjy's looked like a body from which the life had flown when he opened the flower-surrounded door. The stove had gone out and there was a scatter of grey ash around it. Some flowers in a jar on the table drooped dead and sere. Hannah's shawl hung limp from the hook on the back of the door and the baby's empty basket lay on the floor by the bed. He stood on the threshold and put his hands in front of his eyes as if to shut out the sight, but then he pulled himself together and went in, hauled a box from beneath the bed and quickly took things out of it. When he had changed into his best suit, he neatly folded his wet clothes and laid them on the bed. Then he took Naughten's drawing of Hannah down from the mantel-shelf and slipped it into his breast-pocket. After that he walked to the door and stood staring into the little house for a long time before he finally went outside, turned the key in the lock and strode away.

The first place he went was the Abbey, where more bodies had been put in the pit overnight. The gravediggers were extending it and they leaned on their spades when he walked towards them. 'How many are in there now?' he asked.

The first man, who was working with a handkerchief tied across his mouth, shrugged and mumbled, 'About a hundred. They've been bringing them down all night.'

'Who's in charge of this graveyard? Are you – or you?' Tim asked first one and then the other, but they both shook their heads.

'No, it's the beadle who lives in that cottage across the road. He's keeping well away from this, though. He leaves it to the likes of us.'

'What's his name?'

'Thomson, Henry Thomson.'

Henry Thomson was smoking his post-breakfast pipe when the caller rapped on his door and said without preamble, 'I'm Tim Maquire. My wife and daughter were buried here yesterday. I want to put up a stone to mark their graves.'

Thomson assumed a sanctimonious expression but took a step back so that he was well away from the navvy as he said, 'That's sad, but I'm afraid the Church Session has decided that there shouldn't be any headstones on the pit. It's bad for the town to mark it, you see.' In fact Rosewell's dignitaries had decided that the least said about the cholera epidemic, the sooner it would be forgotten. The town newspaper which had appeared that morning carried no news item about the scourge that had hit the navvies and their families.

'You won't let me mark my wife's grave?' asked Tim in a voice of incredulity.

'I've been told there's to be no crosses, no stones with names or dates carved on, nothing to show that the fever's been here. If you try to put one up, we'll just take it away.'

Tim turned on his heel and strode off, leaving Thomson staring after him. Now he went to the camp in search of Sydney but could only find Dr Robertson, who sat smoking in a small open space between two huts. He nodded at Tim and said, 'One hundred and ten people have died already. It's like a massacre. I can't keep up with it.'

'Have you slept?' asked Tim, struck by Robertson's strange, remote air. He seemed like a man who was sleepwalking.

'Oh yes,' was the reply, 'for a little while. Your friend gave me his bed. He's resting there now.'

'I'm looking for him. Is he in Major Bob's?'

Robertson nodded. 'Yes, in the hut where it started. God, I can't believe this. I can't believe that it's not possible to stop it. All those people dying and me not able to do anything to help them!' He seemed to be talking to himself as much as to Tim, who only shrugged and walked away.

Sydney was sprawled fully dressed in bed in Major Bob's hut. There was nobody else there and as he walked in Tim realised with a terrible pang that the hut was empty because his other friends were all dead. Only Sydney had survived, and he lay asleep with his head thrown back on the pillow and his face colourless as if he too was deathly ill, but in spite of that Tim shook him by the shoulder. Sydney groaned, 'Go away.'

'Wake up. I want you to help me,' said Tim, still shaking him.

Sydney opened his eyes. 'For God's sake, Black Ace, I haven't slept for two nights till now.'

Tim's face was unsmiling and unapologetic. 'I need your help and I need it now. Have you still got that horse you borrowed to ride to Maddiston? You've not taken it back yet, have you?'

Sydney sat up. 'God, I forgot all about it. I turned it out in the field next door – I hope it's still there. Has Dicky sent a man for it? Is that what this is about?'

'Who's Dicky? Oh, it doesn't matter. I want that horse. Get up and come with me: I need you too.'

The determined tone of his voice told Sydney there was no point in protesting any longer. He sat up and groped for his boots under the bed, grumbling all the time to himself, 'Can't even sleep for an hour! Bloody awful!'

Tim ignored his protests and stood with his arms crossed like a jailer waiting for Sydney to stand up. 'Now come on. Let's catch that horse,' he said.

For fear of thieves Sydney had hidden its harness beneath his bed and now he lugged it out, shoving most of it into Tim's arms. 'You carry that and I'll catch the horse. I wish you'd tell me what this is all about, Black Ace.' But no satisfaction was forthcoming and they walked in silence to the field next door to the camp where the horse was grazing in a far corner. When Sydney whistled, it lifted its head, turned and came trotting towards him. A docile beast, it stood still while he slipped the reins over its neck and soon had it bridled. Then he looked at Tim with raised eyebrows. 'Where to now?' he asked.

'It's not far – near the bridge. Do you think that horse is capable of carrying a heavy weight?'

'What sort of a weight?'

'A stone, about this high . . .' Tim held his hand about three feet off the ground '. . . and this wide.' He measured out some twelve inches.

'It might not carry it but it'll drag it,' said Sydney, mystified.

Tim seemed satisfied. 'That's all I need. When we get it on to the road, I'll fetch a cart. Come on.'

The railway line was advancing inexorably towards the secret dell that Hannah had shown him. He and Sydney led the grey horse past the track the digging gangs had made. Only a few men were working in a desultory fashion and some of them shouted, 'Hey, Black Ace,' when Tim passed, but he never paused or called back to any of them. When he reached the last working party, however, he let go of the horse and walked across to them. Without a by-your-leave, he lifted two spades and a length of rope off the ground. No one tried to stop him. With a completely impassive expression on his face and his eyes staring straight ahead, he walked back to Sydney, who was suddenly struck by the fear that Black Ace might have gone mad.

Soon they left the dug-up area of ground and headed into a tree-filled glen that was cut through by a stream. The horse flinched as tree branches swept back at it, but Tim pulled it on grimly, saying, 'Give it a jab in the ribs. Don't let it stop. It's not far.'

At last they reached what seemed to be his destination. It was the narrowest part of the glade, where high banks rose on either side of the stream and trees bent down into the water. Tim dropped his hold on the reins and started clambering up a steep incline on the far side of the stream. As Sydney watched in amazement, he disappeared into the middle of a thick-growing tree that clung to the rockface like a limpet.

'Tie the horse up and help me with this,' his voice came back in a few minutes.

Sydney did as he was directed and climbed up the bank too. He saw that his friend was pointing to a carved white stone that stuck out of the bank. 'We'll need the spades to get it out,' was all he said.

They delved and dug for half an hour before they prised it loose. Then it was laid on its side and pushed down into the stream, where it lay with the water bubbling gently over its surface, washing away some of the dirt that stained it. Sydney slithered down and knelt on the bank, gazing at the stone in admiration. 'That's marble,' he said. 'It's quite beautiful. It's a Roman gravestone . . .' He read out the carved words and told Tim what they meant. 'The benefit of a classical education,' he said with a wry smile after he'd translated everything. Then he sat back and asked, 'How did you know it was here?'

'Hannah showed me. I want to take it back to the burial-ground and put it up as her gravestone. It's got a mother and a bairn on it too.'

Sydney nodded. 'Yes, Flavia and Corellia. Now it'll mark Hannah and Kate as well. What an excellent thing to do, Black Ace. Most suitable, most poetic.'

Tim shot him a glance as if he suspected him of sarcasm, but Sydney was very serious. 'The beadle in charge of the churchyard said there's to be no headstones on the pit,' Tim said as he stood up and started making loops in the rope to go round the stone.

Sydney looked up. 'I know. I heard that yesterday when we took one of the burial parties down. They're trying to pretend none of this is happening, and when it's over they'll pretend it never took place.'

Tim groaned, 'I wish to God it hadn't, but I'm determined Hannah's going to have her stone. I thought if I didn't carve any new names or dates on this one, they'd leave it be.'

Sydney shook his head. 'Rules are rules for people like the burghers of Rosewell, I'm afraid, and the minute you're out of sight, they'll do what they like. But I think I can do something about their rules. I've a friend who's their superior; he has them in his pocket. I'll have a word with him.'

Now it was his turn to say, 'Come on.' They looped up the stone, tied it to the harness and the horse obligingly pulled it out of the glen for them and over the rough ground to the road.

'I'll go and fetch a cart from the site,' said Sydney, and ran off downhill towards the half-built bridge. Several carters were standing around gossiping after having unloaded more stone from the quarry and he spoke to one urgently. Money changed hands and the man grabbed his horse by its bridle and turned his cart back up the hill to where Tim and the grey waited with its gleaming burden. The stone was quickly lifted on to the cart-bed, and while Tim directed the driver to take him with it to the Abbey, Sydney jumped on the grey's back and rode off for the Duke's mansion on the other side of the hill.

The stone-carrier's cart lumbered along slowly, and when they reached the Abbey gate, Tim asked the driver to help him lift off the marble stone and carry it to the gravepit. They were soon interrupted in their labours, however. 'And where do you think you're going with that?' Thomson the beadle stood with folded arms, blocking their way as Tim and the other man were struggling to bear the slab.

'I'm putting it up on my wife's grave,' was Tim's reply.

'I've already told you the rules about gravestones on that pit.'

'You've told me and I'm not listening. Get out of the way or I'll knock you down.' Tim was large and threatening, the beadle small. There was no doubt about which of them would give way. When the stone was eventually dumped on the earthen mound that covered the already-buried bodies, Tim said to one of the watching grave-diggers who were obviously enjoying the beadle's defeat, 'Give me a spade.'

It didn't take long before the slab was set upright in the earth, which he stamped down firmly all round. Then he stood back and surveyed the stone, which glittered icily in the autumn sunshine. Because it had to be firmly sunk in newly-dug earth, only the upper halves of Flavia and her child were visible, but the look of love exchanged between them was still heartbreakingly obvious.

The beadle was not touched by its melancholy, however; he was prancing about with rage on the grassy sward that surrounded the other graves. 'That can't stay there. It'll be away by tonight,' he shouted, but at that moment another man came in through the gate and rapped out, 'Don't make such a fuss, Thomson. The Duke's given his permission for the slab to stay. It's an ancient stone of historical interest, apparently.'

Anthony Frobisher, the Duke's man of business, came hurrying over the grass. He nodded to Tim and grasped the beadle by the arm to lead him away, talking earnestly in a low voice. Thomson nodded as he listened and then, without looking back at Tim who was still standing on top of the mound, walked quickly out of the graveyard. Frobisher came back and said to the shirt-sleeved figure guarding the stone, 'Come off there, please. The Duke of Allandale has sent orders that the gravestone is to remain where you've set it up in your wife's memory, but he'd appreciate it if you'd stop making trouble. There is also no question of more carving being put on the stone. Apart from its value as a Roman artefact, he has to respect the feelings and fears of the townspeople.'

'That's fair enough,' said Tim, climbing down. 'So long as Hannah's stone stays where it is.'

Frobisher clapped his shoulder. 'I understand – your friend explained the situation to us, and it will stay. Around here the Duke's word is law. Now push off out of here, man. We don't want to stir up trouble.'

'I'll go, but there's one thing I've got to do first,' said Tim, and he climbed back to the stone, kneeling by it and laying his face against its cold surface. 'Goodbye Hannah, goodbye Kate,' he whispered. The watching men, even the gravediggers, turned away so that he could take his final farewells in privacy. No one moved or spoke as he walked with dignity past them to the gate and disappeared up the narrow road.

He was sitting in *Benjy's* with his elbows on the table staring bleakly into space when Sydney found him. 'What are you going to do?' he asked.

Tim looked at him from bloodshot eyes. 'Thanks about the stone. I don't know how you did it, but it worked. I'm thinking out what I'll do now.'

Sydney walked in and sat down. 'Don't let it be anything rash. I know it sounds impossible but life goes on, and in time the pain softens. My mother died when I was quite young and I thought I'd never get over losing her because she was the only person I loved and the only one who loved me, but I did – almost. I still think of her but it doesn't hurt so badly now.'

Tim looked at the bland face with a flicker of interest. The mysterious Sydney was not given to revealing things about himself, and to be told so much was a great concession. 'I was thinking about how to kill myself,' he said, returning confidence for confidence.

'I thought that was it: don't do it. Hannah wouldn't want you to die as well. Tomorrow morning the sun will rise, and again the day after. The world goes on. I'm not going to tell you that killing yourself is a sin because I don't believe in that sort of thing, but what I am going to tell you is that it would be a terrible waste. You're a good man, you've got a great future before you. Don't waste it.'

'But I can't stay here. Everything reminds me of her. Even the hills remind me of Hannah. She was the spirit of this place. If I stay my heart will burst in two.' Passionately he put a clenched fist in the middle of his chest. It was not like him either to reveal himself so rawly to another man. The only person to whom he'd ever talked of his innermost feelings was his dead wife.

Sydney nodded in sympathy and said, 'I've been putting my mind to your problem and I think I've come up with a solution. I don't know if you've heard, but they're recruiting navvies to go to the Crimea. I read about it in the newspaper. They'll take you because you're good and everyone in the business knows you ... There's a man called Peto doing the recruiting in Whitechapel. Go to London and sign on.'

Tim did not look over-impressed. 'The Crimea – to the war? I don't want to fight in a war, Sydney. It's a hard enough life being a navvy, but at least you're your own master. In the army you're just a slave.'

'Peto's not recruiting men to fight, but to build a railway between the port and Sevastopol. He only wants the best and he's getting them. If you don't go down there fast, you'll have missed your chance.'

'It sounds as if you're wanting rid of me,' said Tim with a wry smile, his first for a long time.

Sydney saw it and grinned back. 'Of course I am. No, seriously, if you can't stay here where else will you go? There's not much work available anywhere apart from here. Or have you made enough to return to Ireland? Could you go there?'

Tim shook his head vigorously. 'No. That dream died long ago. Anyway, I'm going to give Hannah's mother most of my savings. I've no use for money now and she's lost her only child. There'll be no one to care for her when she's older. Hannah loved her Mam. I'll see to it that she has a bit of money put by for when she needs it.'

'In that case, go to the Crimea and make more.'

'Are you going too?' Tim asked curiously, wondering why Sydney was so keen on the idea. But the answer was a shake of the head.

'No. I'd like it, I think, but this bridge has got hold of me in some way. I want to stay and see it finished.'

Tim said slowly, 'I thought I did, too, but what's happened has ruined it. When Mr Wylie died I was sad, but now that I've lost Hannah and Kate I've completely lost heart. Maybe there is a curse on the bridge after all. That mad farmer cursed it, you know.'

Sydney stood up. 'In spite of what we've just been through, I still don't believe in curses any more than I believe in divine retribution. I'll stay – but you should go.'

Tim did not say whether he would or not but he did concede, 'I'll think about it.'

Sydney was pulling on his hat. 'Robertson says the cold weather's going to kill off the cholera. He's still got some patients very ill, though. I'm off to help him. That man's worked like a slave through this. He thinks he's done nothing, but I know that a lot more people would have died if he hadn't come to help us. None of the other doctors would even set foot in the camp.'

'What's the death-toll?' asked Tim bleakly.

'It's hard to believe it, but this morning it was one hundred and twenty-eight. So many people in less than a week! I find it impossible to comprehend. I keep expecting to turn a corner and walk into Naughten or Major Bob.'

Tim shivered. 'They've all gone. I wonder why we didn't die too?'

'There must be a reason. Either the man up there doesn't want us, or he's got something else for us to do,' said Sydney in his old irreverent tone of voice.

'You're the master of the cover up, aren't you? What's your story – why are you here in a navvy camp? Are you just amusing yourself?' asked Tim.

Sydney, at the door by this time, turned and glared

back. 'It may have begun like that, but it isn't that way now. My story's my business, Black Ace. I might tell it to you some day when we're both old men and meet in our clubs, because you'll get to the top. I've a good facility for picking out men who make it.'

'Is that how you persuaded the Duke to lend you his horse and send his factor to make sure Hannah's stone stayed on the grave?' asked Tim curiously.

'It might be,' Sydney's voice shouted as he went away.

Emma Jane's days went by very fast, but as she hurried around the bridge she found that her biggest setback was the unsuitability of her clothes for working on a building site. The long frilled black skirt was a nuisance; the thin-soled shoes a liability. She looked at the heavy boots worn by the navvies and longed to have a pair like them herself. Then the thought struck her: 'Why not?' She'd seen children walking to school in heavy boots, and the women gathering potatoes in the next field wore them too. At midday she walked across to where two women farm workers were sitting in the lee of a hedge eating slices of bread with cheese and onion, and asked the oldest one, 'Would you mind telling me where you buy your boots?'

Big Lily stared down at her sensibly-shod feet and then at Emma Jane's slim ones. 'I buy them from Bob's in the village,' she said.

'Would he have my size?'

'He might hae bairns' bits that wid fit ye,' suggested Wee Lily, who was listening to the exchange with interest.

'Where's his shop?' asked Emma Jane.

'We'll tak ye,' said Wee Lily, jumping up. 'Come on, it's no' far. If you've no' got enough money he'll gie ye tick.'

Emma Jane smiled and patted the side of her skirt. 'I think I've enough money providing they don't cost too much.'

Wee Lily cocked her head and said solemnly, 'A good pair o' bits'll cost you one pound and ten shillin',' she warned.

'But they'll last ten year,' said her mother, who was walking behind her.

'That seems like a good bargain,' said Emma Jane. 'I'd be pleased if you showed me where to buy them.'

The shop was within walking distance and everyone in it seemed to know who she was, for they all asked about Tibbie Mather, referring to her as Emma Jane's landlady. It struck her that it was impossible to keep anything secret or private in a village like Camptounfoot. A pair of boots swinging from the rafters turned out to be the right size for her. Bob swiftly threaded long leather laces through the eyeholes and then everyone stood around watching while Emma Jane tried them on. Holding up her skirt with her hands, she clumped around with a most satisfactory feeling of solidity. 'Oh, they're perfect! I'll take them,' she cried. Bob told her they were a bargain at two pounds and she paid it gladly.

Outside the shop Big Lily pulled a face and said 'You should hae knocked the price done. He was glad to get rid o' them. They're only bairns' boots.'

Emma Jane laughed and hitched up her skirt so that she could admire her new footwear. 'I think they're splendid. They're just what I need. I feel so out of place in my town clothes on the site.'

'That's a bonny skirt but it's awful thin. It'll no' keep the wind out when November comes,' warned Big Lily. 'I'll give you one of mine. It's real thick stuff. The cold doesnae get through it, not even in the middle of winter.'

'Oh, I can't take it from you,' protested Emma Jane, but Big Lily was intent on making her a present of the skirt.

'I've twae o' them. Come on into our hoose and try it on.'

The bondagers' little house was a shock to Emma Jane. The kennel at Wyvern Villa where her father and James used to keep their gun dogs was more salubrious. The thatch was thin and ragged, with broken places where the sky showed through. It was unplastered inside, so the walls were rough unhewn stone and the floor stamped-down mud. There was no chimney, only a hole in the thatch over the open hearth so the room was smoky and it was difficult to see into the corners. Above the fire a round pot like a witches' cauldron was swinging from a hook. The furniture consisted of two chairs, an iron bed and a table – and nothing else. There were no pictures or pieces of china, no colourful ornaments or brass knick-knacks like the items that prettified Tibbie's little home. This was genuine poverty.

The poorness of their surroundings did not seem to worry the two women, who ushered Emma Jane into their house with affability and showered her with hospitality. 'Take some tea? No tea? Then have a mug of ale. It's good ale, we mak it oorsel's.'

The ale was sweet and malty and she drank it with relish. 'It is excellent,' she agreed, and had the greatest difficulty in preventing them from giving her more. The little she had taken had already made her head swim so she knew it was very strong.

Big Lily was rummaging beneath the bed and eventually emerged with a dark swatch of material in her hands. When she opened it out and held it in front of herself, Emma Jane saw it was voluminous and made of black material through which a thick red stripe ran vertically. 'It's a braw skirt. It was my mither's – she wore it for thirty year,' Big Lily announced proudly.

She pushed it towards Emma Jane. It smelt of soap and woodsmoke, 'It's a bit big for me,' said little Emma Jane.

'Put it on. Hitch it up,' cried the Lilies, greatly excited. When she did as she was told, the skirt reached to the tops of her new boots and she had to admit it felt soft and comfortable around her legs.

'You wear that. It'll keep you warm down there by the bridge. We've been watching you and wondering about what you'd do when the winter starts, and it's coming soon. I smell it on the wind,' said Big Lily.

Emma Jane tried to give them her old skirt in exchange, but they laughed at the very idea. 'What wid we do wi' a skirt like that, wi' frills on the bottom and everything?

You wear our yin when you're at the bridge and let us have it back when you're finished with it,' said Wee Lily.

'Now all you need is a good thick shawl and you'll be set up for work as good as any bondager,' added her mother, and it took all Emma Jane's strength of will to stop them giving her Big Lily's dead mother's shawl as well.

'I've a good shawl in my bag at Mrs Mather's. I'll wear that,' she promised.

'See and wear it the right way then, crossed over your breast and knotted at the back, not thrown over you like a lady,' was Big Lily's advice.

When she left, they showed her a quick way to reach the bridge site by clambering down a steep hill behind their cottage and following a river path downstream to the site. They wouldn't go with her because they had work to do on the farm. Feeling much more businesslike and efficient, Emma Jane planted her big boots firmly in the slippery ground and slid to the lower level. She was halfway along the path before she saw that someone was sitting by the river bank in front of her. It was Tim Maquire, and he had not heard her approach. To her distress she saw that he was hunched up like a hurt child, weeping into his crossed arms on to which his head was bent.

It was impossible to pass him without being heard so, very quietly, she backed away and retraced the precipitous path up the hill to the road, hoping that the Lilies would not see her. She returned to the bridge by the normal route, but was unable to drive the memory of the grieving navvy out of her mind.

That night, after taking supper with Tibbie, she went early to bed and was lying in the dark relaxing her aching muscles between cool linen sheets. Her eyelids were beginning to droop when the sound of voices coming from the room below woke her again. It was impossible not to hear what was being said because the floor was very thin and Tim Maquire's voice was loud and very audible. He was saying, 'I'm off, Tibbie – I'm leaving. It's not possible to stay here after losing Hannah and the bairn. I'd do myself an injury if I stayed.'

Tibbie's voice murmured something. It was obvious that she was consoling him for he went on, 'That's good of you, but I'm worried about you. Who'll look after you now Hannah's dead?'

More murmurs and then Tim again. 'I know your brother's here and that your neighbours are good but you've not much money, have you? I want you to take this. It's my savings. They're as much Hannah's as they are mine because she was my wife, and I'm giving them to you because that's what she would want.'

Protests from Tibbie were so loud that this time they could be heard. 'I canna take your money, lad. You'll need it yourself.'

Then Tim was saying, 'No, I'll not take it back. What about the bridge? It'll be finished by someone – the railway company'll see to that. You've the girl staying here, haven't you, but I don't think she'll be with you for long. She's not up to it.. It's just a whim she's got. She'll give up, but the bridge'll be built. It doesn't need me.'

When she heard this, Emma Jane put her hands over her ears in an effort to cut out the sound of his words. The pity she felt for his evident sorrow and suffering was lessened a little by her anger at his dismissal of her. 'How dare he talk about me like that! How dare he dismiss me as if I was a child playing games! He knows nothing of my circumstances, nothing of how much I've got to drive myself to do this but I'll finish it,' she wore to herself. 'I'll finish it and show you that I'm serious, Tim Maquire!'

As she was finally dozing off she heard the door opening on to the street and Tibbie's voice ringing out clearly in the midnight air. 'God bless you, laddie. My Hannah loved you dearly and I'm sure she'll watch over you wherever you go.'

He didn't say anything, but Emma Jane thought she heard him sobbing after Tibbie closed the door.

*

Later that night, when Alex Robertson and Sydney had done their last round of the remaining cholera sufferers, they totalled up the number of deaths so far; it came to one hundred and thirty, and there were still four people grievously ill and unlikely to survive. Dog tired, they were making their way back across the half-deserted camp to Major Bob's old hut, when suddenly to their horror they saw that a hut was blazing over by the far wall.

As they ran towards it, Sydney gasped out, 'It's *Benjy's*! It's Black Ace's hut! My God, I hope he's not inside.'

The tiny house that Hannah had loved so much was well alight, with flames leaping like dervishes to the sky from its wooden roof. As they watched, the glass of the little window exploded outwards with a terrible bang and the glare from inside lit up its gap and the open door so that it looked like a peepshow of a scene from hell. If a devil had suddenly appeared, prancing in the middle of the orange glow, the two men would not have been surprised.

The fire had attracted a little crowd which stood clustered together out of range of the flying sparks and blast of heat thrown out by the burning of the tinder-dry wood. 'Is Black Ace in there?' gasped Sydney as he ran up, but the man he spoke to shook his head.

'No, but I saw him start the fire. He filled the house with straw and set a light to it. He waited till it was well alight and then he just walked away.'

Sydney and the doctor stood staring at the burning house till the walls fell in and it became a flickering heap of firewood, just another bonfire. Then they went to bed. In the morning, when Sydney walked back to the place where *Benjy's* had stood, the only sign that it had ever existed was a smouldering heap of grey ashes.

CHAPTER

Fourteen

Dr Robertson's prediction that the first frost of autumn would kill off the cholera, proved correct. After Tim left, nature showed clemency by sending a succession of mornings that dawned bright and crisp; frost silvered the tops of walls and shone like silk on cobbles. Ice covered the puddles between the huts and water kept in buckets by the doors froze overnight. The cold, combined with Robertson's efforts to make the inhabitants clean up the camp, defeated the scourge. The doctor stayed ten days after the last death to be sure the disease was definitely burned out, but on the day he left to ride back to Maddiston, one hundred and thirty-four people – eighty-one men, thirty women and twenty-three children – had died.

Miraculously, the infection had not affected the outside population to any great extent. When cholera did appear in Rosewell, the weather was about to turn. Five people died in the town but the cause of their deaths was kept secret, and Dr Stewart officially listed them as having succumbed to enteric fever. Their burials took place beside their forefathers in the Abbey grounds, with headstones and full panoplies of grief. The mourners attending those interments looked with interest at the white marble stone that jutted out of the top of the navvies' burial mound, but few of them were sufficiently brave to go close enough to look at the carvings on it.

A group of grateful men saw Robertson off at the camp gate. Because he had not shaved for many days, a light brown beard covered his chin and he looked tired and ill. One by one the navvies shook his hand, and when it was Sydney's turn, Robertson asked him, 'What'll happen to the widows and orphans?' His gaze swept up the hill to the bedraggled camp, which looked even sadder and shabbier than it had done before. Its population was cut by thirty per cent through desertions and fever, and more would soon be leaving, for in many huts, women and children mourned the deaths of their breadwinners.

'The men who're still at work will take a collection for them, but there's so many that it'll be the Poor Law or charity for most, I'm afraid,' was the reply.

Robertson shook his head sadly. 'I feel I've failed. I never want to have to cope with anything like this again. So much death!'

Fervently Sydney told him, 'Without you, my friend, it would have been worse, much worse. Everyone in this camp will be eternally grateful to you.' He knew that the navvies had collected money to make a presentation to Robertson, who had given his services for nothing although he was little better off than the people to whom he ministered. The man who was to present the doctor with a purse of ten sovereigns, now stepped forward and handed it up with a few words of gratitude. Robertson stared at it and tried to give it back. 'I can't take it. I don't deserve it. Give it to the people who have been widowed or orphaned.' But the men would not take their gift back. For Robertson to refuse this token of respect and thanks would be an insult, so he had to accept it. 'If any of you ever need a doctor, just send for me. I'll come at any time, for anything, and I won't expect a fee,' he promised them before he rode away.

After the doctor left, Sydney walked to the bridge. It was the first time he had been there since the fever began and, as people always did, he paused on top of the rise after Camptounfoot and stared down at the river valley. Tall pillars were lined up like an avenue of storm-broken trees, the ground was covered with piles of stone and bricks, and the embankments at both ends were rising like giant molehills. Though there were a few advances, the difference was not very striking because, during the fever, the workforce had been too depleted and too dispirited to be very active.

Jopp stood in the field beside a group of men who had been brought down from Maddiston to augment the Rosewell force. As Sydney walked towards them he recognised Bullhead among them, as large and bestial-looking as ever. Trust him to survive plague and pestilence. Trust Bullhead to have got out of the camp before the cholera began, Sydney thought angrily. Then his attention was caught by a man whom he thought was a stranger – a gaunt and shivering wreck standing beside the big bully. It took a few moments before recognition dawned. This unsavoury-looking specimen was a horribly transformed Jimmy-The-New-Man. In a few months he had changed from a fresh-faced, happy youth to a piece of human flotsam. From his appearance he could have been of any age between thirty and sixty. His eyes were pouched and red-rimmed, his cheeks unshaven, his body hunched and thin and he was shuddering like a distempered dog as he stood beside Bullhead listening to what Jopp was saying. Though Sydney was six feet away, his nostrils were assailed by the smell of stale alcohol. It was obvious that Jimmy had become a drunk, and was now in what looked like the last stages of alcoholic decay.

'Good God, what's happened to you?' asked Sydney, putting a hand on the quivering shoulder.

For a second Jimmy stared at him without recognition and then remembrance slowly dawned. 'Oh, hello Sydney,' he said in a toneless voice.

'What's happened to you?' Sydney asked again, deeply concerned.

Bullhead turned round and growled, 'Nothing's happened to him. He's all right, aren't you, lad?'

Jimmy was clapping his arms around his chest as if he was freezing cold, and his teeth were chattering, but he nodded and after a few seconds managed to ask, 'Where's Black Ace?'

'He went away. His wife and child died in the sickness and he left,' Sydney told him.

Jimmy nodded, apparently unconcerned, wrapped up only in his own misery, but Bullhead said with a leer, 'Black Ace's no loss. Jopp's the boss here now.'

'Is he?' asked Sydney with interest. 'I thought Wylie's girl had taken over the contract.'

He looked at Jopp as he said this and the fat little man glared back. 'Miss Wylie's running her father's share of the work, but I've been called in by the company to help her and to make sure everything's done the right way.'

'Really? Who's hiring here today, then? I'm looking for work again,' drawled Sydney.

'I'm hiring. On my terms,' said Jopp.

'And those are?'

'Four shillings a day and half of it in truck tickets.'

Sydney leaned slightly to the side as he pondered this. 'Not very good terms, are they? Wylie paid five shillings and no truck.'

'Things have changed since he died. Now you take my terms or you don't work for me. I'm bringing more men down from Maddiston tomorrow and I don't need trouble-makers.' Jopp was bristling like an angry terrier.

'I think I'll leave it, then,' said Sydney and strolled away. He walked over to the site hut and looked in through the open door. A girl with brown hair was sitting facing the door on a high stool before a table on which large sheets of paper were spread. Her head was in her hands and her brow was lined in thought. Sydney tapped discreetly on the door and she lifted her head, staring at him with large golden eyes. 'Yes?' The eyes were guarded if not outright hostile.

Sydney smiled. 'I was wondering if you're hiring any men, Miss Wylie? I worked for your father but I've not been on site during the fever.'

'Jopp's doing the hiring for me,' she said flatly.

Sydney stepped inside the hut and said in a quiet voice, 'If I may offer a piece of advice, Miss Wylie, don't let Jopp do your hiring. Your father paid five shillings a day, which is a good wage, and it was repaid by good work. Jopp's paying four and insists that the men take half of it in truck. You won't get good men for that. You'll get drunks like Bullhead and Jimmy-The-New-Man, who wouldn't be taken on anywhere else.'

She listened to him attentively but remained unsmiling. 'I told Jopp I'd pay five shillings. I don't know anything about truck – what is it?'

'It's the iniquitous system by which men are paid with food tickets that they can only exchange in a shop owned by their employers. Truck food is nearly always bad. It causes a lot of trouble. Jopp's a past master at the truck system. The profits go into his own pocket.'

She nodded. 'I understand. I should hire my own men, then.'

'If you want to finish this job, I'd advise that.'

'You're looking for work, aren't you?' she asked.

'Yes, I am. The bridge fascinates me. I was here when your father started the project and I want to see it finished.'

'So do I,' she said fervently. Then she nodded briskly and said, 'All right, I'll hire you. Do you know any more men I should hire for my own squad? Good men, I mean.'

'A lot of the good men are dead and the best one of all has gone away, but I'll ask in the camp. I'll tell them to come to you and not to Jopp.'

'Can't you hire for me?' she asked. 'I'm a woman – they might not take me seriously.'

Sydney said very firmly, 'No, I can't. I'm not one of them. I'm an outsider, even more of an outsider than you are. You're Wylie's daughter: they'll respect you for that and if you play fair with them, they'll respect you even more. Find yourself a good assistant among the men and make him your mouthpiece if you like. I'm far too frivolous for the task, I'm afraid.'

As he walked away she remained staring after his departing figure. 'What a strange man!' she thought, but felt glad to have him on her side.

It was nearly time to finish so she gathered up her papers and prepared to walk back to Camptounfoot. As she stepped out of the hut, it struck her that the plans stuck under her arm represented a pipe dream. The enormity of the task she'd taken on was only now becoming apparent to her. In her head she had the idea of a lovely bridge soaring over the river valley, but the reality was a half-built skeleton. To make one into the other she had only an army of ragamuffins and swaggerers. Whom could she trust? How was she going to turn her orders into action? For a brief moment she wished Tim Maquire hadn't gone away, but then she pulled herself together and determined to do the best she could. She pulled her shawl over her shoulders, remembering Big Lily's advice about crossing it over her breast, then clumped out into the field in her big boots. Jopp was still standing in the middle of his crowd of men. She marched across to him and asked, 'Are you hiring men today, Jopp? I need a squad of fifty good workers to help the masons because we must move fast now. The piers all have to be completed up to brick level by the time the bad weather sets in, and that'll be any day now.'

His voice was like honey as he turned to her and said, 'Oh, I've got fifty good men here, Miss Wylie.'

'How much are you paying them?'

'What you told me.'

'How much is that?'

'Four shillings and truck.'

She frowned. 'For that money we'll only get poor workers. I'll pay five shillings and no truck.'

As she spoke she turned to look at the gathering, who stared back at her with a variety of expressions ranging from loathing to reluctant liking on their faces. Her eye ran over them. Some were decent enough, but most looked like the occupants of a prison hulk. She could tell that there were few she'd choose to employ.

'I want to see every man that's hired for my squad. Anybody who thinks they're up to my standards can apply to me directly,' she said and clumped away, a stiff little figure in black.

She was halfway up the hill when she heard running feet behind her and a young lad whom she knew to be

Robbie Rutherford caught up with her. His hair was flying in a boyish way and he smiled unaffectedly as he drew up at her side and asked, 'Can I walk with you, Miss?'

'Of course. I'm going back to Mrs Mather's now. You live on the other side of the road, don't you?'

He was pleased to be recognised. 'I do that. My family have lived there for hundreds of years. They're weavers.'

She shot a look at him. 'How do they feel about this upheaval that's going on at their doorsteps?' she asked.

Robbie considered. 'They weren't happy about it in the beginning, but like most folk they've got used to it now. A lot of the men are like me, working on the line or the bridge and earning more money in a month than they used to earn in a quarter.'

She lifted her eyebrows. 'A quarter?'

He laughed. 'Three months, you'd say. I think a quarter sounds better.'

She laughed back. 'So do I, but seriously, isn't the village upset about us? I remember when I was here before there was a strange feeling in the street. I sensed that people were avoiding me. My father felt the same way.'

The boy at her side gave her a sharp look and said, 'They didn't like it at first: there was a lot of trouble. My own mother and father were against the line coming through here, but when I got work . . . and the other men got work . . . things changed a lot. Look, I'll take you down to the shop with me and you'll hear what they're saying now.'

'But I've been in the shop already,' Emma Jane said. 'I bought my boots there.'

Robbie grinned. 'Then you were only a customer. If you come in with me, you'll be a villager. Come on – you'll see what I mean.'

In the evenings, Bob's shop became the chief meeting place of the village. When Robbie pushed open the door and the little bell pinged, the shop was crammed full of men buying clay pipes and tobacco, and women making purchases of food for the evening meal. They all knew

Robbie and greeted him by name. He stepped in and gestured towards Emma Jane, who was at his back. 'I've brought Miss Wylie down to meet you. She's building the bridge now,' said he. It was an unnecessary introduction, for they all knew who she was and what she was doing, but they looked either surprised or interested and nodded their heads. 'Oh aye . . .' they said.

Bob leaned forward on his counter and enquired, 'How's your bridge doing then, Miss?' as if it was an invalid on the mend.

'Very well, thank you,' she smiled. 'And so are your boots.' She stuck out one foot to show that she had them on and someone chuckled and said, 'It wouldna' dae tae walk through the glaur in fancy shoon, wid it, Miss?'

The speaker was the widow Bella Baird, who had terrified Jo out of his midnight prowls. She had been one of the villagers who was against the railway, and the fact that she'd even spoken to Emma Jane was a gesture of acceptance, though the girl did not know it.

Robbie said in a loud voice, 'Miss Wylie was wondering how the village is taking to the railway.'

A hush fell for a few minutes and then someone said gruffly, 'You ken how they're taking it, Robbie. You're working there, aren't you?'

Robbie turned to the speaker, a man in his middle age, and replied, 'And so're you, Willie.'

Willie grinned, 'And I'm no' the only yin. Most o' the men in this village are working on the line.'

Bob interrupted with, 'It's been good for the village. It's brought money in. Even the folk that were wild against it in the beginning have changed their minds . . . even Tibbie Mather.'

Tibbie's sister-in-law Effie was in the shop and she piped up, 'Tibbie's no' changed her mind but she's accepted it – that's different. There's others like her. They're sorry things are going to change but they realise there's nothing they can do about it.'

Emma Jane raised her voice to say above the hubbub, 'I'm sorry if we've caused an upset here. This is a lovely village and it must have been very quiet and peaceful before we came.'

The village schoolmaster had been listening to the exchange and he pushed his way through towards her and said, 'Miss Wylie, this village'll not change, not really. It's come through worse than this in its time. Camptounfoot is the oldest village in Scotland, you know. It's survived wars and pestilence, famines and feasts, and the fact it's still here shows its sticking power.'

'I hope it goes on surviving, and that when the bridge is built and the navvies move away, life here will return to normal,' said Emma Jane solemnly.

'It will, it will,' Mr Anderson assured her. 'The trouble's almost over now. There's only one or two folk still wild against the railway. Craigie Scott's the worst one, and he's half-demented anyway. Don't you worry about Camptounfoot, Miss Wylie. It'll still be here, going about its business, when railways have all disappeared.'

As she was walking back up the hill with Robbie, Emma Jane asked him, 'Why didn't you become a weaver like your father, Robbie?' She liked him because he was obviously highly intelligent and willing and she felt that this was a boy who could go a long way.

He paused in the middle of the road and stared at her. 'It was because of your father. I used to watch him going back and forward to the bridge from the Jessups', and I wanted to be like him. I want to be an engineer – I want to build bridges and railways like he did.'

She felt tears prick her eyes as she whispered, 'He was a poor boy, poorer than you when he started, you know.'

Robbie was gazing up the long street with a rapt smile on his face. 'I'm going to be rich and famous, Miss. I'm set on it.'

Now they were at Tibbie's door, but before she went in, Emma Jane said, 'Would you like to help me? I'm needing an assistant I can trust.'

Robbie's eyes were shining as he looked at her. 'You can trust me,' he said.

She thrust the plans at him. 'Go home with these and

take a look at them. Bring them back tomorrow and tell me what you think. I know you're not an engineer or anything like that, but just tell me how they strike you. And don't talk about them – they're very secret.'

Next morning, Robbie was waiting for her at the end of St James' Wynd with the precious plans neatly wrapped in white linen. 'Did you look at them?' she asked.

'Aye, I did, and there's some things I'd like to say.'

She looked around at the other figures toiling up the hill in the half-light of early morning. 'Tell me when we get to the hut,' she cautioned him.

When the plans were at last spread out on her work-table, Robbie put a finger on the extreme left-hand side of the first page and said, 'I'm worried that the first landfall bastion's not going to be strong enough, Miss Wylie. Maybe you should build it up with more stone, make a buttress around it.'

She leaned over and examined the plan. 'I think you're right, Robbie. It's going to have to bear the weight of the arches, after all. But Father must have thought of that.'

'He didn't see the earth dug out. I think he assumed there was solid rock under the surface soil but there's a lot of shale there too. I went down and looked at it last night.'

Emma Jane frowned. 'You went down specially?' Robbie nodded. 'If you're right, we'd better strengthen it then,' she said, impressed.

Robbie was pleased, but he cautioned her: 'We'll have to work fast because when the really hard frost sets in, we won't be able to do any more stonework. And it won't be long now. This valley's bad for frost – it lies here a long time, too. The buttress should be up before spring, though, because then you'll be able to start on the arches. I've had an idea about that as well. You should build a big scaffolding and put spars across between the piers so they can all be done at once. It'll need a lot of bricklayers, but they'll come if the money is good and it would be cheaper in the long run.'

His voice was strong with excitement and enthusiasm, which made her look at him with respect and admiration.

'How old are you, Robbie?' she asked. If he had started to shave, it was only necessary for him to do so once a week.

Colour flooded his cheeks like a girl when he answered. 'I'm nearly eighteen, Miss Wylie, but I know I'm wee for my age. My mother says I'm the runt of her litter.'

Emma Jane laughed and patted his shoulder. 'I know what it's like. I was small when I was growing up, too, and everybody thought I was a child even when I was a woman. Some of them still do! Never mind – what you lack in size you make up for in brains. I'll take your advice and if you have any more ideas, don't forget to tell me.' It didn't strike her that she was talking like a woman of forty and not a girl of twenty-two.

Their conference was interrupted by the arrival of several men asking to be hired by Emma Jane. She took some but rejected others, including, had she known it, Bullhead and Jimmy. Her rejection of him infuriated Bullhead, who stormed away muttering, 'Bloody bitch of a woman. Who does she think she is?'

Jopp took him back, however, because Bullhead's capacity for bullying and terrifying other men could come in handy at times. Jopp made him a ganger and told him to form a squad to work on the embankment. 'You can all go and live in one of the empty huts at Rosewell camp,' he said.

Jimmy, who was trailing Bullhead like a disconsolate shadow, shuddered and groaned, 'Aw no, not back there.'

The others stared at him and Jopp sneered, 'Scared of fever, are you? It's all past now.'

'It's not that. I just don't want to go back to that camp. It's a bad place, with bad memories,' muttered Jimmy.

Bullhead grabbed his arm and gave him a push. 'You'll come with me. I'll watch you.' It was almost as if he was afraid to let Jimmy out of his sight.

When work began again on the bridge, the navvies noticed that old Colonel Anstruther and his pretty daughter-in-law did not come each morning to watch what was going on. They were unaware that the Colonel had been summoned to Edinburgh to give an account of the state of the bridge to the railway company directors, all of whom had taken great care to keep well away from the district during the cholera outbreak, and were still chary of visiting there.

The Colonel was away for a week, and when he returned he went stumping into Bella Vista calling loudly for a burra peg, then, glass in hand, he roamed the downstairs rooms in search of someone to keep him company and hear about his trip north. He was glad to find Bethya sitting reading by the library fire.

'I've met some villains in my time, Begum,' the old man began, 'but that Miller's worse than any of them in spite of his smooth manners. He's a blackguard!'

Anger had been building up in him for hours. She looked up, surprised but pleased to hear this, but there was no time for private discussion because at that moment her mother-in-law came bustling in, summoned by the noise of her husband's return. As the Colonel's wife was alert to every nuance of Bethya's expression when Miller's name was mentioned, she kept her tone jocular as she enquired, 'Why, what's he done?'

The Colonel was not joking, however. 'I went up to the city to tell them about how the cholera had affected the men, but neither Miller nor any of the other directors cared a jot. All they wanted to know was did I think the bridge would be finished on time? None of them have been down here since the fever started, you'll have noticed. I tried to explain what a tragedy it's been, but nobody cared.'

His wife sat down in a chair by the window and said dismissively, 'Why should they, Augustus? The people who died were only navvies.'

The Colonel swallowed his whisky down. 'Oh hell, Maria, don't say that. You've not seen the camp. I have, and I'm not easily shocked, but those people have had a terrible time. More than a hundred and thirty died in ten days, and when I asked Miller if the company couldn't start a fund to help them in their distress or do something for their families, he said to forget all about it. The hold-up in building has cost us enough already, said he.'

'Business is business,' said Mrs Anstruther calmly, but Bethya stood up with her eyes blazing.

'How typical of Miller!' she cried out passionately. 'We should do something ourselves. The weather's so cold now – we could open a soup kitchen at least.'

Mrs Anstruther sneered, 'I thought you'd have had enough of good works after the Corn Exchange fiasco.'

'This is different,' said Bethya, more to the old man than to his wife. 'We'll be doing something practical, not preaching. If you'll provide the money, Bap, I'll ask my friends to help.'

'Your friends?' sneered Mrs Anstruther in a voice that insinuated Bethya's friends were insignificant.

Bethya ignored her, although the tone rankled for she knew very well that Gus' mother thought she was aspiring above her proper place in life. A chi-chi girl from Bombay was lucky to have any well-bred friends, and if they knew the truth about her, she wouldn't keep them for long. The reminder that she came from a class as reviled and discriminated against as the navvies, made Bethya's mettle rise even higher, however. 'I'll do it, Bap!' she promised vehemently. She had seen the camp since the fever struck, and had been horrified by the state of the women and children, some of whom were like walking skeletons. 'Somebody ought to help them because they can't help themselves,' she went on in a tone that was unfeignedly sincere. She had been quite unprepared for the misery of the people she saw slinking about between the huts. They brought to mind the beggars of Bombay who used to wring her heart when she was a girl, and the memory of them could still make her feel guilty if she recalled how little she had done to help them.

Mrs Anstruther was angry that the girl and her husband were conducting a dialogue between themselves, so she stood up to walk over and stand between them. 'Don't call him Bap,' she instructed Bethya. 'It's very native.'

Her husband did not take his eyes off Bethya's face.

'How much do you think you'd need to provide them with good soup till they get back on their feet?' he asked.

'How about ten pounds? I'll ask people to arrange for their cooks to make the soup, then we'll take it up to the camp and serve it out to them. And perhaps we could start a fund for the widows and children,' she suggested.

Infuriated at being shut out, Mrs Anstruther sneered, 'Children, indeed. You'd do better to have some children of your own.'

Bethya turned on her like a tigress. 'If I haven't any children, you should ask your son why – don't accuse me!'

'Did you hear that, Augustus? Did you hear what she said?' squealed Maria Anstruther, but her husband was not listening. He was pulling out his pocket-book.

'Here's ten pounds,' he said to Bethya. 'See what you can do with that, my dear. If you need more, come back and tell me.'

'Thank you,' she said, planting a kiss on his cheek and running out of the room.

As she went she heard her mother-in-law starting to scold the old man. 'How can you let that girl twist you round her finger like that? Did you hear what she said about Gus? There's nothing wrong with him but there's something very strange about her, I'm convinced of it. She has an extremely odd relationship with that maid of hers, and she's a very funny one.'

Though she had left the library, Bethya stopped dead in the hall to listen to what was being said about her. Mrs Anstruther did not trouble to lower her voice. It was as if she wanted to be overheard. Bethya stood trembling with passion as she heard the clink of glass. That was the Colonel having another whisky. Then she heard his voice saying, 'Oh Maria, you've always had a very nasty mind. The girl's lonely and Gus doesn't pay her any attention. You'd better face up to it, our son's the odd one, not his wife.'

Maria burst into tears. 'His own father! How can you say such a thing? He's not in love with her any more, that's what's wrong, and who could blame him if she's up to something unspeakable with her maid? There are women like that, you know, especially among her kind.'

Burning with anger, Bethya rushed upstairs to her bedroom. Francine was there, of course, and came across the carpet, eager to help with whatever it was that her mistress required. Bethya stood with her back against the door and stared at the French girl. 'Oh God,' she thought, 'that horrible woman. I shouldn't listen to her but there *is* something very peculiar about Francine. But not that . . . surely not that?'

'You are upset, madame. Do you want to lie down?' asked Francine.

Bethya shook her head. She did not want to be influenced by Gus' horrible mother, for Francine was the only person in the house apart from the old man that she even liked, far less could talk to. She said in a trembling voice, 'It's that awful woman again. I don't know why I let her annoy me so much. You'd think I'd be used to her by now, but she's really clever at getting under my skin.'

'There are people like that,' agreed Francine, thinking of Jessie and Madge in the kitchen, who continued to tease her unmercifully.

Bethya walked into the room and went to stand in the window bay. 'She asked me why I had no children with Gus. She blames it on me.' As she spoke she wondered if she should tell Francine about the insinuation Gus' mother had made about them, but decided to hold that back.

'Does she not know about him?' asked Francine. 'If she doesn't, she's the only person here that is in ignorance.'

'I think she only sees what she wants to see. Perhaps we all do that,' said Bethya slowly. She hated the idea that her ease and friendship with Francine might have to end, but knew in her heart that from now on it would: Mrs Anstruther's poison dart had struck home.

Few of the ladies of Rosewell and district were as enthusiastic about manning a soup kitchen at the camp gate as Bethya. Several of the people she approached pleaded family commitments, illness or an unexpected absence from home as their reasons for opting out. She knew perfectly well that they were not telling the truth, but pretended to believe them. 'It's quite safe now, you know,' she assured them and they all nodded, saying, 'Of course,' but their voices lacked conviction.

Dread of what her mother-in-law would say if she failed in her intentions spurred Bethya on, and by dint of passionate pleadings and unashamed manipulations, she eventually recruited five other young women into the scheme. Some of the older ladies, who were not able to serve soup themselves because of various frailties, sent money, and as the subscription list was headed by the Duke's mother, who contributed ten pounds, everyone in society wanted their name on it as well. Money flowed in, and within two days Bethya was in receipt of over a hundred pounds. She took great delight in announcing this at dinner when both her husband and his mother were present.

Gus grunted, 'They'll only drink it. You might as well convert it into porter and send that to the camp.'

Bethya smiled most tenderly at him, as she always did on the rare occasions they spoke to each other. He found her unfailing sweetness disconcerting and she knew it. 'Do you think so, dear?' she trilled. Inside she was saying, 'Well, you should know, you oaf. A hundred pounds wouldn't keep you in drink for long.'

'What are you going to do with all that money? It won't cost a hundred pounds for a few plates of soup. The whole idea is madness anyway. You'll all catch cholera. Well, I hope you don't bring the infection back here,' said Mrs Anstruther sourly. She didn't care if Bethya fell sick. What worried her was the risk to herself – or so she pretended.

Bethya shot her a glance. In that instant she knew it was her mother-in-law who had been undermining her efforts for the soup kitchen. It was she who had been spreading scare stories about the virulence of cholera and the danger of infection to frighten off possible volunteers.

'It's perfectly safe,' she said.

'How can you say that? A hundred and thirty-four people died up there in ten days!'

Bethya switched on her most dangerous smile. 'If there's one thing my Bombay background is good for, it's knowing about cholera,' she said. 'If there have been no cases for ten days after the last death, the danger's past. And in cold weather, you're safe as well. Both of those things apply in this situation. Perhaps you'll remember to tell that to your friends, the next time you talk about it. We start serving soup tomorrow and we'll go on serving it for as long as it's needed. Then we'll decide what to do with the hundred pounds – and we won't be turning it into porter, either.'

The weather during November became bitter, so Bethya expended some of her hundred pounds on fuel, warm clothes and invalid food for people recovering from the fever and the families of those who had died. Though her mother-in-law scoffed and said such philanthropic enthusiasm would not last, Bethya became the driving force behind a group of women who wrapped up warmly and stationed themselves at the camp gate in a makeshift booth erected by their servants. From there they dispensed soup to anyone who wanted it or looked in need of it. Some of the helpers only appeared occasionally, but Bethya was there every day except Sunday, when she had to attend church with the rest of the Anstruthers.

At first the people of the camp were suspicious and prickly, fearing that they were being patronised, but the soup smelt delicious and there was a real need among them for nourishing food. On the second day, the ladies disposed of their entire supply in half an hour, and resolved to step up the quantity in future.

'But when will we stop?' asked one of Bethya's helpers plaintively, for she did not relish month after month of good works. She was told, 'When they don't need it any more.' As long as there were pinch-faced children and red-eyed women waiting for the soup to arrive every day, Bethya would go on serving it. She did not really know why she was so fired with zeal for the work, but fired she certainly was. For her stints over the soup cauldron she always wore a long cloak of green velvet lined with grey squirrel fur. It had a hood that surrounded her face with a flattering fringe and gave her skin a translucent glow, highlighting her brilliant eyes. Many of the people who stopped and accepted her offer of a mug of soup did so because they were dazzled by the look of her, and worshipping children were always waiting at twelve o'clock for 'the lady in the cloak' to arrive. She was very sweet to them, always gave extra to the thin and scantily-clad, and sometimes slipped a copper coin into the hands of the most dejected.

Most of the soup-kitchen patrons were women and children because the men were at work during the day, and were also too proud to take what they considered to be charity. After all, were not navvies the aristocrats of the working classes?

On the eighth day of Bethya's visits to the camp, however, snow began to fall at eleven o'clock and the soup-kitchen ladies were surprised by a sudden increase in demand for their offering. Chilled, wet men coming back from the site where work had been suspended were halted at the gate by the smell of soup, and for the first time accepted the proffered bowls. The supply ran out quickly, and Bethya was scooping up the last dregs in her pot when she heard a voice saying, 'G'morning, mum.' The mocking note alerted her to its owner, and she looked up defensively to see Sydney standing before her. He grinned at her confusion and asked, 'Temperance soup, is it? No brandy or anything in it? I won't let strong drink pass my lips now.' He had seen her at the gate and her beauty astonished him but, being Sydney, he was not going to give her any sign of his admiration and would have died rather than let her know how often he had made a detour or an unnecessary visit back to the camp at midday, simply to catch a sight of her in her green cloak.

'Of course there's no brandy in it. It's soup, not grog,'

she snapped and then, recollecting herself, asked, 'Would you like some?'

He looked cold, and she held the last steaming bowlful towards him but he backed away, shaking his head and saying, 'No thank you. Give it to someone more deserving.'

She could not tell whether he was spurning her offer or whether he really felt there were others more in need, which of course was true for though he was cold and wet, he was well-enough nourished and looked very strong. He strode off and left her standing with a full bowl in her hand and when she looked around for a recipient, her eye fell on two approaching figures – a young lad and a girl with a black shawl drawn up over her head, a red and black striped skirt and enormous boots on her feet. The girl's companion, who looked as if he might be her younger brother, was wearing a tight black jacket and trousers the seams of which seemed in danger of splitting. He had grown out of them, Bethya deduced as she observed him. Those clothes must have been bought when he was younger and smaller.

'A drop of soup will warm you up,' she said to the young woman, who paused, looking surprised at the offer. Thinking she was reluctant to accept charity, Bethya urged her, 'Take it. The people in the camp have all had theirs. I'll get another mug and you can share it with your brother.'

The face beneath the snow-covered shawl smiled and seemed to come alive. 'That's very kind of you,' said a gracious, ladylike accent. The hands which took the cup were covered with the fingerless gloves local women called 'palmies', which had been knitted for Emma Jane by Tibbie and were being worn for the first time that day.

Surprised and flustered, Bethya found another bowl and passed it to the young woman's companion who was Robbie Rutherford, accompanying Miss Wylie into the camp in search of a workman from whom Emma Jane wanted advice about whether or not to go on laying concrete in such cold weather. Trying not to upset the well-meaning lady, they solemnly stood side by side spooning the soup up till it was all finished. Then Emma Jane handed back her mug and said, 'That was truly delicious. Soup is very welcome on a day like this.'

Inadvertently, she sounded as if she were congratulating the hostess of a successful tea party. When she heard her own voice, she flushed but blundered on, 'It's very kind of you and your friends to take so much trouble for the people in the camp. I've been told how much my men appreciate what you're doing.'

When the gracious girl went away, Bethya looked at her helpers in astonishment and exclaimed, 'My men! Can anyone tell me who that was?'

Only one woman thought she knew. 'I think she's the daughter of the man who had the contract to build the bridge. He died and they say she's taken over the work on his behalf.'

'But she's only a girl!' gasped Bethya, staring up the path at the dwindling figure. She'd heard Colonel Anstruther talking about Wylie's daughter and had imagined a huge, Amazon type in middle age at least – not a little thing with fingerless mittens who looked like a working-house waif.

'Oh, no one really thinks she'll do it,' said her informant lightly. 'But it's amazing she's even trying, isn't it?'

Bethya bent down and started putting used mugs and spoons into a big basket at her feet. When she straightened she said, 'I think we've done all we can here now. The hardest-hit people have left and the men are all at work and earning money again. We'll have to stop some time and I think that time has come.' She was right: the crisis was over.

Next day, when Sydney made an unnecessary walk back to the camp at noon, he was disappointed to see the wooden booth empty and no beautiful half-caste woman smiling behind the swirling steam from the soup pots. What a pity, he thought. Today, if she had offered him soup, he'd have taken it.

CHAPTER
Fifteen

When Emma Jane returned from her visit to the camp, she went straight home to Tibbie's and was happy to find the little cottage glowing with welcoming comfort. 'How lovely to come home to a warm fire,' she exclaimed, hurrying across to the hearth where she stood with her mittened hands held out to the flames. Her fingers and toes were so cold that she feared blood would never run in them again.

'Oh dear me, you shouldn't have been out in that weather,' exclaimed Tibbie, who was rolling out pastry dough on the table. 'The snow's blowing off the hill and when it comes from that direction it always cuts into your skin like a knife. Sit down by the fire. I'm making a pie for your tea.'

Emma Jane shook her head. 'I can't wait for it, I'm afraid. There's a carriage coming to take me to Maddiston. I'm going back to Newcastle tonight.'

Tibbie's hands went very still and her voice became quiet as she asked, 'You're going away?'

Emma Jane turned back from the fire and patted her on the shoulder. 'Not for good, Tibbie, certainly not. If you'll still have me, I'll come back when the thaw sets in. I didn't know I'd have to leave so soon, but a letter arrived at the site this morning from my Aunt Louisa saying that my mother's not well and there's trouble over our house. I've got to go and this is a good time because today we stopped work. It's so cold there's no point in trying to build. We're ahead of schedule, so that's all right.'

'I'll miss you,' said Tibbie softly. Since Hannah's death

she had lost weight and her face looked much older, but at last her depression was beginning to lift. The company of Emma Jane had proved to be a great solace to her. Their relationship had developed gradually and almost without either of them noticing, but now it was strong, a genuine friendship between different generations, a loving sympathy between women.

This had started the day after Tim went away. In the morning Emma Jane had got up and told Tibbie, 'I'll leave – I'll find other lodgings. I can't impose myself on you.'

But Tibbie had looked so frightened, for she was in deep sorrow and dreaded being alone for hour after hour with only her thoughts for company. She clutched Emma Jane's arm in entreaty. 'Don't go. I'd value it if you stayed,' she said.

So they had worked out an arrangement between them. Emma Jane paid a modest but fair sum for her lodging and the food which was provided in such lavish quantities. As the weeks passed it became a pleasure for Tibbie to see how sleek and healthy-looking her lodger was becoming, in spite of the hard work she did and the many miles she walked every day.

When Emma Jane said she was going back to Newcastle, Tibbie's heart sank at the prospect of day after day without her companion. The girl sensed what she was feeling and told her, 'I'll come back as soon as I can, but there's things I must see to in Newcastle. Believe me, I'd rather not go but I have to.'

'Of course you do. I'm just being silly. I'll have to be on my own one day, but you've been a real comfort to me, lass,' said Tibbie. 'Come on, I'll help you pack your bag.'

As they bustled about stuffing clothes into the portmanteau, Emma Jane diverted Tibbie by telling her the events of the day. This was something she always did when she came home, and her landlady looked forward to the recital, adding comments of her own or giving advice if she thought it helpful.

Emma Jane gave a little laugh when she described the

scene at the camp soup kitchen. 'The lady in charge thought Robbie and I looked hungry and she gave us soup. It was good as well, but not as good as yours of course,' she said to Tibbie.

'Didn't she know who you are?'

'Oh, I didn't mind. Why should she know me? Robbie said she was Colonel Anstruther's daughter-in-law. She was only being kind and she's done a very good job with the soup kitchen. A lot of people in the camp really needed it.'

Tibbie nodded. 'Aye, that'll be young Mrs Bethya. Hannah used to talk about her. She said she's awfu' bonny but a bit flighty. She's got a French maid with a funny name.'

'She didn't have a maid with her today,' said Emma Jane, 'but you're right, she *is* lovely. She was wearing the most beautiful cloak I've ever seen, all lined with grey fur. It made me feel warm just to look at it.'

'Oh, that's another thing Hannah said. Mrs Bethya was aye sending to London for fancy clothes. They came up by the cartful but nobody blamed her because they thought she needed some comfort, being married to that Mr Gus. He's a terrible man, apparently.'

Emma Jane was interested. 'In what way? What's wrong with him?'

Tibbie was pushing a last piece of clothing into the bag and attempting to snap the lock. 'He drinks like a fish, he's never sober. And they don't live together, if you know what I mean. Folk do say he's one of the kind that takes up wi' other men.'

'What a pity,' sighed Emma Jane, remembering Bethya's beautiful and glowing face.

'You never can tell what people's lives are like from the outside,' Tibbie warned her sententiously.

'*You never can tell what people's lives are like from the outside* . . .' Those words echoed in Emma Jane's head as she sat in the lurching train carrying her from Maddiston to Newcastle. 'I wonder if anyone could possibly guess from my appearance that I'm building a bridge?' she asked herself with secret pride and glee, smoothing down the cloth of her black skirt. She was once more wearing her stays and the hated travelling clothes, black bonnet and all, which felt strange and constricting after weeks of freedom going bare-headed and clad in Big Lily's voluminous skirt, with its generous drawstring waist. She wished she could have travelled in the mixed compartment next door, for it reeked of tobacco from cigar-smoking men. The smell reminded her of the navvies, who smoked strong black cheroots between arduous bouts of work. She liked the scent of those cheroots and sometimes longed to smoke one herself. That would not have been proper behaviour for a respectable young woman, however, and neither would travelling in a train compartment with strange men! Here she was, confined in the ladies' compartment with a prim woman whose pursed mouth indicated that she suffered from a dyspeptic condition. She did not reply to a remark from Emma Jane about the terrible weather, and not a word was uttered between them for the whole journey.

As they approached Newcastle, close-packed streets of workers' houses could be seen through the window, and Emma Jane's heart sank progessively deeper. Her old doubts and worries took over. She felt guilty at having been happy in Camptounfoot, for while she had been so busy, she had almost laid aside her grief about her father's death. It was not that she had forgotten him – more that she had not been obsessed by grieving. But now sorrow engulfed her; her legs ached and her head began to throb; her whole outlook changed. She was afraid that all her new lightness of heart and optimism would disappear, and hopelessness would creep up on her again if she stayed at home too long.

Haggerty was waiting at the station, for she had sent a telegraph message to say she was coming. His face showed such astonishment when he saw her that she demanded in a panic. 'Is everything all right, Haggerty?'

He nodded. 'Yes, of course, miss. It's just that you look

different, somehow. I almost didn't recognise you. Imagine! And I've known you since you were a bairn.'

She made no comment about that but next asked, 'How is Mama, Haggerty?'

He turned in his seat beside the driver on the box. 'She came back from Harrogate yesterday with your aunt, miss. She doesn't seem much better if you ask me. They're waiting for you now.'

Inwardly Emma Jane groaned and sat back in the seat with her eyes closed. Haggerty observed her anxiously. 'She hasn't changed so much after all,' he thought. 'Poor lass, she looks tired and drawn.'

Though it was late and past their normal bedtime, Mrs Wylie and her unsmiling sister Louisa sat on opposite sides of the drawing-room fire with lace caps on their heads and open prayer books in their hands. Aunt Louisa had also been recently widowed, and since her husband's death had indulged herself in a fervour of piety with which she had infected her impressionable sister. Arabella had always done what Louisa told her.

Now it was Louisa who rose to embrace Emma Jane when she came into the room. 'Your mother's not able to get up. She's very weak,' she whispered, but loud enough to be heard by the invalid who raised suffering eyes that swam with tears as she looked at her daughter and held out beseeching hands.

When they had embraced, Mrs Wylie asked in horror, 'Oh my dear Emma Jane, what's happened to your face?'

The girl put a hand to her cheek in surprise. 'Has something happened to my face, Mama?'

'It looks terrible – it's all freckled! What on earth have you been doing? You must wash in lemon juice or you'll be ruined for life.'

Emma Jane walked up to the looking glass that hung over the fireplace and stood on tiptoe to peer into it. What her mother said was true – a thick scattering of brown freckles covered the bridge of her nose and the tops of her cheeks. She had not noticed them before because the only looking glass in Tibbie's was a tiny square, not big enough to see your whole face in, and she had been too busy for staring into mirrors anyway. She smiled as she turned and said, 'Oh, they'll go away. It's just because I've been working outside.'

'Without a bonnet?' asked her aunt in horror. Emma Jane decided not to answer that question and wondered what their reaction would be if they could see her working boots, crossed shawl and thick skirt. This thought made her giggle inside and she began to feel a little less oppressed.

Her mother's voice sounded fluttery as she asked, 'You're not going on with this nonsense much longer, Emma Jane, are you?'

The girl turned to stare at her. 'What nonsense, Mama?'

'This bridge nonsense. You'll hire a man to do the work for you now, surely?'

'Oh no, it's not nonsense, Mother. It's very serious. Both of our futures depend on what I'm doing.'

'Oh, darling. You could hire a man, an engineer or something. Men are better at that sort of thing. It's not work for a woman. No decent man will ever marry you if you labour outside like a farm-woman. Your aunt and I have been talking about it. Who's going to look after me if you're up in Scotland for months on end?' Her hands were shaking as she held them out to her daughter in entreaty.

Emma Jane shot a look at her aunt who was nodding grimly. Louisa had been fostering and feeding her mother's worries, she knew. 'I won't have to stay in Scotland forever, Mama, only till the bridge is finished next summer – and it's going very well,' she said reassuringly.

Her mother sobbed, 'What if I lose you, just like I've lost James and Christopher? What will I do then?'

Emma Jane said firmly, 'I'm stronger than I look Mama. You're not going to lose me.'

Her mother tried again. 'But I'm lonely. I need your company, my dear.'

'I'll hire you a companion, Mother,' Emma Jane offered.

The sisters stared at each other in horror 'A companion!

When your mother has an unmarried daughter whose duty it is to take care of her. What a scandalous suggestion!' snapped her aunt.

'I have something else to do. I've to build the bridge,' said Emma Jane calmly.

'I think you've gone mad. I've been telling poor Arabella that she should call a doctor to you,' said her aunt angrily as Emma Jane's mother began weeping into her cupped hands.

Emma Jane kept calm and tried to reason with them. 'Aunt Louisa, I want to finish Father's bridge and I know I can do it. If I don't, my mother will be penniless. I don't think you appreciate how bad our financial position is.'

Louisa was furious. Her cheeks were flaming red as she turned on her niece. 'And that's another reason why we had to come back here in this terrible weather. That is why I sent for you to come home. Your mother has had a letter from that awful Amelia asking what furniture she wanted sent over to the cottage. She said you're selling this house and your mother will have to live in the cottage in future. I've advised your mother to consult her lawyer about this. You can do nothing without her agreement. Remember that, young lady.'

Exasperated and angry, Emma Jane turned to walk from the room. 'I'd be only too glad for you to discuss the matter with Mr Johnstone. You might listen to what he has to say,' she called back angrily.

Next day, she went to see Amelia who had arrived in the cottage to clear it of her own effects. 'I didn't know you'd written to Mother about moving out of Wyvern Villa,' she said to her sister-in-law.

Amelia looked up from packing curtains in a big box. 'The lawyer said I should. Apparently the bank's pressing for their money and Wyvern Villa will have to be sold soon. I thought it would save moving costs for you if, when I moved out, Dan brought your mother's things in. I only wrote her a little note but it seems to have caused all sorts of trouble. I'm sorry.'

Emma Jane shrugged. 'It can't be helped, 'Melia. We'll

just have to try to soothe things down, but Aunt Louisa's set on making as much trouble as possible.'

Amelia grimaced. 'She's a bitch, is that Louisa. I never liked her and she's not improving with age!'

Mr Johnstone, the lawyer, arrived next afternoon for a consultation and brought Munro the banker with him. Both men sat solemnly on the spindly chairs of the drawing room and listened while Mrs Wylie, urged on by her sister, talked about how peculiarly her daughter was behaving by driving her out of her home and attempting to sell it over her head.

At the end of her speech she leaned forward in her seat and said to Munro, 'Mind you, I don't really blame the poor girl. It's not her fault – she's only trying to do her best. My daughter has some sort of fixation about finishing her father's bridge. Her aunt thinks she perhaps slightly deranged.'

Munro raised his eyebrows and glanced across at a silent Emma Jane, who was sitting very still staring down at the folded hands in her lap. 'That seems a rather extreme opinion, Mrs Wylie,' he said. 'Miss Wylie has taken on the contractual responsibilities left by your late husband and I wouldn't describe her as deranged, far from it.'

Aunt Louisa sat forward and hissed, 'Not deranged? Selling her father's house without her mother's leave! Telling her she's got to go to live in that miserable cottage, going off to build a bridge with a gang of navvies who don't even speak the Queen's English. Do you seriously think that's normal conduct for a sensible girl?'

Munro fixed his eyes on her face. 'It may be rash and very unusual, but it's also rather noble. And anyway, Miss Wylie is *not* selling this house. My bank is selling it because it owns Wyvern Villa, lock, stock and barrel.'

At that moment Emma Jane lifted her eyes and looked at him with gratitude, then she glanced across at her mother, whose face had gone a worrying shade of grey. 'Are you all right, Mother?' she asked.

'No. No, I'm not,' was the mumbled reply. Louisa was

immediately at her sister's side, chafing her hands, and Emma Jane rose to go to her as well.

'Mother,' she said, bending over the chair. 'Listen to what Mr Munro has to say. I've been wondering how to tell you about this. Now you *must* listen.'

She turned to Munro and gave a small gesture to encourage him to go on. He did so with admirable clarity, detailing all Wylie's debts, telling his widow about the restrictive contract, and leaving absolutely no doubt about the family's financial position. 'It is only through the goodness of heart of your daughter-in-law that you have a house to move into, Mrs Wylie,' he ended up by saying.

That was the last straw. Arabella Wylie burst into hysterical tears and the men withdrew in embarrassment. Emma Jane saw them to the door and, as he shook her hand, Munro said, 'I've heard what you've been doing up at the bridge and I'm most impressed, Miss Wylie. I hope you succeed.'

'But you don't think I will, do you?' she asked solemnly.

'Let me say that I hope against hope that you do, even though my colleagues would not be pleased to hear me telling you that,' was the banker's reply.

Emma Jane stood very still in the hall when the door closed on the visitors and a mutinous look came over her face. 'Just wait and see, wait and see,' she whispered through clenched teeth.

She longed to be back at her bridge, back at Camptounfoot with the knowledge that when work was done she would be received by the peace of Tibbie's cottage, but first there were things she had to do. She raised her chin and walked back into the drawing room.

'Now, Mama,' she said, 'we must decide which pieces of furniture you want to take to the cottage with you, and tomorrow I'll go into Newcastle to an employment agency and find a companion to live with you while I'm in Scotland.'

Her Aunt Louisa looked up balefully. 'That won't be necessary, Emma Jane. Your poor mother will come back to Harrogate with me. At least I won't abandon her. How can you possibly expect her to accept the charity of that terrible girl who was married to your brother?'

Emma Jane sighed. 'Aunt Louisa, Father bought the cottage and gave it to Amelia because he was afraid this would happen . . .' The face that looked back at her was stony, however, and she could see that no matter what was said, Louisa had closed her mind to facts and would persuade her sister into the same way of thinking. To argue with her was like battering against a stone wall. The girl walked to the window and stared out at the orderly garden. It would be a relief, she realised, to get out of Wyvern Villa for ever.

'When I've built the bridge, Mama, you'll be able to buy another house,' she said placatingly.

Her mother moaned, 'Oh, what's to become of us? Why did Christopher die and leave us in this mess?'

Her sister fluttered round her, saying, 'Christopher was always too taken up with his work. I've often said he didn't consider you enough, Arabella.'

To hear her father criticised for dying at the wrong time made Emma Jane furious. She turned round stiff-faced and asked, 'When are you returning to Harrogate, Aunt Louisa? There's a lot to do before I go back to Scotland and it's time I got started.'

'That goes, this stays . . . That goes, this stays.' Emma Jane was walking from room to room in Wyvern Villa putting little tickets on the things that were to be taken over to the cottage. Surprisingly, she found that she was enjoying the task. Every now and again the work was interrupted by her Aunt Louisa who would say, 'Your mother will want to keep the escritoire. Don't send away the davenport – it's so comfortable for Arabella's poor back . . . and on no account must you sell the needlework carpet.' She walked along behind Emma Jane, lifting the tickets and questioning her decisions. Rather than argue, Emma Jane found it easier to nod and then do exactly as she pleased after her aunt had gone away, which was usually quite quickly, for her stamina and enthusiasm did not last long.

Mrs Wylie had not yet left for Harrogate but lay sadly upstairs, tended by the solicitous Louisa who made all the decisions. 'Your mother is still far too unwell to travel. All this fuss about leaving her old home has undone the improvement she's made since she came to live with me. It would be better if you delayed all this, Emma Jane,' said Louisa. It was impossible to make her acknowledge that moving to the cottage was not a whim but had been forced on the family by harsh realities. Through speaking assertively in private to her mother's doctor when he made one of his expensive daily visits, Emma Jane had learned that Arabella's condition was nothing like as perilous as she seemed to believe, and she was sufficiently reassured by this to adopt a firm line with her troublemaking aunt.

'The house is being given up on the last day of the year,' she told her. 'If Mama's too ill to leave her bed, I'll make arrangements for her to be carried in it down to the cottage.'

The anticipated recriminations and protests followed this announcement, spiked with venom. 'How can you do this to your mother? What's the matter with you? You've always been strange. I thought so when you were a little girl but now I'm beginning to suspect that you're very evil! It's those eyes of yours. You can't hide what's in those eyes,' Aunt Louisa upbraided her niece. When Emma Jane attempted to speak directly to her mother, she found the patient in a state of nervous indecision. Louisa had a strong hold over Arabella, but she loved her daughter too so she took refuge in tears and illness.

There was nothing to do but persist in the course that Emma Jane knew was best. Little by little the house was emptied of the things the Wylies wanted to keep, and the rest was marked for despatch to the saleroom in Newcastle. Amelia's muscular Dan made trips to and fro with his long cart, carrying kitchen equipment, armchairs, beds, looking glasses and, most important of all as far as Emma Jane was concerned, her father's huge desk and chest of plans. She only kept his technical books, reluctantly deciding that there was not enough shelf-space at the cottage for the leather-bound works of literature that had lined his library shelves, but which, she had to admit, he never read.

December 31st dawned bitterly cold, and Emma Jane woke in her almost-stripped room with a strange thrill of excitement – so strong, that it made her skin prickle. She sat up against the pillows as the thought struck her . . . *'Today is a watershed in my life. This is the day I cast off the past and start the future.'* She jumped up and went running over to the window to look out on a frost-gripped world. The house was silent because the only servant left was Mrs Haggerty, who would be busy in the distant kitchen preparing morning trays for Emma Jane's mother and Louisa. Only in their bedrooms were morning fires lit. Emma Jane's room was so cold that her breath rose in front of her like a wisp of smoke so she hurried around in search of warm clothes. When she was dressed, she paused to examine her image in the little looking glass on the dressing table which was not accompanying her to the cottage. The face that stared out from its grey depths startled her. Her eyes looked enormous and very defiant. Surely they hadn't always been that funny agate-yellow colour? They looked like cat's eyes, strange and challenging. Her aunt's cruel words came back to her, but her eyes, she knew, were not evil. If they were mirrors of her soul they must show that she harboured no hate against anyone. She had dislikes, of course, and Aunt Louisa was running high amongst them, but she also had burning desires and a determination that was almost ruthless. Perhaps that was what showed in her eyes; perhaps that was what Aunt Louisa found frightening.

There was no time for deep ponderings, however. First she ate a light breakfast and then hurried down to the cottage which was glowing and comfortable. The furniture brought from Wyvern Villa was all in place, the fires were lit and the pieces of silver and brass her mother loved so much, were polished and gleaming. Amelia had worked very hard with Mrs Haggerty to make it perfect. She was waiting with Dan and her children for the arrival of the Wylies. When the new occupants were installed, Amelia's family would set off for Hexham. Arbelle, grown much taller and greatly improved in manners, was in a state of high excitement, running about plumping up cushions and encouraging the already-blazing fire wtih a brass poker.

'Everything's ready,' she squeaked, grabbing Emma Jane's hand and pulling her into the red-curtained parlour. 'Isn't it pretty, Aunt? Look, we've put all the things Grandmama loves best in here.' The room smelled of beeswax polish and lavender, and Arabella's favourite sofa, her footstool, needlework pictures and fringed silk cushions were all prominently displayed.

'I think it's perfect,' exclaimed Emma Jane sincerely, turning to hug first her niece and then Amelia. To her sister-in-law she said fervently, 'You've been wonderful. You didn't need to give this cottage up, you know, 'Melia. There was nothing written down. It was yours to keep if you wanted.'

Amelia hugged her back. 'Bless you, I love this little place but it's not my home. My home's with Dan. Anyway, I promised your father I'd hold on to it for your mother and you. I hope it changes your luck, Emma Jane, I really do. Now come upstairs and I'll show you what I've done about the big bedroom. It'll be your mother's. A fire's been burning in there for two days and it's as warm as a bread oven. Your aunt won't find anything to complain about there.'

'Is that possible?' asked Emma Jane with a laugh.

It was impossible, however, not to feel pity for her mother as, white-faced and visibly wobbling, Mrs Wylie was driven the short distance from her old home to the cottage. She sat between Emma Jane, who held her hand tightly and tried to console her, and her sister Louisa, who seemed to be bent on upsetting her with utterances like: 'How sad to be leaving the house where you lived with dear Christopher. Don't look back, Arabella. Don't look back at it.' Of course Arabella looked back and of course Arabella wept.

When they alighted at the cottage door, Louisa stared around and keened, 'Oh, what has your mother come to? If only Christopher could see this!'

Accustomed by this time to the smallness of Tibbie's home, Emma Jane looked around the wide hall with four solid panelled doors opening off it and said, 'But it's a lovely house! It's more than big enough for Mother and me. Come into the parlour, dear Mama, and see what Amelia and Arabella have done with it.'

The door swung open and beneath her sister's baleful gaze, Arabella slowly walked over and stood on the threshold, looking all around. Emma Jane felt her heart-rate accelerate with tension as her mother's eyes moved from the gleaming brass coal-scuttle beside the fire to the cushioned sofa, from the vase of silk flowers on the table to the walls covered with her favourite pictures and samplers. Aunt Louisa sniffed but Arabella tottered forward and collapsed on the end of the sofa. Her head drooped beneath the black lace mourning cap. Emma Jane was thinking of something comforting to say ... something like, 'One day I'll buy Wyvern Villa back for you, Mama!' when her mother's head raised and tear-filled eyes were fixed on her daughter's face. 'Darling, it's lovely. You've tried so hard, and you've made it beautiful,' she sobbed, and then sank back against the cushions in a half-faint.

Her sister chipped in, 'It's very poky but don't worry, my dear, I'll take you back to Harrogate with me tomorrow.' Louisa lived in the large and impressive practice house of her late husband, the doctor. Her son had taken over the practice from his father but as he was unmarried, his mother still held sway at home though she had the uncomfortable feeling that any day now her son would take a wife. The girl he had in mind was as formidable as his mother, and there were already signs that a power struggle was brewing in the practice house.

As they all stood staring anxiously at her, Arabella

showed the first signs of resolution since her husband's death. She shook her head. 'No, dear Louisa, I'll stay here. I like this little house – it makes me feel safe. And Emma Jane's right, we must adapt to our new circumstances.'

Louisa's jaw dropped but she was not going to be done out of her position as saviour of her sister. 'If you insist on staying, my dear, of course I'll stay with you until your health improves or your daughter is able to return and take care of you.' Though she would never admit it, she did not particularly want to return to Harrogate, and her sister's illness was an excellent excuse for staying away.

Emma Jane said briskly, 'That's good of you, Aunt Louisa. If you're going to stay with Mama, I'll be able to get back to Camptounfoot sooner than I thought. Now come, Mama, let's help you upstairs so you can see your bedroom. It's just as pretty as the parlour, you'll see.'

Arbelle popped up under Emma Jane's arm and said brightly, 'Yes, do come, Grandmama. I want you to see all the pretty things I've put in there for you.'

Mrs Wylie gave a heartbreaking sob and said, 'Oh poor Arbelle, you're such a sweet child!'

Amelia opened her mouth to protest about the use of the adjective 'poor' but thought better of it because even she was mollified by the way her mother-in-law had taken to the cottage. She had not expected the transition to go so smoothly. As a kind of peace offering she said, 'Dan and I will have to be off now if we're to get home before dark, but if you like, Arbelle can stay with you till Dan comes down to the market next month.'

This was accepted with joy by everyone concerned, and when Emma Jane and her niece saw the carter's family off, even the baby waved gaily as Dan gave the reins a shake to urge on the horse. Amelia turned in her seat and called to Emma Jane: 'Now you go back and build that bridge – and do-ant forget to invite us to the opening ceremony, will you?'

'I won't!' cried Emma Jane, raising her hand high over her head like a soldier about to go into battle.

Now the way was clear for her to return to Camptoun-foot and she could hardly wait to leave. She'd have gone right there and then, but she knew there were still a few things to do, and was surprised to realise that one of them was to see Wyvern Villa again for the last time. Sending Arbelle inside with instructions to read to her grand-mother, Emma Jane hurried the short distance between her new home and her old one. At the gate, she paused and gazed over the expanse of frost-whitened lawn to the empty, staring windows that seemed to look back at her with the same accusing expression she had seen on her aunt's face when she made the cruel remarks about Emma Jane's eyes.

Now she remembered that tomorrow was the first day of the year 1855. She counted back the years since she'd come to live in the house that glared with such hostility at her now. Slowly she walked over the crackling gravel of the drive, remembering the sound it had made beneath the carriage-wheels on the first day her father had driven his family to their new house. She'd only been a little girl, and how thrilled she had been! She remembered that James had been particularly impressed by the turret. Now the house still looked imposing and grand, but the life seemd to have left it; it resembled an empty husk. Soon another family would move in, however, and fill its rooms, warm themselves before its fires, drive out its sorrows. She stood gazing at the tarnishing knocker on the front door and then turned away, glad to go, glad to know that it was no longer her home because within its walls she had suffered grief, loss and the annihilation of her self-esteem. Miss Emma Jane Wylie of Wyvern Villa had been a shy, withdrawn person who was too frightened to go out or even contemplate leading a life of her own, too scared to attend a tea party without her mother. Now she was free to forge her own future. The thought was so exciting that she remembered how it had been when she got slightly drunk at Amelia's wedding. She felt giddy, light-headed and full of the belief that anything was possible.

At the gate she turned for the last time and looked back.

'Don't be afraid,' she told the old Emma Jane who, she imagined, was peeping out of one of the upstairs windows. 'Don't be afraid. Even if I fail, at least I'll have tried.'

Next morning she set off again for Camptounfoot and took a tearful farewell of her mother. 'You'll get better, Mama, you really will and when I've finished the bridge, we'll have money again. Then you can do anything you like – travel, buy a new house, anything. I promise.'

Her mother nodded but was obviously not completely convinced, for Louisa had spent the previous evening filling her mind with fear and doubt. Emma Jane knew the only thing to do was to get on, finish the bridge and present her mother with a *fait accompli*.

'It'll be finished by August,' she promised.

'I might be dead by then,' sobbed Arabella.

Her daughter looked stricken and turned to her aunt to say, 'You'll keep me informed of how Mama progresses, won't you?'

Louisa nodded grimly. 'Of course. She couldn't have better attention. Poor dear Arabella . . .' Comfortingly she patted her sister's hand and then added briskly, 'Goodbye, Emma Jane. I only hope you're making the right decisions and don't come a cropper.' Her baleful tone of voice made it clear that she had no confidence in her niece but, thought Emma Jane, that was hardly a surprise. Louisa was just another of the Doubting Thomases, who would be surprised when the great project was finished. 'Don't doubt yourself,' she scolded inwardly. 'You can't afford doubt. Not now . . .'

CHAPTER
Sixteen

After Tim Maquire went away, Syndey Godolphin, the man of many secrets, was left with no real friend among the navvies. He had many acquaintances – people who were happy to talk or joke with him – but no one whom he admired or with whom he felt in tune. He also knew that the other navvies did not really understand or trust him as Maquire had done. As he had told Emma Jane, he was an outsider.

'Why do I stay here?' he asked himself as he walked between the huts of the camp one bitter morning during the Christmas season. Because of the frost the navvies were not working and prostitutes had come from far afield to ply their trade among the idle men. One of them, a big black-haired woman, stepped out from the shadows and hung on to his arm, beseeching him to go with her. 'Only a florin,' she whispered. He shook her off and walked away, apparently deaf to the shouted insults that followed him. 'What's wrong wi' you? You're a queer . . . you fancy bastard!'

It had become his habit, if the weather was dry, to take solitary walks along the river bank or through Camptounfoot to the bridge, which glimmered eerily beneath a coating of frost that had covered it for many long and bitter days. 'Why do I stay here?' he asked himself again, staring at the gunmetal-coloured river rippling round the truncated piers. The answer to his question escaped him. Was it only because he wanted to see the bridge finished? Yes, that was part of it, for he had a hatred of leaving things half-done and besides, he could not think of anywhere else he wanted to go. There was another, almost inexplicable motive for his inability to leave, and the only way to explain it was that he felt as if he was waiting for something to happen – though he had no idea what that something would be. It was the same feeling he used to have just before he threw dice or lifted a hand of cards – a feeling so exciting that it made the blood surge in his ears. One of Sydney's secrets was that he had a dangerous taste for gambling. Only sheer strength of will, coupled with the fact that he liked to play for higher stakes than navvies' wages, kept him out of the camp card-games.

From time to time, during the long lay-off that occurred while a bitter frost gripped the Tweed Valley during late December, he hired a horse and rode to Maddiston to spend the evening with Dr Robertson in his little parlour. There they smoked cheroots or drank the brandy which Sydney took with him, for he knew that Robertson had no money for such luxuries.

The physician liked to talk, as young men do, about his hopes for the future. Sydney did not join in much, and when questioned said his plans were vague. 'A bit of travel perhaps,' he'd say and laugh lightly.

Robertson sighed and gazed into the fire. 'I'd like to find a wife one day. My dream is to live a quiet family life and raise a houseful of children, but I doubt if I'll ever be able to afford it.'

Sydney tapped the glowing end of his cheroot into the fireplace and said briskly, 'But doctors aren't paupers, old man, At least, I've never met one who was.' He was disturbed by the depths of the man's melancholy. 'If there's a black side to anything,' he said jokingly to his new friend, 'you'll be sure to find it.'

Robertson shook his head. 'I should have realised why this practice was so cheap – there's three doctors in the town already. The only patients I get are poor people who can't afford to go to the others.'

Sydney frowned. 'And I'll wager you treat them for nothing.'

'How could I take their money? Some of them are starving.'

'What you need are a few rich patients to balance out the poor ones, don't you?' said Sydney, and Robertson nodded.

'That would help.'

'Well, you can be sure of one thing. There'll never be a sick navvy that doesn't send for you,' Sydney told him, and Robertson shuddered.

'Oh my God, I hope I never have to go through anything like that cholera again. I wasn't lying when I said that I felt insufficient. I wanted to save all those poor people, but they went on dying in spite of me.'

His face was sad as he looked at Sydney, who only shook his head and said, 'Have another brandy.' He pushed the bottle across the table at the doctor and told him, 'I think you've picked the wrong profession. You're far too soft-hearted to be a doctor. I may not be a medical man, but I've got a prescription for you, my friend. Get yourself a woman – go courting. There must be lots of eligible young ladies – and maybe even some with respectable dowries – around here who'd want to marry a doctor. Get yourself out amongst them and you'll be amazed at how much you'll cheer up.'

"That's a good idea,' said Robertson, brightening a little as the brandy coursed into his bloodstream. By the time Sydney left, the bottle was empty and they were both quite cheerful again.

On a day that was unremittingly cold but bright, Sydney decided to explore Rosewell, and he walked its streets and narrow alleys, peering up at the carved stones above the doors of the old houses. Eventually he found his way to the Abbey and walked over the green grass that floored the ruins, gazing with interest at the grinning gargoyles and foliate carvings. He stopped in the middle of the roofless vault of the nave and stared up at an icy-blue sky showing between the fretted arches of broken stone. They reminded him of the half-built bridge, for they represented man's desire to soar and dominate, to leave his mark on the world in defiance of mortality.

Emerging from the Abbey into the street, he was

suddenly and violently knocked back against the wall by the speed of a passing barouche drawn by four cantering grey horses. Its hood was down and sitting alone in the back was the Duke of Allandale, who bawled out to his coachman, 'Stop, stop!' Then he turned round and called, 'Sorry about that. Get in, Godders.'

Ignoring the scowls of the coachman and outriders who recognised him as the man who'd stolen the Duke's horse and kept it for three days, Sydney climbed into the carriage and settled down with a sigh of pleasure into the deep cushions opposite the owner of this grand equipage. 'You do yourself proud, Dicky,' he said with a grin.

'It's expected,' the Duke grinned back. Then he leaned forward and said, 'I'm glad to see you again. I've been to London, and when I was there I saw your father—'

Sydney glared at him. 'You didn't say where I was, did you?'

'No, of course I didn't, but I'm longing to hear what this is all about – navvying, living in that camp, causing a fracas in the town hall and ruining my mother's efforts at good works, wandering about by yourself like a lost dog. Hiding from your family . . . what's going on?' He stuck his thumb back at the Abbey and said, 'Now I find you coming out of there. Have you got religion or something? Is that it?'

Sydney looked shocked. 'You should know me better than that!'

The Duke laughed. 'Yes, I think I do. In London I heard that you'd bolted a couple of years ago, but people think you went to France.'

Sydney nodded coolly. 'Let them go on thinking that. I did go to Paris but I didn't think much of the people so then I went to India. I liked the girls there but not the climate so I came back and joined a navvy gang. I thought I wanted a mindless and muscular way of earning money, and it was time I saw how other people live. By God, I've found out.'

'Your father's sick,' said the Duke tentatively.

'Is he? That doesn't make any difference. I'd appreciate it if you don't tell anyone where I am.'

'The last time I saw him he was looking very ill.'

'Good,' came the retort, 'but don't worry – he won't die. I doubt if even the devil's anxious to make *his* acquaintance.'

'I know he's difficult but you tried his patience rather badly. He was always paying your debts and pulling strings to keep you out of prison if I remember rightly,' said the Duke.

Sydney laughed as if he was being complimented. 'Yes, I did make life rather difficult for him, didn't I? It was getting to be a strain though, thinking of sins that would madden him enough. I'd done most things.'

'To hear that you're in a navvy gang would probably give him apoplexy,' suggested the Duke, but Sydney shook his finger in warning.

'No, no, none of that. We'll keep this between ourselves, shall we? At least for the meantime. I used to dream that if I heard he was on his deathbed I'd hurry home and stage a scene in which I told him that I was going to gamble away the entire family fortune the moment he died, but now I don't think I'll bother.'

'You mean you're going to stay like this?' The Duke spread out his hand to indicate Sydney's fading coat and battered hat.

The reply, spoken with a devilish grin, was, 'I might. Would you still stop and give me a ride in your barouche if I did?'

His friend groaned, 'You know perfectly well I would, but how can you stand a life like the one you're living – when you don't have to? Isn't there anything you miss?'

'I miss pretty, cultivated women. And I miss sport. If you're not too fussy you can always find a prostitute, but I am fussy.'

'There are plenty of eligible young ladies round here,' said the Duke, who was the quarry of almost all of them.

Sydney laughed. 'And can you see them receiving a navvy as a suitor? No, I think I need a rather special

453

woman and I've not met her yet. At least, I don't think so
. . . I want a woman with a bit of spice about her – a bite.'

His eyes were abstracted as he spoke and his friend
looked at him with curiosity. 'You sound doubtful,' he
said. 'Have you found the ideal lady here?'

Sydney shook his head. 'No, no I haven't. It's just that
life's beginning to pall a bit, Dicky. I don't know what to
do next.'

'Well, I can provide you with some sport. I'll give you
a good day's hunting any time you want it. You used to
be keen on the chase.'

Sydney's hooded eyes glittered. 'Now that's something
I *do* miss – a fast run on a good horse over difficult
country! That'd shake some of the doubts and worries out
of my head.'

'Let's do it. My stable's full of the best horses you ever
saw. You can have your pick. We'll hunt the Three Sisters
behind my place, just the two of us.'

'When?'

'Tomorrow if it doesn't snow. If it's frosty the scent'll
be strong. You're not worried about breaking your neck
so we could have a fine run. Come up to the stables now
and we'll pick out a horse for you and tomorrow morning
we'll make an early start.'

The stables behind Greyloch Palace were big enough to
house ten families and still leave space over. The unexpected arrival of the Duke caused consternation. Grooms
and stableboys ran hither and thither, rubbing cloths over
horses' flanks and wetting down their own forelocks with
hands dipped in the water-trough. The riding horses were
stabled in a building like a mansion with Grecian pillars
on the façade. It was divided into a dozen large loose-
boxes, each one more spacious than Tibbie Mather's
kitchen. On the door of each box was a brass plaque
inscribed with the name of the horse that was housed
within it. The grooms and stableboys followed in an
anxious procession as their employer showed his horses off
to his friend, peering through the iron railings that topped
the half-wooden walls of the boxes, first at a stallion called

Achilles, then at a mare named Rosalie, and finally at an enormous black gelding that stood behind a plaque announcing him to be Siegfried. At each one Sydney shook his head. 'Not my sort; too heavy in the heel; looks a bit lazy; too big in the belly . . . Surely you've got something better than this, Dicky?' he said, to the scandal of the grooms who resented such criticisms of their master's bloodstock.

When he reached the last three boxes in the line, the Duke warned him, 'You'd better not say anything bad about the next ones, Godders. They're my best.'

The first horse was a chestnut with a distinctive head and a sharp eye who raised his head and whinnied in recognition as he saw his owner. The Duke opened the box and clapped the animal on the shoulder. 'This is Ajmeer. He's the fastest thing on two legs.'

Sydney nodded in appreciation. 'Very fine, very fine.' Then he bent and ran a hand down the horse's foreleg. 'He's had a bit of a bump, hasn't he?'

The head groom, who was behind them, jumped forward with an anxious look on his face. 'That's an old bump, sir. It doesn't affect the horse in any way.'

'It might in time,' was Sydney's laconic comment as he straightened up.

The next animal was a finely-bred bay mare with beautiful conformation. The veins were raised beneath her silken skin and she shivered with maidenly apprehension when they stepped in beside her. The Duke cupped his hand under her black muzzle and said, 'This one's a fine hunter. She's as brave as a lion but she's not up to a lot of weight, are you, Pompadour?'

'You're trying to put me off, aren't you?' Sydney complained. 'I can see you don't want me to pick her. D'you plan to ride her yourself tomorrow?'

The last horse was dark grey, so dark it looked like polished metal. A broad white blaze ran down the middle of its face and two short, forward-pricking ears showed its keenness and intelligence. 'At last,' said Sydney, nudging his friend. 'This is really something. You've kept this to the end hoping I wouldn't see him, haven't you? Here is the one I want to ride.'

'I knew you'd pick him,' the Duke laughed. 'You and this horse suit each other very well. He's wild and wily and can't be trusted an inch, just like you. But for the man who can master him, he'll run all day and jump any obstacle.'

Sydney turned to look at the shining brass plate on the door and read out, 'Knave of Hearts. I'll ride him tomorrow, won't I, old boy?'

He was rubbing a hand over the horse's gleaming shoulder when the head groom stepped forward and said anxiously, 'It's a wild horse this one, sir, and it's not been out much recently because the only man who can ride it has been sick.'

The Duke intervened, 'Oh, that's all right. It'll put you on your mettle, Godders, won't it?'

Behind him the stableboys nudged each other, anticipating a come-uppance for the cheeky devil who'd said he wasn't too impressed by the Duke's horses. They all wanted to be chosen as whippers-in for the next day so that they could see Sydney defeated by Knave of Hearts.

The festivities of the Christmas season for Rosewell society were greatly enlivened by a round of entertainments hosted by the Anstruther family at Bella Vista. It was generally agreed that the most charming, lively and enchanting of all the ladies of the district was beautiful Bethya, who danced, flirted, laughed and teased with incomparable style. Everyone talked about her and she provided plenty of gossip-fodder, for they discussed over and over again how she had come to marry the lumpen Gus, and when that topic was exhausted they talked about her high-spirited beauty and the glory of her clothes.

No one except her maid Francine knew that Bethya was only acting, but with as much panache and style as any famous stage idol. Beneath the polished exterior and the dimpling smiles, she was utterly miserable.

On New Year's Day she wept bitterly when she woke, sobbing as if her heart would break. She was crying because of the wretchedness of her existence and her longing for her family in Bombay. Through the tears streaming down her face, she sobbed over and over again, 'I hate this place, oh how I hate it. I hate the cold and the greyness. I hate the people . . . you've no idea how much I hate these people. The only one I care for at all is Bap – and you, of course, Francine.'

Her misery was worse because she could imagine what was happening at home in Bombay at that very season. Her parents and sisters would be preparing to ride out in two gharris, all packed in tight on seats that sprouted straw stuffing from huge holes. Laughing and giggling, they would be on their way to visit her aunt's family who lived in a shabby, rambling bungalow on Colaba Point. It was always there that the family's New Year dinner was held. They'd eat spicy chicken, tongue-sizzling lamb curries, folded naan bread, lady's fingers, fried pomfret, a favourite sticky pudding made from carrots, rosgullas in hot sugar syrup, mangoes and tiny red bananas, the kind Bethya loved best. Her taste buds ached for the spices that she missed so much and she wept again. 'I shouldn't have done it. I should never have married Gus. I thought he'd take me into London society. I had dreams of becoming a famous hostess, marrying another man, having children. I never thought he'd bring me here and leave me stranded. Oh, how I wish I could go home . . .'

Francine had heard all this before and knew there was no use contributing anything to it. She was preparing Bethya's morning bath, pouring hot water from the huge jugs carried upstairs by the maids into a prettily painted hip-bath that stood on spread-out towels before a blazing fire. When she saw that her mistress was preparing to rise, she seized the poker and rattled it in the bars of the grate to make the fire leap higher and throw out more heat. Dropping her nightgown from he shoulders as she walked, Bethya came across the floor like Venus. 'Stop making that terrible din,' she snapped irritably. 'And you're very quiet this morning. Are you sulking?'

Francine glanced up with her black eyes flat and expressionless. 'No, madame, I'm not sulking.'

Bethya stepped into the bath and sank down in the warm water with a pleased sigh. Some of her misery was beginning to lift though the core of it would always remain. 'You've been very odd recently, Francine,' she commented.

The maid handed her a cake of rose-petal-scented soap. 'In what way have I been odd?'

'Silent, not speaking, not smiling . . . odd.'

In fact Francine had sensed a drawing back in her mistress and she was right, because after Bethya had overheard Mrs Anstruther's remarks to the Colonel the words had taken root in her mind and she had resolved to be more formal with her maid. Now that the subject had been raised, however, Francine's own pent-up feelings came to the surface and she burst out, 'Do you want me to leave you, madame?'

Astonished, Bethya looked up. 'Leave me? Of course not! What on earth would I do without you?'

'So you're satisfied with my work?'

'More than satisfied. You're indispensable to me as a friend as well as a maid.'

Tears appeared in the French girl's eyes. 'Then why do you not talk to me like you used to do?'

'Damn Gus's horrible mother,' thought Bethya. 'She's ruined the only friendship I have in this place.' But she assumed her actress front. 'You're being silly, Francine. Of course I still talk to you. I've been talking to you this morning, haven't I?'

'But not in the old way, not as you used to do,' sobbed Francine.

Suddenly embarrassed, and very conscious of her nakedness, Bethya stood up in the bath and reached for an enormous towel that lay on a nearby chair. Wrapping it tightly around her and knotting it on her breast, she stepped out of the water and told Francine: 'I'm very fond of you, Francine – you're like a *sister* to me – but I'm not able to show it openly because Gus's mother thinks that we're too familiar with each other. I overheard her saying so to the Colonel. That's why I've not been as open as before.' The word 'sister' was used deliberately, but as she said it Bethya knew it was partly true. She adored her real sisters but she was fond of Francine and felt remorse and pity when she realised that the French girl's life must be as isolated and lonely as her own. She had no companion or confidante in Bella Vista either. They needed each other for support and succour.

'I want to give you a New Year present. We always give them to each other at home. We think New Year is more significant than Christmas, you see,' she said.

'But you gave me ten guineas at Christmas,' said Francine in surprise. On Christmas Day the mistress had presented her maid with a purse containing an unusually generous amount of money.

Bethya nodded. 'Oh, that.' In Bombay it was the custom of her parents to give the servants gifts of money on major feast days, and she had only done what she considered proper, though she knew that the money she was giving was really too much. In a way it was reparation for having been cool with Francine. She did not tell the maid this, however, and hoped that Francine was sufficiently discreet not to talk about her mistress' liberality below stairs because, if Mrs Anstruther Senior got to hear about it, she might take it as another proof of an unsuitable relationship between mistress and maid.

'No, no,' she went on, shaking her head. 'That wasn't your real present. I want to give you something special. Now I know you like my garnet brooch – so I want to give you that.'

Francine's expression was shocked. 'But the Colonel gave you that last Christmas! If he or his wife see me wearing it, they'll think I've stolen it.'

Bethya laughed. 'So they would, wouldn't they? And she'd not hesitate to say so, either. Don't wear it when you're near the Anstruthers, that's all – but you must have it. It'll suit you very well.'

Tripping on her towel in her eagerness, Bethya ran over

to the chest and pulled out the top drawer. Inside was her velvet-lined jewel box, and in the top tray she found the brooch. It was made of circles of matching deep-red garnets, set in gold with tiny diamonds dotted here and there like stars against the glowing colour. It must have cost a great deal of money because it was two inches across – a brooch the wearer would find hard to conceal from sharp eyes like Mrs Anstruther's.

Francine received it with a look of wonder. 'It's lovely,' she whispered.

'Put it on,' said Bethya. When the brooch was pinned to to the maid's bodice, she clapped her hands in delight. 'It's perfect! It suits you just as much as I knew it would.'

'Thank you very much. I will treasure it all my life,' said Francine, putting her cupped hand over the brooch. Her eyes were shining as if she'd been given the most wonderful gift in the world, for it represented more to her than monetary value; it represented an affirmation of Bethya's esteem and affection.

Colonel Anstruther was sitting at the breakfast table with his rubicund face shining when his daughter-in-law appeared. There were only the two of them in the room so she could be as natural as she liked and treat him as she would her own father.

'Happy New Year, Bap,' she said, pausing by his chair and planting a kiss on the top of his bald head.

He looked up in delighted surprise. 'And the same to you, my dear,' he exclaimed.

Her hands were behind her back and she brought them forward to put a little parcel by his plate. 'A gift for you. At home we always give presents on New Year's Day to the people we love best,' she said. She delighted in giving presents but could not bring herself to buy one for Gus or his mother, only for Bap.

He opened it with careful fingers, as pleased as a child, and revealed a jeweller's box. From the other side of the table Bethya was watching him attentively. She wanted him to like her gift. From the box the Colonel drew out a beautiful little jewelled pencil made of gold with a circle of emeralds around its middle and a green silken tassel at one end.

'What a pretty thing!' he exclaimed, and dashingly used it to write his name on the stiffly starched linen tablecloth. If his wife had been present he would have been well and truly scolded for that alone. Then he repeated with a delightful grin, 'What a pretty thing – thank you, my dear. I'll always carry it and when anyone asks me where I got it, I'll say it was given to me by a beautiful young lady.'

He walked round the table to kiss her cheek and his pleasure in the gift was so obviously genuine that she kissed him back, pleased with her success. 'It was difficult to find a gift for a man who owns so many lovely things,' she told him.

'You made an excellent choice,' he assured her, then stood up and folded his napkin. 'Drink your tea and I'll take you to see something *I've* bought for *you*. I wanted you to start the year with it, and it came last night. It's waiting for you now.'

She gulped a cup of tea hastily and stood up. 'Oh, let's go now, Bap. I love presents. What is it?'

'Wait and see,' he said mysteriously as he ushered her to the door. The present was waiting in the stable, groomed and shining. It was a lovely bay mare.

Bethya clasped her hands in delight at the sight of it. 'What a lovely horse – but it's very big, isn't it? Do you think I'll be able to manage it?'

Her father-in-law looked at her in approval. 'You're a superb horsewoman and you know it, so don't come that little girl act with me, young lady. I got you this horse because I could see that your grey's too placid for you now. You need something with more spirit – an animal to put you on your mettle. I thought you could take her out hunting, because the man I bought her from said she's the boldest jumper he's ever ridden.'

'What's her name?' asked Bethya, going up to the mare and stroking her face.

'He called her Jess, but that's an awful name. You can call her anything you want,' the Colonel said.

Bethya turned with her lovely face vibrant and said fervently, 'You're so kind to me, you really are. If it wasn't for you, Bap, I'd have gone away from here long ago.'

His shrewd little eyes were sad as he looked back at her. 'I know that, my dear, and I also know you'll go one day, but in the meantime I have the pleasure of your company. Why don't you take your new mare out now? It's a fine morning – I'll come with you.'

The groom who was holding the horse frowned. 'If you go out, sir, don't go up on the hill. I heard horns coming down from there a little while ago. There's hounds running and this horse is keen: it might take off with Mrs Anstruther. Perhaps I should ride out with you?'

But Bethya shook her head. 'I'll be all right,' she said. 'Come on, Bap, Let's go and change and then we can be off.'

The mention of hounds running on the Three Sisters excited her, for the thought of galloping over their vastness on a spirited horse was exactly what she needed to drive away her still-lingering melancholy.

She and the old soldier cantered off down the drive in high spirits and of course, as soon as they were out of sight of the stable, she persuaded him to head for the hill. Bethya was dressed in her winter riding habit of dark green topped by a shiny silk top hat of the same colour and a broad-meshed eye veil. The Colonel eyed her appreciatively as they rode along. She was fearless on a horse but he felt he ought to warn her.

'Take care, my dear,' he cautioned. 'She's not like your other mare. Don't do anything rash – keep her on a short rein. They are hunting up there and from the sounds of it, they're running.'

He might as well have saved his breath. The sound of the hunting horn made Bethya even more determined to gallop up the hill. 'Come on, Bap, I'll outrun you,' she called, and set off at a gallop. The new mare was as eager as her rider to be out on the hill. For too long she had fretted in a loosebox with her only exercise being lunged round and round on a long rope by grooms who were

462

afraid to ride her, for as soon as she sensed their fear she started bucking and kicking, and always succeeded in throwing them off. Bethya was not afraid, however, and the mare responded to her confident handling with good behaviour. They quickly struck up a rapport – a sort of communication and understanding between woman and horse. They had a lot in common: both of them were beautiful and wayward, but both also longed to be loved.

Freedom exhilarated them. The air was crisp, and as soon as the mare felt soft turf beneath her hooves, she gave three tremendous bucks and kicked out wildly. Instead of responding with panic, Bethya laughed and tightened her hold on the reins. 'On you go, then. Let's see what you can do,' she said, leaning forward and urging the horse into a gallop. With the Colonel panting behind them, they tore up to the summit of the first hill and then paused while he caught up. The sparkling countryside spread all around them in a breathtaking panorama. In the far distance was a bluish-coloured line of snow-covered hills that marked the border between England and Scotland. Between them and the hill-top was a winter world of frost-whitened smaller hills, leafless woods, farmhouses with grey trails of smoke rising from their chimneys, glittering rivers, empty, neatly-ploughed fields that looked like squares of chocolate ... a beautiful, open world inviting them to ride on and explore it. Bethya was smiling when her father-in-law drew rein at her side. 'Isn't this wonderful?' she exulted.

'Maybe, maybe, but I'm too old for it,' he gasped. 'I'll have to go back.'

'Oh Bap, not yet,' she pleaded. 'I'm only just getting a taste for it. You go back but I'll ride on. I'll be quite safe, I promise. I'll return in an hour.' She dimpled prettily at him and he gave in.

'Oh, all right – but do take care. I can see you've got that mare under control, but stay away from those hounds.'

In the distance they could hear the sound of a hunting horn, crisp in the frost-sharp silence. The mare heard it, too, and bent her neck to bite on the bit but Bethya held her still until the old man rode away down the hill again. Then she sat down firmly in her side-saddle, looked around and said out loud, 'Which way, which way?' As she gazed over the farthest slope she saw them, four tiny figures galloping behind a pack of hounds that raced along in a straight line with their noses to the ground. Far off in front of them, a red-brushed fox loped in the direction of a thick covert. It didn't seem to be hurrying. Bethya laughed, drove a heel into her horse's side and they slithered down the slope to join the hunters.

The Duke of Allandale was leading the field on his chestnut horse Ajmeer. As he galloped along, he blew on a silver horn because today he was hunting the hounds himself. Two of his grooms were acting as whippers-in and his friend Sydney Godolphin was close beside him on the grey Knave of Hearts. They were all galloping flat out and the Duke knew that if he could raise the fox out of the covert for which it was heading, there was a chance that it would run for at least six or seven miles. 'Whoo-oop!' exalted Sydney at his side and glanced at his friend with an expression of pure delight. 'He's running, he's running, let's hope he goes on,' he cried.

They were aiming for a gate, intending to jump it, when the youngest whipper-in rode up beside them and called out, 'Someone's joined in, sir!'

'Damned cheek! Go back and say this is private. It's my pack and this is my hill. Tell whoever it is to go away. It must be some crazy farmer out for a bit of sport. These fellows just get in the way,' called the Duke.

The whipper-in's face was concerned. 'It's not a farmer, sir, it's a woman.'

Both Sydney and the Duke stared at him in alarm. 'A woman? My God, her horse must have bolted with her! Go back and stop it. She'll probably break her neck if you don't. Send her home. She shouldn't be hacking on this hill anyway.'

The man turned his horse and galloped back, but when the Duke and Sydney were checked at the covert gate listening to the hounds inside working the wood, he came back looking even more worried. 'She won't go home, sir. She's asked if she can ride along with you. She says she won't cause any trouble.'

'But dammit doesn't she know this is man's sport? We don't want women in on this. What if she falls off? Someone'd have to pick her up and catch her horse. Where is she? I'll send her back myself,' said the furious Duke.

'She's on the other side of the wood. She said she'd wait there to help watch in case the fox comes out on that side,' was the groom's reply.

At that moment a shrill cry rent the air, 'Gooone Awaaay!' The second whipper-in was telling them that the fox had broken covert. The men turned their horses and rode round the edge of the wood to the other side, where the hounds were once more coming out and giving tongue. To the chagrin of Sydney and the Duke, at least a field's length in front of them was the woman on the bay horse. The only consolation they could find was that they did not think she would be able to stand the pace or cope with the obstacles that stood in her way. 'Let her alone. We'll lose her quick enough and if she falls, don't stop to pick her up,' the Duke rapped out to his companions.

The ground beyond the wood was rough and needed watching, but the woman in front maintained her lead and her pursuers began to wonder if her mount was in fact bolting, for it charged along with its head down and its legs covering huge lengths of ground at each stride. Yet she sat up in the saddle and appeared to be enjoying herself. There was no sign of panic or hauling on the reins as she surely would have done if the horse really was running away with her.

When the hounds reached the rising slope of the second hill they began nosing in and out of whinbushes making a great din but the Duke drove his horse down a bank of slippery shale to bring them together and set them on the right line again. Once more they were off, streaming along behind the dark-red blur that was the fox. It, too, was travelling faster now and the pace became furious. The

Duke and Sydney, who were riding stirrup to stirrup, caught up with the woman but ignored her and spurred their horses on, setting them at the most dangerous places without trying to find safe routes. From time to time they noted with surprise that the woman was still with them, taking the same frightening jumps with total aplomb. In the end they covered six miles, ending up at a hill-top cairn where the fox went to ground in a hole that it knew well. It just managed to slip into its sanctuary a few feet in front of the slavering jaws of the leading hound, an old veteran called Bellman who'd lost many a fox there before. Bellman looked up at the Duke with puzzled and sorrowful yellow eyes when he rode up. 'Yes, he's done it again, he's got away,' agreed the hound's master, slithering out of the saddle and standing on the heap of stones beside the panting dogs.

Sydney rode up, too, and rested with both hands on his knees and his head down while he fought to get breath back in his lungs. 'What a run he gave us. He deserves to get away,' he gasped.

Then the woman came clattering up, mud-spattered and pink-cheeked with her hat on the back of her head. 'That was wonderful,' she cried. 'I hope you didn't kill it!'

Sydney turned and looked at her in astonishment at the same moment as she recognised him. Her expression froze. 'It's you! What are you doing here?' she exclaimed.

He assumed a mock Irish accent. 'Sure amn't I doing a bit of whipping-in for his Grace the Duke here.' His friend looked at him in astonishment but Sydney silenced him with a significant look and said in a more normal voice, 'This is Mrs Anstruther. Her father-in-law the Colonel is one of the directors of the railway company, Your Grace.'

He knew the Duke was still against the railway. He had never softened his opposition, for there was no reason to drop his prejudices and objections, but courtesy had been bred in him and he doffed his hat to Bethya, saying, 'You ride very well, Mrs Anstruther, but I feel I must point out that this is private land and today I'm hunting my hounds purely for my own amusement.'

She flushed even pinker. 'Oh, I'm sorry. My mare was so excited I couldn't stop her . . .'

Sydney butted in, 'That's not how it looked. As far as I could see you were urging her on.'

'I got interested,' Bethya snapped back, giving her most haughty stare and thinking, 'What right has a navvy to question my word?' Every time she came up against this man he caused her trouble.

The Duke tried to defuse the situation. 'All right, let's go back now. The horses and the hounds are tired. Follow us, Mrs Anstruther. We'll show you the way.'

When Colonel Anstruther built his house, he told the architect that all the reception-room windows and those of the main bedrooms must look up to the mysterious trio of hills. The Three Sisters fascinated him, and they were the reason he had chosen to build a house on that site. After he returned from his ride he stationed himself in the morning-room bay window with a spyglass to his eye, watching for his daughter-in-law to come riding down the slope. He'd known she would go towards the hounds. By telling her not to, it dawned on him later, he was as good as issuing a challenge. Though she did not know it, he'd turned around halfway down the hill and watched her cantering through the thick gorse-bushes, sitting up easily in the saddle with her top hat shining in the winter sun. 'She's no fool. She'll be all right,' he had told himself in reassurance, but now he was watching to see her come safely home.

Gus was lounging in a chair with a newspaper up before his face. 'What are you looking for, Pa?' he asked.

'Your wife. I gave her a new horse today and she's ridden out on it. She's going up the hill.'

Gus lowered his paper to reveal a debauched face as he said in surprise, 'You gave her a horse? But she's got one already, hasn't she?'

'I gave her a better horse,' said his father, who was still standing staring out of the window with an anxious look on his face. 'I hope I didn't make a bad choice. It's very highly bred.'

Gus laughed nastily. 'Well, well, no wonder you're worried. With any luck your little pet'll break her neck.'

The Colonel turned and looked at him with scorn. 'I don't know how I managed to father you,' he said as he stomped from the room.

He need not have worried about Bethya. At that moment she was riding along behind Sydney and the Duke who were trying to show her how unwelcome she was in their hunting party by pointedly talking together and comparing their runs. Piqued by their neglect but still thrilling with the excitement of the headlong chase, she rode behind. She knew she'd acquitted herself well. Leaning forward, she patted the mare's sweat-stained neck and told her, 'Well done, well done. I'm going to call you Boadicea.'

When they were on the last slope, and Bella Vista could be seen lying among its gardens and lawns beneath them, two grooms came cantering up in their direction. The leader was her own head groom, who called out in relief at the sight of her: 'Oh, thank goodness you're safe, ma'am. You've been away for so long we thought there'd been an accident. The Colonel's in a terrible lather.'

Bethya said coolly, 'I'm perfectly all right, and so's my mare. I've been hunting.'

At this point Sydney spoke to the groom. 'I think you'd better tell the lady's husband that he ought to take greater care of her and not let her out on these hills alone in future.'

She was furious and spat at him like an angry cat. 'I'm perfectly capable of riding alone. I can outride you any day!' Then she cantered away, stiff-backed.

The Duke looked across at his friend and grinned. 'Well, she told you off good and proper, didn't she, my lad? That's some lady, Godders.'

Sydney was smiling too as he watched her go. 'I wouldn't call her a lady, Dicky – she's an altogether different kind of creature. And she's dangerous, if you ask me. Any woman who takes her fences like that must be half-mad.'

CHAPTER
Seventeen

Emma Jane was back at Tibbie's for ten days before the thaw set in, but on every morning of inaction she walked to the bridge and stood beside the piers, laying her hand on the stone and wondering when the frost would be sweated out of them. At last it was and work recommenced.

During the lay-off, the navvy camp had looked bleak and empty, but when the frost began to lift, life returned to it. It was never again to be as crowded as it was before the cholera epidemic, for not only had death cut down the population but many frightened families had moved away. As the year 1855 got under way, however, word spread around via the navvying grapevine that there was work at Camptounfoot, and men came back. Once again women gossiped at the water burn; children played and fought in the cleared area where *Benjy's* had stood; dogs yapped and ran about as skinny and undisciplined as ever. Sydney still slept in the hut that had been Major Bob's, but now it was looked after by the wife of one of the new occupants – a lanky lad from Derry called Lucky Jim for no reason that he or anyone else could explain. He'd been given the name on the first job he got after leaving Ireland, and had used it ever since. Mrs Jim was a good plain cook, better than Major Bob, and she was sober too, so living conditions in the place improved, but Sydney remembered the old days with a strange nostalgia as if it had been a golden age. He realised that his time as a navvy was coming to an end, and hoped Miss Wylie would finish the bridge before he could stand the life no longer.

Jimmy-The-New-Man was living again in the camp in

the hut that used to be kept by Squint Mary, another cholera victim. Its new châtelaine was even more degenerate-looking and drunken than Mary had been, but was just as terrified of Bullhead, the boss of the hut. Jimmy was seldom seen without the big man by his side and so inseparable were they, that tongues began to wag. Bullhead saved his own reputation by having a succession of women living with him, though Jimmy never seemed to be with anyone in particular and anyway he was nearly always staggering drunk. His behaviour still perturbed Sydney, who tried from time to time to speak to him privately, but never with any success, for Bullhead always seemed to pop up and stand between them.

During the lay-off, Jopp had gone among the workforce spreading rumours about Emma Jane. He told them that she was about to run out of money and wouldn't be able to go on paying wages past the spring. He also said that the railway company had asked him to take over the contract when she gave up, and that it would be in every man's interest to throw in his luck with him at once and not wait till the end came, when all his vacancies might be full.

As a result, on the day she began recruiting again, Emma Jane was surprised to see how few navvies turned up to apply. By contrast, Jopp, high on his embankment, had a crowd of applicants around him. Standing beside Emma Jane was her helper Robbie, who was proving invaluable because of his ability to pick up stories and rumours. He soon discovered the reason for the defection of the men from Emma Jane, and told her what Jopp had been saying.

'But that's nonense!' she protested. 'I'm not going to run out of money. I sold my house in Newcastle to satisfy the bank and they're not going to pressure me for any more money until the bridge is finished. I've Munro's promise on that.'

No matter what she said, however, the seeds of doubt had been sown. When work began again in the spring, she only had thirty navvies to work with her bricklayers and masons, who were all men from Camptounfoot who had thrown in their lot with her. This force was not sufficient to finish the bridge in the time left, so she was forced to go to Jopp to ask him to hire twenty of his men to her. He agreed with suspicious alacrity but made the stipulation, 'They're my men, and they're on my pay roll. You pay me and I'll pay them.'

She knew what was happening. She paid Jopp five shillings a day for each man and he passed on four of them to the navvies, but part of that was in truck-tickets.

She was not in a position to argue, for she needed to concentrate on the work in hand. To do them justice, the men all worked hard at first and the piers were quickly erected to the height where it was necessary to start building the brick arches. Emma Jane stood beneath them and stared at their dizzying height. Up there, the masons were laying the last stones. On the day the final pier reached its maximum height, she said to Robbie, 'Now we'll have to put up the linking scaffolds. We'll build them along the top of the piers like a walkway as you suggested, and the bricklayers can work from them.'

Twenty loads of long timber planks had been delivered to the site the previous day and more were expected. They had to be put up as soon as possible, so the most intrepid men were detailed to go up the pillars with ropes tied round their waists and set them in place. This job was going to take at least two weeks, but Emma Jane gave instructions for the scaffolders to start at the southern, lowest end of the bridge and as they moved along, the bricklayers could come in behind them. The planning, the working out, the mathematical minutiae of the task pleased her, and she discovered she had a talent for it. She really began to feel that success was within her reach on the day that the first arch rose between the southernmost pair of piers in a pale salmon-coloured semi-circle. She could not look at it enough, for it filled her with optimism.

It was a mistake to tempt fate, however, as she soon found out.

When she was in her hut that afternoon she heard

shouting, and went out to see a crowd of men standing around a body on the ground. She hurried over and to her horror saw Robbie lying in a crumpled position, his face contorted with pain. 'I've broken my leg, miss,' he groaned from between clenched teeth. He'd been helping to pass bricks up to the men on the scaffold, had jumped on a waggon to load more bricks on to the flat trays that were used to hoist them overhead, had missed his footing and fallen over backwards.

Sydney knelt beside him and ran his hands down the twisted leg. 'It's a bad break, I think,' he said, looking up at Emma Jane. 'I'll ride over to Maddiston for Doctor Robertson. He's the one who helped at the time of the cholera.'

The other men agreed. 'Yes, get Robertson. He's a good man . . .' they chorused.

Distraught for her young friend, Emma Jane knelt on the grass and held Robbie's hand. 'Yes, do go and get the doctor,' she urged. 'Tell him to come at once. In the meantime we'll carry Robbie into my hut.'

They didn't realise that it was dangerous to move him, and his agony and groans were terrible as they lifted him up and carried him into Emma Jane's hut, where he was laid on the floor and covered with her shawl. When one of the men gave him a generous swig of brandy – the first he had ever tasted, for the Rutherfords were abstainers – his groans grew less so they kept administering alcohol till Robertson and Sydney arrived back.

As soon as the doctor stepped into the hut, Emma Jane was struck by the sympathy and humanity that emanated from him. This was a very different physician from any she'd previously encountered. She stepped back from Robbie and watched as Robertson examined the leg and then set it straight, using spars of wood brought down from the bridge. 'I think it's broken in two places,' he said when he stood up.' 'There's a break in the ankle and also in the femur, but fortunately both in the same leg. He must have taken a bad tumble.'

Robbie, only semi-conscious because of the brandy, slurred, 'How long till I walk again, Doctor?'

A strained look, which did not go unnoticed by Emma Jane, passed over Robertson's face. 'I should think about two months,' was all he said, and then he added quickly, 'But first we'll have to get you home to your mother, my lad. It's going to be a bit of a shock for her. I'll need to borrow a cart and some strong men ... can that be arranged?'

Emma Jane nodded, put a hand on his arm and gestured to him to step outside the hut with her. 'I'm the contractor on this bridge,' she told him, 'and Robbie, the lad with the broken leg, is my friend and one of my most valuable assistants. Why did you look so odd when you told him how long it would take to walk again?'

Robertson's eyes searched her face as if he was making up his mind whether he could talk freely to her or not, and the verdict must have been in her favour for he said, 'The ankle break's a very bad one – the bone's smashed. It might mean that he will never walk again.'

Emma Jane stared back at him in consternation before she said, 'Whatever you do, don't tell that to Robbie. He's got to think he's going to be all right. He's only a boy, and if he was told he was going to be crippled, he might give up.'

Robertson's eyes showed interest in her. He'd heard a girl had taken over the bridge and had been intrigued by the idea. This little scrap of a thing didn't look anything like he'd imagined a female contractor to be, however. All he said was, 'I won't tell him, and anyway I may be wrong. I often am.'

The accident to Robbie was the first in a catalogue of troubles that beset Emma Jane during the dark days of early spring. Worries and irritations, both major and minor, besieged her so that she was too distracted to notice the world around her. All she was concerned with was keeping warm, keeping dry, making sure the work went on and defusing disputes among the men – the greatest of her most recent troubles. Since work had begun again, the force was riven with an undercurrent of resentment, and she had no Robbie to bring her information about what was causing it.

One blowy morning as she was walking to work with her head down against the wind, she suddenly sniffed something in the air that made her look up and stare around. She'd caught the smell of spring – a fresh, clear scent that made her blood rise. Then she saw the signs that she had been missing – red buds beginning to swell on the black branches of the trees; grass looking green again and losing its dead, sere look and, most wonderful of all, snowdrops spreading like rippling sheets of white silk over the banks beneath the trees. As she gazed at them she felt optimism rising. They gave her hope.

At the bridge, however, that hope was driven away very quickly because work had stopped and a huddle of navvies stood under the middle pier. This was not the first time that work had been held up by arguments and protracted discussions so, with anger rising in her, she walked up to the men and said shortly, 'Why aren't you working? There's a lot to do and I can't afford to pay slackers.'

They were all men she'd hired from Jopp, and one turned to her to say, 'And we ain't going to work today unless we get the same money as the other men.'

'I pay all my labour at the same rate,' she told him.

'We're doing the same job but your men have five bob a day and we're lucky if we end up with three.'

She faced up to him. 'I pay Jopp five shillings a day for each one of you. If you leave him and come to me, you can get that money direct.'

The malcontents looked at each other. One or two muttered behind their hands and then their spokesman stepped forward to ask, 'Have you the money to finish this job, Miss?'

She looked him straight in the eye and said, 'I swear to you I have.'

Then another man stepped up and said, 'All right, Miss, we'll join your gang. We should have known Jopp was a liar.'

She knew it would not be long before word got back to Jopp that she'd poached his men, and she was right. Half an hour later he came storming into her hut and demanded, 'What do you think you're doing, taking away my workers?'

She gave him her most quelling glare and said,'They were working for me and giving a lot of trouble because you're cheating them out of their wages. My concern is to get this bridge finished on time, and so I'm going to pay them direct in order that they work with a will. If you've any complaints about that, take it up with the railway company. What you've been doing to those men is a kind of robbery.'

Jopp's face went pale but he kept his temper. 'It's not robbery, Miss Wylie, it's what's called sub-contracting. You needed men, I provided them and I took my payment for doing it.'

Standing up behind her table, she put her fists on the wood and leaned forward at him. 'Jopp, you're a rogue!' she shouted. 'And you're a villain, too. I don't trust you an inch. I'm watching you, I'm watching every move you make. Now get out – and make those men of yours work or I'll tell them so much about you that they'll want to lynch you.' Her tone was ferocious.

He stepped back with a shocked look and exclaimed, 'Miss Wylie, when you first came here you were a nice, polite young lady. What's happened to you? You sound like a fishwife.'

'Good, good,' yelled Emma Jane, pointing at the door. 'Now get out and do what I say or I'll make sure the railway directors hear what's going on. I'll tell them you've been deliberately trying to hold up the work, and I'll force them to move you away from here.'

Secretly she knew she had no such power, but she sounded as if she had and Jopp backed away. She had hit him on a raw spot because he was deeply in awe of Miller and the other directors, and although they knew he peculated a little, they did not know by how much. Her biggest strength, however, for the moment at least, was the fact that she was the only one who knew exactly what was still to be done – and even more importantly, *how* it was to be done – to finish the bridge. The railway company needed her until the project was past a certain stage. After that, thought Jopp viciously as he hurried away, after that she'd have her come-uppance. He'd enjoy witnessing that . . .

Before Emma Jane went back to Tibbie's that night she rolled up all her plans and hurried to the Rutherfords' house. Robbie lay in the downstairs room beside his father's constantly clattering loom, and his bed was surrounded by mounds of books because Emma Jane had written to the Haggertys with instructions that her father's engineering library be packed up and sent to the boy to help pass the time of his convalescence. He read the books avidly and every day she looked in on him, he had something new to tell her that was relevant to the bridge. His recovery was slow and, as Robertson had predicted, the leg was not healing well but he did not complain and was always glad to see Emma Jane because she brought news of the work. He wanted to hear about every brick and stone that was laid. When she told him about her row with Jopp, he said, 'He's a cunning little rat.'

She nodded in agreement and laid the plans on his bed. 'I think he's not to be trusted, so I've brought you the plans. I want you to keep them, and no matter who asks to see them, pretend you don't have them. You and I will go over them alone when I need to check on anything.'

The precious plans were stacked under Robbie's bed and then Emma Jane asked, 'Did the doctor come to see you today?'

Robbie's face darkened. 'Yes, he did. I think he's worried about my leg. I should have been able to stand on it by now but I can't. It's still all swollen and sore. I hope I'm not going to have to lie here for the rest of my life.'

Emma Jane sat down beside him and took his hand. 'You won't. You'll get better – I know you will. You've got to make up your mind. I didn't really think that I had much of a mind to make up before I started this bridge, but I'm working on it every day and I want you to do the same. We'll both make up our minds, Robbie.'

He smiled at her and squeezed her hand. 'I'll take your prescription because I don't think Doctor Robertson's is doing much good,' he said.

When she left the Rutherfords' noisy cottage where the loom never stopped until darkness fell – for Robbie's father worked even while he ate – Emma Jane crossed the road to peace and tranquillity, where a good meal and a warm bed awaited her. Tibbie was still subdued and sad because every turn of the year, every change of the weather, every dish in her kitchen or ornament on her shelves made her think of Hannah, but she was glad to have the distraction of Emma Jane. When the girl came home, tired and mud-stained, she bustled about, eager to take care of her. It stopped her thinking about her grief. Before they went to bed she and Emma Jane liked to talk and sometimes sat up till late discussing things that Tibbie had never heard of before. It struck her as strange that she had become so involved with the building of the railway which had caused her such anxiety and fear when it started. Now she knew how many tons of stone Emma Jane needed to finish her bridge; how many sleepers and how many yards of metal line would have to be laid before a train could pass across. Emma Jane's enthusiasm infected even Tibbie, and she began to look forward to the completion of the project as she and the eager girl gazed into the heart of the fire and saw in imagination the arches of the bridge glowing there like a wonderful vision. Tibbie's secret dread was that her companion would go away and she'd be lonely again, but she resolved not to think about that till it happened. The summer was a long time away.

When Emma Jane returned to the site next day she was not surprised to find that her hut had been broken into and the contents strewn about the floor. Nothing was missing, and she smiled wryly as she sorted out the chaos because she knew what the intruder had been looking for and was glad that she'd had the sense to spirit the plans away. She was in excellent spirits and even smiled at Jopp as she walked out to begin her round of inspection.

Gentleman Sydney, working with the gang that was loading bricks on to hoists, watched her as she walked around and reflected on the change that had come over her. Miss Wylie had been a plain little thing when she first arrived, but as the months passed she was gaining in confidence and even, it seemed, in stature for she stood straighter, walked more freely and held her head up as she moved from group to group. Even in her working clothes she had a striking air of dignity and competence. She was not a girl whom you would take lightly or overlook any more.

As he turned to go back to loading again, his eye went up to the roadway, to the spot where the old Colonel and his daugher-in-law usually sat on their horses in the mornings watching what was going on. Today they had not come and he wondered where they were. The sight of Bethya in one of her many smart riding outfits brightened his day, and as he knew it annoyed her greatly if he acknowledged her presence, he always made a point of doffing his hat and bowing in a most exaggerated manner whenever he encountered her. She glared furiously back, eyes flashing and mouth tightening. Then he would laugh and she'd turn her horse to ride away, often making it rear or kick out in her haste. He always made sure there was a good distance between them before he started his teasing because he wouldn't put it past her to try to ride him down. He knew why she was so furious. The Duke had written a stiff letter to Colonel Anstruther pointing out that while he had no objection to the young Mrs Anstruther exercising her horse on the hill, he did not want her participating in his private hunts in future. For her own safety of course, he added.

Now every time this impudent navvy removed his hat and bowed to her, Bethya felt murderous, for she was sure he knew about the Duke's letter and was jeering at her. What was he doing in a navvy gang anyway – a man like that? She remembered how confidently he rode, and how he looked like a gentleman but acted like a villain. 'How he annoys me,' she said to herself. Yet, every time she went to the bridge with Bap, she found her eye searching the working parties for him. If he wasn't there, she wondered why, and was not really at ease until she saw him again.

Sydney was distracted from searching the road for a sight of Bethya by a sudden yell behind him. He whipped round quickly and saw two men swaying to and fro, grappling with each other ferociously, and swearing while the other navvies, who always enjoyed a fight, laid down their spades and cheered them on. The combatants were Jimmy-The-New-Man and Bullhead. Both of their faces were contorted with rage and they were staggering and slithering around on the slope where neither was able to find a sure foothold. After a few moments Bullhead got free of Jimmy and put both hands round the younger man's neck with the obvious intention of strangling him. This was more than just an ordinary fight, this was about to become murder, so the men standing nearest jumped in to separate the fighters. Even the most bloodthirsty of them couldn't stand aside and watch the pathetic Jimmy being slaughtered. They pulled Bullhead off him and pinioned the big man's arms behind his back while Jimmy got up off the ground with his hands round his own throat and a look of terror on his face. Bullhead's eyes were burning red like coals and he was shouting, 'I'll kill you! I'll kill you, you bastard . . .'

'What's it all about?' Sydney asked the man beside him.

The answer was a shrug. 'Dunno, they're been fighting off and on for a week. Some private business apparently. Jimmy's asking for money off Bullhead. He wants to go away and he reckons Bullhead owes him. He's not getting anywhere though. You know what Bullhead's like about money. He'd rather give blood.'

Sydney watched with interest as Jopp arrived and started sorting the fighters out. 'You should be working, not fighting,' he bawled at Bullhead. 'You're on the pulley-gang at the top of the pier, aren't you? Get back up there and start pulling up loads or you're off this site for good. I'm sick of you.'

Then he turned to Jimmy and ranted, 'And you're on your last warning. Get up there, too, and start working or hit the road.' He pointed to the top of the tallest pier where men were looking down from the dizzying scaffold.

'Don't send him up there, he's drunk,' protested Sydney, for Jimmy was incoherent and reeling but Jopp yelled angrily, 'Mind your own business! I'm the boss here. You' – to Jimmy – 'get up there and start working.'

Jimmy staggered across the grass to the rickety-looking ladder that led to the bricklayers' work-platform. Bullhead was up there already, for Sydney saw his bullet-head looking down. Things were quiet for the rest of the morning, but shortly after work began again following the midday break, the air was rent by a terrible scream as a body came hurtling down from the platform to the ground. While men stopped work and stared up in horror, the awful screaming trailed on until the body hit the ground with a terrible thud. There it squirmed as if it was trying to get up, but then it lay still with the limbs spread out like a stranded jellyfish. Everyone rushed across to the sprawled man. Jimmy-The-New-Man lay with his eyes staring up at the sky in speechless agony and his mop of fair hair matted with blood.

'Christ, he's still alive,' said one man, staring down at the white face on the ground. The eyes flickered in response. Up above their heads, shocked faces were peering over the platform and someone was scrambling down the ladder to see what had happened. 'Get a doctor,' he said, kneeling beside Jimmy who was groaning and obviously so badly hurt that no one wanted to touch him. To Sydney another man said, 'You got the doctor when the laddie broke his leg. Fetch him again.'

A carter's horse was commandeered and once more Sydney set off across country to Maddiston, riding flat out. He did not really think that Jimmy would still be alive when he got back and he was furiously angry because he was sure that Bullhead had killed the poor lad.

When he and Robertson arrive back on site, however, Jimmy had not died – though it might have been better if he had. He was alive, in agony, bloodstained, misshapen and groaning on the floor of Miss Wylie's hut with her standing beside him, white-faced and frightened. Robertson ran in and stopped short. 'Dear God!' he exclaimed at the sight of the injured man.

'He fell from there . . .' Emma Jane, whose teeth were chattering, pointed to the top of the bridge pier. It was at least a hundred feet high.

Robertson looked from the bridge to the broken man, shook his head and knelt down beside Jimmy, laying a hand on the bloodstained brow while Sydney seized Emma Jane's arm and led her out of the hut. 'Go home,' he advised. 'The men won't work any more today after an accident like this. I'll send you a message to tell you what happens.' He could see that Jimmy had not long to live and did not want the girl to be there when he died. To his relief, she knew why he was anxious for her to leave and she walked away, pulling her shawl tightly over her shoulders as she went.

Back in the hut, Robertson looked up and said to Sydney, 'He wants a priest. Can you send for one?'

A man standing in the doorway offered, 'I'll fetch him from Rosewell – I know him.'

Sydney squatted beside Robertson and asked, 'Can you do anything?'

The answer was a shake of the head. 'No. He's broken his back, and other bones as well. The internal organs are damaged, too. He'll not be with us long.'

Jimmy did not seem to be conscious but as this was said his eyes opened and he looked up into Sydney's face. 'Where's Black Ace?' he whispered.

'In the Crimea, I think,' Sydney told him, but the words meant nothing to the dying man who licked his lips and whispered, 'I want to tell him something.'

'Tell me and I'll pass it on,' said Sydney. He put his head down beside the bloody mouth the hear the words.

Jimmy's breath was rasping in his throat as he croaked, 'Tell him he was right about Mariotta. Bullhead killed her – and I helped him carry the body away. Now he's done for me . . .'

Sydney looked from the dying man on the floor to the doctor standing at the table rummaging in his bag. 'Did you hear that?' he asked sharply.

Robertson looked around, surprised. 'Hear what?'

'Did you hear what he said?'

'No, I didn't. I hope that priest doesn't take hours to come. He's not got much longer.'

Sydney gestured to him to come and kneel by the dying man again and he urged Jimmy on: 'Tell the doctor what you told me, Jimmy.'

But his injuries were too severe. Jimmy was far gone; now he could only groan and before the priest arrived, he was mercifully dead.

When the body was carted away by Jo, Sydney said to Robertson, 'He was murdered, you know. Bullhead did it. What can we do?'

'We'll have to go and tell the policeman in Rosewell,' Robertson replied grimly.

Sydney was still furious. 'Jopp shouldn't have sent him up to the platform. He was drunk – but that wasn't why he fell. He was pushed. He said so, but we'll probably never be able to prove it.'

They fetched the policeman and sent for Emma Jane to come back again. The navvies crowded around her hut. Some of them had already started to drink, which was the navvy's usual response to trouble. Bullhead was among the drinkers. While the policeman was painstakingly writing the fact of Jimmy's death in a notebook, Sydney walked up to Bullhead and pulled him forward by the neck of his shirt. 'Where were you when Jimmy fell off the bridge?' he demanded.

'Having a piss,' said Bullhead coarsely.

'Did anyone see him?' Sydney asked the others, but

they all hung their heads. At times like this they knew it was advisable to have seen nothing, good or bad. When the policeman questioned them he found that every man had gone conveniently blind when Jimmy fell. No one on the platform or the ground had anything to contribute and no one could say where Jimmy was standing before he plunged to his death. The first any of them knew of the accident, they said, was when he started to scream as he plummeted to the ground.

But Sydney was not satisfied. He shoved Bullhead towards the policeman. 'He pushed him,' he shouted in fury. 'Jimmy said he pushed him.'

'You're mad. Prove it! Go on – prove it,' was Bullhead's reply. The veins were bulging in his forehead and his eyes were raging mad. Sydney knew that if Bullhead could have attacked him then, he would have killed him but he did not back down. 'You did it,' persisted Sydney.

Bullhead looked at him out of evil eyes. 'And why was that then?' he sneered.

'Because of Mariotta. Because he knew you killed her and he was going to tell the truth about it.'

Bullhead pushed Sydney hard in the chest, sending him flying. 'I've heard enough about that useless bitch,' he snarled. 'That's finished. It was your friend Black Ace who killed her. His coat was on her – that's why he took off. If you can prove anything else, just try. Just you try . . . you toffee-nosed bastard. And watch yourself or you'll be sorry . . .'

Like Mariotta's death, the killing of Jimmy-The-New-Man was officially listed as an accident. Again the authorities were prepared to let the navvy community look after itself – it was easier that way. The boy from Inverness was buried in one of Jo's coffins in an unmarked grave by his workmates, and since there was nothing among his meagre possessions to give any clue of where he had come from, or if he had left any family behind to mourn him, his clothes were divided among the men in his hut and in a few days he was almost forgotten. Some of the older navvies were not altogether displeased by his death, for they believed that every big project, especially a bridge, always demanded human blood before it could be finished. Jimmy was a kind of ritual sacrifice which allowed them to breathe more freely, for it meant that the odds against them being killed were lessened.

When spring really began, the days lengthened and there was more heat in the sun. Parties of tourists and hopeful antiquaries drove out to look at the bridge, which was becoming a talking point for miles around. They even came from as far afield as Edinburgh, and among them were Sir Geoffrey and the new Lady Miller, who arrived to stay at Bella Vista.

To Bethya's delight Sir Geoffrey's second wife turned out to be old, gaunt and extremely tall – almost six feet in height – and as thin as a lathe. Towering over her husband in every way, she was very short-tempered and dismissive, addressing him as if he were an unruly dog. She was also very voluble, with opinions on every matter under the sun, and if her husband tried to interrupt her flow of words, he was quickly put in his place with a sharp, 'Do be quiet, Miller.'

Bethya sat wide-eyed and smiling, encouraging Lady Miller to more and more conversational excesses while secretly exulting in the duplicitous Sir Geoffrey's downfall. From time to time she dimpled at him and was rewarded by the anguish in his eye. When he attempted to put a hand on her arm going into dinner, she neatly lifted it off as if he had committed an act of gross over-familiarity.

It was arranged that the Millers and the Anstruthers should make a trip to the bridge to inspect work in progress. Though Sir Geoffrey received regular reports from Jopp and other informants, including Falconwood, he had not been to Camptounfoot in person since the cholera epidemic, so was eager to see for himself what Miss Wylie had achieved. By all accounts and against all expectations, she was doing very well – but he was not prepared to allow that to deflect his purpose. To him, Emma Jane Wylie was only an instrument towards an end. She was to be allowed to go as far as possible, for as long as she was useful, and then to be thrown aside at the end.

Only Colonel Anstruther and Bethya accompanied the Millers on their tour of inspection, for Gus never rose before noon and Mrs Anstruther avoided expeditions that bored her, and the bridge bored her very much. Sometimes she felt as if it was being built in her drawing room, and she would be very glad when the whole thing was finished and forgotten.

For the outing, Bethya was dressed in a very becoming pale-green gown with a back-tilted bonnet lined in the same colour and decorated with lilies of the valley. She'd taken a lot of trouble with her toilette that morning, and was pleased to see that Lady Miller was garbed in a garish gown of dark-green tartan and a bonnet that could have done duty for a coal scuttle. Colonel Anstruther, bouncing with excitement and enthusiasm, was clapping his hands together and exclaiming, 'Let's go, let's go. They'll have been working for hours already. They're joining up the piers, you know. Magnificent sight, magnificent sight!'

It was a good day for an outing. The sky was pale-blue and the air as heady as champagne. Transparent green leaves festooned the trailing branches of the beech trees which lined the curving drive of Bella Vista, and the party rode along with the carriage top down so that they could admire the beauty of the Three Sisters, on which shoots of sweet green bracken were beginning to uncurl above banks of primroses.

'What a fine day to be alive,' exulted the Colonel, and beamed at his daughter-in-law who smiled unfeignedly back. She loved to see him happy.

Everyone drew in breaths of surprise and admiration when they caught their first sight of the bridge boldly rising across the broadest part of the valley. The piers in the river, even the one floated on wood, had withstood the onslaught of the winter floods and were in the process of being built up to match the others in the field. In all, nineteen tall, tapering and elegant needles of red sandstone seemed to sway and shimmer with deceptive fragility in the spring sunshine. The first six piers were joined together by high arches faced with pale-pink bricks so it was now possible to appreciate the impact the finished bridge would have. 'Well, well, well. Who would have thought it? Quite Roman, really,' said Sir Geoffrey, his eyes shining.

His wife interrupted him, 'More Venetian, Miller. The colour's Venetian, I think.'

He glowered at her. 'Quite so, my dear.'

Colonel Anstruther was pointing to a group standing in the field beneath the shadow of the pillars. 'There's that girl – an amazing young woman I'd say, wouldn't you, Miller? I never thought she'd get this far. She's been on site every day, all through the bad weather. I must say I admire her.'

He had not been taken into Sir Geoffrey's confidence or told about the plot being laid for Emma Jane. 'Anstruther's too soft-hearted in spite of all his bluster to make a really effective businessman,' was Miller's private assessment. In his opinion, it was one thing fighting wars against rebellious Indians, and quite another taking on ambitious entrepreneurs.

They dismounted from the carriage and made their way down the slope. Emma Jane had seen Sir Geoffrey from a distance and walked towards him warily, but he greeted her with apparent enthusiasm though his eyes were coldly summing her up. 'I don't think I've ever seen such a change in anyone in such a short time,' he was thinking. The middle-class, decent-looking young woman he'd met before had become a ragamuffin with a freckled face and hair all a'straggle. She wasn't even wearing a bonnet! However, she had a presence now that had been missing before, so his tone towards her was more deferential than in the past as he enquired, 'My dear Miss Wylie, how are you coping with this enormous undertaking?'

To her he sounded as affable as a vicar opening a fête. 'Well, I think,' she said cautiously. Since the day when she'd fallen into the trap of being optimistic and Robbie had had his accident, she'd avoided open expressions of hope or enthusiasm, so much so that sometimes she felt afraid that she was affected by an attitude of continual pessimism.

Miller was walking around staring at the bridge with barely concealed surprise. 'You've done more than well, more than well. Take us round and show us everything,' he cried.

During their tour of inspection, they passed groups of navvies who paused in their work and gazed insolently at the visitors. Sydney, as usual, doffed his hat to Bethya in appreciation of her gown but registered the thought that he wouldn't want to have to foot her dressmakers' bills. She flushed at his salute and saw Lady Miller shooting her a sharp glance. Nothing missed that woman. Bullhead was in Sydney's working party, and when he saw Bethya he gave a low groan. As soon as the party moved on, he leaned on his spade and told his companions in gloatingly pornographic detail what he'd like to do to her. Sydney who, from a sense of self-preservation, had given the bully a wide berth for weeks, stood up straight and snapped angrily, 'Watch your tongue!' The words came out without premeditation, brought on by his feeling that to have Bullhead lust after Bethya, even from a distance, was to defile her.

His companions roared with laughter while Bullhead mimicked him. 'Watch your tongue! It's not my tongue I'd be watching if I could get my hands on her. Got your eye on her yourself, have you? Is that what's wrong? I thought you didn't go in for women . . .' The jeers went on and on in the hope of rousing Sydney to violence, but he tried to ignore them. When they did not stop, he threw down his spade and walked away for he knew that Bullhead was trying to incite him to a fight in which he would certainly come off worst. He was not foolhardy.

'Why do I stay in this damned place? Why don't I walk away? I'm not forced to stay here,' he asked himself continually, angry thoughts running through his head in confusion as he climbed the hill behind the site and sat on

487

its upper slope staring out over the countryside. In time its beauty and tranquillity soothed him.

It was dark when he went back to the camp, threw himself into bed and slept like a log, only to be wakened at dawn by the sound of a terrible rainstorm. Overnight the weather had changed and rain was teeming from a pewter-coloured sky. Most of the men were huddled in their huts gloomily watching the downpour through the open doors, but Sydney braved the onslaught and walked to the site where he found the ground awash. Rivulets were running over the field and the river was rising at a terrifying rate. Emma Jane was there, draped in a waterproof cape and staring fascinated at the remorseless flow of water. When Sydney stood beside her she glanced up with anguished eyes and said, 'I hope it stops soon. I hope it doesn't cause too much damage. Everything was going so well . . . I should have known!'

'It'll stop,' he assured her. 'It always does. Go home and wait for the storm to pass. You can't do anything standing here, and nobody can work in this.'

It rained without cessation for two days. During that time the men in the camp turned as usual to drinking, gambling and fighting among themselves. The worst brawler was Bullhead. After the men in his hut combined forces to throw him out when he caused a fight after losing money in a card-game, he stamped off. He didn't know where he was going or what he was going to do, but he wanted to cause trouble, to hurt somebody. First of all he sought out Sydney, who fortunately could not be found for he had gone back to the bridge to watch the brown tumbling waters breaking round its truncated piers.

Thwarted, Bullhead wandered into Rosewell. 'I'll find a woman,' he told himself, but none of the local prostitutes would take him on because he had abused them all in the past. By now he was raging with lust. The memory of Bethya Anstruther was vivid in his mind and because Sydney had defended her, he was even more eager to take revenge on womankind. In Rosewell women fled at the sight of him and, getting more and more angry, he went on walking till he reached Camptounfoot. The village street was deserted. Water flowed like a burn over its cobbles. The alehouse's door was closed, so he hammered loudly on the wooden shutter which covered a hatch recently cut in the side wall for the serving of navvies. Some of them caused too much trouble if they were let inside. The hatch was thrown open and the alehouse proprietor's face glared out. 'What do you want?' he asked truculently, because he recognised Bullhead as one of the worst offenders.

The big man snarled, 'Ale. That's what you sell, isn't it?'

'I know you. You're barred – you're a trouble-maker. Go away. I'll sell no ale to the likes of you.' And the shutter was slammed shut. No amount of angry hammering with both fists could get it opened again.

As Bullhead turned away in frustration he saw a figure come running out of a side alley and go hurrying up the street. It was a girl – he couldn't believe his luck. Slinking like a predatory cat along the high wall, he followed her. She was scurrying in the direction of the farmsteading. Bullhead crept at her back. She turned into a shed and he could hear her rattling something within. Anger and lust rose in him as he stepped up to the open door and looked in. A young woman in bondager's costume was pouring corn into a big metal bowl. He jumped into the shed, pulled the door closed behind him and moved towards her. She turned with guileless eyes wide and asked, 'What do —?' but before she could finish the question, he clapped a hand across her mouth and threw her on her back on the ground.

Wee Lily was a strong girl and she fought back furiously, but she was no match for Bullhead who grunted as he held her down, 'Shut up, or I'll kill you.' His bloodshot eyes glared crazily into hers, and she knew he meant what he said. His hand was pressed against her mouth and though she bit into it, the palm was like leather from years of wielding shovels and she could not make him let go. He tore her skirt off and like a raging animal

489

penetrated her, brutally and repeatedly. When he finally rose, spent, she lay with her head turned on the ground and tears running down her face. Buckling his belt, the big navvy laughed mockingly, kicked her in the side with his booted foot and strutted away.

Emma Jane, wrapped in her waterproof cape, was on her way back from a visit to the bridge when she met a distraught Big Lily in the street. 'Have you seen my lassie? Have you seen Wee Lily?' she asked, rushing up and laying a hand on Emma Jane's arm.

'No, I've not seen anybody. The whole place is deserted, thanks to this rain.'

'I sent her out two hours ago to feed the hens and she's not come back. I've been to the steading and the hen corn's all scattered over the shed floor and her shawl's there, but she isn't. I'm feared something's happened to her.'

'Oh, nothing'll have happened to her. I'll come with you and help you look. Where would she go? She might have called in to see somebody. Did you ask Tibbie?'

'I've been at all the neighbours but she's not there. It's no' like her . . .'

'Have you been at the farm?'

'Craigie's sisters won't let her in. They've aye been jealous about me and Wee Lily, because of Craigie . . . and they've nae bairns of their ain, ye see.'

'Let's go to the farm, then. It's the only place left,' said Emma Jane sensibly, taking hold of Big Lily's hand. 'Come on – I'll go with you.'

They rapped on the farmhouse door and after a long wait it was opened by a wizened little woman who looked like an aged fieldmouse. She stared at Big Lily with hostile eyes and said, 'He's in his bed. Just get on with the work. You know what's to be done – go and do it.'

Emma Jane spoke up. 'We've come to ask if you've seen Wee Lily.'

The tiny eyes switched to her but the gaze did not soften. 'No, why should I?' Then the door was slammed shut.

The two disappointed women were about to walk away when Big Lily suddenly stopped. 'I hear her, I hear her. She's in the wash-house,' she cried.

At the side of the farmhouse was a low-built, stone-walled structure where the women washed clothes. The door stood ajar and from within came a little voice crying, 'Oh Mam, oh Mam ... help me, Mam.' They ran over and Big Lily burst in to find her daugher huddled in a corner, half-naked with the ragged remnants of her skirt held in front of her and her torn blouse revealing bruised plump breasts.

'Dear God, Lily, what's happened to you?' cried the anguished mother, dropping to her knees beside the weeping girl.

'Oh Mam, he came into the shed and grabbed me. He did terrible things to me and then he kicked me.' Wee Lily put a hand on her side where her ribs ached, for Bullhead had broken one of them.

Big Lily stood up with her face thunderous. 'Oh bairn, it wasnae Craigie, was it?' Emma Jane, listening with horror, wondered about the circumstances in which Big Lily had conceived her child.

Wee Lily groaned, 'No Mam, not Craigie, yin o' thae navvies. I've seen him at the bridge – a big one with a red face. He smelled something horrible.' Then she started crying again.

They lifted her to her feet and covered her nakedness with Emma Jane's cape. 'Come on home, bairn, come on home. Dinna hide in here, you've no' done anything wrong,' Big Lily told her grimly.

'I just want to dee,' sobbed Wee Lily, but she stood up and leaned on her mother. Between them they guided her back to the bondagers' bothy and as she staggered along, she sobbed, 'He said he'd kill me. "I'll kill you, you bitch, I'll kill you" – that's what he kept on saying all the time. Oh Mam, I was that feared and it hurt so much. Why does it hurt so much?'

'Watch here a minute, I'm going to ask the smith to fetch the doctor to her. He might have hurt her bad,' said

Big Lily to Emma Jane, when they got the girl inside the house. She ran off in the direction of the smithy and Emma Jane sat holding Wee Lily's hand, listening to her terrible description of the rape. The girl couldn't stop talking about it.

'He jumped on top of me, he had me round the throat. "I'll kill you, you bitch!" Oh God, it's sair!'

When Big Lily came back she nodded to indicate that William was on his way to Dr Stewart's and then she said urgently to Emma Jane, 'Go and bring Tibbie – she'll ken what to do.'

When Tibbie heard the awful tale, she ran straight out of her cottage without even taking off her long apron, and burst into the bondagers' bothy. Wee Lily looked up, saw her standing in the doorway and began her story all over again. 'He threw me doon among the corn . . . he was grunting like a pig . . . After he got up he kicked me. It's so sair . . .'

Tibbie nodded as she listened and then she said, 'I'll make up a brew for her just in case – you know – but let's hope nothing's happened. Has she had her bleeding recently?'

Big Lily shrugged hopelessly. 'About two weeks ago. She only started last year. She was late, like me.'

'Then this is the worst time. But I'll make her a potion and we'll see what we can do.'

'The doctor's coming,' said Big Lily. 'Maybe he'll do something.'

'I doubt it,' replied Tibbie drily.

Dr Stewart did not want to go out in the rain, but he could not refuse William Strang for he sent his carriage horses to Camptounfoot for shoeing and Tibbie's brother was the best smith in the district.

'Are you sure it's an emergency?' he asked, and the black-bearded smith nodded firmly.

'A lassie's been attacked. She needs your help, Doctor.'

William stood his ground, solemn and strong, so Stewart had to go with him. When he was shown into the bothy, the physician's nose wrinkled and he stared around

492

in disapproval, for this was not the sort of house he liked to visit. Lily was by this time in bed and slightly calmer, but she cowered back like a scared animal as the doctor leaned over to look at the bruises on her body. The pain in her ribs made her cry out when he tried to turn her over.

'She's been beaten,' he said.

'She was raped,' Big Lily told him indignantly.

'Raped?' He raised a sceptical eyebrow. 'She's a big girl. Most females who say they've been raped co-operate, you know. I've never heard of a genuine case of a woman being taken without her consent. A strong girl can fight a man off if she wants.'

'He said he'd kill me,' sobbed Wee Lily as her mother bristled in her defence.

'She's only fifteen and she was a virgin, as innocent as a lamb,' she shouted.

Stewart frowned in disapproval of such impolite behaviour. 'Did she know the man?' he asked.

'Of course not.' Big Lily was so angry she looked as if she wanted to hit him.

'How do you know? Were you there?' asked the doctor.

'Of course I wasn't! You don't think I'd let a man rape her if I was, do you?' He said nothing and Big Lily, angered beyond endurance, burst out with, 'Like I said, my lassie was a virgin till this happened and I'm feared that he's given her a bairn.'

Stewart straightened up from the bed. 'I can do something for her broken rib and for her bruises, but if she's pregnant, she'll just have to bear it. There's nothing I can do about that.'

Before he left, Craigie Scott came bursting in, for William had gone to fetch him. Tibbie had not seen Craigie for many months, and was astonished by the sight of him. His hair had grown so long that it was nearly at his shoulders, and a beard covered most of his face. His eyes were the same though, mad and raging.

'Is it true? Has some navvy hurt Wee Lily?' he asked, looking around at the women in the house.

'Aye, she was raped,' Tibbie said heavily. 'The doctor says she's got a broken rib as well. He's bandaged it up for her.'

Craigie glared at Stewart. 'How much is your fee?' he demanded.

'Five shillings,' was the reply.

'Here — take it,' grunted Craigie, reaching into his pocket and bringing out some coins. When Stewart had gone, he looked at Big Lily and said, 'Which navvy did it?'

'The big one with the red face. The folk in the alehouse say he was in there asking for beer before he found Wee Lily in the shed. It's the one they had to bar for fighting. He's on the bridge gang and he aye wears a red scarf round his neck. Bullhead's his name . . .'

Craigie nodded. 'I know the one. Leave it with me.' Then he went away and the people left behind stared at each other in amazement at how calm and rational he sounded.

It went on raining all night, teeming down with relentless fury, battering against the window glass and filling the burns and wells. Craigie Scott sat in his farmhouse listening to the fury of the storm and drinking whisky. He was not normally a liquor-drinking man, for he resented what he called pouring money down his throat. Usually his refreshment was the watery ale his sisters brewed and which local people said would drown you before it fuddled you. There was, however, a line of big, brown earthenware jars full of whisky in his cellar and occasionally when people called he would unbend sufficiently to offer them a glass from his secret store. It was one of those jars that he hauled up when he came back from seeing Wee Lily, and all night long he sat drinking from it while his frightened sisters, who did not sleep either, peeped round the edge of the door at him, pleading with him to stop drinking and go to bed. He didn't answer, for by that time he was carefully taking apart and oiling his shotgun. His sisters clung together in despair and whispered to each other.

First one and then the other tried to stop him, but Craigie ignored them and went on with his task.

At dawn Emma Jane was wakened from sleep by a tremendous hammering at Tibbie's front door. 'Miss Wylie, Miss Wylie, get up! The embankment's slipping!' It was Jopp's voice and he was in a panic. He had arrived in a dogcart and she climbed in beside him for a pell-mell ride round by Rosewell to the north side of the bridge.

He was right. The terrible rain had washed away at the end of the piled-up northern embankment. Only the stone pier that had faced it stood stark against the side of the hill with a huge, washed-out void behind it. Obviously it would not stand there for long before it came crashing down as well, because a cascade of water was running round it towards the river far below.

Emma Jane looked aghast at the sight. 'The bridge-end's gone. The embankment's not packed hard enough.'

Jopp was in a panic because he was afraid the railway directors would blame him for this collapse. The embankment was his responsibility, and if its fall held up the progress of the bridge, that could not be blamed on Emma Jane, and might in fact earn her extra time to finish her contract. He turned on her in a fury. 'It's not my fault – it's the rain. It wasn't full finished before the rain got it. Don't blame me.'

She stared hard at him. 'I'm not blaming you. What we've got to do now is to stop the whole thing from sliding away. We must call out the men and divert that flow of water.'

Jopp was beside himself. 'I've sent for them, I've sent for them. They're coming. Oh my God, when's this damned rain going to stop!'

For two hours they worked, digging, heaving, ditching . . . The men sweated so heavily that their soaking shirts steamed on their backs, but they could not stop the inevitable. At half-past nine there was a tremendous crash and the first pier, the one that was meant to bear the weight of the whole bridge, crashed into the river. When the noise died away and the splashing subsided, Emma Jane, standing high on the embankment, stared down on the ruin of her hopes, sunk her face in her hands and began to cry.

The men around turned to give her support, especially Gentleman Sydney who said, 'Don't worry, Miss Wylie. We'll build it up again and we'll build it better next time.'

He put out a hand to help her off the embankment, but as she was clambering down they were both almost knocked over by a man who came running up from the field below. His hair was flying and he was only wearing a shirt and a pair of working trousers belted round his waist. In his hand he carried a gleaming gun. Emma Jane clutched Sydney's arm. 'It's Craigie Scott, the farmer from Camptounfoot,' she gasped.

Craigie paid no heed to her or to Sydney. It was a figure standing in a group on the top of the pile of earth that drew all his attention. Bullhead turned when the man walked up behind him and shouted, 'Which one's Bullhead? Are you Bullhead?'

The big man looked him up and down insolently. 'I'm Bullhead,' he said. 'Who wants me?'

Craigie Scott didn't answer. Instead he raised the rifle, took careful aim and shot Bullhead full in the face from a range of five feet. Blood and brains spattered in all directions as his victim screamed and put his hands up to his shattered head. Very slowly he sank to his knees with blood spurting out between his fingers. Then he fell over sideways and lay still.

'Oh my God, don't look, don't look,' cried Sydney and grabbed the girl, pulling her towards him and burying her face in his wet shirt-front.

Bullhead was killed outright, and Craigie Scott lowered his rifle with a strange abstracted look on his face. The man standing next to him, a quiet and responsible fellow, put out a hand and said very gently, 'Give me the gun.' Without argument it was passed over. 'Come and sit down,' said the man in the same tone, and he led the dazed Craigie away.

When Sydney saw them go he loosened his grip on Emma Jane, who had been shaking and quivering against his chest. 'He's gone,' he said, releasing her fully.

She looked up at him with agonised eyes, not daring to look around. 'Is Bullhead dead?'

'Yes.'

'It's in revenge, because he raped Wee Lily, Craigie's daughter, last night,' she explained.

Sydney was not surprised. Whatever Bullhead had done to deserve his final retribution, it had been coming to him for a long, long time. Craigie Scott was only the instrument of Nemesis.

'You're soaked and you're shocked. I'll take you home,' he told the shuddering girl.

When he handed her over to Tibbie, who listened horrified to the tale he had to tell, he drove to Maddiston to fetch Alex Robertson. There was nothing the young doctor could do for Bullhead except write the death certificate, but Sydney thought he might be able to help Emma Jane, who was on the verge of hysteria though she had not yet realised it.

Half an hour later, a frightened-looking Tibbie opened her cottage door to Robertson and solemnly pointed up the stairs to Emma Jane's room. 'She's up there and she's bad. She can't stop crying,' she said distractedly.

Sydney entered the house behind his friend and stood in the hall while the doctor climbed the stair. Then he turned to Tibbie and asked, 'Have you heard anything from your son-in-law? Do you know where he is?'

She nodded. 'He's in a place called Balaclava. He sent me a letter to say he's in the Crimea.'

'That's what I thought. Thank you,' he said.

CHAPTER
Eighteen

The navvies were working on a steeply rising gradient of land called Frenchman's Hill, when a young fresh-faced ensign came galloping up. 'Which one's Maquire?' he called out.

For a moment Tim did not respond. He had grown so used to being addressed as Black Ace, which was the name he had given to Peto when he signed up at Whitechapel, that now he responded to nothing else.

'Which one of you is called Timothy Maquire?' repeated the ensign irritably. In his hand he held a slip of paper that fluttered in the breeze. He was resentful at being ordered by his Colonel to deliver a telegraphic message to a navvy, for the ensign was a prim young man who regarded those brawling, outrageous characters as little better than heathens.

Tim straightened up from his work and called out, 'I'm Maquire. What do you want?'

The ensign wheeled his horse and said haughtily, 'It's not what I want – a telegraphic message has come for you. My Colonel ordered me to bring it over.'

The telegraph line between London and Balaclava was the most recent modern miracle. It has been completed only weeks before, and was used exclusively by the Army or by people with influence like the correspondent for *The Times*. The men looked at Tim with awe and one of them said, 'You must have friends in high places.'

He rubbed his head in bewilderment. 'I don't know who could have sent it, but let's have it.' He walked over to the impatient ensign and accepted the paper that was thrust at him. '*Tim Maquire in the navvy gang at Balaclava*' was written along the top.

'Yes, it's for me,' he told his companions. Then he read the rest of the message silently to himself. '*Come back at once. Crisis at bridge. All arranged for you to leave. Godolphin.*'

Godolphin? Gentleman Sydney was called Godolphin, wasn't he? That was what he'd put on Tim's wedding certificate. Why was he sending telegraphic messages? Was it some kind of a joke?

He crumpled up the paper and put it into his pocket. One of his friends asked, 'Not bad news, I hope?'

Tim shook his head. 'It's a joke, I think.' But he knew it wasn't. He had some hard thinking to do.

That night when work was over, Tim and his companions walked the six miles back to the neat lines of huts where they had lived for four months while building a railway between the port of Balaclava and the fort at Sebastopol, which was under siege by the Allied forces. The Army needed a constant line of supply, and the navvies were working flat out to build eight miles of railway line to take it to them. They had worked so hard that they had broken all records and laid seven miles of line in seven weeks. Only one mile remained to be completed.

The navvy camp above the port was neater and more orderly than any Tim had lived in before. That was because the men Peto recruited were hand-picked. They were there to work and work hard. Trouble-making ruffians had not been taken on. In spite of that, there were, of course, outbreaks of fighting and disorder from time to time, because navvies were navvies and to keep them sweet their employers not only paid over-the-odds wages of eight shillings a day, but issued a free rum ration four times a day as well. Some of the men were never sober – but they said they worked better that way. Others, like Tim, drank the rum because they believed it made them immune to the terrible fevers that ravaged the Army camps – and they might have been right, for the navvies lost far fewer men to fever and illness than the military.

As Tim walked into the main street running past the hut doors, he saw James Beatty, Chief Engineer of the line, waiting outside the hut where he was billeted. Beatty saw him coming and walked quickly towards him. 'I've had a message about you,' he said. 'You've to go back to England by the next available ship.'

'What if I refuse?'

Beatty frowned. 'Nothing was said about that. I was just told to release you. Some trouble at home, I understand. The order came from Peto – he says you're to be let out of your contract. There's only a month of it left to run anyway. I'll be sorry to lose you, Black Ace, you're one of my best men, but orders are orders.'

'I can't understand this. I haven't any family at home, only a mother-in-law. She wouldn't be sending orders to Peto.'

'The Duke of Allandale contacted the War Office, apparently, and they got on to Peto. Strings have been pulled in high places,' shrugged Beatty.

'I got a message too,' said Tim, handing it over.

Beatty read it and wrinkled his brow. 'What bridge? And who's Godolphin?'

'He's a navvy like me. I'm just hoping he's not making some hare-brained joke.'

'He'd better not be. If he has involved the War Office in his joke, he'll end up in the Tower. But I'd go if I were you. You might find you've inherited a fortune,' grinned the engineer.

Tim laughed. 'No risk of that!'

'There's a ship going back from here tomorrow night on the tide. You've a berth on her, as I understand it – that's been arranged, too. Some guardian angel has an eye on you, Black Ace. If you come to me tomorrow I'll pay you what's due. As I said, I'm sorry you're going but we must obey the orders of our betters, mustn't we?'

'Must we?' said Tim grimly. 'I'll have to think about this. I like being here – I might not want to go back. What's there to go back for, anyway?'

'There's this bridge – whatever's wrong with it. They want you for that, I believe.'

Tim nodded. 'Yes, there's the bridge. I'll think about it, Mr Beatty. I'll let you know tomorrow.'

He lay awake most of the night staring out through the open hut door at a black velvet sky that sparkled with stars. It was warm and the air smelt sweet, for they were high above the port and surrounded by trees. He smoked black cheroots while he pondered. 'Will I go? There's trouble at Wylie's bridge, obviously. Why should that bother me?'

Then he remembered Christopher Wylie's burning vision of the bridge, how he talked about it with shining eyes. He'd infected Tim with his enthusiasm at the time, but poor Wylie had died and Tim's world had crashed around him. Who cared about a bridge any more when you were dead or broken-hearted?

But Wylie's words came back: '*I want to build a bridge with such impact that it'll take people's breath away.*'

Tim thought of the Wylie girl. As he had anticipated, she must have come a cropper. It probably meant that all Wylie's money would be lost. Everything gone . . . Everything Wylie had worked for dissipated and nothing left behind, not even his dream of a bridge. He recalled what Wylie had told him of the contract into which the railway company had manoeuvred him, and it seemed to Tim as if the old man was calling out to him. 'You were good to me, Mr Wylie,' he said aloud. 'I know I owe you this.'

He turned on his side and stubbed out his cheroot. Anyway, the Crimea contract ended in May. In only a few weeks he'd be wandering the world again. He might as well go back and finish the job he'd started. Beneath his thin pillow he felt the crackling of the paper on which Naughten had drawn Hannah. He always kept it there. The reason he'd fled from Camptounfoot was because everything reminded him of her, but he'd discovered that travel didn't take away memories. Even in Balaclava the vision of her still haunted him.

Next morning he stood in Beatty's office and received

his wages in gold. It was more money than he'd ever possessed at any one time in his whole life, because Beatty did not work the truck system and was an honest man who acted as a bank for navvies who did not want to dissipate all their earnings. Tim, who had worked every available day for five months and spent little, had over fifty pounds to his credit. Feeling rich, he went to the wharf to put his bag on board the ship that was to carry him home.

The port was bustling with labourers unloading ships, and carts drawn by mules or oxen were lined up along the quays. Among them wandered men in native dress and scarlet-coated soldiers on furlough, who gazed longingly at the troopships being loaded up with their comrades who were lucky enough to be wounded or ill.

Tim had been allocated a place on a clipper called *Wildfire* – the same vessel that had carried Peto's band from Birkenhead. The captain recognised him and called down from the bridge, 'Going back with us, are you? You're lucky the weather's good. We should be in Birkenhead in two weeks if this wind keeps up.'

On his last afternoon in Balaclava, Tim went to the huge market that had grown up near the navvy camp. The men called it Donnybrook Fair, and in its thickly-packed alleys you could buy almost anything from anywhere in the world . . . cigars and cheroots, exotic alcohol, silks, gold and silver, spices, strange sweetmeats, beautifully-wrought brass and copper vessels, carpets and rugs, jewellery, pet animals ranging from monkeys to snakes, parrots which talked and toys for children . . . With a pain in his heart he remembered Kate and wished he had a child to buy presents for as he walked from stall to stall, picking up things and looking at them. The money in his pocket clinked and he was back in memory to that wonderful day with Hannah, buying food for *Benjy's* after their first night together. How Hannah would have relished this place, he thought, and reeled again from the painful realisation that she was dead. 'How long will it take before it stops hurting?' he asked himself miserably.

In the end he bought a pair of piratical-looking gold earrings for himself, and submitted to the ordeal of having his ears pierced by the vendor, who performed the operation with an enormous needle and a piece of cork which he held behind Tim's earlobe with dirty fingers. 'I'd better rinse my ears with my rum ration tonight,' was his chief thought when the needle stabbed through the soft flesh.

He wanted a gift for Tibbie, too, and spent a long time pondering over what she would like, finally choosing a long scarf of finest silk interwoven with gold and silver. It was graded in shimmering shades of violet, purple and mauve and he was sure that no one in Camptounfoot would have ever seen anything like it. He was sorely tempted to also buy her a parrot in a brass cage that cocked an eye at him and said, '*Bonjour*', but decided against it. He'd travel lighter if he had no baggage that couldn't be dropped by the wayside. He was still not entirely sure that he was really going back to Camptounfoot.

When he bade farewell to his friends, they clapped him on the back and told him that they'd be sure to meet again on some navvying job in the future. One of them offered to give him a shave, for his beard had grown while he was in Balaclava and was now a thick, curling beaver that glistened blackly round his chin. He was quite proud of it in fact and put a hand protectively on it. 'No, I'll keep it.'

'Yes, you keep it,' said one of the other men. 'With those earrings and that beard you look like Morgan the Pirate.'

On his way to the ship that night, flushed with rum and friendship, he suddenly stopped, turned back and ran to Donnybrook Fair where he bought the talking parrot.

To Tim's surprise, Gentleman Sydney was waiting on the platform at Maddiston station when he alighted from the train. He strolled towards Tim, as negligent-looking as ever, and said as casually as if it was only yesterday since they had last met, 'Where have you been? I've met every train from the south for two days. The *Wildfire* arrived at Liverpool four days ago.'

Tim did not tell him that two days, and more importantly two nights, had passed very pleasantly in the company of the daughter of the proprietor of the inn where he'd put up on arrival at Birkenhead. She'd taken a tremendous shine to him and it had been difficult to drag himself away. It was the first time he'd made love since Hannah died, for he didn't relish prostitutes, and the happy experience had lifted some of his gloom. Sydney didn't need telling, however. 'A woman, eh? Well done, that's what you need. But what's that on your face and what's all this?' He indicated first the beard and then the parrot.

Tim laughed, white teeth flashing beneath the beard. 'Don't you like my beard? And that's a parrot for Tibbie. I call it Napoleon because it speaks French.'

Sydney sighed and lifted up the cage by the ring in the top. 'Well, well, travel *does* broaden the mind, doesn't it?' he said sarcastically.

He had a dogcart waiting with a driver at the reins of a workmanlike-looking cob. Tim raised his eyebrows when he saw that the man was wearing livery, but Sydney only said, 'Get in, there's a lot to tell you.'

'The first thing I want to know is what's this all about? Then I'd like to hear how you managed it. Sending telegraph messages to Balaclava can't be easy.'

Sydney laughed. 'It is if you've the right friends – that's another advantage of an expensive education. But seriously, I sent for you because you're the only person I could think of who has a chance in hell of finishing that bridge in time for poor Miss Wylie. I can't, and Jopp won't. She doesn't deserve what's happening to her. She's tried so hard.'

Tim stared at his friend's face. '"Poor Miss Wylie"? It sounds as if you're smitten with her.'

But Sydney shook his head. 'No, I'm not, though our friend the doctor is, poor devil. If I were a better person I might have been, but nice girls don't appeal to me in that way, I'm afraid, and Emma Jane Wylie is a very nice girl indeed. Things are desperate, Black Ace. She needs your help.'

Tim said flatly, 'Why should I help her? I didn't like her much.'

'But you liked her father, and what she's doing is because of him. I don't think for a moment she'd be plodding through mud every day if it wasn't for that. She's trying to salvage something from the ashes of his hopes.'

'Very poetic,' commented Tim. 'What's gone wrong exactly? And give it to me in plain language, please.'

'What's gone wrong is that Jopp's out to make her fall down on her part of the contract – the bridge itself. He's succeeded in stirring up discontent among the workforce. They strike, they go slow, they fight among themselves . . . you know, the usual things when men are fed up. They need someone to pull them together and they need to see that the job's going to end soon. It's gone on too long. And then there was the trouble with Jimmy and Bullhead.'

Tim didn't know about that and had to be told. He was sorry about Jimmy, but the death of Bullhead seemed to him to be well-deserved, especially when Sydney explained about Mariotta and Wee Lily. 'I'd have thought that bastard being blown away would make things better, not worse. What happened to the man who shot him?' he asked.

'Oh, they shut him up. He's raving mad. They didn't hang him because Bullhead had raped his daughter and he was taking primitive vengeance. Local opinion is very much on his side,' said Sydney.

'There's been a lot of drama in Camptounfoot since I went away,' Tim commented wryly. 'They can't have had so much excitement there since time began. But Bullhead getting shot hasn't stopped the bridge being built, has it?'

'No,' Sydney agreed, 'but you haven't heard it all yet. The rain swept the north embankment away and took the pier with it. The railway company's hopping mad because that's their responsibility, not Miss Wylie's. She can't finish the bridge though, until it's built back up. That's where we were working when the farmer shot Bullhead.'

Tim gaped. 'The north pier swept away? That was the first one that Mr Wylie and I built, and we thought it would stand till Doomsday.'

'It would have done if it hadn't been affected by the collapsing embankment.'

'But Jopp was building the embankment, wasn't he?'

'That's what I'm telling you. He was in a terrible state in case his bosses in Edinburgh blamed him for the collapse. They've had to give Miss Wylie another few weeks' grace because of it, and that makes them mad. The point is, it fell down and took the bridgehead with it. Even though she's got extra time, it's only three or four weeks, and the project will be months overdue unless there's a miracle. I thought you might be that miracle.'

Tim sighed, 'August the first's the original finishing date, and three weeks or so takes you to the end of the month. Today is May the twentieth. If there's a whole pier to build up again, I don't see how it can be done. How far has the rest of the bridge got? Is it almost completed?'

Sydney nodded. 'Yes, amazingly it is. All but the spans over the river are finished and it's a good job they weren't up or they'd have come down too. Once they're in place, only the superstructure has to be erected and the track laid—'

'In two months? Impossible,' said Tim categorically.

'Try it,' urged Sydney. 'Go on – try it. What this project needs now is new energy and enthusiasm. Everybody's tired and dispirited. Even the girl is tired and I'm so sick of the whole thing that I've only been waiting for you to come before I leave. I'm off tonight.'

Tim stared at him. 'Tonight? That's quick. What's your hurry?'

'I told you, I've been hanging on waiting for you. But I've also had a death in my family. I've got to go back. My runaway days are over, I'm afraid.'

'I've always wondered about you, but you don't give

much away, do you? Have you a wife somewhere that you're trying to dodge? Is that what this is all about?' Tim asked curiously.

'Oh no, no wife. But I've a father – or at least I had a father. He's the one who has died and that is why I've to go back. I have a younger sister and brother, you see. Well, a half-sister and brother by two different mothers. My father was a serial marrier. My mother was the first. She stood him for twelve years before she died. That's the longest any of his wives survived.'

Sydney's voice was hard and Tim could tell that this was not a subject that ought to be pursued. 'I hope we don't lose touch when you've gone,' he said, and Sydney grinned.

'Oh, I'll always keep in touch with you, Black Ace. Didn't I tell you once how I pride myself on recognising men with potential? You're going places in spite of the beard and the parrot. We'll meet again – don't worry about that.'

When they drove into Rosewell, Tim turned to his friend and said, 'Drop me at the Abbey first. I want to see Hannah's grave. I want to tell her that I'm back.'

'Of course. I'll take your traps and that awful bird to Mrs Mather's and then I'm off. Goodbye, Black Ace. Do your best for the bridge. I'll come and see it when it's finished.' Sydney stuck out his hand and Tim grasped it. Then they parted.

The ruins of the Abbey looked grim and skeletal beneath a grey sky. Rain was drifting on the wind and the trees and bushes in the burial-ground were bent to the west by its force. Moss-covered gravestones leaned at strange angles, some sideways, some forwards, some deep in the ground as if the inhabitants of the grave were hauling the stone down in beside them. There were no paths and he had to weave his way among the haphazardly-placed stones till he reached the boundary wall where the cholera mound was plainly visible, but mercifully covered now with a carpet of green turf spangled with daisies and wild flowers. The white marble memorial stood at the end where he'd put it, rain-washed and shining. Flavia and her daughter stared at each other with the same look of love. Tim felt tears prick his eyes as he stood looking at them. To his relief, the grief that he felt didn't have the terrible impact on him that he had feared. It was still acute, but also more settled and philosophical. His wound was healing. He'd been right to come back, to stand on the mound and accept that his wife and child were really dead. He would never have been free of grief if he hadn't.

Alex Robertson was in love, and it was making him neglect his work. Almost every evening he could be seen under the first span of the bridge waiting, as if by accident, for Emma Jane when she walked back to Camptounfoot. When she appeared, he would dismount from his horse and walk with her, listening sympathetically as she talked about the day's work. She liked his company so she talked freely to him, more freely than she did to any other man around her, though not quite as freely as she did to Tibbie or Robbie. His gentle nature and slow smile were soothing, and she began to look forward to their evening rendezvous. She had no idea that he was in love with her, but felt that he was nervous in her company and hoped he might relax when he got to know her better.

She always had something fresh to tell him when they met, and on one sweetly-smelling spring evening, she burst out with, 'I had a visit from Sir Geoffrey Miller today.'

'Did you know he was coming?' he asked, but she shook her head.

'No, he just appeared with Jopp. They're very rattled about the embankment collapse. He offered to take the contract off my hands – at least, that's how he put it.'

'If he paid enough you should accept his offer,' said the doctor. 'It's not good for you to be working like this. You'll wear yourself out.' His look was adoring but she wondered if he was dropping a hint about something amiss in her state of health that had so far escaped her.

'I feel quite well,' she said defensively. 'Anyway, Sir Geoffrey's not prepared to pay enough money for the contract. His offer this time is more than it was before, but it's still paltry. I suspect he thinks Jopp can do the rest of the bridge without my plans. He probably could. His big worry now's the north pier, and this will hold up the schedule which will give me more time.'

Robertson asked gravely, 'Are you only doing this for the money? Is that all that matters to you?'

She was surprised. 'Of course not! Anyway, the money's not for me. I've got my mother to consider. From my point of view, the real object is to get my father's bridge built the way he imagined it, and by a member of his family. It's Wylie's Bridge – my bridge too, in a way. It's like my child. Isn't that silly? A child as big as that . . .' She threw her hands up to the piers soaring above her head for they were walking under the first arch at that very moment and though Robertson's heart expanded with love and admiration as he watched her, he felt that she was being too idealistic.

'How much did Sir Geoffrey offer you to give it up?' he asked.

'Three thousand pounds,' said Emma Jane.

'That's a lot of money.'

'No,' she disagreed. 'My father's debts amount to much more than that, and as I've said, there's my mother to consider. She needs an income for the rest of her life.'

'But she must understand that things will have to change for her now that your father's dead.'

Emma Jane looked at him and spoke frankly. 'She's very spoiled and unworldly. Mama closes her mind to anything unpleasant. It's a great gift – I wish I could do it.' The letters that had arrived for her from Aunt Louisa recently said her mother was much recovered in health, but Louisa was still scathing about life in the cottage.

'When you've finished this nonsense with the bridge, you'll have to sell this terrible cottage and buy a decent house for your mother. I've been looking at suitable properties already because I've decided to live with dear Arabella permanently,' she wrote. The thought

of spending the rest of her life with her mother and her aunt together made Emma Jane's toes curl. She'd rather go on building bridges in the rain and mud forever.

By now she and Alex were walking past Craigie Scott's house, which looked grim and blank-eyed now that the owner was in the asylum. His sisters still lived there and the two Lilies went on working the land because they all believed that Craigie would get better and come back one day. The sisters were completely ungrateful to their industrious bondagers, however, never acknowledging that without them the farm would revert to a wilderness, but Big Lily worked on stoically, for she knew what was needed at every season of the year and was prepared to go on doing it without thanks.

At Tibbie's door Emma Jane said to the doctor, 'Tie up your horse round the back and come in for a cup of tea. Tibbie won't mind, she likes company.' He didn't need asking twice. 'I'll let you in at the back door,' said the girl, slipping into the little hall. When she opened the door to the kitchen, however, she was surprised to see that Tibbie had company already. A tall, black-bearded man was sitting at the table drinking tea. Beside him on the floor stood a huge brass cage with a green and yellow parrot in it. The bird looked up at Emma Jane with a beady eye and croaked: '*Bonjour, ma belle.*'

The man laughed and looked at her too. When their eyes met she felt as if she'd been punched in the solar plexus; the breath was driven out of her body and she had to fight to collect herself. Tim Maquire was staring at her and he was looking as dashing as a dandy, dressed in a short jacket with black braiding round it, a white shirt and a floppy bow tie made of scarlet silk. Beneath the jacket was a waitcoat of red and gold brocade with glittering buttons. What made him even more eye-catching was the fact that his skin was very brown, his beard very thick and there were two bright golden rings glittering in his ears. Her legs seemed to have lost the power to hold her up any longer and Dr Robertson, coming in the kitchen door at that moment, saw something was wrong so he rushed over to help her into a chair.

'Sit down – you're exhausted. I've told you this can't go on,' he said warningly.

Tibbie was worried by Emma Jane's reaction, too. 'Oh, did Tim give you a fright? It's that beard. You'll have to shave it off, my lad, it makes you look like a dervish. Doctor Robertson, of course you remember Tim Maquire – my Hannah's man? He's back from the Crimea and he's brought me a parrot and the loveliest scarf you've even seen.'

Proudly she draped a length of shimmering silk between her outspread hands and Emma Jane touched it admiringly, astonished at how fast her heart was beating. She wondered if she was going to faint. 'It's beautiful,' she said politely to Tibbie, but with an effort. She felt Maquire's eyes on her and wondered what he was thinking.

'Are you back on a visit, Mr Maquire?' she asked him in a formal tone. His eyes were still fixed on her face and she felt her own gaze hardening in self-defence.

'Not really. I'm looking for work – I thought you might be able to use me,' he said.

'Oh, indeed I could,' she gasped, and then felt silly at having been so effusive, but for the first time in weeks a glimpse of light appeared in the gloom of her prospects.

He didn't stay long after that. 'I'll have to go and find lodgings in Rosewell. I'm not going back to the camp. I'll spend tonight at the Abbey Hotel and look for something better tomorrow,' he told them as he stood up to leave. Then he put on his big hat, shook hands with Alex and strode away down the street.

Tibbie came back from seeing him off with a starry look on her face. 'That's a grand man – and to think that I didn't like him when he and Hannah got married! If only he could find some other nice lassie and settle down. I wouldn't mind a bit.'

Dr Robertson, also preparing to leave, was standing by the door with his hat in his hand. 'From the look of him I don't think it'll take him long to find somebody. He's a fine-looking fellow,' he said generously.

Emma Jane sat silent, wondering how she was going to cope with the disturbing presence of the dashing Tim Maquire on her workforce. 'Oh dear, perhaps I shouldn't have taken him on after all,' said a little voice inside her head.

'I think I'll go over to see Robbie,' she announced suddenly, getting up and ignoring their protests against going out again. Visiting Robbie was a pleasure, for her faith in her young friend had proven correct. He was getting better every day and now was able to swing around on crutches. To Emma Jane he was invaluable, for he spent his days doing calculations and re-drawing plans and was currently engaged in drawing up specifications for the new bridgehead.

When she arrived at his cottage, out of breath, he had the precious papers spread on a table, waiting for her, and she gradually calmed down as they studied them together.

'I think we should blast back deeper into the rockface and build up another artificial face for ourselves. We'll make it wedge-shaped – a solid wall of stone. The embankment can be laid on the top of it,' explained Robbie, pointing at the north pier with a pencil.

Emma Jane gazed at his drawing with awe. 'It's huge! It'll take tons of stone.'

He nodded. 'I know, but it's the only way. Otherwise every time it rains heavily there'll be the danger of another landslip. Put it to Miller and say that he has to share the cost of the stone with you. He'd have to build it up anyway so it's only fair.'

'But what about time?' she fretted. 'How long will it take to build it?'

His face darkened. 'I was thinking about that as well. I don't know how long it'll take. It won't be easy to do—'

Then she smiled. 'You'll never guess what's happened, Robbie. Black Ace, my father's right-hand man, has come back – and he's going to work for us again!'

Robbie was delighted. 'I remember him, of course –

he's the best! If anybody can get this done, it'll be him. Leave it to Black Ace, Miss Emma. He'll sort out the work, and you and I'll draw up the plans. What luck he's come back now!'

'Yes, isn't it,' she said, but she was not entirely sure that she meant it.

When Emma Jane returned from the Rutherfords' cottage it was almost midnight. The rain had stopped and the sky was clear. A fine mist drifted over the valley and a pale moon was glittering above the shoulder of the nearest Sister. She stopped in the middle of the street and stared westwards up the valley to where the lights of Rosewell glittered like diamonds against the blackness of the hills. Everything seemed bathed in peace and tranquillity until she turned to look southwards and saw a tongue of flame leap like a dancing imp up into the sky from a dark patch of trees on the lowest slope of the hill. The first flare-up was followed by another and another, red and orange devils dancing together against the encircling night. Something was burning and it wasn't a bonfire. It was too big for that . . .

Tibbie was in her box bed by the fire but still awake when Emma Jane ran into the kitchen. 'There's a big blaze on the hill. What's up there?' she gasped, pointing in the direction of the flames.

Tibbie sat up with her grey hair flowing loose over her shoulders and her eyes wide. 'There's only Bella Vista, where Hannah used to work. It's Colonel Anstruther's place.'

'It's burning, it's blazing,' Emma Jane told her agitatedly. 'I wonder if anybody knows about it?'

'We'd better tell somebody. Let's find William – he'll know what to do,' said Tibbie, scrambling out of bed.

'You stay there. I'll go and tell him,' offered Emma Jane, and she ran out of the house again, across the road and up to the smiddy.

William stuck his head out of the window when she hammered on the door and called down, 'Whatever's up, lass?'

When she told him about the fire, his head was quickly withdrawn and soon he was out beside her. 'I'll ride over there,' he announced, 'It's a big house, Bella Vista, and if it's on fire they'll need all the help they can get. You go back to your bed. I'll tell you what's happened in the morning.'

Bella Vista was well ablaze when he reached it, and the Rosewell Volunteer Fire Brigade were already in attendance with their horse-drawn van, brass helmets glittering with the reflection of the leaping flames which were tearing up from the central part of the house, through the roof and into the sky. There was nothing anyone could do to save it, and the men were standing around watching the destruction with tense, awestruck faces.

'Is everybody out?' gasped William when he reached the first group.

The leader of the Brigade turned and said bleakly, 'They think there's still some poor souls inside but it's impossible to reach them. It was burning like kindling by the time we got here.'

William groaned, 'Oh my God, how many are missing?' As he spoke a huge timber from the roof went crashing into the heart of the flames, sending up a dazzling display of sparks.

'I'm not sure yet. The old man and his wife are safely out – the butler rescued them – and so are most of the maids and the cook because they lived in a wide wing. But the son and his wife and her maid and a couple of wee bootboys who lived in the attic haven't been accounted for yet. Mind you, they might have got out on their own and wandered off. People do funny things when they're running away from a fire.'

Behind William, the two maids Madge and Jessie were clinging together and sobbing hysterically. 'Oh, what about Mrs Bethya? Where's she? And Francine? Where's Francine?'

Allardyce the butler was passing them in search of a coat to wrap round the old Colonel and there were tears running down his cheeks when he shouted, 'Don't waste your pity on Francine. She's the one who did this. It's that Francine who set the house alight.'

'How do you know?' asked the chief fireman.

'Because I saw her, that's how I know. I saw her pouring lamp-oil over the furniture and setting fire to it. She was mad – I always thought so.'

The Rosewell policeman had arrived now and stood listening with a bemused look on his face. 'You saw her setting fire to the hoose? Why didnae you stop her?' he asked.

'I tried to but she was raving. She'd already set fire to the first floor by the time I woke up. All I could do was get the Colonel and Mrs Anstruther out and raise the alarm, then the whole of that floor fell in. Oh Christ, what a terrible thing to happen. Bonny Mrs Bethya's still in there. This'll kill the Colonel.' He didn't mention Gus. The loss of the family's dissolute son would only be devastating for his mother.

The Colonel was sitting on the grass with his back against the trunk of a tree. His normally highly-coloured face was ghastly white, and his eyes were staring. Beside him knelt the manservant who had been at his side through many adventures in India. The man was chafing his master's hands and imploring, 'Bear up, sir, bear up. I'll fetch you a drop of brandy in a minute.' Then he looked over his shoulder and called, 'Has anybody a drink on them? Give it to me for the Colonel. He needs it badly.'

William passed over a battered tin flask saying, 'It's whisky.'

The manservant hurriedly unscrewed it and held it to the Colonel's blue lips, whispering, 'Take a sip, sir, take a sip. It'll do you good.'

The Colonel swallowed, shuddered and then asked in a shaking voice, 'Is everybody out? Is the Begum out?'

The manservant lied to him, 'Yes, sir, she's out,' he said.

'Colonel Anstruther, sir, Colonel Anstruther!' Raeburn of Falconwood came running over the lawn with his hands held out in sympathy. He had been wakened with news of the tragedy and had come at once to see if he could render any assistance.

The Colonel stared at him with bleak eyes but did not speak and Falconwood said to the old man's attendants, 'Help the Colonel and his lady into my carriage. I'll take them home with me – they can't stay here.'

After they were driven away, the servants and the firefighters stood together staring with horror at the burning house, which they now knew was a funeral pyre for five people. Buckets of water were carried from the stable-block by a line of willing workers, but nothing could be done except to dowse the snaking tongues of fire that were trying to creep across the stableyard and attack the outbuildings. When dawn broke it was judged safe enough for the exhausted helpers to go and lie down in beds of hay and straw in the hayloft. There they fell into a merciful sleep.

When they woke there was nothing left of Bella Vista but a mound of smoking ruins. The Fire Brigade climbed back on to their cart and went home, and one by one the dispirited spectators drifted away. A feeling of doom and disaster hung over the scene.

'This'll take a few days to burn itself out and cool down, and then we'll come back to look for the bodies – if there's anything left of them, though I doubt it. That was an awful blaze, the worst I've ever seen,' said the Rosewell policeman to Allardyce the butler, who was in a state of shock and couldn't stop talking about what he'd witnessed when he first realised the house was burning.

'I can't believe it, I can't believe it,' he kept repeating. 'That Frenchwoman did it – God knows why. I heard noises and got up to find out what was going on. There she was in the drawing room, setting fire to everything – the curtains, the furniture, everything. I tried to stop her but she started screaming about not being able to trust anybody, about nobody ever loving her, that sort of stuff. She was mad. She didn't care that the fire was going to kill her . . . the last I saw of her was with her dress all in flames. Oh my God, what a sight!'

He sank his face in his hands as the policeman asked, 'Why was she trying to kill herself?'

Allardyce shook his head and jabbered on, 'God knows! God knows, but she's killed other folk too. That's the tragedy of it. And she was laughing . . . laughing like a crazy thing. Oh God, it was a terrible sight.'

A young footman came over to help the distraught man, and he had something to contribute to the story. 'That Francine was acting odd before it happened. I heard her yelling at a man who came to the back door and asked for Mrs Bethya, but he wouldn't go away . . . I think Mrs Bethya went down to see him in the end, but I'm not sure. Aw, poor lassie . . .' He was one of the many who were badly affected by the tragic death of the beautiful Bethya.

The policeman asked, 'What sort of man was this? Did you recognise him?'

The footman shook his head. 'I'd never seen him before. It was dark, but I could tell he was tall, and dressed in a long cloak . . . that's all I saw.'

For three days the ruins smoked and during that time Colonel Anstruther lay in bed at Falconwood House, but on the fourth day he rose to receive an official party from Rosewell.

'I'm afraid your house is completely gutted, sir,' said the Chief Magistrate sadly.

The old warrior fixed him with dead eyes. 'I'm insured. What about my family? Have you found the bodies?'

'No, sir, we haven't but we've made a list of the missing persons. Perhaps you'd like to look at it.'

The Colonel ran his eye down the list: Major Augustus Anstruther, age 30; Mrs Bethya Anstruther, age 24; Mademoiselle Francine Perrot, age unknown but thought to be about 25; Thomas Telfer, bootboy, age 12; Robert Macintosh, kitchen boy, age 15.

'She wasn't twenty-four, she was only twenty-three,' he said bleakly, handing the paper back, and everyone knew to whom he was referring. Then he gave a little sob and asked, 'You're absolutely sure she's dead?'

The policeman stepped forward with something in his

hand. 'We found this on a body, sir.' It was a mangled piece of jewellery, twisted out of shape by the fire.

The Colonel took it and turned it over, then his head dropped. 'Yes, it's hers. It's the brooch I gave her for Christmas two years ago – garnets and diamonds. She thought it was very pretty . . .'

That night the old man was taken ill. In the morning when his servant went to wake him, he found the Colonel lying in bed, his eyes mutely appealing for help. His speech was affected and he could not move his left arm or leg. 'Oh God sir, not that too!' cried the anguished servant, before ringing the bell for assistance. He stayed by the bed, cradling his employer in his arms like a baby, until Dr Stewart arrived.

Next day, a sombre-looking Sir Geoffrey Miller arrived at Falconwood to express his sympathy. Mrs Anstruther was too upset to receive callers, for the terrible succession of tragedies had left her numb and inconsolable. The Raeburn women, who were kindly souls, were at their wits' end about how to help her.

The sick Colonel was in bed but Raeburn took Miller upstairs where they stood together gazing at the old man while Sir Geoffrey spoke some carefully chosen words. 'This is a terrible tragedy, my friend. I've come to express my deepest sympathy and that of my fellow directors to you and your wife. It is almost unbelievable that your son and his lovely wife both lost their lives in the fire. We'll do everything we can to help you.'

The Colonel did not speak but his eyes were bleak. 'I'm going down to the bridge now,' said Sir Geoffrey, speaking loudly and slowly as if to someone who was half-witted. 'It's in trouble too, I'm afraid. As well as the bridgehead being washed away, Jopp now tells me that they've found a crack in one of the piers in the field. That makes it almost certain that the girl won't finish in time. We'll save some money, anyway.'

The Colonel wearily closed his eyes. It was obvious that he had no desire to be told about any other troubles or any plots and plans.

Miller felt relieved when he left the grief-filled house to ride with Raeburn to the bridge. 'It's a pity that pier's cracked because it's beginning to look very fine,' said Raeburn guilelessly as he stared at it.

'It's not fine if it's in danger of falling down. God knows when we can run a service over this line. It's eating up money now. I should never have allowed that girl to keep the contract. I should have bought her out of it – it would have been cheaper in the end,' was Miller's angry reply.

Emma Jane and Tim Maquire were standing in the field beside the third pillar from the south end and a young lad on crutches was with them when Miller and Raeburn rode up. Without dismounting, Miller abruptly asked, 'Which is the cracked pier?'

'This one. There's a long crack on the inner side,' said Emma Jane, laying her hand on the stone. 'We're working out what we should do.'

'I'll tell you what you'll do – you should make it safe as soon as you can before the whole damned thing falls down. I'll sue you for breach of contract if it's not finished by August the first,' bawled Miller.

She flared up at him. 'Don't talk to me like that! The bridgehead fell down because your man Jopp didn't do his job properly. That is what's holding us up, not the crack.'

He was not prepared to listen, however. 'The crux of the matter is that it's cracked. What will go wrong next, that's what I'd like to know? I doubt if we'll have a bridge in a year's time, far less two months. The line's finished and this damned bridge is holding it back from opening. It'll cost you dear. You can't get out of your undertaking now. You'll be paying for it for the rest of your life.'

His rudeness made Tim Maquire's Irish temper rise. 'You listen to me,' he said, walking up and grabbing Miller's stirrup. 'You listen to me. I'll prove you wrong, see if I don't. We'll do it – we'll damned well do it even if we have to work night and day for two months. Your bridge'll be ready on the day it was promised.'

Wrenching his foot out of the navvy's grasp, Miller rode

off, followed by Raeburn. Emma Jane watched them go and then turned on Tim to ask, 'Why did you say that? He's probably right. There's no way we can finish this in time. I'm ruined and I might as well accept it now!'

Robbie looked at her with pity but Tim's eyes flashed fire. 'Don't talk like that. Here's what we do first. We'll make this pier safe and then we'll finish the bridgehead. After that it'll be plain sailing.'

If she had not been so miserable, she would have burst out laughing. To call what they were faced with 'plain sailing' seemed to be plain folly, more like.

Maquire, however, seemed to be infected with some sort of madness. He ran around the field, shouting, waving his arms, gathering men about him. 'We'll buttress it: we'll make it safe. Get started! Build a shell round it, ten feet thick on every side.' Then he ran back to Robbie and demanded, 'Are there any unemployed masons left in Camptounfoot?'

'One or two, and there's a few old men who'll come out and help.'

'We'll hire them. We'll hire every mason for miles around. It doesn't matter what we pay, we've got to finish this.' Hair flying, he dashed off up the hill in the direction of the village where he stopped at the alehouse and issued his appeal for workers before going on to William's smiddy. He burst into the forge, calling out to the labouring blacksmith, 'Stop what you're doing! I want you to forge big metal bars to bolt round the broken pier. We're going to buttress it and then tie it in with iron. That'll stop it shifting: it won't move for a thousand years.'

William, hammer in hand, gazed in astonishment at the madman in his doorway who was saying urgently, 'I mean it. I want iron bars twelve inches thick and as long as you can make 'em. We'll bolt them together. It'll work.'

His urgency and enthusiasm were so infectious that the smith set about forging forty iron bars immediately, while in the field, navvies were digging out the foundations for the new buttress and masons were busy chipping huge lumps of stone into rough blocks. For three days Maquire did not sleep. He went to the quarry and arranged for more stone; he harangued the navvies and kept them working; he supervised the rising buttress and shouted at any man he thought was working too slowly. People feared for his sanity as he dashed from place to place in a state of absolute frenzy.

Emma Jane watched his wild behaviour with disquiet. When he was finally found fast asleep in her hut on the fourth morning, she tiptoed around him and let him lie undisturbed because she had been afraid that he would drop dead with exhaustion if he didn't halt. For her own part she was working harder than she had ever done before, harder and longer than she ever thought possible. From dawn till dark she was on site, supervising, hiring, paying out money, arranging for supplies of stone, sand and concrete and all the time making sure that the building of the brick arches overhead still went on.

She rarely spoke to Tim for he was too busy doing what he considered necessary and relied on her to do the same. Robbie rode down to the site every day on one of the tradesmen's carts and spent hours there, smoothing out structural problems or making useful suggestions. His grasp of building practice was astonishing in one so young and Emma Jane congratulated herself on giving him her father's books.

On the afternoon of the eighth day of their marathon effort, Maquire's head appeared round the hut door and he said shortly, 'We've buttressed the cracked pier. Come and see it.'

The men had been working behind wooden palisades but now these were down and Emma Jane was able to see what had been done. A thick stone skin had been built round the bottom of the narrow, elegant pier and bolted round with bars of black metal. Her jaw dropped. 'But it's spoiled the line. It's thicker than the others. It's spoiled the design,' she gulped.

Tim was walking behind her and he clenched both fists and jumped in the air. 'Is that all you can say? To hell with the design! It's up and it's holding! It'll never fall down. You're a stupid woman, that's what you are – a stupid woman!'

She turned to apologise for she knew she had been wrong. Sacrifice of symmetry was nothing if the pier was going to hold and would not need rebuilding, but Black Ace had charged off across the field towards the river where men were dragging up blocks of stone from the fallen bridgehead. She knew better than to run after him. He was obviously not in the mood for polite conversation.

All through June the sun beamed down. Camptounfoot was full of bustle because almost every able-bodied man was working on the bridge. Emma Jane left home at sunrise and did not come staggering back until late, too tired for one of the fireside conversations with Tibbie, too tired for anything but forcing down a meal and dragging herself up to bed.

Tim still kept a room at the Abbey Hotel though he seldom slept in it, preferring to doss down in Emma Jane's hut because he could not bear to leave the site. Sometimes he went into Rosewell early to hire a gig for expeditions to order more stone or bricks or recruit extra workers. On those mornings he would stop in the pearly dawn at Tibbie's door and rap loudly to waken up Emma Jane. Still half-asleep, she would get dressed, run downstairs and climb in beside him. He'd collect Robbie too and the three of them would clatter quickly down to the bridge where they separated and went about their individual tasks. They didn't talk except about what was to be done that day.

At sunset Dr Robertson still waited in the roadway for Emma Jane, but she often did not come and stayed working in her hut. Then he turned and rode sadly back to Maddiston without seeing her.

Colonel Anstruther did not die, as so many people had expected. Slowly, very slowly, he improved in health. His speech returned and he was able to move a little. His faithful manservant never left his side, nursed him as if he were a child and when the sun shone, pushed him in a wickerwork Bath chair out on to the lawn of Falconwood

House where he sat in the sun with his eyes closed thinking and grieving without weeping. His subdued wife sat beside him holding his hand and talking constantly, but fortunately she had enough feeling and tact not to mention Gus or Bethya. Mostly she talked about India and the people and places they had known there, for she felt it was safest to concentrate on the past.

On the last day of June, Tim was working with a gang of men on refilling the embankment behind the new stone pier, when the post-runner from Rosewell came in search of him.

'I've a letter for you, Mr Maquire,' he said. 'I took it to the Hotel but they said I'd find you here. It's got *Urgent* written on the front of it.'

A large square envelope was handed over. Tim looked at it with curiosity. 'It's from France,' he said. 'Who'd be writing to me from France?'

'You'll no' ken that unless you open it,' said the postman laconically.

The letter was written on a square of thick linen paper with an embossed coronet at the top of the page. The sender wrote in a large confident hand and had used black ink.

'*Dear Black Ace, I suppose by this time everyone will know that when I left Camptounfoot I did not go alone. I'd been infatuated with the lady in question for a long time though I'd done nothing about it. I actually travelled quite a distance before I decided to turn back and speak to her about how I felt. To my surprise and astonishment she felt the same way about me and we decided to go off together.*

'*Of course she left a husband behind, but she wrote a letter for her father-in-law, of whom she's very fond, and put it on his desk for him to find in the morning. She gave him a contact address in London but so far there has been no reply and we are becoming rather concerned because we want to marry. Before we can, of course, there will have to be a divorce. She is worried in case she left a great deal of trouble behind, but neither of us cares about who divorces whom. Her husband can divorce her if he likes – we've given him plenty of cause and hope to continue to do so. Could you be a good fellow and ask around to find out what's happening at Bella Vista? I apologise for involving you, but I can't ask my old friend Allandale because he's in Italy and won't be home till autumn. I want to marry Bethya because my vagabond days are over now. We'd like to be respectable for a change and we can't be that until we marry. At the moment we're in Paris but will be back in London by the time you receive this letter, so address your reply to me at 114 Pall Mall, which is my townhouse. And I have to sound uppish but you should address it to Lord Godolphin. I succeeded to the title on the death of my father. Your old friend, Gentleman Sydney.'*

Tim threw back his head and laughed and laughed. Then, when his first fit of amusement was over, he sobered, for he remembered the fire at Bella Vista and the grief of the old Colonel. 'Poor old devil, he doesn't know the girl's still alive. Someone ought to tell him,' he thought. Sticking the letter in his pocket, he scrambled down the embankment and crossed the low-running river by the ford. Emma Jane was in her hut making minute calculations on scraps of paper, trying to work out if the money she still had available for wages would last until the end of the job. She was surprised when he stepped in out of the sunlight and abruptly asked, 'Do you remember Gentleman Sydney?'

She looked up with a furrow between her brows. 'Yes, of course I do. He was very kind to me, especially when Bullhead was shot. I was sorry when he went away. Why do you ask?'

'Well, you're in for a shock. He's a lord and he didn't go away alone. He took Colonel Anstruther's daughter-in-law with him, so she didn't burn to death in the fire after all.'

Emma Jane clasped her hands. 'Oh, I'm so glad! I used to see her on the road with the Colonel and she was so beautiful. I thought it tragic that she'd died. The Colonel will be delighted – people say he's broken-hearted about her death. He didn't like his son much, but he was very fond of her.' Then she looked puzzled. 'But how do you know all this?'

Tim brandished the letter. 'Sydney's written to me. He obviously doesn't know about the fire and I'll have to write to him about that, but right now I'm going up to Falconwood to tell the Colonel.'

'Let me know what happens. I think it's wonderful,' she said with a brilliant smile, the first she'd bestowed on him for weeks.

It was difficult for Tim to speak to the Colonel but he insisted and stood his ground. 'I've information about the fire,' he said stoutly. 'I've further details about his daughter-in-law, and I won't tell anyone but the Colonel.' In the end he was admitted to the terrace in front of Falconwood House and led across to where the Colonel lay under a thick rug in spite of the warmth of the day.

'Don't expect him to talk much,' warned the manservant. 'Just say what you've got to say. He'll hear you.'

Tim said his piece. He told about Sydney's letter and the startling news it contained. He brought it out of his pocket and held it in front of the Colonel's face so the old man could see what he said was true.

'She's eloped with Gentleman Sydney, who's really Lord Godolphin. They were in Paris last week but now they're back in London. She doesn't know about the fire, or her husband dying, or her maid either,' Tim finished up.

The Colonel's eyes stared at him blankly for a few moments and then it seemed as if a light had been lit behind them. A low chuckle rumbled in the old man's chest and he croaked the first words he'd uttered for a long time. 'Damned good, damned good!'

His servant rushed towards him, terrified in case the astonishing news would be more than his constitution could endure, but he need not have bothered. The Colonel was rejuvenated. By gestures he told the servant to offer Tim money, but this was refused so then he offered him a drink instead, which was accepted. Holding the glass high, Tim toasted the old man before he swallowed the neat whisky it contained. 'I'm glad you're pleased, sir. I'll leave the letter with you and you can decide what you want to do. Good day. I'll have to go now because I'm very busy.'

On his way home the whisky swirled in his brain and made him feel happy and optimistic. 'When I finish the bridge, I'll do something wonderful. I don't know what, but I'll change my life somehow, the way Sydney changed his,' he resolved.

He was still beaming when he stopped at the hut and shoved his head in to inform Emma Jane: 'I told the Colonel. He's pleased as Punch.'

She glanced up with a yearning expression on her face and said dreamily, 'It's so romantic. It's like a miracle, isn't it?'

Tim nodded. 'I've been thinking that, too. I've decided that when the bridge is finished, I'm going to do something wild – take off for somewhere I've never thought of before.' Then he sobered, surprised at having unburdened himself so much to this girl. 'But the bridge has to be finished first, doesn't it? Back to work, back to work,' he said before he disappeared.

There were still many problems, of course. When it looked as if they had cured the cracked pier, they completed the line of elegant arches that joined the whole thing together. Then Jopp pulled his last trick. One dull morning in mid-July, Tim turned up at the site to find only a handful of workers there. He gazed round in astonishment. 'Where is everybody? We're going to start laying the hardcore on the top today. Where are they all?'

'Jopp's men are all out and they've talked most of the rest into staying out with them. It's the money. Jopp's cut their daily rate again and the food's worse than ever. If he doesn't bring in better stuff to the truck-shop, there'll be fever in the camp again. The food he's selling is stinking – you wouldn't give it to a dog,' said an old navvy who was too long in the tooth to go on strike.

'Jopp! Bloody Jopp! I wondered how long it would take before he started his dirty work,' yelled Tim, and he ran off up the road to Rosewell and the navvy camp. It was the first time he'd been in it since he burned down *Benjy's*,

but now he had no time to spare for nostalgic remember-
ings. He went from hut to hut throwing open the doors
and yelling at the men inside, 'Get up off your backsides
and come to the bridge at once. *Get up*! You're not going
to leave it now, are you? This is what Jopp wants you to
do. If you play into his hands you'll all be earning half a
crown a day and no truck. The minute he sees off Miss
Wylie he can do what the hell he likes with you.'

Most of them listened to him and went back to work,
but others stayed sullenly in their huts, grumbling and
complaining. A few even packed up their traps and left
the camp because there was more work available locally
for navvies now. Branch lines were being built off the
main line that was to cross the bridge, and they no longer
had to stay.

Tim headed back for the bridge with any strike-breakers
he could persuade to go with him, and his rage was so
incandescent that when Emma Jane walked out into the
field to ask him what was going on, he spun round at her
and snapped, 'Don't ask what's happened – don't talk
about it. I'll finish it, that's all.'

'Please tell me what's going on,' she said quietly. 'This
is my contract after all.'

He glared at her. 'All right, it's your contract. You talk
to them. You tell them to work and ignore Jopp. I'll leave
it to you.' He stepped back and indicated the watching
men with a sweep of the hand.

She walked past him and stood in front of them, a tiny
figure in her work-clothes, her golden eyes looking from
one face to another as she spoke. 'Is Jopp making trouble
again?' she asked.

'Yes, he is,' said one of them.

She held out her hands in an imploring gesture. 'But
the bridge is almost finished. I've almost done what I set
out to do. Please don't leave me now. Please keep on
working as you have done these last weeks. I've been
watching you. I know how hard it's been and I promise
that if you finish the bridge for me, I'll pay every man a

loyalty bonus at the end, you have my word on it.' Then she walked away.

Behind her, one man cheered and another, then another joined in. She'd swung them behind her. They'd work and they'd go back and persuade the others to work as well.

CHAPTER
Nineteen

'Let me take you for a drive tomorrow. You've been living here for almost a year and you've not been anywhere except Maddiston and Rosewell. There's some lovely places round about and you need a break – just one day,' Alex Robertson pleaded with Emma Jane as they walked up the hill from the bridge to Camptounfoot on a romantic evening when dog roses were blooming in the hedges and the air smelt heady with the scent of hawthorn blossom.

She leaned on his arm, for she was very tired and her big boots weighed down her feet like lead. She gave a disbelieving laugh as if he'd suggested a trip to the moon, and replied, 'Oh Alex, I can't go driving around like a tourist. There's so much to be done and anyway – what would Maquire say if I went off on a jaunt!'

The young doctor laughed. 'You and Black Ace! You're as bad as each other. I think you both see this bridge as your own property and neither of you will go away for even a minute lest the other one takes it over. You're like a pair of children quarrelling over your favourite toy.'

'That Maquire is dreadful and he's getting worse and worse,' Emma Jane complained. 'I was furious today because he shouted at me in front of the men as if I was a servant girl or something, just because I wanted one thing and he wanted another. He really does think he's the boss, Alex. One of the things I'm looking forward to when the bridge is finished is not having to argue with *him* every day.'

'What else are you looking forward to?' asked Robertson tenderly.

She glanced up at him with a little laugh. 'Lying in bed

till eight o'clock and not having to rise at five . . . wearing a proper dress and slippers . . . taking tea from china cups . . . going on drives.'

She didn't say 'with you', he noticed, but smiled as if that was what she meant and the smile was good enough for him. For weeks he had been longing to speak to her of his growing love, but although this would have been the perfect evening to bring the subject up, he knew that she was not yet ready to listen. The bridge and its problems obsessed her. All she wanted to talk about was the work, which was going flat out in order to finish on time.

Both she and Tim Maquire thought of nothing else but the bridge. They even dreamed about it at night when they fell into their respective beds and lapsed into exhausted unconsciousness. Day followed day, task followed task, problem followed problem without them ever lifting their heads and seeing how close they had come to achieving their objective – until the afternoon Sir Geoffrey Miller turned up unexpectedly. Looking as bland as a neutered cat, he announced to Emma Jane, 'Well, Miss Wylie, I think we can safely organise the bridge's official opening for August the eighth, don't you?'

Tim, wild-looking in an open-necked shirt and scarlet throat-cloth, was standing beside her when this announcement was made and he growled, 'What's the date today?' As he spoke Emma Jane realised that she, too, had lost track of time.

Miller looked surprised but he said, 'It's July the fourteenth. That gives you enough time, doesn't it? You're well ahead. All that needs to be done now is for the rails to be laid.'

Tim looked at Emma Jane and gave a huge grin. 'God, girl, he's right, ain't he? We've done it, we've done it!' Then he seized her round the waist and whirled her off her feet. She put a hand on each of his hard shoulders and hung on to him, giggling like a child, while the navvies round about gave a huge cheer and threw their hats in the air. Emma Jane had become very popular among them and they looked on her with a mixture of awe and affection, as if she was some sort of mascot. It was Black Ace they worked for, however: it was he who drove them on.

When Tim dropped her back on her feet, Emma Jane, hearing the men's huzzahs, was suddenly overcome with embarrassment and acute self-consciousness, so she stepped primly away from Tim and told Sir Geoffrey, 'I'm sure we'll finish the bridge on time now. The date you mention is perfectly acceptable.'

That evening, when work was finished, a sort of anti-climax set in. Tim Maquire went off up the hill to the alehouse with a group of navvies and sat on the bench opposite Tibbie's door with a huge mug in his hands, drinking as heavily as any of his companions. He wanted to get drunk and fuddled; he wanted to drive away the memories of the times he'd sat on that same bench waiting for a glimpse of Hannah; he wanted to forget that the project which had engaged his thoughts and energy for so long was almost completed, and he'd have to make a decision about what he was to do next, where he was to go . . .

Emma Jane was similarly affected by a strange tearful-ness, and when Robbie limped off home, she stayed in her hut, sitting on her high stool with her head in her hands staring down at the plans which had now become a reality. Outside, the bridge soared as she had dreamed it would, beautiful and elegant, a fitting memorial for her father. Why then did she want to weep? She was wiping her eyes with the edge of her sleeve when the hut door opened and Alex Robertson walked in. He had been waiting for her on the road, and when she did not emerge, he'd come looking for her.

'Aren't you going home tonight? It'll be dark soon,' he said gently.

She stood up and mumbled, 'Oh yes, I'm coming. I'm a little tired, that's all. I was sitting here on my own thinking – it's hard to think when everybody's milling about around you.'

He lifted her shawl off the back of a chair and draped it

over her shoulders. 'I'm taking you home and I'm going to tell Tibbie to put you straight to bed. If you don't stop driving yourself like this, you'll have a breakdown. You can't keep up with the men, no matter how much you want to.'

Astonished by his firm tone, she gazed up at him and he saw how the freckles that marked her face were so close together that they made her look as brown as an Indian. He wanted to put his finger on them and trace the pattern they made over the bridge of her nose. 'I can't stay at home now. There's still too much to do,' she protested, but he took her firmly by the arm.

'You're going home,' he repeated, 'and I'll tell Tibbie not to let you out tomorrow, even if she has to lock you in.'

She stepped back. 'Did Maquire tell you to do this?' she asked suspiciously, for she thought that Tim wanted her out of the way for some reason.

Robertston was surprised. 'Black Ace? Of course not. I'm a doctor, remember, and I can see that you're in need of a rest. I'm going to make sure you get it, that's all. I met young Robbie on the way here and he told me the date for the opening ceremony's been fixed. If you crack up now you'll not be there.'

Suddenly she felt so exhausted that her legs almost buckled under her. 'I think you're right – I *am* tired. I'll go home,' she agreed.

'Take my arm,' he said in a gentle tone, and she did as she was told. Over their heads, tiny pipistrelle bats were swooping and when they reached the top of the hill, she looked down on the bridge with a returning expression of delight on her face.

'It hasn't spoiled that valley, has it?' she asked him

'On the contrary, it adds to it,' he said.

She smiled. 'Even Tibbie thought we were going to ruin the countryside when we started, but we haven't. Soon we'll all go away and everyone here will forget about us. They'll forget any of this ever happened and they'll become as used to the bridge as they are to the trees and the hills. It'll be part of the landscape.'

'I won't forget you,' he said softly. She said nothing to that so he added, 'What are you going to do now it's finished?'

'I don't know – I haven't had time to think about that yet. All I want to do is to see it through to the end.'

He stopped in the middle of the road and looked at her with great intensity. 'Please listen to what I've got to say. I've fallen in love with you, Miss Wylie. I've not a lot to offer, not what you were used to when your father was alive, but I admire you and I'll really try to make you happy and take care of you forever if you'll let me. Perhaps you'll think about what I'm saying.'

She opened her mouth to speak but he put a hand on her arm and said urgently, 'No, I know it's a surprise. Don't say anything yet. Just think about it and tell me what you've decided when the bridge is opened. I'll wait till then.'

She took his arm and nodded her head. 'Thank you very much for the compliment, Alex. I'll think about it very carefully,' she said solemnly. 'Perhaps I should have called him Doctor Robertson since he called me Miss Wylie,' she thought, but decided to stick to Alex. After all, that was what she'd been calling him for months.

Just before they reached Tibbie's, she saw a noisy group of navvies milling around the hatch in the alehouse wall. Standing tall in the middle of them was Tim Maquire, laughing merrily and obviously drunk. It was the first time she'd seen him like that, though she'd seen plenty of other navvies in a similar condition, but somehow the sight of Tim drunk shocked her deeply and she averted her gaze as she and Alex walked past. But he'd spotted them, and she heard him shout, 'Miss Wylie, Robertson! Miss Wylie, have a mug of ale with us!'

Pretending not to hear him, she hurried through Tibbie's door and pulled the doctor behind her. In the little hall she said angrily, 'Maquire! Isn't he awful? He's always trying to make a fool of me.'

Robertson grinned at her discomfiture. 'I don't think he's doing that, Emma Jane. You mustn't be so critical of him. Everything he does is wrong, according to you.'

She was quite annoyed. 'That's because it usually *is* wrong,' she retorted. From the other side of the closed door she could hear Maquire's big laugh and she was sure he was laughing at her.

Tibbie had a kettle on the hob and food on the table, and she hurried across the room saying, 'I've been boiling water in the boiler so's you can have a bath. You're tired out, you poor wee soul. Come on, you've done enough. You need a rest.'

'That's just what I've been telling her,' Alex commented. 'I'll leave her to you then, Mrs Mather.' Before he went away he turned to Emma Jane and said softly, 'Think about what I said, won't you?'

Tibbie looked from the girl to the man in the doorway and her eyes were sharp. When he had left she said to Emma Jane, 'That's a good man, you know.'

'I know. I like him but —'

'Oh, I'm sorry there's a but. It usually means you've got your eye on somebody else,' was the reply.

After she'd soaked in the big tin bath before the fire and had dried and dressed in her nightgown, darkness had fallen and Emma Jane was walking through the hall on her way to bed when she heard noises outside the front door. Male voices were muttering; someone was laughing, there was a chink of saddlery. It sounded as if a group of men were standing on the doorstep. Surely Maquire was not still out there, poking fun, making trouble! Slowly and quietly she opened the door a crack and peered through the slit. What she saw made her freeze. Just as slowly she closed it again and tip-toed back to the kitchen where Tibbie was tidying up for the night.

'Tibbie, Tibbie, you didn't put whisky in my tea, did you?'

'Of course not!'

'I've just seen the queerest thing at the door.'

Tibbie turned round. 'What?'

'There's three men out there, dressed like Roman soldiers. They're all having a gossip and a laugh – right outside your door! Who are they? I've never seen any of them before.'

Tibbie threw her arms out in delight and grabbed Emma Jane round the shoulders. 'Och lassie, that's grand! They've not gone away, then! I haven't seen them for two years – not since all this started – and I thought they'd gone forever. I've been really bothered about them, but now you've seen them. They're back. It doesn't matter about the railway – things are going to be the same as always. Och, that's grand!'

The parrot was wakened from its doze by the fuss and it croaked in the Scots-French it now affected, '*C'est bon, that's grand, ma belle, that's grand . . .*'

When he left the alehouse, Tim's head was swimming with alcohol and he was filled with a kind of wild rage that needed assuageing. Striding like Colossus, he walked to Maddiston where there was a large hotel popular with navvies. It was crowded when he walked in and the men, all of whom knew him, rushed over to buy him drinks. He asked for brandy and threw back glass after glass, pouring it down his throat as if he was trying to quench a fire inside. Women crowded round him too, stroking his arm, pecking at his bearded cheek and when midnight struck, he staggered off into the darkness with a prostitute on his arm. She lived in a cottage on the edge of town and when they reached it, she guided him indoors like a tug steering a huge ship. He stood swaying in the middle of the floor while she began trying to pull off his clothes, but suddenly he seemed to come to himself and pushed her away. 'Get off me, I'm going home,' he muttered and headed for the door again. Her angry screeches followed him but he did not pause and was heading in the direction of Rosewell when he met Alex Robertson returning from a late call.

The doctor jumped from his horse, grabbed the staggering man and asked, 'Where are you going, Black Ace?'

'Rosewell. I'm drunk, Robertson. I'm going to bed,' Maquire's voice was slurred and he swayed on his feet.

The doctor said, 'It's too far to go in that state. Come back with me and sleep on my sofa. You can go home in the morning.'

This idea appealed to Maquire who said, 'All right, but will you make sure I wake early? I don't want Miss Wylie getting to the bridge before me.'

Robertson snorted with mirth. 'What a pair you are! Don't worry – she won't be there tomorrow. I told her to take a day off.'

Maquire groaned, 'Are you mad enough to think she'll do what you tell her? If she does, you're a better man than I am, Doctor Robertson.'

Maquire was right. Emma Jane was back at the bridge next day, but she was late in arriving, even later than he, and the pair of them stayed well apart. Tim was positioned on the top of the bridge making arrangements for the line-laying. She, tactfully, gave him a wide berth and stayed on the ground.

The last days of the great project continued to be anticlimactic. When the final stretch of hardcore surface was laid and driven down between the shallow stone parapets that edged the top, Emma Jane, in her lady-like black skirt and jacket, walked the length of the bridge for the first time with Robbie limping by her side. He'd abandoned his crutches now, and got around with the help of a stick which he used with a flourish, for he'd accepted that he would always have a marked limp but he'd beaten his disability and proved the doctor wrong. His confidence was great and his ambition unlimited, for already he'd been offered a job with another contractor in London. He was going there when the bridge was completely finished.

The wind was high on the top and Emma Jane's hair escaped from the constriction of her bonnet which she was holding on with one hand. She stopped in the middle of the bridge and stared down at the broad ribbon of silver river running beneath her feet. The view was giddying for there was no guard-rail; only about ten inches of stone parapet projected above the hard surface. It would be horribly easy to plunge over . . .

She placed one neatly-buttoned kid boot on the ledge and Robbie anxiously pulled at her arm. 'Don't go too near, Miss Emma. The wind's strong and it might just catch you.'

She smiled at him but there was a melancholy look in her eye. 'Oh, I won't fall over. I've got to see this opened first, haven't I?'

When they were three-quarters of the way across, they came upon Tim Maquire standing in the middle of a group of navvies. He was making his last examination of the surface before the men moved in to lay the sleepers and then the iron rails. His curly head was bare and he stood proudly with both thumbs stuck in the breast pockets of a bright yellow waistcoat, booted feet firmly planted. It would take a typhoon to blow him off the bridge.

He saw her approaching and turned towards her. 'Well, it's almost finished, then. How do you feel?' he asked.

'I thought it would never happen,' she said solemnly. 'Why,' she wondered, 'do I feel so low? I should be throwing my bonnet in the air . . . How do you feel?' she said aloud.

'Wonderful,' he lied. But there was something in his eye that told her he was sharing her unaccountable dejection. Perhaps he was only happy under stress; perhaps he needed continual excitement, she thought.

'They're having a grand ceremonial dinner in Maddiston on opening night,' he went on. 'Jopp's been here flourishing his invitation card. You'll have had one too, will you?'

She shook her head in surprise. 'No. I've been invited on to the platform for the speech-making, but I haven't heard anything about a dinner.'

Tim grinned. 'You'll hear. You've got more right to be there than anyone. You've done this. It's your bridge, Miss Wylie.'

It was the most pleasing and flattering thing he'd ever said to her and she was surprised at his magnanimity. 'Mr Maquire,' she replied primly, 'I couldn't have done it without you.' That was an enormous concession on her part too.

He laughed and his beard seemed to bristle thicker and curlier than ever. The piratical look was even more marked. 'Well, we've had our fights, haven't we – but that's all over now, I hope,' he said to her.

'Oh yes,' she agreed. 'All over.' Suddenly she felt that she wanted to weep. Turning away quickly, she took Robbie's arm. 'Come, Robbie. I've just remembered that we forgot to take the plans out of the hut. I want to keep them as mementoes of this.'

Robbie's face lit up. 'Can I have one, Miss Emma?'

'Of course you can have any one you want. I couldn't have done it without you either . . .' The wind carried her words far, far away over the trees and the hills and the now-tranquil river.

There was still a week to go before the inaugural day, but already carpenters were erecting the platform for the official party to sit on after they came steaming down the line from Maddiston on the first train to cross the bridge. As she walked past it, the sight somehow increased Emma Jane's depression and she turned her head to the side so that she did not have to look at it. Robbie knew that something was wrong and he asked her, 'What are you going to do now, Miss Emma?'

She frowned. 'I don't really know, Robbie. I'll go home, I suppose. Father used to say that when the bridge was built he would go to Menton and lie in the sun. I might try that.'

She said nothing about the proposal she'd received from Alex Robertson. She had been thinking about it a great deal, weighing the pros and cons. He was an admirable man and she liked him a great deal, but she did not love him – or at least she did not think she loved him, because the feeling she had for him was not exciting. It was placid, and safe. Perhaps lots of people married for reasons of safety and security; perhaps that was a good basis for a life together, but Emma Jane was a romantic who longed for more than that. She remembered Gentleman Sydney and the beautiful Bethya who threw their hats over the windmill when they ran away together. What did they feel for each other? Not a calm liking, certainly. It must have been much more tempestuous than that. Marriage as a way of escaping from life in Newcastle was a great temptation, but she knew that to marry Alex for that reason alone would not be honest. She longed for laughter, for noise, vitality and passion. She longed for adventure. Life with Alex might bring contentment but it was unlikely to prove adventurous.

Robbie, walking by her side, was thinking about Menton and his eyes were starry. 'Menton, that's in the South of France, isn't it? It must be lovely there. I'd like to see it one day,' he sighed, gazing at the greystone cottages which lined the street of the place where he'd been born.

'You'll go there one day,' she promised him. 'I'm sure of it. You'll make a mark on the world, Robbie Rutherford.'

He looked sideways at her and said in a rush of confidence, 'I want to – I really want to succeed. I'm awfy ambitious, Miss Emma. When I make my name it's you and your father I'll thank for it. I'll never forget that the Wylies gave me my start.' His face was changing. He wasn't a boy any more but a young man with a determined line to his mouth and a hardness in his eye that came from suffering and winning. She knew he'd succeed in anything he set out to do, and felt a certain awe of him.

They parted at Tibbie's door, and when Emma Jane went in she found Tibbie and Effie admiring a little framed picture that was propped up on the mantelshelf. 'Look what Tim brought me,' Tibbie said, turning towards Emma Jane and holding out the picture.

It was a naive portrait of a girl with a mass of red hair. Her eyelids were drooping and her mouth curved sweetly. She looked as if she were on the verge of sleep when the artist drew her.

'What a beauty,' sighed Emma Jane. Even though the

artist was unskilled, the girl's loveliness shone out of the picture.

'It's my Hannah,' said Tibbie proudly.

'And it's her to the life. She had that sort of dreamy look about her,' chipped in Effie.

'But she wasn't aye dreamy,' Tibbie said defensively.

'No, no, but she looked as if she was, especially when she was happy,' Effie quickly agreed.

'She was happy right to the end,' said Tibbie softly. The pain was lessening now but she knew that it would never go away completely.

Emma Jane carefully put the picture back on the shelf and Tibbie told her, 'Tim brought it to me today. He said he'd been carrying the paper round with him since she died, but he was afraid it'd get spoiled and so he had it framed. Now that he's going to be off again soon, he's given it to me. He says that he'll always be able to see it when he comes back to Camptounfoot. If he kept it, he might lose it.'

What a fine couple they must have looked, thought Emma Jane – the lovely girl with the red hair and the darkly handsome, vibrant man. What sort of a woman would he find to marry as his second wife? Another beauty, no doubt. She felt very small and mousy again: Miss Emma Jane Wylie, spinster of Newcastle.

'Did he say where he was going after the bridge is opened?' she asked lightly.

Tibbie shook her head. 'He's no idea. He's been invited to visit that Lord Godolphin in London – the one who ran away with young Mrs Anstruther. He might go but he won't stay, of course. He was talking about France, too. There's a lot of railway-building going on there, apparently. Poor laddie, he hasn't a soul in the world.'

'He's got you,' said Effie.

'He has – and he says he'll aye come back and see me. And I'm sure he will,' said Tibbie proudly.

At that moment it struck Emma Jane that Tibbie had no insecurities about the future. She was settled and secure in Camptounfoot, grounded deep in her native village, with family and friends around her; she had no doubt about what was going to happen to her. When the railway-builders went away, her life would go on as it always had. The ghostly Romans would march the street forever. Tibbie would grow old and in time she'd die. In future years someone else like her would live in her cottage, do the same things, have friends like Tibbie's friends and they, too, would grow old and die . . . The awareness of a continuing circle of life and death in the little cottage was very comforting somehow.

'I'm going to Newcastle for a few days,' Emma Jane told them, 'but I'll come back for Opening Day. I hope you'll be there, Tibbie. I've reserved you a seat in the special viewing enclosure – and seats for you and William, too, Effie.'

'Oh, we wouldn't miss it,' they chorused together. Then Tibbie laughed, 'I never thought I'd hear myself say that!'

Emma Jane had been away from the city for months; she felt like a visitor from another world when she got off the train and was met by the faithful Haggerty with a hired cab. When they reached the cottage, she was delighted once more by its homely, cosy appearance. Mrs Haggerty was at the door with a broad smile on her face and she cried out, 'Oh Miss Emma Jane, you do look well! Life up there must be suiting you just fine.'

'I nearly didn't recognise you at the station, Miss. You seem to have grown much taller, Miss Emma.'

'I haven't,' she assured him with a smile. 'My skirt's still too long for me. You've got everything looking so pretty. You've done really well.'

The garden was full of the same sort of flowers that bloomed in Tibbie's – honeysuckle, tightly-furled old roses, tall white lilies, pink and purple phlox, feverfew with its little white flowers and grey-green serrated leaves. Sunflowers were ranged along the cottage wall beside tall pink hollyhocks. It was very different from the regimented trimness of the flowerbeds at Wyvern Villa.

'Your poor Mama's so much better. She and your Aunt

Louisa are out to tea but they'll be home soon,' said Mrs Haggerty as she ushered Emma Jane inside. All of a sudden the girl's spirits plunged and a cloud came over the sun. Only a little time of freedom was left to her.

An hour later Mrs Wylie, restored to health, came bustling in with Louisa stalking behind her. 'Darling, you look so *healthy*, positively rural and almost plump,' she cried at the sight of her daughter. Emma Jane stood in the hall with a smile of greeting on her face as her mother advanced towards her, lips pursed for a kiss. It was never delivered, however, for she stopped dead and gave a gasp. 'Oh heavens, Emma Jane, you've still got those awful freckles! You're like a leopard. I told you never to go out without a bonnet. Oh Louisa, look at her. Isn't it awful? What can be done about her complexion?'

Emma Jane put a hand to her face and stepped back. 'They're not so bad in the winter,' she said defensively.

'This isn't the winter,' moaned her mother. 'Everyone will see you like that when we go to the opening of your father's bridge.'

Emma Jane bristled. 'It's *my* bridge,' she thought, but didn't actually say it because she drove the resentment away in the same manner as she had always repressed her resentments in the past. Her cowardice frightened her. Little by little, she knew, her old weak personality would re-emerge and engulf her if she stayed at home too long. Like a drowning woman she'd have to fight to keep her head above water, fight for survival.

She decided to change the subject. 'The cottage is looking very pretty, Mama,' she said.

Mrs Wylie brightened. 'Yes, isn't it? Louisa thinks it's poky but I love it really. I don't think I'd like to live in Wyvern Villa again.' Emma Jane was surprised at this show of independent thinking from her mother and cheered up considerably.

Aunt Louisa was not so easily defeated, however. She laughed politely and said to Arabella, 'You always did like dolls' houses, my dear. But you really need something bigger, especially when Emma Jane comes home to stay.

We'll move to a better area where there are more eligible bachelors. She might find a nice husband once those freckles fade away.'

Emma Jane had to restrain herself from telling them about Alex Robertson but instead she said firmly, 'I don't think I'll be staying at home for long.'

The two women stared at her. 'Where will you go? What will you live on?' asked her mother.

Of course her father's estate was vested in her mother for life, but at least she had her allowance – £150 per year. She could live on that, Emma Jane said to herself. After all, she had managed on the equivalent of £30 per year at Camptounfoot. 'On my allowance,' she said grandly.

Her aunt and her mother looked at her askance.

'What's happened to you, Emma Jane?' said her mother with a quaver in her voice.

'I've grown up, Mama,' replied Emma Jane.

CHAPTER
Twenty

Before she left Maddiston to go to Newcastle, Emma Jane had reserved rooms in the recently-opened Grand Station Hotel for Mrs Wylie, Aunt Louisa and Amelia's family.

With her mother and aunt, she arrived in the town the day before the bridge opening. Amelia, Dan and the children were to come from Hexham next day. 'I hope you like your rooms,' Emma Jane said to her aunt when they had settled into the hotel, which was decked with flags to honour the opening of the extension of the railway.

'They're adequate. It's a small place, not like Harrogate, of course. They do as well as they can here.'

Mrs Wylie, who was anxious to keep the peace between her sister and her daughter, enquired, 'Is your room comfortable, my dear?'

'I'm not staying here, Mama – I'm going back to Camptounfoot tonight. Mrs Mather's expecting me. I want to walk the bridge: there might be things to do before the opening ceremony tomorrow.'

'Oh dear, this bridge!' exclaimed Mrs Wylie, throwing up her hands as if Emma Jane had been talking about a favourite toy.

'I'll send a carriage to bring you all down tomorrow,' said Emma Jane patiently.

'We'll see you there, then,' replied her mother brightly. 'It's twelve o'clock, isn't it, when the first train crosses Papa's bridge?'

Emma Jane gritted her teeth, 'Why do I get so annoyed? She's not deliberately trying to hurt me,' she thought, then said out loud: 'Yes, it's twelve o'clock, Mama. The carriage will pick you up at eleven.'

She walked the length of the bridge before she went back to Tibbie's, stepping with long strides over the gleaming metal lines and hopping from sleeper to sleeper. The sides of the bridge were draped with huge festoons of red, white and blue interspersed with flags in the railway company's colours of dark-green and gold. Flags fluttered from tall poles on the reception platform, and men in striped aprons were carrying up potted plants and distributing them around the speakers' dais. All the workers were strangers and no one spoke to her, but now she was filled with pride and exultation about her achievement. The melancholy was gone. She stood in the roadway and stared up at her bridge like someone having a vision.

Tibbie's cottage when she reached it was a haven. She sank into her favourite chair by the fire and heard all the gossip. Wee Lily was definitely pregnant, despite the potion Tibbie had made her drink; she was swelling up fast and, amazingly, delighted to be having a baby. She had forgotten all about its terrible begetting.

'She and Big Lily are coming to wave flags tomorrow. They're thrilled. Most of the village is turning out, too – even Jo and Mr Jessup. We're all fair proud of you, Emma Jane,' said Tibbie happily.

She didn't mention Tim Maquire and eventually Emma Jane was forced to ask, 'Is Maquire going to be at the opening?'

'Of course. He's been to London to see Lord and Lady Godolphin and he had a grand time. What tales he has to tell! And you've never seen such braw clothes as he's come back with. He's a great dandy is Tim. He's been in here today telling me all about Mrs Bethya and Gentleman Sydney. Apparently Sydney just turned up at the door of Bella Vista and asked the maid to fetch her mistress. When Mrs Anstruther came down, he asked her to run off with him and she went! Imagine! She thought she was running away with a navvy. It was a real shock to her when she found out she'd eloped with a lord! Sydney told Tim he didn't tell her in case it made her keen to get him. Tim said they're fair daft about each other though.'

Emma Jane nodded. 'Gentleman Sydney is a very nice man in spite of pretending that he isn't. They'll be happy, I'm sure. They didn't know about the fire, did they?'

'Not for a long time. They said the maid went crazy when she saw that Bethya was going away. She shouted and screamed and carried on like a mad thing. They thought she'd calm down eventually, but of course she didn't.'

'Are they coming to the opening?' asked Emma Jane.

Tibbie shook her head. 'No, they said it would be tactless because Mrs Anstruther and the Colonel will be there. The Colonel's much better since he heard Bethya wasn't killed, but his wife's still very bitter. She's the only one who seems to mourn that Mr Gus.'

'Poor man,' said Emma Jane, but Tibbie dismissed Gus with a flick of the hand.

'Och, he wasn't worth much. Now tell me what you're going to wear for the opening. It'll take something to outshine Tim, I can tell you!'

'I wouldn't even try,' grinned Emma Jane. 'I've a purple outfit that was made by a dressmaker in Newcastle, and I've only worn it twice. I was keeping it for something special and I think this could be it.'

The weather gods were kind, for next day dawned bright and fair. The cloudless blue sky told everyone that there would be no rain to disrupt the ceremony and no wind either, because everything was still and golden under a kindly sun. In her nightgown, Emma Jane walked out into Tibbie's garden and sat under the old apple tree. Its branches were heavy with green apples, and a flock of multi-coloured butterflies fluttered past her as she breathed in the gloriously sweet air. She felt utterly tranquil and happy, her mind emptied of all speculation about the future and all regrets over the past. There and then, she made a resolution. 'I'm not going to worry about anything all of today. I'll think about my future tomorrow.'

When she finally went indoors and dressed, Tibbie was overcome with admiration for the purple costume. 'Oh my goodness, don't you look grand! The colour's perfect for you. I've never seen you look so braw,' cried the little woman, fussing around Emma Jane and plucking out her skirt to better effect.

Emma Jane arrived early at the platform. The earthen embankment had been transformed by the men in aprons into a bank of vividly coloured flowers – geraniums, petunias, white daisies, marigolds and roses all set among ferns. On the dais floor stood a lectern like one from a church and a line of fragile-looking gilt chairs. On the seat of each chair was a card telling the name of its occupant. She found hers and sat down on it with her hands folded in her lap. The purple skirt fell in satisfying folds to her feet, the bodice fitted her snugly and the perky little hat made her feel cheeky and self-confident. She blessed Madame Rachelle. Then the unheralded thought came into her head, 'Where's Tim Maquire? I want to see Tim Maquire.'

There was no sign of him or any of the other navvies, however, as one by one the guests started to arrive. Carriages began to roll up and disgorge their occupants. Chattering, jostling people climbed on to the groaning platform. The Raeburn family turned out en masse. Dr Stewart with the Provost and Chief Magistrate of Rosewell all marched on with their wives and sat down stiffly. Colonel Anstruther's Bath chair was pushed on by his servant, and placed beside Emma Jane. The Colonel was alone because at the last moment his wife had decided she could not face the festivities. The chair's occupant was beaming, however, and he turned to Emma Jane to say, 'Well done, Miss Wylie. You must be a proud young woman today.'

'I am,' she told him, and he beamed even more broadly.

'D'ye remember my daughter-in-law Bethya – "Begum" I called her. I've had a letter from her. She's Lady Godolphin now, so it's well done to her too. She didn't even know this navvy feller was a lord when she went off with him. Did you know that?'

'No I didn't but I thought he was a strange navvy,' she admitted.

'There's a lot of queer fish among them, isn't there?' the Colonel laughed. He didn't seem to bear Bethya any resentment for being the unwitting cause of his house burning down and his son disappearing with it. In fact, Emma Jane got the feeling that he was relieved to be rid of Gus.

Then the Wylies arrived. Aunt Louisa and Arabella Wylie were as smart as fashion plates in expensive gowns, paid for by Louisa, but Amelia was pregnant again and looked like an earth mother in loose sprigged muslin and a face-shading straw hat with ribbons on it. Dan was obviously hot and uncomfortable in a suit of brown corduroy but the children looked summery in starched white cotton with blue ribbons. Arbelle had grown into a sweet-faced little girl who did as she was bid without protest. A miracle, thought Emma Jane as she kissed the child.

She had reserved seats for them all in the front row of the first enclosure behind the platform. These were very sought-after seats, but the fact that she was not in the platform party piqued Louisa and her lips tightened: however she accepted a seat with fairly good grace. 'At least she's sitting down,' thought Emma Jane, watching her. The mass of the spectators were standing.

The Wylies were surprised by the number of rough-looking people who were waving to Emma Jane as if they were proud to be her friends. 'Do you *know* those people?' Arabella asked her daughter, who smiled and said, 'Oh yes, they're all my friends. That's Big Lily and Wee Lily, and Bob and Mamie and the Rutherfords ... Oh, and there's Tibbie and her brother and sister-in-law.' She raised her hand high and waved enthusiastically to a group in the far corner.

'Good heavens,' sighed her mother.

At that moment, Alex Robertson, very smart in a dark suit and crisp white neckerchief, walked on to the platform to greet Emma Jane. When she introduced him to her mother, who brightened at the mention of the title 'doctor', he took her hand very solemnly and said, 'I'm very glad to meet you. Has your daughter told you I've asked her to be my wife?'

An amazing range of expressions crossed Arabella Wylie's face, but all she said was, 'Really?' for at that moment there was a scream of a train whistle, a puff of smoke from the far end of the bridge and a huge cheer from the crowd. The first train was about to roll on to the bridge.

Emma Jane stared along its length and, to her astonishment, all she could think was, 'Where's Tim Maquire? I want Tim Maquire to see this.' She frowned and forced herself to concentrate on what was happening but it was difficult. She felt he should have been with her at that moment.

"Wheee!' went the whistle as the train came lumbering slowly on to the line. The front of the engine was like a warrior's shield with concentric golden circles painted round a large brass boss. The short engine was dark-green with straps of gold around the body like belts holding it together, and its tall smoke-stack, out of which a plume of white smoke spurted, was also golden-coloured. It was pulling two eight-wheeled carriages, green as well, with the Company's shield and initials on the doors. Men and women waving handkerchiefs were leaning out of the windows in acknowledgement of the cheering of the crowd. As the train shuddered to a halt alongside the wooden platform, Rosewell Brass Band struck up and a choir of children from Camptounfoot School broke out in song. 'Hail smiling morn, hail, hail, hail, hail . . .' they trilled.

'Where's Tim Maquire?' thought Emma Jane as Sir Geoffrey and Lady Miller, who looked like a gaudily dressed flagpole, stepped out of the first carriage followed by a crowd of other dignitaries from Edinburgh. They were shown to their seats by liveried railway servants and, when the music died away, Sir Geoffrey stood up with a folder covered in green leather in his hand to deliver the inauguration speech. He began with a pious statement of how he and the rest of the railway company directors had felt it was their duty to bring civilisation, industry and prosperity to rural parts of the country and by building their bridge and their railway they had managed to do it. Everyone clapped dutifully and sat back to listen as he launched into a long list of names of the people who deserved congratulation for what he called 'this great achievement'.

'Where's Tim Maquire?' thought Emma Jane again, distractedly searching the crowd with her eyes.

Some old people dozed off when Sir Geoffrey began naming the railway company directors, their backers and bankers, their lawyers and advisers, the quarry owner, the brickmakers, Mr Jopp . . .

'. . . And of course,' he said finally, 'the navvies, the masons and the bricklayers – without whom this bridge would never have been built.'

'Where's Tim Maquire?' thought Emma Jane. She hardly noticed that her name did not appear in Sir Geoffrey's list until Colonel Anstruther patted her hand and said, 'That's a bad show, a bad show. He should have thanked you.' Then she forced herself to listen to the speaker's smug, self-congratulatory voice and a tide of anger rose in her. At that same moment she remembered what Maquire had said about the celebratory dinner. She'd not been invited to that, either. She wanted to get to her feet and shout, 'What about the Wylies?' but of course she couldn't. It wouldn't have been lady-like.

'Oh, where's Tim Maquire?' she inwardly groaned.

At last Sir Geoffrey closed his folder, sat down and the band burst out with *Hail The Conquering Hero Comes*.

All the directors were smiling and nodding to every side and preparing to re-board the train for the return to Maddiston by a circular route, when a tremendous outbreak of cheering was heard from the far end of the bridge. Everything stopped; everyone stared at what looked like an invading army charging towards the platform party over the gleaming new lines. Emma Jane's heart rose when she saw that the crowd was made up of her navvies in their colourful best, hats with tassles, waistcoats of purple, canary yellow or orange, cravats in brilliant hues and highly polished boots. And, most glorious of all, at their head ran Tim Maquire, magnificent in a grey tailcoat with gleaming buttons, grey trousers and a waistcoat striped in all the colours of the rainbow. His flowing bow tie was scarlet silk, a brave contrast with the black beard and glittering earrings and he was shouting as he ran, 'Three cheers for Miss Wylie, three cheers for Miss Wylie. She's the one that built this bridge. Three cheers for Miss Wylie!'

The crowd on the dais scattered in confusion as the navvies rushed upon them but they need not have worried, for the men were in search of only one person – Emma Jane. She was lifted bodily from her chair and carried off like a Sabine woman. Hands closed around her waist, someone hoisted her high in the air and she heard Tim Maquire's voice saying, 'Don't worry, hold on. I won't let you fall.'

She was perched on his shoulders with him holding her hand and the navvy army took her on a triumphal procession along the length of the bridge and back again. With one hand clamped on to her purple hat, for she was determined not to lose it, and the other around Maquire's neck, she bobbed in the middle of them like a laughing doll. 'Hooray for Miss Wylie! Hip, Hip, Hooray,' yelled her escort and the spectators joined in. The brass band started playing again and this time they chose the *Ode To Joy*.

She was breathless, laughing and tearful at the same time when they finally deposited her back on the platform. When her feet were safely on the ground again she called out, 'Thank you very much! I couldn't have done it without you.' Over the top of the men's heads she saw Tim Maquire watching her and she said again, directly to him, 'Thank you, thank you!'

He grinned and shouted back, 'You didn't think we were going to let that prick get away with it, did you?' Sir Geoffrey and everybody else heard him but he didn't care.

People crowded round Emma Jane but her mother stood slightly to the back, wiping her eyes with a lace-edged handkerchief, and when her daughter reached her, she whispered, 'Oh my dear, I was so afraid they'd let you fall. You looked tiny up there on their shoulders.'

Emma Jane laughed proudly. 'Maquire wouldn't let me fall, Mama.'

'Maquire? Is he the one with the beard? My dear, he was the most terrifying of all. Such awful *language*.'

'Language? What language?' asked Emma Jane in genuine puzzlement.

'That *obscene* word he used about Sir Geoffrey. I didn't think such language at all proper in front of ladies, and your poor Aunt Louisa practically fainted. What the young doctor feels about this I hate to think. He must have a reputation to keep up round here. When you marry him you'll have to be much more careful about who you associate with.'

But Emma Jane was too taken up with the mention of obscenities to worry about Alex Robertson. 'What obscene word?' she repeated, bemused. She'd grown accustomed and inured to navvy language and couldn't think of any really serious curses being bandied about.

Mrs Wylie hissed, 'Surely you heard what the man with the beard called Sir Geoffrey Miller? You laughed. I was so ashamed, I didn't know where to put myself.' Once more she wiped her eyes.

'Oh, Mama. What Maquire called Miller is mild, I can assure you,' grinned Emma Jane as she turned away to greet Amelia who was running towards her with arms held out and calling, 'You did look splendid up there on those men's shoulders! And what lovely men. Oooh, if I wasn't married to Dan, I'd be making eyes at that big one with the beard myself.'

Aunt Louisa stepped between them and said stiffly, 'I think we'd better go back to our hotel, Emma Jane. All this might be too much for your mother. She's only just regaining her health, you know. She ought to lie down.'

Arabella, reminded by her sister of her fragile health,

drooped like a lily and Emma Jane was overcome with remorse for having forgotten her mother's delicacy. 'Oh Mama, of course. I'll take you back there now,' she cried, grasping her mother's elbow and guiding her through the dwindling crowd.

Their carriage was still waiting on the road. The driver, who had known her father, grinned broadly when she appeared. 'Well done, Miss! I saw your victory parade,' he said. Her mother gasped and Louisa bristled but as they all climbed aboard, Amelia held back and whispered, 'I hope you're not going to settle back at home with your mother and Louisa. After what you've done, that would be a terrible comedown. Grasp fate, girl, do something outrageous!'

'I love you 'Melia. I really do,' Emma Jane said fondly. She wondered if Amelia would think marriage to Alex Robertson was sufficiently outrageous, but at least it was a way of escape.

During the drive to Maddiston her mother held Emma Jane's hand and said, 'I did like that young doctor, Emma Jane. He's not really a gentleman but he's very respectable-looking and solid, isn't he, Louisa?'

Her sister nodded. 'Quite. It's a respected profession, at least. A doctor's wife has a place in society . . . You're very lucky, Emma Jane. Where did you meet him?'

A sort of devil entered into her and she pretended to ponder. 'I think the first time I met him was when one of my navvies was murdered . . . No, that was the second time. The first time was when young Robbie fell off a cart and broke his leg. He was doctor to the navvies, you see. He looked after them during the cholera epidemic and they always called him out in preference to Stewart in Rosewell. Stewart's a dreadful snob.' She saw her mother and aunt looking at each other is dismay.

'Cholera? Murder?' asked Arabella faintly.

Emma Jane nodded. 'Oh yes. There were several murders in fact.' Christopher Wylie had always shielded his wife from the black side of his working life and this was a revelation to her.

'Oh my dear,' she gasped, leaning towards her daughter. 'I'd no idea you were being exposed to such things. I wouldn't have allowed you to do it if I had.'

Then Amelia chipped in. 'If she hadn't done it, things would be bad for you all now. Emma Jane's saved the family fortunes. Isn't it time somebody thanked her for that?'

'It's a good thing she's going to marry that doctor. He can look after her now but I hope he knows what he's taking on,' was Louisa's contribution. It struck Emma Jane that everyone assumed she was sure to marry Alex, that she must be grateful to be offered the opportunity.

'I haven't made up my mind if I will marry him yet,' she said and Louisa scoffed: 'Of course you will! You'd be stupid if you didn't.'

They were all stiff and formal when they reached the hotel. Mrs Wylie and her sister went off to lie down because they were not returning to Newcastle till the following day, but Amelia and her family were leaving immediately and Emma Jane went with them to the station. Again she thanked her sister-in-law for the gift of the cottage and Amelia smiled as she said, 'At least it gives your mother a place to live. You won't have to worry about her any more. And don't let your aunt annoy you. She wants to stay with your mother – it suits her – and that's all right because it means you can get away. Don't do anything hasty like rushing into marriage, Emma Jane. Take your time. You're still so young and you've been working like a slave. It's time you enjoyed yourself.'

Emma Jane kissed her sister-in-law and said, 'You're so sensible, 'Melia. Father said you were and it's true.'

When Dan, Amelia and the children went away, however, she looked around the station as if she were at a loss. What to do first? Yes, of course, she'd have to go to see Alex. It was time to make up her mind. His house was on the outskirts of the town on the road to Camptounfoot, and she told the carriage-driver to wait for her at the gate while she hopped down and ran up his garden path. Alex was in his consulting room with his stethoscope pressed

554

against the chest of a stout man in a striped working shirt. She looked in the window and watched him for a few moments before he noticed her. His face was concerned and caring as he bent towards his patient. His brown hair was slightly tousled and he looked boyish and young. What a nice, kind man he was, she thought. Any sensible woman would be glad to be his wife.

Then he saw her face at the window and gestured for her to come in so she sat in his tiny waiting room until his patient left. Eventually he appeared, pulling on his jacket, and told her, 'I'm glad you came. I've been thinking about you ever since that business at the bridge.'

'Were you ashamed of me too?' she asked.

'No, of course not, but I was afraid they might let you fall.'

She laughed. 'Oh dear me, Alex, of course they'd not let me fall. You're as bad as my mother – that's what she said.'

He frowned. 'I'm worried about something else. I shouldn't have told your mother that I wanted to marry you. I hope I didn't embarrass you too much.'

'Not at all,' she said gently. 'It was very good for my standing with my mother and aunt. They're afraid that no one'll ever want to marry me, so they're very pleased.'

His anxious look lifted. 'Does that mean you're going to say yes?' he asked.

She stood up from her chair and walked towards him. Gently she grasped his right hand in both of hers and said, 'I like you very much indeed. I think you're a splendid doctor and a superb man. The fact that you want to marry me is very flattering but, dear Alex, I'm sorry. I'll have to say no.'

He seemed to expect it. 'You don't love me,' he said softly, 'I know that. You're in love with —'

She put a finger on his lips and said, 'Ssh, I don't love anyone else. It's just that I'm not ready to marry yet – perhaps I never will be. Building the bridge has shown me that the world's full of possibilities, and I don't want to settle down yet. I know everyone will think I'm very silly to turn you down but that's my decision. There's nothing wrong with you – it's me that's odd. Goodbye, Alex, I'm going away tomorrow. I wish you the very best of luck for the future.'

When they shook hands, she realised with a pang that they'd never even kissed each other. Come to that, she'd never kissed any man. 'I wonder if I ever will?' she thought as she hurried back to her waiting carriage. 'Oh, where's Tim Maquire?' mourned the little devil of a voice inside her.

It was a glorious evening when she reached the river. The setting sun was striking beautiful colours off the bridge; she had not known that stone could shine with so many shades of red.

'Stop, stop, let me off here,' she called to the driver, for she had to take one last walk along the top of the miracle she'd created. It soared above her as magnificent as a dream. Even the thick buttress that Maquire had built around the cracked pier did not annoy her so much any longer, though she still thought it looked like a bandage on the finger of an elegant hand.

'I know, I know,' she murmured as if she were talking to him. 'It would have fallen down if you hadn't.'

There was a line of wooden-edged steps cut into the embankment by the roadside and she climbed up, holding her skirt high so that it would not be marked by the raw earth. The bridge stretched in front of her like a road to infinity, metal rails glittering in the light of the dying day. She walked very slowly to the middle and then stood staring round. Being up so high made the world look very different. Darkness was creeping in and there were midnight-coloured patches of shadow everywhere. She wondered if Tibbie's Roman soldiers were out walking already.

A rising wind whipped her skirt around her legs and made her hold on to her hat. She shivered a little and turned to go but when she looked back along the way she had come, she realised with a tremor of shock that someone was walking towards her. It was a man on his own, his silhouette black and broad-shouldered against the last of the light. She could not see his face.

She stood very still as he came nearer. Her heart was hammering in her throat as Tim Maquire stepped close to her. Without speaking, he gently took off her hat, laying it on the rails at their feet. Then he cupped a hand behind her head and tilted her face up towards his. She stared with wide eyes into his. 'They're blue – I never noticed that before,' she registered in wonder. She could neither speak nor move, for she felt as if her whole body was turning into liquid. Tim kissed her and for a moment she wondered if she was asleep and dreaming. His lips gently brushed against hers and his beard prickled against her skin. She put up a hand to stop him, but only half-heartedly. He grasped the hand and held it tight as he kissed her again, more insistently this time.

As he held the girl in his arms, something woke and expanded like a flower inside his heart. He was a man who yearned to have someone to look after. He'd taken care of Christopher Wylie; he'd tried to take care of Hannah and now, more than anything in the world, he wanted to take care of this little waif-like thing with the yellow eyes and funny freckles. His hand cupped her head gently and as he kissed her she was suddenly not timid any more. She pressed against him, opened her lips and kissed him back.

Time stood still. Neither of them knew if it was seconds, minutes or hours before he stopped kissing her and said in a voice of wonder, 'My God, I didn't think this would ever happen to me again. I love you. You can be one of the most annoying women I've ever met but I love you very much. I didn't mean this to happen. I saw you up here and came to fetch you down to the celebration dinner. Then it hit me.'

'I'm glad you did,' she whispered.

'Glad I did what?'

'I'm glad you kissed me.'

'So am I. Very glad. But we'll have to hurry if we're going to that dinner.'

'But I've not been invited,' she protested.

'I have. I've got the card in my pocket and I'm taking you with me,' he said, grabbing her hand and picking up her hat in one swoop as he started to run along the bridge. Laughing, she ran with him.

The directors of the Edinburgh and South of Scotland Railway were holding their celebration dinner at the flower-bedecked Red Lion Hotel overlooking Maddiston Square. The big dining room on the first floor had three long windows with wrought-iron balconies from which flags and bunting were hanging.

Tim cantered the sweating pony of his hired gig on to the half circle of cobbles in front of the hotel door and turned to look at the exhilarated Emma Jane by his side. Gently he smoothed her hair back from her glowing face, picked up her hat which he'd put at his feet for the ride to Maddiston and carefully set it on her head. Then he adjusted it, leaned back a little to see the effect, adjusted it again, stuck her hatpin in the back so that it was skewered to her thick rope of hair and announced, 'You look beautiful. I love that hat.'

He jumped down, held out a hand and helped her alight from the gig like a princess. Arm in arm they entered the Hotel and climbed the stairs to the first-floor landing where a black-coated waiter stood on guard at the door of the dining room. He tried to stop them, hissing, 'It's an all-male dinner, sir.'

'This lady,' said Tim grandly, 'is the guest of honour. Please stand aside.' The waiter did as he was told.

Emma Jane surprised herself by feeling totally unafraid of a dining room full of men. The strength of Tim's arm gave her confidence. A long top table was set against the top wall facing three other tables which stretched to the end of the room. There was bunting hanging from the ceiling, bottles on the tables, and the air was blue with tobacco smoke. When the interruption occurred, Sir Geoffrey was on his feet making another speech. He stopped in mid-sentence and stared at Maquire striding up the middle of the floor with the Wylie girl on his arm.

Jopp was sitting at the top table, three places down from Sir Geoffrey and next to Colonel Anstruther, still in his Bath chair. Tim walked up and put a hand on Jopp's shoulder. 'Get up. You're here on false pretences,' he said.

'I'm not,' spluttered Jopp, attempting to hold on to his seat, but Tim lifted him up by the back of his collar as if he was a toy. Then, very courteously, he showed Emma Jane into Jopp's chair. All the guests watched in astonished silence as she sat down with a sweep of her skirts.

Colonel Anstruther, who had a taste for pretty women, turned and smiled at her. 'Welcome, young lady. You deserve to be here. Can I offer you some claret?' he said.

'Thank you,' she said.

By this time Tim had taken his own place at the bottom of one of the other tables beside the man who made the bricks and the chief mason. His unwavering gaze sustained Emma Jane and made her glow with love. There was not a man present – except for Miller and Jopp – who did not warm to her.

It was time for the toasts. Colonel Anstruther spoke up before anyone else had the chance to interrupt. 'I'm afraid that my infirmity doesn't allow me to stand, gentlemen, but I'd like to propose a toast to the young lady beside me. Without her we wouldn't have that beautiful bridge to grace our line. I've seen her on site working with the men and I was amazed at what she was doing. Yet here she is as lovely as a rose, and three miles down the line is our bridge. Well done, Miss Wylie!' He raised his glass to her in a storm of clapping.

'Speech, speech,' called someone from the end of the room and with calm aplomb Emma Jane stood up. A hush fell as she began.

'I'm not going to say much, and when I've finished I'll go away and leave you gentlemen to the serious business of toasting the bridge, but I'd like you to know how much I've enjoyed building it. There were times when I was in despair, times when I thought it would never be completed

. . .' she eyed Miller as she said this '. . . but with the help of people like young Robbie Rutherford, who is not here tonight, and my right-hand man Tim Maquire who is, the job was done. Thank you, Tim. You are absolutely invaluable. I couldn't have done it without you.' As she raised her glass towards him, he jumped from his chair to walk up to the top of the room and stand opposite her.

'I'll take you home now,' he said huskily, and then turned to face the gathering. 'Gentlemen, if any of you ever want another bridge or even a railway built, remember us. We're forming a company called Wylie and Maquire, and we'll build anything you want, any place you want it.'

Then he held out a hand to Emma Jane who stood up and walked around the table to take it. Once they were outside the dining room she looked up at him and said with a laugh, 'I think we should call it Maquire and Maquire, don't you?'

He laughed and kissed her on the cheek. 'I was hoping you'd want more than a business alliance. Yes, let's make it legal, Miss Wylie.'

A great giggle rose up in her throat and she leaned on his arm beaming as she told him, 'Oh Tim, I do want to be there when you ask my mother for my hand. I'm longing to see the effect it'll have on dear Aunt Louisa!'